A Noise Downstairs

ALSO BY LINWOOD BARCLAY

Parting Shot

The Twenty-Three

Far from True

Broken Promise

No Safe House

A Tap on the Window

Never Saw It Coming

Trust Your Eyes

The Accident

Never Look Away

Fear the Worst

Too Close to Home

No Time for Goodbye

Stone Rain

Lone Wolf

Bad Guys

Bad Move

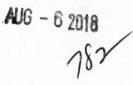
A Noise Downstairs

A Novel

Linwood Barclay

HARPER LUXE

An Imprint of HarperCollins*Publishers*

A NOISE DOWNSTAIRS. Copyright © 2018 by NJSB Entertainment Inc. All rights reserved. Printed in the United States of America. No part of this book may be used or reproduced in any manner whatsoever without written permission except in the case of brief quotations embodied in critical articles and reviews. For information address HarperCollins Publishers, 195 Broadway, New York, NY 10007.

HarperCollins books may be purchased for educational, business, or sales promotional use. For information please e-mail the Special Markets Department at SPsales@harpercollins.com.

FIRST HARPERLUXE EDITION

ISBN: 978-0-06-284564-1

HarperLuxe™ is a trademark of HarperCollins Publishers.

Library of Congress Cataloging-in-Publication Data is available upon request.

18 19 20 21 22   ID/LSC   10 9 8 7 6 5 4 3 2 1

For Neetha

Prologue

Driving along the Post Road late that early October night, Paul Davis was pretty sure the car driving erratically in front of him belonged to his colleague Kenneth Hoffman. The ancient, dark blue Volvo station wagon was a fixture around West Haven College, a cliché on wheels of what a stereotypical professor drove.

It was just after eleven, and Paul wondered whether Kenneth—always Kenneth, never Ken—knew his left taillight was cracked, white light bleeding through the red plastic lens. Hadn't he mentioned something the other day, about someone backing into him in the faculty parking lot and not leaving a note under the windshield wiper?

A busted taillight was the kind of thing that undoubtedly would annoy Kenneth. The car's lack of back-end symmetry, the automotive equivalent of an unbalanced equation, would definitely irk Kenneth, a math and physics professor.

The way the Volvo was straying toward the center line, then jerking suddenly back into its own lane, worried Paul that something might be wrong with Kenneth. Was he nodding off at the wheel, then waking up to find himself headed for the opposite shoulder? Was he coming home from someplace where he'd had too much to drink?

If Paul were a cop, he'd hit the lights, whoop the siren, pull him over.

But Paul was not a cop, and Kenneth was not some random motorist. He was a colleague. No, more than that. Kenneth was a friend. A mentor. Paul didn't have a set of lights atop his car, or a siren. But maybe he could, somehow, pull Kenneth over. Get his attention. Get him to stop long enough for Paul to make sure he was fit to drive. And if he wasn't, give him a lift home.

It was the least Paul could do. Even if Kenneth wasn't the close friend he once was.

When Paul first arrived at West Haven, Kenneth had taken an almost fatherly interest in him. They'd discovered, at a faculty meet and greet, that they had a shared, and not particularly cerebral, interest.

They loved 1950s science fiction movies. *Forbidden Planet, Destination Moon, Earth vs. the Flying Saucers, The Day the Earth Stood Still. The Attack of the 50 Foot Woman*, they agreed, was nothing short of a masterpiece. Once they'd bonded over the geekiest of subjects, Kenneth offered Paul a West Haven crash course.

The politics of academia would come over time, but what a new guy really needed to know was how to get a good parking spot. Who was *the* person to connect with in payroll if they screwed up your monthly deposit? What day did you avoid the dining hall? (Tuesday, as it turned out. Liver.)

Paul came to realize, over the coming years, he was something of an exception for Kenneth. The man was more likely to offer his orientation services to new female hires, and from what Paul heard, it was more intensive.

There were a lot of sides to Kenneth, and Paul still wasn't sure he knew all of them.

But whatever his misgivings about Kenneth, they weren't enough to let the man drive his station wagon into the ditch and kill himself. And it would be *just* himself. As far as Paul could see, there was no one in the passenger seat next to Kenneth.

The car had traveled nearly a mile now without

drifting into the other lane, so maybe, Paul thought, Kenneth had things under control. But there was an element of distraction to the man's driving. He'd be doing the speed limit, then the brake lights would flash—including the busted one—and the car would slow. But then, it would pick up speed. A quarter mile later, it would slow again. Kenneth appeared to be making frequent glances to the right, as though hunting for a house number.

It was an odd area to be looking for one. There were no houses. This stretch of the Post Road was almost entirely commercial.

What was Kenneth up to, exactly?

Not that driving around Milford an hour before midnight had to mean someone was up to something. After all, Paul was out on the road, too, and if he'd gone straight home after attending a student theatrical production at West Haven he'd be there by now. But here he was, driving aimlessly, thinking.

About Charlotte.

He'd invited her to come along. Although Paul was not involved in the production, several of his students were, and he felt obliged to be supportive. Charlotte, a real estate agent, begged off. She had a house to show that evening. And frankly, waiting while a prospective buyer checked the number of bedrooms held the promise of more excitement than waiting for Godot.

Even if his wife hadn't had to work, Paul would have been surprised if she'd joined him. Lately, they'd been more like roommates who shared a space rather than partners who shared a life. Charlotte was distant, preoccupied. It's just work, she'd say, when he tried to figure out what might be troubling her. Could it be Josh, he wondered? Did she resent it when his son came for the weekend? No, that couldn't be it. She liked Josh, had gone out of her way to make him feel welcome and—

Hello.

Kenneth had his blinker on.

He steered the Volvo wagon into an industrial park that ran at right angles to the main road. A long row of businesses, every one of them no doubt closed for the last five hours or more.

If Kenneth was impaired, or sleepy, he might still have enough sense to get off the road and sleep it off. Maybe he was going to use his phone. Call a taxi. Either way, Paul was thinking it was less urgent for him to intervene.

Still, Paul slowed and pulled over to the side of the road just beyond where Kenneth had turned in.

The Volvo drove around to the back of the building, brake lights flashing. It stopped a few feet from a Dumpster.

Why go around the back? Paul wondered. What was Kenneth up to? He killed his headlights, turned off the engine, and watched.

In Paul's overactive imagination, the words *drug deal* came up in lights. But there was nothing in Kenneth's character to suggest such a thing.

And, in fact, Kenneth didn't appear to be meeting anyone. There was no other car, no suspicious person materializing out of the darkness. Kenneth got out, the dome light coming on inside. He slammed the door shut, circled around the back until he was at the front passenger door, and opened it. Kenneth bent over to pick up something.

Paul could not make out what it was. Dark—although everything looked pretty dark—and about the size of a computer printer, but irregularly shaped. Heavy, judging by the way Kenneth leaned back slightly for balance as he carried it the few steps over to the Dumpster. He raised the item over the lip and dropped it in.

"What the hell?" Paul said under his breath.

Kenneth closed the passenger-side door, went back around to the driver's side, and got in behind the wheel.

Paul slunk down in his seat as the Volvo turned around and came back out onto the road. Kenneth drove right past him and continued in the same direction. Paul watched the Volvo's taillights recede into the distance.

He turned and looked to the Dumpster, torn between checking to see what Kenneth had tossed into it, and continuing to follow his friend. When he'd first spotted Kenneth, Paul had been worried about him. Now, add curious.

Whatever was in that Dumpster would, in all likelihood, still be there in a few hours.

Paul keyed the ignition, turned on his lights, and threw the car back into drive.

The Volvo was heading north out of Milford. Beyond the houses and grocery stores and countless other industrial parks and down winding country roads canopied by towering trees. At one point, they passed a police car parked on the shoulder, but they were both cruising along under the limit.

Paul began to wonder whether Kenneth had any real destination in mind. The Volvo's brake lights would flash as he neared a turnoff, but then the car would speed up until the next one. Kenneth, again, appeared to be looking for something.

Suddenly, it appeared Kenneth had found it.

The car pulled well off the pavement. The lights died. Paul, about a tenth of a mile back, could see no reason why Kenneth had stopped there. There was no driveway, no nearby home that Paul could make out.

Paul briefly considered driving right on by, but then thought, *Fuck this cloak-and-dagger shit. I need to see if he's okay.*

So Paul hit the blinker and edged his car onto the shoulder, coming to a stop behind the Volvo wagon just as Kenneth was getting out. His door was open, the car's interior bathed in weak light.

Kenneth froze. He had the look of an inmate heading for the wall, caught in the guard tower spotlight.

Paul quickly powered down his window and stuck his head out.

"Kenneth! It's me!"

Kenneth squinted.

"It's Paul! Paul Davis!"

It took a second for Kenneth to process that. Once he had, he walked briskly toward Paul's car, using his hand as a visor to shield his eyes from Paul's headlights. As Paul started to get out of the car, leaving the engine and headlights on, Kenneth shouted, "Jesus, Paul, what are you doing here?"

Paul didn't like the sound of his voice. Agitated, on edge. He met Kenneth halfway between the two cars.

"I was pretty sure that was your car. Thought you might be having some trouble."

No need to mention he'd been following him for miles.

"I'm fine, no problem," Kenneth said, clipping his words. He twitched oddly, as though he wanted to look back at his car but was forcing himself not to.

"Were you following me?" he asked.

"Not—no, not really," Paul said.

Kenneth saw something in the hesitation. "How long?"

"What?"

"How long were you following me?"

"I really wasn't—"

Paul stopped. Something in the back of the Volvo had caught his eye. Between the headlights of his car, and the Volvo's dome light, it was possible to see what looked like mounds of clear plastic sheeting bunched up above the bottom of the tailgate window.

"It's nothing," Kenneth said quickly.

"I didn't ask," Paul said, taking a step closer to the Volvo.

"Paul, get in your car and go home. I'm fine. Really."

Paul only then noticed the dark smudges on Kenneth's hands, splotches of something on his shirt and jeans.

"Jesus, are you hurt?"

"I'm okay."

"That looks like blood."

When Paul moved toward the Volvo, Kenneth grabbed for his arm, but Paul shook him off. Paul was a good fifteen years younger than Kenneth, and regular matches in the college's squash courts had kept him in reasonably good shape.

Paul got to the tailgate and looked through the glass.

"Jesus fucking Christ!" he said, suddenly cupping his hand over his mouth. Paul thought he might be sick.

Kenneth, standing behind him, said, "Let . . . let me explain."

Paul took a step back, looked at Kenneth wide-eyed. "How . . . who is . . . who *are* they?"

Kenneth struggled for words. "Paul—"

"Open it," Paul said.

"What?"

"Open it!" he said, pointing to the tailgate.

Kenneth moved in front of him and reached for the tailgate latch. Another interior light came on, affording an even better look at the two bodies running length-wise, both wrapped in that plastic, heads to the tailgate, feet up against the back of the front seats. The rear seats had been folded down to accommodate them, as if they were sheets of plywood from Home Depot.

While their facial features were heavily distorted by the opaque wrapping, and the blood, it was clear enough that they were both female.

Adults. Two women.

Paul stared, stunned, his mouth open. His earlier feeling that he would be sick had been displaced by shock.

"I was looking for a place," Kenneth said calmly.

"A what?"

"I hadn't found a good spot yet. I'd been thinking in those woods there, before, well, before you came along."

Paul noticed, at that point, the shovel next to the body of the woman on the left.

"I'm going to turn off the car," Kenneth said. "It's not good for the environment."

Paul suspected Kenneth would hop in and make a run for it. With the tailgate open, if he floored it, the bodies might slide right out onto the shoulder. But Kenneth was true to his word. He leaned into the car, turned the key to the off position. The engine died.

Paul wondered who the two women could be. He felt numb, that this could not be happening.

A name came into his head. He didn't know why, exactly, but it did.

Charlotte.

Kenneth rejoined him at the back of the car. Did the man seem calmer? Was it relief at being caught? Paul gave him another look, but his eyes were drawn back to the bodies.

"Who are they?" Paul said, his voice shaking. "Tell me who they are." He couldn't look at them any longer, and turned away.

"I'm sorry about this," Kenneth said.

Paul turned. "You're *sorry* about—"

He saw the shovel Kenneth wielded, club-like, for no more than a tenth of a second before it connected with his skull.

Then everything went black.

Eight Months Later

One

The old man in the back of the SUV could have been taken for dead. He was slumped down in the leather seat, the top of his nearly bald, liver-spotted head propped up against the window of the driver's-side back door.

Paul got up close to the Lincoln—it was that model the movie star drove in all those laughably pretentious commercials—and peered through the glass.

He was a small, thin man. As if sensing that he was being watched, he moved his head. The man slowly sat up, turned, blinked several times, and looked out at Paul with a puzzled expression.

"How you doing today?" Paul asked.

The man slowly nodded, then slipped back down in the seat and rested his head once more against the glass.

Paul carried on the rest of the way up the driveway to a door at the side of the two-story, Cape Cod–style, cedar shake–shingled house on Carrington Avenue. There was a separate entrance at the back end of the driveway. There was a small bronze plaque next to it that read, simply, ANNA WHITE, PH.D. He buzzed, then let himself in and took a seat in the waiting room, big enough for only two cushioned chairs.

He sifted through a pile of magazines. He had to hand it to Dr. White. In the three months he'd been coming to see her, the magazines—there were copies of *Time* and *The New Yorker* and *Golf Digest* and *Golf Monthly*, so maybe his therapist was an avid golfer— were always turning over. If there was a fault to be found, it was that she wasn't scanning the covers closely enough. Was it a good idea, in a therapist's office, to offer as reading material a newsmagazine with the headline "Paranoia: *Should* You Be Scared?"

But that was the one he opened. He was about to turn to the article when the door to Dr. White's office opened.

"Paul," she said, smiling. "Come on in."

"Your dad's in your car again."

She sighed. "It's okay. He thinks we're going to go visit my mother at the home. He's comfortable out there. Please, come in."

Still clutching the magazine, he got up and walked into the doctor's office. It wasn't like a regular doctor's space, of course. No examining table with a sheet of paper on it, no weigh scale, no eye chart, no cutaway illustration of the human body. But there were brown leather chairs, a glass-and-wood desk that looked like something out of the Herman Miller catalog with little on it but an open, silver laptop. There was a wall of bookshelves, restful paintings of the ocean or maybe Long Island Sound, and even a window with a view of one of Milford's downtown parks.

He dropped into his usual leather chair as the doctor settled into one kitty-corner to him. She was wearing a knee-length skirt, and as she crossed her legs Paul made an effort not to look. Dr. White— early forties, brown hair to her shoulders, eyes to match, well packaged—was an attractive woman, but Paul had read about that so-called transference stuff, where patients fall in love with their therapists. Not only was that not going to happen, he told himself, he wasn't about to give the impression it might.

He was here to get help. Plain and simple. He didn't need another relationship to complicate the ones he already had.

"Stealing a magazine?" she asked.

"Oh, no," he said, flashing the cover. "There was an article I wanted to read."

"Oh, God," she said, frowning. "That might not have been the best one to put out there."

Paul managed a grin. "The headline *did* catch my eye. Otherwise, I might have tried a golf magazine. Even though I don't play."

"Those are my father's," she said. "He's eighty-three, and he still gets out on the course, occasionally, if I can go with him. And he loves the driving range. He can still whack a bucket of balls like nobody's business. A lot less chance of getting lost when you don't actually head out onto the course." She extended a hand and Paul gave her the magazine. She took another glance at the headline as she tossed it onto a nearby coffee table.

"How's the head?" she asked.

"Physically, or mentally?"

"I was thinking, physically?" She smiled. "For now."

"Dr. Jones says I'm improving the way I should be, but with a head injury like I had, we have to watch for any effects for up to a year. And I'm still having some, no doubt about it."

"Such as?"

"The headaches, of course. And I forget things now and then. Sometimes, I walk into a room, and I have no idea why I'm there. Not only that, but I might not even remember getting there. One minute, I'm in the bedroom, the next I'm down in the kitchen, and I've got no idea how it happened. And I haven't gone back to squash. Can't run the risk of getting hit in the head with a racket or running into the wall. I'm kind of itching to get back to it, though. Maybe soon. I'll just take it easy."

Anna White nodded. "Okay."

"Sleeping is still, well, you know."

"We'll get to that."

"My balance is getting pretty good again. And I can concentrate pretty well when reading. That took a while. It looks like I'll be back to teaching in a couple of months, in September."

"Have you been to the campus at all since the incident?"

Paul nodded. "A couple of times, kind of easing into it. Did one lecture for a summer class—one I'd given before so I didn't have to write it from scratch. Had one tutorial with some kids, got a good discussion going. But that's about it."

"The college has been very patient."

"Well, yes. I think they would have been anyway, but considering it was a member of their own faculty who tried to kill me . . . they've been accommodating, for sure." He paused, ran his hand lightly over his left temple, where the shovel had hit him. "I always tell myself it could have been worse."

"Yes."

"I could have ended up in the Volvo with Jill and Catherine."

Anna nodded solemnly. "As bad as things are, they can always be worse."

"I guess."

"Okay, so we've dealt with the physical. Now let's get to my area of expertise. How's your mood been lately?"

"Up and down."

"Are you still seeing him, Paul?"

"Kenneth?"

"Yes, Kenneth."

Paul shrugged. "In my dreams, of course."

"And?"

Paul hesitated, as though embarrassed. "Sometimes . . . just around."

"Have you seen him since we spoke the other day?"

"I was picking up a few things at Walgreens and I was sure I saw him in the checkout line. I could feel a kind of panic attack overwhelming me. So I just left, didn't buy the things I had in my basket. Got in the car and drove the hell away fast as I could."

"Did you honestly believe it was him?"

Slowly, Paul said, "No. I knew it couldn't be."

"Because?" She leaned her head toward him.

"Because Kenneth is in prison."

"For two counts of murder and one of attempted murder," Anna said. "Would have been three if that policeman hadn't come by when he did."

"I know." Paul rubbed his hands together. It had been more than just luck that a cop came. The officer in that cruiser he and Kenneth had driven past had decided to go looking for that Volvo with a busted taillight.

Anna leaned forward onto her knees. "In time, this will get better. I promise you."

"What about the nightmares?" he asked.

"They're persisting?"

"Yes. I had one two nights ago. Charlotte had to wake me."

"Tell me about it."

Paul swallowed. He needed a moment. "I was finding it hard to see. Everything was foggy, but then I realized I was all wrapped up in plastic sheeting. I tried to move it away but I couldn't. And then I could see something through the plastic. A face."

"Kenneth Hoffman?"

Paul shook his head. "You'd think so. He's been in most of them. What I saw on the other side was myself, screaming at me to come out. It's like I was simultaneously in the plastic and outside it, but mostly in, and feeling like I couldn't breathe. I was trying to push my way out. It's a new variation on my usual nightmare. Sometimes I think Charlotte's one of the two women in the back of that car. I have this vague recollection, before I blacked out, of being terrified Kenneth had killed Charlotte."

"Why did you think that?"

He shrugged. "She hadn't come with me to the play. My mind just went there."

"Sure."

"Anyway, thank God Charlotte's there when I have the nightmares, waking me up. The last one, my arms were flailing about in front of me as I tried to escape the plastic."

"Are you able to get back to sleep after?"

"Sometimes, but I'm afraid to. I figure the nightmare's just on pause." He closed his eyes briefly, as though checking to see whether the images that had come to him in the night were still there. When he opened them, he said, "And I guess it was four nights ago, I dreamed I was sitting at the table with them."

"With?"

"You know. Jill Foster and Catherine Lamb. At Kenneth's house. We were all taking turns typing our apologies. The women, they had these ghoulish grins, blood draining from the slits in their throats, actually laughing at me because the typewriter was now in front of me and I don't know what to write and they're saying, 'We're all done! We're all done!' And you know how, in a dream, you can't actually see words clearly? They're all a-jumble?"

"Yes," Anna White said.

"So that's why it's so frustrating. I know I have to type something or Kenneth, standing there at the end of the table, looking like fucking Nosferatu—excuse me—will kill me. But then, I know he's going to kill me anyway." Paul's hands were starting to shake.

Anna reached across and touched the back of one. "Let's stop for a second."

"Yeah, sure."

"We'll switch gears for a bit. How are things with Charlotte?"

Paul shrugged. "I guess they're okay."

"That doesn't sound terribly positive."

"No, really, things are better. She's been very supportive, although having to watch me go through all this has to get her down at times. You know, before all this happened, things weren't exactly a hundred percent. I think Charlotte was going through something, almost a kind of reassessment of her life. You know, ten years ago, is this where she would have imagined herself being? Selling real estate in Milford? Not that there's anything wrong with that, you know? I think her dreams were a little different when she was younger. But my nearly getting killed, maybe that had a way of refocusing things. They're better now."

"And your son? Josh?"

Paul frowned. "It hit him hard when it happened, of course. Thinking your dad might die, that's not easy for a nine-year-old kid. But I wasn't in the hospital long, and while I had some recovering to do—and still am—it was clear I wasn't going to drop dead right away. And he splits his time between his mom and me. So he's not necessarily around when I wake up screaming in the night."

Paul tried to laugh. Anna allowed herself a smile. They were both quiet a moment. Anna sensed that Paul was working up to something, so she waited.

Finally, he said, "I wanted to bounce something off you."

"Sure."

"I talked about this with Charlotte, and she thinks maybe it's a good idea, but she said I should get your input."

"I'm all ears."

"It's pretty obvious that I'm . . . what's the word? Haunted? I guess I'm haunted by what Kenneth did."

"I might have used the word *traumatized*, but yes."

"I mean, not just because he nearly killed me. That'd be enough. But I *knew* him. He took me under his wing when I arrived at West Haven. He was my friend. We had drinks together, shared our thoughts, connected, you know? Fellow sci-fi nerds. How could I not have seen that under all that, he was a monster?"

"Monsters can be very good at disguising themselves."

Paul shook his head. "Then again, there were many times when I wondered whether I knew him at all, even before this. Remember Walter Mitty?"

"From the James Thurber story?"

Paul nodded. "A boring, ordinary man who imagines himself in various heroic roles. Kenneth presented as a drab professor with some secret life as a ladies' man. Except with him, the secret life wasn't imaginary. It was for real. He had this underlying charm that women—well, some women—found hard to resist. But he didn't advertise it to the rest of us. He didn't brag about his latest sexual conquest."

"So he never told you about women he was seeing?"

"No, but there was talk. We all knew. Whenever there was a faculty event, and he'd bring his wife,

Gabriella, all you could think was, is she the only one in the room who doesn't know?"

"Did you know his son?"

"Len," Paul said, nodding. "Kenneth loved that boy. He was kind of—I don't know the politically correct way to put this—but he was a bit slow. It's not like he was somewhere on the spectrum or anything, but definitely not future college material. But Kenneth would bring him out on campus so he could hang out for hours in the library looking at art books. Kenneth'd gather a stack of books for Len so he could turn through them page by page. He liked looking at the pictures."

Paul gave Anna a look of bafflement. "How do I square that with what he did? Killing two women? And the *way* he did it. Making them apologize to him before slitting their . . . I can't get my head around it."

"It's hard, I know. So, you wanted to bounce something off me."

He paused. "Instead of trying to put all of this behind me, I want to confront it. I want to know more. I want to know *everything*. About what happened to me. About Kenneth. I want to talk to the people whose lives he touched. And not just in a bad way. The good, too. I want to understand all the different Kenneths. If it's possible, I'd like to actually talk to him, if they'll let me into the prison to see him. And if *he'll* see me, of course. I guess what I'm searching for is the answer to a bigger question."

Anna tented her fingers. "Which is?"

"Was Kenneth evil? *Is* Kenneth evil?"

"I could just say yes and save you the trouble." She took in a long breath, then let it out slowly. "I could go either way on this. Do you honestly think it will help?"

Paul took a moment before answering.

"If I can look into the eyes of evil in the real world, maybe I won't have to run from it in my sleep."

Two

Anna followed Paul Davis out the door. He continued up the driveway to his own car when Anna
stopped to open the back door of her Lincoln SUV,
careful not to let her father fall out.

"Come on in, Dad."

"Oh, hi, Joanie. Must have nodded off."

"It's Anna, Dad. Not Mom."

"Oh, right. We should get going. Joanie will be
going to lunch soon."

"She's not at Guildwood anymore, Dad," she said
gently. "I'm going to get you some coffee. There's still
half a pot."

"Coffee," he said. "That sounds good."

He turned his legs out the door, then ever so carefully slid off the seat until his feet touched the ground, like some slow-motion parachutist.

"Ta da," he said. He looked down, saw that the laces on one of his shoes were loose. "For my next act, I will tie my shoelaces."

"When we get inside," Anna said, closing the car door and walking with her father back into the house. Once inside, her father chose to sit in one of the two waiting room chairs so that he could deal with his shoe promptly.

"I'll go get you a coffee, then you can go upstairs and watch your shows," she said.

He gave her a small salute. "Righty-o."

Instead of going through the door into her office, Anna took the route that led back into the main house. She went to the kitchen, got a clean mug from the cupboard, and filled it from the coffeemaker.

She heard, faintly, the side door open and close again. She hoped her father hadn't decided to take up residence in the car again. Then it occurred to her that her next client might have arrived.

"Shit," she said under her breath. Anna did not want her father engaging in conversation with her clients, particularly the one who was now due. In her rush to return to her office, she fumbled looping her finger into the handle of the coffee cup and knocked it to the floor.

"For fuck's sake," she said. Anna grabbed a roll of paper towels off the spindle, got to her knees, and mopped up the mess. Once she cleaned the floor and tossed the sodden towels, she poured another cup of coffee and went back to the office.

She found her father chatting with a thin man in his late twenties who had settled into the other chair and was leaning forward, elbows on knees, listening intently to Anna's dad. When Anna walked in, he smiled.

"Hi," he said nervously to Anna. "Just talking to your dad here."

Anna forced a smile. "That's nice, Gavin. Why don't you head in?"

Gavin shook the old man's hand. "Nice to meet you, Frank."

"You bet, Gavin." Frank White tipped his head toward his daughter. "She'll get you sorted out, don't you worry."

"I hope so," Gavin said.

Gavin went into Anna's office as she handed her father his coffee. She looked down at his feet.

"You didn't do up your shoelaces," she said.

Frank shrugged, standing. "I'll be fine. He seems like a nice fella."

You have no idea, Anna thought.

"Are you going to watch TV in your room?"

"I think so. Maybe work on the machine a bit."

"Dad, you already did, like, an *hour* of rowing this morning."

"Oh, right."

She accompanied him as he went into the main part of the house and walked to the bottom of the stairs. She looked at the coffee he was holding, his untied shoelaces, and that flight of stairs, and could imagine the disaster that was waiting to happen.

"Hang on, Dad," she said.

Anna knelt down and quickly tied his shoes. "You don't have to do that," he protested.

"It's no problem," she said. "I don't want you tripping on the stairs. Hand me your coffee."

"For Christ's sake, I'm not an invalid," he said angrily.

Anna sighed. "Okay."

But she stood there and watched as he ascended the stairs, one hand still gripping the coffee mug, the other on the railing. When he'd reached the second floor he turned and looked down at her.

"Ta da!" he said again.

Anna gave him a sad smile, then went back through the house to her office. She found Gavin standing around the back of her desk where her closed laptop sat, admiring the books on her shelves, running his finger along the spines. Gavin wore a pair of faded jeans, sneakers, and a tight-fitting black T-shirt. In addition to being thin, he was scruffy haired and no taller than five-six. From the back, he could have been mistaken for someone in his early to mid teens, not a man who'd soon turn thirty.

"Mr. Hitchens," she said formally. "Please take a seat."

He spun around innocently, then dropped into the same chair Paul Davis had been in moments earlier. "Your father's nice," he said. "He told me he used to work in animation. *And* he said"—Gavin grinned—"that it's time you found yourself a man. But don't worry, I don't think he was looking at me as a prospect."

"Gavin, we need to talk about—"

"But he called you Joanie. Is that your middle name?"

"That was my mother's name," Anna White said reluctantly. She did not like revealing personal details to clients. And that was especially true of Gavin Hitchens.

"Oh," he said. "I see. Is your mother . . ."

"She passed away several years ago. Gavin, there are

certain ground rules here." She grabbed a file sitting on her desk next to the computer. "You are here specifically to talk with me. Not my father, not any of my other clients. Just me. There need to be boundaries."

Gavin nodded solemnly, like a scolded dog. "Of course."

Anna glanced at some notes tucked into the file. "Why don't we pick up where we left off last time."

"I don't remember where that was," Gavin said.

"We were talking about empathy."

"Oh, right, yes." He nodded agreeably. "I've been thinking about that a lot. I know you think I don't feel it, but that's not true."

"I've never said that," Anna replied. "But your actions suggest a lack of it."

"I told you, I've never hurt anyone."

"But you have, Gavin. You can hurt people without physically harming them."

The young man shrugged and looked away.

"Emotional distress can be scarring," she said.

Gavin said nothing.

"And the truth is, someone *could* have been hurt by the things you did. There can be consequences you can't predict. Like what you did with Mrs. Walker's cat."

"Nothing happened. Not even to the cat."

"She could have fallen. She's eighty-five, Gavin. You locked her cat in the attic. She heard him up there, dragged a ladder up from the basement, and climbed it to the top to open the attic access panel to rescue him. It's a wonder she didn't break her neck."

Gavin lowered his head and mumbled, "Maybe it wasn't me."

"Gavin. Please. They weren't able to prove you did that, not like with the phone call, but all the evidence suggests you did it. If we're going to be able to work together, we have to be honest with each other. You get that, don't you?"

"Of course," he said, looking suitably admonished and continuing to avoid her gaze. His eyes misted.

"You're right, I did the cat thing. And the phone call. I know I need help. It's why I agreed to come here and see you. I don't want to do these things. I want to get better. I want to understand why I do what I do and be a better person."

"Gavin, you were *ordered* to see me. It was part of the sentencing. It kept you out of jail."

His shoulders fell. "Yeah, I know, but I didn't fight it. I heard you were really good, that you could fix me. I'm happy to come here as often as it takes to make me a better person."

"I don't fix people, Gavin. I try to help them so they can fix themselves."

"Okay, sure, I get that. It has to come from within." He nodded his understanding. "So how do I do that?"

Anna took a breath. "Ask yourself why."

"Why?"

"Why would you hide a lonely old woman's cat? Why phone a still-grieving father claiming to be his son who died in Iraq?" Anna paused, then asked, "What would make a person do something like that?"

Gavin considered the question for several seconds. "I know," he said slowly, "how those actions might be viewed as cruel or inappropriate."

Anna leaned forward, elbows on her knees. "Gavin, look at me."

"What?"

"I need you to look at me."

"Yeah, sure," he said, allowing Anna to fix her eyes on his. "What is it?"

"Are there any other incidents you haven't shared with me?"

"No," he said.

"Any that you've contemplated but haven't done?"

Gavin kept his eyes locked on hers. "No," he said. Then he smiled. "I'm here to get better."

Three

Driving home, Paul was pleased Dr. White did not actively discourage his idea of delving more into the Kenneth Hoffman business, rather than retreating from it. He'd come to believe that the nightmares rooted in his near-death experience—"near-death" in the most literal sense, since he had almost died—would persist as long as he allowed the event to consume him.

There needed to be a way to turn that horrific night into something that did not own him. Paul could not let his life be defined by finding two dead women in the back of a car, followed by a blow to the head. Yes, it was horrendous. It was traumatic.

But there needed to be a way for him to move forward.

Maybe there was a way to apply what he did for a

living to the situation. Paul taught English literature. He'd studied everything from Sophocles to Shakespeare, Chaucer to Chandler, but more recently, his course on some of the giants of twentieth-century popular fiction, Nora Roberts, Lawrence Sanders, Stephen King, Danielle Steel, Mario Puzo, had proved to be the biggest hit with students, sometimes to the chagrin of his colleagues and the department head. His point was, just because something was embraced in large numbers did not necessarily make it lowbrow. These writers could tell a story.

That was how Paul thought he could approach the Hoffman business. He would take a step back from it, attempt to view it with a measure of detachment, then analyze it as a story. With a beginning, a middle, and an end.

Paul knew much of the middle and the end. He had, literally, walked into the middle of it.

What he needed to do now was find out more about the beginning.

Who was Kenneth Hoffman, really? A respected professor? A loving father? A philandering husband? A sadistic killer? Was it possible to be all these things? And if so, was the capacity to kill in all of us, waiting to break out? Was it possible that—

Shit.

Paul was home.

Sitting in his car, in the driveway, the engine running.

He had no memory of actually driving here.

He could recall getting into the car after he left Anna White's office. He remembered putting the key in the Subaru's ignition, starting the car. He could even recall seeing her next client arrive, a young guy, late twenties, heading in.

But after that, nothing. Nothing until he pulled into the driveway.

Do not panic. This is not a big deal.

Of course it wasn't. He'd been deep in thought on his way home. He'd gone on autopilot. Hadn't this sort of thing happened even before the attack? Hadn't Charlotte teased him more than once about being the classic absentminded professor, his head somewhere else while she was talking to him? His first wife, Hailey, too. They'd both accused him of being off in his own world at times.

That's all it was. No reason to think he was losing his marbles. He was unquestionably on the mend. The neurologist he was seeing was sure of that. The MRIs hadn't turned up anything alarming. Sure, he'd still have the odd headache, suffer the occasional memory loss. But he was improving, no doubt about it.

Paul turned off the car and opened the door. He felt slightly light-headed as he got out, placing one hand on the roof of the car for a moment and closing his eyes, steadying himself.

When he opened them, he felt balanced. Felt—

"I'm sorry about this."

Suddenly, his temple throbbed where Kenneth had struck him with the shovel. He relived the pain, reheard those last words from his would-be killer.

They'd sounded so real.

As if Kenneth were here with him right now, standing next to him in front of his home. Paul felt a chill run the length of his spine as he struggled to get Kenneth's voice out of his head.

Not exactly a sign that my idea is a good one, Paul thought.

No, he told himself. This was *exactly* why he needed to know more. He needed a Kenneth *exorcism.* Grab him by the throat and get him the fuck out of his head.

Paul closed the car door and held on to the keys as he approached the front door. Charlotte's car was not here, and this was not a week Josh was living with them, so he'd have the house to himself, at least for a while. Charlotte was rarely home in the late morning, although as a real estate agent her schedule was erratic. But if she wasn't showing a place to a prospective buyer, or meeting with someone wanting to put their place on the market, she was getting caught up on the paperwork in the office she shared with half a dozen other agents. One of them was Bill Myers, whom Paul had known since before Charlotte joined the agency. Back when Charlotte was getting started, Paul had asked Bill to put in a word with his fellow agents about adding her to the team. He'd pulled some strings, and Charlotte was set.

And working at the real estate agency had given Charlotte the inside track when the house they were now living in came on the market. They were on Milford's Point Beach Drive, which ran right along Long Island Sound. The back of the house looked out over a beautiful stretch of waterfront. They loved the fresh sea air and the never-ending music of the incoming waves.

The house was on three levels, the bottom mostly garage, laundry room, and storage. The middle level was made up of the kitchen and living room areas, and the bedrooms were on top. Both the living room and the master bedroom featured small balconies with views of the beach and beyond.

The property had suffered a lot of damage when Hurricane Sandy stormed ashore back in 2012. The owner had sunk a fortune into rebuilding the place before deciding he no longer wanted to live there. This had been shortly after Paul and Charlotte got married, and the timing was right to move from their small apartment into something nicer. So long as the polar ice caps didn't melt *too* quickly, this would be a great spot for the foreseeable future.

Paul unlocked the front door and climbed the stairs with slow deliberation. Going up, or coming down, could sometimes make him woozy. Given that he'd felt a bit off getting out of the car, he took his time. But when he reached the top, and tossed his keys onto the kitchen island, he felt good.

Good enough for a cold one.

He opened the refrigerator, reached for a bottle of beer, and twisted off the cap. As he tilted his head back for a long draw he caught sight of the wall clock, which read 11:47 A.M. Okay, maybe a little early, but what the hell.

He had work to do.

At one end of the kitchen, on the street side of the house, was a small room the original owners had designed as an oversize pantry—it was no bigger than six by six feet—but which Paul had turned into, as he had often called it, "the world's tiniest think tank."

He'd cut twelve inches off a seven-foot door that had been left in the garage by the previous owner after the reno, mounted it on the far wall as a desk, added some supports underneath, and filled with books the shelves lining two of the other walls that had been intended for canned goods and cereal boxes. By removing a few shelves he'd managed to carve out enough space to hang a framed, original poster for the film *Plan 9 from Outer Space*. He'd found it in a movie memorabilia store in London years ago. As there was no window, he'd lined the wall at the back of the desk with cork, allowing him to hang articles and calendars and favorite *New Yorker* cartoons where he could see them.

Centered on the desk was his laptop. Also taking up space were a printer and several cardboard business boxes filled with lesson plans, lectures, bills, and other files.

Paul dropped himself into the wheeled office chair and set the beer next to the laptop. He tapped a key to bring the screen to life, entered his password.

He stared at the computer for the better part of five minutes. He thought back to when he was six years old and his parents started taking him to a community pool in the summer. It wasn't heated, and Paul couldn't deal with getting in at the shallow end and slowly walking toward the deeper part, the cold water working its way incrementally up his body. It was torture. He took the "ripping off the Band-Aid approach," which was to stand at the edge and jump in, getting his entire body wet at once. The only problem was, the rest of his family could be ready to go home before he'd taken the plunge.

Paul was standing at the edge of the pool again.

He knew what he had to do.

He needed to *understand* what had happened to him. And where there were holes in the story, he'd attempt to fill them in with what *might* have happened. Weren't there photo programs like that? Where the image was grainy or indistinct, the computer would figure out what was probably there and patch it?

What did Kenneth say to these women before he'd reached his decision to kill them? What were their intimate moments like? What lies did Kenneth come up with when questioned by his wife, Gabriella?

Even a partly imagined story would be better than no story at all.

Paul opened a browser.

Into the search field he entered the words "Kenneth Hoffman."

"Okay, you son of a bitch," he said. "Let's get to know each other a little better."

Paul hit ENTER.

Four

Paul thought the best way to begin was with news accounts of the double murder. He'd read many of them before but never with quite the intensity he wanted to devote to them now. He recalled that when Kenneth was sentenced, one of the papers had carried a long feature summing up the entire story. It didn't take long to find it.

The *New Haven Star* carried it. Paul remembered that he had given an interview to the reporter. The story ran with the headline "A Scandal in Academia: 'Apology Killer' gets life in double murder."

He leaned in closer to the laptop screen and began to read:

BY GWEN STAINTON

There are some things even tenure can't protect you from.

So it was that yesterday, longtime West Haven College professor Kenneth Hoffman—the so-called Apology Killer—was sentenced to life in prison for the brutal murders of Jill Foster and Catherine Lamb, and the attempted murder of colleague and friend Paul Davis, bringing to a close not only one of the state's most grisly homicide cases, but also perhaps the most bizarre scandal of academia in New England history.

A lengthy trial might have brought out more details, but Hoffman waived his right to one and pleaded guilty to all charges. It was not difficult to imagine why he might have made that decision. When Hoffman was arrested, he was in the process of disposing of the bodies of the two women, and had just knocked Davis unconscious, striking him in the head with a shovel.

Had he not been discovered by a Milford police officer who'd decided to go after Hoffman's car—it had a broken taillight—Hoffman most likely would have buried all three in the woods. He was in the process of finding a suitable location when police happened upon him.

Paul reached for his beer. *Look at the words. Read them. Don't look away. The man was going to make sure I was dead and then he was going to put me in a grave.*

The point of the exercise was to face this head-on, he told himself. No shying away. It occurred to him, for not the first time, that whoever'd bumped into Hoffman's car in the faculty parking lot and broken that light had effectively saved his life.

After conducting extensive interviews with court and police officials, friends and family of Hoffman and his victims, as well as people from the West Haven College community, the *Star* has been able to put together a more detailed, if no less puzzling, picture of what happened.

Kenneth Hoffman, 53, husband to Gabriella, 49, father to Leonard, 21, was a longtime member of the WHC staff. While his areas of expertise were math and physics, he was perhaps even more skilled in one other area.

Fooling around.

West Haven College was, and remains, a close-knit community, and affairs in academia are hardly unheard of. Hoffman could have taught a course in them. From all accounts, Hoffman did not present as a so-called ladies' man. He was a much-praised professor, admired by his students, and his affairs with college employees, or their spouses, were conducted with the utmost discretion.

There is no evidence he had a sexual relationship with a student. Hoffman seemed to understand behavior of that sort could land him in serious, professional trouble. Nor was he ever the subject of a sexual harassment complaint.

And yet, people knew. Or at least suspected.

"Yeah," Paul said under his breath. He could remember going to Kenneth's office one time, and as he arrived the door opened and a woman came out, tears streaming down her cheeks. You might see a student emerge crying from a meeting with a professor, especially if the prof had found proof of plagiarism, but this woman was a colleague, not a student.

When Paul came in he couldn't help but ask, "What happened?"

Kenneth had been unable to hide his look of discomfort. He struggled for an answer, and the best he could come up with was, "Some sort of personal issue."

Paul, at first, thought he'd heard "personnel" and asked, "Jesus, is she being fired?"

Kenneth blinked, baffled. "If they were going to fire anybody, it'd be . . ."

He never finished the sentence.

Paul read on:

While Hoffman had a pattern of one affair at a time, his statement after his arrest made clear he was seeing Jill Foster and Catherine Lamb simultaneously, although neither knew about the other.

Also apparently in the dark was Hoffman's wife, Gabriella. Interviews with various sources suggest Gabriella was aware of some of her husband's acts of infidelity over the years, but she did not know he was juggling two mistresses in the last few months.

Jill Foster, assistant vice president of student development and campus life, was married to Harold Foster, assistant manager of the Milford Savings & Loan office in downtown Milford. Catherine Lamb, a senior sales manager at JCPenney, was the spouse of Gilford Lamb, director of the college's human resources department.

After his arrest, Hoffman admitted to police he'd become increasingly obsessive, and possessive, where the women were concerned. He wanted them all to himself, to the point of telling them they were forbidden to continue having sexual relations with their own husbands. It was a demand they'd each found impossible to accept, and no doubt, rather difficult for Hoffman to enforce. But just the same, they'd asked him how they were to explain that to their spouses. Hoffman told investigators he felt that for them to be sexually involved with anyone but him amounted to betrayal.

In what one Milford detective called the understatement of the year, Hoffman told them, "Perhaps I was being unreasonable."

"Maybe just a little," Paul said, moving the story farther up the screen.

But it was during this period of "being unreasonable" that Hoffman set a trap for them both.

He invited them one night to his home when his wife and son were out for an extensive driving lesson. (Leonard wanted to work on his skills to improve his chances of getting a job that involved operating a truck.) Both of the women probably expected a private romantic rendezvous and were undoubtedly surprised to discover each other. They were acquainted through college functions and must have wondered if they had been called there for some other reason.

Posing as the perfect host, Hoffman offered the women glasses of wine, which they accepted. The wine, however, had been drugged, and soon Foster and Lamb were unconscious. When they awoke, they found themselves bound to kitchen chairs, an old-fashioned Underwood typewriter on the table before them.

Hoffman demanded written apologies from them for—as he himself described it later to investigators—their "immoral, licentious, whore-like behavior."

With one hand freed by Hoffman, Jill Foster typed: "i am so sorry for the heartache i have brought to your life please forgive me."

When Hoffman released Catherine Lamb's hand, she wrote: "i am so ashamed of what i have done i deserve whatever happens to me."

"Sounds like you dictated what you wanted them to say," Paul said under his breath, shaking his head.

Hoffman took the two sheets of paper from the typewriter, put them in a drawer in the kitchen, and returned with a single steak knife that he used to slit the women's throats.

Hoffman then wrapped the women in sheets of plastic, loaded them in the back of his Volvo. He also placed into the front passenger seat of the car the antique typewriter, which had the victims' blood on it.

North of Milford, he pulled over, thinking he might have found a wooded area suitable for disposing of the bodies. West Haven College colleague Paul Davis spotted his car and pulled over. When Davis saw the bodies in the back of the station wagon, Hoffman tried to kill him with the shovel he'd brought to dig his victims' graves.

"If the police had not come along when they did," Davis said in an interview, "I wouldn't be here now."

Davis could not explain what made Hoffman, a former mentor, commit such a heinous crime.

"I guess there are things we just never know about people, even those closest to us," Davis said.

His comments were echoed by Angelique Rogers, 48, a West Haven College political science professor who went public about an affair she'd had with Kenneth Hoffman four years earlier.

"She was the one," Paul said to himself. "She was the one coming out of his office."

"I can't stop wondering, all this time later, how close I came to meeting the same fate as Jill and Catherine," Rogers said. "Did Kenneth think I had betrayed him at some level, too, by not leaving my husband?" She said Hoffman had not made the same demands of her that he reportedly had of the two women he killed.

(Rogers and her husband have since divorced. She still teaches at West Haven.)

Hoffman himself seemed at a loss to explain his actions.

When asked how he could have slit the throats of the two women, Hoffman reportedly shrugged and said, "Who knows why anyone does anything?"

Paul read the story through a second time. It raised as many questions as it answered. Why did Hoffman make such strange demands of the two women? Expecting them to stop having sex with their own husbands? Seriously? Why invite them to the house together, allow them to meet each other? Okay, they might have already known one another through college functions, but why put them together like that, at his house? What was the point? He must have known from the beginning what he was going to do, but why kill both of them? What had snapped in Kenneth's mind?

And a minor question the story failed to address was that typewriter. The reporter mentioned that Kenneth put it in the car, but not what he had done with it.

At least, where that question was concerned, Paul had a pretty good idea. His memory of events that night had taken time to come back to him, but while recovering in Milford Hospital he did tell the police about Kenneth's side trip into that industrial plaza to throw something into a Dumpster.

He never heard anything more about it after that. He supposed if the police had found it, they would have used it in building their case against Hoffman, had he not confessed and pleaded guilty. But it was more likely that by the time Paul remembered what he'd seen, the Dumpster had been emptied and the typewriter was in a landfill somewhere.

"I'm sorry about this."

Kenneth's voice, in his head, again.

"No, you're not," Paul said. "You never were. Not for a goddamn minute. The only thing you're sorry about is that you got caught."

Paul heard the front door open downstairs.

"Paul?"

Charlotte was home. It wasn't unusual for her to pop by through the day, especially if her evening was going to be taken up with showings.

"Up here!" he shouted. "In the think tank!"

He heard her walking up the steps. No, not walking. More like running.

"Paul?" she said again, her voice on edge.

Paul got up out of the computer chair and went back into the kitchen in time to see his wife reach the top of the stairs.

"Is everything okay?" he asked.

"Who's that guy parked across the street, watching the house?" she asked.

Five

After lunch, Anna White sat at her desk, opened her laptop, and made some notes from her three Friday morning sessions.

Her first visitor was a retired X-ray technician who was having a hard time getting over the death of her dog. It had darted out into traffic, and the woman blamed herself. Anna understood why that was making it difficult for the woman to move on. Anna's second client of the day, Paul Davis, was making some headway. Anna was not yet entirely sold on his idea of writing about Kenneth Hoffman, but he might be onto something. She wasn't going to tell him not to do it. If Paul believed the exercise would help his recovery, she wasn't going to discourage him.

And then there was Gavin Hitchens.

She had her work cut out for her where he was concerned.

He said he wanted to get better, and she wanted to believe that was true, but she had her doubts. She knew the young man was not being entirely open with her. She didn't know that he was outright lying to her, but he was definitely holding things back.

At least he wasn't denying the basic facts about what had gotten him into trouble.

Sitting in a coffee shop, he'd taken from the table next to him the unwatched cell phone of a distracted babysitter and used it to call the father of a soldier who'd died in Iraq. Gavin claimed to be the dead son. Told the dad he'd faked his death so he wouldn't have to return and face the father he hated so much.

Gavin didn't even know the man. He'd seen his name in a newspaper story. He thought it would be fun.

What he hadn't counted on was the surveillance camera.

When the call was traced back to the woman who owned the phone, she swore she hadn't made it. Besides, the caller had been male. She knew she'd been at the coffee shop at the time. Police recovered security camera footage that showed Gavin grabbing the woman's phone when she wasn't looking, then tucking it back under her purse when he was done with the call.

Gavin had tried to dismiss his actions as a "prank," but the authorities didn't see it that way. A look into Gavin's history revealed other, possible "pranks." Sneaking into an elderly woman's home and hiding her cat in the attic was one.

Anna had been trying to get Gavin to search within himself to understand why he perpetrated such cruel hoaxes. He'd been quick to blame a sadistic, unloving father.

Gavin had spun a pretty good tale of abuse and belittling. His father had mocked him for things he was good at (high school theater, sketching, playing the flute) and ridiculed him for things he was not (football, baseball, pretty much anything sports related). His nicknames for Gavin included "flower fucker" and "Janice." Gavin's dad figured if you didn't know how to rebuild an engine block or throw a left hook at somebody in a bar, you were some kind of cocksucking faggot. (Putting that flute in his mouth, Gavin's father maintained, was a clue.)

"I don't know why he hated me so much," Gavin had said in one of their earlier sessions. "Maybe he had low self-esteem. He could have been haunted by how he was mistreated by his own father."

When patients started tossing around phrases like "low self-esteem," Anna suspected them of trying a little too hard.

But Gavin's story didn't end with his childhood.

At nineteen, he left home. Four years later, his mother killed herself after downing a bottle of sleeping pills. Three years after that, Gavin's father was diagnosed with liver cancer, and leaned on his son to move back home and look after him.

Gavin conceded to Anna that he saw it as an opportunity to exact some revenge.

He'd hide his father's reading glasses. Put his pills in a different medicine cabinet. Leave his slippers out on the deck when it rained. Change appliance settings so that when his father made toast it came out burned. Unplug the heating pad Dad sat on as he watched TV.

One time, he added laxative to the old man's soup, and removed the toilet paper from his father's bathroom.

"I know it was wrong," Gavin told her sheepishly. "I think maybe, after he died, I couldn't stop. I had to find others to torment."

Maybe there *was* something to all this business with his father, Anna thought, assuming the story he told was true. She had checked some of the details—the mother's suicide, the father's liver cancer—and they'd turned out to be true. But the story seemed a little too pat, Gavin's excuse too convenient.

It was also possible Gavin had perpetrated those "pranks"—the ones she knew about and the ones she didn't—not because of a miserable father but because at his core, there was something just not right with him.

It was entirely possible Gavin wasn't wired right. Maybe taking pleasure in the pain of others was part of his DNA. It could be that he just got off on finding people's weaknesses and exploiting them.

Sometimes, the reasons were elusive. People were who they were.

She wondered if there might be a way to find out more about his teenage years, if there were things he might have done that no one had—

Hang on, Anna thought.

When she'd sat down to make these notes, she'd had to open her laptop.

But I left my laptop open.

And then she remembered that she'd found Gavin behind her desk, supposedly looking at the books on the shelves, when she'd come into her office.

Six

Paul went immediately to the window that looked down onto the street. He peered through the blinds.

"Where?" he asked. "What car?"

Charlotte dumped her purse onto a chair and rushed over to join him. She looked between the slats.

"It was right—"

"There's no car there," Paul said. "Where was it exactly?"

"Right there. Right across the street. It's gone. It must have taken off."

"Who was he?"

Charlotte stepped back from the window "I don't know. Just some guy. I didn't get much of a look. The windows were tinted."

"What kind of car was it?"

Charlotte sighed. "It was kind of boxy. It was like the car you said you saw out there the other day."

Paul looked at her. "What are you talking about?"

Charlotte raised her eyebrows. "What was it? Saturday? When you said there was someone on the street watching us?"

"I . . . don't . . . Saturday?"

She nodded. "I was sitting right there." She pointed to one of four stools tucked under the kitchen island. "You were looking out the window wondering about a car. A station wagon. You said some guy got out, stood there for a second, and pointed right at you. Shouted your name."

Paul moved slowly back into the kitchen, turned, and leaned against the counter. He ran a hand over his chin. "I don't have any memory of that."

Charlotte approached him slowly. "Okay."

"When I told you this, did you see him?"

She shook her head. "I got to the window fast as I could, but there was no car there. But I couldn't help but remember that when I saw that car, right now."

"But that guy didn't get out?"

"No."

"Was he looking at the house?"

"Actually, not so much." She shrugged. "It could have been anybody. I shouldn't even have mentioned it." She shook her head. "God, you're starting to make *me* paranoid."

Paul visibly winced.

"I'm sorry, I shouldn't have said that," she said. "I totally take it back. It was—"

"Don't worry about it, really."

They said nothing for several moments. It was Charlotte who broke the silence with a tentative question. "How did it go today with Dr. White?"

Paul nodded slowly. "It was okay."

"You told her you're still having the nightmares?"

"Yeah. And I told her about my idea of facing this whole thing head-on."

Charlotte pulled out a stool and sat down. "What did she say?"

"She didn't try to talk me out of it. I told her you were on board with it."

"Did you tell her it was my idea?"

Paul frowned. "I didn't. I'm sorry. I should have given you credit."

She waved a hand. "Doesn't matter. I'm just glad she didn't shoot it down. If she had, maybe *that's* when you'd have told her it was my idea."

That brought a smile. "Anyway, when I got home, I actually got started."

Charlotte looked into his office off the kitchen, saw the open laptop. "That's great."

"I'm starting by reading all the news accounts of the trial. I want to know everything, including the things I forgot afterward. And anything I can't learn, I'm going to . . ."

"Going to what?"

"You know how, in *American Pastoral*, Philip Roth has his alter ego character, Nathan Zuckerman, write about this guy's life—he calls him 'the Swede'—and he starts with what he knows, but then when he gets to the parts he doesn't know, he imagines them? To fill in the narrative blanks?"

Charlotte looked at him and smiled. "Only you would use an example like that to try and explain something. I've never read that book."

"Okay, forget that part. And anyway, I'm no Philip Roth. But what I want to do is, write about this. The parts I know, and even the parts I don't know. Not to actually be published. I don't even know that I would want it to be published, assuming any publisher even cared. I'm thinking that writing it would be a kind of catharsis, I guess. I want to try to understand it, and I think that might be the way to do it. Imagine myself in Kenneth's head, what he said to those women, what they said to him."

"I'm not so sure in Kenneth's head is a place you want to be."

"I said, *imagine*." Paul saw hesitation in Charlotte's eyes. "What?"

"I know it was my idea, but now I'm wondering if it's such a good one. Maybe this is a really dumb thing to do."

"No, it's good," Paul said. "It feels right."

Charlotte went slowly from side to side. "You have to be sure."

"I am," he said. "I . . . think I am."

She slid off the stool, walked over to him, slipped her arms around him, and placed her head on his chest.

"If there's anything I can do to help, just ask. I have to admit, I'm alternately repulsed and fascinated by Hoffman. That someone can present as friendly, as someone who cares about you, but can actually be plotting against you. He didn't come across that way when I met him."

"You met Kenneth?" Paul asked.

She stepped back from him. "You know. From that faculty event we went to a couple of years ago, when

I thought he was coming on to me? How smooth he was? He wanted to read me a poem he'd written that afternoon, about how a woman is exquisitely composed of the most beautiful curves to be found in nature. I thought it'd be creepy, but God, it was actually pretty good, but then, I've never been much of a judge of poetry."

"I don't—when did you tell me this?"

Charlotte shrugged. "I don't know. More than once. Around the time it happened, and then, you know, since . . ."

"You'd think I'd remember something like that, I mean, if it involved you."

"Anyway, it's not like I got a case of the vapors and started going 'Ah do declare, Mistah Hoffman, you are getting my knickahs in a twist.'" She laughed and tried to get her husband to see the humor in it. But Paul looked troubled.

"I'm sorry. It worries me when I can't remember things."

Her face turned sympathetic and she wrapped her arms around him. "Don't worry about that," she whispered. "It's nothing." She squeezed him. "I nearly lost you."

He placed his palms on her back. "But I'm here."

"I feel . . . like I can't forgive myself."

Paul tried to put some space between them to look into her face, but she held him tight. "What are you talking about?"

"Before . . . before it happened, I wasn't a good wife to you. I—"

"No, that's not—"

"Just listen to me. I know I was distant, that I wasn't . . . loving. I wasn't there for you the way I should have been. I could offer all kinds of excuses, that I was all wrapped up with myself, wondering about my choices in life, whether my life was going the way I'd imagined it when I was younger and—"

"You don't have to do this," Paul said.

"All I was thinking about was me. I wasn't thinking about *us*. And then that horrible thing happened to you, and I realized . . ."

She pressed her head harder against his chest. He could feel her body tremble beneath his palms as she struggled not to cry.

"I realized I couldn't just wait around to receive what I thought was owed me. I realized that I had to give, that I hadn't been giving to you. Does that make any sense at all?"

"I think so."

She tilted her head up. Tears had made glistening,

narrow tracks down her cheeks. She wiped them away before managing a smile.

"Josh'll be here in a couple of days. Maybe, while we still have the house to ourselves . . ."

He smiled. "I hear you."

She gave him a quick kiss, broke free, and said, "How about a drink?"

He'd already had a prenoon beer, but what the hell. "Sure."

As she headed for the refrigerator she said, "I picked up a little something for you the other day."

"What?" he asked.

"You'll have to wait and see," she said.

He was about to press for details, but his phone alerted him to a text message. He dug it out of his pocket. It was from Hillary Denton, the dean of faculty at West Haven College, and read:

Sure, any time you want to come in I'm available.

Under his breath, he said, "What the hell are you talking about?" He scrolled up to look at the previous message.

Charlotte had the refrigerator open and was saying, "Did you get the vodka?"

Hillary's text had clearly been a reply to a message from him that read:

Can we talk sometime about my return in September?

Paul stared at the message. He had no memory of sending it.

"Earth to Paul," Charlotte said. "I asked you to pick up a couple of bottles of vodka? The mandarin flavor? I mentioned it last night?"

Paul looked up from his phone. "What?"

"Doesn't matter," Charlotte said. "Beer's fine. You want a beer?"

The drive home. The man in the car. Vodka. A text message to the dean.

Paul wondered what else might have slipped his mind he didn't even know about yet.

Seven

Gavin was breathing so shallowly he was hardly breathing at all.

He didn't want to wake her.

She was sleeping peacefully in her bed. Her name was Eleanor Snyder and, according to Dr. White's notes, she was sixty-six, widowed, and retired from her job as an X-ray technician.

Gavin had very little trouble getting into her Westfield Road home. It was a small, story-and-a-half place shaped something like a barn. He'd waited in the bushes across the street for the upstairs lights to be killed, then gave Eleanor another half hour to nod off.

He crossed the darkened street and peered through the window next to the front door, looking for the telltale red glow of a security system panel. He saw none.

He then tried the front door, but Eleanor had at least been cautious enough to lock it before she retired for the night. Gavin walked around the house until he found an accessible basement window.

Gavin crawled through and dropped down to the floor. He'd brought along a half-filled garbage bag, knotted at the top with a red, plastic drawstring. He worked his way quietly to the first floor, then found the stairs to the second. He took each step carefully. There was always one that creaked.

And sure enough, one did.

That was when he froze, held his breath, and listened. If Eleanor Snyder heard that creaky step, she'd get up and check it out. But Gavin heard no rustling of covers, no footsteps. What he could make out was soft, rhythmic snoring.

He followed the snores.

And now here he was, standing next to Eleanor Snyder's bed, looking down at her. There was enough light filtering in through the blinds to make out her flowered nightie, a copy of the latest Grisham on the bedside table. If only all the people whose homes he snuck into wore eye masks and stuffed those little plugs into their ears.

Could she be dreaming? And if so, was she dreaming about Bixby?

Bixby was not her late husband. Aaron had been her husband's name. Bixby had been her little schnauzer.

According to Dr. White's notes, after Aaron died, Eleanor funneled all her love—and grief—into that pooch. Bixby got her through those difficult times. It was Bixby who got her back out into the world.

Eleanor walked him around the neighborhood three or four times a day. Bixby didn't just keep her sane. He kept her in shape. She'd bought one of those extra long leashes that extended and retracted with the push of a button. That gave Bixby freedom to run in short bursts, which Eleanor was no longer up to.

She blamed herself for what happened. It wasn't really the driver's fault.

There was no way the driver of the Honda Accord could see that slender leash running horizontally out into the street, or that tiny dog that didn't even come up to her front bumper.

That had been six months ago.

Eleanor, so said the notes, could not forgive herself.

Gavin watched Eleanor breathe in and out. He'd tied the drawstring on the garbage bag too tight to loosen it, so he made an opening by ripping apart the plastic. Once he'd made a large enough hole, he reached in and took something out. He wadded up the empty bag and stuffed it into the back pocket of his jeans.

Gavin looked about the room for what he needed. It occurred to him to check the back of the bedroom door.

With a gloved hand, he moved the door three-quarters of the way closed. A bathrobe hung from a simple coat hook.

Perfect.

Gavin removed the robe from the hook, let it fall noiselessly to the floor, then replaced it with the item he had brought.

He slipped out of the room, closing the door behind him, thereby ensuring that the first thing Eleanor Snyder would see when she woke up was the surprise he'd left for her.

A small, dead dog. Hanging by its collar.

Eight

Anna White woke to a repetitive mechanical sound, something metallic sliding back and forth, as well as a television at very low volume. She threw back the covers, slipped on a robe, and went out into the second-floor hallway. She pushed open the door two down from hers, not worried about disturbing anyone.

"Morning, Dad," Anna said.

Her father, wearing blue pajamas and slippers, glanced her way and nodded. He was on a rowing machine, his hands firmly gripping the handles, sliding back, pulling his arms, gliding forward, then repeating the motion. Before him, atop the dresser, was a flat-screen television on which Wile E. Coyote was trying, once again, to catch the Road Runner.

Frank White's eyes were glued to the screen. He

grinned. "It's coming. Where the truck comes out of the tunnel that the coyote painted. It's simply surreal. Ha! There it is!"

The coyote was flattened.

He cackled, looked Anna's way again. "Wish to hell I'd worked on that one." He saw something in her eyes and said, "Did I wake you?"

"It's fine," she said.

"Chuck Jones was a genius, Joanie," he said, looking back at the TV. "I ever tell you what I told Walt when I met him?"

"Yes, Dad," Anna said. She could not be bothered to correct him about calling her by her mother's name. "Shall I put on the coffee?"

"Sure," he said, continuing to row. "I said to him, I said, 'Walt, even Pepé Le Pew could have kicked Mickey's ass.'"

"I know, Dad," she said, and headed down to the kitchen to start the day.

Frank White, Anna had to admit, was something else. Well into his eighties, he was in better shape than she was, at least physically. His arms were roped with muscle and, at 120 pounds, there wasn't an ounce of fat on the man.

If only he were half as fit mentally.

His short-term memory was slipping away, but his

recollections of years past, particularly those youthful ones he spent in California working as an animator at Warner Bros., were rich with detail. He'd retired from that world nearly thirty years ago, at which point Frank and Anna's mother, Joan, returned to Connecticut.

They filled their first fifteen years back with gardening and travel and socializing, but then Joan's health began to fail. It was a slow decline, ending in an extended period in a nursing home and finally a chronic care ward. She'd been dead three years now, and Frank had taken it hard.

Anna insisted her father move in with her.

It was not pure altruism on her part. She'd been on her own after she and her husband, Jack, split up two years before her mother's death. She'd taken back her name and thrown herself into her work, but she'd soon found herself spread thin. Having her father around could actually make her life a lot easier.

During the last few years of Joan's life, Frank had taken over the running of the household. Did the grocery shopping, made the meals, did the laundry, cleaned the house, kept track of the bills and the finances.

Anna made it clear to her father that taking him in was not some act of charity. He could look after *her*. She was so busy with her clients, local charitable causes, plus being on the Milford Arts Council, it would be a relief not to have to worry about domestic duties.

It was rocky at first. Even if Frank had not been grieving, it would have taken them a while to work into a groove. That took about six months. After that, things went great. Frank even had time to go back to golf, bought a rowing machine, renewed a long forgotten interest in gourmet cooking, all while Anna made a living for the two of them by counseling the confused, depressed, and troubled of the world. Well, of Milford and environs, anyway. Frank encouraged Anna to get back out into circulation, find herself a new husband, maybe even have kids—"It's not too late! Almost, but not quite!"—and when she did, he promised her, he'd find a place of his own.

She wouldn't hear of it. Anna liked her life. Maybe she didn't care about a husband and kids. She had her career, she had her dad, she had her house.

It was a stable, safe life.

But then, sixteen months ago, things slowly started to unravel.

Frank had a minor fender bender that could have been much worse—he backed into a Ford Explorer at the Walmart in Stratford, narrowly missing a woman pushing a four-month-old in a stroller. He became confused behind the wheel. One day, at the Stamford

Town Center, he spent four hours trying to find his car in the parking garage. He'd walked past it, Anna figured later, at least a dozen times. He confessed to her later that he'd been looking for the Dodge Charger he'd owned in the late 1960s.

He lost credit cards. One day, he headed out of the house without a shirt on.

More recently, he'd been calling her Joanie, and other times, when he realized who she really was, he asked to be taken to the nursing home to visit his wife. He'd get in the back of Anna's car, expecting to be taken there. So now, Anna was not only back where she was before her father moved in—running a household as well as doing her job—but taking care of her dad as well.

"Such is life," she'd say to herself.

And yet, in the midst of this, there could be moments of great clarity. Frank was often his best first thing in the morning. When he showed up in the kitchen, Anna put a mug of coffee in front of him as he sat down.

"That cartoon channel runs some of the best Warner Bros. stuff in the morning. They had so much more of an edge than that wholesome stuff Disney was doing back then. Wit and sophistication. Cartoons for adults."

Frank reached over to the counter for a pen and notepad that sat by the phone. He did some doodling with one hand, drank from the mug with the other.

"Lots of customers today?" he asked her. He never called them clients or patients.

"It's the weekend, Dad. But I wanted to talk to you about something."

"What's that?"

"It's not a good idea for you to be chatting with the people who come to see me."

Frank looked puzzled. "When do I do that?"

"Not often, it's true. But the other day, you were talking to this one patient. Gavin?"

Frank struggled to remember. "Uh, maybe."

"You were about to tie up your shoes?"

"If you say so, Joanie."

"It's just . . . he's not the kind of person you want to become familiar with."

"Why's that?"

She had been giving a lot of thought to Gavin ever since she'd found her laptop closed. Maybe she was mistaken. Maybe she *had* closed it before he'd arrived for his appointment, but she hadn't been wrong about seeing him behind her desk. Had he been looking in her computer and, when he'd heard her coming, closed it, out of reflex? And only remembered it had been open when it was too late to do anything about it?

She shook her head, ignoring her father's question. "It's just best if you do not engage with my clients."

Still doodling, he said, "Speaking of engaged."

"Dad."

"Come on, sweetheart, we need to talk about this. I'm dragging you down. We can't go on like this. I moved in to help you, and now you're the one helping me."

"Everything's fine here."

"Remember that cartoon where Bugs Bunny's up against Blacque Jacque Shellacque?"

"Uh . . ."

"Anyway, Jacque wants Bugs's bag of gold, but Bugs gives him a bag of gunpowder with a hole cut out of the bottom. The gunpowder leaves a trail, which Bugs lights, and blows up Jacque."

"I don't remember that one."

"Well, it doesn't matter. The thing is, my mind is that bag of gunpowder. A little leaking out every day. Pretty soon that bag'll be empty. You need to find a place for me. You need to start looking."

"Stop it, Dad."

He tore off the sheet of paper he'd been doodling on and handed it to his daughter. "There you go."

It was a poodle, done cartoon-style, with a face that looked remarkably like Anna's. Frank smiled, waiting for her approval.

"That's quite something," she said. "But my tail doesn't look like that."

Frank stared out the window for several seconds, then turned back to look at her. "I think I might hit some balls around in the backyard."

And we're out, Anna thought.

But wait.

He patted her hand and smiled. "What point is there in keeping me around now?"

She felt a constriction in her throat. "Because I love you, Dad."

"You need to get over that," he said, pushing back his chair. He grabbed his mug and left the kitchen.

Anna sat there, picked up the drawing of her as a poodle, looked at it, then got up and went to the counter. She opened a drawer and tucked the sketch in with several hundred others.

Nine

Paul stopped doing some online research when he heard the front door open and his son, Josh, shout: "Dad!"

Paul exited his office and headed for the top of the stairs in time to meet his son. He knew better than to expect a huge hug. Josh, backpack slung over his shoulder, gave his father the briefest of embraces and ran to the fridge.

"How was the train?" Paul asked.

Josh found a can of Pepsi, popped it, and said, "It was good. Mom went right down to the platform with me to watch me get on." He rolled his eyes. "I'm not a kid. I'm almost ten. I've taken the train before."

"She can't help it. She's a mom."

Josh shrugged, then said, "Charlotte got you something. She wouldn't let me put my bag in the trunk when she picked me up in case I saw it."

Charlotte had reached the top of the stairs. "No blabbing!"

"I don't even know what it is," Josh said, taking a drink.

"Just one of those a day," Paul said, pointing to the can. "You don't need all that sugar."

Josh displayed the can. "It's diet."

"Oh," Paul said, then to Charlotte, "What did you get me? Is this the thing you mentioned the other day?"

She smiled devilishly. "I want you and Josh to take a walk. Go down to the beach. Give me five."

Paul exchanged glances with Josh. "I guess we're getting kicked out."

Paul and Josh descended the steps, went out the front door, and rounded the house to reach the beach. The wind coming in off the sound was crisp and cool, but the midday sun cut the need for a jacket. It was early June, and the temperatures had been below average for this time of year. The water would have to warm up a lot before Josh would want to go in.

"How's your mom?" Paul asked.

"Fine."

"And Walter?"

Josh's stepfather.

Josh looked for a stone to throw into the water. "He's okay." He paused. "I like it in the city. There's tons to do."

"Okay," Paul said. It wasn't that he wanted his son to be miserable in Manhattan with his mother and stepdad. He wanted nothing but happiness for the boy. But it pained him some to think Josh had to endure the boring Connecticut suburbs to spend time with him.

"Walter's always getting free tickets to stuff, like baseball games and shows and stuff. In fact . . ."

"In fact what?"

Josh glanced up warily at his father. "Walter got tickets to tomorrow afternoon's Knicks game."

"Great. I hope he and your mom have fun."

"But so, like, they're going to pick me up tomorrow morning. I'd have taken the train but Walter's got some client in Darien he wants to see in person before heading back. So I'm just here for one night. Maybe I wasn't supposed to tell you. Mom talked it over with Charlotte. She's probably going to tell you after she gives you your surprise."

"Maybe *that's* the surprise," Paul said grimly. He shook his head slowly, feeling the irritation build.

This definitely should have been discussed with him. He was expecting to spend the entire weekend with his son. But he didn't want to take his anger out on Josh. He patted him on the back and said, "We'll sort it out."

"But I can go, right?" Josh asked. "I've only been to one other NBA game and I really liked it."

Paul suddenly felt very tired. He glanced at his watch. "I think it's been five minutes," he said.

When they got back to the kitchen, Paul immediately noticed his office door was closed. Charlotte stood before it, a smug look on her face, but it broke when she saw Paul's expression.

"What?" she asked. "You don't look happy."

"Did you know Josh was going back tomorrow?" he asked.

"Hailey mentioned it when she emailed me about when Josh's train would arrive."

"You couldn't have told me?"

She crossed her arms and waited a beat. "Maybe this isn't a good time."

Josh's face fell. "We're not doing the surprise?"

Charlotte stared at Paul. "It's your dad's call."

Paul looked at Josh, quickly sized up the disappointment in his face, and tamped down the anger he'd been feeling. "Sorry," he said. "Surprise me."

"Is it in there?" Josh asked. He looked ready to charge into the small study.

"Stay right there, buster," Charlotte said. Her look softened as she said to her husband, "I wanted to get something to inspire you as you . . ." She looked at Josh and decided against getting into all the details. "I wanted to celebrate your moving forward."

Paul smiled with curiosity. "Okay."

She aimed her thumb at the door. "Go on in."

Josh said, "Can I open it?"

"Yeah, okay," Paul said. To Charlotte: "Should I close my eyes?"

She shook her head.

Josh turned the knob and pushed the door open.

Sitting on the desk, beside the closed laptop and hidden beneath a tea towel adorned with Christmas trees, was something the size of a football helmet, although far less rounded.

"So it's a Christmas present," Paul said.

Charlotte shrugged. "It was the biggest dish towel I had, and it was too awkward to wrap properly. Take a guess."

Paul grinned. "I got nuthin'."

Josh had squeezed himself in front of his father, wanting to reach out and pull the towel away, but knowing he had to let his dad do it.

"Here goes," Paul said, grabbing the corner of the towel and flicking it back like a magician whipping out a tablecloth from a fully set dining room table.

Josh said, "What *is* it?"

"Oh, my God," Paul said. "It's amazing."

"You like it?" Charlotte said, putting her palms together, as though praying, the tips of her fingers touching her chin. "Seriously?"

"I love it."

For a second time, Josh asked, "What *is* it?"

"That," Paul told him, mussing his hair, "is a type-writer."

"A what?"

"You must have needed a crane to bring it in here," Paul said, running his fingers along the base of the machine. "It looks like it weighs a ton."

Charlotte did her best Muscle Beach pose. "Strrrong vooman. Like ox."

Paul dropped his butt into the computer chair and gave the antique a thorough examination.

"This is so funny," he said. "I was just thinking about one of these old typewriters."

"Seriously?" Charlotte asked. "I'm like a mind reader. Why were—"

Paul shook his head to suggest it didn't matter. Besides, he was too busy inspecting the machine to reply.

It was an Underwood. The name was stenciled onto the black metal just above the keys and, in much bigger letters, across the back shelf that would prop up a sheet of paper, had one been rolled in. The machine was almost entirely black, except for the keypad—Paul wondered if that was strictly a computer term—but anyway, all those keys, marked with letters and numbers and punctuation marks, each one perfectly ringed in silver.

"What does it *do*?" Josh asked.

Above the keys, a semicircular opening that afforded a view of the—Paul wasn't even sure what they were called, those perfectly arrayed metal arms that struck paper as one pounded on the keys. But there was a kind of beauty in how they were arranged, like the inside of a very tiny opera house. Those keys were the people, the paper the stage.

"It writes things," Paul said.

"How?"

"Grab a sheet of paper from the printer."

Charlotte said, "I tried it. There's still some ink in the ribbon, but I don't know if you can even buy type-writer ribbons anymore."

"Ribbons?" Josh said, handing a sheet of paper to his father.

"Okay," he said, taking the sheet and inserting it into the back of the machine. He twisted the roller at the end of the cylinder, feeding the paper into the typewriter until it appeared on the other side, just above where the keys would hit it.

"I don't get this at all," Josh said.

"Watch," Paul said. "I'm going to type your name."

He raised his two index fingers over the keys.

Chit chit chit chit.

"God, I love that sound," Paul said.

Josh watched, open-mouthed, as JOSH appeared, faintly, on the sheet of paper. "Whoa," he said as his father pulled the sheet out and handed it to him. "That's cool. But I still don't get it."

"This is what we used before computers," Paul said. "When we wanted to write something, we used this. And you didn't have to print out what you wrote, because you *were* printing it as you wrote it, one letter at a time."

Josh studied the machine. "But how does it go onto the Net? Where do you see stuff? Where's the screen?"

Charlotte laughed. Josh looked at her, not getting the joke.

Paul struggled to explain. "You know how if you want to write something on the computer, like, you use Word or whatever. That's what you would use this for. But that's all it did. You didn't surf the Web with it. There *was* no Web. You didn't figure out your mortgage on it, you didn't use it to read the *Huffington Post* or watch a show or look at cat videos or—"

"But what does it *do*?" Josh asked.

"This machine does one thing and one thing only. It lets you write stuff."

Josh was unable to conceal his disappointment. "So it's kind of useless, then. How old is it?"

Paul shook his head. "I've got no idea."

Charlotte said, "I looked all over it for a date and couldn't find one. But I'm guessing maybe the nineteen thirties, forties?"

Paul shook his head in wonder. "Who knows. But it's older than any of us in this room, that's for sure."

"Even Charlotte?" Josh asked.

"Josh!" Paul said, and shot his wife a look of apology.

"I'll get you for that," she said, giving the boy a grin.

Paul asked Charlotte, "What made you . . . why did you get this?"

She smiled. "I told you, I wanted to inspire you.

How many times have we been in an antique shop and you've stopped and looked adoringly at one of these? I know you love these old gadgets."

His eyes misted. "When I was a kid, we had a typewriter like this, well, it was a Royal, not an Underwood. But just like this, it weighed about as much as a Volkswagen."

"I can attest to that," Charlotte said. "I think there's more steel in that thing than in our stove."

Paul continued. "I liked to write stories, but writing them out by hand took so long. When I was ten, before every house had a computer, I asked my dad to show me how to use the typewriter. I got the world's fastest lesson. Your fingers go here, this one hits this key, this one hits *that* key, and so on. I remember him holding his hands over mine."

He put a hand over his mouth, took a moment to compose himself.

"Anyway, that was it. That was my lesson. Been typing ever since." He smiled wistfully. "All the bad habits I learned at that age, I still have." He ran his hand over the top of the typewriter. "Just think of all the things that may have been written on this. School essays, love notes, maybe letters from a mother to her soldier son fighting somewhere in France or Germany, if she wasn't into handwriting. A machine like this, it has a *soul*, you know?"

"What does that mean?" Josh asked.

Paul struggled to find a way to explain. He turned his son so he was standing directly in front of him.

"You know how—how do I put this—you see things with your eyes"—he pointed to Josh's—"and you take them in, and they're just *there*. Like, watching a bus go by or something like that. But other times, you see things, and you *feel* them in here." He placed his palm on the boy's chest. "Like, a beautiful sunset. Or an eagle, or even when you hear a magnificent piece of music."

Josh stared blankly. "I like buses," he said.

Paul looked at Charlotte with amused dismay.

She smiled. "I wasn't thinking you'd actually write on it. It's not exactly easy to do cut-and-paste with scissors and a bottle of glue. And you could wear out what's left of that ribbon and never get any replacements. I thought of it more like a work of art. Like I said, it's meant to inspire." She cast her eye about the tiny room. "If you can find any place for it."

"Oh, I've got a spot for it. And I like your idea. I'm already inspired. And considering what I've been researching lately, you could have hardly found something more appropriate."

Josh got into the chair and began tapping away madly at the keys.

Chit chit. Chit. Chit chit chit.

"I love you," Paul said, putting his lips to Charlotte's.

"Right back at ya."

Chit chit chit. Ding!

"Whoa!" Josh said. "What was that?"

"You have to hit the carriage return."

"The what?"

Paul reached around his son to hit the lever on the left side of the machine to move the cylinder back to the right. Josh resumed typing.

Chit chit chit chit.

"Where did you find it again?" Paul asked.

"Someone selling their house had a garage sale to clear out their stuff. Less stuff to pack, right? I stopped because, you know, you never know what you might find, and if they haven't found a new place yet, they might just need an agent, so I thought I might hand out my card. And then I spotted this little beauty and immediately thought of you."

"Well, I'm glad you—"

"*Ow!*"

They both turned to see Josh's right hand deep into the heart of the typewriter. His fingers were entangled in a collection of keys fighting to get to the ribbon.

"Everything's stuck!" he cried, looking at the antique as though it were a dog that had bit him.

"Hang on, hang on," Paul said. "The letters got jammed. It's not a big deal. Just let me carefully pull apart those—"

"It hurts!" Josh said. Before Paul could help him, Josh jerked his arm back to free himself. Blood spurted from the index finger of his right hand. The skin was torn on the side, just back of the nail.

"Shit!" Paul said as blood dripped onto the keys and the top of his desk.

"Why did it do that?" Josh asked.

"If you hit too many keys too fast—"

But Josh wasn't interested. He'd turned to Charlotte, who had grabbed a handful of tissues from a box on the desk and was wrapping them around her stepson's finger. "Come into the kitchen. We'll get you fixed up."

Paul watched as they left his cramped office, then at the blood-spattered typewriter.

Josh could be heard saying to his stepmother, "That thing sucks. You should have got him a new computer instead."

Ten

B ill Myers dropped by that evening with a folder full of real estate flyers that Charlotte had forgotten to bring home with her for an open house she was holding the following afternoon.

Paul went down and answered the door to let him in.

"How's it going?" Paul said.

"Good. Can you give these to Charlotte?"

"No problem. Come on in, have a cold one."

Bill hesitated, then said, "What the hell."

Bill was in his early forties, a full head of blond hair morphing into gray. When Paul first met him, back when they both attended UConn—the University of Connecticut—up in Storrs, east of Hartford, Bill was the classic jock and looked the part. Six-foot, lean, one of those classic chiseled jaws. Nearly twenty years later, he wasn't the athlete he once was but remained trim, keeping himself in shape by running five miles most days.

While always friends, they'd barely kept in touch—Christmas cards, the odd email, maybe meeting up for a drink every couple of years—but had renewed their connection since Charlotte joined the real estate agency where Bill worked. Up until Hoffman's attack on Paul, there had been a weekly squash game, and whenever Bill had a new girlfriend he wanted them to meet, the four of them would plan a dinner out.

Paul took two beers from the fridge and guided Bill through the living room to the balcony that looked onto Long Island Sound.

"Charlotte's upstairs, getting ready to head out tonight," Paul said as they sat down on modern Adirondack chairs. He tossed his bottle cap into an empty coffee can he kept nearby. "This one couple, she's shown them at least twenty places, but they want to go back one last time and see some house in Devon just off Naugatuck."

"I know it," Bill said. "Been on the market thirteen months. Handyman's dream. Someone should buy it for the lot, tear the place, and start over."

"Josh and I are gonna watch a movie. How's your weekend looking? Out with Rachel?"

Bill shook his head. "That's kind of cooled off. She thinks a guy who's been married once before is not a good prospect."

"I can't imagine why."

Bill grunted.

The glass door slid back and Josh stepped out.

"Hey, pal," Bill said, gripping the boy's shoulder and giving him a small shake. He spotted Josh's finger and said, "What'd you do there?"

"A typewriter bit me," he said.

Bill raised a puzzled eyebrow. Paul said, "A surprise from Charlotte. An old Underwood. Josh got his finger caught in it."

Bill nodded. "Okay. Old typewriters are becoming a thing. Not that I'd want to use one. I'm a fan of find-and-replace."

"We talking about women now?"

Josh chuckled.

The door slid open again and this time it was Charlotte. "Hey, Bill," she said as Josh scurried back into the house.

Bill turned around in his chair. "Left those flyers for your thing tomorrow on the counter."

"Thanks." She gave Paul an apologetic look. "I hope I won't be too late."

Paul smiled ruefully. "No problem."

Charlotte withdrew, sliding the glass door into the closed position.

"Uh, good-bye," Bill said.

Paul felt obliged to offer an apology. "She's got a lot on her mind. Me, mostly."

"How's it going with the shrink?"

The term brought a sigh from Paul. "Okay."

"Good. 'Cause we don't want you doing anything stupid."

Paul narrowed his eyes. "Christ, I'm not going to kill myself."

Bill leaned back in his chair and raised his palms as though under attack. "Sorry. It's just, you've kind of been on edge. Depressed, the nightmares, forgetting shit. Like the other day, I returned your call, and you're all 'What, I never called you' except you did."

Paul bristled. "Okay, yeah, I admit, the last eight months have not been the best. But I'm working through it. I've got a plan."

"Okay, great, that's all I wanted to hear." He smiled. "What you need is to get that head of yours fixed up so I can beat your ass again at squash. I'm suffering from the withdrawal of humiliating you."

"Fuck off."

Bill grinned. "Truth hurts, man." He paused. "So what's the plan?"

Paul hesitated. "I want to find out what makes Kenneth Hoffman tick."

Bill eyed him amusedly. "I can help you with that."

"Oh, yeah?"

"Yeah. He's a fuckin' psycho."

Later, after Bill had left, Josh hurriedly slid open the balcony door and said breathlessly to his father, "Don't you hear that?"

Paul, who'd been turning the pages of *The New Yorker*, taking in nothing more than the cartoons, said, "Hear what?"

Josh gave him a *"duh?"* look. So Paul listened. The sound had been there the entire time. He'd just been unaware of it. Music. Well, not really music. It was an endlessly repeating jingle.

Dee dee, diddly-dee, dee dee, dee-da, dee-da, dee da dee.

"Ice cream?" Josh said. "The ice cream truck?"

"Right!" he said, springing out of his chair. "I have to get my wallet."

Josh produced it in his upraised right hand.

By the time they hit the street, the truck was only half a block away. It was an old, rusted blue-and-white panel van with rudimentary drawings of ice-cream cones and sundaes and the words THE TASTEE TRUCK painted on the sides. Josh waved a hand to make sure the driver didn't miss them. The truck slowed with a rusty screeching of brakes at the end of the driveway.

"Whatcha want?" Paul asked as Josh scanned the menu board with wonder.

"Chocolate-coated cone," he said.

The driver moved from behind the wheel to the open bay on the side and asked, in a low monotone, "Yeah?"

Paul suddenly found himself unable to speak.

The ice cream man, not much older than twenty, looked like he ate a lot of what he sold. Thick, pudgy arms; a round face with soft, pimpled cheeks; hair cut so close to his head he was almost shaved bald. He was probably six feet tall, but looked even taller, towering over them from the serving window.

The name tag pinned to his ice cream–smeared apron read LEN.

Len asked, slowly, "What do you want?"

"Dad?" Josh said.

"Uh, two cones. Mediums," Paul said. "Dipped in chocolate."

"Okay," Len said.

Paul briefly turned and looked away while Len grabbed two empty cones, held them beneath the soft ice cream dispenser, pulled down on the bar, then gently waved each cone to create a swirling effect. Then he dipped them in melted chocolate, which instantly froze into a shell.

"Mister?" Len said.

Paul turned back. Len looked at him blankly as he leaned over and handed him the cones. Paul gave one off to Josh, then dug into his pocket for his wallet. Paul handed Len a ten.

"One second," Len said, going into a green metal cash box for change.

"Just keep it," Paul said, and led Josh away from the truck.

Len offered no thanks, returned to the driver's seat, and steered the Tastee Truck farther down the street, the jingle heralding his presence to the neighborhood.

"I haven't seen that guy before," Paul said.

"Yeah, he's new this summer," Josh said. "There was a different guy last year."

"I don't think he knew who I was."

"What are you talking about?" Josh asked.

"Never mind," Paul said. "Let's go back and watch a movie."

Josh had long wanted to see the Batman flicks, which Paul felt were a bit too mature and intense for a boy of nine, not counting the Adam West version. All the ones made this century—well, they didn't call him the Dark Knight for nothing—were violent and bleak and occasionally disturbing. But Paul was able to call up the 1989 one starring Michael Keaton, which, while bleak enough, was tamer than the more recent versions.

Josh was very quiet during the part where young Bruce Wayne's parents were murdered in the alley behind a theater.

"I don't think we should ever go out to a movie," he said, leaning into his father on the couch as the final credits rolled.

"It's okay," Paul said, mentally kicking himself for forgetting that central part of the crime fighter's backstory. "We don't live in Gotham City. We live in Milford."

"Bad things happen here," he said. "A bad thing happened to you."

He gave his son a squeeze. "I know."

"I hope I don't get nightmares," he said.

Paul grinned. "You and me both, pal."

Charlotte texted to report that she'd be late. Her clients had decided to put in an offer. Paul said he would say good night for her when he put Josh to bed. As he sat on the edge, about to turn off Josh's bedside table lamp, the boy said, "I'm sorry about tomorrow."

"That's okay."

"I don't even care that much about basketball. But a lot of my friends do, and I wanted to be able to tell them I went to a game."

"It's okay. The next weekend, when you're here longer, we'll do something special."

Josh reached for an iPhone and earbuds next to the bed.

"What are you listening to these days to help you get to sleep?" Paul asked.

"The Beatles."

"Seriously?"

Josh nodded. "They're pretty good. One of them's about a walrus."

"Don't strangle yourself on the cords after you fall asleep."

Josh put a bud into each ear, tapped the phone's screen. Paul leaned in, kissed his son's forehead, turned off the light, slipped out of the room, and closed the door.

As he came down the stairs to the kitchen he heard the front door open. Seconds later, a weary Charlotte appeared.

"Nightcap?" he said, opening the fridge.

"No, thanks," she said. "I just want to go to bed."

"Was the offer accepted?"

She shook her head, exhausted. "We spent nearly two hours on it, sorting out a closing date, inclusions, everything. And then, at the last minute, they got cold feet."

He smiled sympathetically. "Run you a tub?"

She shook her head. "The second my head hits that pillow, I'm dead. How's Josh?"

"We watched *Batman*." He grimaced. "The part where Bruce Wayne's parents die hit a little too close to home." He hesitated. "A weird thing happened."

"What?"

"We went out to the ice cream truck. Kenneth Hoffman's son was driving it."

"That's Hoffman's son? I've bought ice cream for Josh from him, too."

"It just felt . . . strange. I don't think he had any idea it was me. Not that he necessarily should have." He looked down. "I tell myself I want to face this business head-on, but then I see Hoffman's son and I can't look him in the eye."

"Coming to terms with what Kenneth did doesn't mean you have to confront his boy. What do they say about the sins of the father shall not be visited upon the son?"

Paul grinned. "Actually, I think it's the other way around."

Charlotte rolled her eyes. "You get my point."

"I do."

Charlotte sighed, then trudged upstairs. By the time Paul had tidied the kitchen and climbed the stairs to the bedroom, Charlotte was under the covers making soft breathing noises.

Paul slipped under the covers stealthily, taking care not to wake Charlotte. He reached over to the lamp and plunged the room into darkness.

In seconds, he was asleep.

It was just after two in the morning when he heard the sounds.

He became aware of them while he was still asleep, so when he first opened his eyes, and heard nothing, he thought he must have been dreaming.

There was nothing.

But then he heard it again.

Chit chit. Chit chit chit. Chit. Chit chit.

He immediately knew the sound. It was a new one to the household but instantly recognizable. One floor down, someone was playing with the antique type-writer in his cramped office.

He gently ran his hand across the sheet until he felt Charlotte there. So, it wasn't her. As if that would have made any sense, her getting up in the middle of the night to mess about with her gift to him.

That left Josh.

Paul squinted at the clock radio on the table beside him. It was 2:03 A.M. Why the hell would Josh go down and play with the typewriter now? Or at all, given that he'd hurt himself on it and professed to hate the thing.

Paul gently pulled back the covers, put his feet down to the floor, and stood. Wearing only his boxers, he walked out of the bedroom and into the hall, not turning on any lights.

Chit chit.

He went straight past Josh's closed door and down the stairs, keeping his hand on the railing. It wasn't just because of the dark; he was not fully awake and slightly woozy. When he reached the kitchen, the various digital lights on the stove, microwave, and toaster cast enough light that he could see where he was going.

The door to his small study was closed, and there was no sliver of light at the base. He turned the knob, pushed open the door far enough to reach around and flip the light switch, then pushed the door open all the way.

Josh was not there.

No one was there. The chair was empty.

But the typewriter was there.

There was no paper in it. The single sheet with *Josh* typed on it remained on the desk.

Paul stared at the scene for several seconds, then glanced back into the kitchen. The way he figured it, Josh must have heard him coming, ducked out, hid behind the kitchen island, then scooted back upstairs the second Paul stepped into his office.

Sure enough, when Paul went back upstairs and peeked into Josh's room, the boy was under the covers, eyes closed, buds tucked into his ears.

The little bugger.

Paul smiled to himself. He'd conduct a proper interrogation in the morning.

Eleven

P aul had been in his office for an hour, on his third cup of coffee and researching online what made supposedly good people do bad things, when Josh, still in his pajamas, came padding down the stairs to the kitchen.

Paul closed the laptop, came out, went to the fridge, and got out a container of milk. "Cheerios?" he asked his son.

Josh muttered something that sounded like a yes and sat at the table. Paul put a bowl of cereal in front of him, splashed on some milk, and grabbed a spoon from the cutlery drawer. Josh stared sleepily into the bowl as he scooped a spoonful of cereal and shoved it into his mouth.

"How are you this morning?" Paul asked, glancing at the wall clock. It was half past ten.

Josh made a noise that was little more than a soft grunt.

"You really slept in," his father said.

Josh glanced for a second at his father. Paul noticed there was still some sleep in the corner of his eyes. "It's Sunday."

"True enough. But you seem a little more tired than usual."

"I had bad dreams," Josh said, going back to his cereal. "We shouldn't have watched that movie."

"Sorry. I should have picked something else, but the thing is, almost any movie can remind us of something bad that's happened to us."

Charlotte appeared, both hands to one ear, attaching an earring. "Hey, you two," she said.

"Heading out already?" Paul said. "I thought your open house was at two."

"It is. But I have to make sure the house is presentable. Last time I was there the master bedroom floor was littered with laundry and there were half a dozen dog turds in the yard. And I want to pick up some frozen bread, put it in the oven."

Josh perked up. "Why?"

"Old real estate trick. Make the house smell nice."

She pulled out the glass carafe from the coffeemaker and frowned when she found it nearly empty.

"Sorry," Paul said. "I already went through a pot. I was up kind of early. Couldn't sleep." He tipped his head toward the study. "Thought I'd get back to it."

"How's it going?"

Paul shrugged. He slipped into a chair across from his son. Josh yawned, looked at the wall clock, and rested his spoon in the bowl. "I gotta get ready. Mom and Walter will be here soon."

He started to push back his chair but was stopped when Paul reached out and gently grabbed his wrist.

"So you want to tell me what you were up to in the middle of the night?"

"Huh?" Josh said.

"I heard you. Around two in the morning."

"What's this?" Charlotte said, putting a new filter into the coffeemaker and spooning in some ground coffee.

Paul said, "I thought you hated that typewriter, but you got up in the middle of the night to play with it."

"What?"

"I know what I heard," Paul said. "I know it wasn't Charlotte, because she was in the bed right next to me."

"It wasn't me," Josh said. "Why would I play with that stupid typewriter?"

"Come on, pal. You're not in trouble, except maybe for not being truthful with me now."

"I'm not lying," he said.

Paul gave him a look of disappointment. "Okay, Josh."

Charlotte, pouring water into the coffee machine, said, "I don't understand. You heard the typewriter in the night?"

"Yup," Paul said.

Charlotte gave him a quizzical look. "And it's somehow a big deal if Josh was messing around with it? It's built like a tank. He can't break it."

"It wasn't me," Josh said again. "I'm glad Mom is coming." He got up from the table and fled up the stairs to his room.

Charlotte gave her husband a look.

"What?" Paul said.

"Has it occurred to you that maybe you dreamed it? You heard some *tap tap tapping* in your sleep?"

Doubt crept across Paul's face.

"Okay, the first time I heard it, I was in bed, probably half-asleep."

"There you go."

Hesitantly, he added, "But then I got up and heard it again when I was going down the hall."

Charlotte slowly shook her head. "Your mind plays

funny tricks on you when you're half-awake, or half-asleep, that time of night. Maybe you heard something else. Some kind of house noise. A ticking radiator or something."

"This house doesn't have rads."

"Whatever." While the coffee brewed she took a seat at the table. "Look, you've been under an enormous strain lately. Don't take it out on Josh."

Paul ran a hand over his mouth and shook his head.

The doorbell rang.

Paul tipped his head back and shouted to the upper floor, "Josh! Your mom's here!"

"Early, as always," Charlotte said, returning to the coffee machine. "Walter's always in a hurry."

The doorbell rang again.

"Hold your horses," Paul said under his breath.

Then, from the front door one floor below: "Hello?"

Paul and Charlotte exchanged glances. "Did you lock the door when you came in last night?" Paul asked her quietly.

Charlotte grimaced. "I thought I had. Does Hailey have a key?"

Paul shook his head. "Josh does. Maybe she made a copy." He got out of the chair and reached the top of the stairs as Hailey appeared. Five-ten, short blond hair, jeans with artfully arranged threadbare patches, bracelets jangling from each wrist, hoop earrings the size of coasters. She gave Paul's wife a cold stare and said, "Charlotte."

"Hailey."

Paul nodded a silent hello to his ex, then called a second time for Josh. "Coming!" the boy shouted.

Outside, a horn honked.

"Jesus," Hailey said.

"Walter in a bit of a hurry?" Paul asked.

"When isn't he? There's not a damn thing he doesn't do in a hurry."

Charlotte snickered. Hailey, realizing her comment invited more than one interpretation, tried to recover. "Just getting out of the city was a nightmare. Even on a Sunday morning. We were stuck on the FDR for forty minutes. You know Walter and traffic. He totally loses it. And 95 was no picnic, either."

Hailey sighed then regarded her former husband with what seemed genuine concern. "How are you doing?"

"Okay," he said.

"Back to a hundred percent?"

"Getting there."

Hailey smiled. "That's good."

Josh came thumping down the steps, his backpack slung over his shoulder. He was heading straight for the stairs.

"Hey," Hailey said, "you gonna say good-bye to your dad?"

Josh mumbled a "bye" without turning around.

"That was a bit lame," his mother said.

"Dad says I'm a liar," he said, holding his position at the top of the stairs to the first floor.

"What?" Hailey asked. "And what happened to your finger?"

"It's nothing," Paul said. "Josh, I never said you were a liar." Josh glared at him without comment. "I just—look, come here."

The boy moved his way as though his running shoes had lead soles. Paul said, "Maybe I was wrong."

"Maybe?" Josh said, then spinning on his heels and disappearing down the stairs.

Hailey gave her ex-husband a reproachful look but voiced no criticism. "Good-bye, Paul," she said, then, almost as an afterthought, glanced at his wife. "Charlotte."

Charlotte nodded.

Once they'd heard the front door close, Paul shook his head and said, "Shit."

Twelve

While Charlotte hosted her open house, Paul spent much of the afternoon cloistered in his office. He read more articles online about Kenneth Hoffman, and when he thought he'd found pretty much everything on the subject, including several video segments from local news stations, and an item on that NBC show *Dateline*, he broadened his search to include think pieces on why people do bad things.

That covered a lot of territory. Why do people lie? Why do they steal? Why do they have affairs? And, most important, why do they kill?

He scanned articles until he felt he would go blind, and by the end of it, he had no clearer sense of why Hoffman murdered those two women. Paul found Hoffman's motivation to kill *him* the simplest to explain.

Paul was a witness. He had seen those two women in the back of the Volvo. Hoffman had to kill Paul if he was to have any chance of getting away with his crime.

Paul thought he would like to talk to him about it.

Face-to-face.

He thought he was up to it. His reaction to un-expectedly seeing Kenneth's son, Leonard, was not, Paul believed, an indicator of how he'd react to sitting down with the killer of two women, if that could be arranged. For one thing, he'd be prepared.

He was about to do a search on how one arranged a visit with an inmate when his thoughts turned to Josh.

He'd really botched things with his son that morn-ing. There really was no reason for Josh to lie about tapping away at the typewriter in the middle of the night. And it didn't make much sense for him to have done it in the first place. He hadn't gone near the thing since catching his finger in it.

He had to accept that there was only one logical explanation: he'd dreamed it.

Yes, he'd told Charlotte he'd continued to hear the *chit chit chit* as he went down the hallway, but maybe he hadn't shaken the dream by that point. Maybe he was half sleepwalking.

What pained him was that he and Josh had had such a nice—albeit short—time together, aside from the troubling aspects of the Batman movie. And Paul had sabotaged it at the end.

Damn it.

But Paul was pretty sure he could fix things with Josh. He'd make this right. The next time Josh came out from the city, they'd do something really special. Maybe go for a drive to Mystic, check out the aquarium.

Maybe Charlotte would even want to come.

Things definitely seemed better with her. They'd hit a few bumps in the road, but if there was any upside to his nearly getting killed, it was that it had made Charlotte reassess not just their marriage, but also the expectations she had for herself. As she'd told him more than once since the incident, she'd been questioning where she was in her life. Was she where she'd hoped she'd be ten years ago?

While she was doing respectably as a real estate agent, it had never been her goal. She'd entertained, at one time, the idea of a career in, well, entertainment. Living in New York, she'd done off-*off*-Broadway, even had three lines one time as a day care operator in a *Law & Order* episode. (Paul suspected Charlotte had actually gone on a date or two with one of the stars, on the *Law* side, but she would never confirm nor deny.) Sadly, she never got the big break she'd strived for and reached the point where she had to make an actual living. She'd held sales jobs, worked hotel reception. When Paul met her, she was the early-morning manager of a Days Inn. So, where her career was concerned, she had settled.

If there was little glamour in being a real estate agent, there was even less in being married to a West Haven College professor. Yes, it was a decent place to teach, but it wasn't Harvard, and it lived in the shadows of nearby Yale and University of New Haven. If Charlotte had ever viewed what he did as a noble calling—molding young minds into leaders of tomorrow, ha!—Paul doubted she did anymore. Before the attempt on his life, she'd rarely asked him about his work, and why would she? It was boring. What was there for him to aspire to now? Where did one go next? The dizzying heights of department head?

So this was what Charlotte's life had become. Selling houses in a drab Connecticut town, married to a man of limited ambition.

And then there was the baby thing.

Paul had not brought up the subject in a long time, but he'd hoped he and Charlotte would one day have a child. Had he stayed with Hailey, he was sure Josh would have ended up with a baby brother or sister. Hailey had as much as said she and Walter were trying.

But Charlotte had not warmed to the idea of becoming a mother herself.

Well, fuck all that.

This was a new day, Paul told himself. This was the day when he took control. This was the day when he stood up to the demons. This was the day when he would start rebuilding himself and his marriage.

He was going to tackle this Hoffman thing. He was going to write something. He was going to write something beyond the notes he'd already made. He was going to write something *good*. He didn't yet know what shape it would take. Maybe it would be a memoir. Maybe a novel. Maybe he'd turn his experience into a magazine piece.

It had everything.

Sex. Murder. Mystery.

Coming back from the brink of death.

The fucking thing would write itself, once he decided which direction to take it in. This was the key to putting his life and marriage back together. He wasn't doing this just for himself. He was doing it for Charlotte. He wanted her to see that he could be strong, that he could get his life back.

Enough of this sad-sack bullshit.

Maybe he could even be the man she'd want to have a child with.

But hey, let's take things one step at a time.

Paul reflected on how he'd come across these last few months. Christ, even Bill seemed worried he might kill himself. Yes, he'd been depressed. He'd been traumatized not just by the event itself—the nightmares, the anxiety—but also by physical manifestations. Headaches, memory lapses, insomnia. Who wouldn't be depressed?

But suicidal?

Had he come across as that desperate? Maybe.

"See how you are when you've got Kenneth Hoffman visiting your sleep every night," he said to himself.

Shit.

Of course.

The typing he'd thought he'd heard was clearly part of a Hoffman nightmare. Paul must have been dreaming about those two women typing out their apologies. Charlotte's gift of that antique Underwood had triggered a Hoffman dream that zeroed in on that aspect of his crime.

That was the *chit chit chit* he'd heard in the night. Jill Foster and Catherine Lamb tapping away.

Paul got out his phone. Josh was very likely at the game now, so Paul wasn't going to call him. But Josh might see a text.

Paul quickly wrote one.

Hey pal. Luv you. Sorry about this morning. Ur Dad was a jerk. Hope u r having fun at the game.

He sent it. Paul stared at the phone for a long time, waiting for the dancing dots to indicate his son was writing him a reply.

When none came after three minutes, Paul put his phone back into his pocket.

Thirteen

"So, Gavin, how did you spend your weekend?" Dr. Anna White asked as the two of them settled into their respective chairs in her office.

Gavin appeared thoughtful. "Reflecting."

Anna's eyebrows raised a fraction of an inch. "Reflecting?"

He nodded. "About the hurt I've caused, and if there's any way I can make amends."

"Amends."

"Yes. Do you think it would be possible to arrange a meeting with the people I've wronged so that I might apologize?"

Anna eyed him warily. "I don't know that a face-to-face would be the way to go. I think it could end up badly for all concerned."

Gavin, innocently, asked, "How so?"

"I think the woman whose cat you hid would be too fearful, and that father you called . . ." At this point she shook her head. "I hate to think what he might try to do to you if you were in the same room."

"You might be right," he said. "Maybe I should write something instead."

"We'll get to that. But besides reflecting, what else did you do with your weekend?"

"Not much," he said. "Well, I worked Saturday. I usually work evenings at Computer World, but they're not open Saturday night, so I did a day shift."

"Did you work Friday night?"

Gavin nodded. "I did."

"What time did your shift end?"

"Nine," he said slowly. "Why are you asking me?"

Anna hesitated. "A troubling thing happened to someone on Friday night."

"Someone? You mean, someone you know?"

Anna slowly nodded.

"Another one of your patients?" he asked.

Anna studied him for several seconds, weighing how to proceed. She ignored his last question and continued. "Someone did a very sick, very cruel thing to her."

"This person you know who might be a patient," Gavin said.

"Her dog was recently run over by a car. Someone snuck into her house and hung a dead Yorkshire terrier in her bedroom. According to the tag, the dog had belonged to a family in Devon. They were making up the missing posters when the police notified them."

Gavin sat back in his chair and put a hand over his mouth. "Wow. That's pretty sick."

"Yes," Anna said. "It is."

"So, you're telling me this why?" he asked.

Anna hesitated. "The other day, when I came in here, you were standing over there. Behind my desk."

Gavin looked at her blankly, then shrugged. "Uh, I guess."

"What were you doing over there?"

Gavin glanced over to that part of the room. "Just looking at the books."

"You're interested in psychology texts?"

Another shrug. "You don't know what a book actually is until you look at it." He grinned. "You could use a few more graphic novels."

"When you were over there, Gavin, did you look at my computer?"

"Huh?"

"My laptop. Were you looking at my laptop?"

Gavin's eyes narrowed. "Holy shit. Let me guess. This lady with the dead dog hanging on her door, she *is* a patient, and you think I was fucking with her head?"

"I didn't say the dog was hanging from her door."

Gavin blinked. "Yes, you *did*. That's exactly what you said. Jesus Christ, you're actually accusing me of this."

Anna hesitated. "I haven't accused you of anything, Gavin."

"Of course you are. What did I do this weekend? Where was I Friday night? This is unbelievable. I come here for *help*. I come here, *trusting* you to help me deal with a personal crisis, and what happens?" He shook his head. "This is fucking unbelievable. So I guess every time something bad happens to anyone in Milford, I'm immediately the number one suspect. Was there a hit-and-run this weekend? A bank robbery? Did someone steal a candy bar from the 7-Eleven? Do you think I had anything to do with those things, too?"

Anna had begun to look slightly less sure of herself. "You have to admit, Gavin, that what happened to that woman is not unlike the stunt you pulled, the one that landed you here."

"I swear, I don't even know who that woman is. What's her name?"

"I can't tell you that."

"Yeah, well, if you think it's me, you might as well, since I'd already know it, right? But I don't. If I'm the prime suspect, why haven't the police been to see me?"

Anna said nothing.

"So wait, not only are you accusing me of doing this horrible thing, but you think I'm snooping around in your computer? Checking out who comes to see you and what their problems are?" He shook his head and adopted a wounded expression. "Wow. So this is the kind of help and understanding I'm getting. I'm sure going to get better coming to see you a couple of times a week."

"Gavin—"

He stood. "I can't do this."

"Gavin, killing an animal is a sign of a more serious issue than any we've dealt with so far. You need to understand that—"

"Understand what?" he shouted. He jabbed a finger in her direction. "I should report you or something. There must be some kind of ethics commission or something for you people. They need to know!" He stood.

"Gavin, sit down!"

"No, I think I've had just about—"

The door suddenly swung open. Paul Davis stood there, looked quickly at Gavin, then at Anna.

"I'm sorry," he said. "I heard—are you okay, Dr. White?"

She got out of her chair. "We're fine here, Paul."

"I heard shouting and—"

"Whatever your fucking problem is," Gavin said to Paul, "don't expect *her* to help you."

Paul gave Gavin a long look. "You need to calm down, buddy."

"Buddy?" Gavin said. "Are we buddies?" He regarded Paul curiously, as if wondering whether they had met before. "You're Paul? Did I hear that right?"

Slowly, Paul said, "Yeah."

"Well, Paul, good luck."

He started for the door so quickly that Paul didn't have time to step out of his way. Gavin put his hands on the front of his jacket to toss him to one side, knocking Paul's head into the jamb.

"Shit!" Paul said, touching his head for half a second, but just as quickly pushing back. Gavin stumbled from the office to the small waiting room.

"Asshole," Gavin said.

Now they were both pawing at each other, each trying to grab the other by a lapel so as to make it easier to land a punch with a free hand.

"Gavin, stop it!" Anna screamed.

They stopped, looked in unison at her. As each released his grip on the other, Gavin turned and ran for the door.

"Paul, I'm so sorry," Anna said.

He brushed himself off, as though some of Gavin had somehow stayed with him. "I'm okay."

"Your head," she said. "Did you hit your head in the same spot?"

He touched it again. "No, it's okay. I'm fine. What about you?"

"I'm okay," she said, then frowned.

"What the fuck is *his* problem?" Paul asked, glancing at the door through which Gavin had departed. "What was his name? Gavin?"

"I think I just handled something very badly."

"What?"

She shook her head. "Nothing. Mr. Hitchens is my problem, not yours. Do you still want to talk? I'll understand if all this—"

"I'm okay, if you're okay."

"I just need a minute," she said, taking her seat.

"You're shaking," Paul said. "We don't have to do this."

"No, no, we do. What just happened here, it's still nothing compared to what you've been through." She sat up straight, raised her chin, and said, "I'm ready."

"You're sure?"

A confident nod to assure him she was back on track. "So, tell me what's happened since we last spoke."

He filled her in on his online research and how it was having an empowering effect, although it hadn't stopped the nightmares. He told her that Charlotte's gift of an antique typewriter had triggered a bizarre dream that seemed so real, he ended up blaming his son for something he clearly had not done.

"I texted him an apology. It took him the better part of a day to reply." He paused, reflecting. "Do I seem borderline suicidal to you?"

"Why would you ask that?"

"It was something a friend said. He seemed worried I might do something stupid."

"I would say no," Anna said. "But you'd tell me if your thoughts were trending in that direction?"

"Of course." He also told her about not remembering his drive home one day, forgetting about texts he'd sent, other memory lapses.

"When do you see the neurologist again?"

"Couple of weeks." Another pause. Then, "Do you know anything about visiting someone in prison?"

"Not much."

Paul nodded. "From what I read on the state website, the inmate needs to put you on a list. Unless you're, you know, a police detective or a lawyer or something."

"You still want to see Kenneth Hoffman."

Paul bit his lip. "I think so. I know closure is a huge cliché, but a sit-down with him might provide some. You always hear it on the news. How the family of a murder victim gets closure on the day the accused is convicted."

"I'd say that's something of a myth," Anna said. "But I won't stop you from looking into a visit. In the meantime, you can think about what you'd want to say to him. What you'd want to ask him."

"I'd like to know if he's sorry."

Anna smiled wryly. "Would it make a difference?"

Paul shrugged. "If I can get in to see him, I don't want to go alone."

Anna nodded. "You'd want to take Charlotte."

"No. I'd want you to come."

Anna's eyebrows went up. "Oh."

"I don't know if I could come back here and give you an accurate account of what happened. Having you there to observe could be helpful."

Anna appeared to be considering it. "I don't normally do house calls."

Paul grinned. "You mean, *Big* House calls."

When Paul went out to his car, he could not find his keys. Anna said if she found them, she'd let him know.

He called Charlotte, who picked him up at Anna's, drove him home, and unlocked the door. Once he had his spare keys, Charlotte drove him back to Anna's so he could retrieve his Subaru.

That night, over dinner, he told Charlotte about what had happened at Anna's before his session had started.

"Some people," he observed, "are even more fucked-up than I am."

They killed off a bottle of chardonnay while watching a movie. At least, part of one. Halfway through, Charlotte ran her hand up the inside of Paul's thigh and said, "Is this movie boring or what?"

"It is now," he said.

When they turned the lights out shortly after eleven, Paul thought, *Things are getting better.*

And then, at six minutes past three, it happened again.

Chit chit. Chit chit chit. Chit. Chit chit.

Fourteen

Before the sounds of the Underwood reached him, Paul had been dreaming.

In the dream, he has a stomachache. He's on the bed, writhing, clutching his belly. It feels as though something is moving around in there. Something *alive*. It's like that *Alien* movie, where the creature bursts out of John Hurt's chest as the crew of the *Nostromo* eat lunch.

Paul pulls up his shirt, looks down. There's something in there, all right. There's something poking up from under the skin. And then, as if a zipper ran from his ribs down past his navel, he opens up. But there's no blood, no guts spilling all over the place. His belly opens up like a doctor's bag.

Paul looks at the gaping hole in his body and waits.

What come up first are fingers. Dirty fingers with chipped nails. Two hands grasp the edges of his stomach. Something—someone—is pulling itself out.

Holy shit, I'm having a baby, Paul thinks.

Now there's the top of a person's head. It's Kenneth Hoffman. Once his head clears Paul's stomach, he looks at Paul and grins. He's saying something, but Paul can't make out what it is.

It turns out he's not saying actual words. He's making a sound. The same sound, over and over again.

Chit chit chit. Chit chit.

Paul reaches down, puts his hands over Kenneth's face. He doesn't know whether to push Kenneth back inside himself, or try to drag out the rest of him. He feels Kenneth nibbling at his fingers.

Chit chit chit. Chit chit.

Paul opened his eyes. He was breathing in short, rapid gasps. He touched his hand to his chest and found it wet. He'd broken out in a cold sweat. He craned his neck around to look at the clock radio glaring dimly at him from the bedside table.

3:06 A.M.

He didn't want to close his eyes and return to that nightmare. Slowly, so as not to disturb Charlotte next to him, he swung his legs out of the bed and onto the floor.

He decided to take a leak.

As his eyes adjusted to the darkness, he looked at Charlotte. She was sleeping with her back to him, head on the pillow, hand slipped beneath it. He could just barely make out her body slowly rising and falling with each breath.

Dressed only in a pair of boxers, he padded silently across the floor to the bathroom and closed the door. The plug-in night-light glowed dimly.

He lifted the toilet seat, drained his bladder, cringed as he flushed, hoping the noise wouldn't be too disruptive. He rinsed his hands at the sink and dried them, waiting for the toilet tank to refill before opening the door.

The tank refilled, and silence again descended.

As his fingers touched the doorknob, he heard it.

Chit chit. Chit chit chit.

He held his breath.

I am not dreaming. I am awake. I am absolutely, positively, awake.

It was the same sound from the other night. A typing sound.

He waited for it to recur, but there was nothing. Slowly, he turned the knob, opened the door, and took a step out into the hallway. He froze, held his breath once again.

Still nothing.

All he could hear was the distant sound of the waves of Long Island Sound lolling into the beach, and Charlotte's soft breathing. Could something else have made a noise that sounded like keys striking the cylinder? Something electrical? Water dripping somewhere in the house? Maybe—

Chit chit.

A small chill ran the length of Paul's spine. He wanted to wake Charlotte. He wanted her to hear this, too. But waking her would also create a commotion. Whoever was fooling around with that typewriter— and clearly it was not Josh, who was miles away in Manhattan, but it had to be *somebody*—was going to stop once they heard talking on the floor above.

Paul wanted to catch whoever it was in the act.

No, wait. He should call the police.

Right. Great plan. *Hello, officer? Could you send someone right over? Someone's typing in my house.*

Paul reached the top of the stairs, then tiptoed down, one soft step at a time. When the house was rebuilt after Sandy, a new staircase had gone in, and there wasn't a single squeak in the entire flight.

As he reached the second step from the bottom, he heard it again.

Chit chit. Chit chit chit.

He looked across the kitchen to the closed door of his study. There was no light bleeding out from below it. Just like the other night. How was someone supposed to mess around with that Underwood in total darkness?

A miniflashlight. Sure. Whoever was in there wasn't going to want to attract attention by turning on the lights.

Yeah, like that made sense. They were already attracting attention with the typing.

Paul moved barefoot across the floor. As he closed the distance between himself and the door, he wondered whether he needed some kind of weapon. As he sidled past the kitchen island, he carefully extracted a long wooden spoon from a piece of pottery filled with kitchen utensils.

He had a pretty good idea how ridiculous he looked, but the spoon would have to do. You went into battle with what was at hand.

Paul reached the door, gripped the handle. With one swift motion, he turned and pushed.

"Surprise!" he shouted, reaching with his other hand to flick the light switch up.

And just as it was when he thought Josh had been fooling around in here, the room was empty.

The typewriter sat where it had been since Charlotte bought it for him, seemingly untouched. No paper rolled into it.

Paul stood there, blinked several times. "What the fuck," he said to himself. He scanned the room, as if someone could hide in a place that wasn't any bigger than a closet.

Suddenly, struck by an idea, he ran to the steps that led down to the front door. Someone could be making a run for it. Quietly, for sure, but did anything else make sense?

Paul ran his hand along the wall, hunting for the switch. He flipped it up, illuminating the stairs and the door at the bottom.

There was no one there. From where he stood, he could see the dead bolt on the door turned to the locked position.

In his rush, his left foot slipped over the top step and dropped to the next, throwing him off balance. He canted to the right, reaching frantically for the railing to break his fall, but missing it altogether. His butt hit the top step, then bumped down two more, hard, before he came to a shuddering stop.

"Fuck!" he shouted. He suddenly hurt in more places than he could count. Butt, thigh, foot, arm.

Pride.

Upstairs, Charlotte shouted. "Paul! Paul!"

Wincing, he yelled back, "Down here!" He grabbed his right elbow, ran his hand over it delicately. *"Jesus!"*

He heard running on the upper floor, then thumping down the stairs. "Where are you?"

Charlotte sounded panicked.

"Down here," he said, struggling to his feet. His boxers had slid halfway down his ass, and he gave them a tug up, hoping to preserve what little dignity he had left. She arrived in the kitchen, her white nightgown swirling around her like a heroine in a romance novel.

"What's happened? Did you fall? Are you okay? What's going on?"

Instead of telling her, Paul wondered whether there was something worse than nightmares and memory loss.

Going batshit crazy.

Fifteen

The sun wasn't even up, and her dad was at it already.

Anna White, dressed in an oversize T-shirt that hung to her knees, was awakened not by her alarm but by the sound of the rowing machine. She tossed back the covers and padded down the hall to her father's room. She gently pushed open the door. Frank, in his pajamas, was stroking away on the machine, watching the cartoon channel.

"Dad," she said softly, "it's five-thirty."

Anna believed the cartoons put her father into a kind of trance, keeping him from any awareness of how long he had been on the machine. She was convinced he was going to have a heart attack at this rate.

He either didn't hear her, or had chosen to ignore

her. He laughed as Daffy Duck took a shotgun blast to the face, spinning his bill to the other side of his head.

"Dad," Anna said, stepping forward, putting a hand on his upper arm. She was amazed at how hard it felt. Her father's head jerked in her direction.

"What?"

"You should go back to bed. It's too early to be up. It's sure too early to be up doing this."

"This one's not over."

The remote was on the floor. She knelt down to reach it, hit the POWER button. The screen went black.

"Why'd you do that?"

"Dad, please. Go back to bed."

"Not tired. Gotta take a whiz," he said, getting off the machine and walking down the hall. Anna sat on the edge of his bed, waiting for him to return. He wandered back in after a couple of minutes, a dark coaster-size stain on the crotch of his pajama pants.

Always hard to get that last drop, Anna thought.

She stood, allowing her father to get into the bed. Then she plopped herself back down on the edge once he had his head on the pillow.

"You going to read me a story?" he asked.

She felt a twinge of fear. Was he joking, or did he think he was five years old?

"Something raunchy'd be nice," he said, grinning.

Okay, a joke.

"No, I am not going to read you a story," she said. He hadn't called her Joanie, so maybe this was one of his moments of clarity. She hoped so.

"I'm not going to get back to sleep, you know," he said. "I'm usually up by six, anyways."

"Yeah. Who am I kidding."

Frank rubbed Anna's arm affectionately. "Sorry if I woke you up."

"Don't worry about it, Dad." It struck her that he seemed very much with it at this moment. "Since we're both wide awake, let me ask you something."

"Okay."

"You were always my go-to guy when I was wondering what to do with my life."

Frank waited.

"I wonder if I'm in a rut," Anna said. She then added quickly, "And not because of you. This has nothing to do with you. I'm talking about my work. It's interesting, and I like it, but there are times when I need to get out of my comfort zone."

Frank nodded.

"I've got this one patient, doesn't matter who, but he wants to set up a meeting, in prison, with the man who tried to kill him. And he wants me to go with him."

Frank looked intrigued. "Wow."

"Yeah. I'm not sure he's in the right frame of mind for an encounter like that, but he seems pretty determined, so it might be better if I were with him."

"I think you should go," her father said. "Sounds damn interesting."

"Yeah," she said, nodding. "I shouldn't always just play it safe, staying in the office."

Her father blinked at her several times. She wondered whether she was losing him.

"Isn't that why you asked me to move in? To feel safer?"

She gave his hand a squeeze. "It was one of the reasons. A good one, too."

"It made me feel safer, too." He smiled in a way that seemed almost childlike. "I like that feeling. It's a warm feeling."

Anna patted his hand. "I'm gonna have a shower, and then I'll start the coffee."

Her father's brow wrinkled slightly, as though he was considering something.

"What is it?" Anna asked.

"Just wondering if I need to pee again."

She grinned. "I think only you know for sure."

He thought one more second, then said, "No, I'm good."

She looked back at him as she was stepping into the

hall, and his eyes had shut. In two seconds he appeared to have fallen back asleep.

The shower could wait, Anna thought.

She returned to her bedroom and crawled back under the covers. It didn't take her much longer to nod off than it had taken her father.

So she was out cold when the police stormed the house five minutes later.

Sixteen

"So what'd you tell her?" Bill asked, sitting on the lockerroom bench, lacing up his shoes. "What'd you tell Charlotte?"

Paul shrugged, twirling the squash racket in his hand, waiting for Bill to get ready. "I told her I thought I'd heard someone knocking."

Bill chortled. "What, like Girl Scouts going door-to-door selling cookies in the middle of the night?"

"Like someone trying to get in."

Bill shook his head. "Are you sure you're up to this?"

"I want to get back to doing the things I used to do."

"Yeah, but *this*?" Bill held up his own racket. "Doctor gave you the okay?"

"Didn't ask," Paul said. "I want to hit the ball, move

around. I'm not going to do anything heroic. The ball lands in the corner, I'm not going in after it."

"So I'll take it easy on you," Bill said. "Like always."

"Fuck you."

They walked out of the locker room and into the West Haven College athletic facility. They strolled past exercise machines and an indoor track before they got to the squash courts. There were five, all backed with glass walls for the benefit of spectators.

"Does Charlotte know you're doing this?" Bill asked.

"No."

"This is a bad idea."

"I'm telling you, I'm fine."

Two women were playing in the court they had booked. Bill glanced up at a wall clock. "They've still got two minutes. Okay, so Charlotte finds you on your ass on the stairs and you say you heard someone at the door, but there *was* no one at the door."

"Isn't that what I said?"

"Why didn't you tell her the truth?" Bill asked, his eyes on the two women in the court.

"I had already accused Josh of messing with the typewriter in the middle of the night. What's Charlotte going to think if I tell her I heard the same thing again?"

"That you're losing it?"

"Yes, thank you."

"But you're telling *me* what you really heard. Suppose *I* think you're losing it?"

"Do you?"

Bill sighed. "I haven't got any other explanation." He tapped the edge of his racket on the glass. When the women turned around, he pointed to an imaginary wristwatch. The women ended their game and exited. One of them gave a long smile to Bill as she blotted her neck with a small towel.

"You're as bad as Hoffman," Paul said as the woman headed for the locker rooms.

"Hey," Bill said, "that's low. He was married. I'm not."

They ducked through the low door and entered the court.

"So you *do* think I'm losing it," Paul said.

"I'm not saying that," Bill said. He was holding the ball. He tossed it a couple of feet into the air and whacked it against the far wall.

Paul returned the serve. "What are you saying?"

Bill, swinging, said, "You've been totally stressed-out and this is how it's manifesting itself." The *pings* of the ball bouncing off the walls echoed within the court. "There's no evidence anyone was in the house, right?"

Paul swung, hit the ball. "Right."

"The door was locked, you didn't see anyone, you didn't hear anyone running down the stairs."

Paul ran to the right side to hit the ball. "Yeah."

"So no one was there, and you couldn't have heard what you thought you heard. Which means one of two things. You heard something else that *sounds* like that typewriter, or you heard it in your head."

Bill went into the corner for the ball as Paul said, "What else sounds like a manual typewriter?"

"So you dreamed it."

"I didn't. I was awake." He let the ball sail past him.

Bill shrugged. "I don't know what to tell you. Are we stopping?"

"I'm feeling a little light-headed," Paul said, looking ashamed to admit it.

"Then let's stop before I end up killing you."

"Thanks."

The court was still theirs, so they stood there as they continued talking. Bill shook his head, struggling on Paul's behalf for an explanation.

Bill snapped his fingers. "I got it."

"What?"

"Mice." Paul rolled his eyes. "No, hear me out. You've got mice, and they ran over the keys in the middle of the night."

"Even for you, that's pretty dumb. Even if we did have mice, which we don't, a mouse weighs so little, the key wouldn't go down. And you'd need an entire troupe of dancing mice to make as much noise as I heard."

Bill held up his palms in defeat. "Call the Ghostbusters."

Paul ran his hand over the back of his neck. "I didn't even work up a sweat." As they turned for the door, Paul said, "I think I'll move it."

"What?"

"The typewriter. I'll put it in the laundry room or something."

Bill nodded thoughtfully. "That'll make Charlotte happy. Her special gift relegated to the laundry."

"Shit."

"And what, exactly, would that prove? Where's the logic? If you believe someone, somehow, is breaking in, hiding the typewriter isn't the answer. A fucking dead bolt is the answer."

"We've got a dead bolt on the door."

"Windows all secure?"

"Yes."

"You got an alarm system?"

"No."

"Maybe *that* should be your first step. If you still hear

keys tapping in the night after that, well, then maybe you really do need the Ghostbusters." He grinned.

"Who ya gonna call?"

Bill's face lit up. "Here's what you do. Roll in a sheet of paper and see if there's a message in the morning."

"*That's* the strategy of a crazy person," Paul said.

That night, at dinner, Paul said, "What would you think about our getting a security system?"

"Seriously?" Charlotte said, digging her fork into her salad. "What, you're getting me a priceless jewel collection?"

"Just asking."

Charlotte shrugged. "Sure. I can get some recommendations at the agency. But what's prompted this?"

Paul pressed his lips together hard, debating with himself whether to get into it. His mouth was dry, so he picked up his glass of water and took a long drink. "So you know, that thing with Josh? When I said I heard typing noises in the night?"

"Yeah?"

"I heard it again."

"The typewriter?"

Paul nodded slowly. "That's why I was up. I didn't hear someone at the door. I heard someone on the typewriter."

Charlotte shrugged. "So you were dreaming. Or, more specifically, having another nightmare. Was it about Hoffman?"

"It was."

"What happened in it?"

He touched his stomach without thinking about it. "I don't even want to say."

"Okay."

"But . . . but at the end, he was trying to talk to me, but the sounds coming out of his mouth were like typewriter sounds."

"So it *was* a dream."

"But then I got up. I went to the bathroom. I started hearing it again."

Charlotte studied him for several seconds. He could see the skepticism in her eyes. She didn't have to say anything.

But finally, she spoke. "So, if you hear it again, wake me up."

Paul nodded. "Deal."

And that night, there was nothing.

Paul lay awake for hours, staring into the darkness, waiting for the *chit chit chit* to begin.

It did not.

When he rose the following morning—he thought

he'd finally fallen asleep around five—he was exhausted and bleary-eyed, but also slightly relieved.

But the more he thought about his situation, the less relieved he was. If the typing sounds were imagined, even when he was certain he was fully awake, was his head injury to blame? Were there symptoms the doctor had not discussed with him?

Had he been sleepwalking? Had he been in some kind of trance?

At breakfast, Charlotte said, "So, no *tippity-tap* last night?"

"No," he said groggily. "I listened for it all night."

"Oh, babe, you gotta be kidding. No wonder you look like shit."

"Yeah, well, I feel like shit, too."

She went back to the counter and filled a mug from the coffee machine. "I've just renewed your prescription."

He stared into the black liquid and said, "Can you inject this directly into my veins?"

"Look, I gotta go," she said, leaning in to give him a light kiss on the cheek. "Maybe the mystery typist will return tonight and we can all have a drink together."

Paul didn't see the humor in the comment.

"What have you got on today?" she asked.

He shrugged. "Just my project."

After Charlotte had left for work, he continued sitting at the kitchen table, sipping his coffee, hoping the caffeine would kick in. He noticed his hand was slightly trembling.

"God," he said to himself. "You're a mess."

The door to his small study was open, and from where he sat, he could see the black Underwood typewriter sitting atop his makeshift desk, dwarfing the laptop next to it, facing in his direction.

The semicircular opening to the cathedral of keys struck Paul as a kind of garish smile.

"What the fuck are you looking at?" Paul said, and went back to his coffee.

Seventeen

The following morning, more than twenty-four hours after it had all happened, Frank White still found himself trembling at the memory of it.

Anna, who had canceled all her appointments for the previous day but expected to return to work today, was sitting with her father at the kitchen table, stroking his hand. He'd hardly touched the scrambled eggs she had made for him.

"It's okay, Dad."

He nodded, slipped his hand away from hers and picked up his fork. "This looks good," he said.

"There's ketchup there if you want it."

The doorbell rang. Frank's entire body stiffened.

"It's okay. It's someone from the police." She did half an eye roll. "Someone I'm *expecting* from the police. Who can maybe answer a few questions for us. Would you be okay here on your own for a few minutes?"

"Of course," he said, a tiny bit of egg stuck to his lower lip. "I'm not a child."

Anna smiled and, considering what he had just said, resisted the temptation to pick up his napkin and wipe his mouth.

Frank said, "I thought they were going to shoot me. I thought they were going to shoot you."

"I know. But it didn't happen. You're okay and I'm okay."

The doorbell rang again.

"Neither of us has a scratch on us." She gave him another smile, hoping she could coax one out of him. "Never a dull moment around here, right?"

He nodded.

"And there's more coffee if you want it."

Finally, a smile from her father. "I could probably use something a bit stronger."

She got up and left the kitchen. She opened the front door and found a short, heavyset black man in his forties standing there. His bushy black mustache made up for the few strands of hair he had on his head. He wore a sport jacket, dark blue shirt and tie, and jeans. He was ready with a badge to display for Anna.

"Hi," he said. "Detective Joe Arnwright. Milford Police."

"Come in," she said.

"How are you today?" he asked, taking a seat in the living room. It wasn't a polite greeting. He was clearly asking how she was compared to the day before.

"My father's still very upset. *I'm* still very upset."

Arnwright nodded sympathetically. "Of course."

"They *stormed* in here," she said. "We were *asleep.*"

"To be fair, they managed to open a window and came into the house very quietly in an effort—"

"Don't you people do something to confirm that what someone's telling you is true?"

"Dr. White, we've—"

"My father gets up to take a pee and finds men with guns in the hallway. It's a wonder you didn't give him a heart attack, let alone shoot him."

Arnwright nodded patiently. "Their information, as you know, was that a man had already shot his wife and was going to shoot his daughter next. That's what our officers believed they were coming into. They needed to assess the situation as quickly as possible to eliminate any threat. And that threat, they would have presumed, was against you. The daughter."

"You were conned," Anna said.

"I'm not disputing that."

"They made my father lie on the floor and pointed guns at his head!" Anna said through gritted teeth. She managed to convey her anger without raising her voice. She did not want her father to hear all this. "An old man! With dementia!"

"I understand that you're—"

"You *understand*? That's encouraging. My father and I came this close to getting killed."

"I don't believe that's the case. The members of that team are very professional."

Anna took a second to compose herself, to go in another direction. "Have you arrested him?"

"Mr. Hitchens, you mean."

"Who else would I mean?"

"We have interviewed him, yes."

Anna eyed him warily. "And?"

"We've interviewed him and we are investigating," he said. "We believe the 9-1-1 call was placed from a cell phone, a kind of throwaway one they call a burner that—"

"I know what a burner is. I watch TV."

"We're going to try and find out where that burner was purchased, then see if we can determine who the buyer was."

"He didn't have the phone on him? Did you search him?"

"As I said, we are investigating," Arnwright said.

"What did the caller sound like? The one who called 9-1-1?"

"It sounded like an elderly man. But there are all sorts of voice changer apps out there. Did Mr. Hitchens ever threaten to do something like this to you? A crank call of this nature."

"No. But it's his style. My father's suffering from dementia. Hitchens would just love to scare a confused, old man."

"We need a little more than that," Arnwright said.

Anna sighed. "I think he might have killed a dog, too."

Arnwright, pen in hand, looked ready to take down details. "Go on."

She bit her lip. "I can't . . . I don't have any proof of anything."

Arnwright put the pen away and stood. "Again, I'm sorry about what happened here. I'll let you know if there are any developments."

Anna showed him to the door. She went into the kitchen to see how her father was, but he was not there.

"Dad?" she called out.

She went upstairs to his room, expecting to find him on his rowing machine. But he wasn't there either.

She thought she heard a muted *whack*.

Anna went to her father's bedroom window, which looked out onto the backyard. There he was, golf club in hand—it looked like a driver—swinging at half a dozen balls he had dropped onto the well-manicured lawn, except for those spots where he had done some serious divots.

It was him, she told herself. *I know it was him.*

Eighteen

Paul was ready to begin.

He'd typed up plenty of notes, copied and pasted paragraphs from online news accounts of the double murder, but now he was ready to take that leap. To write the first sentence of whatever it was he was going to write. Memoir? Novel? A true-crime story? Who knew?

What Paul did know was that however the story came together, one thing was certain: it was *his* story.

And so he typed his first sentence:

Kenneth Hoffman was my friend.

Paul looked at the five words on his laptop screen. He hit the ENTER key to bring the cursor down a line. And he wrote:

Kenneth Hoffman tried to murder me.

That seemed as good a place to start as any. From that springboard, he jumped straight into the story of that night. How, while returning from a student theatrical presentation at West Haven, he'd spotted Hoffman's Volvo station wagon driving erratically down the Post Road.

About a thousand words in, Paul started finding the process therapeutic. The words flowed from his fingertips as quickly as he could type them. At one point he glanced at the bulky Underwood beside the laptop and said, "Like to see *you* crank out this shit this fast."

When he got to the part where he saw the two dead women in the back of Kenneth's car, Paul paused only briefly, took a deep mental breath, and kept on writing. He took himself to the point where the shovel crashed into his skull.

And then he stopped.

He felt simultaneously drained and elated. He had done it. He had jumped into the deep end of the cold pool, gotten used to it, and kept on swimming.

When Charlotte got home that evening, he could not wait to tell her about his progress.

"That's fantastic," she said. "I'm proud of you. I really am." She paused. "Can I read it?"

"Not yet. I don't know exactly what it's going to be. When I feel it's coming together, I'll show it to you."

She almost looked relieved. She'd had a long day that had finished with an evening showing, and all she wanted to do was go to bed. As she did most nights, she fell asleep moments after her head hit the pillow. She rarely snored—Paul knew he could not make the same claim—but he could tell when she was asleep by the deepness of her breathing.

He turned off the light at half past ten but lay awake, he was sure, for at least an hour, maybe two.

Paul felt wired.

For the first time since the attack, Paul felt . . . *excited.* If he'd ever doubted the wisdom of tackling this whole Hoffman thing head-on, he didn't anymore. But would this change in attitude manifest itself in different ways? Would writing about Hoffman have an exorcising effect? Would the nightmares stop? Maybe not all at once, but at least gradually?

If the writing continued to go well—*Let's not get ahead of ourselves, it's only Day One*—then maybe it would be fun to do it in another location. After all, he could take his laptop anywhere. And he was *not* thinking about the closest Starbucks. More like Cape Cod.

If Charlotte could get a few days off, they could drive up to Provincetown, or take the ferry to Martha's Vineyard. He could even toss a few recent bestsellers into his suitcase, maybe find something worth adding to his popular fiction course.

He'd talk to Charlotte about it in the morning, although he feared her answer. Too much going on, she'd say. You can't sell a house when you're not here. *You* can't work twenty-four/seven, he'd tell her. If he could talk her into taking the time, he could see if Josh wanted to come, too. He could call Hailey, see if she'd be okay with that.

No, maybe not. If he was to have a chance of talking Charlotte into the idea, it had to be just the two of them. It wasn't that Charlotte didn't like Josh. Paul was sure she liked him. But did she *love* him? Was it even fair to fault her for that if she didn't? Josh was not her son, and had been in her life for only a few years.

It was about then, thinking about a Cape Cod getaway, whatever time it happened to be, that he fell asleep.

But it was 3:14 A.M. when he woke up. He didn't wake up on his own.

He was awakened.

Chit chit. Chit chit chit.

———

His eyes opened abruptly. Was it a dream again? Had he even *been* dreaming? Even if it was hard to recall the details of a dream upon waking, Paul could usually tell whether he'd actually been having one.

He did not think so.

And he was sure that he was, at this moment, awake.

He pinched his arm to be sure.

Yup.

He held his breath and listened for the typing sound to recur. There was nothing. For several seconds, all he heard was the pounding of his own heart.

Then, there it was.

Chit chit. Chit chit chit.

This was not a dream. This was the real deal.

What had Charlotte suggested he do the next time this happened? Wake her up. Get yourself a corroborating witness.

He sat up in bed, touched Charlotte gently on the shoulder.

"Charlotte," he whispered. "Charlotte. Wake up. Charlotte."

She stirred. Without opening her eyes, she said, "What?"

"It's happening," he said. "The sound."

"What sound?"

"The typewriter."

Her eyes opened wide. She withdrew her hand from under the pillow, sat up, blinked several times.

"Just listen," he whispered.

"Okay, okay, I'm up."

"Shh."

"Okay!" she said.

"Be quiet and listen."

Charlotte said nothing further. The two of them sat there in the bed, waiting. After about ten seconds, Charlotte said, "I don't hear anything."

Paul held up a silencing hand. "Wait."

Another half a minute went past before Charlotte said, "You must have dreamed it."

"No," he whispered sharply. "Absolutely not. I'm going downstairs."

"I'll come with you."

"Be real quiet. It could start up again at any second."

Together, they padded down the hall to the stairs and descended them slowly. Twice, Paul raised a hand and the two of them froze.

Nothing.

When they reached the kitchen, Paul reached over to

a panel of four light switches and flipped them all up at once. Lights came on over the island and dining table, under the cupboards, and in the adjoining living area.

"We know you're here!" Paul shouted.

Except no one was.

Paul bolted down the stairs that led to the front door, careful to grab the railing this time so he didn't land on his butt.

"Paul!" Charlotte screamed.

The door was locked, the dead bolt thrown. He opened a second, inside door that led to the garage, disappeared into there for fifteen seconds, then reentered the house, shaking his head. He trudged back up the stairs to the kitchen.

"Paul?"

"I thought . . . I thought I could catch whoever it was."

"No one was here," Charlotte said softly.

He headed for his think tank, flicked on the light, and stared at the Underwood. Charlotte slowly came up behind him, rested a hand on his shoulder. Neither of them spoke for several seconds, but finally, Paul broke the silence.

"You think I'm crazy."

"I never said that."

"I know what I heard." Paul bit his lower lip. His

voice barely above a whisper, he said, "This is the third time. Three nights I've heard it."

Charlotte, her eyes misting, said, "Believe me, it's the dreams. Go back to bed. In the morning, things may seem a lot clearer."

"I'm not losing my mind," Paul insisted.

"You're tired and you're stressed and you worked all day writing about—"

"Enough!" he shouted, throwing down his arms and taking a step back from his wife. "I swear to God, if I hear the word *stressed* one more time, I don't know what the hell I'm going to do."

"Fine," Charlotte said evenly. "I'm sorry."

"Bill said the same thing, that I must be dreaming it. But"—Paul was slow to say the words—"he did have an idea."

"You talked to Bill?"

"We met up for a game and—"

"*Squash?*"

"It was a very *gentle* game. I didn't want—"

Charlotte was enraged. "Are you out of your mind? You've had a serious blow to the head and you set foot in a squash court? Have you any idea how stupid that is? You could bash your head—"

"Would you just stop!" he shouted. "Fuck! Just shut up!"

Charlotte took a step back. "I'm trying to help you."

Paul lowered his head and held it with both hands. "I feel like my fucking brain is going to explode."

Charlotte, softly, said, "It's going to be okay." She waited a beat. "You said Bill had an idea."

Paul sighed. "Yeah. I don't know if he was joking, or humoring me, or what."

Charlotte waited.

"He said I should roll some paper in."

Charlotte blinked. "He said what?"

Paul pointed at the typewriter. "He said, if this thing's making noises in the night, put some paper in and see what it's saying."

Charlotte said nothing.

"You think I should do that?" Paul asked.

"That's ridiculous," she said.

Paul shrugged. "He mentioned the word *ghost*. Well, actually, he mentioned the Ghostbusters."

"Jesus. He can be such an asshole." Charlotte rolled her eyes, threw up her hands, and said, "Go ahead."

"What?"

"Do it. Roll in a sheet of paper. If you think you hear something again in the middle of the night, and there's nothing on it, then you'll know."

"Know what?"

She touched her index finger to her temple. "That it really is a dream."

Paul's jaw hardened. He met his wife's eyes for several seconds before breaking away, stepping over to the printer, and taking out one sheet of paper from the tray. He set it into the typewriter carriage and rolled it in, bringing an inch of paper above where the keys would strike.

"Great," she said. "I'm going to bed."

She turned and walked out.

Paul stayed another moment and stared at the typewriter. He ran his fingers along the middle row of letters, depressing the occasional key just enough to see the metal arms bend toward the paper, as if with anticipation.

Nineteen

Later that week, Anna White was at her desk, adding a few notes to a patient's file in her computer before Paul Davis arrived for his weekly session, when she thought she heard a noise from upstairs. The only one up there was her father.

She worried he might have fallen.

She bolted from her chair, ran from the office wing on her house to the living area, and up the stairs as quickly as she could. She rapped on her father's closed bedroom door.

"Dad?"

There was no answer.

She tried the door and was surprised to find she could open it only an inch. Through the crack she could see that a piece of furniture was blocking the door. It was her father's dresser. That was what she had heard. Her father dragging his dresser across the room.

"Dad!"

Frank's face appeared in the sliver. "Yes, honey?"

"What are you doing?"

"Can't be too careful."

"Dad, the police are not coming back. That's not going to happen again."

"They're not getting in here, that's for damn sure."

Anna, her voice calm, said, "You can't stay in there forever, Dad. What are you going to do when you have to go to the bathroom?"

He disappeared, only to reappear five seconds later with a wastepaper basket in one hand, and a roll of toilet paper in the other. "Thought of everything," he said.

"Okay," Anna said. "And when you get hungry?"

"You can bring something up for me."

"And who do you think's going to empty that pail for you? Because I can tell you, it's not going to be me."

"Window," he said.

Jesus, she thought, picturing it. She had one last card to play, and knew she'd hate herself for it. "And what about when it's time to go to the home to visit Joanie?"

Frank stopped and puzzled over that. He clearly hadn't thought through every eventuality.

"Oh," he said. "You've got me there."

"Why don't you put the dresser back where it was, Dad? And put on the TV. Maybe they're running some Bugs Bunny cartoons now."

She heard the dresser squeak as he pushed it back. Anna opened the door wide and watched him move it across the room. She didn't offer to help him. All those hours he spent on the rowing machine, he could probably get a job with the Mayflower furniture movers.

Dresser back in place, he grabbed the remote and turned on the television. He propped himself on the corner of the bed, as if nothing had happened.

Anna, wearily, went back downstairs.

The moment she entered her office, she let out a short scream.

Gavin Hitchens was sitting in his usual chair, waiting for her.

"Jesus Christ," she said.

He made an innocent face. "I never canceled. This is when I come."

"Leave."

He raised his palms in a gesture of surrender but did not get out of the chair. "I came here to tell you I forgive you."

Anna blinked. "You what?"

"Forgive you. For thinking I had something to do with that woman and that dead dog, and with whatever happened here a couple of days ago that made you send the police to see me. I know you probably violated some kind of doctor-patient privilege when you did that, but I'm willing to overlook it."

"I mean it, Gavin. You need to leave."

"Because, you see, I think maybe I deserved that. When you've done the kinds of things I've done, you've got no one to blame but yourself when you find yourself facing false accusations. You've set yourself up. I appreciate that now."

"I'm calling the police."

Gavin's look of innocence morphed into one of hurt. "Does this mean you're not going to be counseling me anymore?"

"You could have gotten my father killed."

"I don't know what you're talking about. Well, yes, I do, because the police told me. It must have been awful, a SWAT team coming into the house like that."

"You're sick, Gavin. I hope someone can help you, but it's not going to be me. Honestly, I don't know that anyone can."

He stood. "If you want to know what I think, I think it's some kind of a copycat. Someone who knows I'm seeing you and wants to frame me. You might want to look at your other patients and see who might be capable of something like that."

Anna strode into the room, past Gavin, and went behind her desk. She reached for the phone. Before she could lift the receiver, Gavin put his hand atop hers, pinning it there.

She looked into his smiling face.

He said, "Did you know, when you sleep, you don't snore, but when you exhale, your lips do this adorable little dance?"

Anna felt a chill run the length of her body. She wanted to scream but couldn't find her voice.

Gavin released her hand and grinned. "Just kidding." He walked to the door but turned one last time before leaving. "Good thing you don't have any pets," he said.

Anna slowly dropped into her chair and gripped the arms to stop her hands from shaking.

Twenty

The first thing Paul did when he got up was head straight to his office. Charlotte was still under the covers when he slipped out of bed and trotted barefoot down to the kitchen in his boxers.

He hadn't heard any more typing noises in the night, but it was possible, he told himself, that he'd slept through them. If the keys of the typewriter had—somehow—been touched in the remaining hours of the night, the evidence would be on that sheet of paper he had rolled into it.

This is crazy, Paul told himself. *Why am I even doing this?*

He swallowed and felt his heart flutter as he slowly pushed open his office door.

The Underwood sat there.

The page was blank.

Paul put a hand on the jamb for support and took a breath. He didn't know whether to feel relieved, or disappointed.

"I really am losing it," he whispered.

In the light of day, the events of the night seemed clearer. As much as he had fought Charlotte's conclusion that he'd been dreaming, what other possible explanation was there?

Think about it. Does it make any sense at all that someone would sneak into your house in the dead of night to tap on the keys of an old typewriter?

Paul knew the answer.

He'd mention it today at his session with Dr. White. He'd ask some questions. Could someone be half-awake and half-asleep at the same time? When he thought he was awake and hearing *chit chit chit* was it possible he was not fully conscious? Could it be a kind of sleepwalking?

That, he had to admit, made more sense than anything else.

He went back up to the bedroom and slid under the covers as Charlotte was waking.

"Hey," she said groggily. She blinked a couple of times, pulled herself up into a sitting position and said, "How are you doing?"

"Good," he said, putting a hand on her arm. "I just wanted to say I'm sorry."

"About what?"

"How I acted last night. I was short with you, and you were only trying to help."

"It's okay," she said. "Don't worry about it."

When he told her what he was going to ask Dr. White, Charlotte nodded with enthusiasm. "That could explain everything," she said.

Paul looked down as his face flushed with embarrassment. "I went down and checked."

"Checked?"

"To see if anything had been typed onto that page."

"And?"

He looked up. "I think you know the answer."

Paul felt optimistic on the way to his session. He couldn't wait to tell Anna White that he not only had made a good start on his writing project, but also had come up with a theory about the noises in the night.

He'd decided to pop into Staples for some printer cartridges and the Barnes & Noble for a quick look at new fiction releases first. He was heading south on River Street when he saw the Volvo.

It pulled out in front of him from Darina Place, just ahead of the underpass below the railroad tracks. The driver either didn't see Paul, or didn't care. Paul had to hit the brakes to avoid broadsiding the vehicle.

Paul didn't get to see who was behind the wheel, but that might have been because he was consumed with looking at the entire vehicle.

The Volvo was a station wagon. It was dark blue. It was the same vintage as Kenneth Hoffman's.

Paul felt his heart starting to race. His hands almost instantly began to sweat. His breathing became rapid and shallow.

As the car settled into the lane ahead of him, Paul looked to see if one of the taillights was broken. But as he tried to focus, he found his vision blurring.

I'm having a panic attack.

I'm going to pass out.

Paul hit the brakes and steered toward the edge of the road. Behind him a horn blared. He got the car stopped under the bridge and huddled over the wheel, his head resting atop it. He closed his eyes, fighting the dizziness.

Suddenly, overhead, the roar of a passing commuter train.

Paul's heart was ready to explode from his chest.

"Breathe," he told himself. "Breathe."

It took him the better part of five minutes to pull himself together. Slowly, he raised his head from the wheel, propped it against the headrest. He released his fingers from the wheel and wiped his sweaty palms on the tops of his legs. When he was confident his heart rate and breathing were back to normal, he continued on his way.

Anna White wasn't in her office.

Paul peeked in from the waiting area and did not see her behind her desk or seated in the leather chair she used when they had their chats.

He allowed a couple of minutes to go by before he poked his head into the main part of the house and said, "Dr. White? Anna?"

He thought he heard the sound of clinking cutlery, as though someone was doing dishes in a sink. He followed the noises to the kitchen, where Anna, her back to him, was standing at the sink.

"Anna?" he said.

She whirled around, her eyes wide and fearful. In the process, a wet glass slid from her hand and hit the floor, shattering into hundreds of pieces.

"Oh God, I'm sorry," Paul said, moving forward. He scanned the floor to assess the level of risk. "Don't move your feet."

Anna surveyed the bits of glass around her feet. "Shit." She looked apologetically at Paul. "You startled me."

As he knelt down to gather up the larger pieces of

glass he said, "When you weren't in your office I . . . I should have just waited."

When she started to kneel down to help pick up glass, he said, "No, I've got this. As long as you don't move you won't step in any of it."

But she ignored him, crouching and gathering pieces around her feet.

"Oh for fuck's sake," she said, holding up her index finger. Blood trickled down the side.

"Hang on," Paul said. "Hold it over the sink. I've got almost all of it."

With a dish towel, he swabbed the floor of any shards that were too small to pick up with his fingers.

Standing, he said, "Where do you keep your first-aid stuff?"

She pointed to a drawer. Paul found a package of Band-Aids and peeled one from its wrapping. Standing shoulder to shoulder with Anna, he gently took her wrist in his hand and ran some water over her bloody finger.

"You're trembling," Paul said.

"I'm . . . a little on edge today is all." She shook her head. "I don't even know why I was doing this. I have a dishwasher. I just . . . needed to clear my head."

Paul turned off the tap and gently dried her finger with a paper towel. He studied the cut closely.

"I don't see any glass."

Paul wrapped the tiny bandage tightly around her finger. "If it's none of my business, you don't have to answer, but what's got you on edge? Is it your father?"

"No," she said. "Well, some."

"What happened?"

"A fake 9-1-1 call. The police came, guns drawn. My father was pretty shook up."

Paul held on to her hand a few more seconds before letting go. "There. You should be okay now."

In the office, in their respective chairs, Anna said, "I really *am* sorry. I should have been in here when you arrived." She took a breath.

"We don't have to do this today," he offered.

She raised a hand, waving away any further debate. "I'm good. Go ahead."

"I actually thought I was going to be late," Paul said. He told her about what had happened when he saw the car that looked like Hoffman's. "I don't know all the symptoms of a panic attack, but I think I might have had one. I know it wasn't Hoffman, and I don't even think it was his car, but seeing it triggered something. I've really felt like I've been moving forward these last couple of days, but that was a real reminder that I've got a way to go."

Anna wanted to be sure that he was okay now, and that he would be okay to drive home. Paul said he was confident that he was.

"But I should tell you . . . it happened again."

"What happened?"

"Those typing noises in the middle of the night. And I was as sure as I could be that I was awake. I got Charlotte up, but she never heard a thing." He tossed out his theory about being awake and asleep at the same time.

"Possibly," Anna said, "but that's not really my area of expertise. But yes, I think it's possible. You were still under the influences of a dream while you presented as awake."

Paul stared at her for several seconds. "I think that has to be it. Unless," and at this point he forced a chuckle, "it's a ghost. That's what Bill—a friend of mine—suggested, although he was joking."

Anna managed a wry smile. "If that's the problem, you're absolutely in an area I don't know much about."

As the session came to its conclusion, Paul again asked Anna how she was.

"Better," she said, holding up her bandaged finger and offering a crooked smile. "You're my new hero."

Twenty-One

"I gave Bill shit today," Charlotte said over dinner.

"What for?"

"Seriously? Letting you get into a squash court with him?"

"Oh, that."

"I don't know who's the bigger idiot, you or him."

Paul smiled. "Tough call."

She gave him a sharp look. "It's not funny."

They moved on to other things. She asked if he had the ticket for the dry cleaning. She'd be going by there tomorrow and could pick it up.

"What dry cleaning?" he asked.

"The dry cleaning I asked you to drop off."

"You didn't ask me to drop off any dry cleaning."

"This morning, I said to you, please drop off the dry

cleaning. I pointed to the bag on the chair in our room. And you said, no problem, you'd do it on the way to your session."

Paul stared at her. "No, you didn't."

Charlotte said, "Maybe this will help you remember. I said, tell them to be careful with that black dress. And you said, the one that looks like it's painted on? And I said, why, you got some paint remover? Does *that* help?"

Paul's face fell. "I don't remember any of that."

Charlotte tried to look upbeat. "It's no big deal. I'll drop it off tomorrow."

To his surprise, Paul slept well. Maybe tackling the Hoffman business was having an impact, Volvo incident aside.

When he woke up at five minutes after seven, he heard water running. He threw back the covers and traipsed into the bathroom. Charlotte stood naked behind the frosted shower door, her head arched back to allow the water to splash across her face.

"Hey," he said loudly to be heard over the water.

She turned the taps off and opened the door far enough to retrieve a towel hanging on a hook.

"When did you come to bed?" she asked. "I waited

for you for about twenty minutes before I finally went to sleep."

"I stayed up for a while, that's all," he said. "I was doing some writing."

Paul studied his face in the mirror, examined his eyes. Charlotte dried off behind the glass, then opened the door and stepped out, the towel wrapped around her.

"But you slept through the rest of the night?" she asked.

"I did," he said. "I feel kind of logy, but I slept pretty good."

Paul knew what she was really asking. Had he heard anything in the night? He ran his hand over his bristly chin and neck. He opened a drawer, brought out a razor and shaving cream.

"You want to start the coffee while I get dressed?" she asked when he was done shaving.

He nodded wearily and, after another look at himself in the mirror, said, "It's gonna take more than coffee to fix this."

He slipped out of the bathroom and headed to the floor below. Charlotte took off her towel, dried her hair as best she could, and retrieved a handheld dryer from the cabinet below the sink. She plugged it in, flipped the switch, the small room suddenly sounding like the inside of a jet engine. She aimed the device at her head and let her hair fly.

Less than a minute later, Paul stood at the bathroom door, his face drained of color. She turned the machine off.

"For Christ's sake, didn't you hear me?" he said.

She waved the dryer in front of him. "With this on?"

"Come downstairs."

"What is it?"

"Just come."

She ducked into the bedroom to grab her robe, threw it on, and quickly knotted the sash. She ran after her husband, who was already halfway down the stairs.

"What's going on?" Charlotte asked.

He led her straight to the small office, stood just outside the door, and pointed to the typewriter.

"Look," he said.

"Look at what?"

"The paper," he said. "Look at the paper."

From where she stood, she could make out the letters. A partial line of them on the sheet of paper Paul had rolled into the machine a few days earlier.

"What the hell?" she whispered.

She slowly stepped into the room, bent over in front

of the black metal typewriter, close enough to read the words that had somehow appeared between the time they'd gone to bed and now:

```
We typed our apologies like we were asked
   but it didn't make any difference.
```

Twenty-Two

"I don't want to alarm you, but it's possible some-one got into the house without our knowing it, so we need to be on our guard. I debated whether to even tell you, because I didn't want to upset you."

Frank White looked at his daughter with weary eyes. "Someone broke in?"

Anna reached across the kitchen table and put both hands over his. "I don't know. He might have been just trying to rattle me."

"Who is this?"

"One of my patients. Well, a former one," she said. "It was something he said yesterday."

"Is he the one you think sent the police here?"

"I don't have any proof, but yes, that's what I think. The police have already talked to him about the other incident. But they don't have any real proof for that one, either. But some things you just know. I've been through the whole house. I've checked the windows, the sliding glass doors, everything, and they all look secure."

Frank nodded slowly, then said, "We need to tell Joanie all this."

"Of course," Anna said.

"But don't make too big a deal of it. I don't want to worry her needlessly."

"I'll look after it."

Her father smiled. "Or I could tell her when we go see her."

She smiled. "Sure."

"What did you do to your finger?" he asked, looking down at the Band-Aid and lightly touching it.

"It's nothing," she said. "I broke a glass yesterday." Anna paused. "There's something else on my mind."

Frank waited.

"It's a bit of a professional dilemma," she said. "I have a feeling that this one patient might be a threat to my others. I'm wondering whether I need to warn them."

Frank's eyes seemed to grow vacant. Anna knew he was unlikely to solve her problem, but airing her concerns out loud might help just the same. "I've already reported this man to the police, and some of what he's done is a matter of public record. So I think the ethical concerns are minimal."

Frank nodded, then pushed himself back from the table and stood. "I'm gonna hit a few balls. Let me know when it's time to go."

She gave him a sad smile. "Okay, Dad."

Twenty-Three

"Oh, my God," Charlotte said, staring at the page in the typewriter, then whirling around to look back into the kitchen. "Someone really *is* here."

"No," Paul said, gripping her shoulders. "No one's here now, and I don't see any evidence that anyone's been here at all. I've checked doors and windows. I've been through the whole place. I'm certain no one got in here after we went back upstairs."

"You don't know that," she said.

"Come with me," he said. He walked her over to the stairs that led down to the front door. "Look."

"What am I looking at?"

"That shoe."

There was a single dark blue running shoe on the floor by the door.

"I've been doing that the last few nights. One shoe, up against the door. If someone opened it, the shoe would have moved."

Charlotte stared, dumbfounded, at the shoe, then at Paul. "So what's going on? I don't understand."

"Where did you get that typewriter?" Paul asked.

"I told you. At a yard sale. Some people were moving, clearing out their stuff."

"Where?"

Charlotte blinked several times, trying to recall. "It was on Laurelton Court. A two-story, three baths, double-car garage. I didn't have the listing, but I drove by, you know, because I like to be aware of the houses in Milford that are on the market, and they were having this sale. I saw that typewriter and knew instantly that you'd like it." She paused. "I sure called that wrong."

"Could you find the house again?"

Charlotte gave him a *"seriously?"* look.

"We need to talk to those people," Paul said.

"Why? Why does it *matter* where it came from? It's just a fucking typewriter! Paul, honestly, you're scaring me."

"I need to know who else has used it. I need to know who has used this machine."

"Hundreds of people could have used it," Charlotte said. "Please, tell me what you're thinking?"

"Read it again."

"What?"

"Go on. Read it again."

He led her back to the small room, grabbed the sheet of paper by the top, and ripped it out of the typewriter. "Just read it."

"I've read it."

Paul read it aloud: "'We typed our apologies like we were asked but it didn't make any difference.' That doesn't mean anything to you?"

"Paul, I swear."

"That's what Kenneth made them do. Before he killed them. Before he killed those two women."

Charlotte stared at him blankly for several seconds, then back to the page in his hand. "This is insane."

"No kidding. You think I don't feel nuts even suggesting it?"

"And what the hell *are* you suggesting?"

He shot her *"seriously?"* look right back at her.

Charlotte said, "Hang on, let me try to get my head around what I think you're saying. You believe those women are sending you a message? Through this typewriter? Paul, listen to yourself."

Paul hesitated. "Look, I know it sounds ridiculous. But what if this . . . what if this is the very same typewriter those apologies were written on?"

"But how could that typewriter end up in a yard sale? Wouldn't the police have it? Wouldn't it be in evidence?"

Paul thought about that. "That's a good question. You'd think it would be. I honestly don't know. It was days later that I remembered Kenneth putting something in that Dumpster. The police might never have found it. Maybe someone else did."

"Okay, so maybe it is, and maybe it isn't the actual typewriter. Regardless, how do you explain this?" She took the sheet of paper from his hand and waved it in front of his face.

"I don't know." He thought a moment. "I'm going to call that woman."

"What woman?"

Paul edged around her, sat in his cheap office chair, and fired up his laptop. "The reporter who wrote the story. I can't remember her name. She wrote a feature with lots of details about the case. It was the first thing I read when I decided to throw myself back into this."

He tapped away on the keyboard, scrolled down through the results of a search. "Here it is. Here's the story. Gwen Stainton. She's the one. At the *New Haven Star*. She seemed to know more about this case than anyone else."

Paul executed a few more keystrokes. "Okay, here's

the *Star* staff list . . . hang on. Yeah, Stainton. I'll send her an email." As he typed, he read his message aloud. "Dear Ms. Stainton, I have read with interest all your stories about the Kenneth Hoffman case, and I have one question. What happened to the typewriter on which the apologies were written? Do the police have it? If you know the answer, I'd be most grateful if you could tell me. If not, please pass along the name of someone who might know."

He turned and looked at Charlotte. "How does that sound?"

Hesitantly, she said, "Fine, I guess."

"What? You don't sound like you mean it."

"I'm worried about you."

He pointed to the typewriter. "I have to know more. You get that, right?"

Charlotte glanced down at the typewritten sheet she was still holding, dropped it on the desk, and looked back at her husband. "Go ahead and send it, I don't care. I've got to get ready for work."

She slipped out of the room as Paul turned his attention back to the laptop. He moved the cursor over the SEND button and clicked.

The email to Gwen Stainton vanished from the screen with a *whoosh.*

"Okay," he said to himself.

His eyes moved to the antique Underwood. He stared at it for several seconds, then took a fresh, blank sheet from the nearby printer and rolled it into the typewriter, positioning it just as he had the other piece.

"Just in case you have anything else you want to say," he whispered.

Twenty-Four

"I 'll drive you to work," Paul said when Charlotte had returned to the kitchen to make herself some breakfast. He had already run upstairs and quickly dressed so that he'd be ready to leave when she was.

"I need a car in case—"

"No, listen, I want to see if we can find the house where you got the typewriter."

Charlotte appeared to wilt. "Paul, listen to yourself."

"I just want to talk to them. The people who had the yard sale. Ask them where it came from, how they got it. Look, if they've had it for fifty years, fine. But if they got in the last eight months, then there's a chance—"

"I need my car," she repeated.

"Okay, fine. We'll take your car, and I'll grab a cab home from your office."

"You think we could get a coffee along the way?"

Paul sighed. "Fine."

Before she descended the stairs, she looked into his study. "You rolled in another sheet of paper."

"Yes."

She began to move in that direction. "You really think—"

He took her arm. "Come on, let's go."

As Charlotte got behind the wheel, she dug her phone from her purse. "I don't know how this is going to go, so let me call the office and tell them I might be a bit late."

"Good idea," Paul said, getting in on the passenger side.

She tapped a number, put the phone to her ear. "Yeah, hi, it's Charlotte. Look, uh, Paul and I are running a couple of errands this morning so it's probably going to be around nine-thirty before I get in." She nodded to whomever was on the other end, then said, "Yeah, sure, the file's on my desk. See you in a bit." She returned the phone to her purse. "Okay, let's do this. And don't forget, you promised me coffee."

Charlotte headed out of the neighborhood, and when

she reached New Haven Avenue, she hung a right. Up ahead was a Dunkin' Donuts. She wheeled into the parking lot and said, "You're buying."

Paul went into the store and returned with two paper cups of coffee. She took a sip of hers, then put it into the cup holder between the seats. She keyed the ignition, backed out of the parking spot, and they were off.

She drove confidently back through the downtown Common, then a series of rights and lefts until they had reached Laurelton Court.

"It's a dead-end street," she said. "An attractive feature if you're selling or buying. Minimum traffic. No one uses your street as a shortcut."

She brought the car to a stop out front of a house with a SOLD real estate sign out front.

"This is it," she said.

Paul had the door open before she had the car in park.

"God, slow down—"

He was already out of the car, heading for the front door. He rapped on it hard before he'd even looked for a doorbell button. When he spotted that, he jammed it with his index finger.

Charlotte wore a worried expression as she watched from the car. She reached for the coffee and took another sip.

Paul knocked on the door again. And for a second time, he rang the bell. No one came to the door. Charlotte watched as he peered through the window in the door, using his hands as a visor to get a better look. His shoulders slumped. He turned and walked slowly back to the car.

"What?" Charlotte asked as he settled into the passenger seat.

"I looked inside. The house is empty. Cleared out. Not a stick of furniture. They're gone."

Charlotte gave him a sympathetic look. "Sorry."

"You could find out, right?" he said.

"What?"

"Who owned the house? And where they went? Do you know the agent who had the listing?"

She nodded. "I do."

"If you can get a name, wherever they've moved to, I could call them."

"Sure," Charlotte said. "I could do that."

Paul frowned. "You don't sound crazy about the idea."

"No, it's fine."

"What? What is it?"

"I *said* I would do it."

"I can tell by your voice you don't want to."

Charlotte said nothing for several seconds, then

shifted in her seat so she could look at her husband more directly. "The thing is," she said, her voice softening, "maybe where the typewriter came from doesn't matter."

"Of course it does."

"The only way it would matter is if we were to accept that—I don't even know what to call it—there was some kind of supernatural or psychic or whatever connection between the typewriter and anyone who might have used it. And Paul, I'm sorry, but that just doesn't make any sense."

"You saw the message," he said, bristling. "You saw those words. We weren't dreaming when we saw them. They were there, on that piece of paper."

"I know."

"And I can't find anything to suggest someone got into the house," Paul continued. "I mean, yeah, Josh has a key, and maybe Hailey has a key, for all we know, but that shoe, Charlotte. That shoe, I'm pretty sure it hadn't moved."

"I know," she said again.

"So what's your solution, then?" he asked her. "If nothing else makes any sense, how the hell do you think those words got on that page?"

She looked away, turned the key, and started doing a three-point turn on Laurelton.

"Answer me," Paul said.

"I wonder, and I don't want you to take this the wrong way, but I wonder if it's possible there's one other explanation," she said.

"What?"

"Did you ask Dr. White if it was possible to be partly asleep and awake at the same time?"

"Yeah," he said slowly. "She said maybe."

"So think about that." She guided the car out of the neighborhood and headed toward her office.

"Just spit it out," he said.

"If you could hear something that really wasn't there, maybe you could *do* something you have no memory of."

"Oh, fuck," he said, turning and looking out his window.

"You stayed downstairs a long time last night before you came up to bed. Maybe you nodded off before you joined me. Or maybe you got up in the night and I didn't hear you."

"You think I typed that note."

"All I'm saying is that you need to consider the possibility."

He didn't speak to her the rest of the way. A block away from her office, she said, "Look, I'll run you home. You don't have to get a taxi."

"Just fuckin' drop me off anywhere."

"Please, I never meant to—"

"Save it," he said.

She pulled into the parking lot of the real estate agency. Paul got out without saying another word and slammed the door.

Twenty-Five

"I'm sorry, I don't have an appointment," Paul said later that morning to Dr. Anna White. "I know I was here only yesterday."

Anna had a surprised look on her face when she found him at her door—everyone had to ring in now, no walking straight into the waiting room—looking distressed. "Paul," she said, "I've got someone coming in five minutes, but what's wrong?"

She invited him in and guided him into her office.

"Sorry to just show up," he said again.

"What's happened?"

He hesitated. "Let me ask you something, and I need you to give me a straight answer."

"Of course."

"Do I strike you as someone who could be totally delusional?"

"What's brought this on?"

"I'm pretty sure Charlotte thinks I'm losing my mind."

"I don't believe that. Why would she?"

"Something really strange has happened and I don't know how to explain it."

"Just tell me."

So he told her about finding the sheet of paper in the typewriter with the message written on it.

"I see," Anna said slowly.

"I don't like the sound of that 'I see' very much," Paul said. "My theory is, well, it's pretty out there, but I think Charlotte has one that's a little more down to earth."

Anna nodded slowly. "That it's you? That you typed it yourself?"

Paul nodded slowly.

"Do you think that's possible?" she asked.

"No," he said quickly. But then he bowed his head, and added, "God, could it be?"

"Talk to me about that."

"Charlotte has never heard the typing in the night.

I'm the only one. I mean, yeah, I suppose it's possible I dreamed it, even though it seemed very real."

"Okay."

"But a message in the typewriter, that's totally different. That's something you can hold on to. It's concrete. Charlotte saw it just as clearly as I did."

"Let's try to look at this logically," Anna said. "If we accept the fact, as I do, that there are no spirits or supernatural forces actually at work in our world, except in the movies and in the pages of Stephen King novels, then we have to consider that the stresses you've been under are manifesting themselves in creative ways you may not even be aware of. And you have, in the last week or so, made a conscious decision to revisit the circumstances of Kenneth Hoffman's attempt to kill you."

"So I typed that note and don't even know I did it."

"I think we have to look at that as a possibility."

Paul ran a hand over his mouth and chin. "Charlotte and I had this entire conversation yesterday about the dry cleaning that I have no memory of. There are texts I don't remember sending. And, of course, those typing noises in the night, before an actual note showed up. But composing a crazy note and not remembering it, that's something totally . . ."

"I could do some research on it," Anna offered.

"People have done some amazing things while sleep-walking. A lot more than walking. People have been known to get in their cars and drive around with no memory of having done it. I think if someone could do that, typing out a few words is not such a stretch."

Paul let out a long breath. "Well, whatever I'm doing while I'm asleep is making me crazy while I'm awake."

Anna looked ready to ask something but was holding back.

"What is it?" Paul asked.

"Is your house secure?" she asked.

He nodded.

"So you don't think it's likely that someone could have entered the house and put that note into the type-writer."

Paul shook his head. "I don't think so. And I can't think of any reason why anyone would."

Anna did not say anything for several seconds. Then, "There's something I need to tell you. I don't honestly think it has any bearing on this, but you know that patient the other day? The one who got angry and stormed out?"

Paul nodded. "Yeah. Gavin, was it? Hitchcock or something?"

"The name's not important," Anna said. "But this

patient may, and I stress *may*, be harassing some of the people I see. I can't prove it, but if he were, it would be consistent with the behavior that sent him to me in the first place."

"What's he done?"

Anna hesitated. "Do you know anything about computers?"

Paul shrugged. "About as much as most people."

"How long would someone need to download files from a computer with one of those little sticks? You know the kind I mean?"

Paul let out a long breath. "I don't know. Not long, probably. Why?"

She shook her head. "You understand this is an awkward situation for me, but I can tell you what's already part of the public record. There was a news item. He called a grieving father, pretending to be his deceased son."

"Jesus. Who would do something like that?"

"He seems to get off on exploiting people's weaknesses."

"Do you think—"

"No," she said quickly. "But I only mention it so that you'll be on your guard. A kind of heightened alert. If you should see him around your house or anything like that, call me, or call the police, even."

Paul didn't want to go straight home from Anna's office. He thought he'd drive around for a while and think.

Just what kind of tricks could your mind play on you? he wondered. Sure, he'd been under plenty of stress, but he'd not had any actual delusions. Okay, once in a while, he heard Hoffman's voice in his head, and for a second, maybe he thought the Volvo that had pulled out in front of him was his former colleague's car.

But those were fleeting illusions, nothing more.

Was it wrong to wonder, even briefly, if the message in his typewriter was actually from the people it purported to be? Were Catherine Lamb and Jill Foster trying to communicate with him?

Don't go there.

That led him to speculate whether he was dealing with something worse than the fallout from a blow to the head. Was he suffering some form of mental illness? Paul had known, over the years, two individuals diagnosed with schizophrenia. They had believed, with absolute certainty, they were the victims of elaborate conspiracies. One was convinced the U.S. government was after him, that the president himself was overseeing a scheme to remove his brain. The second, a mature student at West Haven College who'd attended for only a single semester, was convinced her entire body was being devoured by lesions, yet she had skin as beautiful as a newborn baby's.

I'm not like that, he told himself. *I am aware of my reality.*

And yet, didn't those two people believe they were, too?

After driving around Milford for the better part of an hour, he decided to head for home.

He pulled into the driveway, got out of the car, and stood there for a moment. He took out his cell phone, brought up the number of Charlotte's cell, tapped on it, and put the phone to his ear.

"Pick up, pick up, pick—"

"Hello?"

"Hey," he said.

"Hey," Charlotte said.

"I'm sorry. I really lost my shit this morning."

"It's okay."

"I went by Dr. White's," Paul said. "Kind of barged in. The thing is, I'm willing to consider all the options, even the one you were getting at."

"I never really said—"

Dee dee, diddly-dee, dee dee, dee-da, dee-da, dee da dee.

"It's okay," he said.

"What's that noise?"

Paul glanced down the street at the approaching vehicle. It was the same ice cream truck he and Josh had run out to on Saturday night. The one that had been driven by Kenneth Hoffman's son.

"I have to go," he said.

"I've got a call in to find out who sold that house. When I—"

"Later," he said, tucking his phone away.

Stick with the program. Don't be distracted. You set out to confront this shit, and confront this shit you shall. So there've been some strange bumps in the road. Keep on going.

The truck slowed as two kids from a house half a block away ran out, waving their arms. The truck slowed to a stop.

Dee dee, diddly-dee, dee dee, dee-da, dee-da, dee da dee.

Paul strode down the street. He waited for the two kids to get their orders, then stood up to the window. The heavyset young man with the LEN name tag pinned to his chest said, "What do you want?"

Paul said, "Medium cone, just plain."

No more fear. No more turning away.

As Len began to prepare it, Paul said, "You're Leonard Hoffman, right?"

Leonard turned and looked at Paul. "Yeah."

"Do you know who I am? Do you recognize me?"

Leonard stopped swirling the cone under the soft ice cream dispenser, set it on the counter. "I don't think so," he said.

"I'm Paul Davis."

Realization slowly dawned behind Leonard's dim eyes. "You . . . I know that name."

"Your dad . . . I was the witness. Your father was charged with attacking me, that night. I wondered— I know this may sound odd—but I wonder if I might be able to talk to you about your father."

Leonard's eyes narrowed. "Why?"

"I just . . . it's hard to explain. These last few months have been difficult for me, and I've been trying to— how do I put this—confront the things—"

"You're a bad man," Leonard said.

"What?"

"It's all your fault."

"*My* fault?"

"That my dad went to prison."

"Uh, no, I don't think so, Leonard. It was your dad's fault, because he killed those two—"

"You stopped. If you hadn't stopped, he wouldn't have been arrested."

So maybe this wasn't such a great idea after all.

"Because you stopped, it made my dad stay there too long. And then the police came."

Paul blinked. "If the police hadn't come, I'd be dead. Your father would have finished me off."

"He should've," Leonard said, flicking the ice-cream cone off the counter with the back of his hand. It bounced off Paul's chest, leaving a dripping, white mess on his shirt.

"No charge, asshole," Leonard said. He went back to the front of the truck, put it in gear, and drove off.

He went back into the house for a clean shirt and stuffed the other one into that bag of clothes that he was supposed to have taken to the dry cleaners. It was still up in the bedroom. He'd grab a fresh shirt from the closet.

Mockingly, he said to himself, "Hey there, Leonard. Wanna talk about your killer dad? Sit down, really get into it about your homicidal father?"

He passed through the kitchen on the way upstairs.

Glanced in the direction of his office.

Saw the typewriter on the desk.

Something caught his eye.

"No," he said under his breath.

From where he stood, there appeared to be a black line on the new sheet of paper he had rolled into the machine that morning.

A line of type.

Slowly, he approached the door to the small office and stepped in, as though a tiger might be hiding behind the door. His pulse quickened and his mouth went dry. Paul blinked several times to make sure that what he was seeing was real.

The latest message read:

> **Blood was everywhere. What makes someone do something so horrible?**

He stumbled back out of the room.

I did not do this, he told himself. *I did not do this. I have no memory of doing this. I wasn't even here. There's no way I—*

A loud *ping* rang out from inside his jacket, startling him. He took out his phone, brought the screen to life.

He'd received an email. He opened it, saw that it was from Gwen Stainton of the *New Haven Star.*

It read:

Dear Mr. Davis:

I thought I recognized your name as soon as I saw your email address. I covered the Hoffman double homicide from the very beginning and can tell you that the typewriter used in the case was never recovered. What makes you ask?

Sincerely,

Gwen Stainton

Twenty-Six

P aul's mind raced.

If he had not written this note and left it for himself—as Charlotte would probably theorize if she were here—and if those two dead women really were *not* trying to connect with him, then there remained only one possible explanation.

Someone really was getting into the house.

But the house had been locked when he got back here. He clearly remembered sliding the key in, turning back the dead bolt.

Could someone have come in through the garage, then entered the house through the interior door that connected the two?

Paul ran downstairs, went out the front door, and

tried the handle on the garage door. He couldn't turn it. It was locked as well.

He went back into the house, checked the balcony doors off the living room and the bedroom, in case somehow someone had scaled the wall. But those doors were not only locked, they were also prevented from being slid open by wood sticks in the tracks.

No one could have gotten into this house.

He was sure of it.

He returned to the kitchen, then went back into his study long enough to grab the laptop that was sitting next to the typewriter, which he brought out to the kitchen island. He pulled up a chair. He could not bring himself to remain in his tiny office. He was, at this moment, too freaked-out to be in there with that relic. The very thought of going back into that closet-size space made him feel short of breath.

He thought of that movie, the one with *paranormal* in the title, where they set up the camera in the bedroom. In the morning, the couple living in the house saw all these freaky things happening while they'd been asleep. Covers being pulled off them, doors opening and closing.

Except, Paul reminded himself, *that* had been a movie.

This was for real.

He thought back to the moments before he and Charlotte had left to find the house where she had bought the Underwood. Was it possible he'd written this line on the typewriter seconds before they left? But he wasn't even remotely asleep at that point. He'd been up for hours.

"I didn't do it," he said under his breath. "I'm sure I didn't do it."

He opened the mail program on his laptop to take another read of the message he'd first seen on his phone, the one from Gwen Stainton, saying that the Hoffman typewriter had never been recovered.

"What makes you ask?" she'd written before signing her name.

He found the *New Haven Star* page he'd looked at earlier and called the main phone number.

"*New Haven Star*," a recording said. "If you know the extension you're calling, please enter it now. If you had a problem this morning with the delivery of your paper, please press one. If you would like to register a vacation, suspend delivery, or cancel your paper, press two. If you would like to place an ad, please press three."

"For fuck's sake," Paul said.

"If you would like to be connected to the newsroom, press four. If—"

Paul pressed four, thinking that anyone calling in with a hot tip would probably have given up by now.

"Newsroom," a man said.

"Gwen Stainton."

"Hang on."

The line went dead for nearly ten seconds, then, "Stainton."

"Ms. Stainton, it's Paul Davis. I emailed you this morning about Kenneth—"

"Yeah, the typewriter question. We talked, right? Back when I wrote a feature on the case, after Hoffman pleaded guilty."

"That's right."

"How are you doing?"

"I'm okay."

"I know you got hurt pretty bad, but in a lot of ways, you were pretty lucky."

"I guess you're right about that. So, about the typewriter. I don't think this ever even came up—it wasn't in your story—but the night I saw Kenneth, he tossed something into a Dumpster. I think it had to be the typewriter he made the women write those notes on. But because of my head injury, I didn't even recall that for a few days. I suppose, by then, that the Dumpster could have been emptied."

"Possibly," Gwen said. "Like I said in my email, Mr. Davis, what makes you ask?"

He paused. "Is this off the record?"

A pause at the other end. "Yeah, sure."

"I've been seeing a therapist since the incident. To, you know, deal with the trauma. As a way of confronting it, I've decided to write about what happened to me. A kind of therapy, I guess you'd call it. But reviewing everything about what occurred that night, there's this one, well, kind of a loose end. About the typewriter."

"You sound like a modern-day Columbo," Gwen said.

"Maybe so," Paul conceded.

"You probably know as much or more than I do. After he killed those two women, Hoffman wanted to get rid of the evidence. That being their bodies, and the typewriter, which would have had a lot of blood on it. I imagine it would have been impossible to get the blood out of all the little nooks and crannies in an old machine like that."

From where he was sitting, Paul looked at the Underwood. If this was that typewriter, someone had cleaned it up. Or maybe it had rained after Hoffman dumped it. Nature gave it a good rinsing.

"Sure," he said.

"So, yeah, he tossed it. And it wasn't found. But the police didn't need it to make their case, since Hoffman confessed. I'm sure the police did try to find it, but like you said, it probably was in a dump somewhere, buried under tons of trash, by that time."

Paul couldn't take his eyes off the typewriter. He was unable to shake the feeling that it was looking at him. Except, typewriters didn't have eyes. The old ones, like this Underwood, were nothing more than hunks of metal. They were machines, plain and simple. They could neither see, nor hear, nor talk, or—

Maybe *talk*.

"Mr. Davis?" Gwen said.

"I'm here," he said. "In your story, you said the typewriter was an Underwood. How would you know that, if it was never found?"

Gwen hesitated. "I'm pretty sure one of the detectives told me. He said Hoffman had called it an Underwood."

Paul continued to stare at the machine.

"Mr. Davis? Is there anything else I can help you with?"

"No," he said. "I mean, maybe."

"What?"

"Have you ever spoken with him? With Kenneth Hoffman?"

"Briefly," she said. "It wasn't an interview. But there was an opportunity to have a few words with him one day when he was being brought from the jail to the courthouse."

"What was your impression?"

"He was charming," Gwen said. "Positively charming."

Paul had put the phone down for only a second when he thought to call back Charlotte.

"Why'd you cut me off before?" she asked.

"It was the ice cream truck."

"You cut me off to get an ice cream?"

"You said you were going to ask around about some home security companies?"

"Yeah, it's on my list," she said with a hint of weariness. "That, and finding the former owners of that house. Why? Has something else happened?"

Did he want to tell her that he'd found another note? While he considered how to respond, Charlotte said, "Paul?"

"No, nothing's happened," he said. "I just wanted to remind you, that's all."

"I'll ask around. Listen, there's a call I have to take."

"Go."

He put the phone down on the counter and sat there, thinking.

And then it hit him.

"Fuck," he said.

He got back onto the laptop, opened a browser, and went to Google. He entered several key words. *Gavin* and *dead* and *pretend* and *son* and *father* and *Hitch-cock*.

Paul found the news story, even though he had the last name wrong. It was Hitchens, not Hitchcock. It was as Anna had described. The sick bastard tormented a man by pretending to be his son who had been killed in Iraq.

Paul remembered Gavin Hitchens bumping into him as he stormed out of Anna's office. The brief tussle they'd had.

And then Paul couldn't find his keys.

Twenty-Seven

I t all made sense.

If this psycho had gotten into Anna White's files, as she feared, then he knew all about Paul's history. If Hitchens had googled Paul just as Paul had googled Hitchens, he'd know all about what had happened with Hoffman. He'd know Paul had nearly died. He'd know about the notes Hoffman had made the women write.

He'd know about the typewriter.

Hitchens would know more than enough to fuck with him.

Paul called up the online phone directory and entered Hitchens's name. A phone number and a Milford address popped up. The guy lived on Constance Drive.

"You son of a bitch," Paul said.

He felt rage growing within him like a high-grade fever. He wanted to do something about this bastard.

Right fucking now.

He got out his cell and phoned Anna White's office. The first, logical course of action was to get in touch with her.

Voice mail.

"Shit," he said, and ended the call.

He looked at the screen again, focusing on Gavin Hitchens's address. He closed the computer, grabbed the extra set of keys he'd been using the last few days, and headed for the stairs to the front door.

But wait.

What about the shoe Paul had sometimes been leaving just inside the door? If Hitchens had been in the house, how had he left the shoe there on his way out?

Paul ran down to the front door. He picked up a shoe, opened the door, and stepped outside. He got down on his knees, and with the door open no more than four inches, he snaked his arm in, up to the elbow, then crooked it around and set it up against the back of the door.

It could be done, he thought. He had to admit he'd not checked exactly how close the shoe had been to the door. If it had been sitting out an inch or two, would he have noticed?

But wait.

How would Hitchens even know he needed to set that shoe back in that position? If he'd snuck into the house in the middle of the night, he might have heard the shoe move. The sole might have squeaked as it was pushed across the tile.

Minor details, Paul thought. Somehow, this Gavin asshole had figured it out.

While his rage continued to grow, Paul felt something else. There was *relief.* He'd come up with an answer to what had been going on, and it wasn't that he was crazy.

That was good news.

But he was going to deliver some *bad* news to Gavin Hitchens.

Paul grinned. "I'm comin' for ya, you motherfucker."

The house was easy enough to find. It was a white, two-story house with a double garage. A blue Toyota Corolla sat in the driveway. Paul parked two houses down and started walking back.

He had no plan.

Well, he wanted his goddamn keys back. He had *that* much of a plan.

Paul was still one lot away when he saw him. Gavin Hitchens came out the front door, heading for the Corolla.

Paul picked up his pace. He cut across the lawn, the grass underfoot silencing his approach.

Hitchens reached the driver's door and was about to open it when Paul came up behind him, grabbed the back of his head with his outstretched palm, quickly gripped Hitchens's hair, and drove his skull forward into the roof of the car.

Hitchens let out a cry.

Paul pulled his head back, barely noticing that he'd put a small dent into the roof of the Corolla.

"You bastard!" Paul said, driving Hitchens's head into the car a second time. But he wasn't able to do it with as much force this time. Hitchens was resisting. He managed to do half a turn, wanting to see who his attacker was.

"Fucker!" Paul said, spittle flying off his lip. "You sick fuck!"

Hitchens twisted, freed himself from Paul's grasp. He made a halfhearted attempt to take a swing at Paul, but the blow to the head had disoriented him, and he slid halfway down the side of the car.

Paul brought one leg back and kicked Hitchens in

the knee. Hitchens screamed and slid the rest of the way to the driveway.

Paul stood over Hitchens, who was now bleeding profusely from the forehead. "I know it was you," Paul said. "I know what you did, and I know how you did it."

Hitchens moaned. He looked up blearily and said, "Police . . ."

"Good idea," Paul said. "You can tell them about breaking into my house, trying to drive me out of my fucking mind. Where are my keys? I want my goddamn keys."

Hitchens managed to sit upright, his back against the front tire. "You're in such deep shit," he said.

"Nothing compared to what you're in," Paul said.

His phone started to ring inside his jacket.

"Breaking and entering, that's what they'll get you for," Paul said. "And if there's a charge for trying to drive someone out of his fucking mind, they'll add that to the list."

He felt a pounding in his chest. He wondered if he might give himself a heart attack. The thing was, though, it felt *good*. Paul hadn't felt this good, this empowered, in a very long time.

When he looked down at Hitchens, he saw Hoffman, too.

The phone in his jacket continued to ring.

Paul finally dug it out of his pocket and saw that it was Anna. He put the phone to his ear.

"Yeah?"

"Paul?"

"Yes?"

"It's Anna. You called. But listen, I found them."

Paul blinked. "What?"

"Your keys. They'd fallen behind a chair. I just found them. Drop by anytime to pick them up."

Twenty-Eight

A neighbor saw the whole thing and called the police. Paul didn't see the point in running. He was hardly going to lead the cops on a high-speed chase throughout Fairfield County. He sat on the curb in front of Hitchens's home and waited for them to arrive. They got there about a minute after the ambulance.

The neighbor, a woman in her seventies, knelt next to Gavin, trying to comfort him.

"What kind of monster are you?" she shrieked at Paul. She stayed with Hitchens until the paramedics assessed him. When the police arrived, she pointed to Paul.

"He did it!"

Paul sat, arms resting on his knees, doing his best impression of someone who did not present a threat.

The officers approached. "Sir, would you stand up please?"

Not long after that, he was cuffed, thrown into the back of the cruiser, and on his way to the station.

He was allowed to call Charlotte when he got there.

"Do you know any lawyers?" he asked.

"Tons," she said. "I'm in real estate."

"It's not a real estate lawyer I need."

When Charlotte recovered from his news, she said she would find someone and meet him at the station.

Paul was placed in a cell to wait, which gave him plenty of time to think about a great many things.

Anyone else in his predicament might have been thinking about what charge awaited him. Would it be assault? Would it be something more serious, like attempted murder? Would his afternoon behind bars turn into six months or a year? Or more?

But Paul wasn't thinking about any of that.

He was thinking about the typewriter.

Gavin Hitchens had not taken his keys. Gavin Hitchens had not broken into his house. And Gavin Hitchens had definitely not typed that message.

Which presented what one might call a bit of a mind fuck.

Hoffman's typewriter had not been found. It was

within the realm of possibility that the machine Charlotte had picked up at that yard sale was that typewriter.

And if it was . . .

Paul examined the tiny cell. A bench to sit on, a toilet bolted to the wall. It seemed so . . . restful in here. Charlotte and whatever lawyer she could find could take their time as far as he was concerned.

It was nice to have a place to contemplate things, uninterrupted.

So, if it was the same typewriter, Paul had to decide whether to think the unthinkable.

Were Catherine Lamb and Jill Foster trying to communicate with him through that typewriter? If so, what were they trying to say? What was the message?

What did they want from him?

This is crazy. They'll lock me up, but it won't be in a place like this. It'll be a psych ward.

Why contact him? Maybe they'd have reached out to anyone who possessed this typewriter. (Paul made a mental note: when Charlotte found the previous owners, he'd ask if they'd noticed anything spooky about the Underwood. Maybe that was why they'd sold it.) But making a connection with Paul, who was directly linked to the women through Kenneth Hoffman, had to mean something.

Sitting in the cell, Paul had something of an epiphany. He needed to talk to more people. He needed to talk to everyone connected to this case, or at least try.

The dead women's spouses. Other women Hoffman had affairs with. His wife, Gabriella. The more he learned, the more he might understand why messages were appearing in that typewriter.

Charlotte showed up with a lawyer named Andrew Kilgore, who didn't look as though he'd seen his twenty-fifth birthday yet.

"Mr. Davis, I've arranged for your release but you're going to have to appear for a hearing—"

"Sure, whatever, that's fine," Paul said as the cell door was opened and he was led, along with the lawyer, toward the exit.

"Mr. Davis, I'm going to need to sit down with you to discuss our options. Your wife tells me you've been under considerable strain and that you suffered a head injury eight months ago, which could be very useful to us—"

"I want to get out of here," he said.

He found Charlotte waiting out front of the station. She threw her arms around him. Her smeared eye makeup suggested she'd been crying.

"Are you okay?" she asked.

"Fine," he said, breaking free of her and reaching for the car door. "Let's go."

Kilgore had more to say to him, but Paul wasn't even listening. He had a plan now, and he just wanted to get to it.

Twenty-Nine

When Paul and Charlotte got home—they first had to go over to Constance Drive to fetch Paul's car—she found the latest note sitting in the Underwood:

Blood was everywhere. What makes someone do something so horrible?

"Paul?" she said. "What's this? You didn't tell me about this. What's going on? Why did you attack that man?"

"I have to go out," he said.

"Paul, we just got home. For Christ's sake, tell me what's going on?"

"I have things to do."

"**Is Harold Foster** in?" Paul asked at the Milford Savings & Loan customer service desk.

"Do you have an appointment?" the woman behind the desk asked, flashing him a Polident smile.

"No," he said.

"Um, would you like to make one?"

"If he's here now, I would like to see him."

The woman's smile faded. "Let me check. What's the name?"

"Paul Davis."

"And what's it concerning?"

"It's a personal matter," he said.

"Oh." She picked up the phone and turned away so that Paul could not hear her discussion. After fifteen seconds, she replaced the receiver and said, "Have a seat and Mr. Foster will be with you shortly."

Shortly turned out to be five minutes. Finally, a short, balding man in a dark blue suit appeared.

"Mr. Davis?" He wore a quizzical look.

Paul stood. "Yes."

"Come on in."

He led Paul down a carpeted hallway to an office about ten feet square. The wall that faced the hall was a sheet of glass. Foster went behind his desk and sat while Paul took a chair opposite him.

The man's desk was stacked with file folders. "Excuse all the mess. So much paperwork." He grinned. "Everything has to be in writing, I always say."

"Of course."

"How may I help you? You weren't very forthcoming with our receptionist, but I understand financial matters are very personal. Whether you've got a million to invest, or you owe the same to the credit card companies"—he grinned—"these are all things that aren't anyone else's business."

"It's not that kind of thing," Paul said.

"What could it be, then?"

"I teach at West Haven College. Well, not at the moment. But I'll be going back in the fall."

The three words prompted an almost instantly darker look from Foster. "Oh?" He studied Paul a moment longer. "What did you say your name was again?"

"Paul Davis."

Foster leaned back in his chair. "My God, you were . . . you were there."

Paul nodded. "I was."

"He tried to kill you."

"Yes."

"If you hadn't stopped . . . the police wouldn't have found him." He let out a long breath. "And then we might never have found out what happened to them. To Jill, and Catherine."

"I'm very sorry about your wife. I knew Jill, of course. Not well, but I ran into her occasionally at West Haven. The one I knew much better, or at least thought that I knew, was Ken—"

Foster held up a hand. "Stop right there."

"I'm sorry?"

"Don't even say his name," he said, his voice bordering on threatening. "Do not say that man's name in my presence. Never."

Paul nodded. "I understand."

Foster calmed himself. "Well, what is it you want?"

"I . . . I hardly know how to begin this, but I want to ask you some questions, about Jill, and what happened."

"Why?"

He couldn't bring up the typewriter, but he could tell this man about how he was attempting to deal with his post-traumatic stress.

"I'm . . . writing something. I'm writing about what I went through, about my recovery."

"A book?"

"I don't even know yet. The immediate goal is to get it all out, to face what happened to me. Maybe, at some later date, it'll be a book, or a magazine piece. I don't know what shape it's going to take."

"Oh."

"Yeah, well, anyway, that's why I'm here. To ask you—"

The hand went up again. "Enough," he said.

"I just wanted to—"

"Stop. I'm sorry for what happened to you, Mr. Davis. And I suppose I owe you some thanks. You probably, inadvertently of course, helped bring . . . that man to justice by coming upon him when you did. But I don't want to talk about this. Not with you, not with anyone else. I've no doubt these last eight months have been hell for you. Well, they've been hell for me, too. And your way to deal with it may be to turn it into some creative writing exercise, but I have no interest in baring my soul to you or answering your prurient questions about my wife."

"Prurient? Who said anything—"

Foster pointed to the door.

"Get out or I'll call security."

Paul nodded, stood, and left. Foster trailed him, a good five paces behind, until Paul had left the building.

Thirty

Anna White heard the doorbell ring.

It was the front door this time, not her office door. It was after five, and her last appointment had just left. She met weekly with an obsessive-compulsive man who associated leftward movements with evil. When driving, he would go around a block, making three right turns, so as not to make a left. He tried to use his left hand so little that muscle tone in that arm had degenerated. If he meant to walk left, he would rotate his body three-quarters of a turn, then head off in the direction he had to go. It was all rooted in the Latin word *sinister*, which means "to the left" or "left-handed." Not surprisingly, his politics were right-wing.

Anna was making very little progress with him. She hoped that if Gavin Hitchens had actually managed to download many of her files, that he didn't get hold of that one. A psychopath like Hitchens would have far too much fun with him.

She was about to make some postsession notes when she heard the doorbell. She hurried through the house, wanting to get to the door before her father, should he choose to come downstairs to answer it. But a glance through a window revealed that he was outside, chipping away at the lawn with a nine-iron.

Anna opened the door to a woman she did not recognize.

"Hello?"

"Paul's gone over the edge," she said.

"I'm sorry?"

"I'm Charlotte. Charlotte Davis? Paul's wife?"

"Yes, okay. What's happened?"

"May I come in?"

Anna opened the door wide to admit her.

"They arrested him," Charlotte said.

"They *what*? Who? The police?"

"He attacked some man."

"What man?"

"Someone named Hitchens."

Anna's face fell. "Oh my God no."

"What?"

"I shouldn't have—I wanted to warn him but I never thought—"

"Warn Paul about what?"

"Please, tell me what happened."

Charlotte told Anna what she'd been able to learn from Paul and the police. "He has this crazy idea this total stranger got into our house. Or at least, he did, until he got some call from you."

"I'd found Paul's keys, in my office. He must have thought Hitchens had them."

Charlotte wiped a tear from her cheek. "I don't know how much more of this I can take. Lately, Paul's been so . . . I was going to try and make an appointment with you anyway, to talk about him. But then, when this happened . . ."

"I can't discuss my patients," Anna explained. "Not even with their spouses."

Charlotte nodded quickly. "Of course, I understand that. But I have to tell you what's been going on."

"I really don't know that—"

"Please. I thought Paul was getting better, but these last few days, he's getting worse. He's losing it."

Anna hesitated, then said, "Go on."

"He's hearing things in the middle of the night. Things that *I'm* not hearing. Like someone tapping away on an old typewriter I bought him. And now he's *finding*"—she put air quotes around the word—"messages in the typewriter he thinks are coming from these two women Kenneth Hoffman murdered. And he's already told you about the nightmares, right?"

She replied with a cautious, "He has."

"I don't know what to think. Messages from the dead?" She shook her head, reached into her purse for a tissue, and blotted up more tears from her cheeks, then her eyes. "Unless you believe in ghosts, which I don't, the only possible explanation is that he's writing these messages himself."

Charlotte's chin quivered. "What should I do? I'm so worried about him. He's had such a tough year. The nightmares, the physical recovery. I thought maybe his idea of diving right into what happened to him, writing about it, might help, but it's having the opposite effect. I think writing about it is . . . it's like he's being dragged into some black hole."

"I'll talk to him. I'll bring him in for some extra sessions."

"I'm so worried that he—you don't think there's any chance he'd do anything, you know, to harm himself, do you?"

Anna's brow furrowed. "What have you observed?"

Charlotte hesitated. "I don't know. Nothing I can put my finger on exactly. But he's been down so long, and now, he's having . . . are they delusions? I don't know what else to call them. What's next? That message in the typewriter, it's like a text version of hearing voices. What if the next message tells him to kill himself?"

"If I see anything that leads me to think your husband would harm himself I'll take the appropriate steps."

"I mean," Charlotte continued, "they *are* delusions, right? I mean, are they delusions if he's doing it deliberately?"

"What are you getting at?"

"The noises he claims to be hearing, the typed message, at first I was thinking it was all in his head, that even if he's writing the messages, he's doing it unconsciously, he doesn't know he's doing it. But what if he *does* know? What am I dealing with then? Why would he put on an act like that? Is he trying to make *me* crazy?"

"I can't think of any reason why he would do that," Anna said.

"So then is it a hallucination?"

"I don't know."

"Has he been prescribed something that would be messing with his head? Some kind of weird side effect?"

"No."

Charlotte was shredding the tissue in her hand. "I don't know what to do. I don't know how to help him."

Anna asked her to wait a moment. She went to her

office, grabbed the keys she had been holding for Paul, and gave them to Charlotte when she returned to the front of the house.

"You don't have to take all this on yourself," Anna told her. "That's what I'm here for. To help Paul through this period. We need to give him some time."

"Please don't tell him I was here."

"Why don't *you* tell him? It might actually mean a lot to him, to know that you're this concerned."

"I don't know," she said, more to herself than Anna. "I just don't know."

Charlotte turned for the door, then stopped. "When I said I didn't believe in ghosts, you didn't respond to that. I'm guessing, I mean, I'm sure you've seen everything in your line of work. Have you ever encountered anything that would suggest there's anything to, you know, messages from the . . ." Her cheeks went red, as though she were too embarrassed to complete the sentence. "What I'm trying to say is, you've never seen anyone actually get a message from the *beyond*."

Anna offered a smile. "Not in my experience."

"I don't even know if that's a comfort. If those two dead women really *were* trying to communicate with my husband, well, at least that would prove Paul wasn't crazy, right?"

Thirty-One

Once he'd recovered from his encounter with Harold Foster, Paul found himself at the Connecticut Post Mall.

He needed to walk around, gather his thoughts before he did anything else. So he wandered the shopping concourse from one end to the other, not going into a single store, but finally ending up in the food court, where he bought himself a cup of coffee and sat down to drink it.

He'd had, when he'd left the house, the roughest idea of a plan. Talk to Jill Foster's husband, then Gilford Lamb, spouse of Hoffman's other victim, Catherine. He was also thinking of getting in touch with Angelique Rogers, the West Haven political science professor who'd also had a fling with Hoffman, and had been interviewed in that story by Gwen Stainton.

The meeting with Foster's husband hadn't gone well, but that didn't mean he wasn't going to press on. He knew there was no reason to think that any of these discussions would go well. He might be the *only* one seeking a greater insight into Hoffman's soul. Maybe everyone else just wanted to put the whole nasty business behind them. Foster wouldn't even allow Hoffman's name to be spoken in his presence. Kenneth's wife, Gabriella, Paul feared, might be the hardest to talk to of all of them. If there was anyone who might want to be moving on with her life, it could be Gabriella. And yet, she might, more than anyone else, be the one who held the key to the secrets of Hoffman's personality.

But for now, Paul needed to clear his head. The mall's food court wasn't quite as isolating as a jail cell, but it would do.

As he sat there, watching mothers pushing strollers, teenagers hanging out and laughing, an elderly couple sitting across from each other saying nothing, he wondered whether this quest for understanding was a worthy pursuit.

What guarantee was there that no matter how many

people he talked to, no matter how many questions he asked, he'd ever get his answers?

Sometimes people did bad things. End of story.

But now there was more to it.

Something was not right.

That fucking typewriter.

Paul had exhausted all rational explanations for those messages. As unsettling as it would have been to learn Gavin Hitchens had been sneaking into his house to plant them, it would have been a relief to find out he was responsible.

The only other "real world" explanation? Paul was doing it himself. But he wasn't ready to accept that yet. Sleepwalking was one thing. But inventing messages from the dead and having no memory of it? That was a bridge too far.

That was crazy.

The problem was, the only explanation left to him wasn't any less insane.

Was it possible the typewriter was some sort of conduit for Jill Foster and Catherine Lamb? Were those two women actually trying to talk to him?

No.

Possibly.

Did Paul believe things happened for a reason? If the answer was yes, then some unseen hand had guided

Charlotte to that yard sale. Some force he could not possibly understand told her to get out of the car and check out the junk these people were trying to sell.

And that force knew that when she saw that old Underwood, she'd immediately think it would be the perfect gift for her husband.

The mystical heavy lifting was done.

Once the typewriter was in the house, Jill and Catherine could begin their communication with him.

"God, it's fucking nuts," Paul said.

"You talking to me?"

Paul turned. Sitting at the table next to him was a woman he guessed to be in her eighties, blowing on a paper cup of tea, bag still in, the string hanging over the side.

"I'm sorry," Paul said. "Excuse my language. I . . . I was just thinking out loud."

The woman's weathered, wrinkled face broke into a smile. "That's one of the first signs."

That brought a smile to his face for the first time that day. "In my case, you might be right."

"Are you okay?" she asked, grabbing the string and bobbing the tea bag up and down.

"I'm fine," he said. "Thank you."

"You look like a troubled young man."

He forced another smile. "I've had better days."

The woman nodded. After what seemed a moment of reflection, she said, "I come here every day and have a cup of tea. I look forward to it. It's the high point."

"That's nice," he said, although he wasn't sure whether that was nice, or sad.

"And I watch the people, and I think about their lives, and what they're going through. I used to read books, but I find it harder to concentrate on them now. So I make up stories about the people I see."

Paul thought it was time to move on.

"A lot of times, when I see a man sitting here having a coffee, it's because he's waiting for his wife to finish shopping. But I don't think that's the case with you."

"And why's that?"

"You don't keep looking at your watch, or your phone. So you're not waiting on someone. You're here on your own."

"You're good," Paul said.

The woman nodded with satisfaction. "Thank you." She cocked her head at an angle and asked, "What's fucking nuts?"

It jarred him, his words coming back to him, from this sweet old lady.

What the hell, he thought. It might be easier to ask a stranger this question than someone he knew well.

"Do you think," he asked hesitantly, "that the dead can speak to us?"

The woman reacted as though this were the easiest question she'd ever been asked. "Of course," she said, taking out the tea bag and setting it on a napkin. "I hear from my husband all the time. Do you know what he did?"

Paul waited.

"He died in October. This'd be in 1997. He'd been sick a long time and knew what was coming. So, four months later, a dozen roses arrive at the door. He figured he wouldn't make it to February, so he had ordered my Valentine's Day flowers back in September." She smiled. "How about that?"

"Well," Paul said. "He must have been something."

She took a sip of her tea. "He had his moments."

Paul stood. He tucked his napkin into the empty coffee cup. "You have a nice day," he said.

He dropped the cup into the trash and headed for the escalator that would take him from the food court down to the main part of the mall. He glanced back for one last look at that woman, thinking he would give her a friendly farewell wave.

She was gone.

Thirty-Two

He decided his next stop would be Gilford Lamb.

The one-time director of human resources at West Haven had not returned to work after his wife's murder. His initial time off for bereavement leave had turned into an extended sick leave. From what Paul had heard, he had never recovered emotionally from the loss.

Paul looked up his address online and found that he lived in the Derby area of Milford in a simple two-story house. He pulled into the driveway next to a twenty-year-old rusting Chrysler minivan. As he got out of his own car he took note of the uncut lawn choked with crabgrass, the crooked railing alongside the steps to the front door, the paint flecking off the house.

God, Paul thought. *It's only been eight months.*

When Paul pushed the button for the doorbell, he didn't hear anything. Must be broken.

So he knocked.

Not too hard, the first time. But when no one answered, he tried again, this time putting his knuckles into it.

From inside the house, a muffled, "Hold on."

After ten seconds, the door opened. An unshaven Gilford Lamb looked through a pair of taped glasses at Paul, blinked twice, and said, "Paul?"

"Hi, Gil."

"Well, son of a bitch. What brings you here?"

Paul guessed Gilford was in his midforties, but he looked more like a man in his sixties. His hair had thinned and turned gray, and Paul bet the man was thirty pounds lighter than the last time he'd seen him, which would have been about nine months ago. His plaid shirt was only half tucked into a pair of jeans that looked like they'd last seen a wash when the first Bush was president.

"I was going by, thought I'd drop in. It's been a while."

"Goddamn, yes, it has. Come on in."

He opened the door, and the second Paul stepped into the house he wanted to leave. The place smelled of sweat and piss and booze and old meat. The living room, or what was once a living room, was a clutter of newspapers, magazines, bottles, and, of all things, an oval model train track on the dirty carpet. But the Lionel steam train would have had a hard time making the loop, given that portions of the track were littered with dropped items including a coat and a busted computer monitor.

"You want anything?" Gilford asked.

"No, that's okay."

"Well, I think I will," he said and disappeared briefly into the kitchen. Paul heard the familiar *pfish!* of a pull tab. Gilford returned with a can of Bud Light in his hand. "Gosh, it's great to see you!" His smile seemed genuine. "I was thinking about you the other day, wondering how you were doing."

"Good to see you, too," Paul said, working to hide his shock at how Gil's life appeared to have spiraled downward so severely.

"Grab a seat."

That was definitely something Paul did not want to do, but he could see no way to refuse. He moved aside some old magazines—science journals, train enthusiasts' magazines, even a few comic books—from the stained cushion of a lounge chair while Gilford dropped his butt right onto a layer of newspapers that acted as a couch cover. He crinkled as he got comfortable.

"Not many folks from the college come by," he said. "Well, I guess the truth is, none of them come by. Hear from human resources occasionally, but that's about it. You probably know I'm still on a leave."

"Me, too," Paul said. "But I expect to be going back in September."

"Head's all healed?"

"Getting there. How about you?"

"Oh." He smiled. "I'm never going back. I'll ride out the medical leave long as I can and then quit. I'll never set foot on that campus again."

"How are you . . . managing?" He tried not to look about the room as he asked.

"Oh, it's day by day." He chortled. "I don't much give a fuck."

Paul didn't see the point in avoiding the obvious. "It hit you hard," he said.

"Hmm?"

"Catherine."

Gilford studied him for a moment, stone-faced, then looked away. "Yeah, well." His gaze drifted, as though he could see through the wall to the outdoors. "I guess the guilt kind of ate away at me."

Paul felt a chill. "The guilt?"

"I loved that woman more than anything in the world. I truly did."

Softly, Paul said, "I'm sure. But I don't understand the guilt part. It wasn't your fault, Gil."

He focused on Paul and said, "Wasn't it? I sure as hell think it was."

"It was Kenneth's fault."

"Kenneth," Gil said softly.

"You can't blame yourself."

"Maybe he's the one who slit her throat, but I'm the one who put her there with him," Gil said. "I drove her away. I was . . . I don't know. I'd become distant. I took her for granted. I hadn't remembered her birthday in six years. I know that sounds like I didn't love her, but I did. I just . . . I'd just stopped being attentive in any way whatsoever. I was living in my own world. I see that now, how I sent her into the arms of another man. And not just any man, but a homicidal maniac."

"No one saw it coming," Paul offered. "No one knew Kenneth was capable of something like that."

Gilford shrugged. "Doesn't matter anymore, anyway. So tell me this. What brought you to my door this afternoon? I saw you looking around when you walked in here. I know I look like some kind of deranged hermit, but I'm not so far gone that I don't know when someone is lying to me. You weren't just driving by and decided to say hello."

"That's true."

"So what's up?"

"I've been thinking a lot about Kenneth lately."

"I've never stopped."

"I'm sure. I can't really explain this, but some things that have happened lately have prompted me to look for answers."

"Answers to what?"

"To what made him do it."

"What sort of things?"

Paul hesitated. How did you tell a man his dead wife was sending you messages? He decided to take a chance with Gilford, to at least touch on the more recent developments involving Hoffman.

"Do you think it's possible," Paul asked slowly, "for the things that we use in our everyday lives, for them to—how do I put this—hold some kind of energy, to retain something of us in them?"

Gilford said, "What?"

"I'm not putting this well. But let's say you had something of your grandmother's. Like a mirror. Do you think that mirror possesses some of her soul?"

Gilford drank from his can of Bud Light. "Where might you be going with this, Paul?"

"What if I told you that I've come into possession of something, something that has a particularly dark history, and that individuals who used this item, somehow, in a way that I can't begin to imagine, are trying to communicate with me?"

"I guess I'd say, what the hell are you talking about?"

"It's a long story how it all came to be, but I think I have the typewriter."

Gilford squinted. "The what?"

"The typewriter. The one Kenneth . . . the one he made Catherine and Jill write their apologies on."

Gilford studied him. "You don't say."

Paul nodded.

"That'd be quite something."

"Yeah," Paul said.

"And what makes you think this typewriter you've got is that very typewriter?"

Paul licked his lips, which had gone very dry. "Well, to begin with, it's the same kind. And Kenneth's typewriter was never found by the police. So it's at least possible that this is the same one." He paused. "I've been finding messages in it. Words on sheets of paper that I've left rolled in. Asking why Kenneth did it."

Gilford leaned forward. "And who's doing the asking?"

"Catherine and Jill."

"Well," Gilford said. "That's nothing short of amazing."

Paul waited to see whether he had more to add.

When it appeared he did not, Paul asked, "You have any thoughts or questions?"

He nodded very slowly. "I do."

Paul edged forward in his seat. "Okay."

"All you have to do is look around here and you can tell I'm not doing so well. I'm not like one of those nutcases you see on an episode of *Hoarders* who seems oblivious to their surroundings. I know this is a pigsty. I am aware that I'm living in a hellhole. The thing is, I don't give a flying fuck. I haven't given a shit about anything since that son of a bitch took Catherine away from me. I know the clock is running out on me before I drink myself to death one night or leave something on the stove and burn this place down or maybe one night I just take out that gun I've got in the bedroom dresser and blow my brains out, which is something I give some thought to every single fucking day. It would certainly spare me the humiliation of being that crazy person you see wandering the street pushing a shopping cart full of everything they own."

Gilford Lamb paused to take a breath, then continued. "But never, not once in these last eight months, have I had a notion as ridiculous as the one you just came up with. As bad as things have been for me, I've never lost touch with reality. But that, my friend, sounds like what's happened with you, and you have my sympathy.

I know you've been through a lot, too. What I'd suggest, before it's too late, is that you get help, that you find someone to talk to about this, because I'm guessing you got hit harder in the head than you realize."

"I am talking to someone about this," Paul said.

"A neurologist, I hope."

"Him, too."

Gilford nodded slowly. "Well, that's a good thing, no doubt about it. It's been a pure delight having you drop by, Paul, even though I still don't understand quite why you did. If, the next time you're driving by, you get the urge to visit me again, I hope you won't be offended if I ask you now to just keep on going."

Thirty-Three

Paul was lucky to catch Angelique Rogers when he did.

Paul hadn't needed to look up an address for the West Haven political science professor. A launch for a book she had written about women in the Civil War had been held at her place a couple of years ago, and Paul and Charlotte had attended. A local bookseller was hawking copies, and Paul had bought one. Paul had embraced the idea of a book that examined the role of women during that period in the country's history, but the academic writing style had made it a tough slog. He hadn't been able to make it through the first chapter. The book had sat, ever since, on his study shelf, unread, and while he'd told Angelique he'd thoroughly enjoyed it, he lived in fear she would ask him which chapter was his favorite.

She lived on Park Boulevard in Stratford in a sprawling ranch house with flagstone-style siding. On the other side of Park was a narrow strip of land, and then Long Island Sound. It was a stunning view, Long Island itself nothing more than a sliver of land on the horizon.

There was a green SUV in the driveway, tailgate open. The cargo area was half-filled with luggage and bags. As Paul turned into the drive, Angelique came out of the house dragging a small, wheeled suitcase. Her eyes widened with surprise as she spotted him getting out of his Subaru.

"Paul," she said. "Oh, my."

There was still a trace of her French accent. She had told Paul her history once, about moving to America from Paris when she was only ten. Her parents had both been offered teaching positions at Cornell University. When she spoke, it was evident she was not from around here, but several decades removed from France had made it difficult to pinpoint her origins. She was a petite woman with gray-blond hair that hung in wisps over her eyes.

He waited for her around the back of the car and reached for the case when she got there.

"Let me," he said.

He grabbed the case and tucked it into the back.

"Thank you," she said, "although don't be offended if Charles rearranges it. He packs the trunk like it's a game of Tetris."

Charles, Paul recalled, was not the name of her former husband. Angelique caught his blank expression and smiled. "My new boyfriend. We've rented a place in Maine for the next three weeks."

"Sounds fantastic," Paul said.

"You look well," she said.

He wasn't so sure about that, but he accepted the compliment with a shrug. "Forgive me for showing up unannounced."

She smiled. "No one comes along here by accident. I'm a bit off the beaten path."

He nodded. "No, it's not an accident."

Paul told her, as briefly as he could, about his project but this time leaving out anything to do with the typewriter.

"So you're trying to figure out what makes Kenneth tick," she said.

"In a nutshell. You told the newspaper you were surprised."

"Who wasn't surprised? He is an enigma, our Kenneth. He cast his spell over me for a while. I never thought I'd be the kind to—"

262 • LINWOOD BARCLAY

A tanned, trim, silver-haired man in shorts came striding out of the house. "What happened to you?" he called out to Angelique. "There's still the food to—"

He stopped when he saw that she was talking to someone. "Oh, sorry."

Angelique introduced Charles and Paul to each other. While she mentioned Paul was a colleague, she did not get into what had happened to him.

"I bought this car from Charles," Angelique said.

He smiled. "She came into the dealership, and I thought, I don't care if I sell this woman a car, but I definitely want her phone number."

"Love, just start filling the cooler with the stuff on the right side of the fridge," she said.

If Charles understood he was being dismissed, he offered no clue. "Sure. Nice to meet you, Paul."

Paul nodded. As Charles went back into the house, Angelique said, "If there's something you want to ask, now's your chance."

"Tell me about him."

She cast an eye out over the sound. "Like I said, an enigma. He was a charmer. Did you know he wrote poetry?"

"I'd heard," he said.

"I'd sometimes find, in my interoffice mail, or under my door, a short poem he'd typed up. Little love poems." She grinned. "Quite terrible, actually." She gave Paul a knowing smile. "I would imagine an English professor would be better at that sort of thing, but Kenneth, well, there's not a lot of romance attached to math and physics. But he tried."

"Do you remember any of them?"

She shook her head. "They were forgettable, and at some point I threw them all away. I remember one, about how beautifully shaped women are, one of nature's most glorious achievements." She laughed. "It was embarrassing. I look back and wonder what possible clues there were that I did not pick up, that would have offered a hint to what he was capable of."

The same poem he'd tried out on Charlotte, Paul recalled. Maybe Kenneth had only had one poem in him.

"Let me tell you a story. After our . . . is *dalliance* too precious a word? Although, at the time I may have taken it more seriously than that. Anyway, it was over, and had been for some time, and he and I happened to be in the faculty lounge. Not talking, not interacting at all, and I was aware he was there. It was awkward; I tried to avoid him. I was about to leave when I got a call on my cell that my son, Armand, had been injured. He was eight at the time, and a car had clipped him at a crosswalk by the school. He'd been taken to the hospital. It turned out, thank God, not to be life threatening, but it was serious. I nearly collapsed. My husband was out of the country on business. Kenneth asked what had happened. He took me to the hospital—I was in no condition to drive—and he stayed with me there the entire night. I told him to go home, but he wouldn't leave. God knows what he told Gabriella about where he was, but he kept me company, went and found a doctor when I hadn't had an update in hours. He looked after me. And there was never a hint that he wanted anything in return. He saw I needed help, and he helped me."

She paused. "And that's the man who slit those women's throats."

Paul decided to take another shot at Harold Foster.

He recalled a book he'd once read by a legendary Miami police reporter. Often, when she'd call the family of a murder victim, hoping to add some personal details to her story, she'd get a slammed phone in her ear. So she'd wait a few minutes and try again, saying she'd somehow been cut off. Often, in the interim, another family member would argue in favor of talking to the press, that the world needed to know that, no matter what the cops might say, their dead relative was a decent human being, not some lowlife who had it coming.

Harold's situation was not quite the same, but he might have had a similar change of heart.

After his visit with Angelique, he took a route that went past Milford Savings & Loan. As he neared the bank, there was Foster, coming out the front door, heading for the adjacent parking lot. Paul quickly pulled over to the curb, turned off the car, and got out. The banker was nearly to his car when he saw Paul approaching. He stopped.

"Harold," Paul said, trying to sound agreeable.

Foster was speechless.

"I'm hoping, since we last spoke, you might be willing to reconsider answering a few more questions."

"What the hell is wrong with you? Leave me alone."

"Listen, I'm sorry about this, I really am, but if you don't want to help me now, then I'll be back tomorrow. And if you won't help me then, I'll be back the day after that."

"Mr. Davis, I understand that what happened to you was traumatic. Guess what? What happened to *me* was traumatic. Why can't you get that through your thick, damaged skull?"

"So, I'll see you tomorrow then."

Foster sighed with exasperation. "Fine. What the hell do you want?"

Now that Foster appeared to have surrendered, Paul had to work up his courage to ask his question.

Paul nodded sheepishly. He felt his face flush.

"The truth is, I really have just one question for you, and you're going to think it's a strange one. Or, I don't know, maybe you won't."

Foster stiffened.

"Have you ever, since your wife passed away . . . have you ever felt—this is the strange part but bear with me—that she was trying to connect with you in some way?"

"Excuse me?"

"What I'm wondering is, have you ever felt as though she was talking to you? You know how, when you lose a loved one, in some way they're still with you?"

"A loved one," Harold Foster said flatly.

"Yes."

"You're quite serious."

"I am."

"And you're asking this why?"

Paul hesitated. "I'd be grateful if you indulged me without my having to explain."

"Fine," he said. "I'll answer your goddamn question." A sly grin crossed his face. "Sometimes I *can* imagine

Jill speaking to me. I hear her voice in the back of my head."

"You do?" Paul felt his heart do a small flip of encouragement.

"I do."

"What do you hear her saying?"

"She's saying, 'You lucky bastard. Kenneth Hoffman did you a real favor, didn't he?'"

Paul's mouth opened. He was struck not just by the comment, but also by Harold Foster now being willing to utter his wife's killer's name.

"And you know what I say back to her?" Foster continued. "I say, 'You're damn right.' That's what I say. Hoffman rid me of a two-timing, conniving bitch." He shook his head. "Since she died, if you want to know the absolute fucking truth, I've never felt better. It's like I've been cured of cancer. I feel that I can start my life over."

Paul wondered if he looked as stunned by Harold's words as he felt.

"It was so much easier, honestly, than a divorce. So many times I considered asking her for one, but the thought of the process stopped me. The fights, the recriminations, the lawyers, the sleepless nights, the division of property. It's endless. How easy it would be, to avoid all that, to just kill your spouse. But, of course, I'd never have done such a thing. I'd never even have contemplated it. But what Hoffman did, it makes me realize now, what a magnificent time saver murder is. There are times I wonder if I should write him a check."

Paul couldn't think of a follow-up question.

"Does that about take care of it?" Foster asked. When Paul said nothing, the man unlocked his car, got in, and started the engine.

Paul was still standing there as Foster drove out.

Paul realized, as he turned onto his street, that Charlotte's car was directly in front. She hit her blinker, turned into their driveway, and he drove in right behind her. They each got out of their cars at the same moment.

"Hey," Charlotte said, walking toward him.

"Hey," he said.

She approached him tentatively, eyes down, the way a girl might act if she were asking a boy to dance. But it wasn't shyness. She appeared almost fearful.

"There's something I want to tell you I did, because I don't want you finding out on your own and getting angry, wondering why I didn't tell you."

"What are you talking about?" he said worriedly.

She looked him in the eye. "I went to see Dr. White."

Paul said nothing.

"I'm just so worried about you, Paul," she said. "You're scaring me half to death. I'm not sorry I went to see her. I don't care how mad you get. I had to talk to her."

Paul wasn't angry. He put his hands on her shoulders. "It's okay." He paused. "What did she say?"

Charlotte, eyes brimming with tears, said, "What *could* she say? She's not allowed to say anything. You're her patient. I'm not."

"What did you tell her?"

"I don't know what's happening with you. You assaulted a man! You come home, then you take off. I don't know where you're going, who you're going to see. You think you feel like you're losing your mind? Well guess what? Me, too."

He tried to pull her into his arms, but she resisted. When he pulled a little harder, she allowed him to hold her.

"I'm sorry," he said.

"I need you to listen to me," she said. "I want you to get help. You have to promise me that if Dr. White can't help you, you'll see someone else. You'll get to the bottom of all this. You'll find out why you're . . . why you're doing the things you're doing."

"That's what I've been trying to do. I've been out all day, talking to people."

"What people?"

Paul told her, prompting a concerned sigh.

"Do you really think that's the best thing to do? Getting all those people involved. I mean, the more people you talk to, the more people who are going to think you're—"

She stopped herself.

"The more people who are going to think I'm what?"

"Nothing."

"Crazy? The more people are going to think I'm crazy? Is that what you wanted to say?"

"That's not what—I can't take any more. I just can't."

She turned. Her keys were still in her hand, and she used them to unlock the front door. She went in, closed the door behind her, leaving Paul standing there in the driveway.

I'm losing her, he thought. *If she doesn't believe me, where am I?*

Without Charlotte's support, he wasn't sure he had the strength to get through this. Whatever *this* was.

The front door reopened. Charlotte stood there, crying.

"What's wrong?" he asked. "What is it?"

"It's not funny anymore, Paul," she said.

"What are you talking about?"

"Why are you doing this? Why are you doing this to *me*?"

"Charlotte, what are you talking about?"

She pointed a finger over her shoulder. Paul ran past her and into the house, taking the steps up to the kitchen two at a time. When he reached the top, he froze.

The kitchen floor was littered with paper.

Single sheets. The same kind of paper that was loaded into his printer. At a glance, twenty, maybe thirty sheets. Scattered all over the room.

A line typed on each one.

Paul bent over, started grabbing the sheets, one by one. Reading them. He tried to keep his hands from shaking, but each page in his hands was like a leaf in a windstorm.

```
            Blood everywhere
         Laughter as we screamed
      What did we do to deserve this?
   We were unfaithful but that shouldn't be
              a death sentence
```

Paul lifted his gaze from the clutch of pages in his hand and looked toward the study door.

The Underwood, without a sheet of paper in it, stared back at him.

Paul felt himself being watched and turned to see Charlotte standing at the top of the stairs.

"Just tell me the truth," she said. "Is it you?"

He looked her in the eye. "No. I swear."

She nodded very slowly, turned to look at the typewriter, and said, "Then we have to get that fucking thing out of here."

Thirty-Four

Paul didn't need any time to come up with a plan.

"We take this thing, we put it in the trunk, we drive to the middle of the bridge, and drop it in the goddamn Housatonic."

Charlotte nodded. "We could. We could do that. I *like* that idea."

Paul eyed her skeptically. "I'm hearing a *but*."

"Okay, if that's what you want to do, fine, but you better do it at night. You toss something into the river and you'll be up on some environmental charge. Littering, something. And how are you going to explain yourself if the police come by? Why does a person drop a typewriter off a bridge? What's your story going to be? And even at night, there are probably traffic cameras."

Paul shook his head slowly. "Is there another bridge, another place where—"

Charlotte raised a hand. "Look, for now, let's get it out of *here*. We can talk about where to get rid of it permanently later." She thought for a moment as they stood, shoulder to shoulder, looking at the Underwood. "The garage."

Paul bit his lip. "How does that solve the problem? If there's really something going on with this thing, moving it out of here won't make it stop."

"Neither would dropping it into the river, but whether it's there, or in the garage, you'll stop hearing it in the night," Charlotte said. "This . . . *thing* can type out as many notes at it wants in the garage. If we don't know about it, we don't have to care."

"Okay," he said, a hint of defeat in his voice. "I'm in."

He got his hands under the typewriter. It was, he realized, the first time he had ever moved it.

"This thing *is* heavy," he remarked.

"I told you," she said. "It's a fridge with keys."

Careful not to slip on any of the sheets of paper still on the floor, Paul walked the typewriter across the kitchen and down to the first floor. At the foot of the stairs, at right angles to the front door, was the second door—also fitted with a dead bolt lock—that led into the garage. Charlotte got ahead of Paul, turned back the bolt, opened the door, and held it for her husband. Being an interior door that led to a garage, it had a spring-loaded hinge to guard against possible carbon monoxide mishaps.

She flicked on the light switch. The garage was littered with cardboard boxes, several old bicycles, unneeded furniture.

"That," Paul said, nodding at something in the corner.

Charlotte pointed to a wooden antique blanket box tucked up against the wall. "This?"

Paul nodded, shifting the weight of the typewriter from one arm to the other. "Yeah. Open that up. See if there's anything in it."

The box was about three feet wide, a foot and a half high and deep. Charlotte lifted the lid.

"There's a bunch of old *Life* magazines and *National Geographics* and stuff in there."

"God, why do we have those? They were my *parents'.* Can you shove them over, make enough space for this thing?"

Charlotte got down on her knees and started piling magazines over to one side, creating a cavity on the left.

He leaned over and set the typewriter into the

bottom of the box. When he let go, he flexed his fingers to get the blood circulating in them again. "That is one heavy son of a bitch. Okay, close it."

Charlotte closed the lid of the blanket box as Paul scanned the room.

"What?" she asked.

"Looking for something heavy to put on top."

"Jesus, Paul, it's not the clown from *It*. It's not going to break out and attack us."

Paul had nothing to say to that. He found three liquor store boxes with the word BOOKS scribbled on the side in black marker. He set them on top of the blanket box.

Charlotte linked an arm in his. "Do you think maybe you can relax a bit now?" When he said nothing for several seconds, she said, "Paul?"

"There's one more person I want to talk to."

"Who?"

"Gabriella Hoffman," he said, and saw the doubt in his wife's eyes.

"What can that possibly accomplish?"

"Locking that typewriter in a box doesn't mean I don't still have questions."

"I don't know, Paul. Maybe this has been a mistake. Maybe you need to put all this behind you, stop dredging up everything." She glanced at the blanket box weighed down with the boxes of books. "I never should have bought that thing."

"What if you were *meant* to buy it?" Paul asked.

"What are you saying?"

"What if this is all part of some plan?"

Charlotte looked away, not wanting to listen.

"Hear me out. Whatever the reason for those messages, it's possible that typewriter belonged to Kenneth Hoffman, that this is the machine he forced those women to write their apologies on. What are the odds you'd be drawn to that very yard sale, find that very machine, by chance? To buy something linked to someone I know, to an issue I'd already been thinking I might write about? What are the odds of that?"

Quietly, Charlotte said, "Long."

"Exactly. Incalculably long. But it's a lot more believable if it was somehow preordained. What if there were some sort of force leading you to it?"

"Jesus, Paul. What force? Whose plan?"

"I don't know. Did you find out whose house it was?"

"I told you, I've made calls but haven't heard back yet."

"Maybe it doesn't even matter. Maybe we're not meant to know. The typewriter just *is*. It has no history other than what Hoffman made them write on it. It lives in that *moment*."

"It's like a *Twilight Zone* episode."

Paul couldn't help but laugh at that. "No shit. But I think I'm meant, for whatever reason, to pursue this. And that means talking to Gabriella, and ultimately, Kenneth, who can—"

"Wait, hold it. Kenneth?"

"In prison. I want to talk to him in prison. Maybe Gabriella could expedite that process, if she's willing."

"Why would she?"

"Maybe she won't. But it's worth a try." He took hold of Charlotte's shoulders. "Who knows. Maybe she's as desperate for answers as we are."

"I'll come with you."

He shook his head. "No, it's okay. I think this is something I have to do alone."

Charlotte looked less sure. "I'm worried about you. Out there, asking questions that seem . . ."

"Insane."

She sighed with resignation. They crossed the garage to the door that would take them back into the house. As Paul closed it, he took one final look at the blanket box, then turned off the light.

Thirty-Five

"I was afraid maybe you wouldn't want to see me," Paul said to Gabriella Hoffman.

"Not at all," she said, opening the door for him. "It would seem the least I can do."

Instead of dropping in as he had done with the others he'd wanted to talk to about Kenneth, Paul phoned Gabriella first. She had not asked what it was about, which led Paul to wonder whether she'd always expected he would call, someday.

While Paul and Kenneth had been colleagues, Paul had never been in the Hoffman home. It was a stately two-story in north Milford, set back from the road. Paul was expecting some level of inattention, not necessarily along the lines of Gilford Lamb's place, but when tragedy strikes a household, sometimes other things slide.

But the yard was beautifully maintained. Blooming flower gardens, perfectly trimmed shrubs. He parked alongside a black Toyota RAV4, rang the bell, and was admitted.

Gabriella, tall, thin, with silvery hair that came down to her shoulders, was described as forty-nine years old in the Gwen Stainton article, but she looked older. Despite that, she looked fit, and held her chin high, as though she had nothing in the world to be ashamed about.

She said they'd be more comfortable talking in the kitchen, and led him there. She offered coffee from a half-full carafe and set two mugs on the table. They sat across from each other.

"Many times, I've thought about getting in touch with you," she said.

"You have?"

She nodded. "When you discover you've been married to a monster, you can't help but feel responsible for some of the monstrous things he's done."

"I'm not blaming you. It's never occurred to me to do that."

Gabriella smiled and touched his hand. "That's kind of you. The truth is, I never found the courage to approach you. And as much as I've wanted to offer condolences, something, anything, to Harold or Gilford, I have to admit that I haven't the courage there, either. What would I say? Can I make it all up to them by bringing over a dozen home-baked muffins? I think not. Several times I've tried to write letters to them, and to you, but every time I end up tossing them into the garbage."

Paul did not know what to say.

Gabriella continued, "I was reading one time about a case in Canada. A respected military man who turned out to be a serial killer, and his wife had absolutely no idea. I think about her, and wonder, how does she get up every day, knowing she lived with someone like that, that she didn't see it, and that if she had, maybe she could have done something about it?"

"I can't imagine."

"What Kenneth did wasn't quite as horrific as that, but my God, it came pretty close. If there is anything to be grateful for, it's that you survived."

"Well," Paul said, "I guess there's that."

She put a hand on his arm. "I think we met a few times at faculty events."

"We did."

"Did you know?"

Paul felt a jolt. "Did I know what?"

"That Kenneth was sleeping with anyone who'd let him into her pants?"

The bluntness threw him for a second. He was ashamed by the answer he was to give. "Yes." He paused.

"I suppose everyone did."

"I can't speak for everyone, but I think it's likely," he said. "Now, sitting here, I feel somehow complicit, too. It's not in my nature to be judgmental, but maybe if I'd called Kenneth out on what he was doing, it might have made a difference."

"Oh, I didn't mean to make you feel guilty. I just wondered. Don't feel badly. I certainly knew."

"You did?"

"Oh please," she said. "I knew there was the odd one here and there. I knew what kind of man he was. Although, carrying on with two at the same time, that came as something of a surprise."

"Yes, I suppose it did."

She placed her palms on the table and straightened her spine, as though signaling a change in the conversation's direction. "Kenneth spoke of you often. In fact, he still does."

Paul's eyebrows rose. "Really?"

She nodded. "I visit him every couple of weeks. The man does feel, whether we choose to believe it or not, remorseful. I think he feels especially bad about you. You were a good friend."

"I don't know which I'm more surprised by. That he would mention me, or that you visit him in prison."

"He's still my husband."

"You've never—forgive me, this is probably none of my business—but you've never taken any steps to end the marriage? The affairs alone would be cause for divorce, but since Kenneth did what he did . . ."

As Paul asked the question, it struck him where, exactly, he was sitting.

He was in the kitchen of the Hoffman home. This was where it had happened. His eyes wandered down to the table. Could this be the same one? Was this where the typewriter had sat? Was the chair he was sitting in the one Jill Foster had been bound to? Or Catherine Lamb?

What must it have taken to clean this place up after he'd slit their throats? Was there still blood buried in the grains of this wooden table's surface? Was this where two women pleaded for their lives, where they hoped that a couple of typewritten apologies might save them?

"Paul?" Gabriella asked.

"I'm sorry, what?"

"It looked as though I'd lost you there."

"My mind, it drifted there for a second. What did you say?"

"You were the one talking. You were wondering why I haven't divorced Kenneth."

"I'm sorry. It's none of my business."

She smiled. "As difficult as it may be to imagine, he's a victim, too. A victim of his own impulses. Since he's been in prison . . . he's tried to take his own life. At least once that I know of. Kenneth is my husband. For better or for worse. That was the vow I took. Vows mean something, you know."

"Kenneth took those same vows. About being faithful and forsaking all others."

Gabriella smiled sadly. "He wasn't very good at sticking to those, was he?"

Paul felt a shiver.

"What about the house," he said. "Have you thought of selling it, moving away from Milford?"

"Good luck with that," she said. "Your wife, she works in real estate, doesn't she?"

"Yes."

"She'd probably know all about how hard it is to sell a house where something horrific has happened. In time, maybe, but what Kenneth did, it's far too fresh in people's minds." She paused. "For me, it always will be."

She took a sip of her coffee, set down the mug. "So what was so important that you needed to see me?"

Best to come right out with it.

"I'd like to see Kenneth."

"Oh?"

"I thought it might help if you spoke to him, paved the way, had him put me on a list of accepted visitors."

She considered the request for a moment, then said, "I don't suppose that would be a problem, but I have to ask. Why?"

"At first, I wanted to see him just"—he shrugged— "to talk to him. These past eight months—and I know they've been very difficult for you—but they have been pretty hard on me. I guess what I have is PTSD, post-traumatic stress disorder. I've had recurring nightmares, bouts of memory loss. Even . . . moments where I may be perceiving things I believe are real, but they're not."

Gabriella eyed him with sympathetic wonder. "Oh my, that's awful, but do you think seeing him will help you with any of that?"

"I do. I might be totally wrong, but I do. I think coming face-to-face with him, of turning him back into an actual person, instead of some kind of demon that comes to me in the night, may help."

If she was offended by having her husband referred to as a demon, she didn't show it.

"I'm writing about what happened to me. I don't know what it'll turn into. A memoir, a novel, or maybe just something I write for myself that'll never be read by another living soul. But I think the process is helping me come to terms with what happened. I've been talking to the others touched by Kenneth's actions."

Gabriella put a hand to her mouth. "Oh, dear. You mean, like Harold and—"

"Yes."

She appeared to be deflating. "What have they said to you? How—no, don't tell me. I don't think I'm ready to hear it."

"I understand."

Gabriella took a second to collect herself. "You're seeing a therapist, I presume."

"I am."

"Does he think it's a good idea?"

"She. She's not convinced it's a good idea, but she's not stopping me. In fact, I want to take her with me, if I am able to get in to see Kenneth."

"Well," she said. "You said, *at first.* Is there another reason you want to see him?"

"Before I answer that, I want to ask you something else, something that may seem strange."

"Go ahead."

"Do you ever feel . . . haunted by the women Kenneth killed?"

Her head cocked slightly, as though no one had ever asked her this before. "I suppose I do."

"In what way?"

"I don't know . . . I guess sometimes, I can see them, at this table. Asking me why."

Paul nodded. "Yes. When you see them, how real are they?"

"Far too real. I mean, even though I never saw what happened, I can imagine it, sadly." Gabriella sharpened her focus on him. "Why do you ask?"

Here we go.

"I think it's possible," Paul said, "that I have the typewriter."

Gabriella's face froze.

"I'm sorry, what?"

"I think I have it. The typewriter Kenneth made them write their apologies on."

"That's not possible. The typewriter was never found. How could you have it? Kenneth got rid of it the night of the murders. The police never found it. No, that's simply not possible."

Before he could tell her more, she asked: "What kind of typewriter is it? Describe it."

"It's an Underwood. Very old. Black metal. You know. An antique manual typewriter. My wife acquired it recently at a yard sale."

She appeared to be trying to remember. "It's funny, you see it sitting around the house every day, and now I'm trying to think, was it a Royal? A Remington? An Olympia? All names I remember from my childhood. But I think, yes, I think it's possible our old typewriter was an Underwood. But there are millions of them. You can find one in almost any secondhand shop. What would make you think it was ours?"

Paul had thought about how he would answer. "That's something I would be prepared to discuss with Kenneth."

"You should tell me." Her face darkened. "After all I've endured with that man, surely I'm entitled to know whatever you're holding back."

"I'd like to tell Kenneth first. If he wants to tell you what I've told him, I have no problem with that."

She didn't look pleased with that, but she didn't fight him. She did appear ready to ask him something else, but they were interrupted by what sounded like a truck pulling up to the house.

"My son's home," she said.

"Can you get in touch with Kenneth and ask him if he'll see me?"

Gabriella stood up, evidently eager to greet her son. "I'll see what I can do. Sometimes these things can be arranged more easily than you think. And what's the name of the person you want to take with you?"

Paul told her. She nodded and started walking toward the front door.

It opened before she got to it. Leonard Hoffman, still in his ice cream–stained apron, came into the house.

He looked at Paul and said, "You."

Thirty-Six

"Hello, Leonard," Paul said.

Gabriella was startled. "You know each other?"

"This is the bad man I told you about," Leonard said.

"Wait, what?" she said.

"Leonard sells ice cream on our street quite often," Paul said defensively. "Earlier today, I admit, I mentioned to him that there was, well, a connection."

Gabriella looked as disappointed as she was angry. "Why would you do that? Why would you drag my son into this? Don't you think he's suffered enough from what his father has done?"

"I'm sorry, I—"

"He called me saying some man asked about his father, but I had no idea it was you."

Paul looked apologetically at Leonard. "I'm sorry. I didn't mean to upset you."

"Leonard, why don't you go in and have a snack while I see this man out."

Leonard hesitated, not sure that he was ready to be dismissed. But finally he said, "Okay." He glanced over his shoulder, adding, "Don't come back here again." He disappeared into the kitchen.

"Really, I'm sorry," Paul said to Gabriella.

"Something we never got to," she said, keeping her voice low, "was how hard this has been on Len."

"I can well imagine that—"

"No, you can't. Len's not been the easiest boy in the world to raise. He's got his share of difficulties, but say what you will about Kenneth, he loves his son and was always there for him."

"What's Leonard's—"

"If you were going to say 'problem,' Leonard doesn't have a problem. He was always just a little slower than the other kids, but there's nothing wrong with him. He might not have been college material, but he's got this job now driving that ice cream truck and that's done the world for how he feels about himself. Can you imagine what it's been like for him having a father go to jail for what he did? I just thank God he's years out of school. The other kids would have tormented him to death."

"I should go," Paul said.

"Maybe you should."

But Paul hadn't moved toward the door, and Gabriella guessed why. "I'll still do it for you. I'll get in touch with Kenneth, and the prison."

"Thank you. Can I give you my cell number?"

She went for a pen and a piece of paper. When she returned he gave it to her and she wrote it down.

"Okay," she said.

"When I talked to Leonard," Paul said hesitantly, "he said it was my fault."

"What?"

"Because I came upon Kenneth. Because maybe if I hadn't, Kenneth would have been gone by the time the police came."

"Does that surprise you?" she asked. "I think, at some level, Leonard can't believe it's true. That there must be some sort of extenuating circumstances. His father couldn't have done what they said he's done."

Paul nodded. "Thank you for your time, Gabriella."

It was nearly ten when Paul got home.

He locked the front door once he was inside. As he was about to climb the steps upward, his gaze was drawn to the door to the garage.

Paul reached out for the doorknob, but then pulled his hand back.

There's no need to check, he told himself.

But the longer he stood in that spot, the more he knew he was going to have to prove it to himself. It was like going back into the house to make sure you'd turned off the stove. You knew you'd done it, you knew it was off, but you had to *know.*

He turned back the bolt on the door, opened it, and reached his hand around to flick on the light. He stepped around the various boxes and pieces of furniture until he was in the far corner of the garage, where the cartons of books were piled atop the wooden blanket box.

This is crazy, he told himself. *Of course it's in there.*

He held his breath, listening. If the keys were tapping away in that box, he'd surely hear them.

And he was hearing nothing.

Which was a good sign, right?

And even if there had been anything going on in

that box since Paul put the typewriter in there, he had not left any paper in it. So the machine wouldn't be able to do any communicating.

No, wait.

Not true.

What about those sheets of paper scattered all over the kitchen? How in the fuck had *that* happened?

How did countless sheets get rolled into the type-writer? And how the hell did they get pulled out?

Paul began moving the cartons of books off the blanket box. Once he had it cleared off, he knelt down, slipped his hand into the groove under the lid to allow him to lift it up easily.

Just do it.

Lift it up and look inside.

Paul took a deep breath, and brought the lid up.

"Paul!"

"Jesus!" he shouted, dropping the lid and whirling around. His heart jackhammered in his chest.

The interior door to the garage was open about a foot, Charlotte's head poking in.

"What are you doing?" she said. "I thought I heard you come in, but then you didn't come upstairs."

"You scared me half to death," he said, still kneeling.

"What's going on?"

"Nothing," he said. "I was . . . checking. That's all."

He turned back to the blanket box and lifted the lid, casting light down into it.

The typewriter was there. There was no paper rolled into it, no other paper to be found, not counting the stacks of old magazines.

Paul swallowed, lowered the lid, and stood.

"Well?" Charlotte asked.

"It's here," he said.

"Well, of course it is. For God's sake, come to bed."

He nodded sheepishly and walked across the garage, hit the light, and closed the door as he went back into the house.

Thirty-Seven

P aul was in front of his laptop when his cell phone rang shortly after noon the following day. It was Gabriella Hoffman.

"It's set up for tomorrow," she told him. "For both of you."

"I can't thank you enough," he said. "He's willing to see me?"

"He is."

Then he called Anna White and told her they were set for a prison visit with Kenneth Hoffman, if she was still interested in coming.

"Yes," she said without hesitation. She would have to clear her schedule for the day, and make sure that she could get Rosie, a retired nurse who lived next door who often checked in on her father whenever Anna had to be away for any length of time.

"Why don't I drive," she said.

Paul was going to ask why, then figured, if he were dealing with someone who'd suffered a head injury and from all indications was borderline delusional, he'd want to be the one behind the wheel, too.

"Okay," he said. "I'll come to your place, then we'll head up in your car."

"Was there ever any talk of Charlotte coming with us?" Anna asked as they backed out of her driveway. The prison facility where Kenneth Hoffman was serving his time was near Waterbury. Anna figured it would take the better part of an hour to get there. She entered its address into the in-dash GPS system on her Lincoln SUV. They'd start out by taking Derby-Milford Road up to Highway 34, jogging west, then heading north on 8.

"She knew I was trying to arrange a visit with Kenneth, but when she knew you'd agreed to go with me, she thought that was best. She told me she came to see you."

Anna glanced over. "I told her she should. There

was no reason to keep it a secret. She's worried about you."

Paul nodded. "More now than ever."

"Well, you are going through more now than you were before."

"It's not just that," he said. "She just seems . . . more caring. In between moments where she thinks I'm totally nuts. Anyway, she decided to take a day herself and get out of town. Her mother's in Tribeca, and she hasn't been into the city to visit her in weeks. They're not that close, actually, so I was a little surprised, but anyway, I dropped her off at the station this morning. Knowing Charlotte, she'll also make time to hit Bloomingdale's before catching the train home. I don't know when we'll be back so I told her to take a cab home from the station."

Anna swerved too late to miss a pothole. A loud, metallic rattle came from the rear cargo area. It sounded like it was inside the vehicle. Before Paul could ask, Anna said, "Golf clubs."

"Oh. You play?"

"Some. Every time I play there's at least one club missing. My dad keeps taking them so he can hit some balls in the backyard and never puts them back." She changed topics. "What are you really hoping to get out of this? Seeing Kenneth?"

"I'm not going in with any expectations. I guess I'll see how it goes."

She noticed a manila envelope on his lap. "What's in there?"

"Something I want to show him, if they'll let me."

"You want to show me?"

He slid several pages out of the envelope. They were the messages he had found in the typewriter and scattered across the floor.

Anna glanced over several times as Paul leafed through them for her. "I simply don't know what to make of them, Paul."

"They're proof," he said.

"Of what, exactly?"

He glanced at her. "Maybe you think they're proof that I've gone mad. I think they're proof that Jill and Catherine Lamb are trying to reach me."

Anna decided not to respond.

They drove a few more miles in silence until Paul said, "Tell me about Frank, about your father."

"Well, he's a wonderful man. A retired animator. Worked for Warner Bros., actually knew Walt Disney. Still watches cartoons every single day. He's been living with me since my mother passed away. The last year or so, things have . . . started to happen. Confusion. Sometimes he thinks I'm my mom, his wife. Other times he wants me to take him to visit her. I fear we're on a slippery slope."

"It happens," Paul said.

Her lips compressed before she spoke. "He's been a great help to me for so long. He's been telling me I need to find a place for him. Like he's worried about being a burden to me." The lips pressed tightly together again, as if somehow that would ward off tears. "Says there's no reason for me to be keeping him around."

"Is he laying a guilt trip on you?"

"It's not like that at all. He's genuinely worried about me." She let out a short laugh. "Wants me to get *out there*. You know what he called this trip of ours, to a prison? A fun outing."

Paul laughed.

Anna was silent for a moment. Then, "I don't know what I'm going to do. I mean, eventually. We're managing okay now, but in six months? Hard to say. That visit from the SWAT team shook him up badly." She looked his way and smiled. "You would be amazed at how many therapists' lives are a complete mess. We offer advice to others on how to get their shit together when our own is a total disaster." She laughed self-deprecatingly. "We're the evangelists who get caught with a prostitute while preaching morality to the masses."

Paul smiled.

Anna continued, "We're just people. We're just people like anyone else, with a fancy piece of paper on the wall. At the end of the day, we have the same doubts as anyone else. Are we making any progress? Are we making a difference? Are we really any help to anyone at all?"

"You've helped me," he said.

Her mouth formed a jagged smile. "I hope so. And yet here we are, driving off to meet with a murderer. For the life of me, I don't know that this is going to do you an ounce of good."

"It's a journey into the unknown for us both."

"Yeah, well, I wish this GPS could tell us if we're doing the right thing."

Paul looked at her hands gripping the steering wheel. He didn't see any bandage.

"How's the finger?" he asked.

She flashed him a smile. "It healed up nicely, thank you."

A warm feeling washed over Paul. He wanted to touch Anna, rest his hand on her arm ever so slightly. Make a physical connection, no matter how small. He recalled holding her hand under the running water, their shoulders touching.

They barely said a word the next half an hour. Not until the GPS voice advised Anna to take the next exit off the highway. A few more miles, and a few more turns later, they spotted a facility in the distance surrounded by an unusually tall metal fence with thick coils of barbed wire strung along the top.

"Doesn't look much like a day care center," Anna said.

"No," Paul said. He turned and looked at her as the car approached the gate. "All of a sudden, I'm not sure this is a good idea."

"You don't have to do this," Anna said. "I can turn around and take us back."

Paul pressed his lips tightly together. "We're here," he said. "Might as well check the place out. If they send me here for what I did to Hitchens, maybe Kenneth and I will end up as roommates."

Thirty-Eight

Charlotte had not lied to Paul about going into Manhattan. She hadn't even lied about going to visit her mother. She intended to do that, if she had time. And Paul was right when he had joked as he'd dropped her off at the Milford station that she would try to find time to visit Bloomingdale's.

But she was not going into New York for either of those reasons.

When she got off the train and entered Grand Central Terminal, she exited through the market and flagged down a cab almost immediately on Lexington.

"Sixty-Third and Park," she said as she closed the door.

The taxi moved south, the unshaven, overweight man behind the wheel steering over to the left lane to make a turn onto Forty-First Street. One long block later, he went north on Third while Charlotte struggled with muting the annoying mini–TV screen bolted to the partition in front of her.

"Nice day," the driver said.

Charlotte was not interested in small talk.

Traffic, as always, was heavy, but fifteen minutes later the taxi was slowing on Sixty-Third with Park only half a block away. "Where 'bouts?" the driver asked.

"Anywhere here," she said. "Just pull over."

The cab aimed for the left side of the street. Charlotte slid a ten and two ones into the tray below the Plexiglas divider and got out. As she hit the sidewalk she glanced up to check the numbers. She had never actually been to this address before, but she knew, from checking Google Maps early that morning, that her destination had to be practically right in front of her.

Then she saw the sign.

BENJAMIN MARKETING

It was a subtle bronze marker, not much bigger than a license plate, affixed to the side of a building at eye level, next to a set of revolving doors. Charlotte pushed through and found herself in a small, marble foyer. A security guard at the front desk looked up.

"Help you?"

"Here to see Hailey Benjamin," she said, knowing there was probably no need to add the name of the firm.

"A moment," he said, picking up a phone.

Charlotte had figured this would happen. She was waiting for the question.

"Name?" the guard asked, looking at her.

"Charlotte Davis."

The guard repeated the name into the phone, hung up, and said, "Go on up. Sixteenth floor."

Charlotte got onto the elevator, imagining what Hailey's reaction must have been when she was told who was here to see her. She'd be so dumbfounded the wife of her ex-husband was in the building that she'd hardly refuse to see her just because she didn't have an appointment.

As the elevator passed the fourth floor, Charlotte wondered whether Hailey would notify her husband, Walter, that she was here. Walter Benjamin was the president of Benjamin Marketing, and while his wife technically worked for him, it was, from everything Charlotte had heard, more of a partnership.

When the elevator doors parted on the sixteenth

floor, Hailey was standing there in front of the wall with the firm's name stretched out over twenty feet in big blue letters.

"Charlotte," she said, saying the word as a half welcome, half question.

"Hailey," she said.

"Taking a day off to see the city?" Hailey said, forcing a smile.

"Something like that. Is there someplace we could talk?"

"Uh, sure. What's this about? Has something happened? Is everything okay?"

"Let's get settled first."

Hailey said something quietly to the man on the reception desk before leading Charlotte down a glass hallway to a door labeled CONFERENCE ROOM B.

Inside was a rectangular glass table big enough to sit a dozen people. Hailey pulled out a chrome-and-black-leather chair for Charlotte before sitting herself in the one next to her.

"Can I get you something? Sparkling water? A cappuccino?"

"No," Charlotte said. "Hailey, I know you and I have not exactly been best friends over the years."

Hailey said nothing, waited.

"But this isn't about me. This is about Paul. I know

there's got to be some part of you that still cares about him, and—"

"Of course I care about Paul," Hailey said. "Just because things didn't work out between us doesn't mean I have no feelings for him. We had a child together, for God's sake. What's going on? Is he okay? Is he sick? Is this about what happened?"

"Yes . . . and no. He's not himself. He's—he's believing in things that don't make any sense."

"Like?"

"First of all, he's hearing things."

"What do you mean? Do you mean *voices*? Paul's hearing voices?"

"Not exactly," Charlotte said. "But—"

The door opened. A tall, gray-haired man in a dark blue suit, open-collared white shirt, and no tie stepped in.

"Charlotte?"

"Walter," Charlotte said.

She started to stand, but he raised two palms, as though he could keep her in her seat through some invisible force. "Please, don't get up. How nice to see you. Is something wrong with Paul?"

"Why would you ask that?" Charlotte asked, her voice tinged with suspicion.

"I just—" He cut himself off, looked at Hailey.

"I told Walter you were heading up in the elevator," Hailey said, "and all we could think was that Paul was in some sort of trouble. Has he been back to see the neurologist? Is that what this is about?"

"He hasn't," Charlotte said. "It's a different issue than that. I came here because, I think you need to know that Paul is going through a very difficult time, and I don't know that I can handle it all alone."

Hailey shrugged hopelessly. "Tell me about these voices he's hearing."

"Jesus, hearing voices?" Walter said.

"I never said voices," Charlotte said. "More like sounds, in the night, sounds I don't hear."

"It's a good thing you're telling us this," Walter said. "Thank you."

Charlotte shot him a look. "Thank you?"

"Well, it's good to know," he said. "Because of Josh." Walter glanced at his wife. "Right? If there's something wrong with Paul, we need to know."

"What's that supposed to mean?" Charlotte asked.

Hailey looked apologetically at Charlotte. "It's just, well, if Paul is unstable, I mean, that's something we'd have to take into account when it's your turn to have Josh."

"There's nothing wrong with me," Charlotte said. "And I'm not suggesting Paul's *dangerous*."

"Of course not," Hailey said earnestly. "But I can't help but be concerned about the environment Josh is in. It could be very troubling to him, to be there if his father is having . . . episodes. He was very upset after his last visit to your house."

Charlotte slowly shook her head.

Walter was nodding, as though he'd seen this coming all along. "We know that what's happened with Paul isn't his fault. He didn't ask that man to attack him. It's a terrible tragedy, all the way around. But we have to deal with the fallout from that, whether it's fair or not."

"I don't believe this," Charlotte said.

"Well, if he's delusional," Walter said, "it's simply out of the question that Josh can be spending any un-supervised time with him."

"I have to agree with Walter," Hailey said.

Charlotte pushed her chair back and stood.

"Nice to know you're all so very concerned," she said.

"No, Charlotte, please," Hailey protested, placing a hand on Charlotte's arm. Charlotte shook it off.

"I came here looking for some help, or failing that, some sympathy, maybe even a shred of insight," she said. "But look what you're doing. Seizing on Paul's misfortune as an opportunity to keep sole custody of Josh."

"That's ridiculous," Hailey said.

"How dare you," Walter chimed in.

"That's what you'd like, isn't it? Full custody. Force Paul right out of his son's life. In his current state, he needs the love of his son more than ever. He needs to know people love him."

"That's absurd," Hailey said. "I would never do that to Josh, or to his father."

"Seems to be exactly what you're proposing. Maybe it'd make your whole life easier if Paul just did go ahead and kill himself."

Hailey gasped and recoiled. "Where did that come from? How could you say such a thing? Is Paul *suicidal?*"

Charlotte burst into tears. "I don't know! I hardly know anything anymore." She quickly pulled herself together. "All I'm saying is, it *would* make it simpler for you." She fixed her eyes on Walter. "Then you could stop bitching and moaning about getting stuck on the FDR while coming out to Milford."

"I think it's time for you to leave, Charlotte," Walter said.

"I couldn't agree more."

As Charlotte moved for the door to the conference room, she stopped, as if she'd forgotten something.

She looked at Hailey.

"How did you let yourself in the other day?" she said.

"What?"

"Into our house. You had the door open before anyone could get down there to open it for you. Do you have a key? Did you make a copy of Josh's?"

"What on earth are you implying?" Hailey asked.

Charlotte left without saying another word to either of them.

Thirty-Nine

P aul and Anna were not allowed to take much of anything into the main prison area. Car keys, purse, wallet, even spare change, all had to be checked. The guard asked what was in Paul's envelope and he said "papers." The guard flipped open the end of the envelope and peered inside long enough to see it did, in fact, contain papers and nothing else—Paul wondered if he was expecting to find a couple of joints in there— but did not pull them out far enough to see what was typed on them. Paul was allowed to keep them.

"You got lucky," Anna whispered to him as they were led through two sets of gates.

It had been arranged for them to meet with Kenneth Hoffman in a room separate from the common visiting area. Paul had never set foot in a prison before—Anna said she'd been on a couple of "field trips" to correctional institutions during her training—and he found himself trying to take in everything along the way to their appointment. The cinder block walls painted pale green, the clang of gates closing, the smell of desperate men. It felt, in some strange way, like a high school, except instead of windows, there were bars, and instead of young kids bouncing off the walls, there were people without hope.

Plus, there was the feeling that at any moment, someone would stick a shiv in your side.

Paul had a dozen questions for the guard—the man was built like an armoire—leading them through the prison. Had there ever been a riot? Had anyone escaped? Did people really try to hide metal files inside cakes? But not wanting to look like an idiot, he kept all the questions to himself.

"Here we go," the guard said as they reached a metal door with a small, foot-square window at eye level. He unlocked it and showed them into a drab, gray space about ten by ten feet. The only things in there, aside from a camera mounted up by the ceiling in one corner, were a table and three chairs—two on one side, one on the other. Paul noted the metal ring bolted to the top of the table, and brackets that attached the table legs to the floor with bolts.

"Have a seat," the guard said, motioning to the two chairs that were side by side. "I'll be back." He left, closing the door behind him.

They sat.

After three minutes, Paul looked at Anna and said, "I hope they don't forget we're here."

Eight minutes after that, the door reopened. The guard stepped in, followed by Kenneth Hoffman.

Paul stood and took in his one-time friend, stunned by what he saw. Dressed in a short-sleeved, one-piece orange coverall, Hoffman would probably have been six feet tall, but he had become round-shouldered, as though an invisible boulder were perched at the back of his neck. And a man who had once come in at around 180 pounds didn't look much more than 150. His arms were thin and ropy, and beneath his scrawny gray beard—Paul had always known Hoffman to be clean-shaven—his cheeks were hollow. He'd lost much of his hair, his pink scalp visible through wisps of gray.

All this in eight months.

But what struck Paul most were Hoffman's eyes. There was no sparkle, no depth to them. It was as though they were layered with wax paper.

Dead eyes.

"Paul," Hoffman said, his voice low and leaden.

"Kenneth," Paul said. He was going to extend a hand, but they'd been cautioned about no physical contact.

"And you are?" Hoffman said, looking at a still-seated Anna.

"Dr. Anna White," she said.

"A head doctor, I understand," he said. He smiled, showing off teeth tinged with brown. "You're not here to give me a rectal exam."

"Sit down," the guard said. As he slipped out the door, he said to Paul and Anna, "Need anything, just shout."

Hoffman sat. He hadn't taken his eyes off Anna since she'd introduced herself.

"It seems like the dumbest thing in the world to ask," Paul said, "but all I can think of is, how are things?"

Kenneth smiled weakly. "Just lovely."

"Thanks for seeing us," Paul said.

"I don't get a lot of visitors," he said, and shrugged. "Nice to break the monotony. And you're the first one from West Haven to see me." Kenneth shook his head. "I would have thought you'd have been the absolute last. How are things there?"

"I haven't gone back yet," Paul said. "I've been on a leave." He said it without a hint of irony.

"Oh, yes," Kenneth said. "That." He looked Paul straight in the eyes. "If you've come here looking for an apology, you can have one."

Paul glanced at Anna. Her eyebrows went up a tenth of an inch. She knew Paul was not necessarily expecting one, and even if he had been, she figured he wouldn't have been expecting it this quickly.

"I'm sorry you got dragged into my mess," Kenneth said. "I mean, I did what I felt I had to do at the time, but I wish it hadn't happened that way." He paused. "If I was going to be caught anyway, I'm glad you lived." He smiled wryly. "Getting rid of two bodies was going to be hard enough, but three? I'd have probably died from a heart attack digging a third grave." He smiled, turned over his hands to show his palms. "If not that, the calluses would have been brutal."

Paul sat with his hands clasped in front of him and smiled. "It's nice to catch up."

Anna had spotted something on the inside of Kenneth's left wrist, what looked like a fresh scar.

"I was surprised to hear that Gabriella visits you," Paul said.

"She's a saint, she is."

"I might have thought she'd want nothing to do with you."

Kenneth shrugged. "Go figure." He smiled sardonically. "It must be the hypnotic hold I have over women, even those I've wronged." He looked at Anna. "What do you think?"

"Even Charles Manson had his admirers," she said evenly.

"Ooh, that stings," he said. He looked down at the envelope on the table, and then to Paul. "So why are you here?"

"Three reasons, I guess," he said slowly, building up to it. "It's been a rough eight months. There's the physical recovery of course. That's been hard enough. But there's the mental one, too. You haunt me, Kenneth. You come to me more nights than not. I've been looking for ways to deal with that, and believed one way would be to meet with you. To sit down with you. To remind myself that you're not some, I don't know, all-powerful evil force, but just a man. Nothing more. And seeing you here has helped me already. You're a shell of what you used to be. You don't look like you'd be much of a threat to anyone." Paul leaned forward. "You're broken, Kenneth. You're a sad, broken man who's tried to take his own life. So tonight, when I go to sleep, that's the image of you I'll take with me. Not the man who tried to kill me, but a pitiful, beaten man."

Kenneth held Paul's gaze. "Glad to be able to help in that regard. Number two?"

"I wanted to ask why. Why did a man I thought I knew do something so utterly horrible? What happened?" Paul tapped his own temple. "What snapped in here to make you do what you did? Or do you even know?"

Kenneth appeared to take the question seriously. "You don't think I've asked myself that question a thousand times since it happened? You know what I think? I think that inside of all of us—you, me, even you, Dr. White—is a devil just dying to break out. Most of us, we know how to keep him penned up. We lock him away in a personal jail with bars of morality. But sometimes, he's able to pry those bars apart, just enough to slip out. And if he's been in there a long time, when he does get out, he wants to make up for lost time." He smiled. "Does that answer your question?"

"No," Paul said. "But it's probably as close as we're going to get."

Kenneth smiled. "And number three?"

Anna glanced over at Paul and the envelope under his palm.

Paul said, "Remember yard sales? Driving around the neighborhood, people putting out all their junk to sell."

"Of course. I haven't been in here forever."

"Charlotte picked up something interesting the other day at a sale in Milford."

"Okay."

"An old typewriter. An Underwood."

Kenneth blinked. "So?"

"It was an Underwood that you made Catherine and Jill type their apologies on, wasn't it?"

"Yeah," Hoffman said. "It was."

"I'm going to tell you a story you're not going to believe, but I don't care. You may laugh, but I don't give a shit. The typewriter that's sitting in my house is, I'm certain, the typewriter you made Catherine and Jill use before you killed them."

Hoffman leaned back in his chair and crossed his arms. He looked dumbstruck for several seconds, then chuckled.

"That's not possible," he said. "It was never found."

"Well, someone found it. Not the police, I grant you that. But someone found it."

"Bullshit. I tossed it into a Dumpster. It would have been picked up the next day. It's long gone. It's buried in a landfill."

"No," Paul said.

He turned back the flap on the envelope and pulled out the pages. He set them out for display, one at a time, for Hoffman to read. He studied each sheet as it was placed before him.

"What the hell are these?"

"Messages. From the women you killed."

Kenneth looked up from the pages into Paul's eyes. "What?"

"They've been showing up in that typewriter. All by themselves."

Kenneth tilted his head to the right, then the left, almost in the manner of a dog that can't make sense of what it's seeing.

"This is some kind of joke."

"Not a joke."

Kenneth laughed, but it sounded forced. "No, really. This"—he tapped his index finger on one of the pages—"is complete and total bullshit."

Paul slowly shook his head. He noticed Anna had leaned back some from the table. This was his show.

"I wish it were a joke. I was skeptical at first, too. I heard the typing in the night, when the only ones in the house were Charlotte and me. I'll admit, I had to consider alternative explanations for a while. One, that someone was breaking in and doing it. Two, that I was losing my mind and writing these myself without even realizing it. But I've discounted both those theories.

And I believe Dr. White here is with me on that one, am I right?"

Paul looked at Anna, waiting for a reassuring nod that did not come.

"Anyway," he continued, "I was left with only one possible explanation. That there are powers out there beyond our understanding, and that Catherine and Jill are reaching out. Looking for answers."

"You haven't forgotten what I taught, have you, Paul? Math, physics? I dealt in the world of the rational. And what you're saying is nuts."

"It would be nuts for messages like these to show up in a typewriter that was *not* the one you used."

Kenneth took another look at the pages. He ran his index finger over the typing. "The *h*," he said, little more than a whisper.

"It's slightly off center," Paul said. "And the *o* is a bit faint. Do you remember that from your Underwood?"

Kenneth seemed to be struggling to recall.

"I think I know what's going on," he said.

Paul and Anna waited.

"You and your shrink here are running some kind of game on me. I don't know what it is, exactly, and I have no idea why, but that'd be the theory I'd go with, because I am telling you, one hundred percent, that this is a crock of shit."

"Why?" Paul asked. "Why isn't it just possible something's going on here that's beyond our understanding?"

Kenneth flattened his palms on the table and weighed his response. "I told you. The typewriter. I threw it away."

"Someone must have spotted it in the garbage," Paul said. "Before the trash was picked up. Had no idea how it got there, didn't care. And then it wound up in someone's house, and they put it out one day to sell before they moved away from Milford. Tell me it couldn't have happened that way."

For the first time, Kenneth's face registered doubt. "Maybe, just maybe, that's possible. But these notes? That's nuts." He looked down at them one last time.

"What are you looking at?" Paul asked.

"The e's," he said. "They're a bit filled in . . ." Hoffman seemed to be drifting for a moment, then looked up. "The police don't have the typewriter, but they have the notes . . ."

"The notes you made Catherine and Jill write," Paul said, getting ahead of Kenneth's thinking. "Of course. They could compare these pages to the ones they have in evidence. Back in the day, samples of typing were like fingerprints. They could match them to specific machines."

Paul brightened and looked at Anna. "Why did I never think of that? Do you think the police would let us see that evidence?"

"I don't know," Anna said. "They might."

Kenneth did not share Paul's excitement. He asked, "Is there blood on it? Is there blood on the type-writer?"

Paul thought a moment and said, "Not that I've noticed." There was Josh's blood, of course, from when he caught his finger in the machine, but Paul knew that was not worth mentioning. "But there could be traces, I suppose, down between the keys. I guess whoever was selling it did their best to clean it up. I mean, who'd buy a used typewriter that was covered in dried blood?"

Hoffman's forehead wrinkled. His eyes went slowly around the room, then settled back on Paul.

"What are you going to do with it?" he asked. "The Underwood."

"Why?"

Hoffman shook his head angrily. "I just want to know."

Paul shrugged. "I haven't really thought about that. For the time being, it's going to stay in my house."

"Are you going to give it to the police?"

Paul turned to Anna again. "Should I, if it's evidence?"

She shrugged. Before she could answer, Kenneth said, "What's the point? You want to get my fingerprints off it?" Kenneth laughed. "They've got me. You think they want to convict me again? Instead of getting out in a hundred years, it'll be two hundred."

Forty

Neither Paul nor Anna said a word until they were out of the prison and back in the car. Once the doors were closed they let out a collective breath, as though they hadn't taken one for the last couple of hours.

Anna turned to Paul and asked, "How are you? Are you okay?"

"I'm a little shaky," he said, "but yeah, I'm okay. How about you?"

"I'm fine." She found herself smiling, almost against her will. "It was actually kind of exhilarating. Creepy, but exhilarating."

"Is *creepy* a psychological term?"

She laughed. "Pretty much."

"I don't feel . . . scared of him anymore."

"You made that pretty clear."

Paul was quiet for a moment as Anna started the engine and steered the car out of the prison parking lot. "I almost, for a second there, I almost felt sorry for him. When he was talking about how we all have this devil hiding inside us. I thought that almost made sense, in a way."

"Or else it was just an excuse," Anna said. "Listen, I want to apologize for something in there. When you said I'd come to the same conclusion as you had about the source of those notes, I wasn't exactly supportive."

"I noticed."

"I should have said something."

"Maybe I'm the one who should apologize. I presumed when I shouldn't have."

She hesitated. "I don't think Hoffman was convinced those letters were actually written by Catherine and Jill, that two dead women are speaking to you through that typewriter." Another pause. "I'm having a hard time with that, too."

"You aren't willing to consider that there might—just might—be forces at work in the world that are beyond our understanding? You think it's impossible that something like this could happen? Because, for me, I've pretty much exhausted all other options."

Anna kept staring ahead through the windshield. "It'll be almost dark by the time we get home."

"Isn't that what you call avoidance?"

She glanced his way for a second. "I'm going to tell you something I probably shouldn't."

"Okay."

"Twelve years ago, well, going back even further, my mother was not well. It was a long decline. Life's so unfair that way, you know? Sometimes I think it would be so much better if we went just like that." She took a hand off the wheel and snapped her fingers. "None of this lingering. It can be so hard on everyone."

"Sure," Paul said.

"This is something I've never told anyone. Not my father, not any of my friends, not my ex-husband, although we'd split by this time."

Paul nodded. "Okay."

They were back on the main road, picking up speed.

"It was a Tuesday night, just after three in the morning." She stopped, breathed in through her nose, steeling herself. "I was sound asleep. And I heard my mother speak to me. As clearly as you talking to me now. She said, and I'll never forget this, she said, 'It's time to come and say good-bye.' I woke up, and I could still hear her in my head, saying that. I looked at the clock, and it was eleven minutes after three. I don't want to make too much of this, but my mother was born on the eleventh of March."

Paul nodded slowly.

"She was in a hospital chronic care wing at the time. I knew it was irrational, I knew she couldn't actually speak to me like that, but I felt I had to go to the hospital. I threw on some clothes and drove there as quickly as I could and I went to her room."

The car went over a bump and the golf clubs in the back rattled like old bones.

Paul realized he was barely breathing. "What happened?"

"She was awake. She was looking at the door. It was like she was waiting for me to arrive. She smiled and reached out a hand."

Anna put her own hand to her mouth. Paul could see a tear running down her cheek. She needed a moment before she could continue.

"It was so small. Her hand. Just skin and bone. I took it, and she said to me, I swear, she said, 'I'm glad you got my message.' I know it sounds crazy, but that's what happened." She glanced with moist eyes at her passenger. "Pretty nuts, right?"

Paul slowly shook his head. "No. It's not nuts at all."

"And I sat with her, and twenty minutes later, she was gone."

Paul didn't know what to say.

"I called my father, woke him up, told him a lie, that the hospital had called me. That Mom had passed away. I told him I was on my way." She sniffed. "I couldn't tell him the truth."

"No," Paul said, understanding.

"How could I explain that I was there? How could I tell him that she'd gotten in touch with me, and not him? Why didn't she somehow contact my father, too?"

"Maybe she tried," Paul said. "He just didn't hear her."

Anna hit the blinker and steered the car over to the shoulder. Once it had stopped, she put it in park.

"I need a second," she said. "I'm sorry." She allowed the tears to come. She pointed to the glove compartment. Paul opened it, spotted a shallow box of tissues. He pulled out half a dozen and handed them to Anna.

"God, this is so embarrassing," she said as she dabbed her eyes, then blew her nose. She dropped her hands into her lap. "Not to mention unprofessional. I'm the one who's supposed to be keeping it together."

"It's okay."

I can touch her. It's okay.

Paul reached over and placed a hand on hers. Gently, he said, "By not telling your father, that tells me you believe what happened was real."

She looked at him. "Even if I didn't believe it, even if it really was only a dream, and a complete coincidence that I got to the hospital just in time, I couldn't tell my father because *he* might believe it. And think how hurt he would feel. So I could never tell him."

She took her hand out from under Paul's, placed it on top of his, and squeezed. "It's haunted me all these years. It truly has. It was good to finally tell someone."

Paul fought the urge to put an arm around her. He wanted to do it more than anything.

"So," she said, freeing his hand, putting the car back in drive, and checking her mirror to see whether it was safe to pull back onto the road, "I guess the bottom line is, yes, the jury is still out, but I can't tell you that what's been happening to you isn't really happening. I just don't know."

"I understand," he said.

God, I just want to hold her.

But they were back on the road now, Anna pushing down hard on the accelerator. A few miles later, she said, "I think this trip did you some good. If your only takeaway is that Kenneth Hoffman is no longer the boogeyman you'd built him up in your dreams to be, then it was worth it."

"I suppose. And I got to show him those notes. Maybe . . . maybe I was hoping he'd think they were real. If he had, I'd be able to think, okay, I'm not the only one who's starting to believe in the unbelievable."

"I think they rattled him," Anna said. "Although I'm not sure which troubled him more. The notes, or the fact you'd come into possession of what might be his typewriter."

Paul's phone rang. He dug it out of his jacket, saw the caller's name, and frowned.

"What does she want?" he said, more to himself than Anna.

"Who is it?" Anna asked.

Paul put the phone to his ear. "Hailey, is everything okay? Is Josh—what . . . Charlotte came to your office and what . . . yes, I *have* had a hard time, but . . . I know Josh has a key. Why would she . . . okay, okay . . . okay. Thanks for telling me . . . okay . . . good-bye."

He held the phone, made no effort to put it back into his jacket.

"That was weird," he said, staring straight ahead.

"What's happened?"

"Charlotte said she was going to see her mother but she went to see Hailey, supposedly because she was worried about me, and wanted to get Hailey's take. But then there was something about Josh's key, and . . ."

"What is it, Paul?"

He shook his head, as if that might make things come clear. "Something I'll have to talk to Charlotte about when I get home."

Anna decided not to push it. "Okay."

Anna pulled into her driveway next to Paul's car and turned off the engine. She glanced up at her father's bedroom window, noticed that the light was on.

"Thanks again for everything," Paul said, pulling on the handle of the passenger door.

"You're welcome. Thank *you*. It was quite a day."

Paul held his position. He looked at Anna and knew, at that moment, what he wanted to do. Something he couldn't. Something he wouldn't.

"Time to go, Paul." She smiled. "See you at our next session."

"Right, of course," he said.

He got out, closed the door, found his keys, and unlocked his car. Anna waited until he was out of the driveway and heading up the street before she got out and went into her house.

Driving home, Paul felt awash in guilt.

He'd done nothing wrong, he hadn't acted on his feelings, but the fact he'd had them made him remorseful. Just when Charlotte was being so supportive, sticking by him, helping him through the worst crisis of his life, he finds himself attracted to another woman.

He'd spent so much time lately with Anna. He could tell her things he could tell no one else. She listened.

Of course, you idiot. It's her job.

At an intellectual level, Paul knew that. Her concern for him was rooted in professionalism. He'd be a fool to think she felt anything for him that went beyond that.

Except it didn't change how he felt.

He had to push her out of his mind. Any other kind of relationship with Anna White was a nonstarter.

If there was anything Paul needed to work on, to *reward* and *nourish*, it was his life with Charlotte.

Don't make a complicated life even more complicated.

So he struggled to replace thoughts of Anna with a review of his meeting with Kenneth Hoffman.

Had the encounter been helpful? Was Anna right, that if nothing else, seeing Kenneth face-to-face had diminished his stature? He was, indeed, a broken man. Paul thought the days and weeks ahead would be the test of whether seeing Kenneth was a good thing. Would the nightmares fade? Would he stop hearing Kenneth in his head?

He hit the turn signal indicator, turned down his street, then pulled into the driveway behind Charlotte's car.

Well, there was some good news. He actually remembered driving here.

As he wearily got out of his car, it occurred to him he'd had nothing to eat in hours. On the way up, he and Anna had joked about dining on prison food, but once they were inside, they pretty much lost their appetites. He figured Charlotte was home from New York by now. Maybe she'd made dinner and set aside a plate for—

Oh God.

The front door was wide open.

Forty-One

Paul charged into the house, shouting, "Charlotte!" He threw the door closed behind him and took the stairs up to the kitchen two steps at a time. As he reached the top, Charlotte came around the kitchen island, her face full of alarm.

"What?" she asked.

He put on the brakes. "The door was open. I was worried. I didn't know—"

"I left it open," she said, cutting him off. "You know how you were asking about a surveillance system, getting the locks changed? Well, I found a guy and took the first step today. I'd set up an appointment for late in the day, after I was back from the city. We've got new locks. I'd left the door open a crack so you'd be able to get in. I guess the wind blew it all the way open. God, you're a nervous wreck."

"I'm sorry," he said, glancing back down to the front door to be sure it was closed. "I'll close it now." He scurried down the flight, turned the dead bolt, and returned. Charlotte was standing by the island.

"Give me your keys," she said.

He handed her his set. On the granite countertop was a single key that looked, at a glance, identical to Paul's house key. Charlotte picked up his set and worked the house key off the ring, then replaced it with the new one. She took his old key and tucked it into the front pocket of her jeans.

"You did this because of Hailey?" Paul asked.

"What about Hailey?" Charlotte asked, looking nervous.

"She called me."

"I was gonna tell you," Charlotte said, looking like she'd been caught in a lie. "I knew there was a chance Hailey'd rat me out. But you remember the other day, how she strolled right in here?"

"You don't really think Hailey snuck in here and—"

"I don't know, okay?" she said defensively.

"What did you tell them?"

"I told them I was worried about you. So shoot me. I've been worried sick about you, and honestly, I can't predict what you're going to do next. Not these last few days. Not since I bought that goddamn thing and put it in your think tank."

Paul glanced at the open door to his study, as if to confirm that the typewriter was no longer there. He mentally breathed a sigh of relief to see that it was not. He knew where it was, but he was not going to go into the garage to check this time.

You could take paranoia a little too far.

"Whatever's going on, whatever the cause," Charlotte said cautiously, "I see it driving you to the brink of . . ."

Paul gave her a look.

"Just hear me out here. What if Hailey *is* behind this? She had a key. She could sneak in. What if it's a custody thing? What if she and that smug asshole Walter are somehow setting you up, trying to make you seem mentally unfit, so they could go after sole custody of Josh?"

"No!" he said firmly. "She wouldn't do that! She wouldn't do it to Josh. She wouldn't keep him from me."

"Sometimes," Charlotte said, "you don't know what people are capable of."

Paul sighed, moved his head from side to side sorrowfully. "I just spent the afternoon learning that lesson."

He recounted his prison visit for her.

"Are you glad you did it?" Charlotte asked.

He told her he thought he was, and why.

"Good," she said. "You know what I'd like?"

"What would you like?"

"One night where we don't talk about any of this. Nothing about Hoffman. Nothing about typewriters. Nothing about your legal problems with that asshole Hitchens."

"God, him. There's been so much going on, I nearly forgot I might be going to jail myself." He tried to laugh.

"Stop."

"Okay."

"I want one night that we devote just to ourselves."

"Sold."

"Have you eaten?"

"I'm so hungry, I'd eat airline food."

He perched himself on one of the island stools while Charlotte pulled out an already prepared plate from the refrigerator. She said, "Spinach-and-ricotta-stuffed cannelloni with tomato sauce. Sorry, I had mine about an hour ago. I was starving."

She put it into the microwave, then went back to the fridge and brought out a bottle of red wine. "Got this, too." She found a corkscrew in a drawer, opened the bottle, and filled two wineglasses.

Charlotte handed one to him, raised her glass to make a toast. "To a new beginning. To putting the bad behind us, and looking forward to the good."

Paul, struggling to be enthusiastic, clinked his glass to hers and drank. "I like that."

Charlotte, wineglass in hand, turned back to the microwave to check on the progress of her husband's dinner. "Three minutes."

"I'm gonna wash up," he said, leaving his glass and heading for the stairs to the top floor.

"Be quick," she said.

By the time he returned, his dinner was waiting for him and Charlotte was refilling her glass. "It is my intention," she said with mock seriousness, "to get drunk and make some bad decisions."

Paul smiled as he retook his spot on the stool. "Sounds like a plan," he said, picking up his glass and downing the rest of his wine in a single gulp.

"Hit me," he said, setting the glass back down. Charlotte filled it to the brim, then looked at the trickle left in the bottle.

"Good thing I have more than just this one," she said.

Paul cut into the cannelloni with the side of his fork and blew on it before putting it into his mouth. "This is not bad."

Charlotte smiled as she went to the fridge again. "All I want is for you to be happy," she said. She scowled at the second bottle she had pulled out. "A screw top. Is that too down market?"

"Seriously?" he said. "For me, who doesn't know a Chablis from a chardonnay?"

"Yeah, and really, the more you drink, what does it matter?"

She opened the bottle, set it on the island at the ready. Paul went through his second glass in half a dozen gulps. The moment his glass was empty, Charlotte refilled it.

"Do you forgive me?" she asked.

"For?"

"Talking to Hailey and Dr. White."

He nodded. "I do."

"If the roles were reversed, wouldn't you have done the same thing?"

Paul thought about that. "I guess I would have." He had polished off the dinner and pushed the plate away from him.

"Are you wondering what's for dessert?" Charlotte asked.

"It's okay," he said. "I'm good."

"You should reconsider," she said, setting down her glass, coming around the island, turning his head to face her, and putting her mouth on his.

Paul felt himself instantly responding. He slid off the stool, put his arms around Charlotte, and pulled her in to him, their lips parting. She slid her tongue into his mouth as he cupped his hands on her buttocks.

Charlotte wedged a hand down between them, felt his hardness beneath his jeans. She pulled back slightly, creating enough space between them that she could undo his belt and the button at the top of his zipper. As his jeans began to fall, allowing her to slip her hand into his shorts, Paul freed her blouse from her pants and ran his hands over her bare skin, heading toward her back and the clasp of her bra.

"Are you going to take me here on the island?" she whispered.

"If it were a desert island, maybe," Paul said. "But I think a bed might be more comfortable than granite."

"Well, Romeo, if we're moving this party to the bedroom, you better pull up your pants so you don't trip on the stairs."

"Wise advice."

"Turn off the lights on the way up. And bring that bottle."

When they were done, Paul slipped naked out of the bed, staggered into the bathroom long enough to take a piss, guided by the moonlight filtering through the window blinds. He flopped back down on the mattress, staring up at the ceiling. Charlotte, naked and exposed with the covers down around her ankles, had barely moved since they finished making love. The second wine bottle and two glasses all sat empty on her bedside table.

"Whoa," she said quietly.

"No kidding," Paul said, reaching his hand out across the sheet and touching his fingers lightly on her arm. "You know, I'm not as young as I used to be."

"Welcome to the club."

"What I mean is, four glasses of wine—"

"It was five."

"Whatever. I'm feelin' it."

"Like I said, welcome to the club."

Paul turned onto his side and shifted closer to Charlotte. She found the energy to roll onto her side, too, so that he could tuck in behind her, spoon-style.

"Covers," she said.

Paul reached down for the comforter and dragged it up over them. He put his arm around Charlotte, caressing her breasts, and put his head deep into his pillow.

Within seconds, he was snoring.

He was dreaming, perhaps not surprisingly, about needing to go to the bathroom. As he slowly started to come awake, opening his eyes briefly, he thought that killing off a couple of bottles of wine at bedtime will do that to you.

Paul tried to ignore the urgent message from his bladder and closed his eyes again. The two of them had barely moved. Paul was still tucked up against Charlotte, his arm resting over her hip.

He could hear her breathing softly.

He almost drifted back into sleep, but he was being forced to face the inevitability of his situation. He was going to have to get up. The question was whether he could disentangle himself from Charlotte without waking her.

First, he gently raised his arm from her hip and let the comforter settle back onto her. Then he slowly edged his body toward his side of the bed, trying to keep the comforter from dragging across Charlotte.

At the same time, he turned himself over so that his back was to hers, and he was facing the wall beyond his side of the bed.

The room was dark, and the moon had shifted in the intervening hours, so there was almost no light slipping through the blinds.

He wondered what time it was. He was worried it might be four or five in the morning. He did not want it to be that close to daybreak. He was weary, and hoping for several more hours of sleep once he was back under the covers. One or two o'clock, even three, would suit him just fine.

The clock radio on his bedside table was showing no display.

That led Paul to wonder if the power was off. If it had gone out, and come back on, the clock would be flashing "12:00." But right now, there was nothing. It struck him as an odd time for the electrical grid to collapse. There were no high winds, no storm of any kind.

But hang on.

There was a discernible glow coming from the direction of the clock radio. As if the display were on, but at a tenth of its usual illumination.

Lying on his stomach, he extended his left arm, reaching for the clock.

His hand hit something.

It was as though he'd bumped into an invisible wall.

He felt around. Something cold and metallic sat on the bedside table between him and the clock radio. He gave it a slight push, but it did not budge. His fingers scrabbled across the object. One side was smooth, but when his fingers worked around it, he felt countless round pads that recessed slightly at his touch.

Paul felt a chill run from his scalp to his toes.

No longer worrying about disturbing Charlotte, he swung his legs out of the bed and fumbled in the dark under the shade of the bedside lamp, his fingers struggling to find the switch.

He found it, turned the lamp on.

Paul screamed.

Still screaming, he slid off the side of the bed and hit the floor on his back. His scream had morphed into actual words.

"No no no no!"

Charlotte sat bolt upright in bed, throwing back the covers. "Paul?" She spun around, expecting to see him next to her but seeing only his head above the edge of the bed.

She saw the look of horror on his face, then followed his gaze.

And then she screamed, too.

The typewriter sat there on the bedside table, positioned so that it was facing the bed. Charlotte found three words:

"Oh my God!"

And then the room went silent as the two of them stared at the hunk of black metal.

"Paul," Charlotte whispered.

He did not respond. He did not look at her.

"Paul," she said again.

Slowly, he focused on her. His eyes were wide with shock.

"Paul, there's paper in it."

It was true. A piece of paper was rolled into the machine. There were two words of type on it.

Slowly, Paul got to his knees, then stood and approached the typewriter, as though it were a coiled snake ready to strike.

Without touching it, he peered over the machine to read the message that had been left on the single sheet.

It read:

`We're back.`

Forty-Two

Paul, naked and trembling, took a step back from the typewriter and said, "This is not happening. This is not fucking happening!"

Charlotte was in the middle of the bed, crouched on her knees, staring disbelievingly at the antique writing machine. "Paul, how did . . . how is this possible?"

He turned at her and shouted, "I don't know! This can't be happening. This has to be a nightmare. I have to wake up. I have to wake up. This can't be real!" He put his palms to his temples, as though posing for Edvard Munch's *The Scream*.

"I was asleep," he said. "I was right here. Not two feet away. How could this happen? How did it get in here? It can't be here. It *isn't* here."

"Paul, Paul, listen to me. Paul?"

He looked at her, his eyes wide. "What?"

"This isn't a dream, Paul. That fucking thing is *here*."

"How did it get here? How?" He whirled around.

"Someone's in the house!" Charlotte said. "Has to be!"

Paul was not about to argue for a supernatural explanation at this point. He ran from the room, barefoot. Charlotte could hear him tearing down the stairs, shouting.

"Where are you?"

Charlotte got off the bed and grabbed a long T-shirt from her dresser.

"Come out, you son of a bitch!"

She pulled it on over her head, then picked up Paul's boxers from the floor and ran for the stairs.

"You bastard if you're here I'll find you!"

All the kitchen lights were on by the time she reached it, as well as the light in Paul's small study. But he was not there. She went down the next set of steps. The front door remained locked, but the inside one to the garage was not. She opened it, found the lights already on.

Paul was on the far side of the garage, staring into the open blanket box.

"It was here," he said. "It was *here*." He shook his

head angrily. "Shit! Shit shit shit! I forgot to put the books back on top."

He pointed to the boxes he had lifted off the blanket box during his last visit in here, when he had checked to make sure the typewriter was where it was supposed to be.

"It got out," he said softly with a tone of wonder. "It escaped."

"Paul, listen to what you're saying."

"What?"

"You're talking about it like it was some . . . some animal or something."

"It moved. It *moved*."

"It *can't* have moved! That's not possible! Not by itself!"

"Well then what the hell happened?"

Charlotte took a second to calm herself, then said, "Call Dr. White."

"What?" It was as though there were some invisible barrier between them keeping him from comprehending her words.

She crossed the garage, handed him his shorts. "For God's sake, put these on. It's cold in here."

"It was open," he said. "The box was open when I came in here." He looked imploringly at Charlotte. "How did it do that? How?"

"Paul, I'm begging you."

"The front door was locked," he said. "With a new set of locks!"

"Yes," she said quietly.

He nodded, putting it together. "That pretty much settles it. There was no one in here." He smiled, as though this were good news. "Don't you see? No one got in. It did it. It did it on its own."

"Paul."

His face went red with rage. "What the hell else can it be?"

She took a step back. "Will you call her, please?"

"What are you talking about? This is not a fucking *psychological* problem. I need a goddamn exorcist or something. That thing is *possessed*. There are people that do that. I'm sure of it. They come in, they get rid of evil spirits. It should be easy in this case. It's not a house. It's just that *thing*."

"If you won't call her, I will."

"You're not getting this at all."

"I think I am."

She turned for the door, went back into the house. As she was mounting the stairs, the door behind her opened and Paul started coming up after her.

"You're not calling her," Paul said.

"You can't stop me."

"It's the middle of the night, for Christ's sake!"

"I don't care."

Paul gained on her, grabbed the hem of her shirt to stop her progress.

"Let go!" Charlotte said, stumbling to her knees. Her left one hit the edge of a stair. "Jesus! You're hurting me!"

"Please, please, don't."

He was holding her down, keeping her from moving farther up the stairs. She flung back blindly with her arm, catching Paul in the side of the head. It stunned him enough that he fell over to one side and let go of her. He rubbed at his temple.

"Oh, God," she said, realizing where she had struck him. "Is that the same spot where—"

"It's okay," he said, taking his hand away from his head.

"I'm sorry. But, Paul, you need help."

She got back on her feet and managed to reach the kitchen without him attempting to grab hold of her again.

"I don't need help," he mumbled as he followed her.

"Yes, you do. Help from me, help from Dr. White. We all want to help you."

"Christ, don't be so fucking patronizing. How the hell do you think that typewriter got up two flights and parked itself right next to my fucking head? How do you think *that* happened?"

"What did it do, Paul? Did it walk up? Did it fly? Did it use its tiny fucking keys to turn the knob on the garage door? Did it go through walls?"

"It did *something*!" he said. "If it didn't get itself up here how the hell did it happen?"

Tears were forming in the corners of her eyes. "Please don't make me."

"Don't make you what?"

"Please don't make me say it. I'm here to help you, to support you."

"Did you feel me get out of bed?"

"I was drunk," Charlotte said. "We could have had an earthquake and I wouldn't have noticed."

"Don't give me that. I was right up next to you. I had my arm around you."

"I didn't feel you get up before you found that thing next to your bed. Maybe you got up one other time. I'm just saying, Paul, we have to consider the possibility . . ."

"That I'm losing my mind?"

"I did not say that." She threw her hands into the air. "I don't know what to do! What should I do? You tell me."

"For starters, you can get that fucking thing out of the house."

"Fine. Fine. If that's what you want, I'll do it right now."

She stormed up the second flight, Paul in pursuit. "What are you going to do?" he demanded.

"Just watch me."

She returned to their bedroom, went straight past the bed to the sliding glass doors that opened onto the small balcony. She first drew back the blinds, then unlocked the door and slid it open. Cool air blew into the room, and the sounds of waves lapping at the beach became a soft soundtrack.

"Charlotte?" Paul said, standing at the foot of the bed.

"Get out of my way," she said, pushing past him.

She got her fingers under the typewriter and, with a grunt, lifted it off the bedside table.

"It's heavy," Paul said. "Let me help—"

"I told you, get out of my way."

She had to put her back into it. She arched her spine and tilted her head back as she struggled to carry the machine across the room and out the door. Once she reached the balcony, she took a deep breath and heaved the Underwood up and onto the railing, balancing it there.

Charlotte glanced back at Paul, who stood in the doorway, seemingly mesmerized by her actions.

"If you think this thing is alive, well, I'm about to kill it," she said.

"Wait," Paul said.

She looked stunned. "Seriously?"

"Just . . . wait."

The typewriter teetered precariously on the railing. All she had to do was take her hand away and it would plummet to the cement walkway below.

"I . . . appreciate what you're doing," Paul said. "I do. But what if . . ."

"What if what?"

"What if they have more to say?"

Charlotte closed her eyes briefly, signaling she had reached her limit.

"I know, I know. I'm all for getting it out of here. I am. I'm just not sure it should be smashed into a million pieces."

"What, then?" she asked. Before Paul could come up with a suggestion she had one of her own. "I'll put it in the trunk of my car. And then I'm going to put it someplace where it won't be found. How about that?"

Paul considered the offer. "Okay, yes. Okay."

"But I'm doing it on one condition. You have to call Dr. White."

Paul hesitated. "I don't know. I don't see what she can do."

"I'll let this go," she said, nodding toward the type-writer. "Believe me, I don't care what happens to this thing. I'm happy to see it busted into a billion bits. You should be, too, but I'm willing to do it your way. Pick up your phone and call her."

Paul looked back into the room. With the typewriter off the bedside table, he could see the time. He thought it had to be around three or four but was surprised to see that it was only 1:23 A.M.

"It's late," he protested. "I'll be waking her."

"So what?"

"I'll do it. But let's put that into your trunk first."

"Fine," she said. "But do you think you could carry it? I just about broke my arms getting it this far."

Paul came out to the balcony and carefully took the typewriter from Charlotte. He felt a chill as he took the Underwood into his arms, cradling it as though it were some demonic infant.

"Let's do this quickly," he said.

Charlotte got ahead of him on the stairs, grabbing her car keys from a bowl in the kitchen along the way. She held the front door for him, then hit the button on her remote to pop the trunk on her car. The lid swung open a few inches, and she lifted it the rest of the way.

Paul leaned over the opening and set the machine onto the trunk floor. There was a small tarp rolled up in there, which he took and draped over the typewriter, as though smothering it. Then he slammed the lid.

He dusted his hands together and rubbed them on his boxers, as if somehow touching the machine had contaminated him. He turned and looked at Charlotte.

And fell apart.

"Oh, God," he said, and started to cry. He put his hands over his face. "Oh God what is happening, what is happening, what is happening." The cries turned into racking sobs.

Charlotte took him into her arms and squeezed. "Let it out," she said. "Let it out."

His arms limply went around her. "I can't take it anymore, I just can't."

"It's going to be okay. We're getting rid of it. It's in the car." Charlotte suddenly found herself crying, too. "I'm so sorry." She buried her face in his shoulder. "I'm so, so sorry."

Paul, between sobs, managed to say, "It's not your fault. There was no way you could know."

"I shouldn't have . . . I never should have . . . it was a bad idea," she said, weeping. "At the time . . . it seemed . . ."

"Stop," Paul said. His breaths had turned rapid and shallow. "I feel, I feel like I'm going to pass out."

"Come in. Get in the house."

She got him to the door. Once inside, she locked it, checked that the door to the garage was also secure, and the two of them trudged upstairs. She managed to keep him on his feet until they reached the kitchen table, at which point he dropped into a chair.

He was still crying. He put his elbows on the table, rested his head in his hands.

"Maybe it's some kind of nervous breakdown," he said. "I'm willing to admit that. I don't know what else it could be. I must be . . . I must be doing these things. I have to be."

Charlotte had grabbed his phone, which had been recharging from an outlet by the kitchen sink.

"Dr. White," she said, handing it to him.

He nodded, surrendering. He looked at his hand, which was shaking. "You call her. I can't do it. I don't even know if I could hold the phone."

Charlotte found the number in his contacts, and tapped. "It's gone to message after three rings," she said.

"That'll be her office phone. Keep calling it. She'll hear it eventually from the other part of the house."

She ended the call, entered the number again. The fourth time, it worked.

A frantic Anna White answered, "Yes, who is this? Paul, is this you?"

"I'm so sorry," Charlotte said after identifying herself. "Paul's in a bad way. A *really* bad way."

Calmly, Anna asked, "Tell me what's happening."

"He's shaking, he can't stop crying. You need to come over. He needs to talk to you, he—"

"Charlotte, if he's in a psychotic state, then—"

"What the hell is that? How am I supposed—"

"Let me speak to him."

Charlotte said to Paul, "She wants to talk to you."

He nodded weakly, steadied his hand as he took the phone, and pressed it to his ear.

"Yes?"

"Paul?"

"Yes."

"Talk to me."

Paul didn't say anything. He seemed to be struggling to find the words.

"Paul?"

Finally, with great effort, he said two words before handing the phone back to Charlotte.

"*Help me.*"

Forty-Three

By the time Anna White arrived nearly an hour later, Paul had calmed down some. He'd never been a fan of hard liquor, but he'd knocked back a couple of shots of vodka to calm his nerves.

"I hope that wasn't a bad thing," Charlotte said once Anna was sitting at the kitchen table, talking to Paul. For someone who'd been in bed less than an hour earlier, Anna was alert and attentive. She'd come over in a jogging suit, her hair pulled back into a ponytail, her face devoid of lipstick or other makeup.

"That's okay," she said. "How are you now, Paul?"

"Better," he said.

"Tell me everything that happened."

He told her, even the parts about he and Charlotte killing off a couple of bottles of wine and having sex.

But the story really started with the discovery of the typewriter next to his bed.

"Is it still up there?" Anna asked.

Paul shook his head. "We got it out of the house. It's in Charlotte's car." He gave his head a slow, deliberate shake. "It's not coming back in here unless it knows how to get out of a locked trunk."

Anna didn't say anything to that.

Paul leaned in closer to Anna and whispered, "Either that thing got up here on its own tonight, guided through the house by the spirits of those two women, or I brought it up here and have no memory of it." He sighed. "Which would be worse? And if I did bring it up here, if I wrote all those notes, if I did all that, does it mean I'm crazy, or that I'm somehow possessed by the ghosts of Jill and Catherine? Anna, Jesus, there's no good answer here."

"Sitting here, talking to you, you do not strike me as someone who's detached from reality, Paul."

"Something's crazy. It's either me, or the situation."

Anna took out her phone. "I have to make a quick call to my father. I had to wake him before I left. I didn't want him waking up and not finding me at home."

"Of course."

"Dad?" she said into the phone. "I'm just checking in. Okay. I'll call you again in half an hour, unless you really think you can get back to sleep." She nodded. "Okay. Love you, Dad."

As she put her phone away, Charlotte was getting out hers. "Who are you calling?" Paul asked.

She glanced his way. "Bill."

"Bill? Why are you—"

"He's your friend. Maybe it would help if he came— Bill?"

She turned away, walked toward the stairs where she wouldn't be disturbed by Paul and Anna.

"It might be good to talk to him," Anna said.

"I hate her waking him up in the middle of the night."

Anna managed a smile. "But it was okay for me."

"I'm sorry."

"Kidding. What would you like to do, Paul? If you want, I could have you admitted."

"Admitted?"

She put a hand on his arm. "For observation. For a day or two. And I know you've resisted in the past, but once we have you seen by a psychiatrist, and there are a couple of very good ones I can recommend, there might be a pharmacological approach to treatment that we—"

"Drugs," he said.

Anna nodded. "Yes."

"I don't want to be on drugs."

"You want to just stick with vodka?"

He frowned. "Your point?"

"I'm saying that if you drink, you're self-medicating. There may be other, more productive approaches. But as a psychologist, I can't prescribe for you. That's where an assessment by a psychiatrist could be very helpful."

"That's your answer? Go into the loony bin and get doped up."

"We don't have to do that," she said, her voice steady and measured. "As long as you're not a danger to yourself or anyone else, no one's going to force you to do that."

"I wonder what Charlotte thinks," he said.

"Why don't we ask her?"

Although still within earshot of the others, Charlotte had moved over to the stairs and taken a seat on the top step. She said into her phone, "I hate to call you in the middle of the night, but I thought you'd want to know about Paul."

"What's going—hang on, I'm just turning on the light here—what's happening over there?" Bill asked.

"His therapist just came over. He had a full-blown meltdown." Charlotte sniffed, then said, "He's really messed up."

"Are you crying?"

"Of course I'm crying."

"Okay, okay," Bill said. "What do you want me—"

"Hang on, Paul wants to ask me something."

Paul said, "Do you think I should go into the hospital?"

"The hospital?" she said. "Like, what do you mean?"

"The psych ward," Paul said. "It's an option. They could keep an eye on me and they might give me something. You know, to mellow me out, I guess."

"Shit, no," said Bill, who could hear them both talking.

"Hang on," Charlotte said to Paul. Into the phone, she said, "I'm trying to talk to Paul here."

"Put him on," Bill said.

Charlotte held out the phone to Paul. "Bill wants to talk to you."

Paul held the phone to his ear. "Sorry. Charlotte shouldn't have gotten you up."

"Don't worry about it," Bill said. "What's this about the hospital?"

"I'm talking about it with Anna."

"You do *not* want to go into the hospital. There's no *way* you want to do that."

"But they might be—"

"No, you listen to Bill here. Going into a place like that, it'll only mess you up further. Those places are filled with crazy people, and you are *not crazy.* You hear me? Once you let them lock you up, they'll never let you out."

"I don't know," he said.

"Look," Bill said, "how do you feel right now? Right this second?"

"Shaky."

"But shaky enough to go into a hospital?"

"I don't know. Maybe you're right."

"You bet I'm right. Whaddya say you give it a couple of days. I have to go out of town tomorrow—shit, it's already tomorrow—but when I get back, you and me, we'll get together, do something to take your mind off all these things. But not squash. We're not putting that head of yours at risk. How does that sound?"

Paul nodded slowly.

"Are you there?" Bill asked.

"Yeah," Paul said. "Okay, I'll do that. I'll give it a couple of days and see how it goes. Charlotte's taken the typewriter away."

"There ya go," Bill said. "You hang in there, pal."

Paul handed the phone back to Charlotte and turned to face Anna, who was now standing by the kitchen table.

"You can go home," he told her. "I'll be okay."

Forty-Four

Charlotte stayed up most of the night with Paul, waiting until he finally fell asleep. Rattled as he was, he eventually lost the fight to exhaustion. Once he'd succumbed, Charlotte slipped into bed next to him.

Every time he moved or made a sound, she woke up.

Just after seven, she sensed he was fully awake, and asked, "How are you?"

He said, "Did all that really happen?"

"I'm afraid so."

He quickly turned over and looked at the bedside table. Seeing nothing on it but a lamp and his clock, he said, "I thought it might have come back."

Charlotte had nothing to say to that. It wasn't clear whether Paul was attempting to make a joke. He rolled onto his back and stared at the ceiling. "I'm sorry I put you through all that."

"It's okay," she said, raising up on her elbow and turning to face him. "What does it mean, exactly, that you're saying you're sorry?"

He turned his head slightly to look at her. "I don't know. I guess . . ."

"You guess what?"

"I know I may have looked like I was sleeping all night, but I was awake a lot, too. Thinking."

"Okay." Gently, she asked, "And what are you thinking?"

"That maybe Anna—Dr. White—was right."

"Right about what?"

"That maybe I should be admitted."

"You want to go into the hospital?"

"I don't *want* to, but I'm wondering if it's the only thing that makes sense. But I keep thinking about what Bill said, that once they have you in there, they'll never let you out. If I could go in for, I don't know, a couple of days, maybe that would be long enough to figure things out."

"I guess that's something you could revisit with Dr. White."

He managed a nod with the back of his head still buried in the pillow.

"You seem . . . almost calm," Charlotte said. "Certainly a lot calmer than in the middle of the night."

"There's only one way to explain this," he said. "And now that I've settled on that, I guess I do feel a little more at peace."

"And that way is?"

"Think of all the small memory lapses I've had. Forgetting where I'd driven. Forgotten texts and messages. The dry cleaning. Not remembering seeing that car across the street, nearly blacking out when I saw a car like Kenneth's. I must have gotten up in the night and brought the typewriter up and put it next to the bed. I *had* to. And I don't recall doing it."

"So you've moved past thinking it . . . did it itself."

He gave her a sad smile. "I have." He chuckled. "I mean, try to picture it. A typewriter opening the door. Coming up the stairs. It's comical if you think about it."

"I guess I haven't been able to see the humor in all this," Charlotte said.

He grimaced. "Yeah, well, I don't blame you there."

Charlotte threw back the covers and got out of bed. "I'm going to call in sick today."

"No."

"Yes. Any big house deals come along, someone else can take them."

"No, you don't have to do that. I'll be okay. I'll get

in touch with Dr. White and talk to her about whether to go in for, you know, observation or something."

Charlotte shook her head. "I think you need to listen to Bill on this one. Why don't you give it a couple of days. Then, if you still feel that's what you want to do, then do it."

Paul sat up. "Okay."

"And you need to call that lawyer back."

"Call him back?"

"I told you. He called yesterday. He thinks he can get you off with a suspended sentence or something, that there are extenuating circumstances up the wazoo that the court will be sympathetic to. But you have to get it sorted out."

"When did he call?"

"I told you all about this last night," Charlotte said.

"You see?" he said. He tapped his head with his index finger. "This needs a tune-up."

"And I think you need a break from your project. No more talking to grieving husbands and jilted wives. No more holing up in your study, writing about what happened to you. You need to get out. You need to *do* things."

Paul considered her advice. "I don't even know if I care about it anymore. I've met with Kenneth. Maybe my demons have been exorcised. Maybe it's time to move on. I don't have to turn my experience into a brilliant work of literature." He grinned. "Let someone else win the Pulitzer."

Paul managed to talk Charlotte into going to work. "Honestly," he told her, "I'll be fine."

And up until the time she left for the real estate office, he thought he would be.

But once the house was empty, anxiety rushed in to fill the void. He could not stop certain thoughts running through his head:

1. *It's me. I did it.*
2. *No. I didn't do it. I couldn't have done it.*
3. *Someone broke in and did it.*
4. *No, the locks were changed. No one could get in.*
5. *So maybe I did do it.*
6. *Or maybe . . . the ghosts of Catherine and Jill are REAL.*

He avoided his study. Even if he'd not been considering abandoning his project, he knew he wouldn't have been able to write this morning. He couldn't focus. It would be impossible.

If he couldn't accomplish anything on that score, maybe he could do something practical. He could focus on items 3 and 4. He could satisfy himself, once and for all, that the house was secure.

He checked all the windows, even those up on the third floor that only a human fly could access, for weakness. He found them all properly latched. The main garage door was locked and did not appear to have been tampered with in any way.

Paul grabbed a ladder from the garage and hauled it up two flights of stairs, chipping paint on the wall with the legs as he made some turns, to allow him to reach the one access panel to the attic. Flashlight in hand, he climbed to the top of the ladder and gave the square panel door enough of a nudge to slide it to one side. Then he went up one more step and poked his head into the space.

He turned on the flashlight and did a slow 360-degree sweep of the attic. There was nothing up there but rafters and insulation. They'd never used the space for storage. It was too difficult to get anything up there and then, later, bring it back down.

He returned the ladder to the garage.

Well. So that was that.

Now he almost wished the typewriter was not tucked away in the trunk of Charlotte's car. If it were here, he would place it next to the laptop, look at it, and say, "I'm here. What would you like to talk about?"

At one point, the phone rang. It was Anna.

"I wanted to see how you were doing," she said.

"Okay. Thanks again for coming out in the middle of the night."

"I've an opening at two if you'd like to come in."

Paul thought for a moment. "No, I'm good."

"Are you sure? You weren't so good a few hours ago."

"Don't worry. I think I've come to some sort of . . . realization. An acceptance."

"And what's that, Paul?"

Paul said nothing.

"You there?" Anna asked.

"I'm here," he said.

"Look, I'm going to leave that two o'clock open. If you change your mind, just come in. You don't have to call."

"Okay. Good to know."

Anna said good-bye and Paul put away his phone.

Charlotte was right. He needed to get out of the house.

That didn't mean he had to jump in the car and drive to Mystic. But some fresh air wouldn't be a bad idea. Maybe a walk to downtown. Lunch someplace.

As he came out the front door, he was almost knocked back, as if by a fierce wind, but there was not so much as a breeze.

It was music that nearly knocked him off his feet.

Dee dee, diddly-dee, dee dee, dee-da, dee-da, dee da dee.

It was the Tastee Truck driven by Leonard Hoffman. It was stopped almost directly across the street. Leonard was not behind the wheel. He was more likely at the serving window, but it was on the side of the truck that Paul could not see. Leonard had clearly been stopped by one or more of the neighborhood kids. Paul then noticed one pair of legs, from the knees down, visible through the underside of the truck.

Paul huddled by his front door. He did not want to engage with Leonard. He did not want to see him. He considered going back in the house but concluded he could wait here until the truck moved on down the street.

The truck rocked on its springs ever so slightly as someone moved inside it. And then there was Leonard, settling back in behind the wheel, putting the truck into gear, and pulling forward.

As the truck exited Paul's field of vision, he saw who Leonard's customer had been.

It was a man, holding an ice-cream cone. Late twenties, early thirties. His face was severely bruised and a bandage was wrapped about his forehead. One arm was in a sling.

Jesus, Paul thought. *That guy's had the shit beat out of him.*

And then he realized who he was looking at.

Gavin Hitchens gazed across the street, locked eyes with Paul, smiled, and took a lick of his ice-cream cone.

Paul felt his insides turn to liquid.

He stared back for several seconds before summoning the strength to approach. Crossing the street, he shouted, "What the hell do you want?"

Hitchens held his spot, had another lick. "I wanted an ice cream," he said.

"I'm betting that guy goes through your neighborhood, too," Paul said, stopping within ten feet of the man. "Get the hell out of here."

Hitchens nodded slowly. "Soon as I finish. Can't drive and eat an ice cream with one hand."

Hitchens took one more lick, tossed the unfinished cone at Paul's feet, then turned and walked slowly up the sidewalk to his car, limping severely. He opened the driver's door and gingerly got behind the wheel.

Paul watched until Hitchens had reached the end of the street, turned, and disappeared.

Anna White sat at her office desk and glanced at the wall clock. It was nearly three in the afternoon.

Two o'clock had come and gone.

Paul Davis had not shown up.

Forty-Five

It was almost the time when Charlotte, on a slow day, might have gone home. But then a couple from Boston came into the office without an appointment. They had been driving around Milford when they spotted a house for sale on Elmwood Street, half a block from the sound. It was a beautiful three-story with a strong Cape Cod influence. Cedar-shingle siding, a balcony on the third floor. Two-car garage. And out front, a FOR SALE sign with the name CHARLOTTE DAVIS on it.

Charlotte sent Paul a text to tell him she would be home late. He'd gotten plenty of texts like that before.

Charlotte showed the couple the Elmwood house and drove them around town to check out a few more properties.

It was nearly nine-thirty by the time they were done.

Charlotte had a small briefcase with her that was stuffed with various documents and real estate flyers. She decided to toss it in the trunk of her car, where it would be out of sight.

She got the remote out of her purse and hit the trunk release button. Lights flashed, and the trunk yawned open a few inches. She lifted it up and set the briefcase next to the tarp-shrouded typewriter.

She pulled the tarp back and stared, briefly, at the exposed Underwood. She then pulled the tarp back over it and slammed the trunk shut. She got into the car, turned on the engine and headlights, and pointed the car toward home.

She saw the emergency lights as she turned onto her street.

There were so many, they were almost blinding. It was difficult to tell just how many vehicles there were up ahead. She could see at least two police cars, an ambulance, and what even looked like a fire truck.

They appeared to be clustered either right in front of her house, or just beyond it. Either way, the street at that point was impassible.

A male officer standing in the middle of the road held up a hand to stop her. She powered down her window.

"Road's closed, ma'am," he told her.

"My house is right there." She pointed. "Can I get that far?"

Her words made an impression on him. "*That* house?"

She nodded.

"Okay, go on ahead."

"What's going on?" she asked.

"Just go on ahead."

She put the window back up and crept the rest of the way, edging past a Milford Police cruiser and turning into the driveway behind Paul's car. As she opened her door she found a uniformed female officer waiting for her.

"You live here?" she asked.

"Yes," Charlotte said.

"What's your name?"

"What's going on?" she asked.

"What's your name, ma'am?"

"Charlotte Davis. Could someone please tell me what's happening?"

"Please wait here."

"Can I go inside?"

"Please wait here."

The cop walked off, threading her way between the emergency vehicles blocking the street. Charlotte saw her conferring with someone. A fortyish black man in plainclothes with what appeared, at least from where Charlotte was standing, a badge of some kind clipped to his belt.

The man looked in Charlotte's direction and approached.

"You're Mrs. Davis?" he asked.

"Yes. What's going on?"

"My name is Detective Arnwright. Milford Police."

"No one will tell me what this is all about. Give me a second. I want to let my husband know I'm home."

"What's your husband's name, ma'am?"

"What? It's Paul. Paul Davis."

Charlotte had reached her front door, tried opening it first without a key, and when that did not work, started fiddling with the set of keys still in her hand.

But before she could insert it into the lock, Arnwright said, "Mrs. Davis, I have some difficult news for you. There's been an incident."

Charlotte turned to look at the detective. "What are you talking about? What kind of an incident?"

"There was . . . a drowning," Arnwright said.

"What?"

The detective nodded solemnly. "A man was found on the beach. His body had been washed up."

"Why are you—what are you saying?"

"The man was fully clothed, and his wallet was still tucked down in the pocket of his jeans. We found a driver's license and some other ID in there."

"Oh please, no, no. He couldn't have. He told me he was going to be okay. He *promised* me."

"He told you he'd be okay?" the detective asked.

"It's a mistake," Charlotte said defiantly. "It can't be him."

"Well, I'll want to address that shortly, Mrs. Davis. But you seem to be suggesting that maybe your husband was going through a difficult time."

"He . . . he has been. He's been under a great deal of stress. And . . . other things."

"What kind of other things?"

Charlotte began to ramble. "Dr. White, she talked about admitting him, but he didn't want to go to the hospital, he wanted to see if he'd feel better, and now that the typewriter was out of the house and wouldn't be sending him any more messages he probably thought things really would get better but now if—"

"Mrs. Davis, slow down. What's this about a typewriter? And you said Dr. White? Anna White?"

Charlotte became angry. "Why are you asking me these questions? Whose ID did you find?"

"We found several items of identification for a Paul

Davis in the wallet," Arnwright said gently. "Some with photos. The reason I ask about your husband's state of mind is, as I said, he was fully dressed. He wasn't in a swimsuit or anything like that. It's the early stages of the investigation, but it appears he may have simply walked out into the water."

"Oh, God," Charlotte said again. "No, please, no." She started shaking her head back and forth.

Arnwright put a hand on her shoulder. "Mrs. Davis, I am so very sorry . . ."

"Is that him?" she said, pointing toward the street.

Arnwright spun around. Two male attendants were rolling a gurney to the back of an ambulance. A body was atop it, draped in a sheet.

"Paul!" she screamed, and started running.

"Mrs. Davis, please, wait!" Arnwright said, jogging after her. But Charlotte had a good head start.

"Stop!" she shouted at the attendants. One of the two men looked her way and mouthed *shit*.

They stopped wheeling the gurney as they opened the back doors of the ambulance, allowing Charlotte a chance to come up alongside it and grip it by the side rails.

"Is it him?" she asked, clearly unable to bring herself to pull down the sheet and reveal the face. "Is it?"

The attendants looked to Arnwright for guidance. Everyone went silent as the detective decided what should be done.

He nodded.

The attendant slowly pulled the sheet far enough back to reveal the dead person's head.

It was a man, hair wet and matted, the face dirtied with beach sand. But his facial features were undamaged, and even in this condition, he was easy enough to identify as Paul Davis.

"No!" Charlotte said.

As her knees buckled, she collapsed onto the street.

Forty-Six

When Anna White found Detective Joe Arnwright at her front door the next day she thought he must have more news about Gavin Hitchens. He'd made a brief stop at her office a day earlier to confirm that Paul Davis, who'd been arrested for assaulting Hitchens, was also one of her clients.

Anna was between appointments and making some notes when she heard the doorbell to the main house.

"Detective," she said. "Come in."

He smiled grimly. She did not like that look.

"What's going on?" she asked.

"You recall we talked the other day about Paul Davis," he said. "In connection with Mr. Hitchens."

"Yes," she said regretfully. "A terrible situation all around. Has something happened?"

"I'm afraid he died last night."

"Gavin Hitchens?"

"No, Mr. Davis."

Anna stood stock-still for five seconds. Slowly, she raised both hands and placed them over her mouth.

"Oh, God," she said, lowering her hands and looking for something for support. She moved to a nearby chair and put one hand on the back of it to steady herself. "This is terrible. This is awful. What happened?"

"A drowning. That's what everything points to."

Anna looked dumbstruck. "A drowning? How could he have drowned? I don't even think he owned a boat."

Joe Arnwright said, "It appears Mr. Davis took his own life."

Anna's body wavered. "I need to sit down," she said. "Come to my office." Once they were there, she took the chair she occupied when working with her clients. Joe Arnwright sat across from her.

"This is just . . . I can't believe it," Anna said. She bit on the end of her thumb. "This can't be." She looked imploringly at the detective. "Are you sure it wasn't some sort of accident? Did he fall off the pier? Something like that?"

"His wife told us he'd been seeing you for a period of time, that he'd been deeply troubled about a number of things. And, of course, I know now that he was nearly killed by Kenneth Hoffman eight months ago. That there was a lot of fallout from that."

"Yes," she said. "We even went up to visit him, this week, in prison."

Arnwright looked stunned. "You did? Why?"

Anna explained it as best she could. Arnwright had a small notebook in his hand and was scribbling things down.

"Would that explain why he might be inclined to take his own life?"

"If anything," she said, "I would have thought that the visit helped. I can't . . . this is horrible. How is his wife? How's Charlotte?"

"Extremely distraught, as you can imagine. She was telling me that Mr. Davis was suffering from a delusion of some sort."

Anna reached for a tissue from a nearby box. She dabbed her eyes and wadded the tissue in her fingers.

"I don't quite know how to respond to that," she said. "I suppose the short answer is yes."

"Something about a possessed typewriter," Arnwright said, without a hint of derision or skepticism.

"Yes."

"He believed it was the typewriter Kenneth Hoffman made his victims write notes of apologies on."

"That's correct," Anna said.

"I'm not a mental health expert, but that makes me wonder, had he been diagnosed with schizophrenia?"

"No."

"Was he depressed?"

"He was certainly down, but I did not believe he was clinically depressed."

"But doesn't getting messages from dead people count as hearing voices? Isn't that a symptom of schizophrenia? His wife said he was writing the notes himself, but unaware that he was doing it."

Anna sighed. "I know how that sounds. And now, in retrospect . . ." She could not finish the sentence.

"Were you concerned he might harm himself? That he might take his own life? Could he have received one of these so-called messages telling him to kill himself, to walk out into the sound?"

"I just . . ."

"And I understand you were recently out there? Two nights ago? He'd had an episode?"

"Oh, God, what have I done," Anna said and began to curl in on herself. "What did I fail to do?"

As the tears came, she grabbed for more tissues. "I suggested to him that he go to the hospital, that he be admitted for a short period so that he could be observed. But he wouldn't do it."

"Why not?"

Anna shook her head. "His friend talked him out of it."

"What friend?"

"Bill. I don't know his last name, but I think he works with Charlotte. She's a real estate agent."

Arnwright flipped to an earlier page in his notebook. "Bill Myers?"

"Possibly. Charlotte phoned him when I was there. Bill asked to talk to Paul, and after that Paul said he didn't want to go to the hospital. He might have come to that decision on his own, though. Paul did not believe there was anything wrong with him mentally, although toward the end, he seemed more open to considering the idea that maybe he was responsible."

"Responsible?"

"For the strange things that were going on."

"Do you agree with the wife? He *was* writing them?"

Anna looked at the detective with red eyes. "Yes."

Arnwright nodded and closed his notebook. "So it appears what happened is, Mr. Davis was in a very distressed state of mind, walked out into Long Island Sound with the intention of killing himself, and was successful. Is there anything you can tell me, as a professional who was treating Mr. Davis, that would run contrary to that finding?"

Anna struggled. To say no was an admission that she had not done her job, that she had failed him. To say no was to admit responsibility.

To say yes would be to lie.

"No," she whispered. "No, I can't think of anything that would contradict that finding."

Arnwright offered a slow, sympathetic nod. "For what it's worth, Dr. White, we have all been there. We're all just trying to do the best we can."

"I didn't," Anna White said. "Not even close."

Forty-Seven

"I killed him," Bill Myers said. "I killed Paul."

"I'm sorry?" Detective Arnwright said. "What do you mean?"

They were meeting at The Corner Restaurant on River Street, a cup of coffee in front of each of them. Arnwright had suggested Paul's friend order something to eat, but he'd declined, saying he didn't have much of an appetite. That was when he made what had sounded to the detective like a confession.

"Mr. Myers, I should tell you, that if you're about to admit something here, I'm obliged to inform you that—"

"It's nothing like that," Bill said, waving his hand in the air. "I didn't drag him out into the sound and hold his head underwater, for God's sake, but I might as well have."

He made two fists, opened his hands, then made them again.

"I just . . . I can't believe he did that. I can't. He wasn't crazy." He leaned in closer to Arnwright. "He was going through some shit, he really was, but I never, never thought he would do anything like that. Otherwise, I would have told him to take his therapist's advice, to check into the hospital. But no, I had to talk him out of that." He grimaced. "I have to live with that for the rest of my life. That's what I mean when I say I killed him. I talked him out of getting the help he so clearly needed."

"It's hard to know what's going through people's heads," Arnwright said. "When did you last see Mr. Davis?"

"We met up for a squash game the other day but didn't really play that hard. You know he had a head injury, and I didn't even think he should be playing, but he was sick of treating himself with kid gloves. But after a few minutes, he came to his senses, and we cut our session short."

"How did he seem to you?"

"Upset. You know about the nightmares? The typewriter thing?"

"Yes."

"Well, there you go."

"Were you close friends, you and Paul?"

Bill hesitated. "Friends, for sure. Maybe not super close. We knew each other in university, UConn, and we sort of kept in touch. We both ended up in Milford, and he knew what I did for a living, and when Charlotte was getting into real estate, he asked if there was any way I could help her out. We found a spot for her at the agency."

"So all three of you were friends."

"I guess. Sure."

"Are you married, Mr. Myers?"

"I have been, but not now." He appeared to be considering whether to tell Arnwright something. "Let me tell you a story."

"Okay."

"I had a cousin, she lived in Cleveland. And around the time she was turning twenty, she started believing that she was being pursued by Margaret Thatcher."

"The British prime minister?"

Bill nodded. "She said she was getting messages from her, telepathically. And here's the thing. Her parents, they wanted to *believe* that it was really happening. That somehow, for reasons they could not explain, the prime minister of England was out to get their daughter. You know why?"

"I think so."

"Because the alternative was even more horrible to

imagine. That their daughter was seriously mentally ill. They were in denial about that. But eventually, of course, they had to accept the fact that my cousin Michele was delusional. A delusion became the only rational explanation."

"And that's how you feel about Paul and his obsession about that typewriter."

Bill shrugged.

"What happened to Michele?" Arnwright asked.

"She jumped off the Hope Memorial Bridge into the Cuyahoga River at the age of twenty-four."

Detective Arnwright had to wait nearly a minute for his knock to be answered at Gavin Hitchens's house.

When the door finally opened, Arnwright's eyebrows went up a notch. He knew Hitchens had been seriously injured by Paul Davis, that he'd suffered a blow to the head, that his elbow had been sprained, that one of his knees had been hurt. So the sling, the bandage on his head, and the wrapped knee were to be expected. Arnwright was just expecting Hitchens to be wearing more than a pair of boxers.

"Yeah?" he said.

Arnwright introduced himself. Hitchens nodded knowingly and smiled.

"Let me guess," he said. "That son of a bitch wants

to charge me with harassment or something." Hitchens grinned maliciously. "Fucker puts me in the hospital, and *I'm* supposed to be the dangerous one."

"You're talking about Mr. Davis," Arnwright said cautiously.

"Is that what he did? File a complaint about me? Because if he's saying I did something, I didn't do anything."

"What do you think he might have said?"

"Look, okay, I was on his street. I was looking at his house. But that's all. I was getting an ice cream."

"And when was this?"

Hitchens blinked. "Hang on. Is that why you're here or not?"

"If you think I'm here about Paul Davis, yeah, you're right about that. So when was this?"

"Yesterday, kind of midday."

"You had words?"

Hitchens shrugged. "He told me to move on, and I did. End of story."

"But there's a lot of bad blood between you."

"Wow," said Hitchens. "I can see why you're a detective."

"What's the source of this trouble?"

The young man shrugged. "I've been through this. I gave a statement. This Davis guy is some kind of mental case. Thinks I was trying to drive him insane or something, but believe me, his crazy train had already reached the station."

"Did you speak again with Mr. Davis later yesterday?"

"No, that was it."

"What was your purpose in standing out in front of his house?"

Gavin Hitchens looked away. "I don't know. It was a place to be."

"Were you trying to scare him? Intimidate him? Make him think you were going to get even?"

Slowly, he shook his head. "I mean, he might never even have seen me if he hadn't come out when he did, so you can't really scare a guy if he doesn't know you're there."

Arnwright studied the man for several more seconds.

"Okay," the detective said finally. "Thanks for your trouble."

He turned to leave but Gavin said, "Hey, hold on. That's it?"

Arnwright turned. "That's it."

"Is that bastard going to go to jail for what he did to me?"

"Doubtful," Arnwright said.

Forty-Eight

The following day, Charlotte Davis sat on the bed she had shared with her husband and looked out through the sliding glass doors at the sun reflecting off the waters of Long Island Sound.

There were things she had to do, but she was having a hard time getting started.

Finally, she stood and opened the closet so that she could select a suit for Paul. The funeral home had been asking. Paul had only one good one. As a professor, he could get through almost any function with a sport jacket, jeans, and a tie. Even during graduation ceremonies, when he might be called upon to wear a gown, he could get away with smart casual undercover. The last time Paul had worn a suit, Charlotte thought, was to attend the funeral of a cousin in Providence.

And so he would wear one to a funeral again.

Charlotte pulled a dark blue suit from the hanger, laid it out on the bed. It had not seen any outings since its last trip to the dry cleaners. The tag was still attached. She took the jacket off the hanger, held it up to the light from the window, turned it around.

There was a small smudge on the back that the cleaners had missed, but really, did it matter? Even with an open casket, no one was going to see that. The matching pants, she noticed, had been on the hanger so long they had a crease at the knee, but again, was anyone going to see anything below the waist? Wouldn't only the upper half of her husband's body be viewable, not all of him?

Charlotte hadn't even discussed with the funeral home director the possibility of a closed casket. Was that the way to go? It wasn't as though Paul had been in a bad car accident. Death by drowning had left his face relatively unscathed. He was, in a word, presentable.

She decided she would press the pants, regardless. And at least try to get the spot off the back of Paul's suit jacket. The man deserved that much.

Her cell phone rang.

She'd left it on the dresser. She took a step toward it, looked at the screen to see who it was.

BILL

She held the phone for several seconds, letting it ring six times in her hand before declining the call.

She did not want to talk to Bill. Not now. She'd not spoken to him since the call in the middle of the night, when Bill had told Paul not to go to the hospital. Bill was not the only one from whom Charlotte was not taking calls. She was ignoring calls from Hailey, too.

Except for one.

Paul's ex-wife, her husband, Walter, and her son were coming to the service the next day. Josh, Hailey had told Charlotte, was utterly destroyed by the death of his father. He only stopped crying to sleep, which had only come because he was exhausted from weeping.

"Well," Charlotte said, "the good news is, you and Walter got what you wanted. Full fucking custody."

Hailey had gasped. Before she could respond, Charlotte ended the call. When Hailey tried to call her back, Charlotte did not pick up.

Charlotte set up the ironing board in the small downstairs laundry room and placed the suit pants on it. While she waited for the iron to heat, she went up to the kitchen for a cup of coffee. She had started a pot earlier but had yet to have the first cup. Nor had she bothered yet with any breakfast.

The kitchen island was covered with nearly a dozen empty cardboard liquor boxes. She pushed a couple of them aside to make a working space for herself. She grabbed a small plate from the cupboard and some butter from the fridge. She put a slice of whole wheat bread into the toaster, but before she could push it down, the doorbell rang.

She glanced down at herself. She was only a step up from pajamas—a pair of jeans and a T-shirt, hair pinned back, no makeup. She was not ready for unexpected visitors coming to pay their respects.

She sighed, scurried barefoot down the steps to the front door and peered through the narrow window that ran down the side.

It was Anna White.

Charlotte unlocked the door, swung it open.

"Dr. White," she said.

Anna nodded. "Mrs. Davis. I'm sorry to bother you at a time like this, but would you have a moment?"

Charlotte raised her arms in a gesture of futility. It was far from welcoming, but she said, "Sure, come on in."

"Thanks," Anna said, following her up the stairs.

Once they'd reached the kitchen, Charlotte said, "I've left the iron plugged in, be right back."

Charlotte disappeared downstairs.

Anna looked at the empty boxes on the island. As she turned slowly to take in the rest of the room, her gaze landed on the open door to what had been Paul's minioffice.

Anna felt a chill that ran the entire length of her spine.

There, on the desk, next to the laptop, was the Underwood.

Anna assumed it was *the* typewriter. The machine Paul had believed was sending him messages from beyond the grave. The machine that, one might argue, drove him to the brink of madness. The machine that played a major part in the man's suicide.

It had not been here the other night. Paul had said it was in Charlotte's car, that it wasn't coming back into the house unless it was smart enough to unlock the trunk.

She walked slowly to the office and entered. Cautiously, as though it were electrified, Anna touched the typewriter with the tips of her fingers.

She actually felt something akin to an electric shock

but knew it was nothing of the kind. It was an emotional reaction. The metal casing of the typewriter was cool and smooth to the touch.

Anna was reminded of that movie, the one by Stanley Kubrick, where the ape reaches out to touch the black obelisk. Fearfully at first, then, when he realizes the black slab isn't going to bite him, he runs his hands all over it.

Anna ran her fingers across the keys, gave the space bar a tap.

There didn't appear to be anything ominous about it, but how the hell did it get back up here if—

"Dr. White?"

Anna turned to see Charlotte standing there. "You startled me," Anna said. She nodded in the direction of the typewriter. "I just had . . . to look at it. How did it get back up here? Paul had said it was locked in your car."

Charlotte gave her a quizzical look. "I put it there," she said.

"Oh, well, of course," Anna said.

Paul's wife frowned. "Tell me you didn't think it got up here on its own."

"No, no, I didn't think that," Anna said, her face flushing. "I'm just surprised to see it."

"When I went out to get boxes, I needed the trunk

space, so I put it back in here. When I get around to Paul's stuff"—her voice began to break—"I'll have to decide what to do with it."

"I guess, if it were me, I'd have . . ."

"You'd have what?"

"It's none of my business," the therapist said. "I'm in no position to judge."

"No, tell me."

Anna hesitated. "I think I'd have headed for Stratford, stopped on the bridge, and dropped that thing into the Housatonic."

Charlotte's chin quivered. She took several seconds before answering. "That's exactly what Paul wanted to do. I should have let him."

"You still could," Anna said.

Charlotte nodded slowly, and said, "Maybe I just have to know."

Anna let that sink in but said nothing.

Anna emerged from the office and wandered back to the island, where she stood beside a stool, not wanting to perch herself on it unless invited.

"I was getting his suit ready," Charlotte said. "The pants are wrinkled, and there's some kind of spot on the back of the jacket. Silly, right? Like anyone's going to notice."

"It's not silly," Anna said. "You need to get everything the way you want it. You want to do right for Paul." Anna looked at the empty boxes.

Charlotte didn't wait for the question. "I'm going to have to sort through Paul's things sooner or later."

"This is definitely sooner."

"I was wandering through the house yesterday and everywhere I looked I saw him. His books, his clothes, his CDs. I know the mourning is just beginning, but these reminders, everywhere I turn, are going to make it go on and on. Better to rip the bandage right off."

"I guess that's one way of handling it, but you might be moving a bit fast."

"You don't approve."

"I didn't say that. I know people who've dealt with loss this way. I knew a woman who lost her teenage son in a car accident, and she stripped the house of everything that reminded her of him. A week after he died, you'd have never known he lived there."

"Did it help?" Charlotte asked.

"If you're asking did it make her forget, the answer is no," Anna said.

Charlotte was quiet for a moment. Then, "That detective came by late yesterday. Arnwright."

"He came to see me, too."

"He was here two, three times, asking me about Paul, but I guess yesterday's visit was his last. He had the official coroner's report, which also meant that they were able to release his body to the funeral home. That Paul did die from drowning."

"I'm so sorry."

"He said they couldn't officially rule it a suicide. I mean, we can't know what was in his head, and it's not like he left a note. But based on his behavior the last few weeks, it's the most likely explanation. So they've called it something like 'death by misadventure.'" Her eyes reddened. "Like it was some sort of fun outing that went wrong."

Charlotte sighed. She raised her head and looked squarely at Anna.

"Why are you here?"

The question struck Anna with the force of a slap. She sought some reservoir of inner strength and said, "I'm here to say I'm sorry."

"You said that five seconds ago."

"This sorry . . . is different. I'm sorry I failed Paul. I failed him badly. You came to me. You told me. You were worried he might do something to himself. I should have done more."

Charlotte looked at her, steely-eyed. "I guess you should have."

Anna stood there several more seconds before she realized there was not much else to say. "I shouldn't have come." She stopped on her way to the stairs. "But I'd like to come to the service and pay my respects. It's tomorrow?"

Charlotte nodded. "Two o'clock."

"I'll be there."

"Wonderful," she said with more than a hint of sarcasm. "Now, if you'll forgive me, I have a suit to press."

Forty-Nine

Anna had thought there would be more people. About forty showed up for the funeral, which was held in a small church on Naugatuck Avenue. While Charlotte and Paul were not affiliated with any Milford church, the funeral home had found a minister who was not only amenable to hosting the service, but also willing to say a few words about Paul.

Paul's mother, who lived in a nursing home in Hartford, had been driven down by one of the facility's care workers. In her nineties with twiglike arms and legs, she was wheeled in and given a spot near the front, in the center aisle. She gave every indication of being oblivious to what was going on.

At one point, Anna was pretty sure she caught a

glimpse of Arnwright at the back of the church, but then she lost sight of him.

Several of those attending were evidently from West Haven College. Anna walked in with a woman who, she learned after some brief small talk, was the college president. She introduced Anna to a few of Paul's colleagues. Anna forgot the names as soon as she heard them. When anyone asked how she knew Paul, she said simply, "He was a friend."

She felt ashamed to admit her connection. Everyone, she believed, would know how she had failed him. She felt doubly ashamed that she did not want to admit it.

Not that there weren't people there who knew. Charlotte, of course, and there was Bill Myers, who had been huddled over to one side of the church, reviewing some notes. Anna recognized him from real estate signs she'd seen around town over the years.

Anna also figured out who Hailey and Walter must be. They were the couple with the crying boy. That he was Josh there was no doubt. Anna could see the resemblance. He was a miniature Paul in a brown suit, red tie, and shined-up shoes. He sat with his mother and stepfather in the front pew to the left of the aisle, while Charlotte sat on the right. They did not exchange greetings nor look at one another.

It struck Anna that Charlotte was very alone. She

was on the aisle, so she could only have someone on her right. Anna figured that would be a spot reserved for family, but once he had finished reviewing his notes, Bill took that seat space on the pew. He seemed to know the two women and one man to his right, which led Anna to think they were others from the real estate agency. Bill gave Charlotte a comforting hug, followed by the others.

A work family seemed to be all Charlotte had in attendance. Maybe the trip out from New York was too much for Charlotte's mother.

Anna came up the right side of the church and slipped into a pew at the halfway point. She ended up sitting next to a man in a gray suit who turned and nodded.

"Hello," he said.

Anna nodded.

He extended a hand. "Harold Foster," he said.

"Anna White," she said.

Foster?

There were probably plenty of Fosters in Milford, but Anna was pretty sure that Jill Foster's husband's name had been Harold.

He must have sensed the question she wanted to ask but would not. "Yes," he said. "*That* Foster. My wife worked at West Haven."

"Were you and Paul friends?"

"Not . . . really. But there is, I suppose, a connection." He took a moment to form his thoughts. "My wife, and Catherine Lamb, and now Paul. All victims, one way or another."

Anna could see the reasoning.

"Taking his own life," Foster said, shaking his head. "One can only imagine the torment he was going through."

Anna could only nod. She was relieved to see the minister heading for the pulpit. "It looks like things are about to begin," she said.

The minister took his place. He read several passages from the Bible that Anna did not recognize but assumed were relevant. She'd never been particularly religious, and her parents had rarely attended church. The minister called on Bill Myers to say a few words. Bill stood, gave Charlotte's hand a squeeze, and mounted the steps to the pulpit.

"Boy, this is tough," he said, reaching into his pocket for a folded sheaf of papers that contained his remarks. "If there were two words to describe Paul, they would have to be *good guy.* That's what he was. He was a good guy. But he was more than that. He was a good husband, and he was a wonderful father to his son, Josh."

Bill looked at Josh, sitting on the front row bench, dwarfed between his mother and stepfather, staring down into his lap. The mention of his name brought his head up briefly.

"And the fact that Josh is such a fine young man is a testament to what a good man Paul was. He was also a devoted educator. He cared about his students. I know that all the people here today from the college would say that about him, too."

Bill cleared his throat, shuffled his papers. He seemed to have lost his place. He flipped the pages over, his handwritten scribbles briefly visible for the congregation to see.

"Here we are. Sorry," he said. "I'm a little nervous. I first knew Paul back in our own college days, and we kind of drifted apart after that. Then we both turned out to be living in the same town, and we reconnected. I'm glad I got to know him again, even if it was only for a few years. These last few months were not easy for Paul. He suffered a trauma he clearly could not move past. I think for those of us close to Paul, the signs were right in front of us, but we blinded ourselves to them. We thought things would be okay. There's a lesson here for us all. When we see friends in trouble, we have to be there for them. We have to do everything we can to make them get help. We can't assume they'll pull through." Bill paused. "I failed Paul in that regard, and have to live with that the rest of my life."

There were some murmurs in the church. Someone whispered, "He's being too hard on himself."

Bill shuffled his papers again, and sniffed. He appeared on the verge of tears.

"I got a lot more stuff written down here, but to be honest, I'd be saying the same thing over and over again. We'll miss him." He gazed toward the casket, which had been closed for the service. "We'll miss you, man, we really will."

He stepped down and returned to his spot next to Charlotte, head bowed. She patted his back twice.

When the service was over, Harold Foster got up abruptly and cut in front of other mourners to be among the first out of the church. Maybe he was one of those people, Anna mused, who left the baseball game at the top of the ninth. Wanted to beat the rush getting out of the parking lot.

Anna wanted to get out of there as quickly as she could, too, and scanned the church looking for a less crowded exit path. But before she could settle on one, she heard a voice behind her.

"Sad, huh?"

A chill ran the length of her spine. Anna knew the voice. She turned to find Gavin Hitchens standing there in jeans, a sport jacket that was frayed along the lapels, and a loosened plaid tie.

She'd not seen what Paul had done to him. His arm was in a sling, his forehead bandaged. Anna guessed he was favoring one leg, as he had one hand firmly gripped on the back of a church pew for support.

"Gavin," she said.

"Some cop came by, asking weird questions about Paul, but he never said he was dead. But then I heard about the drowning." He shook his head. "A real tragedy."

"Stay away from me."

She started to turn away when he said, "I've got some good news, though."

Anna held her spot.

"The charges got dropped." Gavin grinned. "They gave that dead soldier's dad three voice recordings to listen to, and he couldn't pick mine out. Plus, the coffee shop surveillance video's time code is all fucked-up. They can't tell for sure when I was actually there. So, there you have it." A broad smile. "I'm an innocent man."

"There's a big difference between not guilty and innocent," Anna said.

"But I was thinking, we could still have our sessions. I liked our little talks."

Anna was about to turn away, unable to endure his smug expression another moment, when she saw Arnwright sidling up behind him. Gavin saw her looking beyond his shoulder and turned to see the detective.

Arnwright exchanged a nod with Anna, leading her to think he wanted to speak with her, but that wasn't the case.

"Mr. Hitchens," he said.

"What's up?" Gavin said breezily.

Arnwright smiled. "Guess whose surveillance system's time code is working just fine? And crystal clear, too?"

"I don't know what you're talking about."

"A house in Devon," Arnwright said.

Gavin started to pale. "Uh, what?"

Arnwright appeared to be struggling to keep the smile from growing into a grin. "Yeah. Seems some folks lost their dog. Got the whole thing on video." Arnwright looked Anna's way. "Nice to see you, Dr. White. You have a nice day."

She felt herself being dismissed, but she walked away with a sense of relief. Maybe Hitchens was finally going to get what was coming to him. Her encounter with him had delayed her enough that she was now among the last to file out of the church.

Anna found herself trailing behind Charlotte and

Bill. They walked with heads lowered, shoulders touching. Soon, they'd be outside, where many were waiting to say a few words, if not to Charlotte, then to Hailey and her son.

She worked to push Gavin Hitchens out of her mind. If she had to, she thought, she'd get a restraining order. She'd talked to Arnwright about that.

Anna had already decided against offering any more words of comfort or regret to Charlotte. Her visit the day before had not gone well. Once Anna had cleared the church doors, she headed for her car. She had left her father in the care, once again, of her retired neighbor, but she didn't like to take advantage.

As she trailed Paul's friend and widow, Anna had her chin down, close to her chest. If she'd been holding her head high, she might have failed to notice Bill reaching out a hand to hunt for Charlotte's.

He found it, and when he did, he did more than simply hold it. He laced his fingers in with hers in a gesture that struck Anna as more than comforting.

There was something almost intimate about it.

Well, it's a difficult time, Anna thought.

Almost as quickly as he had found Charlotte's hand, he let it go and thrust his own hand into his pants pocket.

But then he turned to Charlotte, leaned in closely to whisper something in her ear.

Two words.

Anna was close enough that she was able to make them out, although even as the words were whispered, she questioned whether she had heard correctly.

Yet they had been as clear as if Bill had whispered them into her own ear and not Charlotte's.

"It worked," Bill said.

Fifty

Yes, Charlotte thought. *It did.*

But just because they'd pulled it off didn't mean they could start getting careless. What the fuck was Bill thinking, reaching for her hand like that, whispering in her ear, with people all around them. Sure, he'd be expected to console her, but he needed to dial it back a bit.

This was when they had to be the most on their guard.

Charlotte was already worried that she'd made a mistake, going out and getting all those empty boxes at the liquor store. The way Dr. White looked at them had made Charlotte nervous. She hoped she'd explained herself well. The truth was, she'd been itching to start packing up Paul's stuff from the moment she and Bill had decided what they were going to do.

But they had to be careful.

Which was exactly why she had been declining Bill's calls since Paul's death. It didn't look good for them to be talking. Sure, the occasional phone conversation could be explained, should they ever be asked. But the smarter course was to not talk on the phone at all. That was also how Charlotte had wanted it in the months leading up to Paul's so-called death by misadventure. Even though Bill and Charlotte worked together, only so many calls could be attributed to real estate.

There were plenty of opportunities for them to talk at work. In person. Those kinds of interactions didn't leave a trail.

And, of course, there were all those empty houses.

Not every home that went on the market was occupied. Many people who'd put their places up for sale had already moved. Some were homes that developers had built on spec, awaiting a first buyer.

When you slipped into a house like that for a fuck, you didn't have to worry about the homeowner coming back early.

Most of these empty houses had been "staged." Furniture was moved in to make the place look lived-in. Books were put on shelves. Magazines fanned out on coffee tables. Pictures hung on the walls. A bowl of fruit—preferably plastic—on the kitchen table. Maybe one bedroom was done up as a nursery, another as a teenager's room, with sports posters on the wall. And they'd dress up a master bedroom, too, with a king-size bed and fancy linens and assorted throw pillows.

Charlotte and Bill had access to many such places.

Not only was it a hell of a lot cheaper than going to a hotel—and to play it safe they'd have had to go to one well outside Milford—you didn't have to use a credit card. Nor did you have to worry about why your car was parked out front of your coworker's house.

They often joked about how much more convenient it was to have an affair when you worked in real estate.

The other thing they joked about, at least up until Kenneth Hoffman had nearly killed him, was how nice it had been of Paul to bring them together. Putting in a call to his old college friend, now working in real estate, to see if he had any advice for his wife, new to the whole business of buying and selling houses.

"Send her around," Bill said. "I'll see what I can do."

Charlotte went to the agency for a visit. Bill took an instant liking to her and was very interested to learn that she had been, at one time, an aspiring actress.

"That'll serve you well here," he told her. "You'll find yourself working for a seller and a buyer, working both sides, and they both have to believe all you care about is getting the very best deal you can for them. Some performance skills will come in very handy."

She saw something she liked in Bill, too.

She liked all the things he was that Paul was not. More self-assured, more handsome, in better shape. And even though he had one failed marriage behind him, there were no kids, and his former wife was remarried and living in France. Paul, Charlotte soon came to understand, had enough baggage to fill a 747's cargo hold. There was always something with Paul's ex. Working out the visits with Josh, the plans that were always changing. Having to listen to Paul complain about Walter's superficiality and name-dropping. Paul's real complaint, Charlotte knew, was that Hailey had traded up. She'd found a go-getter, a man with ambitions, a man who did not spend his evenings grading essays and writing next week's lecture on Ralph Waldo Emerson but was out meeting with company bigwigs and sports team owners about how to raise their profiles.

It was Charlotte who now had the guy who spent his evening grading essays and writing next week's lecture on Ralph Waldo Emerson.

And was there anything wrong with that? she sometimes asked herself. Maybe not. Unless you'd suddenly woken up to the fact that you wanted more.

It was Bill who'd reawakened her, who had shaken her out of her complacency.

There was an energy about him. When he wasn't working deals, he was taking a long weekend to London with some woman he'd just met. Or driving up to Quebec to ski and returning with a bad back, and it hadn't been on the slopes where he'd damaged it. Another weekend, with another woman, it was hot air ballooning.

He seemed . . . electric.

God, and the man even owned more than one suit.

Bill was always looking to try something new.

I could be something new, Charlotte thought.

One time, she said to Paul, "Have you ever thought about packing a bag full of Agent Provocateur lingerie and just heading into New York and booking into The Plaza and fucking our brains out?"

And Paul had said, "Agent Who?"

So one day, hosting an open house with Bill where no one had shown up for the better part of an hour, she tried the same question.

He looked at her and said, "Tonight works."

They didn't make it to The Plaza. At least, not that night.

There was the ritual of self-recrimination the first few times. Maybe they thought it was expected of them.

"This did not happen," Charlotte said, splayed across the covers in the oversize master bedroom of a three-thousand-square-foot ranch that was close to schools, had a finished basement, and had dropped ten thousand in price in the last week.

"I know," Bill said. "It just . . . Paul's my friend. I mean, he was my friend. Maybe not so much now. This was just one of those things, right? It won't happen again."

But it did.

One night when Charlotte had told Paul she was showing a condo to a woman from Stamford, but instead was in a darkened empty house with her head in Bill's lap, Bill said to her, "I'd like it to be just you."

She looked up and said, "What? What does that mean?"

"Is there a way? Is there a way that we could do this without having to be in a different fucking house every time? A way where we didn't have to pretend anymore? A way where we could just go wherever we want and do whatever we want? Because if there is, I'd want that. Just with you."

Which would mean, of course, that she would have to leave Paul. That she would have to *divorce* Paul.

It could be done. It would be messy. It would be hateful. It would take time. But it could be done.

Paul had already been through one divorce, and from the tales he'd told her, it had nearly destroyed him. He had not made it easy, he had to admit, for Hailey when she wanted to separate. Lots of pleading. Plenty of late-night calls. Failing to see things as they really were.

Refusing to accept that it was *over*.

"I made a fool of myself," he conceded. "I kept thinking I could win her back when it was clear she'd made up her mind."

He'd been afraid to commit to another marriage, so great was his fear of failing again. "But there's something about you," he told Charlotte. "I'm willing to take a leap of faith."

Leap he did.

And now, Charlotte was going to give him news she knew would destroy him. She'd met someone else. Hey, and guess what? It's your old college pal, Bill!

But she was prepared to do it. It would be horrible, but she told herself, if you didn't seek out your own happiness in life, no one else was going to do it for you.

She wanted to be happy with Bill.

And then Paul nearly died.

He stumbled upon Kenneth Hoffman getting rid

of those two women he'd murdered. Kenneth clubbed him on the head. Paul went down. Kenneth knelt down beside him, ready to finish him off.

Enter the police.

Charlotte was willing to admit, to herself, that her feelings had been mixed. If only Kenneth had gotten away with it. If only that single blow to Paul's head had been fatal. It wouldn't have been her fault. She'd have been blameless. An innocent beneficiary.

So close.

Charlotte wondered, should she feel guilty, thinking that way? Because she didn't. What she felt, overwhelmingly, was *frustrated.* It was a bit like checking your lottery ticket, thinking you have every number, then double-checking and finding that you're off by one.

Paul had lived. Therapy had followed. He had to take a leave from West Haven while he recovered, and that recovery was slow with numerous setbacks. There were the nightmares. Waking up at three in the morning in a cold sweat, screaming.

Paul Davis was a broken man.

"You can't do it now," Bill said. "You can't tell a man who's coming back from a fucking attempted murder that you're divorcing him. Think what it would be like for us. At the agency? In this town? You, the woman who left a guy at his lowest point, when he needed your support more than ever before, and me, the guy you left him for." He shook his head. "I can tell you one thing for sure. We'd never sell another house in this market."

Charlotte considered all of his points. She went very quiet.

"What?" Bill asked her. "What are you thinking?"

"Maybe," she said, "there's another way."

Fifty-One

Anna White kept wondering whether she could have heard it wrong.

Maybe Bill Myers had not whispered the words "It worked" into Charlotte's ear as they were walking out of the church together. But what else could it have been? What sounded similar to "It worked" but was not "It worked"?

Surely not "It sucked." Bill wouldn't have said that about the service, unless he was being self-deprecating about his own words honoring Paul's memory. Yes, perhaps that was it, Anna thought. He believed his eulogy was inadequate. He should have said more. And he'd whispered those two words to Charlotte as an apology. He could have done better. Maybe he was looking for some reassurance, hoping that she would then tell him he was wrong, that his words about Paul were from the heart and that they definitely did not suck.

Yes, Anna thought. That could have been what she heard.

But even if he had said what she initially believed she'd heard, so what. "It worked" could have referred to any number of things. The service *worked*. What the minister had said *worked*.

And yet Anna couldn't shake the feeling the words meant something very different.

If all she'd heard were those two words, she might have been able to let it go. But it was what she saw in the seconds before Bill leaned in and whispered in Charlotte's ear.

The way he took her hand.

He did not simply hold it. He entwined his fingers with hers. Gave them a squeeze.

Anna told herself she was reading too much into the gesture. At times like these, people did strange things. Charlotte had lost her husband. She was grieving. It made sense that she would accept comfort from a friend.

But then Bill Myers did something Anna could not explain. He withdrew his hand quickly and thrust it into his pocket.

It was as if he feared someone might have seen what he did.

Anna continued to walk along behind them as they exited the church. As Charlotte and Bill emerged into the daylight, they encountered people who had been waiting for Charlotte so they could offer their condolences. Charlotte found herself in the arms of one person after another. Bill stepped back, gave her some space.

As Anna came out of the church, she moved slowly past those paying their respects to Charlotte, down the steps, and toward the sidewalk. But instead of heading for her car, she stood close to the street and watched.

She thought more about what "It worked" might have meant.

It means nothing.

Yet Anna could not shake the feeling there was something conspiratorial in the way Bill had said it. That it was their secret.

That they had pulled off something.

No, Anna thought. *I'm just looking for a way to ease my own conscience.*

She'd barely slept since Paul's death. She had not been able to shake the guilt she felt. Paul's suicide was proof she'd failed him. She should have pressured him to go into the hospital that night. She should have told him his friend Bill was wrong to talk him out of—

Bill talked him out of going to the hospital.

"It worked."

The words suggested the successful execution of a plan. What plan? Some kind of plan that would result in Paul's death?

Could you really make a man take his own life?

No, impossible.

Unless you could somehow drive him to it. Push him to the brink of madness. Make him believe something that was unbelievable.

"It worked."

Anna had accepted that there was only one explanation for the notes in that old Underwood. Paul was writing them. He might not have known it, but he was. His memory lapses were evidence that it was possible.

There was, however, something about Paul's typewriter delusion that left her troubled. Simply put, it was insufficiently elaborate. It was not wide-ranging. It was too specific. It did not live up to the standard set by other patients she'd seen over the years who'd endured hallucinations. She'd had clients who'd spun out conspiracies of great intricacy. One man she had seen three years ago was convinced Russian president Vladimir Putin was trying to brainwash him into turning over

U.S. government secrets. Putin was communicating with him through various household appliances, including his toaster oven. That part was strange enough, but why would this man be tapped to hand over top secret information, when he worked at Dairy Queen?

That job was just a cover, he explained to Dr. White. He was, in fact, in touch with people from the CIA and the NSA. That's why it all made sense.

No matter how much she challenged his fantasy with logical questions, there was always an answer. She finally had him see a psychiatrist, who wrote out a scrip to keep his delusions in check.

But Paul, well, Paul was not like that.

His delusion was not immersed in multiple hallucinations and conspiracy theories. It was far from elaborate. It was specific. In every other respect, Paul Davis presented as a completely sane individual.

He didn't fit the pattern.

He didn't behave like a delusional man. Believing that Paul wrote those notes required some forcing of the proverbial square peg into a round hole.

What if, Anna wondered, there was no delusion at all?

The notes were real. But they were not coming from those two dead women.

"It worked."

How would you do it? Anna wondered. How could you make someone believe something so fantastical?

The crowd was breaking up. Word had quietly spread that Paul was to be cremated, so there would be no trip to a cemetery for burial. Everyone who had wanted to pass on a few comforting words to Charlotte was now heading to the church parking lot. Doors opened and closed, car engines came to life.

The minister came out to say a few words to Charlotte. Bill had rejoined her, standing alongside, nodding earnestly as the minister spoke.

And then it was over.

Charlotte thanked the minister and shook his hand, then turned and headed for the parking lot. Bill walked with her. Maybe he was going to drive her home.

No. Charlotte took a key from her purse, unlocked her car. Bill opened the driver's door for her.

A true gentleman.

They were talking. Bill said something that prompted Charlotte to shake her head. Then she seemed to cast her eye beyond them, as if checking to see whether anyone was looking their way.

Anna feigned disinterest. She glanced at her watch. But from the corner of her eye, she observed.

Before getting behind the wheel, Charlotte rested her hand on the top of the door. Bill Myers placed his over it and held it there for a good ten seconds. Then Charlotte pulled her hand away, sat in the driver's seat, and closed the door. Bill stepped back as she keyed the engine, and he turned in Anna's direction.

Quickly, he drew his suit jacket together in front and buttoned it. He then slipped a hand into the front pocket of his pants and started walking across the parking lot toward another car.

Anna was almost certain she knew what he had just done. She couldn't have sworn to it in a court of law. She'd have been laughed at. She'd have been mocked for professing to have astonishing observational skills.

But she was sure he was struggling to conceal an erection.

Not the usual response at a funeral, Anna mused.

Bill got into a car, fired it up, turned left onto Naugatuck. Charlotte had pulled out seconds earlier, heading right.

Anna rushed to her own car and got behind the wheel. She pondered what, if anything, to do now. To head home, she would have turned left out of the lot but found herself heading right.

After Charlotte.

Did she want to talk to Charlotte one more time? Start by telling her again how sorry she was, how she'd failed Paul? And then ask what Bill Myers had meant when he whispered those two words in her ear?

And if Anna were to do that, what, seriously, did she expect to achieve?

It was a stupid idea.

And then it hit her.

She was following the wrong car. Bill Myers was the one she wanted to talk to.

Anna checked her mirrors, did a quick U-turn, and went after the other car.

Fifty-Two

"It would be so much better if he just got hit by a bus," Bill had said to Charlotte one night a few weeks earlier when Paul believed she was helping a retired couple decide how much their East Broadway beach house was worth. In fact, Bill and Charlotte were sitting naked in the hot tub out back of a nice three-bedroom on Grassy Hill Road that was listed at $376,000.

"What did you say?" Charlotte asked, trying to hear him over the bubbling of the jets.

"Nothing," he said. "It was stupid."

"No, tell me."

So he repeated it.

Charlotte said, "It's stupid because you can't wait around for something like that to happen. You can't wait for the bus driver to take his eyes off the road. You can't wait for a pedestrian to make the mistake of not looking both ways." She thought a moment. "The only way it would work would be if you could make someone *decide* to step in front of the bus."

Bill rubbed his feet up against hers under the water. "Well, that's not exactly possible."

She moved closer to him, reached below the water, and took him firmly in her hand. As she stroked, she said, "It doesn't have to be a bus."

She told him her idea. How Paul's current mental state played right into it. She had just about every detail worked out.

"That's . . . pretty *out* there," Bill said, managing to concentrate despite the distraction.

"I don't think so," she said. "But I'm going to need help. A lot of help. Some of it technical."

"Like what?"

"Can you set up a phone's ring to be anything you want? Like, if I recorded something, could I turn it into a ringtone?"

Bill, closing his eyes briefly, said he was pretty sure that could be done.

"And I have to find an old typewriter. In all the stories I read, there was one reference to an Underwood. We need to find one of those. It doesn't have to be an exact replica, but close. The good thing is, it's within the realm of possibility it could still be out there. The real one was never found."

"You're sure?"

Still moving her hand up and down, she smiled. "I called the police. Made up a story about being from some crime museum starting up in New York. Said that typewriter would make an excellent exhibit. Never recovered, they said."

Bill said he would start checking antique shops. He even knew a couple of business supply stores that might have something like that, almost as a novelty item. And there was always eBay and Craigslist.

"Nothing online," Charlotte cautioned. "No trace."

"Hang on," Bill said. He closed his eyes, shuddered, gasped. Charlotte took her hand away.

"This is where the creative part comes in," she said. "Paul has to believe this is *the* machine used in the murders."

They would type up all the messages ahead of time, she said. Bill could feed him the idea of leaving paper in the machine if he didn't think of it himself. Charlotte could hide them in the house and roll them into the typewriter or scatter them about the house as opportunities presented themselves. She'd make Bill a key, so he could sneak into the house and plant them. Or, she could do it herself.

Like the morning Paul wanted to find the yard sale where Charlotte had said she'd bought the Underwood. She didn't call the real estate agency to say she'd be late. She called Bill, signaling that the house would be empty for the next hour or so. He went over and rolled a message into the typewriter. The morning that Paul arose late and found Charlotte in the shower, she'd already been down in his study, putting a message in place.

Over the next week, they worked out the details. With a new phone, she recorded the sounds of typing by banging away at the keys. She turned that into a ringtone. The muted phone would be left atop one of the kitchen cupboards, programmed to ring only when called from Charlotte's personal phone. She'd keep that one under her pillow and make the calls once Paul was asleep.

They did some test runs. Bill held the new phone while Charlotte called it, using her own.

Chit chit. Chit chit chit. Chit. Chit chit.

"Oh my God," he said. "It's perfect."

She'd even be able to do it if Josh were staying with them. He slept with iPhone buds in his ears.

Bill had some ideas of his own. "Remind him of

conversations that never actually happened. Ask him if he picked up things you say you asked him to get, but never did. Reinforce the notion that his memory's faulty."

Charlotte liked that. She said she could tell Paul she'd seen a car parked outside the house, the same one he'd seen days earlier. Except, of course, he'd never mentioned seeing a car. She could send texts from his phone, leaving him baffled when he received the replies.

"And I can visit his therapist, and Hailey. Tell them all the disturbing things I've witnessed. Plant the seed that he's losing it." She smiled. "It's nice to get back to acting. I don't see winning an Emmy, but I'll have you."

Bill came up with what he called *the clincher.*

"One night, we go for broke. You get him drunk, slip something into his drink, show him the best night in bed ever. I sneak in, put that fucking typewriter right next to him. If that doesn't drive him round the bend, he's made of stronger stuff than any of us."

Charlotte said she'd tell Paul she'd had the locks changed, even when she hadn't. He'd be even more convinced there were supernatural forces at work.

They found a suitable typewriter in an antique shop in New Haven. The notes were written.

Bill identified one huge flaw in the scheme.

"This is all designed to drive him crazy, push him over the edge, make him step in front of that metaphorical bus."

"Right," Charlotte said.

"But what if he doesn't?"

Charlotte smiled. "Oh, I have that figured out, too."

Fifty-Three

Anna was not an expert at the whole "following cars" thing.

She'd grown up watching *The Rockford Files* and *Miami Vice* and *Cagney & Lacey*, and it always looked so easy on those shows when the detectives had to tail someone. They didn't have to worry about traffic or red lights or pedestrians texting at crosswalks. The road was always clear for them.

The only way she could keep Bill Myers's car in sight was to practically ride on his bumper.

She tried to back off when she could but was so afraid of losing him that she stuck too close to him. She was sure he'd notice he was being followed.

But maybe that wasn't so bad. Didn't she want to

talk to him? She wasn't tailing him so much to find out
what he was up to as to find a moment to have a few
words with him.

Right.

Except what was she going to say? What was she
going to ask him? Anna was starting to think maybe
she hadn't thought this through.

Myers led her into a nice area of south Milford. He
put on his blinker and turned into a development on
Viscount Drive, a few hundred feet from the beach.
He lived in a collection of attached townhouses, and
turned into the driveway of one of them.

She kept on driving.

She had planned to stop, flag down Mr. Myers for a
conversation, but then lost her nerve. She carried on to
the next stop sign and turned.

Anna circled the block, came back, and parked out
front of Bill's house. She killed the engine, sat there,
frozen by fear and indecision.

Knock on the door or leave?

While she considered what to do, she dug her phone
out of her purse. She needed a distraction. She decided to check and see whether she had any messages.
She'd muted the phone during the funeral. If anyone
had texted, emailed, or phoned her, she wouldn't have
known.

Well, what do you know, there were two emails and one voice mail. She checked the latter first.

It was Rosie, her neighbor keeping an eye on her father while she was out, asking when she thought Anna would be back. The woman had an eye appointment at four. Anna called her immediately and said she would be home soon, long before the woman had to be at the doctor's.

Then she turned her attention to the emails. One was junk, and the other was from someone asking if she was taking on new clients. Anna tapped on the reply arrow and was about to write back when she nearly had a heart attack.

Someone was rapping hard on her window.

Anna was so startled she dropped the phone into her lap and put her hand to her chest. Bending over, his nose pressed up to the glass, was Bill Myers.

"Can I help you?" he asked.

Coming home, Bill Myers was pissed.

He wanted to see Charlotte, *needed* to see Charlotte. Not at the funeral, but privately. She'd been putting him off, and sure, he understood the need for caution. But they hadn't gone through all this to *not* spend time with each other. He needed her. He needed her in every way.

It was this need that made him take her hand as they were leaving the church. To link his fingers with hers. What he wanted to do, right there in the church, was put his mouth on hers, take her in front of everyone.

See the look on their faces.

But he wasn't *that* stupid. And he'd already let her know a few minutes earlier what was on his mind. Sitting in the front pew, next to her, he had taken her hand and subtly shifted it to his lap so that she could feel how hard he was.

Charlotte had given him the tiniest squeeze before withdrawing her hand back to her own lap.

He saw that as a good sign. He'd been hoping for one, given Charlotte's avoidance since Paul's death. Not taking his calls, ignoring texts. Yes, she'd told him, weeks earlier, that whenever it was done, they had to be discreet. They did not want to attract any undue attention.

Fine. He got that. But the thing was, he had questions. Like, how long would they put up with the charade? They did work together, after all. How long before he could stay at her place, or she could sleep over at his? It was nobody else's business what they did now. Paul was dead. Wasn't Charlotte entitled to move on with her life?

But son of a bitch, just like he'd whispered to her, it had worked. Better than he had ever imagined.

He paced the house. Antsy. Anxious.

He happened to glance out the window, saw a Lincoln SUV parked across the street. He'd noticed the car in his rearview driving home. He squinted, tried to see who was behind the wheel.

It was a woman, and she looked familiar. Bill thought he had seen her at the funeral. What the hell did she want?

There was only one way to find out.

He went out the front door, crossed the street, and while the woman was engrossed in her phone, went up to the window and knocked on it with his knuckle. Asked if he could help her. Gave her quite a start.

The woman put down the window.

Bill, thinking maybe she hadn't heard him through the glass the first time, asked again, "Can I help you?"

"Mr. Myers?"

"Yes?"

"I'm Anna White. I was Paul's—"

"I know who you are," he said, nodding. "You were there, the other night, when Paul, you know, when things got really bad."

"I'm sorry to bother you. I'd hoped to talk to you at the service but missed you. And now I've been sitting out here, like an idiot, trying to work up the courage to speak to you. I wasn't sure whether to bother you at a time like this, what with Paul being your friend and all."

Bill studied her for a second. "Uh, well—"

"It wouldn't take long. I just want to have a few words."

Bill shrugged. "Come on in."

She got out of the car, locked it, and walked to his front door with him. "I thought your eulogy was very heartfelt."

He shrugged. "Thanks." He opened the door for her and invited her to sit in the living room.

Anna settled into a soft chair. "How is Charlotte doing?"

"Well, she's devastated, of course," he said.

"I can imagine. I dropped by to see her, after it happened. But I think it was a mistake. Did she tell you I visited her?"

"No," he said. "So, what did you want to talk about?"

"I suppose I wanted to tell you what I told Charlotte. That I feel terribly sorry. That I feel I failed your friend. It's all been weighing heavily on me."

"Yeah, well, you're not the only one. I mean, I guess we all played a role there."

"Did you see the signs?" she asked earnestly.

He nodded slowly. "Like I said in the church, I guess we all did. Charlotte for sure. And anytime I saw Paul, I could tell he was pretty troubled."

"Troubled, yes. But anything that suggested to you he'd take his own life?"

"Well, come on. Look at everything that was going on. The attempt on his life, the nightmares, thinking his typewriter was somehow possessed or something? That must have been some scene the other night."

"It was."

"I don't know how he did it. Without waking up Charlotte."

"You mean . . ."

"Going down to the garage, bringing up the typewriter, putting it right there by the bed. Shit, I still can't get my head around it. You're the expert. Do you think he knew what he was doing? Was it like a split personality or something? One part of him was doing all the typewriter stuff, and another part was scared shitless by it?"

"I don't know," Anna said.

"Well, if *you* don't, given your expertise, I guess we'll never know," he said.

"So, looking back, you're not surprised Paul took his own life?"

"What's the phrase?" Bill asked. "Shocked, but not surprised."

"I get that. So that's why I'm a little puzzled."

"Puzzled?"

"The other night."

"Yes?"

"What puzzles me is what you said to Paul when he got on the phone with you."

"What are you talking about?"

"When the subject came up about him going to the hospital, you advised against it."

Bill was, briefly, at a loss for words. "I don't know that I'd go that far."

"I'm sorry?"

"I mean, I may have pointed out the drawbacks to being admitted to the hospital, but it's not like I told him *not* to do it."

"I got the sense you were quite adamant. You persuaded him not to go."

"I don't see why you're laying this on me," he said defensively. "You're his therapist, for Christ's sake. If you thought he should have been put into a psych ward, you should have overruled me."

"I couldn't force Paul into the hospital against his wishes, not if he didn't present an immediate danger to himself, and I was not sure at that moment he did. But you've just told me that you saw indications that Paul might harm himself. That he *might* take his own life. And you've just told me you believed he was writing the messages himself, moving the typewriter around, *himself.* That one part of his mind was doing all this, while another part was unaware."

"I don't think I said that *exactly.*"

Anna smiled. "You're right, I may have paraphrased slightly."

"I don't get where you're going with all this, Dr. White."

"Let me be clear, I'm not absolving myself of any blame," she stated. "But I don't understand why you talked your best friend out of getting more intensive psychiatric care when, from everything you've told me, you believed he was suicidal and carrying out actions his conscious mind was unaware of."

"It's not like the way you're making it sound," Bill said. "He was my friend. And a lot of it's Monday morning quarterbacking, you know? You didn't realize you were seeing the signs until it was too late."

"Right," she said. "I totally understand."

There was a silence between them.

Bill broke it by saying, "I don't know what else to say." He stood, signaling it was time for Anna to go.

"What worked?" Anna asked, still seated, looking up.

"Huh?" he said.

"In the church, as we were walking out, you said to Charlotte, 'It worked.' I wondered what you were referring to. What was it that worked?"

He stared at her for two seconds and said, "I don't remember saying that. You must have misheard me." Bill smiled weakly as he moved toward the door. Then the lightbulb went off. "Oh, I remember. I *did* say that. I was referring to my little speech. I had it all written up at the office, did it on the computer there, and I couldn't get it to print out. There wasn't a soul there, because everyone else was on the way to the funeral, so I actually called Charlotte about it— like she had nothing more serious to worry about at a time like this—and she said the office printer had been acting up, that it was probably jammed, so I opened the printer up and sure enough she was right. So I cleared it, and then I was able to print out the eulogy. So that was the reference. To the printer. That I got it to work."

Anna nodded. "That makes sense."

He smiled as he opened the door. "You have a nice day."

"You, too," Anna said. She stood, left the house, and headed for her car.

Bill needed to know—right fucking now—what Anna White had said when she'd visited Charlotte. If Charlotte declined his call, he'd show up on her doorstep.

I hope we don't have a problem.

Fifty-Four

Once Anna White was back behind the wheel of her car, and before she turned on the engine, she lightly drove the heel of her hand into her forehead.

"Idiot," she said.

It was as simple as that. A printer that would not print.

And then, with advice from Charlotte, it became a printer that *did* print.

"It worked."

There you had it.

How she'd let her imagination run away with her. She'd gone from zero to sixty in under three seconds. Two simple words and suddenly she had Bill Myers and Charlotte Davis plotting to drive Paul crazy.

Next thing, Anna thought, she'd be believing 9/11

was an inside job, that doctors had a cure for cancer but were keeping it hidden, that there really were aliens at Roswell.

Didn't that kind of prejudging go against everything she'd learned in her professional life? You don't size up your patients in three seconds. You listen to all the facts. You talk to them. You dig below the surface and look for clues that are not immediately evident. What she had done was reach her conclusion first, then look only for evidence that would support it.

"Stupid stupid stupid," she said, and started the engine.

Realizing how seriously she had misjudged the situation made her feel more than just foolish. Ashamed, for sure. But not in any way relieved. If Bill and Charlotte had been in cahoots—boy, there was a word she hadn't thought of in years—then some of the responsibility would have been lifted from her shoulders. Her failure to accurately predict Paul's self-destructive behavior would be mitigated.

As she continued driving back toward her house, she thought that if she'd tipped her hand with Bill Myers, if she'd really let it slip that she suspected something monstrous of him, she'd have felt obliged to write him a letter of apology.

It would be the only decent thing to—

Anna slammed on the brakes.

Behind her, a horn blared.

She swerved the car over to the side of the road. Her heart was racing as she threw the SUV into park.

Write him a letter of apology.

She thought back to the service when Bill Myers was making his remarks about his good friend Paul.

How when he got lost and had to search through his notes, how he'd turned the pages over.

From where she sat, Anna could clearly see pages covered with scribbling.

Handwriting.

He had not printed out his speech.

Bill Myers had lied to her.

Fifty-Five

Back during the planning stages, Charlotte had agreed Bill was right. There was no guarantee, no matter how much they nudged him in that direction, that Paul would kill himself.

"You may have to help him with that," Charlotte said.

Bill and Charlotte weren't in the hot tub for this conversation. They were simply sitting in his car, parked behind a furniture store. He was in the driver's seat, hands gripped tightly on the wheel, even though they were not moving.

"Charlotte," he said.

"You've had to know this was a possibility."

Of course he did. But he'd been trying to fool himself, thinking they could actually accomplish this without getting their hands dirty. Well, *really* dirty.

"Look, maybe he'll actually do it," Charlotte said, looking for a silver lining. "But at some point, we have to—what did my father always like to say?—shit or get off the pot."

Once they'd planted the notes, and Charlotte had spoken with Dr. White and visited Hailey in Manhattan, and Bill had managed to get that typewriter placed on the bedside table right next to Paul, well, fuck, if that didn't send him over the edge, what then?

When Dr. White came over in the night and suggested to Paul that he go to the hospital, Charlotte had panicked. She'd called Bill and told him to talk Paul out of it. They were hardly going to be able to move forward if Paul was in a locked ward.

So Bill had talked him out of it.

The question had always been how to do it. If Paul's suicide was going to need a little help, what was the most convincing way for it to happen? Once Bill got over his initial squeamishness, he actually came up with a few good ideas. His best was to have Paul "jump" from the second-floor balcony, or the one off the master bedroom, one floor higher. But was it enough of a drop? Charlotte wondered. What if Paul survived, and told the police what Bill had done? (It would have to be Bill; Charlotte didn't have the physical strength to heave him over.)

Bill was confident it would work. If Paul survived the fall, Bill would twist his neck.

So when Charlotte learned that Paul had drowned, she didn't have to feign shock when Detective Arnwright gave her the news. Why hadn't Bill told her he'd had a change of plan?

Maybe because then she really *would* look shocked.

She couldn't bring herself to talk to Bill those first few days. Their first conversation had been at the funeral. Play it safe, she kept thinking. Give it time.

Soon, they'd reconnect.

Soon, he could tell her why he'd decided to drown Paul. She wondered how he'd done it. Dropped by after dark, invited him for a walk on the beach? Then suddenly grabbed him, pushed him down into the water, held his head under?

Anyway, it was done.

She and Bill could get on with a life together. She was aching for him as much as he was for her. She hoped she would always want him the way she wanted him right now.

God, I hope I don't get bored with him, too.

No, no, that would not happen. They had a bond that was unlike any other.

It had been an interesting experience, all this. Charlotte had learned a lot about herself, what she was capable of. And she'd learned a lot about Bill, too.

She knew he had more of a troubled conscience than she did. She hoped that would not be a problem down the road.

What had he said to her one night?

"What we're doing, you know it's wrong."

Right. And she'd taken only a second to fire back with:

"If you were going to worry about that you should have said something a long time ago."

Fifty-Six

D etective Joe Arnwright's desk phone rang.
"Arnwright," he said.

It was the front desk. "Got a Dr. White wants to see you."

"Sure, send her in."

It struck Arnwright as oddly fortuitous that Dr. White would choose to drop by at this particular moment. He had, on his desk, and his screen, the report on the death of Paul Davis. Everything about the investigation appeared in order. It was still impossible to say, definitively, that Davis had committed suicide. He had gone into the water, and he had drowned. Had he intended that to happen? In the absence of a suicide note, there was no way to know his state of mind.

One thing seemed certain. He had not gone for a

swim. People did not generally go swimming in jeans, shirt, and shoes.

It was possible he'd fallen off a nearby pier and washed up onshore. There was a dock over by the bottom of Elaine Road. And there was that outcropping of rock at Pond Point to the west. Maybe he'd gone for a walk out there and lost his footing.

But the interviews Arnwright had conducted with the man's current and former wives, friends, and therapist painted a picture of a deeply troubled man.

And yet, there was one small detail that bothered Arnwright. In all likelihood, it didn't mean anything. But it nagged at him just the same. Maybe one more visit with Charlotte Davis was in order. Arnwright would have to think about that. He didn't want to bother a woman who'd recently lost her husband with what might be a totally trivial question.

Anna White appeared at the door to the detectives' room. Arnwright stood and gave her a wave. Anna threaded her way between some desks until she was at Arnwright's.

"I know I should have called, but—"

"That's okay. Sit. Can I get you something?"

Anna declined. They both sat. Arnwright closed the folder that was on his desk and minimized the program on his screen.

"Hitchens giving you more trouble?" Joe Arnwright asked. "Because we've got him good on this dog-napping thing."

"I'm pleased to hear that," Anna said. "But that's not why I'm here." She sighed. "I'm not even sure that I should be here."

Joe waited.

"You know, when you came to see me the other day, I told you how responsible I felt about what happened to Paul."

Joe nodded.

"I told you I felt I failed him, and I still do feel that way, so this thing that's been on my mind, I have to question my own motives. I may be looking subconsciously for a way to lessen the guilt I feel."

"Can't be all that subconscious if you're aware of it," the detective said.

"Yes, well, you make a good point there."

"So what's on your mind?"

Anna took a second to compose herself, and said, "I don't think Paul was having delusions."

"What do you mean?"

"I mean, I don't think there was anything wrong with him. Yes, he'd been depressed. But I don't think he was imagining the things he claimed to be hearing in the night. I think he heard *something*, but I don't know what. And I don't think he wrote the messages he was finding in the typewriter. Not consciously, or subconsciously. I don't think he was having hallucinations. I don't think he was mentally ill in any way whatsoever."

Arnwright leaned back in his chair and took in what Anna White had said. "Okay."

"I do concede that Paul was, during these last few days, extremely agitated because of what was going on at home. And that last night I saw him, he was incredibly distressed."

"So, I'm not sure what you're trying to say here. Are you saying you don't think he committed suicide?"

"I'm not saying that."

"So you think he did."

"I don't know."

Joe Arnwright smiled. "Dr. White, I—"

"I think he *might* have done it. But, then again, I think he might *not*."

"So you're leaning toward this being an accident? Because that's still within the realm of possibility."

Anna White bit her lower lip. "I shouldn't have come in. I'm making a fool of myself."

"No, you're not. What I do, Dr. White, is often based on a hunch, a feeling. Do you have a feeling about what happened?"

"I do."

"And what is that feeling?"

"That if Paul did kill himself, he was driven to it."

"Driven to it?"

Anna nodded. It took everything she had to force out the next few words. "And if he didn't take his own life, someone took it for him." She put her hands in her lap decisively, as though she had just gotten the toughest word at the spelling bee.

"You're saying you think someone might have murdered Mr. Davis?"

Anna White swallowed. "I think it's a possibility."

"What makes you say that?" Arnwright asked.

"Because of what he said," she blurted.

"Something Paul said?"

"No, not Paul. His friend. Bill Myers. I heard him whisper 'It worked' to Charlotte."

"That's it," Arnwright said. "Just those two words."

Anna nodded sheepishly. "When I asked him what he meant by that, he came up with a story about how he got a *printer* to work so he could have a copy of the eulogy he gave. But he didn't read a printed speech. It was handwritten. I saw it. He lied to me."

"Okay," Arnwright said, doing his best to tamp down the skepticism in his voice.

"I also asked Mr. Myers about talking Paul out of

going to the hospital." She paused. "It's like he wanted to make sure Paul was where he could get to him. Almost like he didn't want Paul to get away, to get help."

Arnwright frowned. "Okay, so all these things that happened with the typewriter, you're suggesting it was a setup?"

Anna nodded.

"Why?"

Again, Anna struggled to get the words out. "I think Bill Myers and Charlotte Davis might be having an affair."

"You have any evidence of that?"

Anna hesitated. "Not really."

"So that's just a feeling, too, then."

"It was the way . . . they held hands. And . . . I guess that's all. Body language, I suppose." Another anxious swallow. "I've learned to read that kind of thing over the years."

"Body language," Arnwright said.

"I know. I must sound ridiculous."

"You said you think Mr. Davis was set up. How on earth would they do that?" the detective asked.

"I . . . have no idea." She shook her head. "There's something else."

"Yes?"

"The boxes."

"Boxes?"

"When I visited his wife, after his death, she had all these empty boxes."

Arnwright looked at her, waiting.

"She'd gone out and gotten all these empty boxes to start packing his things. Who does that so fast after someone dies? It's like, it's like she couldn't wait to get at it."

Joe Arnwright took a long breath, put both palms on the desk and said, "Anything else?"

Anna sat there, feeling increasingly ridiculous. "No," she said.

"Well, I want to thank you for coming in. It's all very helpful." He stood, implying the therapist should do the same.

Anna got up. "I know what you're thinking."

"And what's that?"

"That I'm trying to get myself off the hook. That I've come up with this elaborate fantasy so that I won't feel Paul's death was my fault."

"That's not what I'm thinking."

"I didn't know what else to do but come and see you."

"And I'm glad you did. If I need to talk to you again about this, I know how to get in touch."

Dr. White knew she'd been dismissed. She stood and said, "Just about every meeting I've had lately I've regretted immediately afterward. I guess I'll add this one to the list." She nodded her good-bye and walked out of the detectives' room.

Arnwright sat back down and reopened the folder on his desk, as well as the report that had been on his screen.

He read, for maybe the fifth time, what had been found on Paul Davis's body.

There had been the wallet, of course. Despite his body having been tossed about by the waves after he had—presumably—walked out into the waters of Long Island Sound, and then subsequently washed back onto the beach, the wallet had not been dislodged from the back pocket of his jeans. It was solidly in there, and it had taken some effort for the police first on the scene to extricate it from the tight, wet clothing.

His watch, an inexpensive Timex, remained attached to his left wrist. It was still working. His tightly laced Rockport walking shoes remained on his feet. Retrieved from the front pocket of his jeans were a gas station receipt, wadded tissues, three nickels, four quarters, one dime, and a dollar bill.

That was it. None of those things had been washed out of Paul Davis's pockets during his time in the water.

Arnwright had been troubled not by what was in his pockets, but by what was not.

He thought back to that night, when Paul Davis's wife got out of her car and went to the front door of her house.

It was locked. She had her keys in her hand, and used one to open the front door.

How had the door been locked in the first place? Presumably, Paul Davis had locked it as he exited the house, on his way to the beach or to a pier or wherever.

So where was the key?

Why was there no key in his pocket?

Fifty-Seven

Charlotte wasn't surprised to see her phone light up with Bill's name on the screen. Not two hours since the funeral and already he was calling her. So much for discretion. But then again, a guy who puts your hand on his dick in the middle of a funeral service clearly has a problem with delayed gratification, not to mention subtlety.

She figured if she ignored the call, he'd just keep trying. So she accepted it.

"Hello?"

"We need to talk," he said.

"Why, Bill," she said, feigning a casual tone. "It's good of you to call. I know I already told you, but I thought what you said about Paul was lovely. Straight from the heart. He'd have been touched to know how you felt."

Bill paused. It took him a second to catch on. There was either someone in the room with her, or Charlotte thought someone was listening to her calls. She had no reason to believe that was happening, but why risk it? She'd actually gone online, looked up bugging devices and where they were most commonly hidden, and then had searched the house to make sure it was clean.

No fool, she. You didn't hear *her* whispering "It worked" in the middle of a crowded church.

"Yeah, well, thanks for that," Bill said. "Like you said, it was from the heart."

"The house feels so empty with him gone."

"Yeah, right. Uh, like I said, there was something I needed to talk to you about. In person."

Charlotte sighed. Maybe it was time. Besides, there were some things she wanted to discuss with *him*.

"Fine, then," she said. "I'm here."

"See you in a few minutes," he said, and ended the call.

Did he want to tell her how he did it? Was he overwhelmed with guilt and needed to talk about it? Did she even *want* to know every detail? As long as it was done, that was all that mattered.

Charlotte figured it would take Bill the better part

of twenty minutes to come over, but the doorbell was ringing in fifteen. She glanced out a second-floor window before running down the stairs, and while she could not see him at the door, she spotted his car parked half a block up the street.

At least that was smart. She wasn't ready for people to see his car parked at her house yet.

She went down the stairs and opened the door. Bill charged into the house and blew straight past her. As he mounted the steps to the kitchen, he said without glancing back, "We've got a problem."

She hurried up the stairs after him. "What are you talking about?"

He went straight to the fridge, took out a bottle of beer, twisted off the cap, and took a long drink.

"Is there anybody else here?" he asked warily.

"No."

"The way you were talking on the phone, I thought maybe—"

"I was being careful. But the house is safe. Say what you have to say."

He leaned up against the island. "Okay, you're gonna be pissed, because this is my fault, but you're going to have to move past that so we can deal with the situation."

"Just tell me, for Christ's sake!"

His eyes looked upward. He couldn't face her. "Someone heard me. What I whispered."

"Whispered when?"

"In the church. What I said when we were walking out. That what we did, that it *worked*."

"For fuck's sake, Bill! Jesus! Who? Who heard you?"

"The therapist. Anna White."

"How do you know?"

"She came and saw me. She came to my fucking *house*. Started talking about this and that, worked her way around to the fact I talked Paul out of going to the hospital. Asked if that was what I was referring to when I told you it worked."

Charlotte shook her head disbelievingly. "You're an idiot."

"All right, all right, I'm an idiot."

"And putting my hand on your cock in the middle of—"

"Okay!" he bellowed. "I get it! I'm a fucking moron. Can we get past that and deal with what's happening right now?" As he shook his head in frustration, his eyes landed on the typewriter. "Jesus, you brought that back into the house?"

"I needed trunk space," she said, waving her hand at the boxes that still covered up much of the island. "Look, let's think about this." Her voice was calmer.

"What does Dr. White really have? She heard you say two words, and she's suspicious that you didn't want Paul to go to the hospital. It's nothing. It's absolutely nothing. What did you tell her when she asked what you meant?"

"I said it was about getting the office printer to work."

"What?"

"If she asks, I called you about that. That I was trying to print out the eulogy."

Charlotte looked exasperated. "She's supposed to believe that the first thing you told me after the funeral for my dead husband is that you got a printer to work."

"I didn't have a lot of time to come up with something. Important thing is, I think she bought it. I'm more worried about the other thing, about talking Paul out of going to the hospital."

Charlotte was thinking. "No, that's okay. What you said made perfect sense at the time. Why would you want your friend to be locked up in a psych ward? Those places are horrible. You had a natural reaction. You're worrying about nothing. Let it go."

"She said she came to see you, too."

"Yeah. But she came by to say she was sorry, that she misread the signals. She was feeling all guilty. That's probably why she came to see you. She wants to lay this off on you so she doesn't feel responsible."

He took another long pull on the bottle. "I guess. But I didn't like the way she was asking questions. I had a bad feeling about it."

"Well, get over it. Even if she went to the police, what does she have, really? You think Detective Arnwright is going to give a shit about something like that? The medical examiner's report, all the statements from us and the doctor and Hailey? It all points to suicide."

"Yeah," he said. "It does. Okay." He grinned. "And wonder of wonders, that's what actually happened."

Charlotte took a step closer. "What?"

"Well, unless you dragged Paul into the water yourself and drowned him, he really did it. What'd you think I meant when I said it worked? He actually fucking offed himself."

Charlotte stared at him, open-mouthed.

"All this time," she said, "I wondered why you didn't give me any warning that you were going to do it that night. We'd talked about that. So I'd be ready."

"Why do you think I was calling you so often before the funeral?" Bill asked. "I was as stunned as you."

"Oh my God," Charlotte said softly. "You didn't kill Paul. We didn't kill Paul."

Bill grinned. "Sometimes things just have a way of working out."

Fifty-Eight

Anna White walked out of the Milford Police headquarters feeling like a fool.

"Idiot," she said under her breath as she got into her SUV.

She headed home. She'd canceled so many appointments over the last week that there were still clients she'd been unable to reschedule. It was already late afternoon—God, she had to get home so Rosie could make her eye appointment—so she wasn't going to be able to see any of them today. But she could start sorting out the next few days.

Despite being dismissed by Detective Arnwright, Anna still believed something was very wrong. She'd spent her professional lifetime reading people, and the story she believed she'd seen developing between Charlotte and Bill was one of deception.

Paul was not, Anna believed, the only one who'd been deceived.

The number one dupe was herself. Anna now could not help but wonder if Charlotte had been putting on an act when she showed up unexpectedly at the office to tell her how worried she was about Paul.

I was played, Anna thought. *I'm their corroborating evidence.*

If Charlotte and Bill were having an affair, as Anna suspected, and were plotting against Paul, who better to back up their story that Paul was unstable than the dead man's therapist?

But if what Anna suspected was true, what could she do about it? She'd gone to Arnwright with nothing more than a hunch, and it was just as well she didn't mention what Bill was trying to conceal after he saw Charlotte to her car.

Hey, Detective, he had a hard-on. That's proof, right?

It would have been the last thing Arnwright needed to be convinced that she was a nutcase. And sex-obsessed.

So what was there to do? If she couldn't get the police interested in taking another look at Paul's death, was she going to conduct an investigation her-self?

I am not Nancy Drew.

She was not going to snoop about like some amateur sleuth in a hackneyed mystery novel. That wasn't the real world. She had no idea how to go about such a thing. She was not going to try tailing someone again. She was not about to hide microphones in Charlotte's house or Bill's townhouse.

All she knew how to do was talk to people. And more than that, to *listen*. And to watch. That was how you got below the surface, to where the truth was buried.

She wanted to talk to Charlotte again. When she'd last spoken to her, Anna had not held the suspicions she did now. Anna wanted to look her in the eye when she asked her some of the same things she'd asked Bill Myers.

And for sure, she'd ask about his call to her about the printer. What a crock of shit that was.

Anna believed she would come away from a meeting like that knowing, in her heart, whether her suspicions were warranted. If she found they were, she might not have enough for the police to open an investiga-tion, but at least she'd have a good idea what really had happened.

I have to know.

Paul's death would always weigh on her. She would always feel responsible. But there were degrees of responsibility.

When she returned home and gave the neighbor her freedom, she checked on Frank, whom she found in the backyard knocking some more chip shots with a nine-iron. The woods behind the house, Anna imagined, were littered with hundreds of golf balls.

Then she went about rescheduling. Once she was done with that, it was nearly seven, and time to pull something together for her father and herself for dinner.

"Dad," she said, finding him back in his bedroom on the rowing machine, "are you okay with a frozen pizza? I know it's pretty sad, but it's been that kind of day."

"Okay by me, Joanie," he said, sliding back on the machine.

Knowing he'd be okay with it, but still feeling she needed to apologize for it, she had already preset the oven. By the time she got back to the kitchen, it was time to slide the pizza into it.

Half an hour later, sitting at the table with her father, he studied her and said, "What's on your mind, pumpkin?"

His pet name for her since she was a child. So at least for the moment, he knew she was his daughter.

"I have to confront somebody about something," she said. "I'm not looking forward to it."

Frank smiled sadly. "It's okay. I can handle it."

"Oh, God, Dad, it's not *you*," she said, laying a hand on his.

"If there's something you gotta tell me, I can take it."

"It's something else entirely. Really."

"Okay, then."

"I might have to go out tonight."

He nodded. "Sure thing."

"And I need to know you'll be okay if I do. I can't impose on Rosie again."

"Not a problem."

She was relieved that her father no longer seemed traumatized by their visit from the SWAT team. He seemed to have forgotten all about it.

"What is it you have to do?" he asked.

"I kind of have to work myself up to it."

Another nod. "If you decide not to, I was thinking we could go visit your mother tonight."

It never ceased to amaze her how he could drift in and out this way. Be perceptive enough to tell there was something on her mind, and then propose an outing based on a fantasy.

"We'll see," Anna said.

He offered to do the dishes—there was little more than a baking sheet, two plates, and two glasses—so Anna told him that would be great. She wanted him to feel useful whenever possible.

When he was finished and had retreated upstairs to his bedroom to watch the cartoon channel, Anna made some tea. When it was ready, she poured herself a cup and sat at the kitchen table to drink it.

She spent the better part of an hour on it.

"Sooner or later," she said under her breath, "you're gonna have to do this thing."

But that didn't have to mean she couldn't have another cup of tea first while she thought about it.

Fifty-Nine

They felt a celebration was in order.

And why not? Bill and Charlotte never had to be worried about being arrested for murder because— Breaking News, folks!—they had not murdered anyone.

Sure, they might have *driven* Paul to take his own life, but how was anyone ever going to prove that? There was no so-called smoking gun. No fingerprints, no DNA, no incriminating hairs or fibers. None of that stuff you saw on TV.

The pages of faked messages from Catherine and Jill weren't evidence. They'd been written on that typewriter, and so far as anyone knew, Paul had written them. About the only thing Bill thought they needed to address was that extra smartphone with the typewriter ringtone.

He grabbed a chair from the kitchen table and brought it over to the cupboards, stood on it, and retrieved the device that had been sitting up there since they'd put their plan into action. It had been plugged into an outlet near the ceiling that had originally been installed to power accent lighting.

He stepped down off the chair, phone in hand.

"No need to throw this out," he said. "All I have to do is change this ringtone."

He fiddled with the phone's settings for several seconds, then placed it screen down on the island.

"Done," he said. "Consider our tracks covered."

Charlotte had apologized for being so angry about the overheard whisper. "Who cares what Anna White heard? I could have gone down on you in the middle of the church and there wouldn't be a damn thing they could do about it."

"We got what we wanted, but son of a bitch, our hands are clean," Bill said. "I have to admit, I didn't see that coming."

"You," Charlotte said, "are a lot smarter than you look."

"Maybe," he said. "But you were the one who really had to pull it off. You had to be here. You had to play along. You deserve an Oscar."

She'd brought out a bottle of wine from the fridge

and was already on her third glass. Bill was into his fourth beer. No more meeting in empty houses. If anyone came by, his presence here was totally legitimate. He was consoling the widow.

He had some very serious consoling in mind for later.

"It's really—shit, you know—it really was the so-called perfect crime," she said. "You know why? Because there *was* no crime."

"Are there even laws for what we did?" Bill asked. "Even if someone could prove we used that thing"— he pointed to the typewriter—"to mess with someone's head, was it even illegal? We could say it was like a practical joke that got out of hand. Or even better, we were *helping* Paul."

"Helping?"

"No, not helping. *Inspiring.* The same thing you told him when you gave it to him. He wanted to write about what Kenneth had done to him, and what we did was designed to inspire him with that effort. Really get him into it. That's all. We couldn't have known he'd take it the way he did."

"*That's* a bit of a stretch," Charlotte said.

"Anyway, it's a moot point. It's never going to get to that." He became reflective. "I still can't believe he did it. Walked right out into the water. I mean, how would you do that? If you fall out of a boat or something like that, and you can't make it to shore, sure, you drown. There's nothing you can do. But walking in? You'd think, once your lungs started filling up, your natural instincts would take over, you'd try to save yourself, turn around and run back for shore."

Charlotte shook her head. "No, it could happen. I've seen stuff like that on the news." Her face went dark. "God, it must have been awful." She looked at Bill and her eyes misted. "The water is so cold." She mimed shivering, but the chill was real.

It was a rare moment for her. She almost felt sorry for what they'd set into motion.

"Listen," he said. "It's done. We don't look back. We look forward." He pulled her into his arms. "It's all over now. We made our decisions and now we live with them." He tightened his squeeze on her. "We got what we wanted."

"I was worried about you for a while," she said. "I thought you were getting cold feet at one point. That you were having some crisis of conscience."

"Not anymore."

He bent his head down and put his mouth on hers. She placed her hand at the back of his neck and latched onto him.

"That's the spirit," Bill said, breaking free long enough to take a breath. He grasped her around the waist and lifted her onto the island so that her face was level with his. She wrapped her legs around his torso, locked her ankles, trapping him. They explored each other that way for another minute before Charlotte put her hands on his chest and gently pushed back.

"Upstairs," she said.

Seconds later, they were in the same bed where Charlotte and Paul had spent their last night together. If she had any qualms about that, she did not show it. The sex with Bill was fast and animalistic. The second time was slower but no less passionate.

By that time, night had fallen. They lay together in the bed, weary and lethargic. Moonlight coming through the blinds cast prison-stripe shadows across their nakedness.

"This is probably the wrong thing to say," Bill said, glancing at the bedside clock, which read 9:57 P.M., "but I could use something to eat."

"Don't give me straight lines," Charlotte said. "Is this where I say you've been doing that for the last two hours?" She turned onto her side, threw a leg over his, pinning him to the mattress. "Just stay where you are. Close your eyes."

"I might be hungrier than I am sleepy," he said.

"Oh shut up," she said. "I'm exhausted and you should be, too."

"My dick could sure use a nap," he said.

"Close your eyes," she said again.

He did. In less than a minute, he could hear soft breathing from her pillow. And shortly after that, he succumbed.

But it seemed to him that he had been asleep only a few minutes when his eyes reopened. He glanced at the clock. It was only 10:14. He'd been asleep barely fifteen minutes.

Something had woken him up.

A sound.

It had sounded like—

No, no way.

He propped himself up on an elbow and listened. The only thing to be heard was Charlotte's breathing in and out.

It was nothing, he thought. Whatever he thought he'd heard, it had to have been part of a dream.

He put his head back down on the pillow, closed his eyes.

And then immediately opened them when he heard the sound again.

Chit chit. Chit. Chit chit chit.

From downstairs.

Sixty

"Wake up!" Bill whispered to Charlotte.

She grunted, opened her eyes. "What?"

"Shh!" He had a finger to his lips. "Listen."

Chit. Chit chit chit.

She blinked a couple of times. "It's nothing," she said groggily.

"You don't hear that?"

She nodded. "It's the phone. You must not have changed the ringtone."

Bill considered that. "Okay, maybe, yeah. I should have tested it."

"Fix it in the morning," she said, putting her head back down onto the pillow.

"But wait," he said. "Someone has to call it for it to ring."

Charlotte raised her head again, turned to look at her bedside table. "Where the hell—"

She shifted over to the edge of the bed, looked down to the floor, felt around with her hand. "There it is," she said.

"What?"

"My phone. I must have knocked it off the table. I guess it called you."

That placated Bill for only a second. "Your phone's not going to make a call just by hitting the floor."

"What about pocket calls? Isn't that kind of how those happen?"

In the few seconds they'd been whispering, there had been no more sounds of typing.

"Maybe," Bill said.

"Or," she said, "someone else called the phone. It didn't have to be me. You never got a wrong number? Or a telemarketer's call? Even on your cell? They don't have to know your actual number. They just keep dialing and sooner or later they hit yours."

"We planned for that," he reminded her. "We programmed the phone to only ring when you called it. Otherwise, it was on mute."

"Oh, yeah," she said. "So maybe there was a glitch. It's accepting other calls now."

"I'm gonna go down and power it off completely," he said.

She grabbed onto his arm. "Stay here."

He allowed her to hold on to him. He dropped his head onto the pillow and stared at the ceiling.

Chit chit. Chit chit chit. Chit.

"Oh, fuck it," he said, and threw back the covers.

Charlotte sighed. "I really was asleep, you know."

"Since I'm going down, you want anything?" he asked, pulling on his boxers.

"You're still hungry?"

"We didn't exactly have dinner."

"I guess not. Bring me up some crackers and cream cheese or something."

"That's it?"

"Jesus, just go."

She flopped back down on the bed and pulled the covers up over her head. Within seconds, she felt herself falling back to sleep.

And then it was her turn to be awakened by a now familiar sound.

Chit chit. Chit. Chit chit chit.

And then:

Ding!

She opened her eyes and sat up in bed. Charlotte reached over for Bill, but her hand hit mattress. She patted around, confirmed that he was not there.

Ding? she thought.

That was the sound a typewriter made when you reached the end of the line. It was the signal to hit the carriage return. That had never been part of the ringtone programmed into the phone.

That sounded like a real typewriter.

Like the typewriter downstairs.

So what the hell was Bill doing playing with that damn thing at—she looked at the clock—10:34 P.M.

Boy, she'd fallen back asleep quickly. But even though Bill had not been gone long, all he had to do was mute a phone and grab something to eat. Why stay downstairs and goof around with the typewriter?

"God," she said, slipping out from under the covers. As she pulled on an oversize T-shirt, she couldn't help but wonder if she had traded a man for whom she'd lost all love for a man who was an enormous pain in the ass.

"Hey!" she called out as she headed for the bedroom door. "What the hell are you doing?"

As she approached the top of the stairs she noticed there were no lights on in the kitchen.

"Bill?" she called. "What's going on?"

No reply.

"You're freaking me out. Talk to me, for Christ's sake."

She slowly descended the stairs, step by step. Listening.

There wasn't any sound coming from the kitchen. Even the typewriter had gone silent.

"Bill?"

As she went to step onto the kitchen floor, her hand reached for the light switch.

Standing there, directly in front of her, was a very tall, heavyset man. Definitely not Bill. The first clue was that he was fully clothed.

The second was that he was wearing a name tag.

It read: LEN.

"Hi," he said, and then closed his meaty hands around her neck.

Charlotte barely had a moment to scream.

Sixty-One

It took three cups of tea—followed by two glasses of wine—before Anna was ready to do what she knew she had to do.

But now that she'd worked up her courage for a showdown with Charlotte Davis, Anna worried that she had left too late.

It was dark out. It was after ten.

Chances were Charlotte was already in bed. With, or without, Bill Myers.

Whoa, Anna thought.

Why hadn't she considered that possibility? That when and if she went to see Charlotte, Myers would be there.

She had to stop thinking that way. She was looking for excuses not to go.

I am going to do this.

And catching Charlotte off guard, possibly waking her up, well, so what? That might work to Anna's advantage. The thing was, Anna knew *she* wasn't going to be able to get to sleep tonight. So what if she kept someone else up, too?

As for Myers, she'd look for his car. If she drove over there and saw it in Charlotte's driveway, she'd reassess at that point.

Charlotte might not even be home. She could be at Myers's house. Would she go back there? She'd make that decision if and when she had to.

Anna went upstairs and rapped lightly on her father's door.

"Hello?"

She pushed the door open. Frank was under the covers, in his pajamas.

"Sorry," she said. "I'm going to go do this thing I was telling you about. I'll be back soon."

"What time is it?"

"It's late. Go back to sleep."

"Where are you going?"

"I'll tell you all about it in the morning. Rosie won't be here. It's too late for her to come over. You'll be fine for a while, okay?"

Her father said sure.

Back downstairs, she pulled on a light jacket, turned

off a few lights, and decided she would exit the house from the office wing. As she was passing through, she heard the familiar ding of an incoming email. She slipped in behind her desk and discovered not one new email, but five, from patients about rescheduled appointments.

Anna opened the datebook beside her computer, made a note of the new times for her clients, then wrote quick replies to confirm the changes. Then she slipped out the side door, locked it, jumped into her SUV, and headed out.

She rehearsed in her head the questions she was going to ask Charlotte. Were there ways she could trip the woman up? Get her to say things she didn't want to say? While she'd been having her tea—not so much when she was drinking the wine—she'd scribbled some thoughts down on a paper napkin.

Not so much questions, but things to watch for, like the things people do when they lie.

Stalling by repeating a question. Excessive blinking. Long pauses. Coming up with overly complicated responses. Impersonal language—fewer references to *I* or other people by their actual names, so more use of *him* and *her.*

Of course, one of the other possible reactions from a liar would be to attack.

Anna was hoping it wouldn't come to that.

Sixty-Two

Charlotte took a moment to place the large man who had her pinned to the wall with his hands around her neck.

She didn't recognize him at first. She wasn't used to seeing him outside his ice cream truck. But it took only a few seconds to remember him from the times she'd bought a cone from him. She also remembered this was Kenneth Hoffman's son.

Leonard.

What was he doing here? Why was he in her house? Why was he trying to kill her? And where was Bill? What had happened to—

Oh God.

Out of the corner of her eye she saw him. He lay on the floor to the right of the kitchen island. He was not moving, and his head seemed positioned at an odd angle to his shoulders, as though his neck had been twisted.

If he was breathing, Charlotte could see no sign.

She struggled to do any breathing of her own. She wanted to scream, but nothing would come out, so she tried to mouth some words.

"Stop," she croaked. "Please stop . . . can't breathe . . ."

She flailed pitifully against the man, trying to slap him with her hands, but it was like trying to repel a bear with a flyswatter. When Leonard pushed her up against the wall, he lifted her slightly, so her feet were only barely touching the floor. She couldn't get any leverage to kick him.

Charlotte felt herself starting to pass out. Her brain was being starved of oxygen. Her eyes darted about the room, catching movement in the doorway to Paul's small office.

There was someone standing there.

A woman.

"Not her, too, Leonard," said Gabriella Hoffman. "We need to talk to her."

Leonard relaxed his grip on Charlotte's neck. She slid an inch back down to the floor, and as Leonard took his hands away she dropped to her hands and knees, hacking and coughing. As she struggled to get air back in her lungs, Gabriella walked in her direction, stopping in front of her.

Charlotte looked up, her neck already purplish with bruising from Leonard's grasp.

"What have you done to Bill?" she asked hoarsely.

"Don't worry about him," Gabriella said. "Worry about you."

"I . . . I know you."

"I think we met at faculty events once or twice," Kenneth Hoffman's wife said. "I'm Gabriella. And you are Charlotte." Her eyes shifted in the direction of Bill's body. "I don't know him. Who is he?"

"Bill," Charlotte said, her voice shaking. "Bill Myers."

"A West Haven professor? I don't recognize him."

"No. We sell real estate together."

"It looks like you do more than that together," Gabriella said. "This is my son, Leonard."

Leonard nodded.

"Most people call me Len," he said.

Charlotte, fully able to breathe again, asked, "Is . . . is Bill dead?"

"Yes," Gabriella said. "Leonard snapped his neck."

Charlotte slowly got to her feet, then took one step back from Gabriella. Leonard hovered to one side like a pet gorilla awaiting instructions.

"What do you want?" Charlotte asked. "Why are you here?"

Gabriella waved her hand toward the Underwood. "That."

"The typewriter?"

"Yes."

"What . . . what about it?"

"Your husband went to visit Kenneth in prison with some ridiculous story about those women, the ones my husband was convicted of killing, trying to talk to him through this machine."

"Yes," Charlotte said, her voice little more than a whisper.

"Paul gave Kenneth quite a scare. Not because of those messages. Those were laughable."

"I don't understand."

"What I needed to see—to get—was that." Again, she indicated the Underwood. "But when we came before, it wasn't here."

Charlotte's eyes went wide. "You were here before?"

Gabriella smiled. "Your husband said the typewriter was in your car's trunk, but I didn't believe him. But I guess he wasn't lying, because it wasn't here. So we've come back. We were going to ask you for your car keys, but then we saw the typewriter sitting right here."

"You saw . . . Paul?"

"Leonard and I just wanted to talk to him. About the typewriter, and the letters. We met him outside. He'd been out for an evening stroll." Gabriella smiled. "Things didn't quite go right. When he understood my concern, well, he became very agitated. And when Leonard here tried to calm him down, he ran off toward the beach."

"Oh, my God," Charlotte said. She looked at Gabriella's lumbering son. "He didn't kill himself. *You* killed him."

Leonard's look bordered on sorrowful. "I didn't really mean to. I guess I held his head under the water a little too long."

Gabriella sighed. "We took Paul's keys and searched your house, but he wasn't lying. The typewriter wasn't here."

"I still don't . . . I don't understand why . . ."

"As I said, those messages that the typewriter was supposedly spewing out were ridiculous. They gave Kenneth pause, for a moment, he was willing to admit that, but he figured it had to be some kind of joke. A trick. But," Gabriella said slowly, "it is still possible— however remotely—that this is the real typewriter."

"I don't understand," Charlotte whispered.

"Kenneth got in touch after Paul's visit. Said I needed to act before Paul did something like ask the police to compare his notes to the ones Catherine and Jill wrote."

She held some sheets of paper of her own. "So I just was doing a little comparing of my own."

She waved one of them in front of Charlotte. "These are from some notes I made when I audited a West Haven philosophy class some years ago." She smiled. "One of the perks of being married to a faculty member." She looked off almost dreamily at a point in the distance. "I've always liked the feel of a real typewriter. So much more *satisfying* than a computer. Don't you?"

Gabriella ended her reminiscing with a small shake of the head. She pointed to the Underwood. There was a piece of paper rolled into it, and a line of type.

"Remember 'Now is the time for all good men to come to the aid of the party'?" Gabriella asked.

Charlotte shook her head.

"You're too young," Gabriella said. "That's what they'd always have you write to test a typewriter. A nice, crisp sentence. That's what I was doing. That's the noise you heard. I was about to compare my class notes to what I just typed here, but that was when your Mr. Myers came down."

Charlotte struggled to piece together what was happening, how whatever she had set in motion was now blowing up in her face. Her eyes kept being drawn to Bill's lifeless body.

Her mind was able to cut through the panic and confusion to ask, "So what if it's the actual typewriter? What difference does it make?"

"Oh, a great deal," Gabriella said.

Gabriella leaned over and peered into the inner workings of the Underwood. "And it looks as though Kenneth was right to be concerned."

"What the hell are you talking about?" Charlotte asked.

Gabriella raised her head. "Blood. There's dried blood in the keys." She looked at Charlotte. "It's nothing short of amazing that you found it. At a yard sale, yes? What are the odds? Someone must have found it in the garbage before the Dumpster was emptied, or maybe it was found at the dump. Then it ended up for sale in someone's driveway, and of all the people in the world who could buy it, it was you."

"I didn't buy it at a yard sale! And that blood is Josh's!"

"Josh?"

"Paul's son. He got his fingers caught in it. You're right, it would be amazing if this were that typewriter. But it isn't."

Gabriella frowned. "I don't understand."

"I didn't buy it at a yard sale. I bought it at an antique store. We—me and Bill—were trying to find a typewriter like the one Kenneth made those women write their apologies on."

Gabriella's expression was one of genuine puzzlement. "Why?"

A tear escaped Charlotte's right eye and ran down her cheek. "We did a terrible thing. A terrible, terrible thing."

Gabriella, intrigued, smiled and said, "They say confession is good for the soul." The smile twisted into something jagged. "Although Kenneth might not entirely agree with that."

Charlotte gave her the broad strokes of what she and Bill had done.

"Why ever would you do that?" Gabriella asked, her face full of wonder.

Charlotte swallowed hard. "We wanted to make it look like he was losing his mind. And, then, when we . . . when we killed him . . . everyone would think it was suicide. Except we thought he'd actually done it. Killed himself. But it was you."

Gabriella's wonder morphed into one of irritation. "So all our worries have been for nothing?" She ran her fingers along the Underwood's space bar. "This was all something you and your *lover* cooked up?"

"Yes!" Charlotte said with sudden enthusiasm. "You don't have to worry! And I don't even understand why you *are* worried. What is it about the blood? Why were you concerned about that?"

Gabriella glanced at Bill's body, then gazed pityingly at Charlotte. "Every time you think you're done, there's always one more thing left to do."

Sixty-Three

A nna White drove slowly down Point Beach Drive. She had her window open slightly, and she could smell the brisk salt air wafting in from the sound. The last time she'd had to find the Davis house it had been dark, and so it was that again she had to rely on artificial light to check house numbers.

She did recall that the house was near the end of the street, although she couldn't remember any particular characteristics.

But then she spotted Charlotte Davis's car in a driveway and, to Anna's relief, the only other car in the driveway was Paul's. She did not see Bill Myers's car there. If she had passed it coming down the street, she had not noticed it.

Luckily, there was a space on the street directly

out front of the Davis house that she was able to pull straight into. She killed the engine, got out of the car, and closed the door softly. She wasn't sure she wanted anyone to know she was here until she rang the bell.

Her stomach was full of those proverbial butter-flies. Was she doing the right thing? Was this a totally misguided course of action? Hadn't she already been through all this interior debate before leaving her house?

One thing she no longer believed she had to worry about was waking Charlotte Davis. A glance up to the second floor showed that plenty of lights were on in the kitchen area. Surely Charlotte wouldn't have gone up to bed without switching off those lights.

She walked up the driveway and stood at the front door.

Just ring the bell. You're not going to turn back now.

She put her finger to the button, and pushed.

Maybe the doorbell sounded, but Anna did not hear it. It was drowned out, at that very moment, by a much louder noise.

A woman's scream.

A shrill, chilling scream that went through Anna like an icy wind, causing her to shudder.

It would have made sense for Anna to run, to get back into her car as quickly as possible, lock the doors, and call for the police. But Anna would have been the first to understand that people did not always do what made sense in emergencies.

Sometimes, they acted solely on instinct.

And Anna's instinct was to help. She had dedicated her *life* to helping.

She immediately tried the door, in case it was unlocked.

It was.

Anna pushed the door open with such force that it went as far as it could on its hinges, hit the wall, and bounced back. She launched herself into the house and was about to fly up the stairs but had to stop.

Someone was coming down.

Now it was Anna's turn to scream.

Sixty-Four

"We can work this out," Charlotte said pleadingly. "We can solve this. I know we can."

"I don't see how," Gabriella said. She glanced at her son, who took a step closer to Charlotte.

"You can—Leonard here, he's big and strong—can get Bill out of here. Dump him someplace far away! No one knows Bill came to see me tonight!"

"Where's his car?"

"Up the street. You could take it! I'll give you the keys. They're upstairs, in his pants. You get rid of the car and him." An idea struck her. "I could help! I can drive the car! Whatever you need, I can do it."

"And you'll never tell a soul," Gabriella said.

Charlotte brightened. "Yes!"

Gabriella motioned to the table where the typewriter sat. "Sit. Let's talk."

Charlotte was eager to oblige. She pulled out a chair, sat down. Gabriella sat down at an angle to her.

"Why would I tell anyone?" Charlotte said. "I did—I admit this—I did a bad thing. Very bad. If I ever told anyone about what happened here tonight, all that would come out. So I have to keep quiet. Not just to protect you, but to protect myself."

Gabriella nodded slowly. "I did a bad thing, too. When I slit the throats of those two women. But my motivation was pure. It was just. Those women had slept with my husband. They had mocked the sanctity of marriage. What I did was teach them a lesson. That was why I wanted those apologies. In *writing*. I had the law of morality on my side. Oh, I know not everyone would see it that way. You might argue that my husband was no better. But he was *my* husband. I'd taken a vow, as had he. For better or for worse. And he did redeem himself."

Charlotte said nothing.

"And while both of us have done bad things, I think you and I are very different. What you did was so very selfish, so self-centered. You plotted to kill your husband so you could be with that man." She shook her head disapprovingly. "Your bad deeds have been in the service of mocking the institution of marriage. Mine were in its defense."

Any hope one might have seen in Charlotte's eyes was fading. "I know what you're saying, I do. But—"

Gabriella raised a silencing hand. "I don't think you're someone I can trust."

"I am! I—"

"Where's the bathroom?" Len said.

Their eyes turned to Leonard, who was standing at one end of the kitchen island.

He shrugged. "I have to go."

Charlotte sprang to her feet. "I can show you where it is," she said with forced hospitality. She started across the room, pointing. Her path was taking her close to the top of the stairs that led to the front door.

"No!" Gabriella said. The order was meant for both Charlotte and her son.

As she neared the top of the staircase, Charlotte bolted.

"Leonard!"

Despite his size and lumbering nature, Leonard was quick. He turned on his heels and went after Charlotte.

He reached out and managed to grab her by the hair, yanking her back like a puppet on a string. As she was snapped back, he used her momentum against her, propelling her into the wall where he'd first pinned her by the neck.

Charlotte screamed.

Gabriella cocked her head to one side. Was that the doorbell she heard? It was hard to tell with all the other racket. She pushed back her chair and moved toward the struggle.

Leonard grabbed Charlotte by her right arm and flung her toward the steps like a bear flinging a rag doll. Charlotte sailed out into the stairwell, airborne. She didn't land until seven steps down, her head connecting first with a wooden riser, making a sound like the crack of a bat hitting a ball.

Leonard and his mother ran to the top of the stairs and watched Charlotte's lifeless body tumble down the remaining steps.

And the door at the bottom was flung open.

Anna White took two swift steps into the house, froze momentarily as she saw the body hurtling toward her, then screamed.

"Good God," Gabriella said.

Anna's gaze went higher. Saw Leonard and Gabriella looming over her like two vindictive gods.

She backed out of the house and ran.

"Stop her!" Gabriella said to her son.

Leonard ran down the stairs, leaping over the dead

woman. Gabriella followed, but it took her longer to navigate around Charlotte. By the time she was outside and could take in what was happening, Anna had reached the end of the driveway, Leonard only a step behind her.

Anna tripped on the curb and went down in the middle of the deserted street. Her purse fell off her shoulder and hit the pavement, spilling car keys and a cell phone. She tried to scramble to her feet, but Leonard was on her, viciously kicking her upper thigh. She shrieked with pain, fell back, and clutched at her leg.

Now Gabriella was at her son's side, struggling to catch her breath.

"Who the hell is she?" she asked, shaking her head furiously with frustration.

"I don't know," her son replied. "What should I do?"

Gabriella took a quick look up and down the street and was relieved to see it was deserted.

"Kill her," she said.

At which point there was a strange sound. A *whoosh*. Something cutting through the air at considerable speed.

Behind them.

And then a loud *whomp*.

Leonard staggered, nearly stepping on Anna.

Gabriella whirled around and said, "What the—"

Another *whoosh*, followed by a *whomp*.

Frank White swung the head of the club—a driver, more specifically, a one-wood—into Gabriella's temple.

The woman went down instantly, her legs crumpling beneath her.

Leonard was clutching the back of his head as he stumbled a few more steps. Blood was seeping through his fingers. He managed to stop pitching forward, stood a moment to regain his balance, then turned to see what had hit him.

Frank, standing there in his striped pajamas, could see that he didn't have much time.

He swung the club back over his shoulder, then came out with it a third time, putting everything he had into the swing. His arms, molded from hundreds of hours on his rowing machine, were pistons.

Leonard went to raise an arm defensively, but he was too slow.

The club caught him in his upper left cheek, just below the eye. That whole side of his face was instantly transformed into a bloody, pulpy mess.

Leonard went down.

Frank stood there, wild-eyed and frozen, panting, holding the driver like a bat, waiting to see whether he was going to need it again. When Gabriella and

Leonard hadn't moved for fifteen seconds, Frank knelt down next to Anna, dropped the club onto the street and reached out, tentatively, to stroke her hair.

"Are you okay, Joanie?" he asked.

"Yes," Anna said, struggling to hold back tears. "I'm good." She reached an arm up and cupped her father's bristly, unshaven chin.

"I've never been better."

Sixty-Five

Detective Joe Arnwright: Are you okay now, Mr.
Hoffman? Can we continue?

Kenneth Hoffman: Yes, yes, I think so. I needed a
minute.

Arnwright: Of course. I'm very sorry.

Hoffman: It's all my fault. All of it. When you
follow everything back to the beginning, it's the
decisions I made that set the wheels in motion.
Did the doctors have anything more to say about
Leonard?

Arnwright: He's still in a coma. He's in the Milford
Hospital.

Hoffman: So he has no idea his mother is dead.

Arnwright: No.

Hoffman: That son of a bitch. He didn't have to do

that to them. I hope he spends whatever years he has left in jail.

Arnwright: They were going to kill his daughter, Mr. Hoffman. He won't be charged. Mr. White saved her life. And he's an old man, to boot. He'd fallen asleep in the back of her SUV. Thought they were going to visit his late wife.

Hoffman: God, this is so . . . Maybe it'd be better if Leonard never wakes up. He'll face so much trouble if he does.

Arnwright: I don't know what to say to that, Mr. Hoffman.

Hoffman: Gabriella never should have involved him. Not this time, and not that night. At heart, he's a true innocent. All he ever wanted to do was make his mother happy.

Arnwright: I understand, Mr. Hoffman, that while he didn't kill those two women, he was culpable. He helped your wife put them in the chairs and tied them up after she'd drugged them. And he did kill Paul Davis. And he killed Bill Myers. And Charlotte Davis. I don't know that I'd call someone like that innocent.

Hoffman: He wouldn't have done any of this without her telling him to do it. He loved his mother so much. He always wanted to please

her. At heart, he's a gentle boy. That was why
they hired him for the ice cream job. It was
the perfect thing for him. And he was a good
driver. He never had so much as a fender bender.
I know that it's hard to believe, but before
all this, I can't think of any time that he ever
hurt anyone. And God knows, he'd have been
entitled. The way the other kids used to tease
him when he was little. Always a little slower
than the others. They mocked him, called him
stupid, but he isn't really. He's not *book* smart,
not *school* smart, but he's smart enough. He
manages. Well, up to now.

Arnwright: You were close with your son?

Hoffman: Yes, I mean, I loved him very much. I
still do. It's why I did what I did.

Arnwright: Confessing.

Hoffman: That's right. Sure, I ended up protecting
Gabriella. But it was never her I was concerned
about. It was Leonard. He'd never have stood
up to a police interrogation. I had to confess
right away before it came to that. And my God,
I certainly know now that the boy could never
have survived prison. Can you imagine it? What
they'd have done to him if he ever went inside?

A boy like him? Sure, he's big and strong, but he'd be a toy for every sadistic bastard in there. I couldn't let that happen. It really would be for the best if he doesn't wake up. Prison would be worse than death for him. You have no idea what it's like in there.

Arnwright: You've tried to take your own life since you began your sentence.

Hoffman: I'll probably keep trying till I get it right.

Arnwright: Was there no way you could have blamed Gabriella and left your son out of it? She could have been the noble one. It didn't have to be you.

Hoffman: There was the blood, you see.

Arnwright: Tell me about the blood.

Hoffman: Jill bit him.

Arnwright: Jill Foster bit your son.

Hoffman: Gabriella thought Jill was unconscious. She'd kind of drifted off after she'd typed the note Gabriella demanded she write. Gabriella asked Leonard to double-check, and when he reached out, to touch her chin, Jill woke up. All of a sudden. She lunged out and grabbed Leonard's hand with her teeth. Bit hard into the heel of his hand. He pulled back quickly, and his hand landed on the typewriter, and it really started to bleed.

Arnwright: Why don't you take us back to that night.

Hoffman: I came home, saw what Gabriella, with Leonard's help, had done. She'd figured out I'd been seeing both Catherine and Jill. She'd confronted me about it, earlier. I tried to deny things, but I knew she didn't believe me. I couldn't have imagined, not in a million years, what she would do. Inviting those women over, drugging them. Making them apologize to her in writing, actually making them type the words. Gabriella always had a strong belief in the written word, that oral contracts and promises were not worth much. And once they'd typed what she wanted, she killed them. But it was me she wanted to punish. She was doing this to me as much as she was doing it to those women. I got home right after she'd done it. Gabriella, she was almost in a state of catatonia. Leonard, if you can believe it, was eating a sandwich. After he'd bandaged his hand, of course. But Gabriella, she seemed to be in a dream. I don't know how else to describe it. But pleased with herself, too. She was . . . she was a strange woman. Cold. I'm not making excuses for why I cheated, but she was a cold woman.

Arnwright: Right.

Hoffman: So I'd been looking for love elsewhere, for a long time. But I guess I'd always been that way. Not like Paul. He was a good man. A loyal man. I wish, looking back, I could have been more like him.

Arnwright: And yet, look where it got him.

Hoffman: True enough. Have you figured out what his wife actually did?

Arnwright: We're still putting it together. We found a phone, and one of the available ringtones on it was the sound of a typewriter. And we found more sample notes, written on that typewriter, at Bill Myers's townhouse.

Hoffman: Wow.

Arnwright: Yeah. But back to that night.

Hoffman: Yeah, anyway, I came home and saw what she had done. I told her I could fix it. I'd help her cover it up. I got the bodies into the car, the typewriter, too, because it had so much of Leonard's blood on it. If they ever found that, and ran a DNA test, well, that would have been the end of him, wouldn't it? So I got everything into the car and told my wife I'd clean up the house when I got back.

Arnwright: But you didn't get back.

Hoffman: No. I managed to get rid of the typewriter, but the police caught me with the bodies. And with Paul, of course. I'd really thought, if I could have gotten rid of Catherine and Jill, and Paul, too, that we could move on. Be a real family again. I'd change my ways. I'd be a good husband and father. But then I saw the flashing lights, the officer heading my way. I had seconds to call Gabriella on my phone. I said to her, I've been caught. I'm going to tell them it was me. Just me. Talk to Leonard. Tell them you were out driving all evening, helping Leonard practice for his new job.

Arnwright: So you confessed.

Hoffman: Yes. You see, when you look at the big picture, I *was* guilty. It was my behavior that set all these things into motion. I deserved prison.

Arnwright: So you played the part of the murderer. All this time.

Hoffman: Yes. I must be the first accused killer in history to be grateful not to have an alibi. I'd spent the evening alone in my office on campus.

I'm in one of the older buildings. No surveillance cameras, regular keys instead of cards. No one had seen me, I'd talked to no one. No witnesses to come to my defense.

Arnwright: What did you think when Paul Davis showed up at prison with those letters?

Hoffman: Right. The letters . . . they were troubling, I admit. I don't believe in the supernatural, but they gave me pause. They *had* to be bullshit. And yet, I couldn't stop thinking that maybe, somehow, Paul had the actual typewriter. And if the police got hold of it, if they checked that blood, found out it was Leonard's, mixed in with the blood of those women, then all of this would have been for nothing.

Arnwright: You told Gabriella to get it back.

Hoffman: Yes. I just . . . I didn't know it would turn out the way it did. I know I tried to kill Paul that night, but all these months after . . . I never wanted Paul to die. I liked Paul. He was a good man. Bill Myers, I didn't know him. Charlotte I had met once. But Paul . . . I feel badly about Paul. I was something of a mentor to him when he came to West Haven. Did you know that?

Arnwright: Yes.

Hoffman: Maybe Bill and Charlotte got what was coming to them.

Arnwright: If you're looking for a silver lining, I guess there's that.

Hoffman: What happens now? Do you think I'll be exonerated? I mean, I didn't really kill those two women. And what I did to Paul, that was a spur-of-the-moment thing. There was nothing premeditated about it.

Arnwright: Are you saying you're an innocent man?

Hoffman: I guess I wouldn't go that far.

Arnwright: Neither would I.

Sixty-Six

"I like this place," Frank White told Anna. "I do."

They'd been given a private tour of the seniors' residence. They'd seen the dining hall and the recreation center and the exercise room, and the last stop was what might end up being his room. It was spacious enough. There was a bed, and a big cushy chair, and a television.

"And I can put my rowing machine right there," he said. "Look out the window. You can see the water."

"I don't know, Dad," Anna said. She'd been trying hard not to limp throughout the tour. Leonard had nearly broken a bone when he'd kicked her. She was going for physical therapy twice a week.

Her father had seemed remarkably lucid ever since that night. While he'd believed, at one point, that he was saving his wife and not his daughter, since then, he'd shown considerable understanding of what had happened.

He knew he'd killed someone, and put someone else into a coma. And he'd had not a moment's regret.

"You do what you have to do," he said.

But he did see it as a turning point. He'd insisted it was time for him to become independent, at least from Anna. They'd been arguing about it for days.

Now, standing in this oversize bedroom with a flat-screen and a view of the sound, she stated her feelings once more.

"I don't want you to go."

"I've lived with you for as long as I did for a reason," he said. "And now we know what it was. It was to be there that night."

"You don't believe in that kind of thing," Anna said. "You think that's a load of shit, that our lives are somehow preordained."

"You'd be surprised what I believe in."

And that was when he told her.

"The night your mother died, I was sound asleep. And then . . ." He struggled a moment to find the words. "And then she spoke to me, like in a dream, and said I should get to the hospital as quick as I could."

Anna said nothing.

Frank sat on the edge of the bed, ran his palms across the bedspread. "And I didn't pay a goddamn bit of attention, because I didn't believe in that sort of thing. And you know what happened. She passed that night. I should have believed. I should have listened."

Anna, softly, said, "Why have you never told me that story?"

Frank shrugged. "I didn't want to upset you. I didn't want you to know I had a chance to say good-bye and didn't take it."

Anna sat down in the easy chair and looked away. Outside, a cloudless sky made the sound a deep blue.

"Anyway, I bring that up now," her father said, "because your mother spoke to me again."

Anna looked back, blinked away tears, tried to get her father into focus. "When did she do that?"

"After what happened with those people who tried to kill you. Couple of nights later, I guess it was."

Anna wasn't sure she could bring herself to ask. But she had to know. "What did she say?"

Now it was her father's turn to gather his strength.

"Joanie said to me, she said, 'Frank, you saved her life. The only thing more you can do is *give* her her life.' And that was it."

Anna stared at her father. He reached out a hand to her and she took it.

"I guess you think that's a bunch of horseshit," he said.

She shook her head from side to side.

"You believe it?"

Anna stopped moving her head and swallowed.

"I do."

Acknowledgments

At HarperCollins and William Morrow, thanks to everyone for getting *A Noise Downstairs* ready, with a special nod to Liate Stehlik, and my terrific editor, Jennifer Brehl, who kept pushing when I thought we were done. We weren't.

In the UK, I am grateful to David Shelley, Katie Espiner, Harriet Burton, Emad Akhtar, Ben Willis, and the entire Orion team.

As always, thank you to my amazing agent, Helen Heller.

For all manner of support, current and past, thanks go out to Robert MacLeod, Bill Taylor, Douglas Gibson, and Stephen King.

And once again, a huge shout-out to booksellers.

Thank you for everything you do to get writers' works into readers' hands.

Finally, I'm long overdue in recognizing two people who are no longer with us, but to whom I remain immensely grateful all these years later for their encouragement, guidance, and friendship: Margaret Laurence and Kenneth Millar.

4th Edition

The Essential Guide to
Family & Medical Leave

Lisa Guerin, J.D. & Attorney Deborah C. England

FOURTH EDITION	JULY 2015
Editor	SACHI BARREIRO
Cover Design	SUSAN PUTNEY
Book Design	TERRI HEARSH
Proofreading	IRENE BARNARD
Index	SONGBIRD INDEXING SERVICES
Printing	BANG PRINTING

Guerin, Lisa, 1964-
  The essential guide to family & medical leave / Lisa Guerin, J.D. & Attorney Deborah C. England. -- Fourth Edition.
       pages cm
  Includes index.
  ISBN 978-1-4133-2166-1 (pbk.) -- ISBN 978-1-4133-2167-8 (epub ebook)
  1. Leave of absence--Law and legislation--United States--Popular works. 2. Parental leave--Law and legislation--United States--Popular works. 3. Sick leave--Law and legislation--United States--Popular works. 4. United States. Family and Medical Leave Act of 1993--Popular works. I. England, Deborah, 1959- II. Title. III. Title: Essential guide to family and medical leave.
  KF3531.G84 2015
  344.7301'25763--dc23

                           2015003653

This book covers only United States law, unless it specifically states otherwise.

Please note

We believe accurate, plain-English legal information should help you solve many of your own legal problems. But this text is not a substitute for personalized advice from a knowledgeable lawyer. If you want the help of a trained professional—and we'll always point out situations in which we think that's a good idea—consult an attorney licensed to practice in your state.

Acknowledgments

The authors would like to thank all of the folks at Nolo who made this book possible, including:

Alayna Schroeder, for her thoughtful, clarifying, and extraordinarily quick editing.

Sigrid Metson and Kelly Perri, for their insights on managing FMLA leave and for their good cheer and hard work in marketing this project.

Janet Portman and Mary Randolph, for their sustained enthusiasm and support.

Terri Hearsh, for creating a beautiful book design.

Stan Jacobsen, for his research assistance.

The authors would also like to thank their friends, colleagues, and mentors in the field of employment law, including:

Michael Gaitley, senior staff attorney, the Legal Aid Society—Employment Law Center

Everyone at Rudy, Exelrod and Zieff

Patrice Goldman

The Honorable John True.

Dedication

To my father, Jim England, who could have used a leave law while raising four kids. And, to my mother, in loving memory.

Deborah C. England

About the Authors

Lisa Guerin is the author or coauthor of several Nolo books, including *The Manager's Legal Handbook, Dealing With Problem Employees, The Essential Guide to Federal Employment Laws, The Essential Guide to Workplace Investigations, Create Your Own Employee Handbook, The Progressive Discipline Handbook*, and *Nolo's Guide to California Law*. Ms. Guerin has practiced employment law in government, public interest, and private practice, where she represented clients at all levels of state and federal courts and in agency proceedings. She is a graduate of Boalt Hall School of Law at the University of California at Berkeley.

Deborah C. England has practiced employment law in San Francisco for more than 20 years, representing clients in litigation in state and federal courts. In addition to litigation, she regularly advises clients on employment issues and in efforts to informally resolve employment disputes. Ms. England has published numerous articles and essays on employment and civil rights law and has spoken frequently on these topics before legal and employment professional organizations.

Table of Contents

1 An Overview of Family and Medical Leave 1

What the FMLA Requires 3

Your Obligations as a Manager 4

How Other Laws and Company Policies Come Into Play 9

How to Use This Book...13

2 Is Your Company Covered by the FMLA? 17

Calculating the Size of Your Company 19

Joint Employers and the FMLA 22

If Your Company Is Covered...28

Common Mistakes Regarding Employer Coverage—And How to
    Avoid Them..32

3 Is the Employee Covered by the FMLA? 35

Employee Eligibility, Step by Step 37

Keeping Track of Employees' Work Hours...................................46

Common Mistakes Regarding Employee Eligibility—
    And How to Avoid Them...49

4 Leave for a Serious Health Condition 53

Your Role in Identifying a Serious Health Condition 55

What Is a Serious Health Condition?...56

Leave for Employee's Own Serious Health Condition 68

Leave for a Family Member's Serious Health Condition..............69

Common Mistakes Regarding Serious Health Conditions
    —And How to Avoid Them..77

5 Leave for a New Child 79

    Leave for Birth..83

    Leave for Adoption...84

    Leave for Placement of a Foster Child...84

    Parental Certifications...85

    Timing of Parenting Leave...86

    Intermittent or Reduced-Schedule Leave..88

    Substitution of Paid Leave...90

    Parents Who Work for the Same Company...90

    Combining Parenting Leave With Leave for a Serious Health Condition 93

    Common Mistakes Regarding Leave for a New Child—
        And How to Avoid Them...96

6 Military Family Leave 101

    Leave for a Qualifying Exigency 104

    Leave to Care for an Injured Servicemember 113

    Common Mistakes Regarding Military Family Leave—
        And How to Avoid Them...120

7 How Much Leave Can an Employee Take? 123

    Counting the 12-Month Leave Year...125

    How Many Weeks May an Employee Take? 132

    Counting Time Off as FMLA Leave..136

    Intermittent and Reduced-Schedule Leave 138

    Common Mistakes Regarding Leave Duration—And How to Avoid Them...........149

8 Giving Notice and Designating Leave 153

    Counting Time Off as FMLA Leave..155

    Individual Notice Requirements..160

    Employee Notice Requirements..167

    Common Mistakes Regarding Giving Notice and Designating Leave—
        And How to Avoid Them...176

9 Certifications 181

Types of Certifications 183

Requesting Certification 190

After You Receive the Certification 197

Common Mistakes Regarding Medical Certifications—
 And How to Avoid Them 206

10 Managing an Employee's Leave 211

Scheduling Leave 213

Covering an Employee's Duties During Leave 218

Continuing Employee Benefits During Leave 224

Managing Intermittent Leave 231

Requesting Status Reports 236

Disciplining or Firing an Employee During Leave 238

Common Mistakes Regarding Managing Leave—
 And How to Avoid Them 241

11 Reinstatement 245

The Basic Reinstatement Right 247

Fitness-for-Duty Certifications 252

Restoring Pay and Benefits 255

When Reinstatement Might Not Be Required 260

When Employees Don't Return From Leave 270

Common Mistakes Regarding Reinstatement—
 And How to Avoid Them 273

12 How Other Laws Affect FMLA Leave 279

Federal Laws 282

State Laws 294

Common Mistakes Regarding Other Laws and Benefits—
 And How to Avoid Them 305

13 Record-Keeping Requirements 313

    Why You Should Keep Records 315

    Keeping Track of Company Workforce FMLA Data 316

    Individual Employee Records 316

    Medical Records 318

    Review by the Department of Labor (DOL) 321

    Now You're Ready! 322

    Common Mistakes Regarding Record Keeping—
        And How to Avoid Them 322

G Glossary 325

Appendixes

A State Laws and Departments of Labor 333

B Company Policies Regarding FMLA Leave 385

    Family and Medical Leave Policy 387

    How Your FMLA Policy Affects Company Obligations 397

C Using the Interactive Forms 403

    Editing RTFs 404

    List of Forms and Podcasts 405

    Index 409

An Overview of Family and Medical Leave

What the FMLA Requires 3

Your Obligations as a Manager 4

    Ten Steps to FMLA Compliance 5

    The Compassionate Manager 6

    Why You Need to Get It Right 7

How Other Laws and Company Policies Come Into Play 9

    Overlapping Laws 11

    Company Policies 12

How to Use This Book 13

The Family and Medical Leave Act (FMLA) is a law with an undeniably noble purpose: to help employees balance the demands of work with personal and family needs. Since the FMLA was enacted in 1993, millions of employees have relied on it to protect their jobs while taking time off to recover from a serious illness, to care for an ailing family member, or to bond with a new child. The FMLA has been amended several times since its enactment, most notably in 2008 to allow military family leave.

According to responding companies, surveys consistently demonstrate that the FMLA has had no noticeable effect on business profitability or growth. However, surveys also reveal that some managers and human resource professionals have difficulty administering FMLA leave. For example, a 2007 survey by the Society for Human Resource Management reported that more than half of all respondents said it was either "very difficult" or "somewhat difficult" to track intermittent leave, figure out whether a health condition qualifies for FMLA leave, and deal with the FMLA's notice, designation, and certification requirements.

Experience has shown that it can be difficult to apply the FMLA when dealing with employees in the real world. For example, do you know what to do in the following situations?

- An employee who needs leave is also covered by workers' compensation, a state family and medical leave law, and/or the Americans with Disabilities Act—and the requirements of those laws appear to conflict with the FMLA.
- An employee asks for time off but won't tell you why or is reluctant to reveal personal medical information that might entitle the employee to leave.
- An employee wants to take FMLA leave at your company's busiest time of year.
- An employee wants to take time off as needed for a chronic ailment, rather than all at once, and can't comply with your company's usual call-in procedures.
- An employee doesn't give exactly the right amount or type of notice, forgets to hand in a medical certification form, or can't return to work as scheduled.
- An employee decides, after taking FMLA leave, not to come back to work.

Amendments, Regulations, and More

The FMLA is a relatively new law, and it remains in flux. It was last amended in 2010, when Congress expanded its military family leave provisions (which were first added to the law in 2008). The Department of Labor has been busy as well, updating its regulations that interpret the FMLA to include these amendments. As we go to press, the Department of Labor has just issued regulations explaining how legal developments in recognition of same-sex marriage affect an employee's right to take time off to care for a spouse, parent, or child. And, the President's 2015 State of the Union address devoted significant time to paid sick and family leave. It seems the one thing we can count on with this law is change. To keep up, check Nolo's online companion page for this book (see Appendix C for directions on how to find it).

These issues—and many more like them—come up every day, and managers have to figure out how to handle them legally and fairly, while protecting the company's interests. That's where this book comes in: It explains, in plain English, how the FMLA works. It can be tricky to figure out what to do in a particular situation, and this book's step-by-step approach will help you sort things out and meet your obligations.

This chapter will help you get started. It introduces the FMLA's basic requirements, with special emphasis on your responsibilities as a manager. It explains how other laws and company policies can affect your obligations under the FMLA when an employee needs time off for family or medical reasons. And it provides a roadmap to the rest of the book, so you'll be able to easily find the answers to all your FMLA questions.

What the FMLA Requires

In a nutshell, the FMLA requires companies of a certain size to allow employees to take time off to fulfill certain caretaking responsibilities or to recuperate from serious illnesses. If your company is covered by the law, an eligible employee is entitled to take up to 12 weeks of unpaid leave every 12 months to bond with a new child, recover from his or her own serious health

condition, care for a family member with a serious health condition, or handle qualifying exigencies arising from a family member's military duty.

Employees are entitled to take up to 26 weeks of leave, in a single 12-month period, to care for a family member who suffers or aggravates a serious illness or injury in the line of duty while on active military duty. However, this provision doesn't renew every year like the 12-week leave provisions described above. Instead, it is available only once per servicemember, per injury. Employees who are entitled to this military caregiver leave may also take other types of FMLA leave, but they can take no more than 26 weeks off, total, in a single 12-month period for all types of FMLA leave.

FMLA leave is unpaid, although an employee may choose—or the company may require employees—to use up accrued paid leave, such as sick leave or vacation, during this time off. The employer must continue the employee's group health coverage during FMLA leave. When the employee's leave is over, the employee must be reinstated to the same position or an equivalent position, with the same benefits as the employee had before taking time off. Although there are a few exceptions to this requirement, they apply only in very limited circumstances.

> **CAUTION**
>
> **Special rules apply to public employers and schools.** The FMLA imposes slightly different obligations on government employers and schools, which we don't cover in this book. Similarly, in unionized workplaces, a collective bargaining agreement—the contract between the company and the union—might impose different family and medical leave obligations. Because every collective bargaining agreement is different, we can't cover them all here.

Your Obligations as a Manager

The moment an employee comes to your office and says, "My wife is having a baby," "My mother has to have surgery," "My son was injured in Afghanistan," or "I've been diagnosed with cancer," you'll have to figure out whether the FMLA applies, provide notices and meet other paperwork

requirements, manage the employee's time off, and reinstate the employee according to strict rules and guidelines.

Ten Steps to FMLA Compliance

Whenever you're faced with a leave situation that might be covered by the FMLA, you should ask yourself the questions listed below. This checklist will help you make sure that you meet all your legal obligations and don't forget anything important. Each of these topics is covered in detail in this book.

Step 1: Is your company covered by the FMLA? The answer is yes if you've had at least 50 employees for at least 20 weeks in the current or previous year. If your company is covered, it has to post a notice and may have to provide written notice to employees, even before an employee requests leave. Company coverage is explained in Chapter 2.

Step 2: Is the employee covered by the FMLA? An employee who has worked for at least 12 months, and at least 1,250 hours during the year before taking leave, at a company facility that has at least 50 employees within a 75-mile radius, is covered. Chapter 3 explains how to make these calculations.

Step 3: Does the employee need leave for a reason covered by the FMLA? Leave is available for the employee's own serious health condition or to care for a family member with a serious health condition, as explained in Chapter 4. Leave is also available to bond with a new child, which is covered in Chapter 5. Military family leave—for a qualifying exigency relating to a family member's military service or to care for a family member who suffers a service-related illness or injury—is also covered by the FMLA; we explain these rules in Chapter 6.

Step 4: How much leave is available to the employee? An employee is entitled to take up to 12 workweeks of leave, either all at once or intermittently, in a 12-month period: to bond with a new child, handle qualifying exigencies relating to a family member's military service, care for a family member with a serious health condition, or recuperate from a serious health condition. An employee who needs military caregiver leave is entitled to up to 26 weeks off in a single 12-month period. Chapter 7 will help you figure out how much leave an employee may take.

Step 5: Did you and the employee meet your notice and paperwork requirements? The employee must give reasonable notice and provide certain information; you

must designate FMLA leave and give the employee required notices, among other things. Chapter 8 provides the details.

Step 6: Did you request a certification (and if so, did the employee return it)? You can—and should—ask an employee who needs leave for a serious health condition, a serious illness or injury to a servicemember, or a qualifying exigency related to a family member's military service, to provide a certificate. Chapter 9 explains how.

Step 7: Did you successfully manage the employee's leave? You must continue the employee's health benefits, manage and track intermittent leave, arrange for substitution of paid leave, and more. In addition, you have to make sure the work gets done while the employee is out, whether by distributing the employee's responsibilities to coworkers, hiring a temporary replacement, or outsourcing the job. Chapter 10 covers all of these issues.

Step 8: Did you follow the rules for reinstating an employee returning from leave? You must return the employee to the same or an equivalent position and restore the employee's seniority and benefits, unless an exception applies. Chapter 11 explains these rules, as well as what to do if the employee doesn't return from leave.

Step 9: Have you met your obligations under any other laws that apply? Whether or not the FMLA applies, the employee may be protected by the Americans with Disabilities Act, workers' compensation statutes, state family and medical leave laws, and other laws. To find out about your obligations under these other laws, see Chapter 12.

Step 10: Have you met your recordkeeping requirements? If your company is covered by the FMLA, you must keep certain payroll, benefits, leave, and other records, and you'll certainly want to keep proper documentation of your decisions and conversations, in case you need to rely on them later. These issues are covered in Chapter 13.

The Compassionate Manager

One of the challenges of implementing the FMLA is that you must meet your legal obligations within a context that can be emotional. After all, employees who qualify for FMLA leave are undergoing major life changes. On the positive side, the employee may be welcoming a new child, with all the joy and excitement that brings. On the more sobering side, perhaps the employee is losing a

parent or spouse to a terminal illness, caring for a seriously ill or injured child, or suffering through a painful disease. Although you have to follow the law's requirements and make sure your company's needs are met, no one wants to be the hardhearted administrator who responds to an emotionally distraught employee by handing over a stack of forms to be completed in triplicate.

The FMLA recognizes that employees who need time off for pressing family or health concerns might not always be able to dot every "i" and cross every "t." The law provides guidance on what to do if, for example, an employee is too ill or injured to communicate with you, can't return to work on time because of continuing health problems, or doesn't complete forms on time. These rules will help you balance your legal obligations with the natural human desire to be compassionate during a difficult time.

And, as we'll remind you from time to time, you have little to gain from imposing strict deadlines and paperwork requirements on employees who are truly in dire straits. Judges and juries are people, too, and they can find ways to enforce the spirit of the law in favor of an employee who needed its protection, even if the employee failed to meet deadlines, give adequate notice, hand in forms on time, or provide required information.

Of course, people have different comfort levels when dealing with emotional subjects. Some can easily offer support and a shoulder to cry on; others would rather volunteer for a root canal. If you fall on the more stoic end of this spectrum, take heart: You don't need to become a therapist—or the employee's best friend—to show some understanding in a difficult situation. Just remember that a little kindness goes a long way. Acknowledge what your employees are dealing with, cut them some slack if necessary, and work with them to make the law serve its purpose.

Why You Need to Get It Right

Properly managing your FMLA obligations is a win-win situation. Employees win because they get time off when they really need it, with the assurance that their jobs will be waiting for them when they come back. You and your company win because helping employees balance work and family leads to greater employee loyalty to the company and all of the other benefits that flow from it, including better morale, stronger retention, and even improved productivity.

Lessons from the *Real World*

An employee who didn't give notice of need for leave can still sue for violation of the FMLA.

For four years, John Byrne worked as a stationary engineer on the night shift at Avon Products. By all accounts, he was a model employee until November 1998, when a coworker reported finding him asleep in a break room. The company checked its security logs and found that Byrne had been spending a lot of time in the break room lately. So the company installed a camera, which filmed Byrne sleeping for three hours one night and six hours the next.

Byrne's managers planned to talk to him about the problem on November 16, but Byrne left work early. He told a coworker that he wasn't feeling well and would be out the rest of the week. A manager called Byrne's house, where his sister answered the phone and said he was "very sick." When Byrne came to the phone, he mumbled some odd phrases and agreed to come to a meeting at work the following day. When he didn't show up for the meeting, he was fired.

It turns out that Byrne was unable to attend the meeting because he had been hospitalized for severe depression, after relatives convinced him to come out of a room in which he had barricaded himself. Byrne had begun hallucinating and having panic attacks and required two months of treatment. When Byrne felt better, he asked Avon to take him back. The company refused, and Byrne sued for violation of the FMLA.

Avon argued that Byrne never gave adequate notice that he needed FMLA leave, so the court should throw out his FMLA claim. The court didn't see it that way, though. Although Byrne never mentioned the FMLA or said that he needed medical leave, the court found that his marked change in behavior might have been sufficient to put Avon on notice that he needed FMLA leave. The court also found that Byrne might have been unable, because of his mental state, to give notice that he needed leave. Either way, the court found that Byrne should be able to present his claims to a jury.

Byrne v. Avon Products Inc., 328 F.3d 379 (7th Cir. 2003).

That's the carrot; here's the stick: Violating the FMLA can lead to serious trouble. And we don't just mean the morale problems and associated woes that can crop up if employees feel that their needs aren't important to the company. Mishandling family and medical leave issues can also give rise to lawsuits, not just against your company, but against you, individually, as the manager who made the flawed decision. Of course, this is the ultimate worst-case scenario, and chances are good that you'll never have to face it. If you're one of the unlucky few, however, your personal assets—such as your home, your car, and your bank accounts—could be on the line, not to mention your career and reputation.

> **CAUTION**
>
> **FMLA lawsuits and enforcement actions are on the rise.** More employees are filing lawsuits alleging violations of the FMLA than ever before. In 2013, the number of FMLA court cases reached almost 900, three times the number filed in the previous year. And, in 2014, the Department of Labor announced its intent to step up its onsite investigations into potential FMLA violations. Although these workplace visits are often a response to employee complaints, the Department has the authority to audit any employer subject to the law. The upshot for employers is clear: Compliance with the FMLA—and proof of compliance, in the form of records and policies—is more important than ever.

How Other Laws and Company Policies Come Into Play

The FMLA isn't the only law you need to consider when employees need time off for family or medical reasons. Other federal and state laws might also come into play, depending on the circumstances. In addition, a company's own policies often affect family and medical leave by, for example, providing paid sick, vacation, or family leave; requiring employees to follow certain procedures before taking time off; or dictating how seniority, benefits, and other issues are handled when an employee is on leave.

Lessons from the *Real World*

Human resources manager can be sued, individually, for violating the FMLA.

Elaine Brewer worked for Jefferson-Pilot Standard Life Insurance Company for 29 years. In July 2002, she requested leave to have eye surgery, estimating she would be out for one to three weeks. While she was out, she gave status reports on her condition to her direct supervisor and to Felicia Cooper, Jefferson-Pilot's senior human resources manager. After three weeks of leave, Brewer's eyes had not yet healed sufficiently for her to return to work. At that point, for the first time, Jefferson-Pilot gave Brewer notice of her rights under the FMLA.

On July 31, 2002, Cooper spoke to Brewer by phone and asked for the names of her health care providers. Cooper then contacted the health care providers and asked them to submit medical certification forms documenting Brewer's condition. On August 2, 2002, before receiving the certification forms back from Brewer's doctors, Cooper accused Brewer of lying about her condition. Although Brewer said she would be able to return to work on August 5, Cooper fired Brewer for dishonesty and insubordination. On August 5, Brewer's doctor returned the certification form, indicating that Brewer had been receiving medical care during her entire leave.

Brewer sued Jefferson-Pilot and Cooper, individually, for violating the FMLA. Cooper argued that she could not be sued personally because she was not Brewer's employer. However, the court disagreed: Relying on the language of the FMLA and the regulations interpreting it, the court found that anyone who acts in the interest of the employer in relation to an employee could be sued as an employer. Because Brewer claimed that Cooper received her medical status reports, controlled the paperwork relating to her leave, contacted the doctors, and fired her for allegedly lying about her condition, Cooper was a proper defendant in the lawsuit.

Brewer v. Jefferson-Pilot Standard Life Insurance Company, 333 F.Supp.2d 433 (M.D. N.C. 2004).

This possibility of overlap means two very important things to managers:

- Whenever an employee requests time off pursuant to any law or company policy, you must ask yourself whether the FMLA applies.
- The employee isn't required to explicitly ask for "FMLA leave"; it's your responsibility to determine whether the employee's time off is FMLA-qualified. An employee on workers' comp leave, temporary disability leave, parental leave, or even vacation might be protected by the FMLA, if the employee meets all of the criteria. And you will certainly want to count that time off as FMLA leave, not only to make sure the employee's rights are protected, but also to put some limit on the total amount of time an employee can take off in a year.
- When the FMLA and another law or policy both apply, you may have to provide more than the FMLA requires. If other laws or your company's policies give employees additional rights, you must honor them as well. The employee is entitled to every protection available, whether it is provided by the FMLA, another law, or your company's policies.

Overlapping Laws

The basic rule about what to do when the FMLA and another law overlap is easy to state: You must follow every applicable provision of every applicable law. In other words, you may not focus solely on the FMLA and ignore your company's obligations under other state or federal laws. If both laws apply to the same situation, you must give the employee the benefit of whichever law is more generous or provides greater rights.

Here are some of the other laws that might also apply to an employee who takes FMLA leave (Chapter 12 explains each in detail, and you can find information on each state's leave laws in Appendix A):

- **Antidiscrimination laws,** which prohibit discrimination based on certain protected characteristics. The Americans with Disabilities Act (ADA) and similar state laws might come into play if an employee's serious health condition is also a protected disability. Laws that prohibit gender and pregnancy discrimination might also overlap with the FMLA.

- **Workers' compensation statutes,** which require most employers to carry insurance that pays for medical treatment and partial wage replacement for employees who suffer work-related injuries or illnesses. An employee who needs workers' compensation leave almost always has a serious health condition under the FMLA, as explained in Chapter 12.
- **State leave laws,** which require employers to give time off for specified reasons. Certain states may give employees the right to take pregnancy disability leave, parental leave, leave for a family member's military service, or other types of family and medical leave. If the employee takes leave for a reason that's covered by both state law and the FMLA, you can count that time off against the employee's allotment of FMLA hours. However, if state law provides leave that isn't covered by the FMLA, you can't count those types of leave against the employee's FMLA entitlement. This means that the employee might be legally entitled to take more time off than the FMLA allows. (See Appendix A for detailed information on state family and medical leave laws.)
- **State insurance programs,** which provide some wage replacement, usually funded by payroll deductions, for employees who are unable to work due to a temporary disability (including pregnancy and childbirth). A few states, including California, have paid family leave insurance programs, which provide similar benefits to employees who take time off to bond with a child or care for a family member. An employee on FMLA leave might be entitled to some compensation from this type of program.

Company Policies

Company policies interact with the FMLA in a slightly different way. For the most part, your company may give employees more rights than the FMLA provides, but it may not take FMLA rights away. For example, if your company has a family and medical leave policy that allows employees to take up to 16 weeks of parental leave, you cannot disregard that policy and give employees only the 12 weeks required by the FMLA. If your company's policies are less generous, however, the company must follow the FMLA: It

must, for example, give employees a full 12 weeks of parental leave, even if the company's policies provide for only six.

The FMLA regulations make clear that employers may require employees to follow their usual procedures when taking leave, as long as those rules don't violate the FMLA. For example, your company may enforce its usual notice rules—such as requiring two weeks notice to use paid vacation time—for employees who want to use paid leave during their FMLA leave. And, your company may generally require employees using FMLA leave to follow other leave requirements, such as calling a particular person to report an absence, as long as those rules don't require more notice than the FMLA requires. These rules are explained in Chapter 8.

In addition to these general rules, the FMLA also makes explicit reference to particular types of employer policies. For example, the FMLA says that you can fire an employee for substance abuse, even if the employee takes FMLA leave to go to rehab, but only if your company has a policy allowing it to do so.

Because this is a potentially confusing area, we've devoted Appendix B to company policies that can affect your FMLA obligations. This appendix identifies the most common areas in which company policy might come into play and provides some sample policy language that will help you maximize your company's rights. In addition, you'll find policy alert icons throughout the book. These icons let you know that your company's policy could determine your rights and obligations regarding that topic.

How to Use This Book

This book explains every aspect of the FMLA, from figuring out whether your company is covered by the law to reinstating an employee returning from FMLA leave. We cover these topics in the order in which they will generally come up as you administer an employee's leave. In addition, we provide helpful appendixes that explain how your state's laws and your company's policies could affect your company's FMLA rights and obligations.

We strongly advise you to read the whole book, even if you are already familiar with some aspects of the FMLA. Because the FMLA imposes fairly

Lessons from the *Real World*

Employee may sue for FMLA benefits promised in employee handbook, even though employee wasn't eligible for leave.

Steven Peters marketed pharmaceutical products to health care providers for Gilead Sciences, Incorporated. Peters was off work for shoulder surgery from December 5 to December 16, 2002; Gilead sent him a letter identifying his time off as FMLA leave. The letter tracked language in the company's employee handbook, including that employees were entitled to 12 weeks of leave, followed by reinstatement. The letter also described the eligibility requirements for FMLA leave, but didn't include the requirement that the company employ 50 employees within 75 miles. In fact, this requirement wasn't met.

On March 4, 2003, Peters began a second period of leave after he began using neurontin, a drug that can cause serious side effects. Gilead again sent him a letter identifying his time off as FMLA leave but Peters never got this letter. On April 16, Gilead received a letter from Peters's doctor, releasing him to return to work on May 5. On April 21, Gilead offered Peters's position to someone else, who accepted it and began work a week later. On April 25, Gilead sent Peters a letter indicating that it could not reinstate him because he held a "key" position (apparently an effort to use the "key employee" exception, covered in Chapter 11).

Peters sued, and Gilead claimed that he wasn't entitled to FMLA leave because he didn't meet the eligibility requirements. The Court of Appeals eventually found that, although Peters may not have had an actual FMLA claim, he could still sue Gilead for promissory estoppel. Because Gilead's handbook and letter promised that Peters was entitled to reinstatement after 12 weeks of leave, Gilead might be responsible for the damages Peters suffered because of his reliance on the promise in taking leave.

Peters v. Gilead Sciences, Inc., 533 F.3d 594 (7th Cir. 2008).

tight deadlines on employers—and because the way you handle initial issues can affect your company's rights down the road—you'll find it very helpful to understand the whole picture before you have to handle a leave request. Also, there have been significant changes in the law and regulations in the last few years, which will require you to meet some different requirements. Once you've reviewed every chapter, you can use the book as a reference, to quickly look up the information you need.

Each chapter includes features that will help you meet your obligations, including:

- **Chapter Highlights,** which summarize the basic rules covered in the chapter
- **Lessons From the Real World,** which show how courts have handled particular disputes between real employees and real employers
- **Examples,** which will help you understand how to apply the material to real-life situations
- **Sample Forms,** which allow you to request information from, and provide information to, employees about FMLA leave (you'll find blank copies of all forms on this book's companion page at Nolo's website; see Appendix C for details)
- **Managers' Checklists and Flowcharts,** which you can use to make sure you've considered every important factor when making decisions about key FMLA issues, and
- **Common Mistakes—And How to Avoid Them,** which will help you steer clear of legal trouble in applying the FMLA.

Complying with the FMLA can be a challenge, but the materials in this book will help you handle your responsibilities legally, fairly, and confidently. The first step is to figure out whether your company is covered by the law— and, if so, to give employees notice of their rights under the law—using the guidelines in Chapter 2. If you already know that your company is covered and has met its posting and policy obligations, move on to Chapter 3, which will help you figure out which employees are eligible for leave.

Get Updates, Forms, and More on Nolo.com

When there are important changes to the information in this book, we'll post updates online. (See Appendix C for a link to the dedicated page for this book.) And if you notice a useful form in this book, including a letter, checklist, or government form, you'll have access to a digital version via the same companion page. You'll find other useful information on that page, too, such as podcast interviews with the authors and blog posts.

Is Your Company Covered by the FMLA?

Calculating the Size of Your Company 19

    Step 1: Does Your Company Employ 50 or More People? 20

    Step 2: Did Your Company Employ 50 or More Employees
             for 20 or More Workweeks? 20

Joint Employers and the FMLA 22

    Is Your Company a Joint Employer? 22

    Primary and Secondary Employers 25

    Integrated Employers 27

If Your Company Is Covered 28

    Posting Requirements 29

    Written FMLA Policies 30

Common Mistakes Regarding Employer Coverage—
    And How to Avoid Them 32

Chapter Highlights

☆ Your company is covered by the FMLA if it employed 50 or more employees for 20 or more weeks in the current or preceding year.

☆ Employees who count toward the 50 or more minimum include:
  • all full-time employees
  • all part-time employees
  • employees on leave if they are expected to return to work, and
  • employees who work jointly for your company and another company.

☆ These workers don't count toward the 50-employee minimum:
  • independent contractors
  • employees working outside the U.S. or its territories
  • employees hired or terminated during a calendar week (for that week only), and
  • employees who are not expected to return from leave.

☆ For purposes of the FMLA's 20-week minimum, employees are employed by your company in any week in which they are on payroll.

☆ The 20 weeks of employing 50 or more employees don't have to be consecutive, as long as they occur in the current or preceding year.

☆ If your company is a joint employer, its responsibilities under the FMLA depend on whether it is a "primary" or "secondary" employer.

☆ If your company is a covered employer, you must:
  • post general FMLA information at every worksite, and
  • include information about the FMLA in your company's written policies or distribute it to new employees.

Before you get your first request for FMLA leave, you have to figure out whether the law applies to your company. Companies subject to the law are required to post notices about the FMLA and include FMLA information in employee handbooks or other company policies. You don't have the luxury of waiting for an employee to raise the issue; you are legally required to inform your employees of their FMLA rights. If your company doesn't provide this information, it can't deny FMLA leave to employees for failing to meet their obligations under the law (for example, to provide advance notice of the need for leave or a medical certification from a health care provider, confirming the need for leave). Your company could even face a lawsuit for interfering with or denying the employee's FMLA rights.

This chapter will help you figure out whether the FMLA applies to your company. It covers:

- whether your company is directly covered by the FMLA
- whether your company is covered by the FMLA as a joint employer, and
- what actions you must take, right away, if your company is covered.

Calculating the Size of Your Company

Your company is covered by the FMLA if it employed 50 or more employees for each working day during 20 or more weeks in the current or preceding year. The purpose of this 50-employee rule is to exempt small businesses from the FMLA. Congress recognized that these businesses might not be able to afford to provide the leave and benefits—and bear the administrative burdens—mandated by the law.

Most companies won't be splitting hairs: Companies with well more than 50 employees know they are subject to the FMLA, and very small companies know they aren't. However, for companies that are close to that 50-employee dividing line, the details about which employees count toward the minimum become very important. For example, managers sometimes aren't sure whether part-time employees count toward the minimum, or whether to count temporary workers who are placed—and technically employed—by an outside agency. To evaluate whether the FMLA applies to your company, you'll need to know the rules for counting employees.

Step 1: Does Your Company Employ 50 or More People?

It seems like a simple question—anyone can count to 50, right? However, when you're making the calculation, you'll need to include each of these employees:

- every full-time employee
- every part-time employee
- employees on leave, whether paid or unpaid, including medical leave, FMLA leave, vacation, and disciplinary or workers' compensation leaves, as long as your company reasonably expects them to return to work, and
- employees, such as temps, who work jointly for your company and another company (called "joint employees," and discussed below).

> **SKIP AHEAD**
>
> **If your company has fewer than 50 employees.** If your company has not employed 50 people at any given time in the last two years, your company will not be directly subject to the FMLA. However, if you're a joint employer with a company that is subject to the FMLA, you will still have some legal responsibilities even if you don't have 50 employees on your own. (For more information, see "Joint Employers and the FMLA," below.)

If your company has employed at least 50 employees at any time in the last two years, or is a joint employer, keep reading.

Step 2: Did Your Company Employ 50 or More Employees for 20 or More Workweeks?

The FMLA applies only to companies that have employed 50 or more employees for each working day during 20 or more weeks of the current or preceding year. Employees whose names appear on your company's payroll at any time in a calendar week count as employed for each working day of the workweek. However, employees hired or terminated during a calendar week don't count for that week, nor do independent contractors or employees working outside the U.S. or its territories.

> **EXAMPLE:** You are the HR manager of Blue Lagoon Pool Maintenance and Repair Service in Scottsdale, Arizona, which has 34 year-round employees but hires extra part-time employees when pool season comes around. Blue Lagoon hires 25 part-time employees the first week of May. When calculating whether Blue Lagoon has enough employees to be subject to the FMLA, you don't count the new part-time employees for the first week of May, but you do count them for every week they work after that, even if they only work one day a week. As of the middle of October, all the part-time employees still work for Blue Lagoon, so you correctly determine that Blue Lagoon will have at least 50 employees for 20 or more weeks of the year. Blue Lagoon will be subject to the FMLA.

Remember though, that the 20 weeks don't have to be consecutive. For example, if your company is a seasonal employer and has more than 50 employees during all of spring and fall (six months of the year), but only ten employees during summer and winter, your company will be covered by the FMLA. And a company that has reduced its workforce from at least 50 employees to less than 50 employees within the last year is still covered by FMLA if it employed 50 or more employees for any 20 weeks in the current or preceding calendar year.

> **EXAMPLE:** Your company, Razberry Jam Productions, employs 62 field workers from March 15 to May 1 every year, and 53 seasonal cannery workers from June 1 to October 15. The rest of the year, your company maintains a bare-bones staff of 15 shipping and administrative employees. In April, Wendy, a shipping clerk, asks for leave to take care of her husband as he recovers from surgery. Her manager denies the leave, telling Wendy that he has counted back 20 calendar weeks and the cannery was closed for most of that period, so the FMLA doesn't apply to Razberry Jam Productions.
>
> Should you step in and reverse the manager's decision? Yes. The manager should have looked at the entire current and preceding year for the company. If he had done that, he would have seen that your company employed over 50 employees for more than 20 weeks in that period. Your company was covered by the FMLA.

If your company didn't employ 50 employees for at least 20 weeks in the current or preceding year, it isn't covered by the FMLA. But, if your company is a "secondary" joint employer (discussed in "Joint Employers and the FMLA," below), it may still have to comply with certain FMLA requirements.

Covered Companies May Not Have Eligible Employees

To be eligible for leave under the FMLA, it's not enough that employees work for a covered company; they must also meet certain individual eligibility requirements, as explained in Chapter 3. One of these requirements is that the employee must work within a 75-mile radius of 50 or more company employees.

As a result of this rule, a company that's covered by the FMLA might not have a single eligible employee. For example, a nationwide company might have outlets in a hundred major metropolitan areas, each employing 20 to 30 employees. Yet, if none of those outlets are with 75 miles of another, none of the company's employees would be eligible to take FMLA leave. In this situation, the company would still have to post notices and provide information on the FMLA (see "If Your Company Is Covered," below), but it wouldn't have to provide leave.

Joint Employers and the FMLA

Even if it doesn't meet the criteria described above, your company could still be subject to the FMLA if it is a "joint employer." A joint employer shares control with another company over the working conditions of the other company's employees. This happens when your company contracts with temporary agencies or shares employees with a contractor or subcontractor, for example. If, counting joint employees, your company meets the requirements described above, your company is subject to the FMLA. However, its FMLA responsibilities to the joint employees depend on whether it's a "primary" or a "secondary" employer, as we explain below.

Is Your Company a Joint Employer?

There are no hard and fast rules that determine whether your company is a joint employer. Instead, you must look at all the circumstances of the relationship between the two companies to determine whether your company acts like an employer. The main factors to consider are whether your company:

- has the power to hire and fire some employees of the other company
- has the power to set rates and methods of pay for employees of the other company
- has the right to supervise the work and work schedules of employees of the other company, and
- is responsible for maintaining employment records for employees of the other company.

These factors are hallmarks of a joint employer relationship. No one factor or combination of factors automatically creates a joint employer relationship. But as a practical matter, if your company uses temps or employees supplied by another company, it is probably a joint employer.

Lessons from the *Real World*

If your company doesn't control the working conditions of another company's workers, it doesn't have to count them as "joint employees."

Stephane Moreau worked as an assistant station manager for a foreign airline in a major U.S. airport. When his father became ill, Stephane asked for FMLA leave to take care of him. But the airline refused to give him the leave. Even though the airline was covered by the FMLA, Stephane only met individual eligibility requirements if the company employed 50 or more employees within 75 miles of Stephane's worksite. The airline claimed that it didn't.

Stephane knew that ground handling companies serviced the airline's planes at the airport. He argued to the employer that the employees of the ground handling companies were "joint employees," because they provided services to the airline's planes at the airport where he worked. The airline disagreed and told Moreau that he would be fired if he took the time off—and when he did, the airline kept its promise.

Stephane sued, but he lost. The court decided that the airline wasn't a joint employer because, among other things, it didn't have the power to hire or fire the ground crew, set the pay rates for the workers, keep their employment records, set their work schedules, or control their work conditions.

Moreau v. Air France, 343 F.3d 1179 (9th Cir. 2003).

EXAMPLE: Your company, Internet Service Solutions (ISS), operates a customer call center to service the accounts of customers of an Internet service provider, Internet View. To find new customer service representatives, ISS hires temporary employees through a placement service, Techno Temps. ISS supervisors interview prospective Techno Temps candidates for their departments, choose which to hire, and decide how much to pay them. If the supervisor likes the Techno Temp employee's work, the employee might later be offered a job directly by ISS. If a Techno Temps placement doesn't work out, ISS can terminate employment. Currently, 20 of ISS's customer service representatives are Techno Temps employees.

In this situation, ISS is a joint employer with Techno Temps because ISS has the power to hire and fire Techno Temps employees working at ISS, sets their pay rates, and supervises them on a day-to-day basis. As a result, all joint employees have to be counted by both ISS and Techno Temps to determine whether the two companies are covered by the FMLA.

Depending on the circumstances, ISS might also be a joint employer with Internet View. For example, if ISS is a subsidiary of Internet View, and human resources operations like recruiting, payroll, and personnel files are all managed by Internet View, ISS and Internet View are probably joint employers.

Professional Employer Organizations

The FMLA regulations address the increasingly common arrangement by which one company retains another to handle payroll and administrative benefits for the first company's employees on an ongoing basis. The DOL calls the companies that are hired to do this work "professional employer organizations" (PEOs). Although the question of joint employment turns on the "economic realities" of the situation based on all of the facts and circumstances, the regulations make clear that a PEO and its client/employer typically are not joint employers as long as:

- the PEO simply performs administrative functions (such as those related to payroll, benefits, and updating employment policies), and
- the client/employer doesn't have the right to hire, fire, assign, or direct and control the PEO's employees.

If, however, the PEO and the client/employer are joint employers, the client/employer usually will be the primary employer.

Primary and Secondary Employers

Figuring out whether your company is a joint employer is just your first task; it tells you whether you have any obligations under the FMLA. To find out what those obligations are, you must figure out whether your company is the "primary" employer or a "secondary" employer.

Is Your Company a Primary or Secondary Employer?

If your company is a joint employer, use the criteria below to determine whether your company is a primary or secondary employer.

A primary employer has authority to:

- hire and fire the employee seeking leave
- place the employee in a particular position
- assign work to the employee
- make payroll, and
- provide employment benefits.

If your company is responsible for these tasks, your company is the primary employer. If not, your company is the secondary employer. Once again, these factors give guidance but are not hard and fast rules.

> EXAMPLE: Your company has 33 employees on its regular payroll. You also have 21 IT technicians working for you, who are directly employed by IS-2, a temporary agency. IS-2 hires and fires these technicians, issues their paychecks, and provides medical insurance coverage for them. One of the IT technicians, Aaron, needs to take time off for the birth of his child.
>
> Who is Aaron's primary employer? Because IS-2 handles all of the employment obligations for the IT technicians, IS-2 is Aaron's primary employer. Your company is the secondary employer because it uses Aaron's services but is not otherwise responsible for his employment.

TIP

When in doubt, act like the primary employer. If you aren't sure whether your company is a primary or secondary employer, the best practice is to assume that it is a primary employer and give employees the required notices, as discussed below. If a court is later asked to decide the issue, you'll have met your company's obligations either way.

Primary and Secondary Employers' Responsibilities

So what are the responsibilities of the primary and secondary employers? The primary employer's responsibilities are pretty much the same as those of any company subject to the FMLA. It must provide FMLA notices to joint employees, grant and administer their FMLA leaves, and restore them to their jobs when FMLA leave is over. The primary employer can't interfere with employees' FMLA rights or discriminate against employees for asserting those rights or helping other employees assert their rights. We'll discuss how to implement all these requirements in later chapters.

The secondary employer's responsibilities are a little less onerous. As long as the secondary employer is still jointly employing anyone with the primary employer when the employee's leave ends, the secondary employer must let any joint employee on FMLA leave return to the same position he or she held before the leave. Additionally, the secondary employer can't interfere with a joint employee's exercise of FMLA rights and can't retaliate or discriminate against the employee for asserting FMLA rights or for assisting other employees in asserting their rights. Even a secondary employer that would not otherwise be covered by the FMLA (for example, because it employs fewer than 50 employees even counting joint employees) is bound by these obligations.

Figuring Out Your FMLA Responsibilities

If you're a joint employer, it can be confusing to figure out what your FMLA responsibilities are. You may be a primary employer with regard to some of your employees, but a secondary employer with regard to other employees. Or, you may be a secondary employer only, or you may have no obligations under the FMLA at all. The following examples will help you determine which category you fall under. The key is to calculate joint employees in both your company's count and the other joint employer's count. Let's continue with the example from the previous page.

> EXAMPLE 1: Your company has 33 regular employees and 21 IT technicians placed by IS-2. Because you're a joint employer with IS-2, you must count the IT technicians in your total employee count. Your company has a total of 54 employees, which means it is covered by the FMLA. You're the primary employer of your 33 regular employees and the secondary employer of the 21 IT Technicians. This means that you will have different FMLA obligations depending on which employee requests FMLA leave.

EXAMPLE 2: Susan, one of your regular employees, needs time off to bond with her new child. Aaron, one of the IT technicians, needs time off for a serious health condition. What are your obligations?

Because you're the primary employer for Susan, you must follow all FMLA requirements, including providing Susan with the required notices, granting her request for FMLA leave (assuming she meets all eligibility requirements), and reinstating her to the same or an equivalent position at the end of her leave. When it comes to Aaron, you have the more limited obligations of a secondary employer. You don't have to provide notice or administer FMLA leave; those are the responsibilities of Aaron's primary employer, IS-2. But, if you still have any joint employees with IS-2 working for you at the time Aaron returns from leave, you must accept his placement at your company.

EXAMPLE 3: Now, suppose your company has only 10 regular employees and 21 IT technicians placed by IS-2. Because your total employee count is 31, you are not covered by the FMLA. However, IS-2 has 34 other employees, for a total of 55 employees. IS-2 is subject to the FMLA. As a result, you have the more limited obligations of a secondary employer when it comes to the 21 IT technicians. But, you won't have any FMLA obligations towards your regular employees.

Integrated Employers

A parent and subsidiary company or two or more affiliated companies (sometimes called "sister companies") must each count all of the other company's employees, even those who work only for one company, when calculating whether it meets the 50-employee test. These "integrated" companies are viewed under the FMLA as a single employer. Companies are "integrated employers" when there is:

- common management
- interrelation between operations
- centralized control of labor relations, and
- common ownership or financial control.

So, if your company is integrated with another company, it must include all of the other company's employees in the FMLA count—even if your company shares no staff with the other company and has entirely separate work facilities.

CAUTION

A successor in interest might have FMLA obligations to "inherited" employees. If your company bought or merged with another company, the company that's left after the merger or sale may be a "successor in interest." If so, the transferred employees will have the same FMLA rights they would have had if continuously employed by a single company. If your company is not covered by the FMLA and it buys another company that is, it must honor the FMLA rights of the employees of the other company who become its employees after the sale. If you think your company might be a successor in interest, you may want to consult with an attorney to determine your company's responsibilities under the FMLA.

Managers' Checklist: Does the FMLA Apply to My Company?

☐ My company had 50 or more employees on payroll during each of 20 workweeks in this year or the last calendar year.

    ☐ I included all employees on leave in this count.

    ☐ I included all part-time employees on payroll during any workweek.

    ☐ I did not include employees hired or fired during any workweek in the count for that workweek.

    ☐ I did not include employees working outside the U.S. or its territories in this count.

    ☐ I counted all employees jointly employed by my company and a joint employer, including temp agency employees.

    ☐ I counted all employees of my company and any other company that is integrated with it.

If Your Company Is Covered

Once you determine that your company is covered by the FMLA, you must immediately provide information to employees about their rights and obligations under the law (unless your company is a secondary employer only). You'll have to post a notice explaining the FMLA and distribute written information on the law to employees.

Posting Requirements

Employees rely on you to provide them with information about the FMLA. Your obligation begins with the requirement to hang a poster explaining employees' FMLA rights. The poster must be in a "conspicuous" place where it can be readily seen by employees and job applicants, and it must be in writing that is large enough to read easily. The posting requirement applies even if your company doesn't have any FMLA-eligible employees on site: Currently ineligible employees may become eligible under the FMLA at a later date and will need to know their rights.

The FMLA regulations allow employers to post FMLA information electronically. However, you must make sure that it can readily be seen by employees and job applicants. An electronic posting on your company's intranet, for example, wouldn't satisfy the posting requirement unless it could be easily accessed by applicants as well.

Fortunately, you don't have to put together a poster from scratch. The U.S. Department of Labor (DOL) has an approved poster that you can download and use. We've provided links to this poster, in both English and Spanish, at this book's online companion page; see Appendix C for more information.

If a "significant portion" of your company's workforce doesn't speak English, the poster must be in the language in which those employees are literate. The family leave laws of some states may also require a poster written in the language in which a specific number or percentage of your company's employees are literate. Additionally, some states have additional posting requirements under their own family, medical, or pregnancy leave laws. For example, California requires employers covered by its family leave law to post a notice alerting employees to their rights under the FMLA, the state family leave law, and the state's pregnancy disability leave law.

TIP
Post the FMLA information in every language that your company's employees speak, including English. That way, you will not have to worry that some employees are not getting the required information.

If your company doesn't post the general FMLA information discussed above, it can't deny leave to, discipline, or take any action against an

employee because the employee has not complied with FMLA notice and procedural requirements. And, the DOL could penalize your company $110 for each violation of the posting requirement. If your company's failure to post the FMLA information interferes with an employee's FMLA rights, the employee could sue the company.

SEE AN EXPERT

Get legal help with your posting requirements. Consult an attorney with expertise in the laws of every state in which your company employs workers to find out the state-specific poster requirements.

EXAMPLE: Delia has worked for your company for two years. Your company doesn't post FMLA information, even though it is covered by the FMLA. Your company also has its own 16-week maternity leave policy. Delia gets pregnant and requests and takes the full 16 weeks of leave. When she tries to return to her original position after the leave ends, you tell her that you filled her position two weeks earlier because she hadn't returned within 12 weeks, which is all she is entitled to under the FMLA. Delia objects and says that the FMLA protects her right to return to her original job. You point out to Delia that the FMLA does provide for reinstatement, but only following leaves of up to 12 weeks. You tell Delia you have assigned her to a downgraded position. Delia threatens legal action. Should you be worried?

You should be quite worried! You were right about the FMLA protecting employee reinstatement rights only for the 12-week FMLA leave period (as discussed in Chapter 7). But, because the FMLA information wasn't posted for Delia and other employees to see, your company effectively interfered with her FMLA rights.

Written FMLA Policies

Before any individual employee even asks for FMLA leave, your company must notify all employees of their FMLA rights in writing. In addition to the FMLA poster discussed above, your company must include information about FMLA entitlements and employee obligations in its employee handbook or other written guidelines to employees regarding employee benefits or leave.

If your company doesn't have an employee handbook or other written guidelines on benefits or leave that it distributes to employees, it must give a copy of the general notice to each new employee upon hire. The general notice is simply the FMLA poster (WH-1420), available as explained in "Posting Requirements," above.

If your company already has a leave policy, you'll want to make sure that it has all the information that's legally required. We've included a sample FMLA policy in Appendix B, which you can use to draft or modify your own company policy.

If your company fails to include FMLA information in its employee handbook or benefits policies or to provide the information to employees as required, it won't be able to take action against an employee who doesn't comply with the requirements of the FMLA or your company's own leave policies. And, your company may be liable for interfering with employee FMLA rights.

Lessons from the *Real World*

An employer that didn't notify an employee in writing of his FMLA obligations couldn't argue that he failed to meet them.

Invacare Corporation employed Isaiah Taylor in its shipping department. Taylor requested leave to care for his wife after she had back surgery. His supervisor denied the leave, but Taylor took time off anyway and Invacare fired him. He sued Invacare for violating the FMLA.

Invacare argued that Taylor's need for leave was foreseeable and that he'd failed to give 30 days' notice as the FMLA requires. Taylor and a coworker testified that Invacare failed to provide employees with FMLA notice information—including the requirement to provide 30 days' advance notice of foreseeable leave.

Taylor won the case because Invacare had failed to inform its employees of their obligations and rights under the FMLA. As a result, Invacare couldn't fire Taylor for not giving the notice required by the FMLA.

Taylor v. Invacare Corp., 64 Fed. Appx. 516 (6th Cir. 2003).

Your company's handbook or other written policies should include all company leave policies that interact with FMLA rights, such as attendance policies, notice requirements, and the like. We'll discuss these policies, and how they interact with the FMLA, in subsequent chapters.

Common Mistakes Regarding Employer Coverage—And How to Avoid Them

Mistake 1: **Your company is covered by the FMLA, but managers who don't know it deny leave to eligible employees.**

Avoid this mistake by taking the following steps:

- Figure out whether your company is covered by the FMLA.
- Reevaluate FMLA coverage when there is a change in your company's workforce or structure, such as a merger or expansion.
- Count all employees the FMLA requires you to count (for example, employees on leave, part-time employees, and joint employees).
- Count only those employees the FMLA requires you to count (for example, do not count independent contractors).

Mistake 2: **Your company doesn't meet its obligations as a joint employer.**

Avoid this mistake by taking the following steps:

- Keep track of all workers who are joint employees of your company and another company, including all temps and any employees your company shares with a contractor or subcontractor.
- Figure out whether your company is the primary or secondary employer of joint employees.
- Fulfill your company's responsibilities as a primary or secondary employer.

Mistake 3: **Failing to give all employees general FMLA information.**

Avoid this mistake by taking the following steps:

- Immediately post the required FMLA notice in a conspicuous location at every worksite.

- Make sure that your company's employee handbook includes a detailed and accurate description of employee FMLA rights and duties (use the sample FMLA policy in Appendix B).
- Distribute a copy of the written FMLA notice to all new employees as part of their first-day paperwork.

Is the Employee Covered by the FMLA?

Employee Eligibility, Step by Step 37

    Step 1: Are There 50 Employees Within 75 Miles? 37

    Step 2: Has the Employee Worked for the Company for 12 Months? 40

    Step 3: Has the Employee Worked Enough Hours? 42

Keeping Track of Employees' Work Hours 46

Common Mistakes Regarding Employee Eligibility—

    And How to Avoid Them 49

Chapter Highlights

☆ Employees are entitled to FMLA leave if they:
- work for your company at a worksite with 50 or more employees within a 75-mile radius
- have worked for your company for at least 12 months, and
- have worked at least 1,250 hours in the 12-month period preceding the leave.

☆ You must determine whether there are 50 employees within 75 miles on the date the employee requests leave, not the date the employee's leave is scheduled to begin.

☆ Time that counts toward the 1,250-hour minimum includes:
- any hours the employee worked, whether paid or not
- work-related travel time during the workday
- continuing education or other required work-related activities, and
- hours the employee would have worked if not on military leave.

☆ The following hours don't count toward the 1,250-hour minimum:
- time spent on suspension
- travel time from home to work, and
- time on leave other than for military service (unless your company counts leave time for overtime purposes).

☆ Different hours-of-service rules apply to airline flight crew employees, who are eligible for leave if they:
- have worked or been paid for at least 60% of the applicable total monthly guarantee, and
- have worked or been paid for at least 504 hours in the past 12 months.

☆ You must carefully track employees' hours to determine eligibility; if you don't keep accurate records, records kept by the employee will be used to resolve eligibility disputes.

N ow that you know that the FMLA applies to your company, it's time to figure out which employees the law protects. Not every employee who works for a covered employer is entitled to leave. To be eligible, an employee must have worked for your company for at least 12 months, and must have worked at least 1,250 hours during the year preceding the leave. In addition, your company must have at least 50 employees within a 75-mile radius of the employee's worksite.

Keeping records of these numbers can get complicated. There are detailed rules on which hours count toward the minimum, how to measure the 75 miles, and when to make these determinations. And it's not a one-time calculation: An employee who was eligible for—and took—FMLA leave in the past might not qualify later on; similarly, an employee who isn't entitled to FMLA leave today might become eligible in the future.

This chapter explains each part of the eligibility process: how to do the necessary calculations, how to track an employee's eligibility, and how to keep proper records that will allow you to quickly determine whether an employee meets these requirements.

Employee Eligibility, Step by Step

To be eligible for FMLA leave, an employee must:
- work at a worksite with 50 or more employees within a 75-mile radius
- have worked for your company for at least 12 months, and
- have worked at least 1,250 hours in the 12 months immediately preceding the leave.

An employee who doesn't meet all three of these requirements is not entitled to FMLA leave.

Step 1: Are There 50 Employees Within 75 Miles?

To figure out whether a specific employee is entitled to FMLA leave, you first need to figure out whether there are 50 or more employees at the employee's worksite or within a 75-mile radius of the worksite. If your company employs thousands of FMLA-eligible workers, but has several employees who work in a remote satellite office that's more than 75 miles

from any other company worksite, the employees in the satellite office won't be entitled to FMLA leave.

> **TIP**
>
> **Don't forget to count joint employees.** When figuring out whether there are 50 employees within 75 miles of the employee's worksite, make sure to count joint employees. A joint employee's worksite is the primary employer's office where the employee is assigned or reports, unless the employee has physically worked for at least a year at a facility of the secondary employer, which would then become the joint employee's worksite. For more on joint employers, including primary and secondary employers, see Chapter 2.

Measuring the 75-Mile Radius

If your company has a "campus" of buildings grouped together, they count as one worksite. Similarly, unconnected buildings used by your company within a reasonable geographic vicinity (for example, within the city limits) are considered a single worksite. The 75-mile radius can be measured out from any of the buildings in the worksite. If there are 50 employees within 75 miles of any building in the worksite, all employees who work at the worksite meet this part of the eligibility test.

> **EXAMPLE:** Petra has worked full time at the Main Street outlet of your company, the Grande Baguette bakery chain, for the last four years. Grande Baguette employs 20 people at the Main Street outlet and another 20 people at another location in the city, the First Street outlet. It employs another 20 people at an outlet in a suburban mall that's 77 miles away from Petra's outlet but only 72 miles from the First Street store. Petra is pregnant and has requested leave to begin on the date of her scheduled C-section. Is Petra entitled to FMLA leave?
>
> Yes. Even though there are only 20 employees at the Grande Baguette outlet where Petra works, the two city locations count as one worksite. There are 40 employees at the citywide worksite, and an additional 20 employees at the mall outlet. Because the mall outlet is within 75 miles of one of the city locations, those employees count when determining Petra's eligibility—even though they don't work within 75 miles of her actual location. Because there are 60 employees within 75 miles of the worksite under the FMLA definition, Petra is eligible for leave.

To measure the 75-mile radius, you must use the shortest route on public streets, roads, highways, and waterways from the worksite. Although employees have tried to argue that the 75 miles should be measured "as the crow flies" (that is, in a straight line on a map), courts have determined that this distance must be measured using actual routes that could be traveled between worksites.

When to Count the 75-Mile Radius

You must determine whether the company has the minimum number of employees within 75 miles of the employee's worksite on the day the employee requests leave, not the day the employee's leave will begin. If your company had the requisite number of employees on the day the employee requested leave, the employee has met this eligibility requirement, regardless of later reductions in your local workforce.

EXAMPLE: Your company has five stores in downtown Omaha, employing a total of 63 employees. Next month, it plans to close two stores that employ a total of 21 people; after those closures, the company will have only 42 employees. Ted works at one of the stores that will remain open. He asks his supervisor, Margo, for three weeks off beginning six weeks from now, to look after his mother following hip replacement surgery. Margo, who knows about the store closure plans, tells you she is going to deny FMLA leave because there will be only 42 employees when Ted's leave starts.

Fortunately, Margo speaks to you before making this mistake. You correctly point out that the company must determine whether this eligibility requirement is met on the date an employee requests leave, not the date leave is scheduled to begin. Because the company has more than 50 employees in the city at the time Ted makes his FMLA request, he is entitled to leave as long as he meets the other eligibility requirements.

Determining Where an Employee Works

It's not hard to identify the worksite of an employee who works in the same cubicle every day. However, figuring out the worksite for employees who travel or telecommute presents more of a challenge. For employees with no fixed company worksite, the worksite where the employee reports or where

work is assigned to the employee is that employee's worksite for FMLA purposes. This is true even if the reporting worksite is temporary and the company's headquarters are many miles away.

> **EXAMPLE:** You are the Human Resources Manager for Nice Catch, a company that owns several fishing vessels operating out of Dutch Harbor, Alaska. Nice Catch is headquartered in Anacortes, Washington. Nice Catch employs 75 workers on its boats in Dutch Harbor and assigns crews from its small dockside office there. In the Anacortes headquarters, Nice Catch employs 22 people.
>
> Maria works on a fishing boat out of Dutch Harbor and has requested leave to care for a baby that she and her partner are adopting. Richie is an accountant in the Anacortes office and has to have shoulder surgery to repair a torn rotator cuff, which has interfered with his ability to work. Assuming they meet the other eligibility requirements, are Maria and Richie entitled to FMLA leave?
>
> Yes and no, respectively. Because the boat crews are assigned work out of the Dutch Harbor office, that's their worksite for purposes of calculating FMLA eligibility—even if their fishing boats operate hundreds of miles apart. Because Maria works at a site with more than 50 employees, she is entitled to leave. There are only 22 employees at Richie's worksite, however, so he isn't an eligible employee under the FMLA.

Step 2: Has the Employee Worked for the Company for 12 Months?

To be eligible for FMLA leave, an employee must have worked for your company for at least 12 months. These months need not be consecutive. An employee who has put in a total of 12 months meets this eligibility requirement, even if the employee had a break in service, as long as the employee's break in service lasted for fewer than seven years. If the employee had a break in service of seven years or more, the employer doesn't have to count employment prior to the break in service toward the 12-month requirement, unless the break in service was due to National Guard or Reserve military service obligations or was pursuant to a written agreement, including a collective bargaining agreement, indicating the employer's intent to rehire the employee after the break.

EXAMPLE: Horacio works on one of your company's construction crews. He worked eight months for your company last year, from the beginning of April through the end of November, before he was laid off because of lack of work during the winter. The company rehired Horacio on April 1. On August 1, Horacio has a heart attack and takes several weeks off work for treatment and recovery. Has Horacio met the 12-month requirement for FMLA eligibility?

Yes. Although Horacio has only worked for your company in eight of the last 12 months, he has worked 12 months total: eight months during his first stint with your company and four months immediately before his heart attack. He has met this eligibility requirement.

When to Count the 12 Months

The employee must have worked a total of 12 months as of the date that he or she will begin FMLA leave, not as of the date the employee requests leave. Note that this is different from the first eligibility requirement, discussed above: You must determine whether there are 50 employees within a 75-mile radius on the date the employee requests leave, not the date leave will start.

EXAMPLE: Anna began working for your company full time 11 months ago. Anna requests leave to undergo back surgery beginning in one month. Is Anna entitled to FMLA leave because she will have worked for you for 12 months by the time her leave starts?

Yes, Anna is entitled to FMLA leave. If she had needed FMLA leave immediately though, she wouldn't be eligible.

Which Time Counts

If an employee works at all during a week, that week counts toward the 12-month requirement. Unlike the hours-worked requirement (discussed below), the 12-month requirement measures how long the employee has been with your company, not how many hours he or she has actually worked.

When determining whether an employee has worked at least 12 months, you should count every week in which the employee shows up on the payroll. It doesn't matter whether the employee works full time or part time, or whether the employee works intermittently (that is, the employee works

some weeks and not others). Once the employee reaches 52 weeks on the payroll, the employee has met the requirement.

If you have joint employees—that is, employees who are employed both by your company and by another company (such as a temp agency)—count all of the weeks during which they have been employed by either joint company. For example, if an employee of a temporary agency was placed with your company six months ago and worked for the temporary agency for six months before that, that employee has satisfied the 12-month employment requirement.

Time employees spend on leave counts toward the 12-month minimum only if:

- the employee took leave for military service (see Chapter 12 for more information), or
- your company provided compensation or benefits during the employee's leave (such as PTO, group health benefits, and so on).

EXAMPLE: Brett has worked full time for your company for one year but spent two months of that year on company-approved, paid disability leave. Brett now requests leave for a serious health condition. Is Brett entitled to FMLA leave?
Yes, because he has worked at least 12 months, including the paid leave time.

A couple of time periods that do not count toward the 12-month requirement are:

- **Suspensions.** If an employee was suspended, that suspension period doesn't count toward the 12 months.
- **Layoff periods.** If you lay off an employee and then recall that employee later, you don't usually count the layoff period when calculating whether the employee has worked for 12 months.

Step 3: Has the Employee Worked Enough Hours?

In addition to having worked for at least 12 months for your company, an employee seeking FMLA leave must have worked at least 1,250 hours in the 12-month period immediately preceding the leave. As with the 12-month requirement, you must calculate whether an employee has worked 1,250 hours as of the date leave is scheduled to begin—not the date the employee requests leave.

Which Hours Count

You must count every hour (or fraction of an hour) worked toward the 1,250-hour minimum. These include:

- hours worked for which the employee was not paid (for example, overtime hours worked by an employee exempt from receiving overtime pay)
- work-related travel time during the workday (for example, when an employee has to travel from his or her usual worksite to a meeting in another location)
- continuing education or other required work-related activities, and
- hours the employee would have worked if not on military leave (see Chapter 12).

The following hours do not count:

- time during which the employee was suspended
- time the employee spends traveling from home to office and back, unless:
  - your company has an agreement or practice of paying for such time, or
  - state law treats such travel time as paid time (for example, when the employee travels from home to a temporary worksite away from his or her usual worksite)
- time spent on leave other than military service covered by the Uniformed Services Employment and Reemployment Rights Act (USERRA), unless your company counts leave time as "hours worked" for overtime pay purposes. (Learn more about USERRA and how it overlaps with the FMLA in Chapter 12.)

POLICY ALERT

Your company's overtime policies could determine whether employees are eligible for FMLA leave. As noted above, if your company counts leave time as hours worked in determining whether an employee has worked overtime, it must also count leave time toward an employee's total hours worked in the 12-month FMLA period. (See Appendix B for more information on how your company's policies can affect its FMLA obligations.)

Lessons from the *Real World*

An employee who didn't actually work 1,250 hours in the preceding year is not entitled to FMLA leave, even if the employer granted it by mistake.

In May 1995, Jayson Sepe, a builder for McDonnell Douglas Corp., requested and was granted a 12-week leave in connection with the birth of his daughter. Because of medical leave Sepe had already taken in the last year, he had worked only 822 hours in the 12 months preceding his daughter's birth.

While on the May 1995 leave, Sepe worked for an excavating company he and his wife had started a few years earlier, in violation of McDonnell Douglas's policy prohibiting employees from working while on leave. McDonnell Douglas fired Sepe for violating the policy.

Sepe sued the company for, among other things, firing him in violation of the FMLA. McDonnell Douglas argued that Sepe wasn't eligible for FMLA leave and that it had mistakenly granted his request. The court held that because Sepe had not worked the required 1,250 hours in the 12 months prior to requesting leave, the FMLA did not protect him.

Sepe v. McDonnell Douglas Corp., 176 F.3d 1113 (8th Cir. 1999).

Special "Hours of Service" Eligibility Requirement for Airline Flight Crews

The unique challenges faced by airline employers when trying to calculate "hours worked" by flight crew members have led to some changes to the FMLA. In 2010, Congress amended the law to require employers to calculate the "hours of service" for FMLA eligibility in a different manner for airline flight crew employees.

For airline flight crews, which include pilots and flight attendants, the 1,250-hour requirement doesn't apply. Instead, the hours-worked requirement for FMLA eligibility will be met if the flight crew employee has worked or been paid for:

- at least 60% of the applicable monthly guarantee, and
- at least 504 hours.

In 2013, the Department of Labor amended its regulations to define key terms and provide some ground rules for applying the 2010 amendment to the law. The following terms apply to airline flight crews:

- **Applicable monthly guarantee:**
  - For non-reserve flight crew members: the minimum number of hours for which the employer has agreed to schedule the employee for any given month.
  - For reserve status flight crew members: the number of hours for which the employer has agreed to pay the employee for any given month.
- **Hours worked:** the employee's duty hours during the previous 12-month period.
- **Hours paid:** the number of hours for which the employee received wages during the previous 12-month period.

Personal commute time, vacation, and medical or sick leave do not count toward the 504 hours of service requirement for these employees.

If Intermittent FMLA Leave Reduces an Employee's Hours

Some employees use their FMLA leave all at once. For example, an employee might take 12 weeks off after the birth of a new child, or to recover from a serious car accident. Sometimes, however, an employee seeking FMLA leave needs occasional days, hours, or weeks off or reduced work hours (for example, from full time to part time). The employee may be entitled to intermittent or reduced-schedule leave under the FMLA. (Chapter 7 covers this topic in more detail.)

An unintended consequence of taking leave in this manner can be that the employee's hours fall below the 1,250-hour minimum. But you can't deny FMLA leave as a result: As long as the employee still needs the reduced schedule for the same condition that necessitated FMLA leave in the first place, the employee remains eligible.

EXAMPLE: Though her regular schedule requires her to work 25 hours per week, Yvonne has been on an FMLA-qualified reduced schedule of ten hours per week for the past 12 weeks. Yvonne notifies you that she needs to continue her reduced schedule. She has all the necessary paperwork and has not used up all of her FMLA leave time.

In preparation for meeting with Yvonne, you count up her hours for the past 12 months. Because of her reduced schedule, Yvonne has worked fewer than 1,250 hours in the last 12 months. Can you deny Yvonne's request for a continued reduced schedule?

No. As long as Yvonne was qualified when she started leave and needs the reduced schedule for the same condition, she has a right to take the full 12 weeks of leave, as calculated for a part-time employee (discussed in Chapter 7).

The same is true if the employee takes some FMLA leave in a continuous block, then needs more leave for the same condition. Although the employee isn't taking a few hours at a time or working a reduced schedule, this counts as intermittent leave, for which eligibility need not be recalculated in the same leave year.

The rules are different if an employee needs FMLA leave for a different condition. In this situation, you must redetermine the employee's eligibility. If the employee's previous intermittent leave has reduced the employee's hours below the 1,250-hour threshold, the employee is not eligible for leave for an unrelated condition.

> EXAMPLE: Let's go back to Yvonne, whose regular work schedule calls for 25 hours a week, but who has been working only ten hours a week for the last three months. Yvonne needed this intermittent leave to care for her father, who has a serious health condition. Yvonne's father is on the mend, but now Yvonne requests two weeks of FMLA leave so she can have knee surgery. Is she entitled to this leave?
>
> No. In the last 12 months, Yvonne has worked ten hours a week for 12 weeks (120 hours), plus 25 hours a week for 40 weeks (1,000 hours), for a grand total of 1,120 hours. If she needed to stay on her reduced-leave schedule to continue caring for her father, she would still be entitled to FMLA leave. But because she wants leave for an unrelated condition, you must recalculate her hours—and she hasn't met the 1,250-hour threshold for FMLA eligibility.

Keeping Track of Employees' Work Hours

Because employees' eligibility for FMLA leave depends on how long they've worked for the company and how many hours they've worked, you must keep track of all employees' work hours. After all, an employee's eligibility can change over time. A newly hired full-time employee, for example, won't be eligible until he or she has worked for the company for at least 12 months. After a year, however, the employee may be eligible.

And it's not just that employees who weren't eligible can become eligible in the future: An employee who qualified for FMLA leave in the past may not be eligible later on. Maybe the employee hasn't worked enough hours in the previous year or has already used up all his or her FMLA leave.

To make sure that an employee who requests leave is actually entitled to it, keep good records of actual hours worked—and leave taken—for all of your company's employees. If your company's records or a compensation agreement with the employee don't accurately reflect actual hours worked, your company will have to prove that the employee didn't work enough hours to qualify for FMLA leave. Even unpaid time worked by an employee (for example, overtime worked by an exempt employee not entitled to overtime pay) counts toward the 1,250-hour requirement, so it is important to keep thorough records of all time employees actually work, whether paid or not.

Most payroll systems provide a running total of hours worked by employees, so you may already have adequate records. If your company keeps time sheets or requires employees to punch a time clock, these records may provide all the documentation you need.

If you don't have some readily available source of documentation, the best practice is to keep a separate chart of hours worked for each employee. This isn't as complicated as it sounds. You can create a simple spreadsheet, like the one below, and update each employee's hours at the end of each pay period. If you have a payroll system, you may even be able to export those numbers directly. This book's companion page includes a downloadable copy of this form. See Appendix C for the link to the forms in this book.

SAMPLE 1:

FMLA Hours Worked		
Employee Name: _____ Employee A _____		
Start date	Hours worked in the 12 months prior to requested leave	Dates FMLA leave taken
1/14/10	3,000	3/22/14 – 5/10/14

SAMPLE 2:

FMLA Hours Worked		
Employee Name: _____ Employee B _____		
Start date	**Hours worked in the 12 months prior to requested leave**	**Dates FMLA leave taken**
4/25/15	300	Not eligible

Don't forget to track hours worked by employees who aren't entitled to earn overtime pay (called "exempt employees"). Many companies don't routinely record hours worked by exempt employees. After all, these employees are not typically paid by the hour, but instead must put in as many hours as it takes to get the job done.

Unless you have records showing the actual hours worked by exempt employees, however, you must assume that they have worked the required 1,250 hours as long as they've been employed for 12 months. You may also need to know the exact hours worked by an exempt employee if he or she wants to take intermittent or reduced-schedule leave. This type of leave is calculated as a reduction in the hours or days the employee typically works, so you can't figure out how much FMLA intermittent or reduced-schedule leave time an exempt employee is entitled to unless you know how many hours the employee has worked.

TIP

Tracking exempt employees' hours won't change their exempt status. One of the cardinal rules of wage and hour law is to avoid treating exempt employees like nonexempt employees. For example, if you dock an exempt employee's pay for showing up an hour late, you are treating that employee like an hourly worker—and the Department of Labor may require you to pay overtime to that employee and others who hold the same position. When it comes to tracking hours for FMLA purposes, however, you don't have to worry: You can keep records of an exempt employee's hours without inadvertently losing that employee's exemption status.

Managers' Flowchart: FMLA-Eligible Employees

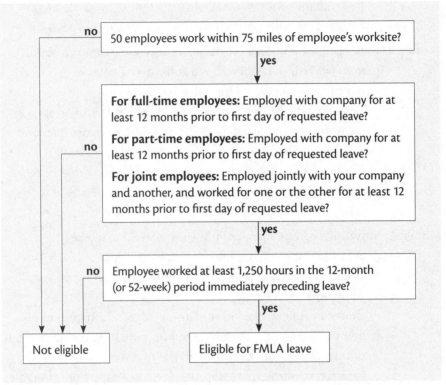

Common Mistakes Regarding Employee Eligibility—And How to Avoid Them

Mistake 1: **Denying FMLA leave to employees who are eligible, or granting it to those who are not eligible, because work hours aren't properly documented.**

Avoid this mistake by taking the following steps:

- Keep accurate records of employee work hours, including all time that counts toward the FMLA hours requirement (military leave, hours for which the employee is not paid, and so on).
- Track hours for exempt employees, even if you don't do so for any other purpose.

- Create a chart that keeps a running total of each employee's hours that count toward FMLA eligibility, if your company doesn't have other records you can use for this purpose.

Mistake 2: Misjudging an employee's eligibility by calculating company size, months worked, and hours worked at the wrong time.

Avoid this mistake by taking the following steps:

- Calculate whether the employee's worksite has at least 50 employees within a 75-mile radius on the date the employee requests leave, not the date the employee's leave is scheduled to begin.
- Compute the months and hours worked by an employee requesting FMLA leave as of the date the requested leave will start, not the date the employee requests leave.

Mistake 3: Miscalculating how many months an employee has worked.

Avoid this mistake by taking the following steps:

- Count any week in which the employee showed up on your company's payroll.
- Count all time worked toward an employee's 12-month minimum; these months don't have to be consecutive, but don't count time worked before a break in service of seven years or more.
- Count time the employee spent on leave as time worked if your company paid compensation or provided benefits during the leave or the employee was on military leave.

Mistake 4: Miscounting hours worked.

Avoid this mistake by taking the following steps:

- Include all hours that count toward FMLA eligibility, including unpaid hours, compensable travel time, and time spent in continuing education.
- Exclude time spent on leave unless the employee was on military leave or your company counts leave time as hours worked for overtime purposes.
- Allow employees whose hours have dropped below the minimum required due to intermittent leave to continue taking leave for the same condition; if the employee needs leave for a new condition, you must redetermine the employee's eligibility.

Managers' Checklist: Is the Employee Eligible for FMLA Leave?

☐ There are 50 or more employees working within 75 miles of the leave-seeking employee's worksite.

  ☐ I counted telecommuting or other employees not physically present at the worksite where they report or where they receive work assignments.

  ☐ I measured the 75-mile radius based on the most direct surface travel routes, like roads, highways, and waterways.

  ☐ I counted all buildings within a reasonable geographic vicinity as a single worksite and measured the 75-mile radius from those buildings.

☐ The employee worked for the company for at least 12 months (or 52 weeks) prior to the first day of the requested leave.

  ☐ I counted the employee as working in any week in which the employee was on company payroll, even if the employee worked intermittently or part time.

  ☐ I counted the employee as working in any week in which the employee was on leave and getting pay or benefits from my company.

  ☐ I did not count the employee as working in any week in which the employee was suspended or should otherwise have been working but wasn't.

  ☐ I didn't count any time the employee worked prior to a break in service of seven or more years, unless the break was occasioned by National Guard or Reserve obligations or was pursuant to a written agreement indicating our intent to rehire the employee after the break.

☐ Company records show that the employee worked at least 1,250 hours in the 12 months prior to the first day of the requested leave.

  ☐ I counted only the hours that the employee actually worked, whether paid or not.

  ☐ Because my company does not count time on leave when calculating hours for overtime pay purposes, I did not count any hours that the employee was on leave.

  ☐ For airline flight crew employees, I did not apply the 1,250-hour rule, but instead made sure the employee worked or was paid for at least 60% of the monthly guarantee and at least 504 hours in the past 12 months.

Leave for a Serious Health Condition

Your Role in Identifying a Serious Health Condition..55

What Is a Serious Health Condition?..56

    Inpatient Care...57

    Incapacity for More Than Three Days Plus Continuing Treatment..............58

    Pregnancy or Prenatal Care..62

    Chronic Serious Health Condition 63

    Permanent or Long-Term Incapacity..64

    Multiple Treatments 64

    Conditions That Are Not Typically Covered 65

Leave for Employee's Own Serious Health Condition 68

Leave for a Family Member's Serious Health Condition......................................69

    Who Is a Family Member Under the FMLA 70

    Proving a Family Relationship 72

    Caring for a Family Member 74

Common Mistakes Regarding Serious Health Conditions—

    And How to Avoid Them...77

Chapter Highlights

☆ The FMLA allows an eligible employee to take time off for his or her own serious health condition or to care for a family member who has a serious health condition.

☆ It's not your responsibility to diagnose employees; you just have to know enough about what qualifies as a "serious health condition" to realize when an employee requests or takes time off that might qualify for FMLA protection.

☆ There are six categories of serious health conditions:
  • inpatient care
  • incapacity for more than three days with continuing treatment by a health care provider
  • incapacity relating to pregnancy or prenatal care
  • chronic serious health conditions
  • permanent or long-term incapacity, and
  • certain kinds of conditions requiring multiple treatments.

☆ To take time off for his or her own serious health condition, an employee must be unable to perform the functions of his or her job.

☆ An employee may take time off to care for a spouse, parent, or child with a serious health condition. In-laws, domestic partners, siblings, grandparents, and other family members don't count under the FMLA (but may under state law).

☆ An employee is caring for a family member when the employee provides physical or psychological care, arranges for care or changes in care, provides necessary transportation, or fills in for other care providers.

Eligible employees are entitled to take FMLA leave for their own serious health conditions or to care for family members with serious health conditions. That sounds simple enough, but this has proven to be a fairly complicated standard to apply. Most of the controversy involves the definition of a serious health condition: which illnesses or conditions qualify, how long an employee has to be incapacitated to be eligible for leave, what happens when a minor problem turns into a serious condition, and so on.

This chapter untangles these complications and explains what qualifies as a serious health condition. We cover the definitions and eligibility criteria, and we provide checklists and charts to help you sort through the issues and figure out whether an employee might qualify for this type of FMLA leave.

Your Role in Identifying a Serious Health Condition

After learning that an employee's (or family member's) health condition must be serious—and that there's a complex legal definition for that word—before an employee can take FMLA leave, some managers start to worry. After all, most managers aren't doctors, and their job responsibilities don't include diagnosing employees, let alone family members of employees. Is every manager going to have to learn how to read X-rays and lab results just to administer the FMLA?

Happily, the answer is no. It's not your job to determine whether an employee really does have a serious health condition; that's for doctors and other health care providers to decide. You simply have to know enough about how the FMLA defines a serious health condition to recognize when an employee asks for or takes time off for what might be an FMLA-protected reason. If the FMLA applies, you'll need to give the employee required notices (see Chapter 8), formally designate the time off as FMLA leave (also covered in Chapter 8), and ask the employee to provide a medical certification from a health care provider confirming that the leave is for a serious health condition (see Chapter 9). But you'll only know that it's time to start this process if you're familiar enough with the categories of serious health conditions to recognize that the FMLA might be in play.

EXAMPLE: Cari tells you that she is pregnant. After congratulations and small talk, Cari says she has been having severe morning sickness and might need to take some time off—or, at least, come in late when she's really feeling crummy. Because you're reading this book, you immediately realize that the time off Cari is requesting could be FMLA-protected. Should your next step be to question Cari closely about her symptoms, so you can decide whether she is truly incapacitated by her morning sickness?

No. You don't have the right to insist that Cari discuss this type of personal health information with you. (It could even be illegal under the laws of some states.) Instead, you should give Cari the required notices and paperwork to designate her time off as FMLA leave and ask her to provide a medical certification from her health care provider.

This doesn't mean that you have to blindly accept whatever the employee and his or her health care provider tell you, however. If, based on the information you receive, you question whether the employee (or family member) really has a serious health condition, you can request a second opinion (Chapter 9 explains how).

TIP

When an employee takes sick leave, workers' compensation leave, disability leave, or leave to care for a family member, always ask yourself whether the FMLA applies. An employee doesn't have to specifically request "FMLA" leave to be protected by the law: As long as the employee is eligible and takes time off for a covered reason, the FMLA applies and you should designate the time as FMLA leave. Chapter 8 explains how much information an employee has to provide and how to designate leave; for now, just remember that an employee who is taking another type of leave might also covered by the FMLA.

What Is a Serious Health Condition?

To qualify for FMLA leave, an employee must have a serious health condition or have a family member with a serious health condition. To be eligible, the employee or family member must have an illness, injury, impairment, or physical or mental condition that involves:

- **inpatient care** at a hospital, hospice, or residential medical care facility
- **incapacity for more than three full calendar days** with continuing treatment by a health care provider
- incapacity due to **pregnancy or prenatal care**
- incapacity or treatment for a **chronic serious health condition**
- **permanent or long-term incapacity** for a condition for which treatment may not be effective (such as a terminal illness), or
- absence for **multiple treatments** for either (1) restorative surgery following an injury or accident, or (2) a condition that would require an absence of more than three days if not treated.

Multiple and Undiagnosed Conditions Count

The FMLA applies to ailments for which health care providers have been unable to offer a definitive diagnosis, as well as to incapacitation that is caused by multiple ailments, even if it doesn't (yet) have a name. As long as someone's medical situation fits into one of the categories above, it's a serious health condition.

Inpatient Care

This is probably the easiest category to recognize as a serious health condition. A condition that involves inpatient care—in other words, an overnight stay—at a hospital, hospice, or residential medical care facility qualifies as a serious health condition covered by the FMLA. An employee is entitled to FMLA leave for the time spent receiving inpatient care and for periods of incapacity or subsequent treatment connected to that inpatient care.

A person is incapacitated by a serious medical condition if he or she is unable to work, attend school, or perform other regular daily activities due to the condition, treatment for the condition, or recovery from the condition. This means, for example, that an employee who was hospitalized for an appendectomy would be entitled to FMLA leave not only for the period of time spent in the hospital before, during, and after the operation, but also for time spent at home recuperating from the procedure.

Follow-up treatment after an inpatient stay is also protected. For example, if a person was hospitalized for surgery, return visits to the doctor for post-operative care would also be covered under the FMLA. The person doesn't have to be incapacitated by the treatment or be out for more than three days: As long as the subsequent treatment is connected to the condition requiring inpatient care, it's covered.

> **EXAMPLE:** Jesse takes a nasty fall while cleaning the gutters on his roof and suffers a major concussion. He goes to the emergency room, where they keep him overnight for observation. He spends the next day at home resting, then returns to work. By midmorning, he has a crashing headache. He calls his doctor, who advises him to come in immediately to be checked for complications. All of Jesse's time off—in the hospital, at home, and at the doctor's office—is covered by the FMLA.
>
> If Jesse had never suffered a concussion but simply got a bad headache at work and decided to go to the doctor, his time off might not be FMLA-protected. Because it isn't subsequent treatment following an inpatient stay, it doesn't qualify as this type of serious health condition. Depending on what the medical cause is, how long the problem lasts, and what type of treatment he gets, however, it might fall into one of the other categories of serious health conditions.

Incapacity for More Than Three Days Plus Continuing Treatment

Someone who is incapacitated for more than three days *and* requires continuing treatment from a health care provider also has a serious health condition under the FMLA. This category of serious health condition has been the most difficult for employers to understand and administer, and it's easy to see why. It covers a lot of gray area because it marks the dividing line between minor ailments such as colds and stomachaches (which are usually not covered by the FMLA; see "Conditions That Are Not Typically Covered," below) and more serious problems that are obviously protected (like a terminal illness or nonelective surgery).

To figure out whether an ailment fits into this category, you must understand how to measure the three-day requirement, who qualifies as a health care provider, and what constitutes continuing treatment.

The "More Than Three-Days" Requirement

To qualify under this category, the employee (or employee's family member) must be incapacitated for *more* than three full consecutive days. The days must be consecutive, but they need not be business days. An employee who is incapacitated Friday through Monday would qualify, for example.

It's not entirely clear what constitutes "more than" three days. Some courts have found that an employee must be incapacitated for at least four days to qualify; others have found that an employee who is sick for any more than 72 hours is covered. Because of this confusion, the best practice is to assume that an employee who is incapacitated for more than 72 hours is covered.

Who Is a Health Care Provider?

Health care providers are defined quite broadly by the FMLA. They include not only medical doctors, but also:

- doctors of osteopathy
- podiatrists
- dentists
- optometrists
- chiropractors (only for manual manipulation of the spine to treat a subluxation of the spine—that is, misalignment of vertebrae—identified by X-ray)
- clinical psychologists
- physician assistants
- nurse providers
- nurse midwives
- clinical social workers, and
- Christian Science providers.

Health care providers who practice outside of the United States also qualify, as long as they are authorized to practice within the laws of the country where they work and the services they provide are within the scope of that authorized practice.

Finally, any health care provider from whom the employer or the employer's group health plan will accept certification of a serious health condition for purposes of substantiating a claim for health care benefits also qualifies. In other words, if your company treats someone as a health care

provider for purposes of allowing or disallowing benefits claims, it must treat that person as a health care provider under the FMLA.

> **EXAMPLE:** Your company's health care plan accepts certifications from chiropractors documenting a wide variety of employee injuries and ailments, including repetitive stress disorders, spinal problems, and neck injuries. Steven sees his chiropractor for pain in his wrists and forearms. After performing a series of tests and physical manipulations, the chiropractor determines that Steven has carpal tunnel syndrome. The chiropractor gives Steven some exercises, gives him braces to wear, and advises him not to do any typing or other activities that will cause strain for three weeks.
>
> Steven asks for FMLA leave and gives you a medical certification from his chiropractor. Because Steven's chiropractor didn't take any X-rays and isn't treating Steven for subluxation of the spine, you intend to tell Steven that he has to get a medical certification from a different type of health care provider.
>
> But wait: Your company's health care plan accepts certifications from chiropractors not just regarding subluxation of the spine, but on a broader variety of conditions and ailments. As a result, Steven's chiropractor qualifies as a health care provider under the FMLA, even though he doesn't meet the usual criteria for chiropractors. If you question whether Steven's condition qualifies as a serious health condition, you are free to request a second opinion (as explained in Chapter 9).

How Much Treatment Is Required

An employee who's out sick for more than three days does not necessarily have a serious health condition under the FMLA. To qualify in this category, the employee's (or family member's) condition must also involve continuing treatment by a health care provider.

Because "continuing treatment" is open to some interpretation, the FMLA regulations provide two definitions. One of the following must be true for the employee or family member to meet the continuing treatment requirement:

- The employee or family member has had at least two treatments by a health care provider, a nurse under the direct supervision of a health care provider, or a provider of health care services under order of, or on referral by, a health care provider. Both treatments must take place within 30 days of the first day of incapacity, absent extenuating circumstances, and

the first treatment must take place within seven days of the first day of incapacity. (Extenuating circumstances might include that the provider has no available appointments within the 30-day period.)

- The employee or family member has had at least one treatment by a health care provider, resulting in a regimen of continuing treatment under the provider's supervision. Again, the treatment must take place within seven days of the first day of incapacity.

For both of these definitions, "treatment" means an actual in-person visit to the health care provider, not a telephone call or email exchange. And, in both cases, the necessity of treatment visits or a regimen of continuing treatment must be determined by the health care provider. In other words, the patient's decision to make a second appointment within the 30-day period doesn't convert a minor ailment into a serious health condition.

A continuing regimen of treatment refers only to treatments that require the participation of a health care provider. For example, taking prescription medications or engaging in therapies that require special equipment (such as an oxygen tank) qualify as a regimen of continuing treatment. However, taking over-the-counter medications or staying in bed does not—even if that's just what the doctor ordered—because you could have made these decisions on your own.

> **EXAMPLE 1:** John has a sore throat, stuffy nose, and cough. He calls his HMO's advice line, and a nurse provider tells him that there's a nasty cold going around and that he should stay in bed and drink lots of water. John doesn't have a serious health condition: he didn't visit the doctor at all, and he isn't following a continuing regimen of treatment.

> **EXAMPLE 2:** Consuela has the same symptoms as John and goes home sick late Tuesday morning. Her symptoms worsen, and she decides to visit her doctor on Thursday. The doctor finds that she has strep throat and prescribes a ten-day course of antibiotics. Consuela is down for the count until Saturday evening, when she starts to feel better. Consuela has a serious health condition: She was incapacitated for more than three days, visited her doctor once, and had a continuing regimen of treatment.

> **EXAMPLE 3:** Because most of her employees have been sick, Marta finally comes down with the dreaded bug. Marta had several bouts with pneumonia as a child, so she goes to her doctor as soon as she realizes that she's sick. The doctor finds

that she doesn't yet have pneumonia, but he also doesn't like the way her lungs sound. Marta doesn't want to take antibiotics unless it's absolutely necessary, so her doctor asks her to come back for a follow-up appointment in several days to make sure her lungs have cleared up. At the second visit, Marta sounds fine; she returns to work after four days off. Marta has a serious health condition: She was incapacitated for more than three days, and she made two visits to the doctor.

Lessons from the Real World

Leave necessary to determine that a condition isn't serious might be FMLA-protected.

James Woodman was a truck driver for Miesel Sysco Food Services. When Woodman suffered chest pains, he went to his doctor, who recommended a series of tests to determine their source and whether Woodman had suffered a heart attack. The doctor also recommended that Woodman take time off until the problem was diagnosed.

Ultimately, the tests showed that Woodman had not suffered a heart attack. His celebration was short-lived, however: Soon afterwards, the company fired him for taking unauthorized leave. Because he didn't have a heart attack, the company said, he also didn't have a serious health condition, so his absence wasn't covered by the FMLA.

The Michigan Court of Appeals disagreed with the company's conclusion, however. The FMLA's definition of treatment includes examinations to determine whether a serious health condition exists, which is precisely what Woodson required, as determined by his doctor.

Woodman v. Miesel Sysco Food Service Co., 8 W & H 2d 619 (Mich. Ct. App. 2002).

Pregnancy or Prenatal Care

Incapacity due to pregnancy or for prenatal care qualifies as a serious health condition. The employee need not be out for more than three days nor actually visit a doctor to fall into this category. As long as she is unable to work or perform other regular, daily activities because of her pregnancy, she

has a serious health condition. For example, a woman who suffers severe morning sickness or is ordered by her doctor to spend the last month of her pregnancy on bed rest qualifies under this part of the definition.

Visits to the doctor for prenatal care also fall within this category. The woman need not be incapacitated or suffering from medical complications to qualify; even routine check-ups qualify for leave.

Lessons from the *Real World*

Back pain, morning sickness, and pregnancy-related migraines add up to a serious health condition.

Charity Wierman claimed that she was fired from her job as manager of a convenience store for taking time off that was protected under the FMLA. Wierman was pregnant and suffered from back pain, morning sickness, and pregnancy-related migraines. The court found that this was sufficient evidence to put her employer on notice that she had a serious health condition, and that her absences might be protected by the FMLA.

Ultimately, Wierman lost her FMLA claim, however. Although she was fired shortly after her employer gave her FMLA paperwork to complete, her employer showed that she was fired not for her time off, but for stealing company property: eating the pastries and fountain drinks that the store sold.

Wierman v. Casey's General Stores, 638 F.3d 984 (8th Cir. 2011).

Chronic Serious Health Condition

Chronic serious health conditions are also covered by the FMLA. A chronic serious health condition:

- requires periodic visits for treatment, defined by regulation as at least two visits per year with a health care provider or nurse acting under a provider's supervision
- continues over an extended period of time, and
- may cause episodic, rather than continuing, incapacity.

These conditions needn't cause incapacity for more than three days, nor must they involve continuing treatment. Instead, this category is intended

to encompass long-lasting conditions that require ongoing management and treatment, such as diabetes, epilepsy, or asthma.

> **EXAMPLE:** Raymond has multiple sclerosis (MS), a disease of the central nervous system that can cause loss of vision, extreme fatigue, muscle weakness, loss of coordination, and other neurological problems. He sees his doctor every three months. He is generally able to care for himself and work, with the help of a cane to walk steadily and medications to control his symptoms. On occasion, however, his symptoms become more severe and confine him to his bed. Raymond's daughter, Cheryl, requests time off to care for her father when his symptoms become exacerbated. Is her leave protected by the FMLA?
>
> Most likely, assuming she meets the requirements for caring for a family member (discussed below). Because Raymond's MS requires periodic treatment, is a permanent condition, and causes episodic incapacity, it qualifies as a chronic serious health condition.

Some mental conditions—such as major depression and bipolar disorder—might also qualify under this category. Often, these conditions are long-term, episodic, and require ongoing treatment but can be largely controlled with medication. Again, you won't have to make the final call; you'll just need to recognize the possibility when the employee requests leave.

Permanent or Long-Term Incapacity

Someone who is incapacitated permanently or for the long term by a condition that is not necessarily amenable to treatment has a serious health condition, as long as he or she is under the supervision of a health care provider. Actual treatment is not required to qualify under this part of the definition; it is enough that the person's care is supervised by a health care provider.

Examples of conditions that might fall into this category are Alzheimer's disease, terminal cancer, or advanced amyotrophic lateral sclerosis (also known as ALS or Lou Gehrig's disease).

Multiple Treatments

Someone who is absent for multiple treatments has a serious health condition if the treatments are for:

- restorative surgery after an accident or injury, or
- a condition that would require an absence of more than three days if not treated.

Examples of conditions that might qualify in the first subcategory include surgery to reset a broken limb or repair a torn ligament. The second subcategory includes treatments for severe arthritis, dialysis for kidney disease, and cancer treatment. (Of course, cancer might qualify as a serious health condition under other categories as well—for example, if hospitalization and/or surgery were required.)

> **EXAMPLE:** Geri has been diagnosed with breast cancer. She had a lumpectomy and is undergoing chemotherapy. Every Tuesday afternoon, she goes in for treatment. The treatment takes several hours, and she often feels too nauseated to return to work afterward. As her therapy progresses, her reaction to the treatment becomes more severe; she sometimes has to take all or part of Wednesday off, and sometimes she even feels sick Monday afternoon and Tuesday morning, in anticipation of her treatment. All of this time—the time she actually spends getting chemotherapy and the time during which she is incapacitated by her treatment—is FMLA-protected leave.

Conditions That Are Not Typically Covered

The FMLA does not create hard-and-fast rules that particular illnesses or diseases are always, or never, serious health conditions. Instead, the facts of each situation are considered individually. After all, one person might breeze through a bout of bronchitis without missing more than a day of work but another with the same illness might have to be hospitalized for complications. In this situation, the first person would not have a serious health condition, but the second would.

Nevertheless, there are certain ailments that don't typically qualify as serious health conditions. These include:

- cosmetic treatments (other than for restorative purposes) unless complications arise or inpatient care is required
- colds and flu
- earaches
- upset stomachs and minor ulcers

- headaches other than migraines, and
- routine dental or orthodontic problems or periodontal disease.

This doesn't mean you can automatically exclude these conditions from FMLA coverage. It depends on the facts. One person's headache might be the result of eye strain or sinus congestion; another's might be a symptom of a brain tumor. Breast enhancement plastic surgery would not be covered if it is purely cosmetic, but reconstructive surgery after a mastectomy or breast reduction surgery necessary to relieve severe back pain, is likely covered.

Substance Abuse

Substance abuse may qualify as a serious health condition, if it meets one of the definitions described above. However, the employee may not take FMLA-protected leave for the effects of substance abuse (for example, because the employee is using drugs or hung over). The company is required to provide FMLA leave for treatment only.

An employee who takes FMLA leave while getting treatment for substance abuse may not be fired solely for taking FMLA leave; that would violate the law. However, if the employer has an established, communicated policy providing that employees may be fired for substance abuse, and it applies the policy consistently to all employees, it may fire an employee for substance abuse even if the employee is out on FMLA leave while seeking treatment. The fact that an employee is using the FMLA may not protect that employee from termination for substance abuse, depending on the employer's policies.

Although the FMLA does not prohibit you from firing an employee for substance abuse even if the employee is seeking treatment, state law may. In California, for example, employers with at least 25 employees must allow employees to take time off to enter rehabilitation treatment as a reasonable accommodation. Before you terminate an employee who is on leave for rehab or other treatment for substance abuse, it's a good idea to get some legal advice.

Is It a Serious Health Condition?		
Category	**Requirements**	**Examples**
Inpatient treatment	Overnight stay in a hospital, hospice, or residential medical care facility	Inpatient surgery Hospitalization Overnight hospital stay for observation
Incapacity for more than 3 days and continuing treatment	Incapacity for more than three days and either: • at least two visits to a health care provider within 30 days, or • one visit to a health care provider and an ongoing regimen of treatment	Pneumonia Migraine Chicken pox Mononucleosis Viral infection
Pregnancy/prenatal care	Incapacity due to pregnancy or prenatal care	Severe morning sickness Doctor's appointments for prenatal care, including OB-GYN visits, sonograms, visits or treatment for complications of pregnancy Medically required bed rest
Chronic serious health conditions	Condition that: • requires periodic visits for treatment (at least two per year) • continues over an extended period of time, and • may cause episodic, rather than continuing, incapacity	Epilepsy Asthma Diabetes Multiple sclerosis Sickle cell anemia
Permanent/long-term incapacity	Permanent or long-term incapacity, under the supervision of a health care provider	Cancer Alzheimer's disease Stroke ALS
Multiple treatments	Treatments for: • restorative surgery after an accident or injury, or • a condition that would require an absence of more than three days if not treated	Arthritis treatment Dialysis Chemotherapy Radiation therapy Surgery to reset a broken bone, repair a torn ligament, or treat burns

Leave for Employee's Own Serious Health Condition

When an employee takes time off for his or her own serious health condition, an additional qualification applies: The employee must not only have a serious health condition as defined above, but must also be unable to perform the functions of his or her job.

An employee is unable to perform the functions of the position if the employee cannot work at all or cannot perform one or more of the essential functions of the job, as defined by the Americans with Disabilities Act (ADA). Under the ADA, essential functions are the fundamental duties of the position: those tasks that the person holding the job absolutely must be able to do.

It can be tough to figure out which job duties are essential, unless you already have a job description that designates those functions. If you don't, you'll need to consider which functions are absolutely necessary to doing the job successfully and which are not.

RESOURCE

Need help drafting job descriptions? For detailed guidance on identifying a job's essential functions and using them to create a legal, effective job description, see *The Job Description Handbook*, by Margie Mader-Clark (Nolo).

The Equal Employment Opportunity Commission (EEOC), the federal agency that enforces the ADA, looks at the following factors in determining whether a function is essential:

- the employer's own assessment of which functions are essential, as demonstrated by job descriptions written before the employer posts or advertises for the position (this caveat is intended to discourage employers from designating essential functions solely to disqualify particular applicants with disabilities from holding the job)
- whether the position exists to perform that function
- the experience of workers who actually hold that position
- the time spent performing that function
- the consequences of not performing that function
- whether other employees are available to perform that function, and
- the degree of expertise or skill required to perform the function.

If an employee must be out of work to receive treatment for a serious health condition (for example, for prenatal care, nonelective surgery, or a doctor's appointment for follow-up care), the employee is considered unable to work for that period of time.

> **EXAMPLE:** Clara tore a ligament in her leg while playing soccer. She had surgery to repair the ligament, and her doctor told her not to walk much on that leg for several weeks. Clara is a receptionist for a large company. Her job involves greeting visitors, answering phones, receiving packages and mail, and so on. Because Clara can perform the essential functions of her job while seated at her desk, she probably isn't eligible to take several weeks off under the FMLA. Although the time she actually spends in surgery and follow-up care would be covered, the weeks of recovery would not.
>
> If Clara's job duties required her to walk around the building—for example, to collect or deliver mail, get refreshments for visitors, and so on—the company would have to decide whether these are essential duties or not, using the criteria listed above. If Clara held a much more physical job (for example, if she worked as a bike messenger or a laborer in a warehouse), she would clearly be unable to perform her job's essential duties and would be entitled to FMLA leave.

RELATED TOPIC

Other laws may apply. An employee's serious health condition might also qualify as a disability under the Americans with Disabilities Act (ADA) and similar state laws, and/or it might be the result of an on-the-job injury that's covered by workers' compensation. Chapter 12 explains what these laws require and how they might overlap with the FMLA.

Leave for a Family Member's Serious Health Condition

An employee is also entitled to take leave to care for a family member who has a serious health condition, as defined above. To figure out whether an employee qualifies for this type of leave, however, you must also understand which family members are covered by this provision of the law and how the FMLA defines "caring for" a family member.

Who Is a Family Member Under the FMLA

An employee may take time off to care for a spouse, child, or parent with a serious health condition. Here is how the FMLA defines these terms for this provision; different definitions apply to military family leave (see Chapter 6):

- **Spouse.** A spouse is a husband or wife to whom the employee is legally married—domestic partners or live-in partners aren't covered. In the handful of states that recognize common-law marriage, a couple that meets the state's requirements may take FMLA leave to care for each other. Same-sex spouses formerly were not entitled to FMLA leave to care for each other. However, this changed in June of 2013, when the U.S. Supreme Court found that the definition of marriage set forth in the federal Defense of Marriage Act (the legal union of "one man and one woman") was unconstitutional. As a result of that decision, the Department of Labor immediately changed the definition of "spouse" under the FMLA to include employees in a legal same-sex marriage if they live in a state that recognizes their marriage (a "place of residence" rule). However, this changed on February 25, 2015, when the Department of Labor amended the FMLA regulations to provide that same-sex spouses are covered if their marriage was valid in the place where it was entered into (a "place of celebration" rule). As long as the employee's marriage was legal at the time and place it occurred, the employee is covered, even if the state where the employee currently works does not recognize same-sex marriage.

  For couples that were married in a foreign country, the rule is slightly different. Their marriage will be recognized, and they will be considered "spouses" for purposes of FMLA leave, as long as (1) their marriage was valid where it was entered into, and (2) their marriage could have been entered into in at least one state.

> **CAUTION**
>
> **The FMLA doesn't cover domestic partners, but state law might.**
> Some states' family and medical leave laws include more family members. For example, the California Family Rights Act (CFRA) allows employees to take

time off to care for a domestic partner. Consider both the FMLA and your state's law when evaluating an employee's request for leave. Chapter 11 and Appendix A cover this issue in more detail.

- **Child.** An employee may take FMLA leave to care for a biological child, adopted child, stepchild, foster child, or legal ward with a serious health condition. (This includes a same-sex spouse's child who became the employee's stepchild through marriage.) An employee may also take time off to care for a child for whom the employee intends to assume the role of parent by providing day-to-day care or financial support. No biological, adoptive, or formal legal relationship is necessary. (In legal terms, this is called serving "in loco parentis," or in the place of a parent.) Children are covered only until they reach the age of 18, unless they are incapable of taking care of themselves because of a physical or mental disability. These criteria must be assessed as of the date leave is scheduled to begin; if the child is under 18 on that day, the employee is entitled to leave.

  > **EXAMPLE:** Sarah's sister, Frances, is a single mother. After being convicted of selling drugs, Frances was sentenced to three years in prison. While Frances is serving her time, Sarah is taking care of Frances's son, Terry. Terry gets the measles, and Sarah asks for FMLA leave to care for him. Because Sarah is Terry's aunt, and nephews aren't covered by the FMLA, you deny her request. Did you do the right thing?
  >
  > No. Although Sarah is Terry's aunt, she is also assuming a parental role while while Frances is in prison. This relationship is covered by the FMLA.

- **Parent.** An employee may take FMLA leave to care for his or her biological parent, adoptive parent, stepparent, or foster parent with a serious health condition. (This includes a stepparent by a same-sex marriage, as long as the parents' marriage was valid in the state or country where it took place (and, in the case of a foreign country, the marriage could have been entered into in at least one state).) This right also extends to time off to care for someone who stood in loco parentis to the employee when the employee was a child, whether or not that person has a biological, adoptive, or legal relationship with the child.

For example, an employee may take time off to care for a grandmother who provided day to day parental care for the employee as a child. In-laws are not covered.

We Are Family—Not!

Contrary to the famous song by Sister Sledge, sisters and brothers do not qualify as family members under the FMLA (unless they are "next of kin" to a covered servicemember, as explained in Chapter 6). This means an employee may not take FMLA leave to care for a seriously ill sibling unless the employee has acted as a child or parent to the sibling. For example, an employee who raised her younger brothers and sisters after their parents died would probably be entitled to take FMLA leave to care for them.

Proving a Family Relationship

Employers are entitled to request reasonable documentation confirming that a familial relationship exists when an employee takes leave to care for a family member. This proof might be in the form of a birth certificate, papers documenting the placement of a foster child, or simply a written statement from the employee (this might be the only documentation an employee has regarding a common law spouse or a child for whom the employee acts as a parent, for example). If the employee provides an official document as evidence, the company must return it to the employee.

We have provided a form you can use to request this confirmation. A sample appears below; you can find an electronic version of this form at this book's online companion page; see Appendix C for information on accessing this material. (The form we provide includes the additional family members for whom the employee may be able to take military family leave; see Chapter 6 for more information.)

FMLA Leave to Care for a Family Member

I, ____Jerry Singer____ , have requested time off work to care for __Melissa Singer__ . I have read the definitions below and I confirm that this person qualifies as my ____child____ .

I have attached a copy of the following documents confirming this relationship:

Birth certificate

(*List any documents you can provide, such as a birth certificate, papers confirming an adoption or foster care placement, marriage certificate, next of kin designation, and so on. If you don't have any documents, please write that in the space provided.*)

Date:____10-10-xx____   Signature: *Jerry Singer*____

Definitions

Spouse: A husband or wife to whom you are legally married.

Parent: Your legal parent, or someone who had day-to-day responsibility for supporting you financially or taking care of you when you were a child.

Child: Your biological child, adopted child, stepchild, foster child, or legal ward, or a child whom you have the day-to-day responsibility to support financially or take care of.

- In the case of leave for a serious health condition, children qualify only until they reach the age of 18, unless they are incapable of taking care of themselves because of a physical or mental disability.
- In the case of leave for a qualifying exigency or military caregiver leave, children of any age qualify.

Next of kin: You qualify as next of kin to a covered servicemember, for purposes of military caregiver leave, if:

- you are a blood relative to a servicemember who has designated you as next of kin for purposes of military caregiver leave, or
- if the servicemember has not designated anyone next of kin and you are the nearest blood relative to a servicemember, other than a parent, spouse, or child. For purposes of determining who is the nearest blood relative, everyone in the highest applicable level of priority qualifies, as follows:
  - blood relatives who have been granted legal custody of the servicemember
  - siblings
  - grandparents
  - aunts and uncles, and
  - first cousins.

Lessons from the *Real World*

Son may take FMLA leave to help his sister decide whether to remove their mother from life support.

Charles Romans was a Fire and Safety Officer at a Michigan home for juvenile delinquent boys. He requested time off under the FMLA to go to the hospital where his mother was a patient and help his sister decide whether to remove his mother from life support. His employer denied him time off, and the district court upheld this decision. The court found that he didn't need to provide care because his sister was already doing so.

The federal Court of Appeals for the 6th Circuit disagreed, however. The Court of Appeals relied on the FMLA regulations, which state that an employee can qualify as "needed to provide care" for a family member, even if other family members are also available to do so. The Court of Appeals also pointed out that FMLA leave is available to make arrangements for changes in care, not merely to provide physical care. As the Court put it, "A decision regarding whether an ill mother should stay on life support would logically be encompassed by 'arrangements for changes in care.' To be sure, this is the kind of decision, like transfer to a nursing home, that few people would relish making without the help of other family members, and the regulations do not force them to do so."

Romans v. Michigan Dept. of Human Services, 668 F.3d 826 (6th Cir. 2012).

Caring for a Family Member

To take FMLA leave to care for a family member, it isn't enough that the employee takes time off to spend with a family member, even if the family member is gravely ill: The employee must actually provide care. For purposes of the FMLA, care includes:

- **physical care** (such as changing bandages, administering medication, preparing meals, helping with hygiene, assisting with physical therapy or exercise, and so on)
- **psychological care** (providing comfort and reassurance to a family member who is hospitalized or bedridden at home, for example)

- **providing necessary transportation** (to doctor's appointments, for example)
- **arranging for care or changes in care** (for example, making arrangements for a family member to move into an assisted living facility or hiring home health care aides to care for a family member), and
- **filling in for others providing care** (an employee might provide care two days a week, when the family member's usual caregiver takes time off, or might share caretaking responsibilities with other family members).

Unless it is needed for the family member's comfort and assurance, simply spending time with a family member does not qualify as care. For example, an employee who takes time off to visit his ailing parents would not be entitled to FMLA leave unless he was needed to actually care for his parents while there.

The employee need not be the only person or the only family member available to provide care. For example, an employee could take time off to care for her son who suffered a serious injury on active duty, even if the son's wife was also available to care for him.

Lessons from the *Real World*

Calling on the phone does not constitute care.

H. Charles Tellis worked for Alaska Airlines in Seattle as a maintenance mechanic. He told his manager that he needed a couple of weeks off because his wife was having difficulties with her pregnancy. The manager suggested that he take FMLA leave and told him to pick up the appropriate forms at the company's benefits office.

Tellis started his leave and requested the forms. The next day, his car broke down. He decided to fly to Atlanta, where he owned another car, and drive back home. This trip took him four days. While he was gone, his wife gave birth; his sister-in-law took care of the family while he was gone. Alaska Airlines eventually terminated Tellis's employment, based in part on his absence.

Tellis sued, arguing that his time off was covered by the FMLA because he was caring for his wife. The 9th Circuit Court of Appeals disagreed: It found that he did not provide any actual care while he was on his trip. Although Tellis claimed that he gave his wife moral support and comfort by phoning her from the road, the court found that this was not what the FMLA means by caretaking.

Tellis v. Alaska Airlines, 414 F.3d 1045 (9th Cir. 2005).

TIP

"Kin care" laws may also apply. Some states allow employees to take time off to care for a seriously ill family member or to take a family member to appointments with the doctor or dentist. Often called "kin care" laws, some of these statutes allow an employee to take unpaid leave for this purpose, while others require employers to allow employees to use their own sick leave for these types of time off.

Managers' Flowchart: Serious Health Conditions

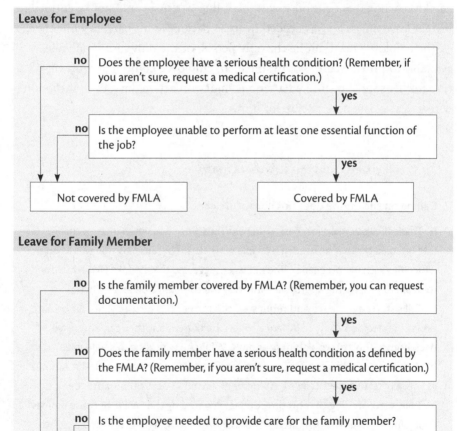

Common Mistakes Regarding Serious Health Conditions—And How to Avoid Them

Mistake 1: Denying FMLA leave for conditions that are covered.

Avoid this mistake by taking the following steps:

- Ask an employee to submit certification (see Chapter 9) whenever a serious health condition might be present. It's not your job to diagnose a serious health condition: Leave that to the health care provider.

- Remember that seemingly minor ailments can be serious health conditions. Even colds, stomachaches, and dental problems can qualify as serious health conditions if they meet the criteria.

- Keep in mind that the "more than three-days rule" doesn't apply to every type of serious health condition. An employee with a chronic serious health condition or pregnancy complications is entitled to leave even if the employee isn't incapacitated for more than three days in a row.

Mistake 2: Denying FMLA leave to care for covered family members.

Avoid this mistake by taking the following steps:

- Ask the employee to provide documentation of the familial relationship.

- Understand that "parents" and "children" refer not only to legal parents and children, but also to those whom the employee takes care of or who took care of the employee when he or she was a child.

- Don't distinguish between biological children and adopted or foster children.

Mistake 3: Failing to designate time off for an illness, injury, or disability as FMLA leave, if appropriate.

Avoid this mistake by taking the following steps:

- Make it your practice to automatically think of the FMLA when an employee takes time off for any physical or mental ailment. If it is a serious health condition, you will want to designate that time as FMLA leave.

- Consider whether an employee who goes out with a workers' comp injury is covered by the FMLA. (The answer will almost always be "yes," for reasons explained in Chapter 12.)

Leave for a New Child

Leave for Birth...83

    Multiple Births in the Same Year...83

    Conditions That Don't Count 83

Leave for Adoption...84

Leave for Placement of a Foster Child..84

Parental Certifications...85

Timing of Parenting Leave...86

Intermittent or Reduced-Schedule Leave 88

Substitution of Paid Leave...90

Parents Who Work for the Same Company...90

Combining Parenting Leave With Leave for a
Serious Health Condition 93

    Pregnancy 93

    Caring for a Child..95

Common Mistakes Regarding Leave for a New Child—
And How to Avoid Them..96

Chapter Highlights

☆ Eligible female and male employees are equally entitled to take parenting leave under the FMLA for the birth, adoption, or foster placement of a child.

☆ Female or male employees who adopt or serve as foster parents of a child may take FMLA leave to:
  • attend adoption or foster proceedings
  • attend counseling sessions
  • meet with attorneys
  • meet with doctors
  • attend court hearings, or
  • attend to other placement-related matters.

☆ You can request documents certifying an employee is a new biological, adoptive, or foster parent before granting parenting leave.

☆ Employees must conclude their parenting leave within one year of the date of birth, adoption, or foster placement of the child.

☆ Married parents who work for the same company are entitled to a combined 12 weeks of leave for the birth, adoption, or foster placement of their child. This limit doesn't apply to unmarried parents, who are each entitled to a full 12 weeks of parenting leave.

☆ Same-sex spouses married in states that recognize same-sex marriage are entitled to leave to care for and bond with a new child, regardless of whether the state where the spouses work or reside recognizes same-sex marriage.

Your professional experience likely confirms what studies show: Providing parenting leave enhances employee loyalty, morale, and productivity. Perhaps this is one reason why the parenting leave provisions of the FMLA have generated so little controversy and have resulted in relatively few complaints to the Department of Labor. Employers and employees alike benefit when employees are able to take some time off to care for a new child.

But, just because nearly everyone agrees on the value of parenting leave doesn't mean that everyone understands exactly how the rules work. The basic parenting leave provision of the FMLA provides that qualifying employees of either sex are entitled to up to 12 weeks of leave for the birth, adoption, or foster placement of a child. As with other parts of the FMLA, however, things get more complicated when you take a closer look at the details.

Some of the confusion surrounds the definition of "parent" and "spouse," while some is a result of the interplay between parenting leave and medical leave related to pregnancy or caring for ill children. For example, a female employee may request leave for the birth of her child, as well as leave for a pregnancy-related medical condition—two different categories under the FMLA, which can affect when the female employee is entitled to take leave. On top of these complications, if a child's parents work for the same company, the FMLA treats married parents and unmarried parents differently.

In response to the confusion on the part of employers and employees about who qualifies as a "parent" under the FMLA, the Department of Labor provides clarification. Under the FMLA, a "parent" includes anyone who stands "in loco parentis." Essentially, this covers anyone who assumes the status of parent toward a child by taking on parental duties. No legal recognition of the parent/child relationship (such as a birth certificate, adoption decree, or foster placement document) or blood relationship is required. In short, if an employee intends to take on the role of parent in a child's life, even a child not related to the employee or to a spouse, that employee is a "parent" for FMLA leave purposes. And, this is true *even if* both of the child's biological or legal parents are present in the child's life. As the DOL puts it, the FMLA regulations do not limit the number of parents a child may have for FMLA purposes!

Who Is a Parent Under the FMLA?

Under the DOL's clarification, a "parent" is anyone who intends to act and/or does act as a child's parent. An employee meeting this definition is entitled to take the birth, adoption, and foster placement leave described in this chapter, as well as leave to care for a child suffering a serious medical condition (covered in Chapter 4). The question of who qualifies as a parent ultimately depends on the particular facts of the situation. The main factors to be considered when an employee claims parental status are:

- the age of the child
- the degree to which the child is dependent on the employee
- the amount of support (either financial, day-to-day care, or both) the employee provides to the child, and
- the extent to which the employee exercises duties commonly associated with parenthood.

This means that an employee whose same-sex partner gives birth to, adopts, or fosters a child may be a parent of that child, in addition to the child's two biological parents, and/or the spouse of the opposite sex biological parent. The key factor is the intent of any of the nonbiological parents to take on the status of the child's parent. Some examples of potential parents for FMLA purposes include:

- unmarried same or opposite sex partners of biological, adoptive, or foster parents
- stepparents of spouse's biological, adoptive, or foster child
- grandparents or other relatives of the child, and
- same-sex spouses whose marriage took place in a state recognizing same-sex marriage, regardless of whether the state where they currently work recognizes their marriage as legal.

Of course, an employee who simply agrees to babysit for his or her partner's child while the partner is on vacation will not be considered a parent under the FMLA if the employee does not generally take on parental duties on a regular (in other words, day-to-day) basis.

This chapter explains the FMLA's parental leave entitlement. It covers leave for birth, adoption, and placement of a foster child; timing requirements; and how to calculate leave rights when an employee needs both parenting leave and leave for a serious health condition. This chapter also describes the rules that apply when both parents work for your company.

Leave for Birth

Any employee defined as a "parent" under the FMLA is entitled to leave for the birth of a child. Parental leave for the birth of a child isn't limited to the birth itself; it's also for bonding with and caring for the newborn. And in contrast with leave for a serious medical condition, employees requesting parenting leave don't have to show that the child is ill or requires care.

At times, it can be hard to distinguish between parenting leave and leave for a serious medical condition, such as when an employee needs leave because of a serious medical condition associated with her pregnancy or childbirth or when a newborn becomes ill. This chapter shows you how to draw this distinction in situations when you might have to do so.

Multiple Births in the Same Year

An employee who has more than one child in the same year does not get additional leave. For example, if an employee gives birth to twins, she does not get 12 weeks of FMLA parenting leave for each child. She gets 12 weeks total.

As discussed further below, employees taking parenting leave are not entitled to intermittent or reduced-schedule leave, so a parent can't divide up his or her leave time, either. For example, a father who had two children at different times in the year (perhaps with two different mothers) can't take six weeks of leave for each birth; he would be entitled only to 12 weeks at once.

Conditions That Don't Count

When an employee's child is stillborn or the mother miscarries, the FMLA does not provide for parenting leave. Of course, if the employee is the mother, she may have serious medical and/or psychological conditions that entitle her to take FMLA leave.

TIP

It's okay to show compassion, as long as you are consistent. When you know that an employee has suffered a loss or trauma, it is both decent and natural to extend sympathetic treatment. Some companies voluntarily offer bereavement leave, for example, even though it isn't required by the FMLA. If your company offers extra leave or benefits in difficult times, such as relaxation of attendance or punctuality rules, just be sure to offer the same treatment to all employees in similar circumstances.

If an employee needs leave to care for a sick newborn or for a wife or partner who is suffering from pregnancy-related illness, that's a request for leave to care for a family member with a serious health condition, not a request for parenting leave. Leave for serious health conditions is covered in Chapter 4.

Leave for Adoption

In addition to biological parents, adoptive parents are also entitled to leave to spend time with a new child (as with a biological newborn) or to deal with the adoption process. Often, an employee in this situation needs time off before the adoption is finalized, for example, to attend court proceedings, meetings with attorneys, counseling sessions, consultations with doctors, or for other matters related to the adoption process. The FMLA allows an employee to take this time off (provided other eligibility requirements are also met). The employee is entitled to adoption leave whether the adoption is conducted through a licensed placement agency, private arrangement, or otherwise.

Leave for Placement of a Foster Child

A new or soon-to-be foster parent is also entitled to FMLA leave to spend time with the foster child and to deal with the foster placement process. Foster care is 24-hour care of a child by someone other than the child's parent or guardian. Foster placement is made either by an agreement between the state and the foster parent or by court order. In either case, the state must be involved for a child's placement to qualify as foster care under the FMLA. Informal custody arrangements, even for emergency child care, don't qualify unless the state plays a role in the placement. (An employee who provides care and

financial support for a child may qualify for leave under the "in loco parentis" provision, though.)

As with the adoption of a child, an eligible employee is entitled to take FMLA leave to attend to matters related to the placement of a foster child with that employee, whether the need for leave arises before or after the actual placement. A foster parent may need time off to attend hearings, examinations, and other proceedings, and that time is protected.

Lessons from the *Real World*

An employee was entitled to FMLA leave when trying to get custody of his biological daughter in an adoption proceeding.

Dwayne Kelley worked for Crosfield Catalysts. He had raised Shaneequa Forbes as his daughter, even though her birth certificate listed Barbara and Michael Forbes as her parents. Kelley "had reason to believe" that the girl was his biological daughter.

When the state child welfare department filed a court action to take custody of Shaneequa away from him, Kelley requested time off work to pursue custody. Crosfield denied the request based on the belief that Kelley could not "adopt" his own child and so was not entitled to adoption leave. Kelley took four days off anyway to appear at the custody hearing. Crosfield fired him, and he filed a lawsuit under the FMLA.

Kelley won the lawsuit. The court of appeals agreed that Crosfield had violated the FMLA. It determined that Kelley was entitled to take leave in connection with an adoption, regardless of whether or not the child in question was his biological child.

Kelley v. Crosfield Catalysts, 135 F.3d 1202 (7th Cir. 1998).

Parental Certifications

When an employee requests parenting leave, you can ask that employee to give you documentation showing that he or she is in fact the parent of a newborn or newly placed child. Such documentation might include:

- a birth certificate
- an adoption decree or court order
- a foster placement certification or court order, or
- a written statement by the employee, showing the employee's intent to take on the role of "parent" as defined by the FMLA.

(See "Proving a Family Relationship," in Chapter 4, for more information on these certifications, including a sample form you can use for this purpose.)

Timing of Parenting Leave

Although a parent is entitled to leave to bond with a new child, the child must indeed be "new." That means the employee must conclude the leave for the birth, adoption, or foster placement of a child within one year of the child's birth or adoptive or foster placement. "Placement" occurs when the parent gets the right to custody of the child. The one-year deadline is not extended when legal or governmental action has delayed the adoptive or foster parent from getting physical custody of the child.

This is a rigid deadline. Even a legitimate need for leave that arises more than one year after birth, adoption, or foster placement will not qualify under this provision of the FMLA. Of course, if the child has a serious health condition that requires the parent's care, the parent may still qualify for FMLA leave to take care of the sick child, even after the first year is over.

EXAMPLE 1: Your employee, Pang, took custody of a foster child on May 2, 2012. On March 28, 2013, Pang asks to take ten weeks of FMLA parenting leave. You grant the request.

You really didn't need to grant that much time because Pang had only a little over four weeks of time left in the one-year period following the child's placement. That was all the time off that she was entitled to within the FMLA deadline for parental leave.

EXAMPLE 2: Your employee Jess and his partner had a baby on March 5, 2012. On March 27, 2013, Jess informs you that he needs to take three weeks off to care for the baby, who has developed severe bronchitis. Because more than a

year has passed since the child's birth, you inform Jess that he has no leave time available for the birth of his child.

You blew it! The baby's illness is not "birth-related" and is not subject to the one-year deadline for such leave. Rather, the baby's illness is a serious medical condition, and Jess may qualify to take FMLA leave as long as he meets other eligibility requirements.

Lessons from the *Real World*

An employee is not entitled to FMLA leave to travel to retrieve adopted children more than one year after adoption.

Bernardo Bocalbos, a naturalized U.S. citizen who was born in the Philippines, worked as an assistant actuary for National Western Life Insurance Co. In 1992, Bocalbos adopted his brother's children, who lived in the Philippines. In March 1995, after finally receiving the necessary visas for the children, Bocalbos requested FMLA leave to travel to the Philippines to retrieve the children. The request was granted. Prior to Bocalbos's departure, his supervisor informed him that he had to take certain actuarial exams by May 1995 or he would be terminated. Bocalbos signed a memorandum stating he understood this requirement. In April 1995, Bocalbos left for the Philippines and returned to work in June 1995. Bocalbos did not sit for the required exams prior to his departure. National Western terminated him for failing to take the exams by May 1995. Bocalbos sued National Western for retaliating against him for taking FMLA leave.

The court of appeals sided with National Western, holding that the leave Bocalbos took three years after the adoption of the children was outside the FMLA deadline for adoption-related leave, so he was not protected.

Bocalbos v. National Western Life Ins. Co., 162 F.3d 379 (5th Cir. 1998).

Foreign adoptions like the one in the above "Lessons from the Real World" are increasingly common. Madonna and Angelina Jolie are the most famous people who have adopted children born in foreign countries, but your company's employees may choose to add to their families in this fashion, too. If an employee must take time off to travel to take custody of

a newly adopted child and does so within one year of the finalization of the adoption, the FMLA protects the employee's right to this leave.

Where an employee has already taken leave for the placement of a foster child and later adopts that child, the FMLA does not give the employee additional leave time for the adoption. The FMLA permits leave only for the "newly placed" foster or adoptive child within one year of the original placement. So even if the adoption doesn't happen for more than a year, the employee can't get additional parenting leave time.

Intermittent or Reduced-Schedule Leave

The FMLA does not require your company to offer intermittent and reduced-schedule parenting leave to employees, with one possible exception: Employees who become foster parents can take leave for each child that is placed with them in the same year. Although such employees still have a maximum of 12 weeks of leave to use in a year, they may take this leave in separate increments if more than one child is placed with them within a single year.

> EXAMPLE 1: Brenda, whose delivery date is December 21, 2012, requests four weeks of parenting leave following the birth of her child. She then plans to return to work for a couple of weeks and wants an additional three weeks of leave to bond with the baby in February 2013. You grant the leave immediately following the birth but deny the additional leave. Have you done the right thing?
>
> Yes. As long as Brenda has a normal pregnancy and delivery and no post-delivery complications, she is not entitled to the February leave, because that would be intermittent leave.

> EXAMPLE 2: Tomas becomes a foster parent on February 1, 2013, and takes six weeks of FMLA leave to spend with his foster child. He enjoys the experience so much that he decides to take in another foster child, who will be placed with him on August 5, 2013. He asks for another six weeks of parenting leave. You deny his request because he has already taken parenting leave during the year, and you don't have to allow him to take intermittent leave for this purpose. Was this the right call?

Not in this situation. Even though parents usually can't divide up their parenting leave, an exception applies when they receive more than one foster child in a year. Although the employee's total leave entitlement doesn't increase, the employee can take this leave in separate parts for multiple foster child placements, each part corresponding to a newly placed child.

However, your company has the option of agreeing to provide intermittent or reduced-schedule parenting leave at the employee's request, even though the FMLA does not require it. In fact, if you have a company policy allowing that type of leave, you should follow the policy. Your company may impose restrictions on this type of leave that are different from those mandated by the FMLA because you're agreeing to provide more than the law requires. For example, although the FMLA requires employers to allow intermittent leave in increments of one hour or less for serious health conditions and military leave, you may require employees who use intermittent leave for parenting to take it in larger increments (for example, a full day at a time).

POLICY ALERT
If your company has a policy of offering intermittent or reduced-schedule leave for parenting leave, follow it. Your company is bound to follow its own leave policies, even if they exceed FMLA obligations.

EXAMPLE: A few years after her first request, Brenda makes a request similar to the one described in the example above, but this time your company has a policy of granting occasional days off or reduced workdays to employees with newborns. Brenda specifically requests FMLA leave in two time segments, one in December and one in February. You deny Brenda the second block of time off because it is not available under the FMLA. Are you correct?
No. Because your company policy allows for intermittent leave for childbirth, you must abide by the policy.

This limitation doesn't apply to a woman who has a serious health condition as a result of pregnancy or childbirth or a spouse or partner caring for a woman with such a condition. In those situations, the leave is not parenting leave, so the employee is entitled to intermittent and reduced-schedule leave. Likewise, if a child has a serious health condition, the employee isn't restricted

by this provision and is eligible for intermittent or reduced-schedule leave (see "Intermittent and Reduced-Schedule Leave" in Chapter 7).

> **SEE AN EXPERT**
>
> **State family and medical leave laws may require your company to provide intermittent or reduced-schedule parenting leave.** Appendix A includes information on each state's family and medical leave laws. If you have questions about how to comply with your state's requirements for parenting leave, consult with an employment attorney.

Substitution of Paid Leave

Your company can require its employees who request parenting leave to substitute accrued paid vacation, personal leave, or family leave under its own policies and to count the time against the employee's FMLA available leave time. So, for example, an employee with two weeks' vacation time on the books could be required to use it up, and that time off would count against the employee's 12-week entitlement to FMLA leave.

However, the rule is different for sick or medical leave, because parenting leave is not "sick" time. So, your company can't require employees requesting parenting leave to use up accrued sick or medical leave. If the leave requested is to care for a spouse, newborn, or newly placed child with a serious health condition, on the other hand, paid sick or medical leave may be substituted if your policy allows sick leave to care for family members.

Even if your company doesn't require an employee to substitute paid vacation, personal, or family leave for parenting leave, it must allow an employee to use this time to get paid during FMLA leave, upon the employee's request, as long as the employee meets the requirements of your paid leave policy. (For more on paid leave, see Chapter 8.)

Parents Who Work for the Same Company

Parents who work for the same company are entitled to parenting leave, but the amount of time they get depends on their marital status. If the parents are

married, they get a combined 12 weeks of leave in connection with the birth, adoption, or foster placement of their child or to care for a seriously ill parent. This rule applies even to spouses who work at different worksites or in different divisions of your company. This rule also applies to same-sex spouses married in states or foreign countries that recognize same-sex marriage, regardless of whether the state where they currently work recognizes their marriage as legal. Spouses are allowed to use the combined leave at the same time.

Spouses who are eligible for military caregiver leave—26 weeks of leave in a single 12-month period to care for a family member who suffered a service-related serious illness or injury (see Chapter 6 for details)—have to share their leave entitlement, as well. These spouses are entitled to a combined total of 26 weeks of leave for parenting, caring for a parent with a serious health condition, and caring for a military family member with a serious illness or injury.

If the parents are not married, they each get 12 weeks of leave (or 26 weeks, for military caregiver leave). This rule seems to favor unmarried couples, but the reason for the rule is actually to avoid discouraging employers from hiring married couples by lessening the burden on those employers when their married employees have children together.

> EXAMPLE: Dan and Anabelle both work for your company and are married to each other. Dan works in the downtown headquarters, while Anabelle works in the warehouse in a nearby suburb. They are both eligible for FMLA leave. Three months ago, Dan and Anabelle adopted a child. Anabelle requests seven weeks of leave in connection with the adoption. You grant the requested leave.
>
> During Anabelle's leave, Dan asks for five weeks off to bond with the child, two weeks of which will overlap with Anabelle's leave. You grant his request. Were you right to do so?
>
> Yes. You accurately noted the time off for each of the parents and calculated the total combined FMLA parenting leave to be taken. Dan was entitled to the five weeks of parenting leave that was left after Anabelle's leave was subtracted from the combined 12 weeks.

Unmarried couples are each entitled to the full 12 weeks of FMLA parenting leave. However, unlike married couples, they are not entitled to FMLA leave to care for each other when one has a serious medical condition. So if

an unmarried pregnant employee needs care for a serious medical condition and you also employ her partner, her partner is not entitled to FMLA leave to provide that care. Your state's family and medical leave law might require you to grant leave to care for a domestic partner, however. (Appendix A provides information on each state's family and medical leave laws.)

> **EXAMPLE 1:** Jared and Betsey are domestic partners who are both employed by your company. The couple has announced that Betsey is pregnant. Before Betsey's due date, Jared requests ten weeks of parenting leave to begin after the baby's birth. You grant his request and wish the couple well.
>
> Shortly after the baby's birth, Betsey calls in and asks for five weeks of parenting leave. You deny that request, telling Betsey that she and Jared get a combined 12 weeks of parenting leave and he has already been granted ten weeks.
>
> Wrong. Because they are not married, Jared and Betsey are each entitled to 12 weeks of FMLA leave in connection with the birth of their child.

> **EXAMPLE 2:** Jared phones in two months after the baby's birth to ask to take two weeks of FMLA leave to take care of Betsey, who has developed severe postpartum depression and been prescribed medication that affects her ability to function.
>
> Because you have read this guide, you know that you can deny this request and tell Jared that unmarried partners are not entitled to leave to care for each other under the FMLA.

In the last example, if Jared and Betsey had been married, Jared would be entitled to the requested leave to care for his spouse during her illness. However, that means that in the first example, Betsey would be entitled to only two weeks of parenting leave, because Jared already took ten weeks.

RELATED TOPIC

State laws may also apply. Several types of state laws might also protect employees who take leave for a new child. For example, some states require employers to offer parenting leave (similar to that provided by the FMLA) to a wider range of employees than does the FMLA. And some state family leave laws cover the same territory as the FMLA, but with additional requirements. Appendix A provides a summary of each state's laws; Chapter 12 explains what to do when a state law overlaps with the FMLA.

Combining Parenting Leave With Leave for a Serious Health Condition

As you've now learned, employees are entitled to two types of nonmilitary leave under the FMLA: leave for a serious health condition and parenting leave to care for and bond with a new child. Sometimes, these two rights may seem to overlap. For example, a pregnant mother may need time off before her pregnancy, when she experiences morning sickness or is confined to bed. Or a newborn may become ill, requiring a parent's care.

Pregnancy

Incapacity due to pregnancy, including leave needed for prenatal care, is considered a serious health condition under the FMLA. In fact, all leave before delivery that a pregnant woman takes because of her pregnancy is leave for a serious medical condition, not parenting leave. (See Chapter 4 for more information on pregnancy leave.)

There are a couple of reasons why it's important to figure out whether an employee is taking leave for pregnancy (a serious health condition) or parenting:

- **Unlike parenting leave, FMLA leave for pregnancy incapacity may be taken on an intermittent or reduced-schedule basis.** If you lump pregnancy and parenting leaves together and deny a request for intermittent leave for pregnancy as a result, you violate the FMLA.
- **If married parents both work for you, they are subject to the combined 12-week "cap" on parenting leave, as explained above.** However, an employee's leave for her own pregnancy doesn't count toward this combined 12 weeks, nor does a husband's leave to care for his pregnant wife. For example, if a pregnant employee took five weeks off due to incapacity, she and her husband would still be entitled to a combined total of 12 weeks off for parenting leave. There is a limitation, though: Each person still has an overall cap of 12 weeks of FMLA leave (or 26 weeks, for military caregiver leave). In this example, the pregnant employee could take a maximum of seven weeks of parenting leave, because she already used five weeks of her annual allotment.

EXAMPLE 1: Back to your married employees, Dan and Anabelle, who took five and seven weeks of parental leave, respectively. A few days after Dan's request for parenting leave, Anabelle asks for three weeks off to care for the child, who has developed pneumonia. You deny this request and tell Anabelle that she and Dan have taken all 12 weeks of parenting leave available under the FMLA.

Oops! Your mistake was assuming that Anabelle's request for time to care for the sick child was part of the 12-week combined parenting leave, instead of leave for a serious health condition. With a medical certification, Anabelle is entitled to the three weeks off. The difference between her total FMLA leave for the year (12 weeks) and the time she actually took off during the combined parenting leave (seven weeks), leaves her with five weeks of FMLA leave for any qualifying reason other than parenting leave.

EXAMPLE 2: A few weeks after returning from his final week of parenting leave, Dan develops a severe cough. He calls in one morning to inform you that his doctor has diagnosed him with bronchitis and ordered him to stay home and off his feet for at least a week to give the antibiotics a chance to work. You ask for a note from his doctor and grant the leave on the condition that you receive the medical certification.

Congratulations! You learned from your earlier error. Dan's illness is an FMLA-qualifying condition separate and apart from the parenting leave he took earlier and he, too, is entitled to 12 weeks of FMLA leave, less the time he actually took off already (five weeks). So, Dan has seven weeks of leave left for any FMLA-qualifying reason except parenting leave.

In addition to granting leave to a pregnant woman incapacitated by a pregnancy-related medical condition, the FMLA also requires your company to allow a husband to take time off to care for his wife who is suffering such incapacitation. As with any other leave for a serious medical condition, the spouse must provide care to the pregnant employee and should provide a medical certification. Of course, this means that a normal pregnancy that doesn't incapacitate the mother doesn't entitle her spouse to take leave to spend time with her.

Because domestic partners and other unmarried couples don't qualify as each other's family members under the FMLA, an employee isn't entitled to take FMLA leave to care for a nonmarital pregnant partner even if she has a serious medical condition. But the employee is entitled to take FMLA leave to care for a newborn child, even if the mother of the child isn't the employee's spouse.

Lessons from the *Real World*

An employee was not entitled to FMLA leave to be with his pregnant wife when she had not suffered medical complications.

After his pregnant wife experienced false labor, Steve Aubuchon orally requested leave from his job with Knauf Fiberglass to be with her. Aubuchon did not inform Knauf that his wife had any medical complications or that she was incapacitated. Knauf denied the request. Aubuchon nevertheless missed several weeks of work, and Knauf fired him for unauthorized absence. He filed a lawsuit claiming that Knauf violated the FMLA.

The court of appeals ruled in the company's favor. Because Aubuchon failed to provide notice to Knauf that his wife had experienced complications during her pregnancy or that she was incapacitated, Aubuchon's leave was not protected and Knauf did not violate the FMLA by firing him.

Aubuchon v. Knauf Fiberglass, GmbH, 359 F.3d 950 (7th Cir. 2004).

Caring for a Child

Leave to care for an ill newborn or newly adopted or foster child is separate and apart from parenting leave because it is to care for a family member with a serious health condition. So if a child becomes ill, you assess the employee's entitlement to leave under the FMLA in the same manner as any other leave request for a serious health condition. (See Chapter 4.)

Lessons from the *Real World*

If an employee wasn't entitled to take FMLA leave to care for his common-law wife, he was entitled to take leave to care for his premature infant.

Ingram Construction Company fired Mark Willard for taking time off to care for his common-law wife and newborn child following the baby's premature birth. Willard sued Ingram for violating the FMLA.

The court of appeals held that, while Willard may or may not have met the requirements of a common-law marriage, he was entitled to take FMLA leave to care for his newborn. The legal relationship between Willard and the mother of the child didn't affect his right to take parental leave.

Willard v. Ingram Constr. Co., Inc., 194 F.3d 1315 (6th Cir. 1999).

Common Mistakes Regarding Leave for a New Child—And How to Avoid Them

Mistake 1: Miscalculating the FMLA leave available to spouses who both work for your company.

Avoid this mistake by taking the following steps:

- Make sure both parents are eligible for FMLA leave in the first place, for example, that they have worked enough hours in the past year. See Chapter 3 for more on these requirements.
- Make sure the two married parents get no more, and no less, than 12 weeks of combined parenting leave.
- Calculate the FMLA leave time each parent has left for other purposes after the combined parenting leave is taken.
- Distinguish between parenting leave and other types of leave that a soon-to-be or new parent might take (for pregnancy disability, to care for a pregnant spouse, for disability relating to childbirth, or to care for a seriously ill new child, for example). Leave for a child's or spouse's serious health condition doesn't count toward the combined 12-week cap.

- Limit spouses who are eligible for military caregiver leave to a combined total of 26 weeks of leave in a single 12-month period for parenting, caring for a parent with a serious health condition, and providing military caregiver leave.

Mistake 2: Denying FMLA leave because the employee has already taken parenting leave.

Avoid this mistake by taking the following steps:

- Allow intermittent parenting leave only if your company's policies allow it or the employee is entitled to separate increments of parenting leave for multiple foster child placements in a single year.
- Recognize the difference between parenting leave and leave for a serious health condition. If a child becomes seriously ill, leave to care for that child does not qualify as parental leave under the FMLA; it's leave to care for a family member with a serious health condition.

Mistake 3: Discriminating against fathers in granting or denying parenting leave.

Avoid this mistake by taking the following steps:

- Grant parenting leave to FMLA-eligible fathers for birth, adoption, or foster placement, just as you would to female employees.
- Make no assumptions about who will or should actually be providing care for a new child. Remember, an employee doesn't have to show that he is required to provide care for a new child, as he would have to show to care for a family member with a serious health condition—and you can't deny parenting leave simply because the child's mother is already at home.

Managers' Checklist: Leave for a New Child

☐ I confirmed that the employee requesting parenting leave is eligible for FMLA leave (see Chapter 3).

☐ I have informed the employee that he or she must substitute paid company vacation, personal, or family leave for unpaid FMLA leave, and

    ☐ I have subtracted the paid leave from the employee's available FMLA leave for the leave year.

☐ I have noted the deadline by which the employee must take the full 12 weeks of parenting leave (one year after birth, adoption, or foster placement).

For Pregnancy Leave:

☐ If the employee is requesting leave for her own pregnancy before delivery, I have:

    ☐ requested medical certification of a serious medical condition

    ☐ designated the leave as leave for the employee's own medical condition and notified the employee, and

    ☐ noted in the employee's FMLA file that the employee may still request parenting leave within the one-year deadline.

☐ If a pregnant employee is requesting leave to begin before delivery, I have:

    ☐ asked if the leave is for her own medical condition (including prenatal care) or for parenting

    ☐ if for her own medical condition, I have followed the steps in the preceding list entry, and

    ☐ if for parenting, I have denied the request for leave prior to delivery.

☐ If an employee is requesting leave to care for his pregnant spouse, I have:

    ☐ requested appropriate certification of a serious medical condition

    ☐ designated the leave as leave for the spouse's serious medical condition and notified the employee, and

    ☐ noted that the employee may still request parenting leave within the one-year deadline.

Managers' Checklist: Leave for a New Child (continued)

For Parenting Leave:

☐ If the employee is requesting parenting leave, I have confirmed that the leave is:

    ☐ to begin after the birth of the child

    ☐ not for the employee's own medical condition, and

    ☐ full time and not intermittent or reduced-schedule leave, unless company policy or state law permits such leave.

☐ I have requested appropriate certification of the parental relationship.

☐ If the employee is requesting parenting leave for adoption or foster placement, I have:

    ☐ requested appropriate certification of adoption or placement, and

    ☐ allowed time off before adoption or foster placement if necessary to attend proceedings or meetings related to placement.

Where Both Parents Work for Your Company:

☐ For parents who are married and are both seeking parenting leave, I have:

    ☐ confirmed in writing to the parents that they get no more than a combined total of 12 weeks of parenting leave and leave to care for a parent with a serious health condition, and

    ☐ subtracted the parenting time from each employee's FMLA time and noted the remainder for use for other types of FMLA leave.

☐ For parents who are not married and are both seeking leave, I have:

    ☐ confirmed in writing to the parents that each parent has a full 12 weeks of parenting leave available

    ☐ subtracted the parenting time from each employee's FMLA time and noted the remainder for use for other types of FMLA leave.

Military Family Leave

Leave for a Qualifying Exigency..104

    Covered Active Duty 104

    Family Members...107

    Qualifying Exigencies...107

    Intermittent or Reduced-Schedule Leave...112

    Substitution of Paid Leave...112

Leave to Care for an Injured Servicemember...113

    Which Servicemembers Are Covered..113

    Covered Family Members 116

    How Much Leave an Employee May Take...118

    Limits on Leave Available to Married Couples...119

    Intermittent or Reduced-Schedule Leave..119

    Substitution of Paid Leave...119

Common Mistakes Regarding Military Family Leave—
    And How to Avoid Them...120

Chapter Highlights

☆ Employees may use their 12-week entitlement of FMLA leave to handle qualifying exigencies arising from a family member's covered active duty in the military.

☆ Qualifying exigency leave is available only if the family member is a member of the National Guard, Reserves, or regular Armed Forces deployed to a foreign country.

☆ Adult children qualify as family members under this provision.

☆ There are eight categories of qualifying exigency:
- short-notice deployment
- military events and related activities
- child care and school activities
- financial and legal arrangements
- counseling
- rest and recuperation
- postdeployment activities, and
- care for a parent who is incapable of self-care.

☆ An employer and employee may agree that other circumstances also constitute a qualifying exigency; they must also agree on the length and timing of the leave.

☆ For some types of qualifying exigency leave, there are limits on how much leave an employee may take or when the leave must be taken.

☆ Employees may take up to 26 weeks of military caregiver leave in a single 12-month period to care for a family member who suffers or aggravates a serious illness or injury on active duty.

☆ For purposes of military caregiver leave, adult children count as family members; siblings, grandparents, or other blood relatives may also be entitled to leave, if they are the injured servicemember's next of kin.

☆ Military caregiver leave is available to care for members of the regular Armed Forces as well as members of the National Guard and Reserves; veterans suffering from service-related injuries or illnesses are covered, too.

☆ Military caregiver leave is a per-servicemember, per-injury requirement; it does not renew every year like other types of FMLA leave.

☆ An employee who is eligible for military caregiver leave may take no more than 26 weeks off in a single 12-month period for all FMLA-qualified reasons, combined.

I n 2008, Congress amended the FMLA to add new leave entitlements for employees with family members serving in the military. As originally passed, these provisions allowed employees to take time off to care for family members who suffered serious illness or injury in active military service; they also created "qualifying exigency" leave, which employees could take to handle certain practical matters arising out of a family member's call to active duty.

In 2010, Congress amended these provisions to expand the reasons employees can take military family leave and the family members for whom they can take such leave. All of these amendments are intended to help employees manage their family responsibilities at a time when our country has significant troops in Afghanistan and elsewhere, and tens of thousands of servicemembers have returned home wounded or ill from their service.

As amended, the FMLA includes two categories of military family leave:

- **Qualifying exigency leave.** Employees may take FMLA leave to deal with certain issues arising from a family member's covered active duty or call to covered active duty in the military as a result of deployment to a foreign country. Although this type of leave was originally available only if the family member was in the National Guard or Reserves, the 2010 amendments extended it to apply to family members in the regular Armed Forces as well. This leave counts toward the employee's total 12-week leave entitlement for serious health conditions and bonding with a new child.

- **Military caregiver leave.** Employees may take up to 26 weeks of leave in a single 12-month period to care for a family member who suffers a serious injury or illness while on covered active duty. The 2010 amendments expand this provision in two ways. First, servicemembers who aggravate a preexisting injury or illness while on active duty are covered. Second, veterans who were discharged (under conditions other than dishonorable) in the past five years and are suffering a service-related serious illness or injury are also covered.

These military family leave entitlements apply only to covered employers (that is, employers who meet the criteria covered in Chapter 2). And, both are available only to employees who are otherwise eligible for FMLA leave: those who work within 75 miles of at least 50 employees, have worked for at least 12 months, and have worked at least 1,250 hours during the previous year, for the employer (these requirements are covered in detail in Chapter 3).

Beyond the basic FMLA coverage and eligibility requirements, however, each of the military family leave provisions comes with its own definitions, criteria, and requirements, not to mention its own certification forms and notice provisions. In this chapter, we explain how these leave rights work, including which employees may use them, the situations in which an employee may take leave, and how much leave an employee may use. In later chapters, you'll find information on how to combine military family leave with existing FMLA leave to determine an employee's total leave entitlement (Chapter 7); notice provisions (Chapter 8); and certification requirements (Chapter 9) that apply to these military family leave provisions, as well as other types of FMLA leave.

Leave for a Qualifying Exigency

Employees may take FMLA leave to handle certain qualifying exigencies relating to a family member's covered active duty or call to covered active duty during deployment in a foreign country. Leave for a qualifying exigency is an additional type of FMLA leave for which an employee may take a total of 12 workweeks off per year, along with leave for the employee's serious health condition (see Chapter 4), for a family member's serious health condition (see Chapter 4), or to bond with a new child (see Chapter 5). In other words, this provision doesn't create a right to additional leave. Instead, it creates another type of leave for which the employee might use some of his or her existing 12-week entitlement.

Generally speaking, the qualifying exigency provision gives employees the right to take time off when a family member's current or impending military service raises particular issues that the employee needs to handle, from child care to legal matters to formal military events and activities. But not every event or issue is covered, nor is every family member nor every type of military service. Each of these terms has been defined in the new law and the revised FMLA regulations, as explained below.

Covered Active Duty

There are many different ways to serve in the military, and not all of them are covered by this type of FMLA leave. Employees are entitled to leave

under this provision only for family members whose service meets the following criteria (explained in more detail below):

- The family member must be a member of the National Guard, Reserves, regular Armed Forces, or, in some circumstances, a retired member of the regular Armed Forces or Reserve.
- The family member must be serving or called to serve on active duty during deployment to a foreign country.
- For those in the National Guard or Reserves only, the family member must be serving or called to serve
  - in support of a contingency operation, and
  - under a federal call or order to active duty.

Members of the National Guard, Reserves, or Regular Armed Forces

Employees whose family members are on active duty in the regular Armed Forces (that is, whose family members are career military personnel) are eligible for qualifying exigency leave. Employees may also take leave for family members who are in the National Guard or Reserves and are called to active duty.

Certain retired military members are also covered. Leave is available for family members who are retired from the regular Armed Forces and are called to active duty. In addition, leave is available for family members who are members of the retired Reserve, are retired after completing at least 20 years of active service, and are ordered to active duty.

Covered Active Duty During Deployment in a Foreign Country

Employees are eligible for qualifying exigency leave only if their family members are on active duty in a foreign country. This also includes deployment to active duty in international waters.

Active Duty in Support of a Contingency Operation

For employees whose family member is serving in the National Guard or Reserves (not the regular Armed Forces), the family member must be on active duty in support of a contingency operation. A contingency operation is a military operation that:

- the secretary of defense has designated as an operation in which members of the armed forces are or may become involved in military actions, operations, or hostilities against an enemy of the United States or an opposing military force, or
- results in the call or order to, or retention on, active duty of members of the uniformed services pursuant to particular sections of the United States code or any other provision of law during a war or national emergency declared by the president or Congress. (You can find a list of the provisions of the U.S. Code that qualify at 29 C.F.R. § 825.126(b)(3).)

Generally, the family member's active duty orders should indicate whether the person is called to serve in support of a contingency operation. You may require the employee to submit a copy of the family member's active duty orders or other official documents about the family member's service along with the employee's certification; see Chapter 9 for more information.

Federal Call to Active Duty

For employees whose family member is serving in the National Guard or Reserves (not the regular armed forces), the family member must be subject to a federal call to covered active duty; a state call to active duty isn't covered unless it has been ordered by the president of the United States in support of a contingency operation.

> **EXAMPLE:** Lawrence works for your company in Northern California. His wife, Saundra, works part time for another employer while their young children are in school; she gets off work at 1 p.m., in time to pick up the kids. Saundra is a member of California's National Guard.
>
> Pursuant to an order by the governor of California, Saundra is mobilized to assist firefighters in evacuating residents and creating firebreaks in response to a wildfire in Southern California. Lawrence requests time off to care for the kids in the afternoon for a week. Because Saundra is in the Guard, you allow Lawrence to take the time off and count it, as qualifying exigency leave, against his 12-week FMLA entitlement. Was that the right call?
>
> No. Although Saundra was mobilized, it wasn't a federal call to active duty, because the president didn't order it in support of a contingency operation. That means Lawrence's time off isn't FMLA leave. Had the fire been so severe that it was declared a national emergency by the president, who mobilized Saundra and other troops in response, Lawrence's time off may have qualified as FMLA leave.

Family Members

As explained in Chapter 4, the FMLA allows employees to take leave only to care for certain family members with a serious health condition. Those family members include parents, spouses, and children who are either under the age of 18 or at least 18 and incapable of caring for themselves.

The qualifying exigency entitlement uses the same categories of family members whose call to covered active duty allows the employee to take qualifying exigency leave, and defines "spouses" and "parents" in the same way as for other FMLA entitlements. However, the term "child" is defined differently. For purposes of qualifying exigency leave, family members include the employee's children regardless of age or incapacity. This change was necessary to make the provision meaningful. Because minors are generally not members of the military (and certainly wouldn't already be retired from military service), an employee would never be able to take qualifying exigency leave to handle matters arising from a child's call to active duty unless adult children were encompassed by the law.

Qualifying Exigencies

The FMLA regulations identify eight categories of qualifying exigencies. For some of these exigencies, the amount of leave available is limited, or restrictions apply to when the employee may take leave. In addition, the regulations create a ninth category for additional activities, which applies to any situation that the employer and employee agree is a qualifying exigency.

Short-Notice Deployment

An employee may take leave to address any issue arising from the fact that a family member is notified of an impending call or order to covered active duty within seven or fewer calendar days before the date of deployment. This type of leave may be taken for only seven calendar days, beginning on the day the family member is notified of his or her impending deployment. Because the regulation refers to calendar days rather than work days, an employee may be entitled to only a few days of FMLA leave pursuant to this provision.

Military Events and Related Activities

An employee may take leave to attend an official ceremony, program, or event sponsored by the military and related to the family member's active duty service. An employee may also take leave to attend family support or assistance programs and informational briefings sponsored or promoted by the military, military service organizations, or the American Red Cross, as long as those programs or briefings are related to the family member's active duty.

Child Care and School Activities

An employee may take time off for the following reasons relating to a family member's call to active duty:

- to arrange alternative child care for the family member's child, if the family member's active duty requires a change
- to provide child care for the family member's child on an urgent, immediate need basis (not regularly or every day) when the need arises from the family member's active duty
- to enroll the family member's child in, or transfer the child to, a new school or day care facility when the need arises from the family member's active duty, or
- to attend meetings with school or day care staff (such as disciplinary meetings, parent-teacher conferences, or meetings with a school counselor) regarding the family member's child, if the employee's attendance at the meetings is necessary because of circumstances arising from the family member's call to active duty.

When an employee takes qualifying exigency leave for child care and school functions, two definitions of "child" are in play. The child who is actually in school or day care must meet the traditional FMLA definition of a child. In other words, the family member's child must be either under the age of 18 or, if the child is older, he or she must be incapable of self-care due to a disability. However, the employee can take time off when an adult child is called to active duty and that adult child's own children need care. In other words, an employee may be entitled to leave to care for a grandchild.

EXAMPLE: Rosalva works for your company. Her son, Carlos, is a divorced parent who shares custody of his young son, Javier, with his ex-wife Nancy. Carlos and Nancy live near each other and cooperate closely on raising their son. Currently,

Carlos takes care of him from Sunday evening until Wednesday evening, while Nancy works. Nancy takes Javier the rest of the week, while Carlos works.

Carlos, a member of the National Guard, is deployed to Afghanistan. Rosalva asks you for time off to rearrange Javier's schedule. Rosalva anticipates that she may need a few days off for a couple of weeks to care for Javier, until she and Nancy can decide whether to enroll him in day care or make some other arrangements. She may also need time to get her home set up to care for Javier. You sympathize with Rosalva's situation, but regretfully inform her that she can't take FMLA leave because the FMLA doesn't cover care for grandchildren.

Although your instincts would have been correct for other types of FMLA leave, here they were misguided. For purposes of qualifying exigency leave, employees may take time off to handle child care and school issues for their adult children's kids.

Financial and Legal Arrangements

There are a number of financial or legal issues that might need attention when a family member is called to active duty. An employee can take time off for things like preparing or updating a will or living trust, preparing or executing financial and health care powers of attorney, transferring bank account signature authority, obtaining military identification cards, or enrolling in the Defense Enrollment Eligibility Reporting System.

An employee may also take time off to act as the family member's representative for purposes of getting, arranging, or appealing military service benefits for the family member. This leave is available while the family member is on active duty or has been called to active duty, and for up to 90 days after the family member's active duty status terminates.

Counseling

An employee may take leave to attend counseling, provided by someone other than a health care provider, for himself or herself, for the family member, or for the family member's child, as long as the need for counseling arises from the family member's call to active duty.

Rest and Recuperation

An employee may take time off to be with a family member who is on short-term, temporary rest and recuperation leave during deployment. The employee may take a maximum of 15 days off for each rest and recuperation leave.

Postdeployment Activities

An employee may take time off to attend arrival ceremonies, reintegration briefings and events, and other official programs or ceremonies sponsored by the military for up to 90 days following the termination of the family member's active duty status. On a sadder note, employees may also take leave to handle issues arising from the death of a family member while on active duty status, such as meeting and recovering the family member's body, making funeral arrangements, and attending funeral services.

Parental Care

In 2013, the Department of Labor issued regulations that created a new category of qualifying exigency leave: time off to assist a military member's parent who is incapable of self-care. This type of leave is available to employees with a military family member (as defined in "Family Members," above) whose own biological, step, adoptive, or foster parent—or person who stood in loco parentis to the military member when he or she was a child—is unable to take care of himself or herself.

A parent is incapable of self-care when he or she requires active assistance or supervision with at least three "activities of daily living" (physical tasks, such as grooming, bathing, hygiene, dressing, and eating) or "instrumental activities of daily living" (basic skills required to live independently, such as shopping, cooking, cleaning, using transportation, maintaining a home, using the phone, paying bills, and so on).

This type of leave is available to:

- arrange alternative care for the parent, if the military member's service necessitates a change in care
- provide care for the parent on an urgent, immediate need basis (similar to the provision for leave to provide child care)
- admit or transfer the parent to a care facility, or
- attend meetings with staff at a care facility, including meeting with social services or hospice providers.

Additional Activities

In addition to the eight categories detailed above, an employer and employee may agree that other events arising out of a family member's call to active

Qualifying Exigency Leave			
Category	Description	Limits on timing of leave	Limits on amount of leave
Short-notice deployment	To address issues arising from call to duty within seven or fewer days of deployment	May be used only for seven calendar days after notification of deployment	Seven calendar days maximum
Military events and related activities	To attend military program, ceremony, or event; or to attend family support and assistance programs and information briefings sponsored by the military, military service groups, or Red Cross		
Child care and school activities	To arrange alternative child care; provide urgent child care; enroll or transfer child to new school or day care; or attend school meetings and conferences		
Financial and legal arrangements	To handle financial and legal matters relating to the family member's absence, such as wills, powers of attorney, and bank account transfers; to act as the family member's representative in hearings on military service benefits	Leave to act as family member's representative may be taken only while family member is on active duty status and for up to 90 days after termination of active duty status	
Counseling	To attend counseling for oneself, family member, or family member's child		
Rest and recuperation	To spend time with family member who is on short-term, temporary R&R leave during deployment		15 days of leave maximum, per service-member's R&R leave
Post-deployment activities	To attend ceremonies, briefings, and events relating to family member's return; to address issues arising from the death of a family member on active duty	Leave for return of family member may be taken only for up to 90 days after termination of active duty status	
Parental care	To arrange alternate parental care; provide urgent parental care; admit or transfer the parent to a care facility; or attend meetings with staff at the parent's care facility		
Additional activities	As agreed upon by employer and employee	As agreed upon by employer and employee	As agreed upon by employer and employee

duty also constitute qualifying exigencies for which the employee may take leave. For this type of leave, the employer and employee must also agree on the timing and the length of the leave.

> EXAMPLE: Duquan works for your company. His father, David, runs a kennel out of his home, taking care of dogs while their owners are on vacation. David, a member of the Reserves, is called to report for active duty in ten days. Duquan asks for time off to help his father with the dogs in his care; some owners are not due back until after David deploys. Duquan will help his father try to contact the owners or arrange other care for the dogs until the owners return.
>
> You recognize that Duquan's request doesn't fall under any of the seven enumerated categories of qualifying exigency leave. However, you decide to grant Duquan's request as an "additional activity." After consulting with his father, Duquan tells you that he will need to take four days off; one to learn the ropes from his father, and the other three to care for the remaining dogs until their owners return. You agree, and designate those four days as FMLA leave for a qualifying exigency.

Intermittent or Reduced-Schedule Leave

Leave for a qualifying exigency may be taken intermittently or on a reduced schedule. As you can see from the categories of qualifying exigency leave above, this type of leave may have to be taken at a particular time, often for just a few hours at a time. For example, parent-teacher night, military ceremonies, or hearings on a family member's benefits take place on a given date and time, typically without regard for the employee's work schedule. But these events won't take more than a few hours.

Substitution of Paid Leave

As for other types of FMLA leave, an employee may choose—or you may require the employee—to use paid leave during FMLA leave. The employee's reason for leave must be covered by your company's paid leave program: For example, unless your company's policy allowed employees to use sick leave to attend school activities, you wouldn't have to allow (and couldn't require) an employee to substitute paid sick leave for time off used to attend school meetings. Also, you can require the employee to meet all other requirements of

your paid leave program, such as having to provide a certain type or amount of notice. For more information on substitution of paid leave, see Chapter 8.

Leave to Care for an Injured Servicemember

The FMLA also gives employees the right to take up to 26 weeks of unpaid leave in a single 12-month period to care for a family member who has a serious injury or illness incurred in the line of duty. Unlike the qualified exigency leave provisions, this caregiver leave entitlement gives employees more leave than they would otherwise have under the FMLA.

The 2010 amendments to the FMLA expand this leave entitlement in two ways:

- An employee can take leave to care for a family member with a serious illness or injury that was aggravated by service in the line of duty. This means that preexisting conditions that are worsened by military service may be covered along with illnesses or injuries first incurred while on duty.
- An employee can take leave to care for a family member veteran suffering a service-related serious illness or injury, as long as the family member was in the service during the five years before the employee's leave.

Like leave for a serious health condition, an employee's right to take leave for a family member's service-connected serious illness or injury depends heavily on medical facts. Military facts also come into play: The illness or injury must be incurred or aggravated "in the line of duty on active duty," a determination that is generally made by the military, not by private employers. This means that, as is true of a serious health condition, your role is not to determine whether an employee's family member has a serious military-related illness or injury, but to recognize when this type of leave might be implicated. Then, you can ask the employee to submit a certification from the family member's health care provider, filling in the necessary blanks. (Certifications are covered in Chapter 9.)

Which Servicemembers Are Covered

Employees may take leave only to care for:

- a covered servicemember
- with a serious illness or injury

- incurred or aggravated in the line of duty on active duty, and
- for which the servicemember is undergoing medical treatment, recuperation, or therapy; is otherwise in outpatient status; or is on the temporary disability retired list.

As you have probably guessed, each of these requirements has its own definition.

Covered Servicemembers

Covered servicemembers include those who are in the regular Armed Forces, the National Guard and Reserves, and members of the regular Armed Forces, Guard, or Reserves who are on the temporary disability retired list. It also includes veterans who were released or discharged from military duty, under conditions other than dishonorable, during the five years before FMLA leave is taken. However, this five-year period does not include the time between Congress's decision to expand military family leave to include veterans (October 28, 2009) and the date when the Department of Labor issued final regulations interpreting these provisions (March 8, 2013). If, for example, a servicemember was honorably discharged in 2010, an employee could take leave to care for that family member up until March 8, 2018.

Serious Illness or Injury

A serious illness or injury is one that may render the servicemember unfit to perform the duties of his or her office, grade, rank, or rating. For a veteran, a serious illness or injury is one that meets one of the following four definitions:

- a continuation of a serious illness or injury (as defined above) incurred or aggravated when the veteran was in the military, which rendered the servicemember unable to perform the duties of his or her office, grade, rank, or rating
- a physical or mental condition for which the veteran has received a Veterans Affairs Service Related Disability Rating (VASRD) of 50 percent or greater, at least in part because the condition requires caregiver leave
- a physical or mental condition that substantially impairs the veteran's ability to obtain or maintain a substantially gainful occupation due

to a disability related to military service (or would create such an impairment without treatment), or

- an injury (including a psychological injury) for which the veteran has been enrolled in the Department of Veterans Affairs Program of Comprehensive Assistance for Family Caregivers.

Note that these definitions differ from the basic definition of a "serious health condition," for which FMLA leave may otherwise be available. Although a serious illness or injury will often also qualify as a serious health condition, that won't always be the case. As explained in Chapters 7 and 8, if an employee's leave qualifies under both provisions, you must designate it only as military caregiver leave.

In the Line of Duty on Active Duty

An employee may take leave only for a family member who is injured or falls ill, or whose preexisting condition is aggravated, in the line of duty on active duty. These are military terms of art that the Department of Labor declined to define in greater detail. Generally speaking, a person is on active duty when serving full-time duty in the active military service of the United States. "Line of duty" is a term sometimes used to differentiate injuries or fatalities for which the servicemember or his or her family may receive benefits (for example, health care or survivor benefits) from those for which benefits are not available. For example, injuries caused by the servicemember's own intentional misconduct or willful negligence may not be considered "in the line of duty." An injury need not be combat-related to qualify as "in the line of duty," though.

For veterans, the injury or illness must also be incurred or aggravated in the line of duty on active duty. However, conditions that arise or manifest only after the veteran leaves active duty, or even after the veteran leaves the military, are covered. For example, post-traumatic stress disorder (PTSD) caused by military duty would be covered if it otherwise met the above definition of a serious illness or injury, even if it did not appear until after the veteran was discharged from military service.

As is true of serious health conditions, this is not a determination you need to make. Instead, the family member's health care provider is asked to

determine whether the injury or illness occurred in the line of duty on active duty when completing the certification form (see Chapter 9). If the health care provider can't make this call, he or she may rely on determinations by an authorized representative of the Defense Department.

Treatment or Recuperation Requirements

An employee is eligible for military caregiver leave only if the current servicemember meets one of the following three criteria:

- the servicemember is undergoing medical treatment, recuperation, or therapy
- the servicemember is otherwise in outpatient status, or
- the servicemember is otherwise on the temporary disability retired list.

A different rule applies to veterans: If the employee wants military caregiver leave to care for a veteran, the veteran must be undergoing medical treatment, recuperation, or therapy for a serious illness or injury.

Covered Family Members

To take caregiver leave under this part of the law, the injured or ill servicemember must be the employee's family member. As is true for all other FMLA provisions, this definition includes the employee's spouse, parent, or child. However, like the qualifying exigency provision, the caregiver entitlement extends by necessity to adult children. If an employee's adult child suffers a serious injury while on active duty, the employee is entitled to take leave under this provision.

Employees are also entitled to leave under this provision if they are "next of kin" to a covered servicemember. If a servicemember has designated a blood relative as his or her next of kin for purposes of military caregiver leave, the designated person qualifies as next of kin. However, if the servicemember has not designated a blood relative, the servicemember's next of kin is his or her nearest blood relative (other than a parent, child, or spouse) in the following order of priority:

1. blood relatives who have been granted legal custody of the servicemember
2. siblings
3. grandparents

4. aunts and uncles, and

5. first cousins.

If the servicemember has not designated a next of kin, all blood relatives within the same level of the highest priority relationship are considered the servicemember's next of kin. For example, if a servicemember has two siblings, and no blood relative has been granted legal custody of the servicemember, both siblings would be considered the servicemember's next of kin.

The purpose of these rules is to make sure that someone, or more than one person, is available to care for an injured or ill servicemember. A spouse, parent, child, and next of kin (or even more than one next of kin) may all take leave to care for the same servicemember, if necessary. However, this probably won't be an issue for most companies, which are unlikely to employ more than one family member.

> **EXAMPLE:** Tory lost a leg and suffered other injuries in a bomb blast while serving in Iraq. She returned home and received inpatient treatment, followed by outpatient care with daily rehabilitation appointments. Tory didn't designate anyone as her next of kin for purposes of military caregiver leave. She is married, her mother lives nearby, and she has three brothers. One of her brothers, Eddie, works for your company and requests military caregiver leave several days a week to take his sister to her rehab sessions and help her with her exercises. He plans to work until 11 a.m., when he will go to his sister's home, help her get dressed, prepare her lunch, take her to her appointment, bring her home, and assist her with her home exercises. He estimates that he'll need to take off five hours a day, three days a week, for a couple of months.
>
> You're planning to tell Eddie that he can take some time off in the next few weeks to help with his sister's care, but only until he uses up his 40 hours of accrued vacation time. After all, Tory's husband can help out, her mother lives nearby and is already retired, and what about those two other brothers? Plus, are siblings even covered by the FMLA? Luckily, you remember the new military caregiver provision: In this situation, and for this type of time off, Eddie is entitled to FMLA leave. As long as he is providing care and the other requirements are met, he may take time off. Tory's husband, mother, and other two brothers are also entitled to military caregiver leave (although none of them work for your company).

As is true of FMLA leave to care for a family member with a serious health condition, you may ask an employee who takes military caregiver leave to provide documentation of a family relationship. For more information, see "Proving a Family Relationship," in Chapter 4, which also provides a form you can use for this purpose.

How Much Leave an Employee May Take

For this provision only, an employee is entitled to 26 weeks of leave, rather than the 12 weeks allowed for other types of FMLA leave. Unlike other types of FMLA leave, however, military caregiver leave isn't an annually renewed entitlement. Instead, it's available once per servicemember, per injury. The employee may take up to 26 weeks of leave in a single 12-month period. The employee may be entitled to another 26-week leave only in one of the following two circumstances:

- The servicemember suffers a different serious injury or illness in the line of duty on active duty. For example, if the servicemember recovered, then suffered another serious injury or illness during a subsequent deployment, the family member would be entitled to a second 26-week leave. If the servicemember later manifested a second injury or illness from the initial event, that would also entitle the employee to a second leave. However, multiple injuries sustained in a single incident don't entitle the employee to more than one leave period.

- A different family member suffers a serious injury or illness in the line of duty on active duty. If, for example, an employee's two children both serve in the military, and the employee takes time off in 2014 to care for one who is injured, the employee would be entitled to an additional 26-week leave period if the other child was injured in 2016.

Even if the employee is entitled to more than one leave period based on these rules, the employee may never take more than 26 weeks of leave in one 12-month period. This limit applies even if the two events entitling the employee to leave occur during the same 12 months. And, the employee's total leave entitlement—for military caregiver leave and all other types of FMLA leave—is 26 weeks in a year. So, for example, if an employee already used six weeks of leave for the adoption of a child, the employee may use only 20 weeks of military caregiver leave in the same 12-month period.

Calculating the employee's leave entitlement is covered in Chapter 7, as are the rules for determining when the 12-month leave period begins.

Military caregiver leave doesn't carry over to a subsequent 12-month period. Any part of the 26 weeks the employee doesn't use in 12 months is lost.

Limits on Leave Available to Married Couples

Spouses who work for the same employer are entitled to a combined 26 weeks. As explained in Chapter 5, you may limit a married couple to no more than 12 weeks of combined leave for parenting and caring for a parent with a serious health condition. This type of limit also applies to military caregiver leave: Spouses who work for the same employer can be required to limit their total leave for military caregiver purposes, parenting, and caring for a parent with a serious health condition to 26 weeks in a 12-month period. See Chapter 5 for a discussion of how much combined leave each spouse may take and how much leave is available for purposes not subject to the combined restriction (such as leave for the employee's own serious health condition).

Intermittent or Reduced-Schedule Leave

Like leave for a serious health condition, military caregiver leave may be taken intermittently or on a reduced schedule when medically necessary. The certification form asks the family member's health care provider to indicate the medical necessity of intermittent or reduced-schedule leave; see Chapter 9 for more information.

Substitution of Paid Leave

An employee may choose, or you may require the employee, to substitute applicable paid leave for military caregiver leave. As is true of other types of FMLA leave, the employee's reason for leave must be covered by your company's paid leave program, and your company may require the employee to comply with your company's policies—for example, requiring a certain type or amount of notice—for using paid leave.

Common Mistakes Regarding Military Family Leave—And How to Avoid Them

Mistake 1: **Failing to recognize employee requests for military family leave as FMLA requests.**

Avoid this mistake by taking the following steps:

- Train yourself to think of the FMLA whenever an employee mentions a family member's military service, past or present, as a reason for time off.
- Ask questions to determine whether the time off might count as qualifying exigency or military caregiver leave.
- Use certifications to determine whether an employee's leave meets the medical and military requirements of military caregiver leave.
- Remember that more family members—including parents of adult children, siblings, and grandparents—may qualify for military family leave than for other types of FMLA leave.

Mistake 2: **Miscalculating how much leave is available for military family purposes.**

Avoid this mistake by taking the following steps:

- Count a qualifying exigency just like any other FMLA leave that is part of the employee's 12-week entitlement; if the employee has already used up his or her FMLA leave for the year, none is available for qualifying exigencies.
- Give employees their full 26 weeks of military caregiver leave. No matter how your company calculates its leave year for other purposes, the clock for an employee's military caregiver leave always starts on the first day of such leave, as explained in Chapter 7.

Mistake 3: **Mishandling qualifying exigency leave.**

Avoid this mistake by taking the following steps:

- Keep track of the limits on timing and duration for particular types of qualifying exigency leave.
- Allow qualifying exigency leave for grandparents, if an adult child is called to active duty and his or her children need care.
- Be consistent in which types of activities your company agrees to count as qualifying exigency leave; if you grant exceptions for some activities and not others, make sure you have a good reason.

✓ **Managers' Checklist: Military Family Leave**

☐ Whenever an employee takes or requests time off relating to a family member's military service, I have determined whether the employee is eligible for either qualifying exigency or military caregiver leave.

☐ If the employee requests time off to care for an injured or ill family member, I have determined whether the employee qualifies for military caregiver leave.

    ☐ I have determined whether the employee meets the general eligibility requirements for FMLA leave.

    ☐ If the employee is not the spouse, parent, or child of the servicemember, I have determined whether the employee is the servicemember's next of kin.

        ☐ I have requested documentation of the family relationship, if appropriate.

        ☐ I have requested the servicemember's next of kin designation, if appropriate.

    ☐ I have asked whether the servicemember or veteran is or was a member of the regular Armed Forces, National Guard, or Reserves.

    ☐ I have provided the employee with a certification form to be completed by the servicemember's health care provider.

☐ If the employee requests time off to handle matters arising out of a family member's military duty, I have determined whether the employee is eligible for qualifying exigency leave.

    ☐ I have determined whether the employee meets the general eligibility requirements for FMLA leave.

    ☐ I have determined whether the employee has any FMLA leave left to use in this leave year.

    ☐ I have determined whether the family member is a current member the National Guard, Reserves, or regular Armed Forces, or a retired member of the regular Armed Forces or Reserves.

    ☐ I have determined whether the employee is a covered family member for purposes of qualifying exigency leave, and I have requested documentation of the family relationship.

Managers' Checklist: Military Family Leave (continued)

☐ I have determined whether the employee's reason for leave may fall within one of the eight categories of qualifying exigency.

  ☐ If not:

    ☐ I have determined whether or not our company will agree to treat the reason for leave as a qualifying exigency.

    ☐ If our company will treat the leave as qualifying exigency leave, we have reached an agreement with the employee on the length and timing of the leave, and we have put this agreement in writing.

  ☐ If so, I have provided the employee with a certification form.

How Much Leave Can an Employee Take?

Counting the 12-Month Leave Year... 125

   Calculating the Leave Year for Military Caregiver Leave.................................... 126

   Calculating the Leave Year for Other Types of FMLA Leave............................ 127

   Choosing a Leave Year Method.. 129

   Applying the Leave Year Consistently.. 131

How Many Weeks May an Employee Take?.. 132

   Employees Who Don't Use Military Caregiver Leave.. 132

   Employees Who Use Only Military Caregiver Leave.. 132

   Employees Who Use Both Military Caregiver Leave
      and Other Types of FMLA Leave... 133

Counting Time Off as FMLA Leave... 136

Intermittent and Reduced-Schedule Leave... 138

   When Can an Employee Take Intermittent or
      Reduced-Schedule Leave?.. 139

   Part-Time Employees.. 144

   Employees Who Work Overtime... 145

   Exempt Employees.. 145

   Administering Intermittent or Reduced-Schedule Leave................................ 146

**Common Mistakes Regarding Leave Duration—
   And How to Avoid Them**... 149

Chapter Highlights

☆ Employees eligible for military caregiver leave may take up to 26 weeks of FMLA leave in a single 12-month period, beginning on the first day of leave.

☆ Employees eligible for all other types of leave are entitled to 12 weeks of FMLA leave in a 12-month "leave year."

☆ The 12-month "leave year" may be measured in one of four ways:
  • the calendar year
  • any fixed 12-month period, such as the fiscal year, the year starting on the anniversary of the employee's hire, and so on
  • twelve months counted forward from the date an employee begins FMLA leave, or
  • twelve months counted backward from the date an employee uses any FMLA leave.

☆ Your company must use the same calendaring method for all employees, except those using military caregiver leave. Your company may change calendaring methods with 60 days' advance notice.

☆ Each week of leave is based on the employee's normal workweek, including any overtime the employee is required to work.

☆ Employees eligible for military caregiver leave may take no more than 26 weeks of combined leave, for all FMLA-covered reasons, in a single 12-month period, of which no more than 12 weeks may be for purposes other than military caregiver leave.

☆ Only leave time the employee actually needs can be counted against the employee's available FMLA leave time.

☆ If needed for any reason other than parenting, FMLA leave may be taken intermittently or on a reduced schedule.

☆ Employees may take intermittent or reduced-schedule leave in the shortest increments of time used for other types of leave or in one-hour increments, whichever is shorter.

Y ou've come a long way. You've determined that your company is covered by the FMLA. You've confirmed that the employee seeking leave is FMLA-qualified and that the reason for leave falls within the FMLA. Now it's time to figure out how much leave the employee has— or has left—to use.

Most provisions of the FMLA require your company to give eligible employees up to 12 workweeks of leave in a 12-month period. But when does that period start and end? What if the employee took leave last December and wants more leave this July—does the employee get another 12 weeks of leave because it's a new calendar year, or does the employee have to wait a full 12 months? How much leave is available to an employee who works odd hours, part time, or overtime? What if the employee wants to take only one day or one hour off a week, rather than 12 weeks at once?

The military caregiver provision, which allows eligible employees to take up to 26 weeks of leave in a single 12-month period, can complicate the calculation. When does this 12-month period start and end—is it the same as for other types of FMLA leave? What does "single" 12-month period mean? What if an employee needs regular FMLA leave after taking military caregiver leave? How do you calculate how much total FMLA leave these employees get?

If you don't know the answers to these questions off the top of your head, you aren't alone. In this chapter, we'll give you the information you need to determine exactly how much FMLA leave is available to your employees. We explain how to measure the 12-month leave year, how to calculate 12 (or 26) weeks of leave in the 12-month leave year, how to handle requests for intermittent leave or reduced-schedule leave, how to calculate leave for employees who work part time, and more.

Counting the 12-Month Leave Year

Each eligible employee is entitled to 12 weeks of FMLA leave in a 12-month period for his or her own serious health condition, to care for a family member with a serious health condition, to bond with a new child, or to handle qualifying exigencies relating to a family member's call to active military duty. Under the military caregiver provision, employees are entitled

to 26 weeks of FMLA leave in a single 12-month period to care for a family member who suffers or aggravates a serious illness or injury on active military duty.

Believe it or not, these two 12-month periods may be different. The 12-month period for military caregiver leave always begins when the employee's leave begins. However, for the other types of FMLA leave (those that allow for 12 weeks off), employers may choose among four different methods of measuring the "leave year" during which an employee may take leave. This means you may have to track two different leave years for a single employee.

TIP

FMLA leave cannot be carried over from one leave year to the next. No matter how your company measures the 12-month leave year, employees can't carry over FMLA leave. An employee is never entitled to more than 12 weeks of any type of leave (or 26 weeks of military caregiver leave) in a given leave year.

Calculating the Leave Year for Military Caregiver Leave

Military caregiver leave is different than other types of FMLA leave in a number of important ways. Perhaps most notably, it allows employees to take up to 26 weeks off, rather than the 12 weeks allowed for all other types of FMLA leave. And, it's not a renewable annual entitlement: As explained in Chapter 6, this is a "per-servicemember, per-injury" right that, absent unusual circumstances, an employee may use only once.

Here's another difference: The 12-month leave year for military caregiver leave always begins on the employee's first day of leave. As the Department of Labor explained in its revised regulations, the purpose of this rule is to make sure that employees can use their full 26 weeks of military caregiver leave. If the 12-month leave year was the same for military caregiver leave as for other types of FMLA leave, the employee may have already used some FMLA leave for other purposes, which would reduce the total amount of military caregiver leave available to the employee. Because military caregiver leave will typically be a one-time entitlement, the DOL wanted to make sure employees get the full benefit provided by law.

Calculating the Leave Year for Other Types of FMLA Leave

The FMLA gives companies four different ways to define the leave year for all other types of FMLA leave:

- the calendar year
- any fixed 12-month period, such as the company's fiscal year, a year starting on the anniversary of an employee's hire, or a year defined by state law
- the 12-month period counted forward from the date that the employee begins FMLA leave, or
- a "rolling" 12-month period counted backward from the date that the employee uses any FMLA leave.

Employers may choose any of these methods. Whichever method you decide to use, it's important to consistently apply the same method to all employees. If you don't, employees can choose whichever method is most advantageous to them.

The Calendar Year or a Fixed-Period Year

If your company chooses to measure the leave year by either a calendar year or another fixed 12-month period (like the fiscal year), an eligible employee is entitled to up to 12 weeks of FMLA leave at any time in the selected leave year. A major disadvantage for companies that use one of these methods is that an employee could take 24 weeks of continuous leave in a row, if the leave spans the end of one year and the beginning of the next. It's difficult for many employers to have an employee out for that long.

> EXAMPLE: Your company measures the FMLA leave year by the calendar year: From January 1 to December 31, each eligible employee is entitled to 12 weeks of FMLA leave. Your employee, Megan, begins her 12-week FMLA leave on October 1. As of January 1, Megan is entitled to 12 weeks of FMLA leave for the new leave year. This means she will be able to take a solid 24 weeks of FMLA leave in a row.

Counting Forward

If your company chooses the third method, an eligible employee is entitled to up to 12 weeks of FMLA leave in the year beginning on the first day that

the employee takes FMLA leave. From that day forward, the employee has 12 months to take the full 12 weeks of FMLA leave. The next 12-month period begins when leave is next taken after the initial 12-month leave year ends. For example, if an employee began leave on February 15, 2015, the employee would have until February 14, 2016 to use up the 12 weeks of leave. If the employee again wanted leave beginning June 20, 2016, the clock would start over. (Note that this is the method required for all military caregiver leave, as explained above.)

This is a relatively simple method for your company to use, because you can administer it easily on a case-by-case basis. However, it may allow employees to take more than 12 weeks of leave in a given 12-month period in the same manner that the first two methods do.

> **EXAMPLE:** Your company counts the leave year by going forward one year from the date FMLA leave is first taken. Megan begins a six-week FMLA leave on December 1, 2014. On October 20, 2015, Megan requests to take her remaining six weeks of leave, returning on December 1, 2015. On January 2, 2016, Megan requests a full 12-week FMLA leave. So, Megan will get 18 weeks of FMLA leave between October 20, 2015 and March 27, 2016.

The "Rolling" Leave Year

A "rolling" year is just what it sounds like—an employee's leave eligibility rolls out throughout the year, as leave is taken. If your company calculates the leave year using this method, an eligible employee is entitled to up to 12 weeks of FMLA leave in the year measured backward from the first day that FMLA leave is taken. Each time the employee takes leave, any part of the 12-week entitlement that was not used in the immediately preceding 12 months is available for future leave.

This is less complicated as it sounds. Essentially, when an employee requests leave, you look back to the last 12 months to see if the employee has already used 12 weeks of leave. Below is a sample worksheet to keep track of hours used under the rolling year method; there is a blank copy (and all other forms in this book) online; see Appendix C for details.

Chart for Calculating Leave Under Rolling Leave Year Method

FMLA Leave Tracking for Jane Edwards

Date Leave Commenced	Amount of Leave Taken	Eligibility for Additional Leave
2/12/13	4 wks.	Currently eligible—8 wks.
4/22/13	4 wks.	Currently eligible—4 wks.
9/07/13	4 wks.	Eligible beginning 2/12/13
3/20/14	4 wks.	Eligible beginning 4/22/13
7/17/14	2 wks.	Currently eligible—2 wks.

The main advantage of this method is that it does not allow employees to take FMLA leave totaling more than 12 weeks in any 12-month period.

EXAMPLE: Jane comes to you on February 7, 2015 asking for two weeks of FMLA leave. You look back to the last twelve months, from February 7, 2014 to February 7, 2015 to see how much FMLA she has used. Jane used four weeks on March 20, 2014 and two weeks on July 17, 2014. Because Jane has used six weeks of FMLA leave in the last 12 months, she still has six weeks of available FMLA leave. You should grant her request.

Choosing a Leave Year Method

For military caregiver leave, the 12-month leave year always begins on the first day an employee takes leave; your company can't choose the leave year. For all other types of FMLA leave, however, your company may choose among the four options discussed above. Be sure to define the "leave year" in your company's written FMLA policy and clearly describe which method the company will use. (See Appendix B for a sample FMLA policy.) If your company's chosen method is not stated in its policies, employees will be allowed to use the method most favorable to them, whether or not it's the best method for the company.

If, after reading this, your company decides to choose a new calculation method, it can do so. However, if employees are on leave or have requested leave, the company must provide 60 days' notice of the change of method to all employees. During that 60-day period, the employee can continue to utilize the method of his or her choice. Once the 60 days has passed, your company may begin using its selected method for all FMLA leaves.

Lessons from the *Real World*

Employees are entitled to rely on old leave year calculation method if their employer doesn't give 60 days' notice in writing of change in method.

Carl Thom, Jr., worked for American Standard as a molder. After he injured his shoulder off duty, he requested FMLA leave for surgery and recovery from April 27, 2005, returning to work on June 27, 2005. American granted his request in writing. At the time Thom made his request, he believed that American used the calendar year method for calculating the leave year, which meant his leave entitlement did not expire until July 14, 2005. However, unbeknownst to Thom, American had changed its leave year calculation method to the rolling leave year method on March 1, 2005, but provided no notice to Thom of the change. Under the rolling leave year method, Thom's leave entitlement expired on June 13, 2005.

On June 14, American called Thom because he had not returned to work on June 13. When Thom tried to give American a doctor's note that he would be returning to work on June 18 (still well before the agreed return date), American told him he was fired for unexcused absences after June 13.

The court found that American hadn't given proper notice (60-days' notice in writing) to Thom of the change in its leave year calculation method. And, the court found that American had not acted in good faith because it applied the rolling leave year method after allowing Thom to rely on its prior calendar-year method. Then it used Thom's ignorance of the changed policy to terminate him. Thom won the case and the court instructed the jury to award double damages against American for violation of the FMLA.

Thom v. American Standard, Inc., 666 F.3d 968 (6th Cir. 2011).

POLICY ALERT

Your policy determines the leave year. If your company does not select a leave year calculation method, uses different methods with different employees, or changes methods without proper notice, each employee will get to choose his or her favored method.

Applying the Leave Year Consistently

Regardless of which method your company uses to calculate the leave year, it must use the same method for all employees who request FMLA leave. It cannot choose different methods for different employees. If one department uses a different method from another and an employee sues to challenge the method used, a court will use the method most beneficial to the employee.

Military caregiver leave is an exception to this rule. Employers must use the "counting forward" method to calculate the leave year for this type of leave, as explained above. However, this doesn't mean employers must use the counting forward method for other types of FMLA leave. As long as employers choose one method for all other types of FMLA leave and use it consistently, they don't lose their right to choose the leave year calculation method.

Another exception applies to certain employers who do business in more than one state. Some states require employers to use a particular method for calculating the leave year under their own medical leave laws. If your company has employees in a state with this type of law, it must apply the method required in that state. However, if your company does business in other states that don't have this same requirement, it is free to use a different (but uniform) method for employees in those other states. In this limited situation, using two different methods to calculate the leave year—one in the state where it is mandated and the other in all other locations—won't give employees the right to choose whichever leave method works best for them.

SEE AN EXPERT

Multistate employers may need some expert help. You can find information on each state's family and medical leave laws in Appendix A, but if you have to integrate various state laws with the FMLA, you'll appreciate some advice from a lawyer.

How Many Weeks May an Employee Take?

Employees are entitled to 12 total weeks of FMLA leave, unless they need military caregiver leave, for which they can take up to 26 weeks off. If an employee needs both types of leave within a single leave year, the calculations can get a bit more tricky.

Employees Who Don't Use Military Caregiver Leave

Employees are entitled to a combined total of 12 weeks of FMLA leave to care for a family member with a serious health condition, for their own serious health conditions, to bond with a new child, or to handle qualifying exigencies relating to a family member's call to active duty. If an employee needs leave for more than one qualifying reason during the 12-month leave year, all of that leave counts toward the employee's 12-week total. In other words, the employee gets 12 weeks of leave per year, not per qualifying reason.

> EXAMPLE: Your company uses the calendar year method for measuring the leave year. Max takes three weeks of FMLA leave in March to recover from hernia surgery. In August, he takes nine weeks of FMLA leave after his wife has a baby. In November, Max's father, a retired member of the Reserves, is called to active duty in Afghanistan, and Max requests FMLA leave to help him get his legal and financial affairs in order. You tell Max that he has no FMLA leave available until January, but Max replies that he should still have 12 weeks available, because he hasn't used any FMLA leave for a qualifying exigency.
>
> Nice try, Max! Employees get 12 total weeks of FMLA leave in a 12-month period, for all qualifying reasons (except military caregiver leave, for which employees can take up to 26 weeks). They don't get 12 weeks for each type of FMLA leave.

Employees Who Use Only Military Caregiver Leave

Employees are entitled to up to 26 weeks of leave in a single 12-month period for military caregiver leave. As explained above, the 12-month "clock" starts on the first day of an employee's leave. Any leave the employee doesn't use during the 12-month leave year is lost; the employee can't take it later.

An employee is entitled to only one 26-week leave per servicemember, per injury. Unless another family member suffers a service-related injury, or the same family member suffers a different service-related injury, this is a one-time-only entitlement. Even an employee who is in the unfortunate position of qualifying for two periods of military caregiver leave may take no more than 26 weeks off in a single 12-month period, regardless of when the employee became eligible for the second period of caregiver leave.

> EXAMPLE: Ellen comes from a military family. Her father served in the Army, her husband serves in the Marine Corps, and, although none of her children are career military, all three are members of the National Guard. Ellen requests FMLA leave to begin May 5, to care for her husband who was seriously injured on active duty in Iraq. Ellen takes 22 weeks of leave and returns to work on October 6.
>
> On February 1, Ellen's son Craig, who had been called to active duty in Afghanistan, is returned home after contracting malaria. Craig is severely weakened by the disease; his doctor predicts that he'll be hospitalized for at least several weeks, after which he will need assistance with daily tasks until he regains his strength. Ellen asks you for another eight weeks of leave. Because she is one of the unlucky few to have more than one family member suffer a serious illness or injury on active duty, you begin a new 12-month leave clock and inform her she is entitled to another 26 weeks of leave. Were you correct?
>
> Nope. Although Ellen is entitled to another "single" 12-month period for her son, she may not take more than 26 total weeks of leave in 12 months. Ellen has four weeks of her original 26-week entitlement remaining, and that's all the FMLA leave she may take until May 5, when her first "single" 12-month period ends.

Employees Who Use Both Military Caregiver Leave and Other Types of FMLA Leave

What about an employee who needs military caregiver leave and FMLA leave for a different purpose—such as the employee's own serious health condition—in the same leave year? These employees may not take more than 26 total weeks of FMLA leave, for any purpose, in a 12-month period. And, no more than 12 of those weeks may be used for all other types of FMLA leave combined. In other words, an employee's eligibility for military

caregiver leave doesn't give that employee more than 12 weeks to use for other FMLA-qualifying reasons.

> **EXAMPLE 1:** Benito's wife was seriously injured while serving in the military. He has taken 20 weeks of leave, starting on September 1, to care for her. His son now has a serious medical condition requiring surgery and rehabilitation. Benito requests ten weeks of leave, starting on April 15, to care for the boy. Do you have to grant that request under the amended FMLA?
>
> No. As the spouse of an injured servicemember, Benito is entitled to a maximum of 26 weeks in a 12-month period for all FMLA leave. That 12-month period began on September 1, and he's used up 20 weeks of it. So, Benito has only six weeks of any type of FMLA leave left until September 1 of the following year.

> **EXAMPLE 2:** Now assume that Benito has taken only eight weeks of leave to care for his wife since she was injured on September 1. Benito provided care for the first few weeks after her injury, then his mother-in-law took over as the primary caregiver. Benito has taken a few days off here and there, when his mother-in-law was unavailable. When Benito's son requires surgery, he asks for 16 weeks of leave, to begin April 15. Must you grant this request?
>
> Still no. Even though Benito has used up only eight weeks of his 26-week entitlement for military caregiver leave to care for his wife, he is still entitled to only 12 total weeks of FMLA leave for all other purposes. His request for time off for his son's serious health condition is subject to this 12-week limit. Although he would be entitled to 18 additional weeks to continue caring for his wife, if necessary, he may not use all of this leave for other FMLA purposes.

If this doesn't already seem complicated enough, remember that two different leave years may be in play. For military caregiver leave, the leave year begins on the date the employee first takes leave. For all other types of FMLA leave, your company may use a different leave year. These situations can turn into brain teasers, although the basic rules remain the same:

- Employees who are eligible for military caregiver leave may take no more than 26 total weeks of FMLA leave in the single 12-month period. No more than 12 of those weeks may be for all types of FMLA leave other than military caregiver leave.
- Employees may not take more than 12 weeks of FMLA leave for all purposes other than military caregiver leave in the leave year.

- FMLA leave, whether military caregiver leave or any other type, does not carry over from one year to the next. Leave that is not used during the leave year is lost.

Here are some examples that illustrate how to calculate leave entitlements when two different leave years are in play. As you read these examples, keep in mind that time off must be designated either as military caregiver leave or as another type of FMLA leave, but not both. In many instances, military caregiver leave would also qualify as leave for a family member's serious health condition. However, the revised regulations state that this time must be counted and designated as military caregiver leave only, to give employees the full benefit of this time off. (Chapter 8 explains this rule—and how to designate FMLA leave—in more detail.)

EXAMPLE 1: **Calendar Leave Year.** Josie's company uses a calendar year for FMLA leave. Josie takes eight weeks of leave when she adopts a new child, starting February 15. On August 1, Josie starts taking military caregiver leave to care for her brother, who has returned from Iraq with serious combat-related injuries. (Josie is his next of kin.) She is entitled to 26 weeks of leave in the 12-month period beginning on August 1. But, through December 31, Josie is entitled to only four additional weeks of FMLA leave for any other purpose.

Starting on January 1 of the following year, Josie will begin a new leave year for all other types of FMLA leave, and will again be entitled to 12 weeks. However, the 26-week limit for all types of leave will continue to apply to the 12-month leave year for military caregiver leave. For example, if Josie uses her entire 26-week allotment of military caregiver leave, she won't be entitled to any more FMLA leave for any reason until August 1 of the following year. At that point, she will once again be eligible for 12 weeks of FMLA leave for other purposes for the remainder of the regular FMLA leave year.

EXAMPLE 2: **Counting Forward.** Terrence's company uses a counting forward method to calculate the FMLA leave year. Terrence hasn't used any FMLA leave in years. On May 1, he begins taking military caregiver leave to care for his daughter, who contracted a serious illness while on active duty. He takes 20 weeks off to care for her, returning to work on September 18.

On December 15, Terrence's mother has a heart attack. Her doctors decide that she needs surgery, for which she is hospitalized for two weeks. She is

immobilized and needs care for a couple of months afterwards. Because Terrence's company uses the counting forward method, he is entitled to 12 weeks of FMLA leave for other purposes (including his mother's serious health condition) in the year that begins on December 15. However, he only has six weeks of leave left to use in the 12-month period that ends on May 1 of the following year, because he already used 20 weeks of military caregiver leave. Terrence may use six weeks now to care for his mother; on May 1, he will become entitled to use his remaining six weeks, if necessary.

EXAMPLE 3: **Rolling Leave Year.** Caroline's company uses a rolling leave year for FMLA leave. Caroline took ten weeks of FMLA leave for childbirth and caring for her new child, starting on January 1. She returned to work on March 12. Her husband was seriously injured while on active duty, and Caroline took ten weeks of military caregiver leave starting on June 1.

On October 1, Caroline asks for four weeks off to care for her baby, who needs surgery. Because her company uses the rolling leave year, however, Caroline has only two weeks of FMLA leave to use for other purposes. She already used ten weeks of leave in the past 12 months, and she won't be eligible for more FMLA leave until January 1. If Caroline needed that time to continue providing military caregiver leave for her husband, however, she would have 16 weeks of leave left.

Counting Time Off as FMLA Leave

Under the FMLA, eligible employees are allowed to take off 12 workweeks (or 26 workweeks for military caregiver leave) in the 12-month leave year. If an employee takes FMLA leave all at once, you won't need to consider the employee's hours or schedule in determining how much leave is available. Whether the employee works part time or full time or puts in plenty of overtime, an employee who takes a whole week off at once has used up one week's worth of FMLA leave (subject to the rules set out below).

If an employee takes intermittent or reduced-schedule leave, however, you'll need to figure out how many total hours of FMLA leave are available to the employee. In this situation, the employee's work hours determine how much leave the employee can take. We explain how to make these calculations in "Intermittent and Reduced-Schedule Leave," below.

Whether an employee takes FMLA leave all at once or a little bit at a time, you'll need to know what time off counts as FMLA leave. Here are the rules:

- **Time spent working is not FMLA leave.** If an employee is on full-time FMLA leave but continues to work (perhaps putting in a few hours at home), the hours worked don't count as part of the employee's FMLA leave time. This is true even if your company does not require the employee to work on leave, but the employee voluntarily does it anyway. So, be sure that employees on FMLA leave are not working. Follow up with managers and supervisors to make sure they understand the rule and they tell employees not to work on leave.

- **Extra time taken off at your request isn't FMLA leave.** If the employee agrees to take off more time than he or she actually needs—for example, if an employee agrees to take a full day rather than a couple of hours so that you can hire a temporary employee to perform the employee's duties for the day—you can't count the difference between the time off and the time actually needed against the employee's FMLA leave entitlement. These extra hours were a convenience to you and can't be held against the employee. But, if it's not possible for the employee to leave work or return to work midshift, the entire period of absence counts as FMLA leave. For example, it would be impossible for an employee who works as an airline attendant to rejoin a flight in midair; in this situation, the entire shift counts as FMLA leave, even if the employee didn't need all of that time off.

  > **EXAMPLE:** Hal usually works an eight-hour shift, five days a week. Hal requests three hours off every Tuesday to care for his sick father. You instruct Hal to take all of Tuesday off, so that your company can put a different employee into his original schedule. You log Hal's eight hours off as FMLA leave. Was this correct?
  >
  > No. Only the three hours off that Hal needed can be counted as FMLA leave time. The other five hours may be designated as paid time off or other leave under your company's policies but do not reduce Hal's available FMLA leave time.

- **Holidays don't affect the count for full weeks of FMLA leave.** All full workweeks are counted; it doesn't matter that a holiday falls within one of the weeks that an employee is out on FMLA leave. However,

if an employee takes less than a full week of leave, a holiday that falls within that partial week of leave is not counted against the employee's available FMLA time.

- **If the company is closed for at least a week, that time doesn't count as FMLA leave.** If your company shuts down operations entirely and employees are not required to come to work for a week or more, that week will not count as one of the employee's FMLA leave workweeks. For example, a company that closes its doors for two weeks in August can't count those weeks as FMLA leave for any employee.

Counting Time Off for Airline Flight Crews

In 2013, the Department of Labor adopted regulations regarding leave entitlement and calculating leave usage for airline flight crew employees. Under the regulations, airline flight crew employees are entitled to 72 total days of FMLA leave during any 12-month period. Eligible airline flight crew employees are also entitled to 156 days of military caregiver leave in a single 12-month period. These entitlements are based on a uniform six-day workweek, regardless of time actually worked or paid, multiplied by the FMLA 12-week leave entitlement (or the 26-week leave entitlement for military caregiver leave). For example, if an eligible pilot took six weeks of leave to care for her sick child, the pilot would use 36 days (6 days x 6 weeks) of her 72-day entitlement.

Intermittent and Reduced-Schedule Leave

Sometimes an employee doesn't need a full workweek off at a time or doesn't need to take all of his or her FMLA leave at once. An employee may, for example, request permission to take hours or days off "as needed" to care for an ill family member when the usual caretaker is unavailable. This "intermittent leave" is allowed under the FMLA. Intermittent leave is leave taken in separate blocks of time for a single qualifying reason, such as a course of treatment spread over months or flare-ups of a chronic illness.

An employee may also need a reduced work schedule, for example, during recovery from surgery or illness. The FMLA allows an eligible employee to take "reduced-schedule" leave when he or she needs to work fewer hours per week or per day than usual, typically while the employee or a family member is recovering from or being treated for a serious health condition.

When an employee uses one of these types of leave, figuring out how much leave the employee is entitled to and how long it will take to use up the 12-week or 26-week allotment can be challenging. It gets especially tricky for part-time employees or those with irregular work schedules because you have to measure the leave taken based on the employee's normal workweek. In this section, we explain how to calculate intermittent and reduced-schedule leave for employees working all types of schedules.

RELATED TOPIC

See Chapter 10 for information on managing intermittent leave, including rules that allow flexibility in scheduling. When Congress passed the FMLA, it recognized that providing intermittent leave could impose a significant burden on employers. The law gives companies a couple of options for easing the load, including the right to transfer an employee who needs intermittent leave to a different position and the right to require employees to schedule foreseeable intermittent leave in a manner that isn't unduly disruptive. These rules—and tips for making sure employees don't abuse the right to take intermittent leave—are covered in Chapter 10.

When Can an Employee Take Intermittent or Reduced-Schedule Leave?

An employee may take intermittent or reduced-schedule leave if it's medically necessary for a serious health condition (the employee's own or that of a family member). Employees may take military caregiver leave on an intermittent or reduced schedule if it's medically necessary. Employees may also take intermittent or reduced-schedule leave to handle qualifying exigencies arising from a family member's call to active duty. As explained in Chapter 5, the FMLA doesn't require you to provide intermittent or reduced-schedule parenting leave, but you're permitted to do so as long as you do it consistently.

Here are some examples of conditions that qualify for intermittent or reduced-schedule leave:

- **An employee is receiving chemotherapy and radiation treatment for cancer.** The weekly treatment renders him unable to work, so he reduces his schedule by one afternoon per week to receive treatment and recover afterward.

- **An employee's mother has multiple sclerosis.** Some days, she is able to care for herself; other days, she needs assistance. The employee can take intermittent leave to care for her mother when necessary.

- **An employee has back surgery to repair a herniated disk.** The employee returns to work part time for several weeks, until he is strong enough to work full time. Afterward, the employee takes a couple of hours off each Friday to go to physical therapy, as well as an hour every other week for a doctor's appointment to check his progress. This employee is using both reduced-schedule leave and intermittent leave.

Lessons from the *Real World*

An employee suffering from flare-ups of a chronic condition is entitled to intermittent leave.

Kathleen Victorelli, an employee at Shadyside Hospital, requested leave when she experienced an episode of stomach pain, nausea, and vomiting as a result of peptic ulcer disease that her doctor had diagnosed two years earlier. The hospital refused the request. Victorelli took the leave anyway, and the hospital fired her. She sued, claiming that Shadyside had violated the FMLA.

The court held that Victorelli's peptic ulcer disease was a chronic medical condition that entitled her to intermittent leave when her condition flared up. *Victorelli v. Shadyside Hosp.*, 128 F.3d 184 (3rd Cir. 1997).

Leave Must Be Necessary

An employee may not take intermittent leave simply because that's what he or she prefers. It must be medically necessary or necessitated by a qualifying

exigency arising from a family member's call to active duty. Qualifying exigency leave may often be intermittent. For example, if an employee must attend counseling sessions, school functions, or military events, those activities will probably take up only a few hours at a time. This time will count as intermittent FMLA leave.

Intermittent leave is available for a serious health condition or for military caregiver leave only if medically necessary. This means that the employee must need the leave in separate increments rather than all at once.

How can you tell whether intermittent leave is medically necessary? By getting a medical certification. On the certification form, the employee's (or family member's) health care provider must state that intermittent leave is necessary. The provider must also indicate the expected duration of leave and, if intermittent leave is necessary for medical treatment, the dates and duration of the treatment. For more on the medical certification form, see Chapter 9. Chapter 10 explains how to use the information in the form—and in subsequent recertifications, if necessary—to make sure an employee uses intermittent leave appropriately.

> **EXAMPLE:** Eric tells you that he needs to reduce his work schedule from 40 hours per week to 30 hours per week to recover from surgery. You request medical certification and give him a preliminary designation of the leave as FMLA-qualified, subject to withdrawal if the certification is inadequate (see "Counting Time Off as FMLA Leave" in Chapter 8).
>
> When you get the medical certification, you discover that the surgery is elective cosmetic surgery to reduce eyelid puffiness. You withdraw the preliminary FMLA designation and deny Eric's request for FMLA leave to recover from this surgery. Have you violated the FMLA?
>
> No. Elective surgery and recovery from it don't count as serious health conditions under the FMLA.
>
> Eric has the surgery on a Saturday and returns to work on Monday, a little bruised and bandaged but able to work. However, on Wednesday, Eric calls in to explain that he has a postoperative infection and his doctor has placed him on a regimen of antibiotics and a restricted work schedule of 25 hours per week for two weeks.
>
> Because you have read this book, you send Eric notice that this reduced-schedule leave may qualify as FMLA leave, because the postsurgery complications are FMLA-qualified (even though the initial surgery wasn't).

Employees Must Be Able to Perform the Essential Functions of the Job

Because an employee on intermittent or reduced-schedule leave continues to work, the employee must still be able to perform the essential functions of his or her job. (See Chapter 4 to learn what an "essential function" is.) In contrast, an employee who takes FMLA leave all at once for a serious health condition must be unable to perform an essential job function. These opposing requirements are based on the different types of leave: An employee on intermittent leave must still be able to do the job while at work, but an employee on full-time FMLA leave won't be working at all.

Lessons from the Real World

An employee who cannot perform the job's essential functions is not entitled to intermittent leave or reinstatement.

Minnie Hatchett worked as a business manager for Philander Smith College. A skylight fell on her head, injuring her to such a degree that she couldn't perform certain essential functions of her job. She asked permission to continue working part time, but the college refused the request and told her she had to go on full-time leave. At the end of her FMLA leave, Hatchett still could not perform all the essential functions of her job, so the college offered her some alternative positions. She rejected them, so the college terminated her employment. Hatchett sued the college for violating the FMLA.

The court sided with the college, finding that an employee who cannot perform the essential functions of her job is not entitled to reduced leave schedule or reinstatement under the FMLA.

Hatchett v. Philander Smith Coll., 251 F.3d 670 (8th Cir. 2001).

Applying the 1,250-Hour Eligibility Requirement

An employee on intermittent or reduced-scheduled leave doesn't become ineligible for FMLA leave if his or her hours drop below the 1,250-hour requirement (because of the FMLA-protected schedule). As long as the

employee worked 1,250 hours in 12 months at the time of initially requesting the intermittent or reduced-schedule leave, the employee's leave is protected for absences relating to the original condition requiring intermittent leave. In other words, you don't recalculate the employee's eligibility.

This rule applies only to intermittent leave taken for the same condition. If an employee properly qualifies for intermittent leave and then needs FMLA leave for a different reason within the same 12-month period, you should recalculate the employee's eligibility at the time of the second request. In doing so, you needn't count the employee's leave hours as hours worked. The odd result of this rule is that an employee might be eligible for one type of FMLA leave (intermittent leave that began when the employee met the eligibility requirements) but not for others.

> **EXAMPLE 1:** Telly, one of your company's part-time employees, has worked 25 hours per week for five years. For the first 12 weeks of 2013, Telly needs to reduce his hours to 20 per week so he can care for his wife, who is receiving cancer treatment. Your company uses the calendar leave year calculation. In July of 2013, Telly's wife takes a turn for the worse, and he asks to resume his reduced leave schedule effective July 1. You count up his time for the last 12 months and discover that he's only worked 1,240 hours. Should you deny his leave request?
>
> No. Because Telly needs intermittent leave for the same condition, you can't redetermine his eligibility during the leave year. Although his hours have dropped below the eligibility threshold, he is still entitled to leave.

> **EXAMPLE 2:** Now assume that Telly needs to take time off, starting July 1, 2013, for his own serious health condition. May you deny this request?
>
> Yes. Because Telly is requesting leave for a different condition, you must redetermine his eligibility. He hasn't worked 1,250 hours at the time his leave is scheduled to begin, so he isn't qualified to take this leave.

And, the employee must meet the 1,250-hour test at the start of each FMLA leave year. Once the employee has used up his or her FMLA leave, you will need to recalculate the employee's leave eligibility as of the next request for leave. When making this calculation, the employee's leave time does not count as hours worked.

Part-Time Employees

Under the FMLA, a part-time employee or an employee with variable hours is entitled to leave in proportion to the amount of time he or she normally works. In other words, the leave time allowed for those employees is prorated. Usually, you will not need to calculate the pro rata time unless the employee is requesting intermittent or partial leave: whether an employee normally works 15 hours in a workweek or 50 hours, an employee who takes a whole week off has used one week's worth of leave time. On the other hand, if the employee uses only a few hours here and there, you have to figure how much total leave time the employee has available.

> **EXAMPLE 1:** Leslie, who normally works 30 hours per week, needs 15 hours off each week due to a serious medical condition. Because Leslie is reducing her schedule by 50%, she will take half a week of FMLA leave each calendar week and will use up all her FMLA leave in 24 calendar weeks.

> **EXAMPLE 2:** Keith usually works the same shift, six days a week. He takes four calendar weeks and two days of leave. The four calendar weeks count as four full weeks of FMLA leave. In the last week, Keith is taking two days of leave out of his normal six-day work schedule, which equals a one-third workweek of leave. If Keith's regular schedule was four days a week, he would be taking half a week of leave in the last week.

If a part-time employee's schedule varies from week to week, you should measure the FMLA workweek by calculating the average weekly hours worked in the 12 months prior to the start of the FMLA leave. You can use the employee's timesheet or payroll records to come up with this figure. Make sure the employee agrees to the weekly average in a signed document.

> **EXAMPLE:** Manny works between 20 and 35 hours per week, depending on your company's needs. He requests intermittent leave for his asthma, which flares up periodically. You add up Manny's hours for the past 12 months, which total 1,456 hours. Dividing that by 52, you come up with a weekly average of 28 hours for the past year. Manny signs an agreement that his weekly average is 28 hours. Using that as Manny's average workweek, you track his FMLA leave. So, when Manny's asthma acts up at work and he takes four hours off, he has used one-seventh of a workweek of FMLA leave.

> CAUTION
>
> **Make sure part-time employees are eligible for leave in the first place.** As explained in Chapter 3, part-time employees must work 1,250 hours in the preceding 12 months to be eligible for FMLA leave. This works out to a bit more than 24 hours a week, 52 weeks a year. You won't have to do the math on intermittent leave availability unless your part-time employees can meet this initial eligibility requirement.

For employees who work irregular hours, the best practice is for you to sit down with the employee and reach an agreement as to the employee's "average" workweek. Calculate the weekly average for the 12 months immediately preceding the start of the leave. Put the calculation into a written agreement and have the employee sign it.

Employees Who Work Overtime

If your company requires an employee to work overtime, the overtime hours are considered part of the employee's normal workweek for purposes of calculating the amount of leave time an employee is entitled to. If an employee chooses to work overtime but is not required to, the overtime hours don't count as part of the employee's normal workweek.

> **EXAMPLE:** Claire and her coworkers all have to work four hours of overtime a week, in addition to their regular 40 hours. In this situation, Claire's usual workweek is 44 hours, and she's entitled to 528 total hours of FMLA leave per year (assuming she's otherwise qualified).
>
> If Claire's overtime was voluntary—that is, the company didn't require it but she decided to work it anyway—then she would have a 40-hour week for purposes of calculating her available FMLA leave.

Exempt Employees

It can be tricky to figure out what constitutes a normal workweek for exempt employees—employees who are not entitled to overtime pay. Most companies don't routinely track hours worked by exempt employees, because those employees don't get paid for putting in extra time. However, an exempt employee's FMLA entitlement is based on the hours the employee usually works, just like any other employee.

Because a salaried, exempt employee usually does not "clock in" or "clock out," when an exempt employee requests this type of leave, your company and the employee must agree in writing on the length of the employee's workweek. If you can't reach agreement, your company must track the exempt employee's hours to calculate how many hours are available for leave.

> EXAMPLE: Manny is an exempt manager who regularly works 60 hours per week. His FMLA workweek and intermittent time off are calculated according to a 60-hour workweek. When Manny takes four hours of FMLA intermittent leave one week, that counts as 1/15 of a workweek of his overall entitlement.

TIP

Pay docking rules don't apply to FMLA leave. Generally, employers may not dock the pay of an exempt employee for absences of less than a full day (for example, because the employee is tardy or leaves early). Employers who violate this rule might lose the right to exempt these employees from overtime—and, as a result, have to pay them time-and-a-half for every extra hour worked. There are a few exceptions to this rule, however, and one of them is for FMLA leave. You can track—and not pay an exempt employee for—FMLA leave taken in increments of less than a full day without losing the exemption.

Administering Intermittent or Reduced-Schedule Leave

Because intermittent and reduced-schedule leave differs from full-time FMLA leave in several ways, it must be administered more carefully. After all, you'll have to keep track of how much protected time an employee is using and how much time that employee has available. Here are some of the notable differences:

- **Record keeping.** Because the calculations and calendaring required by intermittent and reduced-schedule leave are more complicated than those required by full-time FMLA leave, it is essential to keep accurate and regularly updated records of these leaves. Below is a sample worksheet for keeping track of this leave; you can find a blank copy (and all other forms in this book) at this book's online companion page;

see Appendix C for details. Note that this worksheet is completed for employees who are *not* using military caregiver leave.

Calculating Intermittent/Reduced-Schedule Leave

A	B	C	D	E
Employee	Regular Workweek	Total Hours Available for FMLA Leave (column B x 12)	Hours of Leave Needed Per Week	Total No. of Calendar Weeks of FMLA Leave Available (column C ÷ column D)
Employee A	30 hrs./wk.	360 hrs.	20 hrs./wk.	18 weeks
Employee B	25 hrs./wk.	300 hrs.	9 hrs./wk.	33 weeks
Employee C	62 hrs./wk.	744 hrs.	21 hrs./wk.	35 weeks

- **Fitness-for-duty reports.** As explained in Chapter 11, you may ask employees who have been out for their own serious health condition to provide a fitness-for-duty report before returning to work. However, you may not ask employees on intermittent or reduced-schedule leave to provide fitness-for-duty reports unless you have reasonable safety concerns about the employee's ability to perform his or her duties due to the serious health condition for which leave was taken. A reasonable safety concern is a reasonable belief of significant risk of harm to the employee or others, considering the nature, severity, and likelihood of the potential harm. Even if you have a reasonable safety concern regarding an employee's return to work from intermittent leave, you may request a fitness-for-duty report only once every 30 days and only in connection with an absence.
- **Minimum increments of time.** Employees may take intermittent or reduced schedule FMLA leave in one-hour increments or the shortest periods of time that your company's payroll system uses to account for other types of leave, whichever is shorter. So, if your company clocks its employees' leave time by the minute, then an employee's

intermittent or reduced-schedule leave could be measured in minutes. If your company uses different increments of time for different types of leave, it must use the smallest of the increments to measure an employee's intermittent FMLA leave. An employer cannot require an employee to take more FMLA leave than the employee needs for the purpose of the leave. But, if the employee cannot arrive at or leave work midshift, the entire period of absence counts as FMLA leave. In 2013, the Department of Labor issued regulations clarifying that the physical impossibility provision (when an employee is unable to start or end work mid-way through a shift) is to be applied in only the most limited circumstances, and the employer bears the responsibility of restoring the employee to the same or an equivalent position as soon as possible. If it chooses to, an employer may grant intermittent or reduced-schedule FMLA leave in shorter time increments than it grants for other types of leave.

- **Scheduled time versus time actually taken.** If an employee taking intermittent leave returns to work early, only the time the employee actually takes off counts as FMLA leave (even if more time was initially granted).

- **Required overtime versus voluntary overtime.** If an employee on intermittent or reduced-schedule leave is unable to work mandatory overtime, the unworked overtime hours count as FMLA leave time and reduce the employee's total FMLA leave entitlement by the overtime hours not worked. However, voluntary overtime hours don't count.

    > EXAMPLE: Your company requires Manny to work eight hours of overtime each week, so his FMLA workweek is 48 hours. If Manny requests a reduced schedule of 40 hours per week, he is taking one-sixth of a workweek of FMLA leave each week.

- **Special rules apply to teachers.** See 29 C.F.R. § 825.601 for special rules that apply to school employees seeking intermittent or reduced-leave schedules.

- **Special rules apply to airline flight crew employees.** An airline employer must account for an airline flight crew employee's intermittent or reduced-schedule leave using increments no greater than one day. For example, if an eligible flight attendant needs to take FMLA leave for

a two-hour physical therapy session, the airline employer may require the employee to use a full day (but no more) of FMLA leave.

Flexible Schedules Versus FMLA Leave

Sometimes, an employee who has a medical condition or caretaking respon-sibilities might request a flexible schedule. In this situation, the employee isn't asking for time off work; instead, the employee wants to work the same total number of hours, but on a different schedule than usual. Because such an employee won't be taking any time off, this does not count as a request for FMLA leave.

> **EXAMPLE:** Your employee Bud normally works a 9-to-5 workday. He has recently requested a change in his work schedule to 11-to-7 because the antidepressants he is taking make him groggy in the morning. Is this a request for FMLA intermittent/reduced-schedule leave?
>
> No, because Bud is not taking any time off and the schedule change is not needed for medical treatment. However, keep in mind that, if Bud's depression is a disability, you may have to accommodate the schedule change under the ADA. (For more information, see Chapter 12.)

Common Mistakes Regarding Leave Duration—And How to Avoid Them

Mistake 1: Using inconsistent methods to measure the "leave year."
Avoid this mistake by taking the following steps:
- Use the "counting forward" method to measure the single 12-month leave period for all employees using military caregiver leave.
- Make sure everyone in your company uses the same leave year method for all employees seeking other types of FMLA leave.

- If your company changes leave year methods, provide 60 days' written notice to all employees before implementing the change. You must allow employees who already started or requested leave prior to your announcement to use whichever method of calculating the leave year is most beneficial to them.
- Apply the new method to all employees as soon as the 60-day notice period passes.

Mistake 2: Failing to accurately count the leave time taken by employees.

Avoid this mistake by taking the following steps:

- Calculate the total amount of available FMLA leave at the beginning of leave.
- Track all leave time the employee takes—not including time the employee actually spends working, additional time off taken for your company's convenience, and weeks during which your company is shut down.
- Subtract all leave time taken from the employee's available FMLA leave time.

Mistake 3: Failing to accurately calculate available leave time for employees who need intermittent or reduced-schedule leave.

Avoid this mistake by taking the following steps:

- Calculate available leave time based on the employee's usual workweek. Employees who work part time or work overtime hours are entitled to a prorated amount of leave based on their usual hours worked.
- Keep good records of employee work hours, including hours worked by exempt employees.
- Come up with the average hourly workweek for employees with irregular schedules, based on the 12-month period before they start their leave.
- Get written agreements of average workweek hours from employees with irregular schedules and exempt employees who request FMLA leave.

✓

Managers' Checklist: Duration of Leave

For All Employees Requesting Leave:

☐ I confirmed that my company's method for defining the FMLA leave year is in writing, in our FMLA leave policy.

☐ If our company has not yet defined its leave year or has decided to change methods of defining the leave year, I either

    ☐ provided all employees with notice of this change at least 60 days before they requested leave, or

    ☐ gave employees the benefit of whichever leave year calculation method provided them with the most leave.

☐ I calculated the FMLA leave time available to the employee requesting leave according to my company's leave year method.

☐ For military caregiver leave, I calculated the employee's entitlement using the "counting forward" method.

☐ I recorded all FMLA leave the employee has taken, but I have not included the following types of time off as FMLA leave:

    ☐ time the employee actually spent working

    ☐ time taken off for the company's convenience, and

    ☐ weeks during which the company was shut down.

For Employees Requesting Intermittent or Reduced-Schedule Leave:

☐ I determined that the employee's requested intermittent or reduced-schedule leave is medically necessary, or necessary for a qualifying exigency.

☐ I determined that the employee is able to perform the essential functions of his or her job.

☐ If the employee works the same number of hours each week, I used that schedule to calculate the FMLA leave available to the employee.

☐ If the employee's hours are irregular, I calculated the average hours worked per week by the employee requesting FMLA leave, and

    ☐ I have a written agreement of the average workweek signed by the employee, and

    ☐ I calculated the pro rata time off that the employee is entitled to under the FMLA.

Managers' Checklist: Duration of Leave (continued)

☐ If the employee is exempt from overtime, the employee and I reached an agreement as to the employee's average weekly hours, and

    ☐ I have the employee's sign-off on this average.

☐ I included all mandatory overtime hours in the workweek hours of the employee requesting FMLA leave.

Giving Notice and Designating Leave

Counting Time Off as FMLA Leave 155

    Substituting Paid Leave for FMLA Leave 156

    Designating FMLA Leave Retroactively 159

Individual Notice Requirements 160

    General Notice 160

    Eligibility Notice 161

    Rights and Responsibilities Notice 162

    Designation Notice 164

Employee Notice Requirements 167

    Methods of Employee Notification 167

    Getting More Information From the Employee 170

    How Much Notice the Employee Must Give 171

    Your Company's Leave Notification Rules 174

    Employee Failure to Give Notice 174

    Notice Based on Employer Observations 175

Common Mistakes Regarding Giving Notice and Designating Leave—
And How to Avoid Them 176

Chapter Highlights

☆ Your company must provide individualized FMLA information to each employee requesting leave who may be FMLA-qualified, explaining the employee's rights under the FMLA and the effect of the employee's failure to comply with the FMLA and company rules, and designating the employee's leave as FMLA leave.

☆ Employees requesting FMLA leave must give you 30 days' notice of the need for foreseeable leave, unless:
- the leave is not certain in time
- there is a change in circumstances, or
- as a result of medical emergency, the 30-day notice is not practicable.

☆ An employee requesting FMLA leave that is not foreseeable must provide notice as soon as practicable, usually the same or next business day after learning that he or she needs leave.

☆ Your company is allowed to discipline an employee for failing to provide proper notice of FMLA leave and can delay the leave.

☆ Employees may choose, or your company may require them, to use accrued paid leave during their FMLA leave, but only if the reason for the employee's leave is covered by your paid leave policy.

☆ Your company may require employees to follow its usual procedures to use paid leave during their FMLA leave, but an employee's failure to follow these procedures only limits the employee's right to use paid leave, not the right to use FMLA leave.

☆ The employee requesting FMLA leave must give you sufficient information to determine that the FMLA may apply, but the information doesn't have to be detailed or even refer to the FMLA (unless the employee has already used FMLA leave for the same qualifying reason).

This chapter covers the FMLA's notice requirements: what information you and the employee must each provide when an employee takes or requests time off that might be protected by the FMLA. The heavier informational burden lies with you, and for good reason: Many employees don't know what the law is or what their rights are. In fact, your employees may never have heard of the FMLA. This means that employees may come to you requesting leave, without knowing their legal right to take it or their legal obligation to give you information so that you can properly determine whether the FMLA applies.

Your company's informational requirements begin with hanging an FMLA poster and providing general information about the law to employees; Chapter 2 explains how to comply with these obligations. Once an employee requests leave, however, additional requirements kick in. You must know enough about the FMLA to figure out whether it applies and ask the employee for more information if necessary. You must give the employee three separate notices about the FMLA: an eligibility notice, a rights and responsibilities notice, and a designation notice. These notices, mandated by the 2008 revisions to the FMLA regulations, provide employees with detailed information about the law and your company's requirements for FMLA leave. You must also designate the leave as FMLA leave and notify the employee that you've done so.

Sounds like a lot of meetings and paperwork, doesn't it? While it is a significant responsibility to comply with all these requirements, there are ways to streamline the process. We tell you how below and give you some approved forms to use.

Counting Time Off as FMLA Leave

When an employee comes to you requesting medical, parenting, or family military leave, the first important duty that you have is to figure out whether the leave might qualify as FMLA leave. If the leave qualifies, you must give the employee the required notices (see "Individual Notice Requirements," below), including a notice that designates the leave as FMLA leave.

If you don't give notice and designate an employee's time off as FMLA leave in a timely fashion, and your error causes the employee harm, your company may be liable for damages, including lost compensation and benefits that the employee has suffered as a result. The employee may also be entitled to other remedies, including reinstatement, promotion, or other relief for the harm caused by your actions.

Of course, if an employee comes to you and says, "I need FMLA leave," or the employee's leave clearly qualifies under the FMLA, you can proceed to giving your required notices and designating the leave. This section covers a couple of situations that can get complicated: substitution of paid leave for FMLA leave and designating FMLA leave retroactively.

Substituting Paid Leave for FMLA Leave

The FMLA allows employees to substitute paid time off provided under the employer's policies—such as vacation, sick, or personal leave—for unpaid FMLA leave, as long as the reason for leave is covered by the employer's policy and the employee meets the other requirements of the employer's paid leave program. It also allows employers to require employees to make this substitution, even if the employee doesn't want to.

In addition, you should designate any time off for which the employee is paid from another source as FMLA leave, if it meets the requirements. For example, an employee who suffers an on-the-job injury and takes time off while receiving workers' compensation benefits is probably also qualified for FMLA leave—and you should designate that time off accordingly.

Paid Leave Provided by Your Company

Whether company-provided paid leave can be used during all or part of an employee's FMLA leave depends on your company's policies. Employees may use, or you may require them to use, any applicable accrued paid leave during their FMLA leave. However, the type of leave must be covered by your paid leave policies. Employees may not choose, and your company may not require them, to use paid leave for reasons that are not covered by your company's paid leave program.

> **TIP**
>
> **It's really overlap, not substitution.** Although the law refers to "substitution" of paid leave, that's not exactly accurate. The employee isn't using paid leave *instead* of FMLA leave, but is using the two types of leave at the same time.

EXAMPLE 1: Your company has a paid sick leave policy that allows employees to take paid leave to care for ill children and spouses. Your employee, Kurt, has asked for a two-week leave to care for his father following surgery to treat prostate cancer. You provide Kurt with the necessary FMLA notices and inform him that he must use accrued paid sick leave under your company's policy.

Bad move. Because your company's paid sick leave policy does not cover care for a parent, you can't require Kurt to use paid leave during his FMLA leave. The effect is that Kurt has the right to take unpaid FMLA leave to care for his father, and he retains his accrued paid sick leave under your company's policy.

EXAMPLE 2: Lourdes is eight months pregnant and requests four weeks of leave following the birth of her child. She also requests to use paid sick leave under the company's sick leave policy. You deny her request, because your company's paid sick leave policy does not cover time off to bond with a new child.

Not so fast. Lourdes might need the postdelivery leave for her own serious health condition, which would mean she is entitled to use accrued paid sick leave. Your company may also require her to use it.

Your company may require employees to follow its usual paid leave procedures to get paid for their time off, but you may not deny them unpaid FMLA leave for failing to follow those procedures. An employee's failure to follow company policies for paid leave affects only their right to paid leave, not their right to unpaid FMLA leave.

EXAMPLE: Your company requires employees to give at least one week of advance notice before using vacation time. Tim's wife is seriously injured in a car accident while commuting to work on Monday morning. Tim calls you from the hospital and tells you about the accident. He tells you that his wife is in surgery and is expected to recover quickly. He asks about using vacation time while he is out. You tell Tim that he can't use vacation time until a week has passed, because of the company's advance notice rule, but that he is entitled to unpaid FMLA leave. You prepare the necessary notices and send them to Tim's home. Did you do the right thing?

Yes. Your company can require employees to follow its usual paid leave procedures to use paid leave, but it cannot deny them the right to take unpaid FMLA leave if they are otherwise entitled. Tim provided as much notice as is required for unforeseeable FMLA leave (as explained below), so he is covered by the FMLA. If he has to be out for more than a week, he is also entitled to start using accrued vacation time once he has met the one-week notice requirement.

Paid Leave From Another Source

When an employee takes any type of time off to care for a family member, for parenting, for military family leave, or for the employee's own health, you should always consider whether the FMLA applies—and, if so, provide the necessary notices and designate the leave accordingly. Some types of leave slip through the cracks because the employee is covered by another law or program. But any type of leave that falls within the FMLA's parameters should be designated as such and counted against the employee's entitlement, no matter how many other laws apply.

Here are some examples:

- **Workers' compensation.** As explained in Chapter 12, an employee who suffers a work-related illness or injury may be entitled to partial wage replacement while off work to recuperate. This time will almost always also qualify as FMLA leave.
- **Temporary disability.** The laws of a handful of states provide some income to employees who are temporarily unable to work because of a disability. This time may also qualify as FMLA leave.
- **Paid family leave.** In a few states, employees can receive some income for time they take off to care for a family member, which might also qualify as FMLA leave.
- **Disability insurance.** If your company provides disability insurance for employees, they might have the right to replacement income while they are out of work. This time off may also be covered by the FMLA.

If an employee is entitled to some compensation from another source, paid leave typically may not be substituted for this time off, nor may your company require employees to use paid leave during this time. After all, the employee is already receiving some pay. However, your company and the employee may agree that the employee may use some paid leave to supplement benefits from

another source. For example, workers' compensation and state disability insurance typically replace only a portion of the employee's wages. If you and the employee agree, the employee may use paid leave to complete his or her pay.

> EXAMPLE: Ted is on workers' compensation leave, and is receiving two-thirds of his usual compensation as wage replacement. Because Ted has a serious health condition, all of his time off counts as FMLA leave. You and Ted agree that Ted may use accrued sick leave to make up the remaining third of his preinjury wages. Ted was working 36 hours a week before being injured, so he takes—and your company pays him for—12 hours of sick leave per week while he is receiving workers' compensation benefits.

Designating FMLA Leave Retroactively

Often, an employee takes vacation or sick leave for a reason that's covered by the FMLA, but you don't know about it. For example, an employee who needs time off to care for a dying parent might simply request vacation time, without revealing the reason for the time off. Or, the employee might develop a need for FMLA leave while on paid leave, for example, because the employee becomes very ill while on vacation.

You can designate FMLA leave retroactively if, after an employee has started or even returned from leave, you learn that the leave is FMLA-qualified. You may make a retroactive FMLA designation as long as the employee agrees to it or your late designation doesn't cause harm to the employee. When making a retroactive designation, you must give the employee all of the notices discussed under "Individual Notice Requirements," below.

You can also retroactively designate FMLA leave when circumstances change so that a leave that wasn't originally an FMLA-qualifying leave becomes qualified. The rules for how much of the original time counts as FMLA leave depend on whether the FMLA-qualifying event developed out of the original reason for leave (for example, when a minor illness takes a serious turn) or not (for example, when an employee suffers an accident during vacation). In the first situation, you may designate all of the employee's time off as FMLA leave; in the second, only leave taken after the FMLA-qualifying event can be designated as FMLA leave.

EXAMPLE 1: Your employee, Ravi, caught a cold that turned into bronchitis. Ravi requests sick leave to recover from the bronchitis. Four days after going out on sick leave, Ravi calls in and says that he's gotten worse and his doctor has diagnosed him with bronchial pneumonia. How do you handle this change of circumstance?

Because you have read this book, you correctly realize that Ravi now has a serious health condition. Because it grew out of Ravi's original health condition, the entire time he has taken off counts as FMLA leave for a serious health condition. You provide Ravi with the required notices and give him a written designation after learning of the diagnosis of bronchial pneumonia.

EXAMPLE 2: Selena requests two weeks' vacation time to go snorkeling in Belize. You grant the request. One week into the vacation, Selena calls to report that she took a nasty spill on her motorbike and had to be hospitalized for a concussion and broken arm. Does the accident change Selena's leave?

Yes. Selena's leave changed from vacation to FMLA leave for a serious medical condition as soon as she got hurt. Only the time off after her injury counts as FMLA leave. The initial week of time off was true vacation time, and does not count against Selena's available FMLA leave.

Individual Notice Requirements

There are four types of notice an employer must give to an employee who requests FMLA leave. We discuss each in turn and refer to the forms and documents that are available online; see Appendix C for details.

General Notice

The first type of notice that you have to give employees requesting leave, the "general notice," is the same notice you have to post in the workplace and distribute to all employees explaining FMLA rights, discussed in Chapter 2. You can use the FMLA poster for this purpose (see Appendix C).

If your company includes the general notice information (that is, the information contained in the DOL FMLA poster) in its employee handbook or in some other written policy that it distributes to all employees and applicants, it has satisfied the general notice requirement. If your company doesn't include the general notice information in its handbook or other

disseminated, written policies, it must give each new employee a copy of the general notice information in writing at the time of hire.

You can distribute the general notice information electronically on your company's intranet system or in its electronic handbook. But, all *employees and applicants* must have access to it. (This applies to the general posting requirement discussed in Chapter 2, as well.) If the electronic information is not accessible by all employees and applicants, you have to give the general notice information to them in writing or post the information in a conspicuous place where employees and applicants can readily see it.

Lessons from the *Real World*

An employer can be liable for failing to give an employee information on the FMLA.

Marria Saroli was the controller for Automation & Modular Components, Inc. ("A&M"). Upon learning that she was pregnant, Saroli notified A&M and requested leave. A&M didn't respond or provide Saroli with any FMLA information. Instead, A&M told Saroli that it was hiring a man to manage her department and take over her duties.

Saroli's doctor placed her on immediate leave due to a medical condition related to her pregnancy. She again requested pregnancy leave. This time A&M wrote to her, telling her that she could take only six weeks of leave. Saroli had to extend her leave twice, so it exceeded six weeks. When Saroli tried to return to work, A&M told her that the only job she could return to was one with diminished duties. Saroli resigned and sued A&M for interfering with her FMLA rights.

The court ruled that A&M's failure to give Saroli information about her rights under the FMLA and its failure to respond to her requests for information about pregnancy leave interfered with her FMLA rights.

Saroli v. Automation & Modular Components, Inc., 405 F.3d 446 (6th Cir. 2005).

Eligibility Notice

When an employee requests leave that may qualify under the FMLA, you must tell the employee whether he or she is eligible for FMLA leave. This

"eligibility notice" is required at the start of the first leave taken in the leave year and must be provided, for each qualifying reason, within five business days after an employee requests leave, absent extenuating circumstances. For example, an employee requesting leave to care for a spouse injured while on active military duty should get an eligibility notice for FMLA military caregiver leave. If the same employee later requested leave for her own pregnancy, you would have to issue a separate eligibility notice as to that qualifying reason. The eligibility notice may be written or oral, and may be distributed electronically.

If an employee is not eligible for FMLA leave, you have to give the employee a written notice stating at least one reason why the employee is ineligible (for example, that the employee has not worked 1,250 hours for the company in the previous 12 months). If the employee's eligibility for leave for the reason requested changes during the leave year, or the employee requests leave for a different reason, you have to give the employee a new eligibility notice upon his or her next request for leave in that leave year.

> **EXAMPLE:** Dev requested three weeks of leave earlier in the year to care for his new baby when the baby was kept in the hospital for a medical complication following birth. He has recently requested another six weeks of leave to bond with the baby. Do you have to give him another eligibility notice for leave for the same child in the same leave year?
>
> Yes, because the reason for the original leave—the child's serious medical condition—is different from the reason for the current leave request—bonding.

You can use the DOL's *Notice of Eligibility and Rights & Responsibilities* form (Form WH-381) to satisfy the obligations described in this section. (See Appendix C for details on how to access this form.)

Rights and Responsibilities Notice

At the same time you give the eligibility notice to the employee requesting leave, you must also give the employee a written "rights and responsibilities" notice that lays out the employee's rights and obligations under the FMLA, as well as the consequences if the employee doesn't fulfill his or her obligations. The written rights and responsibilities notice must tell the employee, as appropriate to the employee's circumstances:

- that the leave may count against the employee's available FMLA leave time
- whether your company requires the employee to provide certification and, if so:
  - what those requirements are, and
  - the consequences of failing to provide required certification
- that the employee has the right to substitute paid leave for FMLA leave, if applicable
- whether your company requires the employee to substitute paid leave for FMLA leave and, if so:
  - any conditions relating to substitution of paid leave, and
  - the consequences of failing to meet those conditions
- that the employee has the right to continue benefits during leave and have them restored upon return to work
- whether your company requires the employee to pay for health insurance benefits during leave and, if so:
  - how the employee's payment for health insurance benefits during leave is to be arranged
  - the consequences of the employee's failure to pay for health insurance benefits during leave, and
  - the employee's liability, if any, for the cost of benefits payments if your company pays them during leave and the employee fails to return to work
- key employee information, and
- that the employee has the right to return from FMLA leave to the same or an equivalent job.

You can fulfill your notice obligations by providing the employee with the DOL's *Notice of Eligibility and Rights & Responsibilities* form (Form WH-381). You may, but don't have to, provide a certification form to the employee along with this notice. (See Chapter 9 for more information on certifications.)

If the information in the rights and responsibilities notice changes, you have to notify any employee who subsequently requests leave of those changes within five business days of learning of the employee's need for leave.

EXAMPLE: Dev requested leave to bond with his new baby, which your company granted, and you gave him the eligibility and rights and responsibilities notices. He's been on leave for a week and the company just instituted a new policy

requiring employees to substitute paid leave for FMLA leave. You've added the new policy to your employee handbook, which is available to employees via the company's intranet. Do you have to give Dev a new rights and responsibilities notice laying out the details of this new policy?

Not necessarily. You must give him notice of the changes in some form. If he can access the policy while on leave, you can just send him a notice referring to the policy and telling him he can review it in the electronic handbook.

Designation Notice

Within five business days of receiving enough information to determine that a leave request does or does not qualify for FMLA coverage, you must give a written "designation notice" to the employee requesting leave. As with the eligibility notice, you may have more time to give this notice in the event of extenuating circumstances.

The designation notice must contain the following information:
- whether or not the employee's leave is approved as FMLA leave
- how much time will be counted against the employee's available FMLA leave time; if the amount of leave needed is unknown at the time of the designation notice (for example, because the employee will take leave intermittently, as needed), the notice doesn't have to include this information, but
  - the employer must give the employee an accounting of how much time has been counted against the employee's available FMLA time upon the employee's request
  - this accounting doesn't need to be given more often than every 30 days
  - the accounting may be oral, but if so must be confirmed in writing no later than the next payday, and
  - the written confirmation of the accounting may be a notation on the employee's pay stub
- whether the employer requires paid leave to be substituted
- whether the employee has requested that paid leave be substituted
- whether the employer requires a fitness-for-duty certification for return to work (this information may be given orally if the employer's written policies set forth the fitness-for-duty requirement), and

- whether the employer requires that the fitness-for-duty certification cover the employee's ability to perform essential functions of his or her job. If so, the employer must include a list of the essential job functions with the notice. (Fitness-for-duty certifications are covered in Chapter 11.)

You can use the DOL's *Designation Notice* form (Form WH-382) for these purposes; see Appendix C to access an electronic copy. As mentioned in Chapter 7, when an employee requests military caregiver leave, the request often also falls under the FMLA category of leave to care for a family member with a serious health condition. However, that FMLA category allows only the usual 12 weeks of leave per leave year. The DOL regulations require you to designate leave to care for a seriously injured or ill servicemember as military caregiver leave only, to give the caregiver the full benefit of the FMLA. That way, an employee who uses less than 26 weeks of military caregiver leave still has some leave left for other FMLA-qualified reasons.

> **EXAMPLE:** Johnny's wife is injured in combat, and Johnny takes 20 weeks of military caregiver leave. Having read this book, you designate that leave as military caregiver leave only. Assuming he hasn't used FMLA leave for any other purpose in the leave year, Johnny still has six weeks of leave left to use for any other FMLA-qualifying reason, such as for his own serious health condition.
>
> Absent this rule, Johnny's leave could have been counted as both military caregiver leave and leave to care for a family member with a serious health condition. Johnny could use his remaining six weeks only for military caregiver leave; he wouldn't have any of his 12-week entitlement left. This is exactly what the DOL is trying to avoid by requiring employers to designate qualifying leave as military caregiver leave, and only as military caregiver leave, in the first instance.

You have to give the employee only one designation notice per qualifying reason per year, even if the employee takes the leave intermittently during the year. But, if the information in the notice changes, you have to give the employee a written notice of the change within five business days of receiving the employee's first request for leave after the change is made. Also, as noted above, an employee who is using intermittent leave may request an accounting of how much FMLA leave has been used every 30 days. If you choose to give this accounting orally, you must follow up in writing; the written statement may appear as a simple notation on the employee's pay stub.

If You Don't Designate Within the Time Allowed

If you know that an employee's time off is for an FMLA-qualified reason, you are required to provide the designation notice within five business days. Even if you don't designate the leave within this time limit, however, the FMLA regulations allow your company to count an employee's time off as FMLA leave, as long as the employee is actually eligible for FMLA leave and the leave is taken for an FMLA-qualifying reason. However, if the employee is harmed by your late designation, your company may be liable for damages caused as a result. As discussed above, you may be able to avoid this problem by retroactively designating leave as FMLA leave, as long as this doesn't harm the employee, or the employee agrees to the retroactive designation.

Likewise, if you mistakenly designate an employee's time off as FMLA leave when it's not—because the employee is ineligible or the reason for leave isn't covered by the FMLA, for example—that doesn't convert the employee's leave to FMLA leave. In other words, the employee can't claim FMLA rights based on your mistake if the employee isn't eligible for FMLA leave. However, if the employee relies on your failure to properly designate the leave in a way that harms the employee's interests, the employee may still have a valid legal claim.

EXAMPLE: Abdul took eight weeks of leave to help his adult son rearrange his children's care and custody, handle his legal and financial affairs, and deal with other qualifying exigencies when his son's Reserve unit was called to Iraq. Several months later, Abdul asked for time off to care for his wife after hip replacement surgery, scheduled in a couple of months. You told Abdul that he'd have his full 12 weeks of FMLA leave time to care for his wife, because the leave for his adult son wasn't FMLA-qualified. Just before Abdul's wife has her surgery, you realize your error and tell him that he only has four weeks of FMLA leave left because his leave for his son counts as qualifying exigency leave. Now Abdul says that he and his wife will incur a lot of expenses hiring a home-care aide that they could have avoided if you'd properly designated his leave. Had he known that he only had four weeks to use, his wife's sister could have planned to care for her. Because Abdul thought he had time off, however, his wife's sister has taken a new job and is unable to help out. Your error doesn't mean that Abdul is entitled to extra FMLA leave; however, your company could be on the hook for the added expense that Abdul will incur as a result of the misdesignation.

Employee Notice Requirements

While most of the obligation to administer FMLA leave falls on you, the employee bears some responsibility. Primarily, an employee requesting leave that may be FMLA-qualified must give you enough information so that you can determine whether the FMLA applies. If the employee doesn't provide you with the necessary information, you may deny the employee's leave request.

If an employer and employee disagree as to whether a leave request is FMLA-qualified, the revisions to the regulations indicate that the dispute should be resolved through discussions, which the employer must document along with the resolution of the dispute.

Lessons from the Real World

An employee only has to give enough information for the employer to conclude that the employee may need time off for a serious health condition.

Samuel Cavin worked as a production associate in the assembly department of Honda of America Manufacturing, Inc. Cavin had an accident while riding his motorcycle. He called Honda and told his supervisor about it, explaining that he was in the hospital. Honda claimed that this wasn't enough information to notify the company that Cavin had a serious health condition covered by the FMLA and fired him. Cavin sued Honda for violating the FMLA.

The court ruled that Cavin had provided enough information for Honda to conclude that he had a serious health condition entitling him to FMLA leave.

Cavin v. Honda of America Manufacturing, Inc., 346 F.3d 713 (6th Cir. 2003).

Methods of Employee Notification

The employee's notice may be either oral (including by telephone) or in writing (including by fax or email). An employee's spokesperson may give the notice if the employee is incapacitated or otherwise unable to give the notice.

What does the employee need to tell you? Not much: only enough information to let you know that the need for leave may be covered by the

FMLA. Generally, the employee doesn't have to mention the FMLA or the particular rights protected by the FMLA. Nor does the employee have to give you any medical information when making the initial request for leave: It's enough if the employee's notice reasonably informs you that the leave is for a serious health condition, parenting, or military family obligations.

Lessons from the *Real World*

An employee's statement to her employer that she needed time off because she "didn't feel good" wasn't sufficient notice of a serious health condition.

Shortly before Jill Beaver was scheduled to return from an approved vacation to her job at RGIS Inventory Specialists, Inc., she called in and reported to her supervisor that she was ill, "didn't feel good," and that her doctor had ordered her not to fly or return to work for "a couple of days, a few days." RGIS viewed Beaver's extra time off as unauthorized and fired her. Beaver sued RGIS for terminating her while on FMLA leave.

The court sided with RGIS because Beaver hadn't provided sufficient information to alert her supervisor that the FMLA applied to her leave. Beaver's statements to her supervisor were too general for her supervisor to conclude that she might have suffered from a serious health condition.

Beaver v. RGIS Inventory Specialists, Inc., 144 Fed. Appx. 452 (6th Cir. 2005).

It's up to you to recognize the possibility that the leave is covered by the FMLA. For example, if you know that an employee suffers from a chronic medical condition and the employee requests leave without specifying why, you should ask for more information so you can determine whether or not the leave is FMLA-qualified. Your knowledge of the chronic medical condition and the leave request amount to notice under the FMLA. Likewise, if an employee's behavior shows that the employee is suffering from a serious health condition, that may be enough to put you on notice of the need for FMLA leave. Again, you should ask the employee for more information, so you can determine whether the leave qualifies for FMLA protection.

The rules are different when an employee seeks additional FMLA leave for an FMLA-qualifying reason for which he or she has previously taken leave. In this situation, the employee must specifically refer to either the qualifying reason or the need for FMLA leave. This rule recognizes that employees who have already used the FMLA and know their situation qualifies for FMLA leave can be expected to know the rules and provide more extensive notice.

When the employee asks to use accrued paid leave, such as vacation leave, the employee might not tell you the possibly FMLA-qualifying reason for the leave request. As with any request for possible FMLA leave, you are entitled to find out if the type of leave falls within both your company's paid leave policy and the FMLA. If the employee doesn't give you this information, you can deny the employee's request for leave and the employee must then give you sufficient information to establish that the need for leave falls within the FMLA. Otherwise, the employee hasn't shown that he or she is entitled to FMLA-protected leave. For example, if an employee says, "I'd like to take a couple of personal days off," but doesn't indicate what the time off is for, the employer may ask if there is a family or medical need for the leave. While an employer cannot demand detailed medical information, it does have the right to find out if the leave is possibly FMLA-covered.

Lessons from the Real World

An employee's statement that he did not want to apply for FMLA leave "at this time" is not an explicit waiver of FMLA rights.

Robert Righi sent his supervisor at SMC Corp. of America an email explaining that, due to his mother's medical emergency, he needed to take "the next couple of days off" to arrange for her medical care. Righi stated, "I do have the vacation time, or I could apply for the family care act, which I do not want to do at this time."

SMC Corp. argued that Righi had waived his FMLA rights by the latter statement. The court disagreed and held that because Righi's email "left open the *possibility* that Righi might want to use FMLA leave" at some point, the email was sufficient to alert SMC Corp. to the potential that Righi would need FMLA leave.

Righi v. SMC Corp., 632 F.3d 404 (7th Cir. 2011).

Although an employee doesn't have to give detailed medical information when requesting leave, it is not enough for the employee to simply call in "sick" without more information. An employer may request additional information in response to such inadequate notice.

Employees can notify you after returning from leave that they took leave for an FMLA-qualified reason, if that's as much notice as is practicable under the circumstances. Generally, however, it should be practicable for an employee to give notice the same business day or the next business day after the employee learns of the need for leave. If the employee fails to give you enough information to determine that the FMLA applies, then the employee can't later claim that the leave was covered by the FMLA or entitled to the law's protections.

Getting More Information From the Employee

If you need more information than the employee gives you to figure out if the FMLA applies, ask for it. Also ask for certification (covered in Chapter 9) and, if applicable, proof of a family relationship (see Chapter 4).

If the employee fails or refuses to tell you why he or she needs leave, you can deny FMLA leave. After all, you won't have enough information to determine whether the leave is FMLA-qualified, and it would be unfair and inconsistent to grant FMLA to some employees even without proper documentation, while denying it to others.

Even an ambiguous notice from an employee suggesting that the employee may not want to exercise FMLA rights triggers the employer's duty to inquire further about the leave request in order to determine whether or not the leave is FMLA-qualified.

CAUTION

Don't assume an employee is waiving rights based on an ambiguous leave request. Courts have ruled against employers who assumed employees waived FMLA rights by saying they did not wish to invoke the rights "at this time," or making similar statements. If you are not sure whether or not an employee's leave request is FMLA-qualified, follow up with the employee to get more information. And, ask when the employee will return to work, or get their best estimate of a return date.

Lessons from the *Real World*

An employer may deny FMLA leave when the employee didn't provide enough information for the employer to determine whether he had a serious health condition.

Lee Brenneman worked in the pharmacy department of MedCentral Health System for 27 years. Brenneman had diabetes and needed time off because of a medical problem related to using his insulin pump. He informed MedCentral that he was "having trouble" with his insulin pump, but didn't otherwise explain the problem. Brenneman then took time off.

MedCentral didn't designate his leave as FMLA leave and terminated him for unexcused absence. Brenneman sued MedCentral for violating the FMLA.

The court ruled that Brenneman's request for leave didn't adequately notify MedCentral of a serious medical condition, since his statement that he was having trouble with his insulin pump didn't give his employer enough information to indicate that he had a serious medical condition.

Brenneman v. MedCentral Health System, 366 F.3d 412 (6th Cir. 2004).

How Much Notice the Employee Must Give

Sometimes employees need time off for conditions or events that are foreseeable, such as a scheduled surgery or the birth of a child. Other times, the need isn't foreseeable, such as a hospitalization and treatment following a heart attack. While the FMLA allows employees to take leave in either case, it requires different amounts of notice.

Foreseeable Leave

When the need for leave is foreseeable, an employee requesting FMLA leave must give at least 30 days' notice of the need for leave. An employee who fails to give at least 30 days' notice of the need for FMLA leave has to respond to the employer's request for an explanation of why such notice wasn't practicable.

There are several exceptions to the 30-day notice rule:

- **When the need for leave isn't certain in time.** This situation may arise, for example, where an adoption date isn't certain. In this situation, the employee must give notice as soon as is "practicable," which usually means the same business day or the next business day after the employee learns of the need for leave.
- **When there is a change in circumstances.** This situation may arise, for example, where a medical procedure is changed to accommodate a hospital's schedule. In this situation, the employee must give notice of the change as soon as he or she learns of it, even if he or she already gave notice of the original procedure date.
- **When your company elects to waive the FMLA notice requirement.** Your company may allow employees to give less notice than the FMLA requires.
- **When the employee needs qualifying exigency leave.** For this type of leave, the employee need only give such notice as is practicable, even if the need for leave is foreseeable.

How much notice is "practicable" depends upon the particular circumstances of each employee's situation. Generally, it should be practicable for an employee to provide notice either the same business day or the next business day after the employee learns of the need for leave.

An employee also has to make reasonable efforts to arrange medical treatment so as not to unduly disrupt the employer's operations. If an employee fails to do so, the employer may initiate discussions with the employee and tell the employee that he or she must try to make such arrangements, subject to the approval of the health care provider. Employees who are seeking leave to care for an injured servicemember must also try to work out a schedule for intermittent leave that doesn't unduly disrupt the employer's operations. (See Chapter 10 for more on these requirements.)

Unforeseeable Leave

If the employee's need for FMLA leave is not foreseeable, different notice rules apply. An employee must give notice of the need for unforeseeable leave as soon as practicable, which typically means the same business day or the

next business day after the employee learns of the need for leave. Generally, it should be practicable for the employee to give you notice within the deadlines set out in your company's usual and customary leave notice rules, absent unusual circumstances.

Even where an employee's need for FMLA leave is unforeseeable, you are entitled to ask when the employee expects to return to work. The employee may not be able to provide that information immediately, but does have a duty to tell you once an actual or estimated return date is known. And, the employee must respond to your efforts to get more information while the employee is on an unforeseeable leave after giving limited information in the leave notice.

Lessons from the *Real World*

An employee on unforeseeable leave can't simply ignore his employer's repeated attempts to reach him during leave.

For more than a week after Robert Righi went out on leave to see to his mother's emergency medical needs, his supervisor left numerous telephone messages on his cell and home phones asking Righi to call in to tell the supervisor how long Righi would be out and when he expected to return to work. Righi ignored all but the last message, nine days after he went on leave. His employer fired him the next day for violating its leave policy. The court upheld the termination based on Righi's failure to fulfill his notice obligations.

Righi v. SMC Corp., 632 F.3d 404 (7th Cir. 2011).

The FMLA regulations relax employee notice requirements in "extraordinary" circumstances (such as when an employee is physically unable to respond to the employer's efforts to get more information for some period of time). And, when the employee's need for leave is unforeseeable, the employee may not know the exact date of return to work. But, the employee still has an obligation to tell you that the date of return is not yet known.

Your Company's Leave Notification Rules

Your company can require employees to follow its usual and customary leave notification rules, as long as those rules don't discriminate against employees taking FMLA leave and don't require more notice than the FMLA requires. However, your company may require compliance with its usual notice requirements only if there are no unusual circumstances. For example, let's say your company requires employees to call in by 8 a.m. if they are going to be absent that day. You may not deny FMLA leave to an employee who has a heart attack during the night and misses work because he is hospitalized. As long as the employee gives notices as soon as is practicable—all that's required by the FMLA for unforeseeable leave—the employee is entitled to FMLA leave. If an employee doesn't comply with the usual notice rules, and no unusual circumstances are present, you may discipline the employee and delay or deny FMLA leave.

Notice that this contrasts with the rules for using paid leave, discussed above. To substitute paid leave for unpaid FMLA leave, an employee must follow your company's usual notice rules for paid leave. If the employee fails to do so, your company may deny the request for paid leave. Even in these circumstances, however, your company must grant the request for FMLA leave as long as the employee met the FMLA's notice requirements.

Employee Failure to Give Notice

As mentioned above, an employer may delay the start of leave if an employee fails to give adequate notice within the applicable notice period. However, the extent of such a delay depends upon the facts and circumstances of the particular leave request. According to the revised FMLA regulations, the appropriate delay is the difference in time between when the employee gave notice and when the employee should have given notice.

> EXAMPLE: Lila informs you that she is adopting a baby and is scheduled to take custody of the baby in 15 days. You ask her why she didn't give you 30 days' notice and she says it slipped her mind. Because she gave inadequate notice, you can delay the start of Lila's leave by 15 days, to the date 30 days after she

gave notice. You are entitled to delay her leave because her failure to give you the required notice was not due to unusual circumstances.

Notice Based on Employer Observations

Sometimes an employee's behavior, appearance, or other facts will alert an employer to the employee's need for FMLA leave. When observable indications, combined with an employee's request for leave, reveal that an employee may have a serious health condition, you should designate the leave as FMLA leave. You can ask the employee for more information if you aren't sure whether the FMLA applies.

Lessons from the *Real World*

An employer had notice of an employee's serious health condition because the employer had ordered the employee to participate in an employee assistance program.

William Moorer was the administrator and CFO of Baptist Memorial Health Care System, where he had worked for 17 years. Moorer's boss smelled alcohol on Moorer's breath and noted that his performance had started to slip, he was "fidgety" at meetings, and, at one point, slumped in his chair. His boss ordered Moorer to attend the company's employee assistance program, which would require several weeks of leave. Moorer underwent the program and ceased drinking. Nevertheless, Baptist Memorial fired him during the leave. Moorer filed a lawsuit claiming that the company had violated the FMLA by terminating him during an FMLA leave. Baptist Memorial argued that Moorer had never requested FMLA leave.

The court ruled that Baptist Memorial could not claim that it had no notice that the leave it placed Moorer on was FMLA leave. Baptist Memorial had recognized Moorer's serious health condition of alcoholism and need for leave, because it had ordered him into treatment for the condition.

Moorer v. Baptist Memorial Health Care System, 398 F.3d 469 (6th Cir. 2005).

SEE AN EXPERT

Consult an attorney when you make an FMLA designation based on employee behavior. It's always a bit dangerous to make assumptions based on an employee's actions. For example, you could be accused of treating the employee as if he or she has a disability, which constitutes disability discrimination under the Americans with Disabilities Act. (See Chapter 12 for more information.) Talking to an attorney can help you make sure you're doing the right thing.

Common Mistakes Regarding Giving Notice and Designating Leave—And How to Avoid Them

Mistake 1: Failing to count FMLA-qualified leave taken as FMLA leave.

Avoid this mistake by taking the following steps:

- Consider whether the FMLA applies whenever an employee takes or requests time off for parenting, military family obligations, illness, or a family member's illness.
- Consider whether the FMLA applies if an employee requests time off and the employee's behavior suggests that he or she might have a serious health condition.
- Ask the employee to provide more information if you aren't sure whether the FMLA applies.
- Count paid leave as FMLA leave, if the reason for leave qualifies under the FMLA. Don't forget workers' compensation leave, disability leave, and paid family leave.
- Count time off (such as vacation or sick leave) as FMLA leave when a new FMLA-covered event occurs during the leave.

Mistake 2: Denying FMLA leave because the employee has not followed company notice rules.

Avoid this mistake by taking the following steps:

- Understand the different rules that apply to paid leave and unpaid leave: As long as the employee provides adequate notice under the FMLA, you may not deny FMLA leave; you may, however, deny paid leave if the employee doesn't follow the notice requirements of your paid leave program.

- Don't enforce the company's notice rules if they require more notice than is practicable for unforeseeable leave.
- Rather than denying FMLA leave, delay leave for the 30-day notice period if the need for leave was truly foreseeable and it was practicable to give more notice. (Chapter 10 explains how to do this.)

Mistake 3: Failing to give individualized FMLA information to employees who need FMLA leave.

Avoid this mistake by taking the following steps:

- Give each employee requesting FMLA leave the three required notice forms for eligibility, rights and responsibilities, and designation.
- Provide the notices in a language the employee understands.
- If the employee is sensory impaired, give the individualized information in a form that the employee can receive and understand.
- Make sure the notice information is tailored to the employee's particular situation (for example, telling the employee that he or she can substitute paid leave, or that he or she must pay health insurance premiums during leave).
- Provide a new notice form whenever the employee will be required to follow different rules (for example, to provide a medical certification or fitness-for-duty report).

✓ Managers' Checklist: Giving Notice and Designating Leave

☐ The employee requesting leave received a general notice in our handbook, in our written policies, or upon hire.

☐ Within five business days of the employee's request for leave, I have given the employee a ☐ written ☐ oral ☐ electronic eligibility notice stating:

  ☐ that the employee is eligible for FMLA leave, or

  ☐ that the employee is ineligible for FMLA leave and providing at least one reason for the employee's ineligibility.

☐ At the same time I provided the eligibility notice, I gave the employee a rights and responsibilities notice in writing informing the employee:

  ☐ that the leave will count against his or her available FMLA leave time

  ☐ any certification requirements the employee must satisfy

  ☐ the consequences of failing to satisfy the certification requirements

  ☐ (if applicable) that the employee has the right to substitute paid leave for FMLA leave

  ☐ (if applicable) that the employee must substitute paid leave for FMLA leave, the conditions relating to substitution of paid leave, and the consequences of failing to satisfy those conditions

  ☐ that the employee has the right to continue benefits during FMLA leave and upon return to work

  ☐ (if applicable) that the employee is required to pay health insurance premiums during leave, how the employee's payments will be arranged, and the consequences of failing to pay the premiums

  ☐ (if applicable) the employee's liability, if any, for the cost of benefits payments if the employee does not return to work after leave

  ☐ key employee information, and

  ☐ that the employee has the right to return to the same or an equivalent job after returning from FMLA leave.

☐ Within five business days of receiving enough information to determine that a leave request does or does not qualify for FMLA coverage, I have given the employee requesting leave a designation notice informing the employee:

  ☐ whether the leave is approved as FMLA leave

Managers' Checklist: Giving Notice and Designating Leave (continued)

- ☐ the amount of time that will be counted against the employee's available FMLA leave time, if known
- ☐ (if applicable) that the employee has requested that paid leave be substituted
- ☐ (if applicable) that the employee is required to substitute paid leave
- ☐ (if applicable) that a fitness-for-duty certificate must be submitted by the employee for return to work, and
- ☐ (if applicable) that the fitness-for-duty certificate must cover the employee's ability to perform the essential functions of his or her job, which I have provided to the employee.

☐ If the amount of leave needed was unknown when the employee requested leave, I have given the employee a written accounting of how much time has been counted against his or her available FMLA leave, upon the employee's request.

Certifications

Types of Certifications 183

   Certification of the Employee's Own Serious Health Condition 183

   Certification of a Family Member's Serious Health Condition 185

   Certification for Military Caregiver Leave for Current Servicemembers 185

   Certification for Military Caregiver Leave for Veterans 188

   Certification of Qualifying Exigency 189

Requesting Certification 190

   Why You Should Always Request Certification 190

   Procedures and Deadlines for Requesting a Certification 193

   Employee Deadline for Returning the Certification 195

After You Receive the Certification 197

   Certifications in a Foreign Language 198

   Incomplete or Insufficient Certifications 198

   Verifying a Certification for a Qualifying Exigency 199

   Authenticating or Clarifying Medical Certifications 200

   Second Opinions 201

   Third Opinions 203

   Recertifications 203

Common Mistakes Regarding Medical Certifications—
And How to Avoid Them 206

Chapter Highlights

☆ A certification is a document verifying an employee's need to take leave for a serious health condition, military caregiver leave, or qualifying exigency leave.

☆ A certification for a serious health condition must be completed by a health care provider.

☆ A certification for military caregiver leave must be completed by a health care provider in the case of current servicemembers. For veterans, family members may submit documentation from the Department of Veterans Affairs.

☆ A certification for a qualifying exigency relating to a family member's call to active duty must be completed by the employee.

☆ To request a certification, you must do so in writing within five business days after learning of an employee's need for FMLA leave.

☆ The employee must return the certification within 15 calendar days, unless you allow the employee more time or it is not practicable for the employee to do so under the circumstances, despite the employee's diligent, good faith efforts.

☆ Once you receive a certification, you may grant FMLA leave or deny it based on the information on the form. If the form is insufficient or incomplete, you must tell the employee in writing and give the employee at least seven calendar days to provide a complete, sufficient certification. You may take steps to clarify or authenticate a certification for a serious health condition or military caregiver leave.

☆ If you have reason to doubt a medical certification for a serious health condition, you may ask the employee to get a second opinion, at your company's expense. If the first and second opinions conflict, you may request a third opinion, again at the company's expense.

☆ You may verify the information an employee provides in a certification for qualifying exigency leave only by contacting the Department of Defense to verify the family member's duty status and contacting third parties named in the certification as people with whom the employee will be meeting.

☆ You may request a recertification only after the duration of the condition identified in the original certification expires or only once every 30 days, unless the employee requests an extension of leave, circumstances have changed significantly, or you have reason to suspect the continuing validity of the certification.

☆ For chronic or lifelong conditions, you may request certifications once every six months, in connection with an absence.

When an employee requests time off for his or her own health problem, to care for an ailing family member, or for any reason connected to a family member's military service, you should immediately think, "FMLA." But what if you aren't sure whether the employee's situation qualifies for FMLA leave, or you need more information?

In that situation, you may request a certification: a written statement, completed by the employee, a health care provider, or both, that provides some basic information about the employee's need for leave. You may ask the employee to provide a certification for all types of FMLA leave except leave to bond with a new child. In that situation, you may require the employee to provide proof of a family relationship, as explained in Chapter 4.

This chapter explains what certifications are, how and when to request them, when an employee must provide them, and what to do if the certification is late, insufficient, or incomplete (or never shows up at all). We also explain your options for challenging or verifying a certification of a serious health condition by asking for a second or even a third opinion, as well as the rules about requesting a recertification of the same condition.

Types of Certifications

There are four types of certifications:

- certification of the employee's own serious health condition
- certification of a family member's serious health condition
- certification of a family member's serious illness or injury entitling the employee to take military caregiver leave, and
- certification of an employee's need to take qualifying exigency leave.

As explained below, each type requires different information, and most must be completed by a health care provider, at least in part.

Certification of the Employee's Own Serious Health Condition

A certification of the employee's own serious health condition must be completed by a health care provider, and must include the following information:

- the name, address, telephone number, and fax number of the health care provider, along with the health care provider's practice or specialization
- the date the serious health condition began
- how long the condition is expected to last
- a statement of medical facts regarding the health condition for which leave is requested, such as information on symptoms, diagnosis, hospitalization, doctors' visits, medication, referrals for evaluation or treatment, or any regimen of continuing treatment, and
- information sufficient to show that the employee cannot perform the essential functions of the job (except for intermittent or reduced-schedule leave), information on any other work restrictions, and the likely duration of the inability or restrictions.

If the employee needs intermittent or reduced-schedule leave, the certification must state that intermittent leave is medically necessary. For intermittent leave for planned medical treatment, the certification must estimate the dates and duration of such treatment and any recovery period. For intermittent leave for a condition that may require unforeseeable absences, the certification must give an estimate of the frequency and duration of the episodes of incapacity.

The Department of Labor has created a form, *Certification of Health Care Provider for Employee's Serious Health Condition* (Form WH-380-E), which employers can use to gather this information. The form is designed to be handed to employees, who can then ask their health care providers to complete and sign it. Using this form is optional, but if you develop your own form instead, you cannot ask for more information than Form WH-380 requests.

CAUTION

State law may prohibit you from using Form WH-380. Some states have strict laws that protect the privacy of medical records. If your state's law prohibits employers from requesting certain types of medical information, you must adhere to those restrictions, even if the FMLA allows you to have that information. And, because Form WH-380 asks the health care provider to give details about the employee's serious health condition, you may not be able to use that form in some states. Before you adopt Form WH-380 or any other medical certification form, talk to a knowledgeable employment lawyer in your state to make sure that it doesn't violate your employees' medical privacy rights.

RESOURCE

All certification forms (and other FMLA forms) are available online.
You can find all of the forms we discuss in this chapter, along with many other FMLA forms, podcasts, and more, at this book's online companion page. See Appendix C for the link to this page.

Certification of a Family Member's Serious Health Condition

The certification of a family member's serious health condition is similar to the certification of the employee's serious health condition. All of the same information must be provided by the family member's health care provider, with the following differences:

- The certification need not address essential job functions or work restrictions.
- The certification must provide sufficient information to establish that the family member needs care (as defined in Chapter 4), and must estimate the frequency and duration of leave necessary for the employee to provide that care.
- If the employee requests intermittent or reduced-schedule leave, the certification must state that such leave is medically necessary to care for the family member and must estimate the frequency and duration of the leave.

The DOL has created an optional certification form for this purpose, *Certification of Health Care Provider for Family Member's Serious Health Condition* (Form WH-380-F).

Certification for Military Caregiver Leave for Current Servicemembers

The certification for military caregiver leave must be completed by the employee and by the family member's health care provider. You can request this information using the DOL's optional form, *Certification for Serious Injury or Illness of Covered Servicemember—for Military Family Leave* (Form WH-385).

Information to Be Supplied by Employee

The employee must complete the following information on the certification form:

- the name of the employee, the name of the family member for whom the employee will be providing care, and the name and address of the caregiver's employer
- the employee's relationship to the family member
- whether the family member is a current member of the Armed Forces, the National Guard, or the Reserves, and the family member's military branch, rank, and current unit assignment
- whether the family member is assigned to a military medical facility as an outpatient or to a unit established for the purpose of providing command and control of members of the Armed Forces receiving medical care as outpatients (such as a medical hold or warrior transition unit), as well as the name of the treatment facility or unit
- whether the family member is on the temporary disability retired list, and
- a description of the care to be provided and an estimate of the leave necessary to provide it.

Information to Be Supplied by Health Care Provider

The family member's health care provider must also complete part of the form. For purposes of military caregiver leave, the following health care providers may complete a certification:

- a Department of Defense (DOD) health care provider
- a Department of Veterans Affairs health care provider
- a DOD TRICARE network authorized private health care provider (TRICARE is the military's health care program)
- a DOD non-network TRICARE authorized private health care provider, or
- any health care provider recognized by the FMLA (see "Who Is a Health Care Provider?" in Chapter 4 for more information).

The health care provider must complete the following information on the certification form; if the health care provider is unable to make any of the required military-related determinations, he or she may rely on the decisions of an authorized DOD representative (such as a DOD recovery care coordinator):

- the name, address, and contact information of the health care provider, the type of medical practice and specialty, and whether the health care provider falls into one of the categories listed above
- whether the family member's injury or illness was incurred or aggravated in the line of duty on active duty
- the date on which the injury or illness commenced and its probable duration
- a statement of medical facts regarding the family member's injury or illness sufficient to support the employee's leave request, including classification of the family member's medical status; whether the injury or illness may render the family member medically unfit to perform the duties of his or her office, grade, rank, or rating; and whether the family member is receiving medical treatment, recuperation, or therapy
- information sufficient to show that the family member is in need of care
- whether the family member will need care for a single continuous period of time, and if so, the time necessary for treatment and recovery, along with an estimate of the start and end dates of the need for care
- if the employee requests intermittent or reduced-schedule leave for follow-up treatment, information on the necessity of periodic care and an estimate of the treatment schedule, and
- if the employee requests intermittent or reduced-schedule leave for another reason, information on the necessity of periodic care and an estimate of the frequency and duration of the periodic care required.

If the Employee Receives an Invitational Travel Order or Authorization

Sometimes, the Department of Defense issues a family member an invitational travel order (ITO) or invitational travel authorization (ITA), to travel immediately to the bedside of a seriously ill or injured servicemember, at the Department's expense. You must accept an ITO or ITA in lieu of a certification form for the time period specified in the order or authorization. The ITO or ITA is considered sufficient certification for that time period, and it entitles the employee to take continuous leave or intermittent leave. The employee need not be the family member named in the ITO or ITA.

You may ask the employee to provide proof of a family relationship to the servicemember, as explained in Chapter 4. If the time specified in the ITO or ITA runs out, you may require the employee to provide a certification then.

Certification for Military Caregiver Leave for Veterans

The certification for military caregiver leave to care for a veteran must be completed by the employee and by the family member's health care provider. When the Department of Labor issued its final regulations implementing the new provisions of the FMLA allowing for this type of leave, it also created an optional certification form to be used for this purpose, *Certification for Serious Injury or Illness of a Veteran for Military Family Leave* (Form WH-385-V).

Information to Be Supplied by Employee

The employee must complete the first part of the form by providing:
- the name of the employee, the name of the veteran who needs care, and the name and address of the employer
- the employee's relationship to the veteran
- information on the veteran's service and discharge
- whether the veteran is in medical treatment or therapy or is recuperating from a serious illness or injury, and
- the care to be provided to the veteran and an estimate of how much leave the employee will need to provide it.

Information to Be Supplied by Health Care Provider

For veterans, the health care provider must give the same information on the certification form as required for a current servicemember. However, the form for veterans uses a different definition of a serious illness or injury for veterans. The new definition recognizes that these individuals are no longer serving in the military and that their incapacity must be measured by something other than their inability to perform their military duties. Chapter 6 explains how the 2013 regulations define a serious illness or injury for veterans.

If the Veteran Is Enrolled in the Department of Veterans Affairs Program of Comprehensive Assistance for Family Caregivers

There are four ways for an employee's family member veteran to qualify as having a serious illness or injury, for purposes of military caregiver

leave (see Chapter 6 for details). One way is the veteran's enrollment in the Veterans Affairs Program of Comprehensive Assistance for Family Caregivers. If you request a certification from an employee who needs FMLA leave to care for a veteran, you must accept evidence of such enrollment in lieu of a certification form. This is true even if the employee is not the caregiver named in the documentation.

However, you may ask the employee to provide proof of a family relationship to the veteran, as explained in Chapter 4. You may also ask the employee to provide proof of the date the veteran was discharged and that the discharge was not dishonorable.

Certification of Qualifying Exigency

The certification for qualifying exigency leave is to be completed by the employee only. You may ask the employee to provide the following information:

- a statement of facts regarding the qualifying exigency sufficient to show that the employee needs leave, including information on the type of exigency and any available documents supporting the request for leave, such as a meeting announcement or copy of an appointment schedule
- the date when the qualifying exigency began or will begin
- the start and end dates of leave requested for a single, continuous period of time
- the frequency and duration of leave requested on an intermittent or reduced schedule, and
- contact information for any third parties with whom the employee will be meeting as part of the qualifying exigency, along with a brief description of the purpose of the meeting.

In addition to the certification, you may require the employee to provide a copy of the family member's active duty orders or other military documentation indicating that the family member is on covered active duty or call to active duty status, and the dates of the family member's service. You may require the employee to provide this documentation only once, unless the employee needs leave arising out of a different call to active duty or a different family member.

If the employee is requesting leave to spend with a family member who is on short-term rest and recuperation leave during deployment, you may request additional documentation. You may ask the employee to provide a copy of the family member's Rest and Recuperation orders or other paperwork issued by the military indicating that the family member is on leave and the dates of that leave.

You may request this information using the DOL's optional form, *Certification of Qualifying Exigency for Military Family Leave* (Form WH-384).

Requesting Certification

Although you have the right to request a certification when an employee takes leave for any reason except bonding with a new child, you aren't required to. Because it's optional, some managers don't request a certification, or request one only occasionally (for example, if the employee has a history of unexcused absences). The best practice, however, is to request a certification every time an employee wants time off for a covered reason, regardless of the circumstances. This section explains why and provides information on how and when to request a certification.

Why You Should Always Request Certification

You shouldn't pick and choose which employees or conditions will require a certification. Instead, you should always request one whenever an employee requests leave for a covered reason. Here are three good reasons why.

The Condition Might Not Qualify

Unless you ask for a certification, you don't know whether the employee or family member has a condition qualifying the employee for FMLA leave. Remember, it's not your job—or right—to diagnose a serious health condition or serious illness or injury. Once an employee tells you that he or she needs time off, you can't simply say, "You don't look that sick to me," or "I'm sure your wife will be up and around in no time." If you want proof, the only way you are legally allowed to get it is through the certification process.

As a practical matter, once an employee requests leave for a covered condition, you have three options: grant the request outright, deny the request outright, or ask for a certification. If you grant the request without proof, you'll never know whether the employee or family member really had a qualifying condition; you may have provided job-protected leave and continued benefits when you didn't have to. If you don't request proof and don't grant FMLA leave, you are inviting a potentially ruinous lawsuit if the employee's request was legitimate.

Requesting a certification every time is the best way to make sure that you provide the leave required by the FMLA, no more and no less.

You Might Want to Challenge the Employee Later

If you don't ask for certification, some courts have held that your company can't later claim that the employee or family member didn't really qualify for FMLA leave. This could deprive you and your company of an important argument if the employee sues for violation of the FMLA. The lesson here is use it or lose it: If you don't ask for a certification, you may have conceded this point. After all, it might be impossible for anyone to conclusively determine whether or not a person actually suffered a claimed illness months or years later, when a lawsuit finally gets to court.

Inconsistency Leads to Discrimination Claims

Some managers pick and choose which employees have to submit certifications and which do not. A manager might ask only employees who have a history of attendance problems to get a certification or might request a certification only for ailments that are not immediately apparent.

The problem with this approach is that it can lead to discrimination claims. Any time a manager decides to treat employees differently, there is a risk that the manager will be accused of discrimination. If, for example, you ask only pregnant employees to provide a certification, you could be accused of gender discrimination. If you ask only employees who have chronic or permanent conditions—as opposed to a one-time need for surgery or time off for an injury—to provide a certification, you could be accused of disability discrimination. To avoid this problem, you should always request a certification.

Lessons from the *Real World*

Company that didn't request a medical certification can't later dispute the employee's serious health condition.

Katherine Thorson worked in the packing and shipping department of Gemini, Inc., a company that manufactures plastic signs. The company had a policy that employees who were absent for more than 5% of their scheduled hours in a rolling 12-month period could be fired for excessive absenteeism.

Thorson left work and went to the doctor on Wednesday, February 2, complaining of stomach cramps and diarrhea. She came back to work the following Monday, February 7, with a doctor's note saying "no work" until February 7. After a few hours, she returned to the doctor with stomach pain. The doctor suspected a peptic ulcer or gallbladder disease and ordered some tests for that Friday. The following Monday, February 14, Thorson returned to work, again with a doctor's note saying "no work" until the 14th. That Friday, she was fired for excessive absences. She was eventually diagnosed with several stress-related conditions.

When Thorson sued for violation of the FMLA, Gemini argued, among other things, that Thorson didn't have a serious health condition because she was not incapacitated. In other words, she didn't really have to miss work because of her condition. The court found that Gemini wasn't entitled to contest this issue because it failed to request a medical certification at the time. Thorson's own doctor's notes said "no work"; if Gemini doubted this statement, it was entitled to request a certification. Because it didn't exercise this right, the court refused to credit evidence that another physician, whose opinion was sought months after the fact for use in the lawsuit, said there was "no obvious reason" why Thorson had to miss work.

Thorson v. Gemini, Inc., 205 F.3d 370 (8th Cir. 2000).

EXAMPLE: Maggie, one of your employees, has bipolar disorder. She and her doctor have been experimenting with a new medication. Unfortunately, before she and her doctor figure out the correct dosage, Maggie has a manic episode and must be hospitalized briefly. Her brother calls you about the situation and says

that Maggie will have to stay in the hospital for at least a couple of days, then will be released to be cared for by her family until she's able to return to work.

You usually don't require employees to submit a medical certification. In this situation, though, you think you might ask for one. "She had to be hospitalized for getting overexcited? It sounds like someone just wants some time off work. I don't grant FMLA leave for 'mental health' days, and I bet she'll come back to work pretty quickly once she knows that." Because the FMLA allows you to request a certification, you're well within your rights to make this your first, aren't you?

Not quite. Maggie might claim that your request is discriminatory, because it's based on negative stereotypes about people with mental disabilities (that they are "faking it" or could control their conditions with a little will power, for example).

Procedures and Deadlines for Requesting a Certification

As soon as an employee requests leave for a serious health condition or military caregiver leave, you should request the certification, in writing. The regulations interpreting the FMLA say that employers "should" request a certification within five business days of learning that an employee needs leave, either because the employee has requested leave or because the employee has taken leave for an unforeseeable purpose (emergency surgery, for example). The regulations give you the right to request certification later if you "have reason to question" the duration or appropriateness of the leave. The best practice is not to rely on this language, but instead to give your notice and request a certification right away, every time.

Although the FMLA regulations allow employers to make an oral request in limited circumstances, you want written proof of your request for a certification, including the date you made it. The written request must state not only that you are requesting a medical certification, but also the deadlines for providing the certification and the consequences of failing to provide it.

You may request a medical certification as part of the rights and responsibilities notice you must give to an employee who has requested leave for a purpose covered by the FMLA (see Chapter 8 for more information on this notice). If you instead choose to give the employee a separate written request for a medical certification, you can use our form, "Request for Medical Certification." A sample of this form is below (see Appendix C for an electronic copy).

To: Sarah Beadle

From: Rayna Harmon

Date: August 23, 2015

On August 22, 2015, you informed us that you need to take leave for a serious health condition.

You must submit a medical certification of a serious health condition from your health care practitioner. The certification form is attached to this letter. Please note that you must complete a portion of the form if you are seeking leave to care for a family member.

You must return this form to us by September 7, 2015. If you fail to return this form on time, we may delay the start of your leave, or postpone the continuation of your leave, until we receive your certification. If you are unable to return the form on time due to circumstances beyond your control, please contact me right away.

Feel free to contact me if you have any questions about this requirement.

Sincerely,

Rayna Harmon   *August 23, 2015*

Rayna Harmon   Date

CAUTION

A written policy isn't enough. Many employers have policies explaining FMLA leave in their employee handbooks. (For information on what your FMLA policy should include, see Appendix B.) Typically, these policies cover medical certifications, including the information you must give the employee when you request one. If your company has this type of policy, however, it doesn't take the place of a written request and notice to the employee, made when the employee tells you that he or she needs leave. Courts have found that employers who don't make a specific written request to the employee cannot later challenge the employee's certification (or failure to provide one).

Employee Deadline for Returning the Certification

You must give the employee at least 15 calendar days to return the completed certification form, unless it is not practicable for the employee to meet this deadline under the circumstances, despite the employee's diligent, good faith efforts. You may give more than 15 days, if you wish.

If the employee can't meet this deadline despite reasonable, good-faith efforts to do so, the employee must return the certification as soon as it's reasonably possible. You may delay the start of leave if the employee misses the deadline and hasn't made reasonable, good-faith efforts to meet it. If the employee never provides you with a medical certification you properly requested, the leave is not protected by the FMLA.

Even though you have the right to penalize an employee for missing the deadline to return a certification, that doesn't mean you should exercise it. You must act very carefully—preferably, after talking to a lawyer—if you choose to enforce these rules. If an employee is clearly entitled to the FMLA's protections, some courts have been lenient about these requirements. Particularly if your actions cause the employee harm—for example, because the employee had to delay a medically necessary treatment program—you should anticipate the possibility that a court might take the employee's side.

The best practice, both to avoid legal trouble and to provide leave when your employees need it, is to work with your employees on this issue. Remind employees that you need a certification. If an employee misses a deadline, get in touch with the employee or a family member and explain how important the certification is. Put a note confirming this contact in the employee's FMLA file and be sure to include the name of the person you contacted, the date, and the substance of your discussion.

Rather than immediately taking drastic action, such as postponing or ending an employee's FMLA leave, be a little more flexible about getting the documentation you need. Although you might need to wait a little longer, this is the safest and most humane approach.

Lessons from the Real World

An oral request for a medical certification doesn't start the clock.

Ralph Cooper worked for Fulton County, Georgia, for almost 20 years. During his tenure, Cooper had a number of health problems, including depression, for which he was repeatedly absent from work. He was disciplined, suspended, and twice threatened with termination for failing to provide proper medical documentation and contact his supervisor in connection with his absences.

In June 1998, Cooper was absent for several days because he was experiencing chest pains. He was given a letter informing him that he had to provide a doctor's excuse for each day of his absence. On July 8, Cooper provided a doctor's note that accounted for his absences and said he could return to work on July 13. He returned to work as scheduled, only to go home ill several hours later. He told his supervisor he was too ill to work; she reminded him orally to provide a doctor's excuse.

On July 14, Cooper faxed his supervisor a request for leave because he was suffering from blurred vision, having extreme headaches, and passing out. His supervisor called him and again told him to provide a medical excuse. On August 4, the county delivered a letter to Cooper, advising him that he had to provide a medical excuse for his absences by August 10. Cooper got the required excuse from his doctor several days later, but did not immediately deliver it. On August 10, Cooper was sent a letter stating that his employment was terminated effective August 12; Cooper then submitted his medical excuse.

Even with his lengthy history of unexcused absences and failure to comply with employer policies, Cooper won this lawsuit. Why? Because Fulton County didn't give him 15 days' written notice to return the certification. Although the county repeatedly asked him for a doctor's excuse, it did not do so in writing until August 4. Therefore, Cooper had until August 19 to return his certification. By firing him before the time limit expired, Fulton County violated Cooper's FMLA rights.

Cooper v. Fulton County, Georgia, 458 F.3d 1282 (11th Cir. 2006).

After You Receive the Certification

Once you receive a certification, you have several options. You may decide, based on the information provided, that the employee is entitled to FMLA leave. In that situation, you should make sure you've provided the required notices and move on to structuring the employee's time off. (See Chapters 8 and 10.)

The information you receive might lead to the opposite conclusion: that the employee is not protected by the FMLA. This is not as common, but it does happen. For example, the health care provider might describe the condition as a minor ailment which does not incapacitate the patient or might indicate that the employee does not need time off work. In this situation, the employee has not submitted the required proof and is therefore not entitled to FMLA leave. You don't have to request a second opinion; you can simply deny leave based on this information.

TIP
Tell the employee what's wrong with the form. If the information in a medical certification doesn't show that the employee qualifies for FMLA leave, let the employee know. That way, the employee can make sure that the doctor didn't make a mistake in completing the form and will understand why you are denying the leave request. If the employee subsequently gives you a new form indicating that there is a serious health condition, you can always request a second opinion (see "Second Opinions," below).

Even if the form indicates that the employee qualifies for FMLA leave, you may still have doubts. You may wonder whether the illness or ailment described on the form really qualifies as serious. You may doubt that the employee is really using qualifying exigency leave to attend meetings with a child's teacher or a counselor. You may question the employee's inability to work due to a serious health condition. Perhaps the form is incomplete, or you simply can't read the doctor's handwriting. Later on in this section, we explain your options if you need or want more information after receiving a certification.

> ### Where to Keep Medical Certifications
>
> Employees have a right to privacy in their own medical information and that of their family members. Although you can request limited medical information so you can fulfill your obligations under the FMLA, you still have to maintain the confidentiality of this material by storing it in separate files (that is, not in employees' regular personnel files) and restricting access to it. (For more information, see Chapter 13.)

Certifications in a Foreign Language

You must accept a medical certification from a health care provider who practices in another country, if the employee or family member is visiting there, or the family member lives there, when a serious health condition develops. You must also accept second and third opinions from foreign health care providers; these procedures are described below. If the certification is in a language other than English, the employee must give you a written translation of the certification, upon request.

Incomplete or Insufficient Certifications

If the employee returns a certification that is incomplete or insufficient, you must tell the employee and give him or her a reasonable opportunity to fix the problem. A certification is incomplete if one or more of the required entries has not been completed. For example, perhaps the health care provider didn't fill in some of the blanks on the form, didn't sign and date it, or didn't indicate the duration of the employee's condition. A certification is insufficient if it is complete but the information provided is vague, ambiguous, or nonresponsive.

In these situations, you must tell the employee in writing that the certification is incomplete or insufficient, and you must explain what additional information is necessary to make the certification complete and sufficient. You must give the employee at least seven calendar days to hand in a complete, sufficient certification, unless it isn't practicable for the employee to meet this deadline under the circumstances, despite the employee's

diligent good faith efforts. Remember, this rule applies only if the employee hands in a timely certification form. If the employee doesn't provide a certification at all, that isn't considered an incomplete or insufficient certification; it's a failure to meet the certification requirement.

Lessons from the Real World

Employer can't deny leave based on inadequate medical certification if it doesn't give the employee a chance to correct it.

Curtis Sims drove a bus for the Alameda-Contra Costa County Transit District (AC Transit) for 25 years. Starting April 18, 1994, he took a couple of weeks off work because of a back injury. He went to two doctors and a chiropractor during this time and was prescribed medication and physical therapy. He returned to work on May 4 and handed in three medical slips, one from each practitioner. Together, the doctors' slips said he was unable to work through May 1; the chiropractor's slip said he could return to work on a trial basis on May 4.

AC Transit placed Sims on a five-day, unpaid suspension following this absence. In July, Sims took two days off for an illness and was fired.

Sims sued, claiming that his FMLA rights were violated when AC Transit counted his April absence against him. AC Transit argued that Sims was not protected by the FMLA because, among other things, the chiropractor did not qualify as a health care practitioner, and therefore the last two days of Sims's absence were not FMLA-protected. The court found that AC Transit might be right, but it didn't matter: Because AC Transit didn't tell Sims what was wrong with his certification and give him an opportunity to correct it, they couldn't deny him FMLA leave based on that deficiency.

Sims v. Alameda-Contra Costa Transit District, 2 F.Supp.2d 1253 (N.D. Cal. 1998).

Verifying a Certification for a Qualifying Exigency

A qualifying exigency certification is completed by the employee only. As long as the certification is complete and sufficient, you may not ask the employee for additional information. However, if the employee's qualifying exigency

involves meeting with a third party, you may contact that third party to verify that the meeting took place, or is scheduled to occur, and the nature of the meeting (for example, that it is a parent-teacher conference or counseling session). You may also contact an appropriate unit of the Defense Department to verify that the employee's family member is on covered active duty or call to active duty status; you may not request any additional information. If the employee is requesting time off to be with a family member who is on short-term rest and recuperation leave during deployment, you may ask the employee to provide a copy of the family member's Rest and Recuperation orders or other paperwork issued by the military indicating that the family member is on leave and the dates of that leave.

You don't need permission from the employee to verify the information in the certification. The form requires the employee to provide contact information for third parties with whom the employee will be meeting.

Authenticating or Clarifying Medical Certifications

Even after you receive a complete, sufficient medical certification, you may need to seek clarification or authentication from the health care provider. You may not ask for more information than the certification form requires, but you may ask for:

- clarification (to make sure you understand the health care provider's handwriting or the meaning of a response on the form), or
- authentication (that the health care provider verify that he or she provided or authorized the information on the form and signed it).

These procedures are available only for medical certifications: those for an employee's or family member's serious health condition, or for a family member's serious illness or injury entitling the employee to military caregiver leave.

However, you may seek clarification or authentication only after giving the employee an opportunity to cure any problems with the certification, as explained in "Incomplete or Insufficient Certifications," above. To seek clarification or authentication, someone from your company may contact the health care provider directly. Because the law protects the confidentiality of health-related information, you must follow these rules to make contact:

- You may only seek authentication or clarification, as defined above; you may not seek more information than the form requires.

- Only a health care provider, human resources professional, leave administrator, or management official may contact the health care provider. The employee's direct supervisor may not contact the health care provider.
- You must follow the requirements of the Health Insurance Portability and Accountability Act (HIPAA), which, among other things, may require the employee to provide a written authorization allowing his or her health care provider to discuss the employee's health information with a third party (including an employer requesting clarification of a certification). If the employee won't authorize the discussion, you may not contact the health care provider, but you may deny the employee's request for FMLA leave, if the certification is unclear. Ultimately, it's the employee's responsibility to clarify the certification, if necessary.

> **SEE AN EXPERT**
>
> **Get some help with HIPAA requirements.** One of the purposes of HIPAA is to protect the confidentiality of personal health information. The law imposes strict rules about any waiver of this right to confidentiality. For example, the employee's authorization must be in writing, describe the information that may be disclosed, and include an expiration date or event for which the authorization is valid. The regulatory provision allowing companies to make direct contact with a health care provider is relatively new, and there may be some kinks to work out. Our best advice is to talk to a lawyer to make sure your authorizations are legally valid and complete.

Second Opinions

What if an employee returns a complete and legible medical certification indicating that the employee or family member has a serious health condition, but you still have doubts? For example, the certification might say that the employee has a minor ailment (such as a cold or headache) or that the employee will need to be out of work for a long time for something that doesn't sound serious. In these situations, you have two options. You can accept the certification at face value and provide FMLA-protected leave, or you can require the employee to get a second opinion: another certification, from a health care provider of your choosing.

Second opinions are not allowed for qualifying exigency leave. They are also not allowed for military caregiver leave, unless the employee's certification was completed by someone other than a military health care provider.

CAUTION

You can't use the "company doctor." Although your company can choose the health care provider who provides the second opinion, you can't require the employee to see someone who is regularly employed by your company. This includes not only practitioners who are on the company payroll, but also practitioners whom your company regularly uses, unless access to health care in your company's area is extremely limited.

Your company must pay the costs of the second opinion, including the employee's or family member's reasonable travel expenses. You generally cannot require the employee or family member to travel beyond regular commuting distances, absent very unusual circumstances.

In some situations, the health care provider giving the second opinion will need to review medical information pertaining to the employee's or family member's serious health condition. If the employee or family member doesn't authorize his or her health care provider to release this information, and the second health care provider is unable to render a complete and sufficient second opinion as a result, you may deny the employee's leave request.

While the second opinion is pending, the employee is provisionally entitled to FMLA benefits. If the employee asks for a copy of the second opinion, you must generally provide it within five business days, absent extenuating circumstances.

SEE AN EXPERT

If the second opinion contradicts the first, proceed with caution. The FMLA gives you the right to get a third opinion if the first and second certifications differ (see "Third Opinions," below). Some courts have said that you must provide FMLA benefits unless you get this tie-breaking third opinion; others have said that you can deny benefits in reliance on the second opinion (although you might, of course, face a legal challenge from the employee, claiming that the first opinion was correct and that you improperly denied FMLA protections). Based on this conflict, the safest course of action is to go ahead with the third opinion. If you're considering denying FMLA benefits based on a second opinion, talk to an experienced employment attorney.

Third Opinions

If the first and second certifications contradict each other, you may ask the employee to get a third opinion, which will be binding on everyone. The provider who gives the third opinion must be agreed upon by the company and the employee, and both must act in good faith when choosing the provider. The penalty for failing to act in good faith is that the certification favoring the other party will be binding. For example, if you fail to act in good faith in choosing a provider, the initial certification—which presumably found that there was a serious health condition—rules. (Once you reach an agreement on who will provide the third opinion, put it in writing.) The employer must again pay the costs of this process, as well as travel costs. As with the second opinion, you must give the employee a copy of the third opinion, upon request, within five business days.

Recertifications

In some circumstances, you are allowed to ask an employee to provide a recertification of a serious health condition. (You may not request recertification of a qualifying exigency or of a serious illness or injury entitling the employee to military caregiver leave.) This process is intended to help employers fight abuse by employees, particularly employees who take leave periodically either because of a chronic condition that occasionally requires time off or because of a need for intermittent leave for medical appointments or other treatment.

You must give an employee at least 15 calendar days to return the recertification form (you can use the initial certification form for this purpose). You cannot request a second or third opinion for a recertification. How often you can request a recertification depends on the circumstances of the employee's leave.

TIP
You can ask for a new certification every year. You have the right to request an entirely new medical certification—not a recertification—every year, if the employee's or the family member's serious health condition lasts for more than a year. Even if you already requested a certification or recertification, you can request a new certification after the employee's 12-month leave period expires. Unlike a recertification, you can get a second or third opinion on this new year certification.

The general rule is that you may request recertification only in connection with an absence and no more often than every 30 days. If the certification indicates that the serious health condition will last for more than 30 days, you must wait until the duration indicated on the original certification expires before requesting recertification. In all other cases, including chronic conditions with no end date, you may request recertification every six months, in connection with an absence.

> **EXAMPLE:** Preston has asthma, for which he typically needs a couple of days of FMLA leave every month. His original certification indicates that the condition is chronic and is not expected to improve. You require Preston to submit a recertification every time he uses FMLA leave, as long as it's been at least 30 days since you last required recertification. Are you following the rules?
>
> No. Because Preston's condition is lifelong, you may not require recertification every 30 days. Unless one of the exceptions discussed below applies, you have the right to request recertification every six months and only in connection with an absence.

In some circumstances, you may require recertifications more often than every 30 days for short-term conditions, and more often than every six months for long-term conditions. You may request more frequent recertifications if:

- the employee requests an extension of leave
- the circumstances described in the previous certification have changed significantly (for example, the employee has suffered complications or has been absent more often or for a longer period of time than was stated on the previous certification), or
- the employer receives information that casts doubt on the employee's stated reason for the absence or the continuing validity of the certification.

> **EXAMPLE:** Brenda suffers from migraines. She has submitted a medical certification from her doctor, indicating that her migraines qualify as a chronic serious health condition. The certification also indicates that her migraines will cause her to miss several days of work each month, on average. Brenda has been taking about this much leave for the past six months.
>
> Brenda attends an after work "happy hour" event to send off a coworker who is leaving the company. After Brenda orders a glass of red wine, her friend John asks her, "What's going on? I've never seen you drink red wine before; I thought

it triggered your migraines." Brenda says, "I know! My doctor gave me this new medication that has totally changed my life! I've been eating chocolate, drinking red wine, and doing all kinds of things I never used to be able to do, and I haven't had a migraine for two months now."

Unbeknownst to Brenda, you—her manager—were standing behind her and overheard the conversation. The next day, you ask Brenda to recertify her health condition. You are well within your rights, as you have information that casts doubt on the continued validity of the certification.

RELATED TOPIC

You can request a fitness-for-duty certification when an employee returns to work. The FMLA allows you to ask an employee to provide a statement from a health care provider, indicating that the employee is medically able to perform the job, before reinstating the employee. (For more information, see Chapter 11.)

Lessons from the *Real World*

Taking every Monday or Friday off might be enough to justify a recertification.

In response to a question from an employer, the Department of Labor (DOL) issued an Opinion Letter (an interpretation of the law) regarding recertifications based on suspected abuse. The employer asked whether a pattern of Friday or Monday absences might qualify as information that casts doubt on an employee's reasons for leave. The DOL agreed that it might, as long as there was no evidence of a medical reason for this pattern.

Many employers were heartened not only by this guidance, but also by the DOL's suggestion—now codified in the revised regulations—that the employer may present this information directly to the health care practitioner in seeking a recertification. The regulations now state that the employer "may provide the health care provider with a record of the employee's absence pattern and ask the health care provider if the serious health condition and need for leave is consistent with such a pattern."

29 C.F.R. § 825.308(e); Opinion Letter FMLA2004-2-A (May 25, 2004).

Common Mistakes Regarding Medical Certifications—And How to Avoid Them

Mistake 1: Denying FMLA leave inappropriately—that is, when the employee is actually entitled to leave.

Avoid this mistake by taking the following steps:

- Request a certification whenever an employee seeks leave for a serious health condition, military caregiver leave, or qualifying exigency leave. Do this as soon as possible, but within five business days, of the employee's request for leave. Don't make a decision without getting the information you need.
- Verify, authenticate, and clarify the certification as necessary.
- Get a second opinion if you doubt the employee's certification. Rather than disregarding a certification confirming a serious health condition, require the employee to get a second certification from a different health care practitioner.
- Get a third opinion—or talk to an attorney before taking action—if the first and second opinions conflict.

Mistake 2: Violating an employee's (or family member's) medical privacy rights.

Avoid this mistake by taking the following steps:

- Leave the diagnosis to the doctors. Rather than asking an employee for details about his or her medical condition, give the employee a certification form and have the health care practitioners give you only the information to which you are entitled.
- Check with a lawyer before choosing a medical certification form. Some states don't allow employers to request all of the information allowed by the FMLA (and by the Department of Labor's optional medical certification form).
- Follow all the rules to talk directly to the employee's health care practitioner. Only certain company representatives may talk to the health care provider, and then only to clarify information on the form and only with the employee's permission.

- Keep separate, confidential files of medical records. Never put medical certifications and other health-related information in employees' personnel files.

Mistake 3: **Failing to give employees proper notice or enough time to get a certification.**

Avoid this mistake by taking the following steps:

- Use dated written requests for certifications that explain what employees must provide, the deadlines for getting it back to you, and the consequences of failing to return a certification. Unless you put it in writing, you won't have proof of when you requested the certification.
- Give employees at least 15 days to return a certification (or more time, if they have a plausible reason for missing the deadline). Don't try to shave a few days off, even for employees who are chronically absent or should already know the rules.
- Work with employees to get the certification in rather than strictly enforcing the deadline. In the real world, courts often recognize that employees who are seriously ill or caring for a sick child or family member might reasonably need more time, especially because they have to rely on health care practitioners, who may be busy, out of town, or simply forget to complete the form.
- Let an employee know if a certification is incomplete or doesn't support the request for FMLA leave. If you don't tell an employee what's wrong with the form, you won't be able to rely on it as a valid reason to deny the employee's leave request.

Managers' Checklist: Certifications

☐ I requested a certification as soon as I learned that the employee was seeking leave for a potentially serious health condition, leave for a qualifying exigency, or military caregiver leave.

    ☐ I made the request in writing, dated and signed.

    ☐ The request included a deadline at least 15 days away and explained the consequences of failing to return the certification on time.

    ☐ I gave the employee a certification form.

    ☐ I did not request any information that goes beyond what's required by the form.

☐ I worked with the employee to get a complete certification.

    ☐ If the form was not returned on time, I contacted the employee immediately to find out why and explain the importance of getting the form in.

    ☐ If the form was returned incomplete or insufficient, I explained that to the employee, in writing, told the employee what additional information was necessary to make the form complete and sufficient, and gave the employee at least seven days to cure the deficiency.

    ☐ If the form was in a foreign language, I asked the employee to provide a written translation.

☐ I followed the appropriate procedures to verify a qualifying exigency certification, if necessary.

    ☐ I contacted any third parties named in the certification to confirm that the employee is meeting with them and the purpose of the meeting.

    ☐ I contacted a representative of the Defense Department to confirm the family member's active duty or call to active duty.

    ☐ I asked for documentation if the employee is requesting rest and recuperation leave.

    ☐ I did not request any additional information from the employee or anyone else regarding the certification.

Managers' Checklist: Certifications (continued)

- ☐ I followed the appropriate procedures to seek authentication or clarification of a medical certification, if necessary.
  - ☐ I got written authorization from the employee for a company representative to contact the health care provider, if necessary.
  - ☐ Only a health care provider, human resources professional, leave administrator, or management official contacted the health care provider—not the employee's direct supervisor.
  - ☐ No one sought additional information from the health care provider, beyond authentication and clarification.
- ☐ I requested a second opinion if I had doubts about the initial medical certification.
  - ☐ I sought a second opinion only of a certification of a serious health condition or military caregiver leave authorized by a health care provider outside of the military.
  - ☐ I did not send the employee to a health care practitioner who is regularly employed by my company.
  - ☐ While the second opinion was pending, I provided FMLA benefits to the employee.
  - ☐ I provided a copy of the second opinion to the employee, within five days after receiving his or her request.
  - ☐ Before acting on a second opinion that contradicts the first, I consulted with an attorney.
- ☐ I requested recertifications as appropriate.
  - ☐ I requested recertification only every 30 days or when the employee's initial certification expired for short-term conditions, or every six months for long-term conditions, unless an exception allowed me to request one more often.
  - ☐ I requested recertification whenever the employee's situation changed or I learned information that cast doubt on the employee's reasons for leave.
- ☐ I placed the medical certification(s) and any recertifications in confidential medical files, not the employee's regular personnel file.

Managing an Employee's Leave

Scheduling Leave.. 213

    Postponing the Start of Leave.. 214

    Rescheduling Leave.. 217

    Unforeseeable Leave.. 217

Covering an Employee's Duties During Leave 218

    Available Options.. 219

    Talk to the Employee 221

    Handle Logistics.. 223

Continuing Employee Benefits During Leave................................... 224

    What Is a Group Health Plan?... 225

    Other Types of Benefits... 227

    Premium Payments.. 228

Managing Intermittent Leave... 231

    Scheduling.. 231

    Transfers.. 232

    Tips to Prevent Abuse... 234

Requesting Status Reports... 236

Disciplining or Firing an Employee During Leave........................... 238

Common Mistakes Regarding Managing Leave—

    And How to Avoid Them.. 241

Chapter Highlights

☆ You may postpone the start of an employee's leave if the need for leave was foreseeable and the employee could have provided you with 30 days' notice.

☆ Most employers cover an employee's workload during leave by asking coworkers to pick up the slack; other methods of handling work for an employee on leave include hiring temps, using consultants, outsourcing the work, or picking up some of the work yourself.

☆ You must continue an employee's group health benefits while the employee is on leave.
  - You may require the employee to pay his or her usual share of the premium, in one of several ways allowed by the FMLA.
  - If the employee is more than 30 days late in making premium payments, you may cut off insurance coverage, but only after providing written notice to the employee and at least 15 additional days to make up the payments.
  - Employees must make reasonable efforts to schedule foreseeable leave for planned medical treatment so it does not unduly disrupt your company's operations.

☆ You can temporarily transfer an employee on intermittent leave to another position, with equal benefits and pay, that better accommodates the need for leave.

☆ You may request periodic status reports from employees on FMLA leave regarding any changes in their planned return dates or their intent to return at all.

☆ You may discipline or even fire an employee who is on FMLA leave, as long as your reasons for doing so are entirely unrelated to the employee's leave. Before you do so, however, you should consult with a lawyer.

B y the time an employee actually starts using FMLA leave, you've already done quite a bit of work. You've dealt with coverage and eligibility requirements, handled paperwork and notices, and perhaps even had to do some math to figure out how many hours the employee has worked, how much leave the employee can take, and so on. At this point, you might be thinking that most of your work is done.

There are, however, a few more things on your FMLA to-do list. You'll need to provide continued health care benefits while employees are on leave, follow the rules for employees on intermittent leave, and make sure that you'll be ready to reinstate employees upon their return.

In addition to these legal requirements, a number of practical considerations come to the forefront when employees go out on leave. How can you make sure the employee's work gets done? How often should you communicate with an employee on leave to find out how things are going and when the employee intends to return to work? What can you do to ensure a smooth transition to and from leave? And can you ever discipline or replace an employee on FMLA leave? This chapter explains how to manage FMLA leave and provides practical strategies for minimizing disruptions to your company.

Scheduling Leave

When an employee requests time off, you should calendar the employee's leave. (Typically, you'll want to do this as you complete the employee's notice forms, covered in Chapter 8.) Mark the date when the employee plans to start leave, how long the employee expects to be gone, and when the employee intends to return. If the dates are uncertain—for example, the employee doesn't know exactly when she'll have to stop working before having a baby or how long a parent will take to recuperate from surgery—make your best guess based on what the employee tells you and the information in the certification, if applicable.

As you calendar the employee's leave, keep in mind the basic scheduling rules set out below. Now is the time to determine, for example, whether you will postpone the start of the employee's leave or ask the employee to reschedule leave. If you decide not to allow the employee to take leave on

the dates requested, you should tell the employee right away so he or she can make appropriate arrangements.

> ⚠ **CAUTION**
> **Raise scheduling issues in writing.** If you decide to postpone or reschedule the employee's leave, let the employee know in writing when you provide the designation notice form. That form doesn't explicitly address this subject, but it does indicate the dates for which the employee requested leave. If you provide the notice form without telling the employee that you aren't granting leave for the exact dates the employee requested, the employee will be understandably confused and might make plans based on his or her original request. The best practice is to put your scheduling decision in writing and attach it to the notice form, then discuss it with the employee.

Postponing the Start of Leave

As explained in Chapter 8, employees must give 30 days' advance notice if they need leave for a foreseeable reason. Examples of foreseeable leave include time off for scheduled, nonemergency surgery; for the birth or adoption of a child; or to care for a family member who has treatment scheduled well in advance. An employee who can't give 30 days' notice of foreseeable leave— for example, because the employee learned of the need for leave only a few weeks ahead of time—must give as much notice as is practicable under the circumstances. If the employee fails to give this notice, you can delay the start of the employee's leave until 30 days have passed since the employee gave notice.

> ⚠ **CAUTION**
> **You can delay the start of an employee's leave only if you have informed the employee of the duty to provide the notice required under the FMLA.** This information should be included in your company's written FMLA policy and in workplace FMLA posters, as explained in Chapter 2.

If an employee doesn't give 30 days' notice of foreseeable leave, you may ask the employee to explain why it was not practicable to do so. You should put your request in writing and ask the employee to write out his or her response.

You may not delay an employee's leave when the employee has given adequate notice under the FMLA rules covered in Chapter 8, even if the employee hasn't provided as much notice as your company usually requires. For example, if your company requires employees to schedule planned absences three months in advance, you may not penalize an employee who gives the 30 days' notice required by the FMLA for missing your company's notice deadline. However, your company may require employees to comply with its other notice requirements—for example, that employees must contact a particular person or put their leave request in writing—unless unusual circumstances prevent the employee from doing so.

Of course, you shouldn't delay an employee's leave just because you can. You'll have to carefully weigh the facts to decide whether to exercise this right. The reason for caution here is simple: An employee whose leave is delayed may challenge your decision in court, especially if the employee is harmed by the delay. What's more, you will look like the bad guy to other employees who report to you. You will also have poisoned your relationship with the employee who needed leave earlier (and will return to work at some point).

Here are a few things to consider when deciding whether to postpone leave:

- **Why the employee needs leave.** If delaying FMLA leave could cause someone to suffer physical harm, you have good reason to be lenient. For example, if the employee or a family member requires surgery for a life-threatening condition, it's best to allow the employee to take scheduled leave, rather than insisting on a full notice period.

- **How difficult it would be for the employee to reschedule.** In some cases, an employee or family member can reschedule a medical procedure relatively easily, but other times, canceling could mean waiting months for another opportunity. Or, the employee might need leave for an event that can't be rescheduled, such as the birth of a child. The harder it is for the employee to postpone taking leave, the more likely you are to face problems if you insist on 30 days' notice.

- **Your company's needs.** If you really need 30 days' notice for business reasons—for example, because it will take that long to cover the employee's accounts or because your company's busiest season will be over by then—then it makes more sense to delay leave if the employee hasn't give sufficient notice.

- **The employee's reason for failing to give notice.** Remember, the employee has to give only as much notice as it practicable under the circumstances. If the employee had a plausible reason for not giving notice on time, it's best to grant leave without a delay.

EXAMPLE: On May 1, Cora tells you, her manager, that she needs to take several days off, starting May 10, to have surgery to remove a cancerous lump from her breast. Cora's surgeon is a renowned physician whose services are in high demand, and she only found out that she'd been scheduled (after a cancellation) on May 1, the day she notified you. Can you require Cora to delay her leave until June 1?

No. Although Cora knew that she would need time off at some point, she didn't know the exact date of her surgery until the day she gave notice. Under the FMLA, this constitutes as much notice as is practicable under the circumstances, so you cannot require her to delay her leave.

Now assume that Cora actually scheduled her surgery more than a month ago but didn't tell you about it until May 1. Should you require her to delay her leave? It's risky. Cora didn't give the required notice, but she needs surgery for a potentially life-threatening condition. If you require her to miss her scheduled appointment, she might have to wait a long time to get a new date. Although you have the right to require her to wait for 30 days, it doesn't seem like a good idea to exercise it here. If delay could lead to serious medical problems, it's probably best not to require it.

If Cora's surgery was for something less urgent—for example, to remove her tonsils—the balance would shift. You would be well within your rights to require a full 30 days' notice. A delay wouldn't cause Cora any harm, and she has no excuse for failing to give notice as required, so you are on safer ground if you require her to delay her leave.

If you decide, after considering all the facts and circumstances, that you will insist on 30 days' notice, put your decision in writing (including the earliest date the employee's leave can begin) and talk to the employee about it. Listen carefully to the employee's response; you may learn something that could change your mind. If so, simply provide a new designation notice form.

Rescheduling Leave

In addition to the 30-day notice requirement for foreseeable leave, there are a couple of additional timing issues to consider. They are:

- **One-year limit on parenting leave.** As explained in Chapter 5, new parents must conclude their parenting leave within one year after the child is born or placed with them. Review this requirement when you sit down with the employee to discuss his or her time off to make sure the employee understands it.

- **Scheduling foreseeable treatment to avoid undue disruption.** Employees are obligated to make reasonable efforts to schedule foreseeable leave for planned medical treatment so as not to unduly disrupt the employer's operations. This is true whether the leave will be taken intermittently or all at once. And, for all intermittent leave for a serious health condition or military caregiver leave, employees must work with you to come up with a schedule that meets the employee's needs without unduly disrupting company operations. This means you can ask the employee to reschedule planned treatment or to work around the company's needs. However, any changes must be approved by the employee's health care provider. If the health care provider insists that treatment must begin immediately, for example, you can't make the employee wait until your company's annual reports are filed. (See "Managing Intermittent Leave," below, for more information.)

Unforeseeable Leave

As explained in Chapter 8, an employee who needs leave for an unforeseeable reason—emergency surgery or premature labor, for example—need give only as much notice as is practicable under the circumstances. If the employee has a true emergency, you might receive notice only after the employee has already missed work. How can you work out scheduling issues in this situation?

The answer depends on the circumstances. If the employee needs leave for reasons other than his or her own serious health condition—for example, because the employee's family member has been in an accident or the employee's wife has delivered a baby prematurely or been called to active military duty—you should be able to spend a few minutes on the phone

with the employee. You should ask how long the employee expects the situation to last; if the employee doesn't know, tell the employee that you'll call again in a few days to check in.

If the employee is unable to talk to you personally—for example, because the employee is in a coma, recovering from surgery, or simply too weak to attend to work details—talk to a close family member. Under the FMLA, you may talk to the employee's spokesperson (typically, an adult family member) if the employee is unable to give notice personally. In this situation, you should again ask about the condition and how long it's expected to last. If the family member doesn't know, ask to be kept in the loop and call back in a few days to follow up.

> CAUTION
> **Compassion is the order of the day.** An employee who needs emergency leave is typically facing a very tough situation such as a sudden injury or illness or a difficult birth. Although it's important to fulfill your notice obligations, don't go overboard trying to get the employee to do the same. Be sensitive to the employee's situation, and do what you can to get the information you need without being demanding or intrusive.

Covering an Employee's Duties During Leave

As a manager, you're responsible not only for administering an employee's FMLA leave properly, but also for making sure the employee's work gets done. If you're wondering how other managers do it, here's the answer: According to a 2007 survey conducted by the Society for Human Resource Management, almost 90% of employers covered the work of an employee on leave by assigning it to coworkers, at least in part; some employers (23%) hired temporary replacements to help cover the workload. And, for the most part, coworkers were not resentful about having to take on this extra work: A nationwide survey conducted in 2000 revealed that 85% of employees said that a coworker's use of FMLA leave had a positive or neutral impact on them.

One likely reason many employers simply divvy up the work of employees on leave is that employees tend to come back fairly quickly. The 2000 survey

showed that the median length of FMLA leave was only ten days, the equivalent of a two-week vacation.

When it's time to decide how to handle an employee's workload during his or her leave, these statistics provide some reassurance. As we all know, however, statistics give only a general picture. Every situation is different, and you'll have to consider all of the facts and circumstances when trying to figure out how to get the work done.

Available Options

There are a number of ways to get an employee's work done while he or she is on leave. In some cases, you'll be able to use just one of these strategies; other situations might call for a combination of approaches. Here are some commonly used options:

- **Rely on coworkers.** This strategy makes good sense, especially if other employees do similar work: The coworkers already know how to do the job. Your role is to figure out what changes might need to be made (if any) to allow the employee's coworkers to take on extra work, or how to divide the work amongst several employees. In some instances, you might even handle some higher-level work yourself, such as supervising employees or handling key transactions or relationships.

   EXAMPLE: Jody is a customer service representative in a call center staffed by 12 employees. All of them do the same job: answering phone calls from customers who have questions about the company's products, processing orders and returns on a same-day basis, and contacting customers who have purchased the company's products to assess their satisfaction with the experience.

   When Jody takes three weeks of FMLA leave, her manager, Leticia, realizes that it will take too long for a temporary replacement to learn the ropes. By the time a temp gets up to speed, Jody will be back at work. Instead, Leticia decides to ask Jody's coworkers to handle her calls. To make sure the workload doesn't get overwhelming, Leticia makes answering and returning customer calls the top priority but allows orders and returns to be put off until the following day, if necessary. And, Leticia asks two of the company's summer interns to take over the customer satisfaction surveys

until Jody returns from leave. By making these minor adjustments, Leticia ensures that her short-handed team will still be able to get its work done.

- **Hire a temporary replacement.** Whenever coworkers won't be able to take on the employee's job duties—maybe they're too busy or don't have the necessary skills—it's time to look outside the company. Just make sure that any temp you hire understands that the job is for a very limited time; otherwise, you might be faced with a legal claim when the time comes to let the temp go.

- **Hire a consultant.** If you need to replace someone who does highly creative or technical projects, consider hiring an outside consultant: an independent contractor who specializes in particular types of work. If the work is specialized and really can't wait, it might be worth the expense to hire a pro for specific tasks like rolling out a new computer system or designing new company branding or collateral.

- **Outsource the work.** It sometimes makes sense to hire an outside company to do an employee's work (for example, if no one in-house has the skills but an outside agency offers the same service).

> EXAMPLE: Sanjiv works in the bookkeeping department and spends a few days each month processing payroll. The rest of his time he collects accounts receivable. Sanjiv plans to take ten weeks of FMLA leave when his daughter is born. Although his coworkers can pick up his accounts receivable work, only his manager, Brenda, knows how to do the payroll. Unfortunately, Brenda will be preparing the company for an audit while Sanjiv is out and won't have any time to devote to handling the payroll.
>
> Brenda decides to use an outside payroll service while Sanjiv is out. It costs significantly less than hiring a replacement or training another employee to do the payroll. And, Brenda knows that the outside service knows how to handle deductions, withholdings, and other wage adjustments, which assures her that the company won't run afoul of wage and hour or tax laws while Sanjiv is away.

No matter which option(s) you choose, you'll probably have to undo any changes when the employee returns to work because you're required to reinstate the employee when his or her leave is over. (Chapter 11 explains these requirements in detail.) This is why it's important that you explain to

the people who will do the employee's job, whether they are the employee's coworkers or outside temps or contractors, that the situation is temporary. You don't want replacements believing they've received a promotion or landed a permanent position with your company.

Talk to the Employee

Before you decide how to handle an employee's workload during leave, you should talk to the employee about it, if possible. Of course, if the employee takes leave for a medical emergency, you may not get this opportunity. You'll have to patch something together quickly until you get a chance to speak with the employee and figure out how long he or she will be gone.

The employee is your best source of information about exactly what he or she does every day, which job duties are top priorities, which coworkers might be able to step in and handle certain tasks, and so on. The employee also has a vested interest in making sure his or her work is handled properly during leave. After all, nobody wants to return from leave to find a pile of unfinished work, strained relationships with customers or clients, missed deadlines, and other problems. Employees who take pride in their work and value their place in the company will be eager to collaborate with you on a strategy for a smooth transition from work to leave and back again.

But you also have to proceed with caution when talking to an employee about handling his or her work. The FMLA prohibits you from interfering with an employee's right to take leave, which includes discouraging the employee from using the FMLA. If you pressure the employee not to take leave, imply that the employee's opportunities to advance might suffer if the employee takes leave, or require the employee to work when he or she is on leave, you could run into legal trouble.

EXAMPLE: Luisa is a salesperson for a company that produces office supplies. She handles some of the company's largest accounts. Luisa is planning to take a full 12 weeks of FMLA leave when she has a baby. You meet with her to talk about handling her workload. You start the conversation like this: "You know, Luisa, our back-to-school business in August and September is huge, and you're planning to be out until September. If you could come back a few weeks early, we wouldn't have to assign your accounts to someone else. Of course, you

can take a longer leave if you want, but I can't guarantee that you'll get those accounts back if we have to move them."

Oops! You've basically said that you will punish Luisa for taking the full leave to which she's entitled. Here's a better way to start the discussion: "Congratulations, Luisa! I'm so excited for you. As you know, you'll be out during the biggest sales period of the year, so I want to get your ideas about how we should handle your accounts while you're gone, especially Office Club and Binders 'n' More. I really want to work with you to figure out how we can keep these customers happy, and keep our sales high, even though you won't be here. Do you think it makes sense to hire a temporary replacement, or can the other salespeople pick up the slack?"

Your conversation with the employee will depend on the facts, including what the employee does, how long the employee will be out, whether the employee supervises others, and so on. Here are some pointers that will help you in your conversation:

- **Always start by acknowledging the employee's situation.** Congratulate or offer sympathy to the employee as appropriate. Rushing straight into a discussion of work details appears insensitive to the employee's needs, and your conversation may be strained as a result.

- **Briefly state the facts.** Review what you know about the employee's job and leave to make sure you've got the details right. For example, you might say, "I'd like to get your feedback on how to cover your work while you're out, and make sure your transition to leave and back to work is a smooth one. I understand you'll be out for five weeks and that one major project milestone will come up during that time. Is that right?"

- **Learn the priorities.** Ask what the employee has on his or her plate, focusing particularly on projects, deadlines, meetings, and deliverables that need to be handled while the employee is out. For example: "What are the most important things that we need to take care of while you're gone? What can wait until you return?"

- **Discuss options.** Ask whether the employee has any ideas or concerns about job coverage, such as which coworkers might be able to pick up the work, whether to hire a temp, or whether some matters would

best be handled by you or another higher-up at the company. You might say, "When Jane took parental leave, I called on her two major accounts and the rest of the team divvied up the others. Do you think that approach will work for your leave? Are there any accounts that you think I should cover?"

- **Ask what to say.** Find out how the employee would like you to position his or her absence with third parties (vendors, clients, customers, and so on) and coworkers. Some employees want others to know what's going on, while others prefer to keep things private, and you should respect the employee's wishes. For example: "I'll tell the outside auditors that you'll be on leave for four weeks. I know some of your coworkers already know about your father's condition; would you prefer that I announce that you'll be taking leave to help care for him, or would you rather I simply say that you'll be out?"

- **Recap your strategy.** After you've talked through the options and developed a plan, review it with the employee. If either of you will have to gather more information before you can make a final decision, schedule another brief conversation. For example, you might say, "I'm going to ask Mark about his workload, and you're going to try to reschedule the in-house trainings until after you return from leave. Let's meet again on Thursday to see where we are. If everything works out, we'll plan to have Mark and Stacey cover your IT calls, and I'll free up some of their time by bringing in a part-time temp to handle the departmental paperwork."

Handle Logistics

After you've developed a plan to cover the employee's work, it's time to execute it. If you'll need to hire a temp or consultant, make the necessary arrangements. If coworkers will be taking on part of the load, talk with them and find out whether they'll need additional resources or help to handle the additional work. Tell the employee's outside contacts—such as clients, suppliers, and so on—that the employee will be out, and give them the name of someone else to call if they have any questions or concerns.

Lessons from the *Real World*

Company that pressures employee to take fewer days off interferes with the employee's FMLA rights.

Vanessa McFadden was a legal secretary at a law firm when her husband was diagnosed with cancer. She asked for leave to take care of him and was granted some time off, but said she was misinformed about her FMLA rights and pressured not to take as much time off as she needed. She said that the human resources manager at the firm told her that missing work on days when her husband had medical appointments was going to be a problem. Because she felt that she had to report to work, McFadden arranged for her sister to care for her husband on those days and paid her for doing so.

The D.C. Court of Appeals found that McFadden had the right to go to trial on her claim that the law firm interfered with her FMLA rights. Based on the facts, the Court found that a jury could reasonably conclude that McFadden had to pay her sister to take care of her husband because the firm (and the HR Manager, sued in her individual capacity) had led her to believe that she could not take time off to care for him herself.

McFadden v. Ballard Spahr Andrews Ingersoll, LLP, 611 F.3d 1 (D.C. Cir. 2010).

Continuing Employee Benefits During Leave

While an employee is on FMLA leave, you must continue the employee's coverage under your company's group health plan, just as if the employee did not take leave. If the employee usually has to contribute toward the premium, you may continue to require that contribution, but your company must continue to pay its share of the premium as well. Whether you have to provide other types of benefits during leave depends on your company's policies.

The employee is entitled to continue the same type of coverage and benefit levels as before the leave. For example, if the employee's family was covered, then the continuation must include family coverage. However, any changes to the benefits plan, new plans, premium increases, and so on still apply to the employee. And, employees on leave have the same right to change their coverage as they would have had if they were employed. So an employee

on leave during an open enrollment period has the same right to change coverage as employees who are actually working during that period.

Employees do not have to continue their benefits during FMLA leave if they don't want to. However, because you must restore the employee's benefits when you reinstate the employee—and you must do so immediately, without any waiting period, physical examination, or other requalification procedure—you might have to continue the benefits and seek reimbursement later from the employee. (Chapter 11 covers benefits restoration when an employee returns to work.)

What Is a Group Health Plan?

A group health plan is any plan of, or contributed to by, an employer to provide health care to employees, former employees, and their families, including self-insured plans, vision plans, dental coverage, and other health care plans, whether they are components of a single health care plan or administered separately.

A group health plan does not include an insurance program providing health coverage under which employees purchase individual policies from insurers if all of the following are true:

- The employer makes no contribution.
- Employee participation is voluntary.
- The employer's role doesn't go beyond allowing the insurer to publicize its plan to employees, collecting premiums through payroll deductions, and sending them to the insurer.
- The employer doesn't receive any compensation or other benefit from the program, other than reasonable payment for the cost of collecting and remitting premiums.
- The employee's premium does not increase if the employment relationship ends.

Cafeteria Plans

Some companies provide benefits through a cafeteria plan: a benefit program through which employees choose from a menu of benefits, such as health coverage, life insurance, disability insurance, and so on. Employees are allotted a certain number of dollars or "points" to spend on the options; if

they choose not to spend the entire amount, they can typically receive the remainder as compensation.

Employers must continue making cafeteria plan payments toward group health insurance premiums (including dental and vision benefits) while an employee is on FMLA leave. If other benefits—such as life insurance or child care coverage—are paid through a cafeteria plan, the employer is not required to continue the portion of the payment that goes toward these benefits, unless it does so for employees on other types of unpaid leave. (See "Other Types of Benefits," below, for more information.)

Flexible Spending Accounts

A flexible spending account (FSA) allows employees to set aside pretax income for medical expenses not paid by health insurance (such as co-payments, premiums, and expenses that are outside of the employer's plan) or for dependent care expenses. The employee determines how much to set aside each year (typically, through payroll deductions), within limits set by law.

FSAs are funded entirely by employees, so there aren't any employer contributions to be continued during FMLA leave. Employees on leave must be given three options for dealing with their FSAs:

- continue making payments as if they were still working
- continue their participation in the plan but stop making payments during leave, or
- stop participating in the plan while on leave.

If the employee either stops making payments or pulls out of the plan altogether during FMLA leave, the employee has a choice upon reinstatement: return to the previous coverage level or choose a prorated coverage amount that doesn't include payments for the time spent on leave.

> EXAMPLE: David has an FSA and decides to commit $1,200 to it for the year. His employer sets aside $50 from David's twice-monthly paychecks and deposits it in his FSA. David is out for two months on FMLA leave. He decides to continue his coverage but suspend his payments during that time.
>
> When he returns, David would have to make higher payments to set aside a total of $1,200. Because he missed $200 worth of payments while on leave and there are eight pay periods left in the year, he would have to have an additional $25 set aside each pay period, for a total pretax contribution of $75, if he

wanted to set aside the whole $1,200. Alternatively, he could continue setting aside $50 per paycheck and reduce his total coverage for the year to $1,000.

Multiemployer Health Plans

A multiemployer health plan is a special type of health insurance coverage unique to unionized companies. At least two employers contribute to a multiemployer plan, which is maintained pursuant to one or more collective bargaining agreement(s) between unions and employers.

Employers who contribute to these plans must follow the same benefits continuation rules as other employers. For example, they cannot provide less coverage or charge the employee a higher premium to continue benefits than the employee would have had to pay if working. However, there are a couple of different rules for multiemployer plans:

- If the plan contains special provisions for maintaining coverage during FMLA leave (for example, through pooled contributions from all employers subject to the plan), the employer may follow those provisions rather than continuing to contribute the same amount as would have been due if the employee were continuously working.
- Employees who receive health care coverage through a multiemployer plan cannot be required to use "banked" hours during FMLA leave. Typically, an employee banks hours when he or she works more hours than are necessary to maintain eligibility for health care coverage; the employee can then use these banked hours to maintain eligibility when the employee's hours drop below the minimum threshold for eligibility. This provision relieves employees of the obligation to use banked hours to maintain eligibility during periods of FMLA leave.

Other Types of Benefits

For all other types of benefits, your company must follow its usual policies for employees on the same type of leave (that is, paid or unpaid). If your policies do not provide for other benefits to continue or accrue during leave, you do not have to continue them or allow them to accrue during FMLA leave. For example, if your company typically does not allow paid vacation leave to accrue while an employee is on unpaid leave, you do not have to

allow it to accrue while the employee is on unpaid FMLA leave. The same is true of seniority and benefits based on seniority.

> **CAUTION**
>
> **Apply paid leave policies if employees use paid time off for FMLA leave.** If an employee uses paid time off for FMLA leave, you must follow your company's policies for paid leave. For example, if you allow employees to continue to accrue seniority or sick and vacation leave while using paid time off, you must also allow them to accrue these benefits while using paid time off for FMLA leave.

You have no legal obligation to continue other insurance benefits—such as life or disability insurance—while an employee is on FMLA leave unless you continue these benefits for other types of leave. But as a practical matter, you may be required to continue these benefits to make sure you'll be able to restore the employee's benefits upon reinstatement. As you'll learn in Chapter 11, you must give a returning employee the same benefits, at the same levels, that the employee had before taking leave, and you cannot require the employee to requalify for benefits. If your programs would require an employee who drops coverage and then picks it up again to requalify, you might have to keep the employee enrolled to avoid violating the FMLA. (If so, you can seek reimbursement for the employee's share of the premiums when the employee returns to work; see Chapter 11.)

Premium Payments

The FMLA provides several ways to collect the employee's share of the premium for group health coverage. If the employee substitutes paid leave for FMLA leave, the employee's share must be collected as it ordinarily would be for any other type of paid leave (typically, through payroll deductions). If the employee uses unpaid FMLA leave, the employer may collect the premium in any of the following ways:

- The employee makes the payment at the same time it would ordinarily be due through payroll deduction. In other words, the employee would have to pay the premium every payday.

- The employee makes the payment at the same time it would be due if the employee were receiving continuing coverage through COBRA.
- The employee pays the premium in advance to a cafeteria plan (at the employee's option).
- The employee pays according to the same rules that apply to other employees on unpaid leave, as long as those rules don't require the employee to pay the premium before leave starts or require the employee to pay more than he or she would have to pay if employed.
- The employee pays in any manner agreed to by employer and employee. For example, you might agree that the employee can prepay the premiums by having a larger amount deducted each pay period prior to taking foreseeable leave.

Whichever method you choose, you must give the employee advance written notice of how and when the payment must be made and the consequences of failing to pay. You can provide this notice as part of the employee's rights and responsibilities notice, covered in Chapter 8.

If the employee's premium payment is more than 30 days late, you may terminate the employee's coverage. However, you must send the employee written notice of your intent to do so. The letter must state that the payment has not been received and that the employee's coverage will terminate if payment is not received by a certain date; this date must be at least 15 days after you send the letter.

POLICY ALERT
The date the employee's coverage officially terminates depends, in part, on your policies for other types of unpaid leave. If your company has an established policy that allows it to terminate coverage retroactively to the date of the missed payment, it may do so. If it does not have this type of policy, it may terminate coverage effective 30 days after the missed payment.

Here is a sample letter telling an employee that health insurance coverage will terminate unless payment is received; see Appendix C for a template.

Sample Notice of Termination of Group Health Coverage

March 28, 2014

Corinne West

123 Main Street

San Francisco, CA 94910

Dear Corinne,

As I informed you by written notice when you first requested FMLA leave, you are required to pay your share of the premium for group health insurance. We agreed that you would pay these amounts by getting a check to me, in the amount of $36.45, on the 1st and 15th of every month. I have attached a copy of the written notice explaining this requirement, for your reference.

You submitted a check on February 15 and March 1. However, I did not receive a check from you on March 15. I am writing to inform you that we are going to terminate your health insurance coverage if we do not receive your March 15 payment by April 14, 2014. You must continue to make your other premium payments on time.

Please take care of this right away. If you have any questions, feel free to call me at 415-555-1212.

Sincerely,

Jim Ramey

HR Director

Although you have the legal right to terminate coverage for a late payment, you also have a legal obligation to restore the employee's health benefits when he or she returns to work. You cannot require the employee to reapply, take a physical exam, or otherwise requalify for benefits. This obligation applies even if you terminate coverage because the employee fails to pay the premium. As a practical matter, you may have to continue the employee's coverage in order to reinstate benefits as the FMLA requires, even if this means you have to pay the employee's share of the premium. If you find yourself in this situation, you can require the employee to reimburse you for his or her share once the employee returns to work; Chapter 11 explains how.

Managing Intermittent Leave

Intermittent or reduced-schedule leave poses some unique managerial challenges. You and the employee might not know how long the employee's need for leave will last, when the employee will have to take time off, or even whether the employee will show up for work the next day. This can present some challenges when you're trying to make sure that the work gets done.

Scheduling

Employees who need intermittent or reduced-schedule leave for a serious health condition or to act as a military caregiver must try to schedule leave in a way that does not disrupt your company's operations. If the employee knows he or she will need intermittent or reduced-schedule leave, the employee should give you a proposed schedule of leave and try to arrange to take time off in a way that accommodates the company's needs. Of course, this will be easier when the employee needs leave for scheduled treatment rather than for episodic flare-ups of a serious health condition.

This doesn't mean that the company has the right to veto an employee's leave schedule, however. The employee's health care provider will ultimately decide whether treatment or leave can be rescheduled or not. If the health care provider won't approve a change, you may not insist on it.

> **EXAMPLE:** Marcos needs weekly physical therapy for neck injuries from a car accident. Marcos tells you that he needs to be out for two hours every week for at least 12 weeks. You and Marcos agree that he will try to schedule the therapy for the late afternoon, when plenty of his coworkers will be available to handle his workload.
>
> When Marcos calls to schedule his treatment, he learns that there are no available late afternoon slots for a couple of months. Marcos's doctor says that he must begin physical therapy immediately or risk permanent damage. In this situation, can you insist that Marcos wait for an afternoon appointment?
>
> No. Marcos's doctor has the last word, and treatment must start immediately. You should work with Marcos to figure out which of the available time slots would be least disruptive for the company.

When an employee needs leave for an episodic problem, such as migraines, asthma, or any other condition that comes on suddenly or waxes and wanes in intensity, it can be very difficult to manage the employee's time off. After all, the employee typically can't predict when the condition will flare up. If the condition is unpredictable, you cannot insist that the employee take leave only according to a set schedule. As long as the employee is otherwise entitled to leave and either is taking military caregiver leave or has (or is caring for someone who has) a serious health condition, the employee has the right to take unscheduled time off if it's medically necessary.

> **EXAMPLE:** Caroline suffers from Crohn's disease, a chronic condition that causes inflammation of the intestines. On occasion, the disease flares up and she has severe abdominal pain and vomiting that makes it impossible for her to work. If she qualifies for FMLA leave, Caroline is likely entitled to take intermittent leave when her condition incapacitates her, even if she can't give any notice or "schedule" this time off.

Transfers

If an employee has a foreseeable need for reduced-schedule or intermittent leave for planned medical treatment or if your company agrees to allow intermittent or reduced-schedule parenting leave, you may transfer the employee to another position that better accommodates the employee's leave schedule or change the employee's original position to better accommodate the employee's need for leave, as long as the employee still receives the same pay and benefits. If transferred to an alternative position, the employee must be qualified for the position.

The alternative position need not have the same job duties as the employee's original position. However, the company cannot transfer the employee to a less desirable position that could discourage the employee (or others) from taking leave. For example, a change that dramatically increases the employee's commute or moves the employee from the day shift to the night shift violates the FMLA. If the alternative position is a clear and obvious demotion, it won't fly.

Lessons from the *Real World*

An employee must make reasonable efforts to reschedule foreseeable intermittent leave that would result in understaffing.

Scott Kaylor was a CT technician at Fannin Regional Hospital. During his employment at the hospital, Kaylor saw his doctor regularly for treatment for a degenerative back disease.

On December 27, 1994, Kaylor was hospitalized for a flare-up of his back injury. He spent three weeks on FMLA leave, then returned to work. On January 31, Kaylor told his supervisor that he had an appointment with his doctor on February 3. This appointment was one of his regular treatments and had been scheduled before he was hospitalized. Kaylor's supervisor told him he could not take the day off because it would leave them short-staffed and asked him to reschedule the treatment.

After hearing from other employees that Kaylor planned to call in sick on February 3, his supervisor asked him whether he intended to show up. He said that he would come to work. On the 3rd, however, he called in sick, claiming to have a stomach virus. But he still went to his doctor's appointment for back treatment. The doctor said that Kaylor could have gone to work that day, and the doctor's notes didn't mention a stomach virus.

Kaylor was fired for abuse of sick leave. Kaylor sued, claiming that he had a legal right to take intermittent FMLA leave on February 3 and could not be fired for doing so. The court disagreed, finding that Kaylor had an obligation to make reasonable efforts to reschedule his leave after his supervisor told him that it would cause staffing problems. Because he didn't follow the rules for intermittent leave, Kaylor wasn't protected by the FMLA.

Kaylor v. Fannin Regional Hospital, 946 F.Supp. 988 (N.D. Ga. 1996).

EXAMPLE: Roger is a human resources manager for a large hotel chain. He reports to the company's headquarters but travels two or three days each week to conduct trainings for employees in other cities. Roger's doctor certifies that he will need to spend four hours per day caring for his son during a ten-week cancer treatment regimen.

The company needs to continue its trainings during Roger's leave, and Roger can no longer travel. The company would be within its rights to transfer Roger to a different position with the same pay and benefits. For example, it might require Roger to handle compensation and benefits issues, to coach other representatives so they can handle the out-of-town trainings, or to help the company revise its nationwide hiring standards, if Roger is qualified to do those tasks. However, if the company tried to transfer Roger to work at the front desk of one of its hotels or process reservations in a call center, that would violate the FMLA.

Once the employee's leave ends, you must return the employee to his or her original position or an equivalent one (see Chapter 11).

Tips to Prevent Abuse

Some managers worry that employees who qualify for intermittent leave will abuse that right to take time off whenever they want, and that the company just has to sit back and take it. This isn't quite true, however. Although employees have a right to take intermittent leave if it's medically necessary or for a qualifying exigency, this doesn't mean that they are free to use that time off for any purpose. If you think an employee might be abusing intermittent leave—for example, by taking unscheduled intermittent leave only on Fridays or calling in sick whenever a major deadline is looming— here are a few things you can do:

- **Check the certification.** As explained in Chapter 9, you should always get a certification when an employee takes FMLA leave. On the form, the health care provider and/or employee must give certain facts about the need for leave. For example, the certification for qualifying exigency leave asks the employee to estimate a leave schedule, including the frequency and duration of appointments, meetings, and other events; the employee also must provide the names and contact information of those with whom the employee will meet. The medical certification forms ask the health care provider to give similar information, such as a treatment schedule, the frequency and duration of absences for appointments, and so on. If the employee's time off doesn't jibe with these predictions, you can seek recertification of a serious health condition (Chapter 8 explains how) or contact the third parties the

employee names in a qualifying exigency certification to make sure those meetings are taking place as claimed.

- **Get a new certification if the employee's reason for leave changes.** For example, if an employee takes time off every week for scheduled treatment for an injury, then claims to need additional leave for another condition, require a certification of the new condition. This will help you pin down exactly what the employee needs and why.

- **Let the doctor review the employee's schedule for a serious health condition.** The FMLA regulations allow you to provide a copy of the employee's absence pattern to the health care provider when you request recertification of a serious health condition. You can ask the provider whether the serious health condition and the employee's need for leave is consistent with the pattern of absences. A doctor who sees that an employee is gaming the system—by always taking leave on Fridays, for example—may be willing to place some limits on the certification.

- **Require employees to adhere to a schedule for foreseeable intermittent leave.** If an employee needs intermittent leave only for scheduled treatment (not for a condition that might worsen suddenly), you can ask the employee to stick to the schedule. Of course, the employee's doctor might have to cancel every once in a while, but if the employee seems to be taking a lot of unscheduled time off, you should ask the employee what's going on and seek recertification.

- **Require employees to talk to a manager for every absence.** One of the toughest challenges that arises from intermittent leave is properly recording and designating the time off. It's especially difficult if an employee takes a lot of unscheduled time off in small increments. This is why it's a good idea to require employees using intermittent leave to call in and let a manager know why they're taking time off; the manager can then record the leave as FMLA leave or pass the message on to the person responsible for managing the FMLA in your organization. If the employee is unable to call in ahead of time for health reasons, make sure the employee provides notice as soon as possible.

In the past, there was some confusion over whether companies could enforce their own notice rules when employees use FMLA leave. The 2008 revisions to the FMLA regulations provide the following guidance for employers:

- **An employee who gives the amount of notice required by the FMLA is entitled to use FMLA leave.** As long as the employee gives 30 days' notice for foreseeable leave and as much notice as is practicable for unforeseeable leave, the employee is entitled to the protections of the FMLA.
- **You may require employees to follow your company's other notice procedures.** If your company requires employees to give written notice or call their supervisors for all absences, for example, you can require employees taking FMLA leave to do the same.
- **You may require employees to follow your regular procedures for using paid leave if the employee wants to substitute paid leave for FMLA leave.** As long as the employee gives the notice required by the FMLA, the employee is entitled to use unpaid FMLA leave. However, an employee who wants to use accrued paid leave during that time may be required to follow your usual procedures, even if they require more notice than the FMLA. For example, if your vacation policy requires employees to give six weeks' notice to use paid vacation, an employee who gives only 30 days' notice may not use paid vacation until six weeks have elapsed; however, the employee is still entitled to unpaid FMLA leave for those six weeks.

Requesting Status Reports

The FMLA gives employers the right to require an employee on leave to provide periodic reports on his or her status and intent to return to work. This rule serves a couple of purposes: For one, it helps employers manage the employee's workload and plan for a smooth reinstatement. As explained in Chapter 11, employers must reinstate employees immediately upon their return from leave, as long as employees provide at least two business days' notice of the intent to return. Knowing when the employee plans to return to work helps employers prepare for the transition.

For another, requiring status reports also gives an employer notice if the employee won't return to work. If the employee tells the employer, unequivocally, that he or she will not return to work, the employer can replace the employee permanently or make any other necessary changes. If the employee voluntarily chooses not to return—for example, to stay home

with a healthy baby—then the employer can also discontinue the employee's health benefits and seek reimbursement for any premiums already paid. (These rules are explained in Chapter 11.)

If you require status reports, tell employees what you expect. Your request must be reasonable, considering the facts and circumstances of the employee's leave. If you ask for reports too frequently or request too much detail, especially of an employee who is struggling with a serious health condition, you could run into legal trouble. The Department of Labor has said that employers who take advantage of this limited right to communicate with employees on leave by making disruptive or burdensome requests could violate the law. At some point, an employer who is too persistent could appear to be punishing the employee for taking leave or trying to bully the employee to either return to work or forfeit his or her health benefits.

How often you should request a status report depends on how long the employee will be on leave and how definite the employee's return-to-work date is. If the employee will be on leave for 12 weeks and has a scheduled return-to-work date, you might ask for a status report once a month, then check in with the employee a week or two before the planned return date, to make sure that the employee is still coming back as scheduled. If the employee doesn't know how long he or she will have to be off, you might reasonably request more frequent status reports. And for a shorter leave, you might simply ask the employee to check in a week before returning, to make sure everything is still going according to plan.

You should ask for two pieces of information in the status report: whether the employee still intends to return to work and, if so, when. Don't try to use a status report requirement to get medical information; that's governed by the recertification process explained in Chapter 9.

You can request that employees make status reports orally or in writing. These days, it may be easiest to have employees email you with their status updates. But some employees may prefer to use the phone. If you allow oral status reports, however, you must document any changes to the employee's leave dates or intent to return to work. If the employee calls and tells you that he or she is no longer planning to come back, for example, you should put that in writing immediately. The best practice is to also send a confirming letter or email to the employee right away, to make sure you got it right.

Lessons from the *Real World*

Weekly phone calls are too frequent, but it doesn't matter unless it keeps the employee from exercising his or her FMLA rights.

Regina Terwilliger was employed as a housekeeper at Howard Memorial Hospital. She requested, and granted FMLA leave for necessary back surgery and recuperation afterwards. While she was out on leave, her supervisor called her every week to ask when she was returning to work. During one call, Terwilliger asked whether her job was in jeopardy; her supervisor replied that she should come back to work as soon as possible. Terwilliger returned to her job after 11 weeks of leave, not the 12 weeks she had planned to take. She sued for interference with her right to take FMLA leave.

The court issued two opinions in this case. In the first, it ruled for Terwilliger, finding that her supervisor's weekly phone calls discouraged her from exercising her FMLA rights. In a second opinion, however, the court changed its mind. Terwilliger's doctor released her to return to work after 11 weeks. Therefore, the court found, Terwilliger hadn't actually been denied any benefit to which she was entitled. As she no longer had a serious health condition at 11 weeks, she was no longer entitled to FMLA leave. Whether or not the supervisor's calls were appropriate, they didn't have the effect of denying any of her rights. (Had Terwilliger felt so pressured that she came back to work while she still had a serious health condition, however, the outcome would have been different.)

Terwilliger v. Howard Memorial Hospital, 770 F. Supp. 2d 980 (W.D. Ark. 2011).

Disciplining or Firing an Employee During Leave

You may fire or discipline an employee who is on FMLA leave, as long as your reasons are entirely unrelated to the employee's use of the FMLA. This is easier said than done, because it might be hard to prove that the employee's FMLA leave played no part in your decision. This is particularly true if you are disciplining or firing the employee for poor attendance. Even if you consider only absences that were not covered by the FMLA, chances

are good that the employee will claim to have been fired in retaliation for taking legally protected leave.

The best practice is to make absolutely sure that you'll be able to prove that you had independent reasons for acting. You'll be on safest legal ground if you initiated discipline or termination proceedings before you knew that the employee might need FMLA leave. That way, the employee will have a tough time showing any relationship between the leave and your decision. If you are imposing discipline for excessive absenteeism, you must be very sure that you aren't counting any protected absences against the employee.

Even if you have entirely legitimate reasons for disciplining or firing an employee, you might find yourself on the wrong end of a lawsuit if you take action as soon as the employee asks for FMLA leave. Perceptions matter to the employee, the lawyer(s) whom the employee consults about filing a lawsuit, and the judge and jury. If you act right after the employee requests leave, it's probably going to look like you acted because of the request, even if that's not the case. Although you might eventually win in court (if the jury believes your side of the story), you and your company will spend a lot of time and money getting to that victory. You should consult with a lawyer whenever you are considering disciplining or firing an employee who has requested or taken FMLA leave.

TIP
You might need to talk about reasonable accommodations. If an employee who is out for his or her own serious health condition expresses concerns about being able to do the job after returning from FMLA leave, consider the possibility that the employee might have a disability as defined by the Americans with Disabilities Act (ADA). If so, your company has a duty to begin a conversation about whether and how you can make it possible for the employee to perform the job by providing a reasonable accommodation. It's best to start talking about possible accommodations as soon as you learn that the employee might have a disability, to give you time to make any necessary adjustments before the employee is ready to return. (See Chapter 12 for more on the ADA.)

Lessons from the *Real World*

An employee can be fired for previous performance problems discovered during FMLA leave.

Candis Smith worked as an Administrative Secretary at the Memorial Foundation of Allen Hospital. She was responsible for sending a receipt and thank-you card to hospital donors. In December 1998, Robert Justis, the Executive Director of the Foundation, told Smith that he had received complaints from donors who had not been acknowledged for their contributions. Smith told him that she would try to send out acknowledgments as soon as possible.

Smith took FMLA leave starting January 1, 1999, to adopt a child from Romania. She left a stack of donor receipts that had to be sent out and wrote a note asking another employee to type thank-you cards and mail them, along with the receipts, to donors. One week into Smith's leave, another employee found another pile of donor receipts in Smith's work area. There were approximately 400 receipts, for donations totaling more than $350,000, going back a couple of months. One of the receipts was for a gift of $136,000, from one of the donors who had complained about not receiving a receipt.

Justis and Richard Seidler, the CEO of the hospital, decided to terminate Smith's employment immediately. On January 14, when she returned from Romania, they called her in for a meeting and fired her for failing to send out the receipts.

Smith sued, claiming that she was fired illegally for taking FMLA leave. As evidence, she pointed out that she was fired just two weeks after starting her leave and that she was fired for problems that came to light only because she took leave. The court didn't buy these arguments. Instead, the court noted that Smith was fired shortly after she started her leave because the Foundation didn't know how serious the problem was until it discovered the unsent receipts, which put the Foundation in a difficult position with its donors. In light of these facts, the timing of the decision did not demonstrate that Smith was fired for taking leave.

Smith v. Allen Health Systems, Inc., 302 F.3d 827 (8th Cir. 2002).

Common Mistakes Regarding Managing Leave—And How to Avoid Them

Mistake 1: Requiring employees to give more notice than the FMLA requires.

Avoid this mistake by taking the following steps:

- Don't require an employee to give more notice than is practicable under the circumstances.
- Delay the start of an employee's leave only if you have the right—and a good reason—to do so. If the employee could have given 30 days' notice, delaying the employee's leave won't harm the employee, and your company really needs the employee at work in the next 30 days, consider asserting your rights.
- Ask employees to give you written reasons why they were unable to give 30 days' notice of foreseeable leave.
- Require employees to follow your paid leave policies to substitute paid leave for unpaid FMLA leave, while recognizing that you can't deny them the right to take unpaid leave if they meet the FMLA's requirements.

Mistake 2: Overloading coworkers when an employee takes FMLA leave.

Avoid this mistake by taking the following steps:

- Plan ahead if you know an employee will need leave (to have a baby, for example). Talk to the employee and coworkers ahead of time about your plans for getting the work done.
- Cross-train your employees. It will be much easier for employees to cover each other's work if they already know how to do it.
- Get extra help, if necessary. You might need to bring in a temp or consultant to help you get the work done, especially when an employee takes an extended leave.
- Take on important tasks yourself. It doesn't help your company to have inexperienced folks handling major clients or projects. Make time in your schedule to handle these key tasks.

Mistake 3: Mismanaging intermittent leave.

Avoid this mistake by taking the following steps:

- Seek recertification of a serious health condition, if necessary. If an employee is taking leave beyond what the certification anticipated, ask for another one.

- Make sure that every qualified absence is designated as FMLA leave. An employee who takes a lot of intermittent leave may also take time off for other reasons, such as vacation or minor illnesses. You need to know which absences count as FMLA leave, so ask these employees to talk to you or another manager every time they need time off.

- Require employees to stick to their treatment schedules. If an employee needs intermittent leave for scheduled treatment, the certification should state when that treatment will be. You can ask the employee to reschedule, with the doctor's approval, to avoid undue disruption to the company's operations.

- Transfer the employee, if necessary. You are entitled to transfer the employee temporarily to a position that better accommodates his or her need for intermittent leave (except for a qualifying exigency). Just make sure that the transfer isn't a demotion in disguise.

Mistake 4: Firing or disciplining an employee for taking FMLA leave (or appearing to do so).

Avoid this mistake by taking the following steps:

- Consult with a lawyer every time. Because it's so easy to get in trouble here, you should always talk to a lawyer to make sure that you've made the right decision before taking action.

- Make sure you have a very compelling reason to fire the employee. Even if your company is an at-will employer (as most are), this isn't the time to exercise your right to fire without a very good reason.

- Fire only if you can prove that you would have taken the same action if the employee hadn't taken leave. This means, for example, being able to document that termination proceedings were in the works before the employee requested leave or that you discovered truly egregious problems that warrant immediate firing.

- Don't count FMLA absences against an employee with an attendance problem. You can't consider FMLA leave when deciding whether an employee has missed so much work that termination is warranted.

Managers' Checklist: Managing FMLA Leave

Scheduling:

☐ I calendared the start and end dates of the employee's leave, if I know them.

☐ If the employee did not give 30 days' notice of foreseeable leave, I considered whether to require the employee to delay the start of his or her leave.

☐ If the employee did not give 30 days' notice of foreseeable leave, I asked the employee to give me a written statement of the reasons why such notice wasn't given.

☐ If I didn't let the employee take leave on the date requested because the employee didn't provide enough notice, I put that decision in writing and gave it to the employee.

☐ If the employee is taking parenting leave, I made sure the employee's leave will be complete within one year of the child's arrival.

☐ If the employee's foreseeable leave will cause undue disruption to the company's operations, I asked the employee to try to reschedule (subject to the approval of his or her health care provider).

☐ If the employee had to take unforeseeable leave, I made initial contact with the employee or a family member to gather information and made plans to follow up in a few days.

Handling the Employee's Work:

☐ If the employee was available, I talked to the employee and came up with a plan to cover his or her job duties during leave.

☐ If the employee's coworkers will pick up some extra work, I made any changes necessary to ensure that they will not be stretched too thin.

☐ I determined which, if any, of the employee's responsibilities I will handle and made the necessary arrangements to do so.

☐ If we will bring on temporary help, I made the necessary arrangements to hire a temp.

☐ If we will be using an outside consultant or company, I took any steps necessary to start the process.

☐ I informed everyone who needs to know about these arrangements, such as my manager, the employee's coworkers, vendors, clients, and so on, after asking the employee about his or her preferred characterization of the leave.

Managers' Checklist: Managing FMLA Leave (continued)

Benefits:

☐ I made arrangements to continue the employee's group health benefits—including medical, dental, and vision coverage—during FMLA leave.

☐ I applied any benefits changes to the employee, just as if he or she were not on leave.

☐ If the employee chose not to continue benefits, I made sure that we can reinstate those benefits immediately, without any requalification requirements, when the employee returns to work; if not, I continued the employee's benefits, arranged to pay the employee's share of the premium, and sought reimbursement from the employee after his or her return to work.

☐ I collected the employee's share of the premium as permitted by the FMLA and provided written notice, in advance, of how and when to make these payments.

☐ Before terminating the employee's coverage for failing to pay the premiums, I sent the employee written notice, including the following information:

    ☐ The employee's payment hasn't been received.

    ☐ The company intends to terminate the employee's coverage if payment isn't received by a specified date, at least 15 days after the date I sent the letter.

☐ Before terminating the employee's coverage for failing to pay the premiums, I made sure we could reinstate the employee's coverage without any requalification requirements. Or, if not, I continued health care coverage for the employee and sought reimbursement.

☐ For the continuation of other benefits during leave, I followed my company's usual policies for employees on paid or unpaid leave, depending on whether the employee is using paid leave during FMLA-qualified time off.

☐ Before discontinuing any life, disability, or other insurance benefits, I made sure that we could reinstate the employee's coverage without any requalification requirements; if not, I continued the employee's coverage, arranged to pay the employee's share of the premium, and sought reimbursement from the employee after his or her return to work.

Reinstatement

The Basic Reinstatement Right 247

    What Is an Equivalent Position? 247

    Deadlines for Reinstatement 251

Fitness-for-Duty Certifications 252

    Contents of the Certification 253

    Notice and Deadlines 254

    Special Rules for Intermittent and Reduced-Schedule Leave 254

Restoring Pay and Benefits 255

    Pay 255

    Benefits 258

When Reinstatement Might Not Be Required 260

    Employee Would Have Lost the Job Regardless of Leave 260

    Employee Cannot Perform an Essential Job Function 263

    Fraud 264

    Key Employees 265

When Employees Don't Return From Leave 270

    When You Can Seek Reimbursement for Benefits 270

    What Your Company Can Recover 272

    How to Seek Reimbursement 272

Common Mistakes Regarding Reinstatement—
And How to Avoid Them 273

Chapter Highlights

☆ An employee returning from FMLA leave is entitled to reinstatement to his or her former position or an equivalent position, unless an exception applies.

☆ An equivalent position must be virtually identical to the employee's former position in pay, benefits, job duties, worksite, shift, schedule, and other job terms and conditions.

☆ The employee must be reinstated immediately upon returning from leave, as long as the employee gave at least two workdays' notice.

☆ You may require a returning employee to provide a fitness-for-duty certification from a health care provider.

☆ When you reinstate an employee, you must also restore the employee's pay and benefits, including any automatic raises that occurred during leave.

☆ Employees are entitled to the same insurance coverage benefits and may not be required to take a physical, wait for open enrollment, or otherwise requalify for coverage.

☆ You may not be required to reinstate an employee under the FMLA if any of the following are true:
  • The employee cannot perform the essential duties of the position (however, the Americans with Disabilities Act may require your company to make a reasonable accommodation).
  • The employee's job was eliminated through company restructuring or layoffs, and the employee would have lost the job if he or she hadn't taken leave.
  • The employee was fired for reasons unrelated to taking FMLA leave (such as poor performance or misconduct).
  • The employee was hired for a limited term or project, which has ended.
  • The employee obtained FMLA leave fraudulently (for example, by submitting a forged or altered medical certification).
  • The employee stated an unequivocal intent not to return to work.
  • The employee is a key employee (among the highest-paid 10% of employees within 75 miles) and reinstatement would cause substantial and grievous economic injury to your company.

☆ If an employee chooses not to return to work following FMLA leave, you may recoup your company's share of the premium spent to continue the employee's health care coverage, as well as amounts you paid to cover the employee's share of premiums to continue other benefits.

The FMLA provides employees with job-protected leave, which includes the legal right to be reinstated to the same or an equivalent position once leave ends, unless an exception applies. The right to reinstatement gives meaning to the right to take leave: It ensures that employees will have jobs to return to when their leave is over.

This chapter will help you manage an employee's return to work. It covers every aspect of reinstatement, including what position you must restore the employee to, deadlines for reinstatement, how to handle employee benefits when an employee returns to work, and exceptional circumstances when you might not be legally required to reinstate an employee. It also explains your company's rights if an employee cannot, or decides not to, return to work after using up his or her allotment of FMLA leave.

The Basic Reinstatement Right

An employee must be reinstated to his or her former position or an equivalent position upon returning from FMLA leave. Although there are a few situations when an employee's right to reinstatement is limited (see "When Reinstatement Might Not Be Required," below), these cases are the exception rather than the rule. The employee is entitled to be reinstated even if your company made changes to accommodate the employee's absence, such as replacing the employee or restructuring his or her job.

What Is an Equivalent Position?

Although you are legally required to reinstate an employee returning from FMLA leave, that doesn't mean the employee has a right to be put back in exactly the same position he or she held before taking time off. Employers may reinstate the employee to his or her former position or to an equivalent position. In practice, however, this doesn't give employers much leeway: The equivalent position must be virtually identical, in every important respect, to the employee's former position.

TIP

If the employee's position has changed substantially due to company restructuring, different rules apply. See "When Reinstatement Might Not Be Required," below, to find out what your obligations are.

An equivalent position is one with equivalent pay, benefits, and other terms and conditions of employment. Here are some of the things courts will look at when determining whether a position is equivalent to the employee's former job:

- **Pay.** An employee is entitled to receive his or her former salary or hourly compensation, as well as any opportunities to earn extra money (through overtime, a shift differential, or bonuses based on performance, for example) that were previously available. (For more information, including how to handle bonuses and raises, see "Restoring Pay and Benefits," below.)
- **Benefits.** The equivalent position must offer the same benefits, at the same levels, as the employee's previous job. (For more information, see "Restoring Pay and Benefits," below.)
- **Job duties and responsibilities.** An employee is entitled to "substantially similar" job duties and responsibilities. Minor alterations (such as a change in the employee's reporting structure or job title) are allowed, but make sure the employee's new position is just as desirable—and has the same status in the company—as the employee's former position. If the new position looks like a demotion, the company could find itself in legal trouble.
- **Shift and schedule.** Ordinarily, an employee is entitled to be returned to the same shift and to the same or an equivalent schedule.
- **Worksite.** An employee must be reinstated to the same worksite or one that is geographically proximate to the employee's old worksite. A job at a different worksite is not an equivalent position if it significantly increases the employee's commute in time, distance, or both.

CAUTION

The Americans with Disabilities Act may require you to return the employee to the same position. Under the ADA, a qualified employee with a disability is entitled to the same position with a reasonable accommodation, unless it would pose an undue hardship on the employer. If both the FMLA and the ADA apply, you may not be able to return the employee to an equivalent position. (See Chapter 12 for more details on the interaction between the FMLA and the ADA.)

Lessons from the *Real World*

Taking away an employee's responsibilities for work does not violate the FMLA's right to reinstatement.

Phyllis Smith was the Assistant Supervisor of School Accounts for the East Baton Rouge Parish School Board. She assisted school principals and staff with bookkeeping, which included travel to the parish's schools to provide bookkeeping training and support to school officials.

Smith took parental leave under the FMLA. When she returned to work, her job description was revised. She no longer traveled to assist school officials onsite; instead, she audited the schools' books from a central office location. Smith agreed that her pay was the same and that her job duties were largely similar. However, she filed a lawsuit claiming that her new job was not equivalent to her old position because of the elimination of her travel responsibilities.

The court disagreed. It found that she was doing essentially the same work for the same pay before and after she took time off. The court also decided that eliminating travel from her job duties was only a minimal, intangible change, not a significant enough difference to support a lawsuit.

Smith v. East Baton Rouge Parish School Board, 453 F.3d 650 (5th Cir. 2006).

The FMLA doesn't prevent you from giving a returning employee a promotion or some other additional benefit, as long as the employee wants it. Similarly, if the employee asks to be restored to a different position, you can grant the request. For example, if an employee returning from FMLA leave is planning to move soon and requests a transfer to a different facility, you may grant the request without running afoul of the law. If the employee feels pressured or coerced to take a different position, however, that could violate the law.

EXAMPLE: Charlotte works as a sales associate in the juniors section of a large department store. She receives a base salary plus commissions based on her sales. She takes FMLA leave to care for her husband while he undergoes treatment for leukemia. When she returns, her boss, David, tells her that he would like to promote her to a position in the home furnishings department. David explains that she'll receive the same base salary, plus the opportunity to earn much more in commissions, because furniture is more expensive than junior clothing and accessories.

Charlotte thanks David but tells him she wants to return to the juniors department. She explains that she enjoys keeping up with fashions and trends and feels her sales record is driven by her interest in this market. She doesn't think she'd do very well selling furniture.

David responds, "You know, Charlotte, opportunities for advancement don't come along here very often. I'm telling you that we need you in home furnishings. You're free to say 'No, I'll only work where I want to, not where the company needs me,' but I can't guarantee that there will be other opportunities down the road for someone who displays this kind of attitude." Charlotte decides that she'd better accept the move.

Did David violate the FMLA? You bet. Although the company is free to restore Charlotte to a different position if she voluntarily agrees, it isn't free to pressure her or threaten her job opportunities if she doesn't accept the new position. Here, Charlotte wasn't free to make a voluntary decision: She was told that refusing the new position would affect her future opportunities. This violates her legal right to reinstatement.

Deadlines for Reinstatement

An employee is entitled to immediate reinstatement once he or she reports for duty. In some situations, you'll know well in advance exactly when an employee will return to work. For example, if you and the employee agreed that the employee would take six weeks of leave, and the employee's time off goes as expected, the employee will simply report back once his or her leave is over.

> EXAMPLE: Barbara is pregnant and requests time off. She decides to take the full 12 weeks of leave all at once. Her first day off work is Monday, June 1. She takes three weeks of leave for a serious health condition (pregnancy and childbirth), and the remaining nine weeks as parental leave. She returns to work on Monday, August 24. Her employer is legally obligated to reinstate her to her former position (or an equivalent one) that same day.

Sometimes, however, an employee's return to work is delayed or accelerated. Typically, this happens when the employee's or family member's serious health condition takes an unexpected turn. Even in this situation, you must reinstate the employee immediately upon his or her return to work. However, you may require the employee to give you at least two business days' notice of the date he or she plans to come back. If the employee just shows up unexpectedly at work, and you are unable to reinstate the employee immediately, consider that your notice and reinstate the employee within two workdays.

> EXAMPLE: Calvin requests FMLA leave to care for his father, who has to have hip replacement surgery. Because the doctor predicts recovery will take a couple months, Calvin requests eight weeks of FMLA leave. Instead, Calvin's father recovers in five weeks. Calvin lets his manager know that he will return to work right away. If the company can reinstate Calvin immediately, it should. If not, then Calvin is entitled to reinstatement within two workdays.

TIP

Ask the employee to keep you in the loop. You have the right to ask for periodic updates on the employee's plans to return to work. (Chapter 10 explains how.)

Lessons from the *Real World*

A company must reinstate an employee within two workdays or face the consequences.

Lori Hoge worked at a Honda production plant. Honda assigned her to a "door line" position, which accommodated her work restrictions based on a back injury.

On May 11, 2000, Hoge began taking FMLA leave for planned abdominal surgery. She reported for work on June 27. She said this was the agreed-upon date for her return to work; Honda said that it didn't expect her to return until sometime in July.

When Hoge reported for work, Honda told her it did not have an available position that accommodated her work restrictions because of changes to its manufacturing process. On July 31, 2000, she was reinstated on a part-time basis to a position on the engine line, and she didn't receive a full-time position until September 18.

Hoge sued Honda for failing to reinstate her when she was ready to return to work. Honda argued that it was entitled to take a "reasonable" amount of time to find an appropriate job, both because it didn't know when Hoge was returning to work and because her former position had changed.

The court sided with Hoge. The FMLA says employees are entitled to reinstatement upon their return to work, not within a reasonable time after they return. If Honda didn't know that Hoge was returning to work on June 27, it was entitled to take two days—the amount of notice Hoge should have given—to reinstate her to an equivalent, full-time position. Because Honda took several months to fully reinstate Hoge, it lost the case.

Hoge v. Honda of America, 384 F.3d 238 (6th Cir. 2004).

Fitness-for-Duty Certifications

If an employee takes leave for his or her own serious health condition, you may require the employee to provide a fitness-for-duty certification: a signed statement from a health care provider indicating that the employee is able

to return to work. However, you may require this certification only if your company has a consistently applied practice or policy of requiring employees to provide a fitness-for-duty statement. The company need not require every employee to provide a fitness-for-duty certification, but it must require all similarly situated employees (that is, employees in that position and/or with that serious health condition) to provide one. For example, a company might require all employees in positions that require manual labor to provide such a certification following time off for an injury of any kind.

POLICY ALERT

Include fitness-for-duty certification requirements in your written policies. If your company has a uniform policy or practice of requiring certifications from similarly situated employees, it must include this information in its employee handbook or any other written material it provides to employees about the FMLA. (See Appendix B for more information on company policies that affect your rights or obligations under the FMLA.)

Contents of the Certification

A fitness-for-duty certification is a written statement, signed by the employee's health care provider (see Chapter 4 for information on who qualifies as a health care provider), that the employee is able to resume work following an FMLA leave. The employer may request certification only for the serious health condition that necessitated FMLA leave, not for any other illness or impairment.

You may require that the employee's certification specifically address the employee's ability to perform the essential functions of the job. To impose this requirement, you must give the employee a list of the essential job functions by the time you give the designation notice, and the designation notice must indicate that the fitness-for-duty certification will have to address the employee's ability to perform those functions. (See Chapter 8 for more on the designation notice.)

RESOURCE

Need to know more about essential job functions? You'll find lots of information on identifying job functions, determining which of them are essential, and writing them in a clear, descriptive manner in *The Job Description Handbook*, by Margie Mader-Clark (Nolo).

You may follow the procedures described in Chapter 9 to authenticate or clarify a fitness-for-duty clarification. However, you may request clarification or authentication only regarding the serious health condition for which the employee took leave. Unlike with a regular certification, you may not request a second or third opinion with a fitness-for-duty certification.

Notice and Deadlines

If you require fitness-for-duty certifications from employees returning from leave, you must include that requirement in the rights and responsibilities notice you give to each employee who requests leave. (See Chapter 8 for more information on this notice.)

You may postpone an employee's return to work until you receive the fitness-for-duty certification. Though you may clarify the employee's certification through contact with the employee's health care provider, you may not delay the employee's reinstatement while waiting for a response.

Special Rules for Intermittent and Reduced-Schedule Leave

Generally, you may not require an employee to submit a fitness-for-duty certification each time the employee returns from using intermittent leave. However, you may request a fitness-for-duty certification up to once every 30 days if reasonable safety concerns exist regarding the employee's ability to perform his or her duties, based on the serious health condition for which the employee took leave. Reasonable safety concerns are defined in the regulations as a reasonable belief of significant risk of harm to the employee or others, considering the nature, severity, and likelihood of the potential harm.

If you are going to rely on this exception, you must tell the employee, when you issue the designation notice, that the employee will be required to submit a fitness-for-duty certification for each subsequent use of intermittent

leave, unless the employee has submitted one within the past 30 days (or a longer interval chosen by your company; 30 days is the shortest period of time you can use). You may not fire the employee while waiting for the certification.

> **EXAMPLE:** John has epilepsy, for which he occasionally uses FMLA leave. Lately, his seizure activity has increased, leading his doctor to change his medication to one that can cause dizziness, weakness, and drowsiness. John's work as a carpenter requires him to use power tools, climb ladders, and perform other activities that could pose significant risks to himself and others were he to have a seizure or suffer some of the side effects of his medication while working. John's company asks him to submit a fitness-for-duty certification every 30 days, in connection with his intermittent leave. Once John's doctor indicates that his condition and medications have stabilized, the company plans to lift the fitness-for-duty requirement.

Restoring Pay and Benefits

When you reinstate an employee, you must also restore the employee's pay and benefits. The requirements for restoring benefits depend on the type of benefit and your company's policies.

Pay

Whether you reinstate an employee to his or her former position or to an equivalent one, you must restore all components of the employee's pay including base wage or salary, plus the same opportunities to earn bonuses, a shift differential, overtime, commissions, and other extra compensation that he or she enjoyed before taking leave.

> TIP
> **You can restart an exempt employee's pay midweek.** An exempt employee (who is paid on a salary basis and is not entitled to earn overtime) is usually entitled to a full salary for any week in which he or she does any work. FMLA leave is an exception to this rule. If an exempt employee returns to work midweek, you can pay a prorated share of the employee's weekly salary. For example, an employee who

returns to work on Wednesday morning is entitled to three-fifths of his or her usual weekly salary. (29 C.F.R. § 541.602.)

Raises

A returning employee is also entitled to any automatic raises that took place while the employee was out on leave. So if your company provides an annual cost-of-living raise to all employees, you must provide that same raise to an employee returning from FMLA leave.

If the raise is not automatic but is instead based on the employee's performance or seniority, the rules depend on your company's policies and practices. Generally, you must treat employees on FMLA leave just as your company treats employees who take unpaid leave for any other reason. If unpaid leave doesn't count toward an employee's seniority for purposes of awarding seniority-based raises, for example, then you don't have to count FMLA leave toward an employee's seniority.

> **CAUTION**
>
> **Employees substituting paid time off are not on "unpaid" leave.** As explained in Chapter 8, in certain circumstances an employee (either voluntarily or per company requirements) substitutes accrued paid time off for unpaid FMLA leave. If an employee is using paid time off for FMLA leave, you must treat that employee just like any other employee who is taking paid time off. Often, this means that at least certain benefits (for example, vacation or sick days) continue to accrue.

Bonuses

Your company's employees may be eligible to earn bonuses for certain behavior or actions, such as productivity, attendance, performance, safety, or customer service. If a bonus or other discretionary payment is based on achieving a certain goal, such as reaching a specific sales target, and an employee doesn't meet the goal because of FMLA leave, you don't have to provide the bonus unless you provide it to employees who miss the goal because of leave that doesn't qualify for FMLA protection. In other words, you can't treat employees who take FMLA leave worse than employees who take other types of leave.

Lessons from the *Real World*

An employer may prorate a production bonus to account for FMLA leave.

Robert Sommer worked as a financial administrator for The Vanguard Group. Sommer took eight weeks of FMLA leave, from December 7, 2000 to February 4, 2001.

Vanguard had a partnership plan that paid employees an annual bonus based on company performance that year. Each employee's bonus factored in the employee's position, how long the employee had worked for the company, and how many hours the employee worked during the year. Employees who worked fewer than 1,950 hours during the year received a prorated bonus; hours spent on unpaid leave didn't count as hours worked.

Vanguard gave Sommer a prorated partnership plan bonus for 2001 because his FMLA leave brought his total hours worked for the year below the 1,950-hour threshold. Sommer received $1,788.23 less than he would have gotten had he worked the requisite number of hours.

Sommer sued Vanguard, arguing that it unfairly penalized him for taking FMLA leave by reducing his bonus. The court disagreed with Sommer's argument. It found that the partnership plan bonuses were productivity bonuses and that hours worked provided the basis for measuring productivity. Because the bonus was performance-based, the company could legally provide a lesser bonus to recognize the time he was out on FMLA leave.

Sommer v. Vanguard Group, 461 F.3d 397 (3rd Cir. 2006).

EXAMPLE: FunCo offers employees an incentive for perfect attendance. Employees who have no absences for an entire year receive $1,500. Kara has no absences until November, when she takes two weeks of FMLA leave to care for her son while he recovers from mononucleosis. Kara then returns to work and has no more absences for the rest of the year. FunCo may deny Kara the perfect attendance bonus, as long as it also denies a bonus to employees who miss work for other reasons. If FunCo allowed employees to take two weeks of vacation in a year without jeopardizing their attendance bonus, it would have to give the bonus to Kara as well.

Benefits

You must restore an employee's benefits, at the same levels, when the employee returns from leave, subject to any changes in benefit levels that took place while the employee was on leave and affected the whole work force. For example, if a company offers life insurance to its employees and increases the benefit from $30,000 to $35,000 while an employee is on leave, that employee is also entitled to the increased benefit amount.

The specific rules for restoring benefits depend on the type of benefit.

Insurance Coverage

An employee is entitled to restored insurance benefits, including life insurance, disability insurance, health benefits, and so on. As explained in Chapter 10, you must continue the employee's health insurance coverage while he or she is on leave, though you may also require the employee to pay any portion of the premium for which he or she is usually responsible. While your company can cut off an employee's health care benefits if the employee is more than 30 days late paying his or her share of the premium, those benefits must be restored, at the same level, when the employee returns from leave. An employee who chooses not to continue benefits during leave is also entitled to restoration.

Employees may not be required to requalify for benefits, wait for an "open enrollment" period, undergo a physical examination, be subjected to new preexisting conditions limitations or exclusions, or go without benefits during a waiting period. This is true even if the employee's coverage lapsed while he or she was on leave. To comply with this rule, your company may have to keep an employee enrolled in certain benefit programs during the employee's leave. In this situation, you may recover the employee's share of the premium for this coverage from the employee after he or she returns to work.

If there are changes to a benefit plan while the employee is on leave, these changes apply to the employee as well. If, for example, premiums increase, coverage changes, or a new benefit becomes available, the employee must be treated as if he or she had been working continuously.

If a benefit is available only to employees who work a minimum number of hours each year, hours spent on FMLA leave do not count as hours worked. This means that, as a practical matter, an employee may be ineligible to receive certain benefits because the employee took FMLA leave.

Retirement Benefits

Just like other benefits, retirement benefits must be restored at the same level when an employee returns from leave. A few special rules apply to these benefits:

- FMLA leave cannot be treated as a "break in service" for purposes of pensions and other retirement benefit plans.
- If a retirement benefit requires an employee to be employed on a particular date to be credited with a year of service for vesting, contributions, or participating in the plan, an employee who is on FMLA leave is considered to be employed during that time.
- FMLA leave does not have to be counted as time in service or hours worked for purposes of vesting, accrual of benefits, or eligibility.

EXAMPLE: Hal began working at Jefferson's Tool and Die on January 1, 2014. The company allows an employee who has worked at least one year and is employed as of January 1 to participate in the 401(k) plan for the coming year. When Hal becomes eligible, he contributes monthly. The company matches his contributions up to $3,000 a year. Hal is always fully vested in his own contributions to the account; the company's contributions vest over three years, one-third each year.

Hal takes FMLA leave for all of December 2015 and January 2016 to bond with his new daughter. While Hal is on FMLA leave, his 401(k) account must be treated as if he is still working. The company may not close his account or otherwise treat his time off as a break in service. The company must also treat him as if he were employed on January 1 for purposes of participating in the program for the coming year. However, Hal's time off does not have to be counted toward the three-year vesting period. In other words, Hal might have to wait an additional two months to vest employer contributions that had already been made when he took leave.

Other Benefits

Many companies allow employees to accrue certain benefits, such as sick leave, vacation days, or other paid time off. Employees on FMLA leave are entitled to earn these benefits only if employees on other types of unpaid leave are. However, an employer may not take away benefits the employee has earned: If the employee had accrued paid time off before taking FMLA

leave and did not substitute that time for FMLA leave, the employee is entitled to have that accrued paid leave available upon returning from FMLA leave.

The same rules apply to seniority. The company does not have to count FMLA leave toward an employee's seniority unless it counts other types of unpaid leave. However, the employee is entitled to the same seniority upon reinstatement that he or she had when starting leave.

When Reinstatement Might Not Be Required

There are several circumstances in which an employee might not be entitled to reinstatement after taking FMLA leave. Reinstatement may be denied if:

- The employee would have lost the job even if he or she hadn't taken FMLA leave.
- The employee can't perform an essential function of the job.
- The employee takes FMLA leave fraudulently.
- The employee fits within the "key employee" exception, which gives employers the right to deny reinstatement to certain highly paid employees, if returning them to work would cause substantial harm to the company.

Employee Would Have Lost the Job Regardless of Leave

An employee has no greater right to reinstatement than he or she would have had if not for taking leave. If the employee would have lost the job even if still employed, the FMLA does not guarantee reinstatement.

Restructuring and Layoffs

If the employee's job has been eliminated, the employee is not entitled to reinstatement. For example, let's say the company outsourced the work of the employee's department or closed the facility where the employee worked. In this situation, the employee would have lost his or her job whether the employee took FMLA leave or not, and the employee has no right to be reinstated.

However, this rule applies only if the restructuring is unrelated to the employee's leave. Changes made to accommodate the employee's leave—such as hiring a temporary replacement or shifting some job responsibilities

around—don't relieve the company of its obligation to reinstate the employee. And, if the company made structural changes because it wanted to avoid reinstating an employee who took leave, that would violate the FMLA's prohibition against retaliation.

> EXAMPLE 1: Alexander takes FMLA leave to bond with his newborn son. While on leave, his company implements layoffs. The 50 employees with the least seniority lose their jobs, and Alexander is one of them. Alexander has no right to reinstatement.

> EXAMPLE 2: Now assume that Alexander's company didn't have major layoffs. Alexander's manager, Maya, is upset about his leave. Maya doesn't think Alexander should use the full 12 weeks of FMLA leave. After all, his wife doesn't work, and she can stay home with the baby. Maya decides to eliminate Alexander's position so she doesn't have to reinstate him. She has already redistributed his work while he is on leave; she figures she'll just wait a while, then hire someone under a new job title to pick up the slack.
>
> Maya's actions violate the FMLA. The only reason Alexander has no job to return to is because Maya wanted to punish him for exercising his legal right to take FMLA leave. What's more, Maya's sexist reasoning could leave her company open to a discrimination lawsuit.

Termination for Cause

As explained in Chapter 10, you may fire an employee who is on FMLA leave only for reasons entirely unrelated to the employee's use of the FMLA. If you have sufficient, independent grounds to terminate employment, you do not have to reinstate the employee. In this situation, as when the employee's job is eliminated in a layoff or restructuring, the employee would have lost the job whether or not he or she took FMLA leave.

> CAUTION
>
> **Don't rely on the right to fire at will.** Most employees work at will, which means that they can be fired at any time, for any reason that isn't illegal. But you should not exercise this right when firing an employee on FMLA leave. To successfully defend against an employee lawsuit (an all-too-common scenario when an employee is fired while on leave), you'll have to prove that your reasons for firing the employee

were not related to the employee's use of the FMLA. As a practical matter, this means you must have a different reason for firing the employee, one that is compelling enough to convince a jury that your actions were justified.

You may also discipline an employee who takes FMLA leave, but only for independent reasons. If your discipline will make the employee's position less than equivalent (for example, the employee will be demoted, will have more onerous reporting requirements, or will lose some independence and job perks), that's okay, even though it would normally violate reinstatement requirements.

SEE AN EXPERT

Always get legal advice before firing or disciplining an employee on leave. As explained in Chapter 10, even though you believe you have entirely independent and sound reasons for firing an employee on FMLA leave, chances are very good that the employee will see things differently. This is the most likely basis of an FMLA lawsuit, so it's a good idea to talk to a lawyer before you take any action.

Temporary Employment

If the employee was hired for a set period of time only (for example, for two years), and that time runs out while the employee is on leave, the employee isn't entitled to reinstatement. Similarly, if the employee was hired to work on a discrete project and that project is completed while the employee is on leave, the employee isn't entitled to reinstatement. In both of these situations, employment would have been terminated even if the employee hadn't taken leave. In effect, the employee has no job to return to because the work or employment term is complete.

Employee Announces Intent Not to Return

If an employee states that he or she will not return from leave (in other words, the employee quits), your company is no longer obligated to continue the employee's health benefits or reinstate the employee. However, the employee must give clear and unequivocal notice of the intent not to return to work. If, for example, the employee says, "I'm afraid I might not be able to come back" or "I'm not sure we can afford to pay for day care," that's not good enough.

When you hear that an employee won't be returning from work, you should confirm it in writing. (See "Requesting Status Reports," in Chapter 10, for more information.)

Employee Cannot Perform an Essential Job Function

An employee who can't perform the job's essential functions once his or her leave runs out has no right to reinstatement under the FMLA. The FMLA provides only for reinstatement to the same or a similar position: It doesn't require an employer to provide a different position that the employee might be able to do. Therefore, if the employee can no longer do the job—even if that inability is due to the serious health condition for which the employee took leave—there is no right to job restoration under the FMLA.

You Must Allow the Employee to Requalify for the Position

Sometimes, an employee is physically able to do the job but is no longer qualified for the position as a result of taking leave. For example, the employee may have been unable to complete a necessary course, fulfill a certification requirement, or meet a service standard (such as a minimum number of hours in training). In these situations, you must give the employee a reasonable opportunity to fulfill any necessary qualifications after returning to work.

That's not the end of the story, however. If the employee has a disability as defined by the Americans with Disabilities Act (ADA), your company may be obligated to provide a reasonable accommodation: a change to the workplace or job that will allow the employee to do the essential functions of the position. In this situation, you would no longer have a reinstatement obligation under the FMLA, but you might have a legal duty to return the employee to a modified position under the ADA. (Chapter 12 explains the ADA in more detail.)

You might also have an obligation to give the employee more time off. Extended leave might qualify as a reasonable accommodation under the ADA, if it allows the employee to do the job upon return. If the employee is receiving workers' compensation, state law might also require you to hold

the employee's job for a longer period of time. Although the employee has no further rights under the FMLA—and, therefore, has no valid legal claim against your company for failure to reinstate—the employee might still have rights under these other laws. (See Chapter 12 for more information.)

Fraud

If an employee obtains FMLA leave through fraud, the company is not obligated to reinstate the employee. This sometimes occurs when the employee submits false documents (such as a fake or altered medical certification) to get FMLA leave. In some cases, companies find out about the fraud only accidentally, when another employee happens to see the leave-taking employee engaged in activities that seem incompatible with the reason for leave.

Dealing With Employee Moonlighting

Some managers assume that an employee who works another job while on FMLA leave is committing fraud against the company. After all, if the employee has the time and ability to work, he or she should be working at your company, not taking leave. Right?

Not necessarily. According to FMLA regulations, employees may moonlight while on FMLA leave unless your company has a policy prohibiting all employees, on any kind of leave, from working another job. An employee's ability to work a different job doesn't necessarily prove that the employee took leave fraudulently, and you can't deny reinstatement on that basis alone unless you have a uniformly applied policy against moonlighting.

POLICY ALERT

Prohibit moonlighting by employees on leave. You can avoid having employees continue their health benefits—and perhaps even receive paid time off, if they substitute paid leave for FMLA leave—while working for another company by adopting a strict policy that prohibits moonlighting while on leave. (See Appendix B for more information on policies that affect FMLA rights and obligations.)

Lessons from the *Real World*

Employee may be fired based on employer's honest suspicion—supported by surveillance—that she was abusing leave.

Diana Vail worked the night shift for Raybestos Products Company, a manufacturer of car parts. Vail suffered from migraines and took intermittent FMLA leave when she was unable to work due to a migraine. Vail's absences picked up markedly in the summer of 2005; from May to September, she took 33 days of leave. Raybestos suspected she might be abusing leave because it knew she worked part time for her husband's lawn-mowing business during the day, and she tended to take time off during the weeks when he was scheduled to work for his cemetery clients, which required mowing during the workweek.

Raybestos hired an off-duty police sergeant to conduct surveillance of Vail. Vail took FMLA leave due to a change in her medication one evening; the next morning, she spent the day mowing lawns. That evening, she again called in sick, saying she was getting a migraine. Raybestos fired her for abusing FMLA leave.

Vail sued, claiming that her termination violated the FMLA. The court disagreed, however. It found that the employer had an honest suspicion, based on the surveillance and the pattern of Vail's absences, that she was abusing her leave. The court indicated that, although hiring someone to conduct surveillance "may not be preferred employer behavior," the information revealed by the surveillance allowed the company to fire her without violating the FMLA.

Vail v. Raybestos Products Co., 533 F.3d 904 (7th Cir. 2008).

Key Employees

Your company has a legal right to deny reinstatement to certain highly paid employees (called "key employees") if returning them to work would cause the company substantial and grievous economic injury.

Who Is a Key Employee

A key employee is a salaried employee who is among the highest-paid 10% of the company's employees within 75 miles of the employee's worksite. Here's what these terms mean:

- **Salaried employee.** The definition of a salaried employee comes from the Fair Labor Standards Act (FLSA). A salaried employee earns the same amount each week, regardless of how many hours the employee works or the quality or quantity of work performed. To be salaried, the employee must earn at least $455 per week.
- **Highest-paid 10%.** To find out whether an employee is in the highest-paid 10% of the workforce, divide the employee's year-to-date compensation by the total number of weeks worked in the year, including any weeks during which the employee took paid leave. You must include wages, premium pay, incentive pay, and bonuses. You don't have to include any amount that will be determined only in the future (such as the value of company stock options awarded during the year).
- **Company employees within 75 miles of the employee's worksite.** In determining which employees work within 75 miles, you should use the same rules used to determine an employee's eligibility for FMLA leave, explained in Chapter 3. Count all employees, whether they are eligible for FMLA leave or not.

You must determine whether someone is a key employee as of the date he or she requests leave.

Initial Notice to Key Employee

If you believe that you might deny reinstatement to a key employee, you must notify the employee, in writing, that he or she qualifies as a key employee and might not be reinstated if the company determines that reinstatement will cause the company substantial and grievous economic injury. You must provide this information with the rights and responsibilities notice, discussed in Chapter 8. If you need some time to determine whether the employee is a key employee, you must give this notice as soon as is practicable. If you don't, you must reinstate the employee no matter what damage it causes your company.

Notice of Determination of Substantial and Grievous Economic Injury

In addition to the above requirements, you can deny reinstatement to an employee only if reinstatement would cause your company substantial

and grievous economic injury. And you must provide another written notice to the employee if you determine that such injury will result from reinstatement.

The FMLA and its regulations don't provide much guidance on what constitutes a substantial and grievous economic injury. Perhaps because few employers rely on this exception to deny reinstatement, there have been very few court cases on the issue. A few things are clear:

- The injury must stem from reinstatement, not from the employee's absence.
- You don't have to show that the whole company will go under.
- You must show more than minor inconvenience or "undue hardship," as defined by the Americans with Disabilities Act.

Once you determine that substantial and grievous injury will result from reinstating the employee, you must tell the employee in writing. This second notice must include all of the following:

- a determination that reinstating the employee will cause substantial and grievous economic injury to the company
- the reasons for that determination
- a statement that the company may not deny FMLA leave to the employee
- a statement that the company intends to deny reinstatement to the employee once his or her FMLA leave is finished, and
- if the employee is already on leave, a deadline for the employee to return to work to avoid being denied reinstatement. You must give the employee a reasonable amount of time to return, considering the circumstances.

If you have already determined, when you give the employee his or her rights and responsibilities notice, that reinstating the employee will cause substantial and grievous economic injury, you can use that notice to provide this information. However, you will have to add more details than the form allows space for, so you'll have to attach an additional document. We have included a sample "Notice to Key Employee of Substantial and Grievous Economic Injury" below (see Appendix C for an electronic copy).

Lessons from the *Real World*

Failure to give key employee second notice—and a date by which the employee can return to work—violates the FMLA.

Elizabeth Neel worked for Mid-Atlantic of Fairfield as a licensed nursing home administrator. She requested FMLA leave after suffering neck injuries in a car accident. Her request was approved, and Mid-Atlantic informed her, in the rights and responsibilities notice, that she was a key employee to whom job restoration "may be denied." The company also checked the box indicating that "We have determined that restoring you to employment at the conclusion of FMLA leave will cause substantial and grievous economic harm to us."

Neel notified Mid-Atlantic that her physician had released her to return to work in a few weeks. After receiving this notice, Mid-Atlantic sent Neel a certified letter, stating that the company had found a replacement for her who would be starting work soon. When Neel informed the company of her firm return-to-work date, Mid-Atlantic responded that her position had been filled and that she was considered separated from the company.

The court found that Mid-Atlantic had not met its obligations under the key employee exception. Although it had warned Neel that she might be denied restoration, not sending the required second notice, explaining the basis for its decision that reinstating her would cause economic injury and giving her a date by which she could return to work, "deprived her of an opportunity to weigh whether taking FMLA leave was in her best interest." Because Mid-Atlantic didn't give Neel the required information, it wasn't entitled to rely on the key employee exception. Therefore, its decision to terminate her employment and hire a replacement violated the FMLA.

Neel v. Mid-Atlantic of Fairfield, 778 F.Supp.2d 593 (D. Md. 2011).

Even if you intend to deny reinstatement, you must continue the employee's health benefits while the employee is on FMLA leave. The employee's FMLA rights continue unless and until the employee gives unequivocal notice that he or she doesn't intend to return to work or you actually deny the employee reinstatement at the conclusion of his or her FMLA leave. Also, you will not be able to recover your company's share of health care premiums paid while the key employee was on leave.

Notice to Key Employee of Substantial and Grievous Economic Injury

To: Carlos Sandoval

As indicated by written notice dated <u>February 22, 2015</u>, you are a key employee of this company. This means that you can be denied reinstatement following FMLA leave if such reinstatement would cause substantial and grievous economic injury to the company.

We have determined that reinstating you would cause substantial and grievous economic injury to the company, because <u>we have been unable to find a temporary replacement who is qualified to take over your responsibilities as Chief Financial Officer. To complete all of our annual financial filings by the end of March, we will have to hire a permanent replacement and commit substantial resources to bringing that person up to speed quickly. The company cannot afford to pay both you and your replacement to do this work, and we have no alternative positions available</u>.

We cannot deny you the right to take FMLA leave, or discontinue your health benefits, based on this determination. However, we intend to deny you reinstatement once your leave is finished.

If you wish to avoid these consequences, you must return to work no later than <u>March 1, 2015. This is the latest possible date that will enable us to operate without hiring a replacement and give you enough time to complete the annual reports. If you do not return to work by March 1, 2015</u>, we intend to replace you and deny you reinstatement.

Please contact me immediately if you have any questions.

Sincerely,

Carol Singh

Director of Human Resources

Dated:

Handling a Key Employee's Request for Reinstatement

Even if you notify a key employee that he or she will be denied reinstatement and the employee doesn't return to work, the employee still has a right to

request reinstatement after using FMLA leave. If the employee makes this request, you must redetermine, based on the facts available to you at that time, whether reinstatement would cause substantial and grievous economic injury.

If you conclude that such injury would result from reinstating the employee, you must notify the employee of this conclusion in writing. (You can modify the sample form above for this purpose.) If you reach a different conclusion—that is, you decide that the company won't suffer such an injury—then you must reinstate the employee according to the usual rules.

> **EXAMPLE:** Let's consider Carlos, the employee who received the sample notice of substantial and grievous economic injury, above. When Carol sent this notice, she had determined that reinstatement would cause such an injury. If Carlos doesn't return to work by the deadline Carol imposed, but instead requests reinstatement when his leave ends, Carol must again determine whether reinstating him would injure the company.
>
> If the company already hired a permanent replacement and paying both Carlos and the replacement would significantly harm the company's finances, Carol could justifiably conclude that she doesn't have to reinstate Carlos. On the other hand, if Carol were unable to find a replacement, and the company received extensions on its filing deadlines, reinstating Carlos might not cause such an injury. In fact, it might be exactly what the company needs. In this situation, Carol may not refuse to reinstate Carlos. Instead, she must reinstate him according to the rules explained in "The Basic Reinstatement Right," above.

When Employees Don't Return From Leave

When an employee is unable to, or decides not to, come back to work after taking FMLA leave, your company might be able to recover at least some of the money it spent to continue the employee's benefits.

When You Can Seek Reimbursement for Benefits

The company has a right to reimbursement only if the employee chose not to return to work. The purpose of this rule is to avoid heaping more problems on employees who are already losing their jobs due to circumstances out of their control.

You cannot recover any money spent on benefits continuation if the employee can't return due to:

- **The continuation of the serious health condition, illness, or injury for which the employee took leave.** This applies whether the employee is too ill to return to work or the employee's family member continues to require care after the employee's FMLA leave ends.

- **Other circumstances beyond the employee's control.** This exception applies if an employee cannot return to work for other reasons, such as: The employee needs time off to care for new child with a serious health condition; the employee's spouse is transferred to a location more than 75 miles away from the employee's worksite; the employee is needed to care for a relative who has a serious health condition but doesn't qualify as a family member under the FMLA; the employee is not reinstated due to the "key employee" exception (see above); or the employee is laid off while on leave. This exception doesn't apply if the employee chooses to stay home with a new child who is healthy or to stay with a parent who no longer has a serious health condition.

TIP

Request a certification for continuing health conditions. If an employee can't return to work because of a continuing serious health condition, illness, or injury, you are legally entitled to ask the employee to provide a medical certification. Like regular medical certifications, it's a good idea to request this form whenever an employee claims that a serious health condition prevents his or her return to work; otherwise, you might be giving up your right to reimbursement unnecessarily. The employee must return the form within 30 days after you request it. If the employee doesn't return the form on time, or the form indicates that the employee or family member no longer has a serious health condition, you may seek reimbursement.

You can't seek reimbursement if an employee returns to work. An employee who comes back for at least 30 days has returned to work, even if the employee later quits. Similarly, an employee who goes directly from FMLA leave to retirement or retires within 30 days after reinstatement is considered to have returned to work.

What Your Company Can Recover

If the employee doesn't return to work and neither of the exceptions described above applies, your company may recover the following amounts:

- **Health insurance costs.** The company may seek reimbursement for its share of the premium of the employee's health benefits. If the employee failed to pay his or her own share while on leave, the company may seek reimbursement for that as well. Self-insured employers can recover what the employee would have had to pay to continue health insurance benefits under the Consolidated Omnibus Budget Reconciliation Act (COBRA), which allows employees to continue their health insurance benefits for a period of time, at their own expense, after leaving a job. Although employers are allowed to charge employees an additional 2% under COBRA to cover the administrative expenses of continuing benefits, you cannot recover this additional amount under the FMLA.

CAUTION

Your company can't recover its own premiums if the employee is on paid leave. As explained in Chapter 8, sometimes employees may—voluntarily or by company requirement—substitute accrued paid leave, such as sick or vacation time, for FMLA leave. If an employee does this and does not return to work, your company may not recover its share of the premium for health benefits while the employee was on paid leave.

- **The employee's share of premiums for other benefits.** If you continue any other benefits while an employee is on leave, like life or disability insurance, you may seek reimbursement of the employee's share of the premium only, not for your company's share. (As explained above, your company might choose to do this to make sure that it will be able to reinstate these benefits when the employee returns).

How to Seek Reimbursement

The best way to start is simply to ask the employee to repay the money. If that doesn't work, your company can collect the employee's debt through

deductions from amounts still owed to the employee (such as commissions, unpaid wages, or unpaid accrued vacation time), if allowed by law, or in the worst case, through a lawsuit. However, your company's right to seek reimbursement does not give it the right to cut the employee off entirely. For example, your company is still obligated to pay any claims the employee incurred while on FMLA leave (if it is self-insured) or to provide continuing coverage under COBRA.

> CAUTION
> **Some states don't allow deductions from amounts owed to the employee.** Talk to a lawyer before you start deducting the cost of providing benefits from compensation your company owes the employee.

State law may require you to get an employee's written consent before taking a deduction to repay money the employee owes the company. If your company operates in a state that imposes this type of requirement, get the employee's written consent *before* the employee starts FMLA leave. Include a deduction authorization form in your standard FMLA paperwork, and ask the employee to sign it. Experience shows that it's much easier to get this type of consent up front, before the employee owes you any money.

Common Mistakes Regarding Reinstatement— And How to Avoid Them

Mistake 1: Failing to reinstate employees on time.

Avoid this mistake by taking the following steps:

- Check in with employees who are on leave. Ask employees to update you periodically on their plans to return to work. (See Chapter 10.)
- Keeping track of employees on leave. Remember, you'll have to save an equivalent spot somewhere for returning employees. You can't wait until they're ready to come back to start looking for one.

Mistake 2: Mishandling benefits when an employee returns.

Avoid this mistake by taking the following steps:

- Don't require employees to requalify, reapply, or wait to restart their benefits. Remember, you can't make returning employees do anything in order to get their benefits back.
- Maintain employee benefits during leave, if necessary to ensure immediate reinstatement. Even if the employee chooses not to continue disability or life insurance while on leave, you may have to so you can reinstate it.
- Seek reimbursement when legally entitled to it. If you continued benefits that were not legally required, you can recoup the employee's share of the premium once the employee returns from leave.

Mistake 3: Mishandling reinstatement of key employees.

Avoid this mistake by taking the following steps:

- Properly identify key employees in the first place. If more than 10% of your workforce are key employees, you didn't get it right.
- Provide all necessary notices. If you're going to refuse to reinstate a key employee, you have to provide two written notices (and perhaps a third, if the employee requests reinstatement when the leave is over).
- Allow leave and continue benefits. You can't simply fire a key employee who requests FMLA leave. While a key employee is on leave, he or she is still employed by your company, and you have to allow leave (including substitution of paid leave) and continue the employee's health insurance coverage.

✓ **Managers' Checklist: Reinstating an Employee**

If the Employee Was Reinstated:

☐ I reinstated the employee to the position he or she held prior to taking leave or to an equivalent position.

    ☐ The position has the same base pay, and the same opportunities to earn extra pay, as the former position.

    ☐ The position offers the same benefits, at the same levels, that the employee used to receive.

    ☐ The position has the same or substantially similar job duties as the employee's former job.

    ☐ The position has the same or a substantially similar shift or schedule as the employee worked before taking leave.

    ☐ The position is at the same worksite, or one that is geographically proximate to, where the employee worked before taking leave.

☐ I reinstated the employee immediately upon his or her return from leave or within two working days of receiving notice of intent to return to work from the employee.

☐ I restored the employee's pay, including base pay, opportunities to earn extra pay, and any across-the-board raises (such as cost-of-living increases) that became effective during the employee's leave.

☐ I restored the employee's benefits, including any across-the-board changes that took effect during the employee's leave.

    ☐ I did not require the employee to requalify for benefits, take a physical exam, wait a certain period of time, or do anything else to receive benefits.

    ☐ I did not count the employee's FMLA leave as a break in service for purposes of our pension plan.

    ☐ I counted the employee as "employed" while on leave if our pension plan requires employees to be employed on a particular date for purposes of contributions, eligibility, or vesting.

    ☐ I restored the employee's seniority-based benefits.

    ☐ If our company's policies allow employees to accrue seniority-based benefits while on unpaid leave, I added these accrued benefits to the employee's total.

Managers' Checklist: Reinstating an Employee (continued)

☐ I required the employee to provide a fitness-for-duty certification, but only if:

    ☐ I gave the employee notice that a certification would be required.

    ☐ Company policy requires it for all similarly situated employees.

    ☐ I gave the employee a list of the essential job functions, if the fitness-for-duty certification must address the employee's ability to perform them.

If the Employee Was Not Reinstated:

☐ I did not reinstate the employee because one of the following occurred:

    ☐ The employee was unable to perform an essential function of the position.

        ☐ I researched our company's obligations under the Americans with Disabilities Act and/or workers' compensation law.

    ☐ The employee's position was eliminated, for reasons unrelated to his or her FMLA leave.

    ☐ The employee was fired for reasons unrelated to his or her FMLA leave.

        ☐ If the employee was fired for attendance problems, I made sure that the employee's FMLA leave was not counted against him or her.

        ☐ I talked to a lawyer to make sure that we are on legally safe ground in taking this action.

    ☐ The employee's job or work was temporary and has been completed.

    ☐ The employee committed fraud in obtaining FMLA leave.

        ☐ If the employee was not reinstated because he or she worked another job while on FMLA leave, I made sure our company policies prohibit moonlighting.

    ☐ The employee gave unequivocal notice that he or she did not intend to return from FMLA leave, and confirmed this in writing.

Managers' Checklist: Reinstating an Employee (continued)

☐ The employee is a key employee, and reinstating him or her would cause our company substantial and grievous economic injury.

  ☐ The employee is among the highest-paid 10% of employees within a 75-mile radius.

  ☐ I notified the employee, when he or she requested leave or shortly thereafter, of this key employee status.

  ☐ I notified the employee when the company determined that reinstatement would cause substantial and grievous economic injury, stated the reasons for this determination, and gave the employee a reasonable time frame to return to work.

  ☐ If the employee requested reinstatement, I reevaluated whether reinstating him or her would cause substantial and grievous economic injury and notified the employee of my conclusions.

Managers' Checklist: If an Employee Doesn't Return From Leave

☐ I determined why the employee did not come back to work.

☐ If the employee did not return to work because of the continuation of a serious health condition, illness, or injury, I

  ☐ asked the employee to provide a medical certification, and

  ☐ did not seek reimbursement for premiums the company paid to continue the employee's health insurance.

☐ I did not seek reimbursement for health insurance premiums if the employee could not return to work for reasons beyond the employee's control.

☐ If the employee's failure to return from leave was voluntary, I determined what amount (if any) we can recover from the employee for what we spent on benefit premiums while the employee was on leave.

  ☐ I included in this amount our company's share of the premium for health insurance continuation during the employee's leave.

  ☐ If the employee did not pay his or her share of the premium for health insurance, I included any part of the employee's share that we paid during the employee's leave.

  ☐ If we continued any other insurance benefits (such as life or disability coverage), I included any amounts we paid toward the employee's share of the premium during the employee's leave.

  ☐ I did not include the company's share of the premium for any other insurance benefits.

☐ Regardless of whether or not we are entitled to seek reimbursement from the employee, I offered the employee continued health care coverage under COBRA and, if we are self-insured, paid any claims the employee incurred while on FMLA leave.

☐ Before seeking reimbursement via deducting from money we still owe the employee, I made sure that this is allowed by state law.

How Other Laws Affect FMLA Leave

Federal Laws...282

    Americans with Disabilities Act (ADA)..283

    Consolidated Omnibus Budget Reconciliation Act (COBRA)......................290

    Title VII of the Civil Rights Act...291

    Uniformed Services Employment and Reemployment Rights Act

      (USERRA)...293

State Laws..294

    State Family and Medical Leave Laws..294

    Workers' Compensation 302

    Light Duty...303

    State Disability Insurance and Paid Family Leave Programs...........................305

Common Mistakes Regarding Other Laws and Benefits—

  And How to Avoid Them..305

Chapter Highlights

☆ An employee covered by the FMLA and other employment laws is entitled to every protection of every applicable law. If the laws call for different approaches to the same situation, you must apply whichever law is more beneficial to the employee.

☆ An employee who has a serious health condition under the FMLA may also have a disability under the Americans with Disabilities Act (ADA).

- Only qualified employees with disabilities—those who can perform the essential functions of the job, with or without a reasonable accommodation—are protected by the ADA.

- Employers must provide reasonable accommodations to allow employees with disabilities to do their jobs. This may include more time off than the FMLA requires, changes to the job, or a transfer to another position.

☆ An employee who does not return to work at the end of FMLA leave may be entitled to continuing health benefits pursuant to the Consolidated Omnibus Budget Reconciliation Act (COBRA).

☆ Federal antidiscrimination laws prohibit employers from discriminating based on race, color, national origin, religion, sex (including pregnancy), age, or genetic information in any aspect of employment, including providing leave.

☆ Time an employee spends on leave to serve in the armed forces counts as time worked when determining the employee's eligibility for FMLA leave. State laws also give employees the right to take time off for a variety of reasons, including family and medical leave, military family leave, adoption, and pregnancy.

- Some of these laws cover smaller employers, have more lenient eligibility requirements for employees, allow longer periods of leave, allow leave to care for a broader range of family members, or allow leave for different purposes from the FMLA.

- If an employee takes leave that is covered by both the FMLA and a state law, that leave counts against the employee's entitlement pursuant to both laws.

- If an employee takes leave that is covered by the FMLA or the state law but not both, the employee may be entitled to more than 12 weeks of total leave.

☆ An employee whose serious medical condition comes from a workplace injury or illness is probably also entitled to workers' compensation benefits; an employee who is out on leave for a workers' comp injury or illness almost always has a serious health condition covered by the FMLA.

- An employee who is on FMLA leave does not have to accept a "light duty" position; however, an employee who rejects such a position may no longer be entitled to workers' comp benefits.

- Most state workers' compensation laws do not require employers to hold an employee's job for the duration of his or her workers' comp leave; this might come into play if an employee uses up his or her FMLA leave and still needs time off.

T he FMLA is not the only law that might protect an employee who needs time off for family or medical reasons. Depending on the employee's condition and/or situation, other federal laws may also apply. For example, other laws may protect the employee from disability discrimination or provide for continued health insurance. And that's not all: state laws that provide for family and medical leave, pregnancy disability leave, workers' compensation, or temporary disability insurance might also come into play.

Sometimes, these laws cover the same territory as the FMLA. How do you know which to follow? The basic rule when employment laws overlap is this: The employee is entitled to every benefit available under every law that applies. If the FMLA and another law both cover the employee's situation, the employee is entitled to the protections of both laws. If both laws apply and provide different rights, the employee is entitled to the protections that are most beneficial in the circumstances.

This chapter explains how to apply this rule when more than one law protects an employee who takes family and medical leave. This is a topic that many managers dread, and it can be a bit daunting. But, understanding the purpose and requirements of each law will help you figure out what to do.

TIP

Consider each law separately. The easiest way to make sure you meet all of your legal obligations when laws overlap is to think of each law as a separate protection. Run through the laws that might apply, think about what each requires or prohibits, then make sure you offer or provide those protections to the employee. You can use the chart at the end of this chapter to figure out which laws apply.

Federal Laws

A handful of federal laws other than the FMLA might protect an employee who takes family or medical leave. These laws, which are covered in detail below, include:

- the Americans with Disabilities Act (ADA), which protects disabled employees from discrimination and requires employers to make reasonable accommodations to allow employees with disabilities to do their jobs

- the Consolidated Omnibus Budget Reconciliation Act (COBRA), which requires employers to provide continued health insurance to employees and former employees
- Title VII of the Civil Rights Act, which prohibits discrimination on the basis of race, national origin, sex (including pregnancy), and religion, and
- the Uniformed Services Employment and Reemployment Rights Act (USERRA), which requires employers to provide certain rights and benefits to employees who take military leave.

Americans with Disabilities Act (ADA)

If an employee's serious health condition under the FMLA also qualifies as a disability under the ADA, both laws apply. Here, we explain some basic ADA concepts and how the ADA and FMLA might overlap.

TIP
The ADA and FMLA have different purposes. Although the ADA and FMLA both are intended (in part, at least) to help employees with physical or mental ailments, they have different goals. The goal of the ADA is to bring qualified workers with disabilities into the workforce—and keep them there—by requiring employers to make reasonable changes to allow them to do their jobs. The goal of the FMLA's medical leave provision, on the other hand, is to allow workers who are unable to do their jobs to take time off for family or health reasons.

ADA Basics

The Americans with Disabilities Act (ADA) prohibits employers with 15 or more employees from discriminating against employees with disabilities who can perform the job's essential functions with or without a reasonable accommodation. An employee has a disability for purposes of the ADA if the employee:

- has a long-term physical or mental impairment that substantially limits a major bodily function or a major life activity, such as the ability to walk, talk, see, hear, breathe, reason, work, or take care of oneself (short-term or temporary impairments—such as pregnancy—

are not covered by the ADA, although state law may include pregnancy as a disability.)

• has a history of such an impairment (for example, the employee suffered cancer or depression in the past), or

• is perceived by the employer as having a disability. This sometimes comes up when an employee has an obvious impairment (such as a limp or speech impediment) that is not actually disabling.

Employers are required to make reasonable accommodations to allow employees with disabilities to do their jobs. A reasonable accommodation is assistance (technological or otherwise) or a change to the workplace or job that allows the employee to perform its essential functions: the job's most fundamental tasks. Examples include providing voice-recognition software for an employee with carpal tunnel syndrome; altering the height of a desk for an employee in a wheelchair; providing a distraction-free environment for an employee with attention deficit disorder; or allowing a diabetic employee to take more frequent breaks to eat and drink, take medication, or test blood sugar levels.

Under the ADA, an employer does not have to provide a reasonable accommodation if doing so would create an undue hardship. Whether an accommodation creates an undue hardship depends on a number of factors, including:

• the nature and cost of the accommodation

• the size and financial resources of the business and the facility where the employee works

• the structure of the business, and

• the effect the accommodation would have on the business.

An accommodation that would be extremely costly (for example, adapting technical equipment that would eat up months' worth of company profits) or would change the character of the business (for example, installing bright lighting in a previously dimly lit, romantic restaurant) could create an undue hardship.

Rules for Handling Medical Records

Under the FMLA, employee medical records must be handled confidentially, kept in secured files (separate from personnel files), and released only to limited people in limited circumstances. These rules also apply to medical records covered by the ADA. (You can find a description of these rules in Chapter 13.)

Overlap Between the FMLA and the ADA

The FMLA and the ADA overlap only if an employee has both a serious health condition under the FMLA and a disability under the ADA. Although many ailments—such as cancer, multiple sclerosis, HIV/AIDS, stroke, and diabetes—likely qualify under both laws, some do not. For example, an employee who is pregnant, has a broken bone, or has suffered a temporary serious injury is covered by the FMLA but not the ADA. An employee who is blind or hard of hearing and can perform the job's essential functions with an accommodation has a disability but perhaps not a serious health condition.

An employee who is protected by both the FMLA and the ADA is entitled to the rights provided by both laws: up to 12 weeks of job-protected leave with benefits continuation under the FMLA, and a reasonable accommodation to enable the employee to perform the job's essential functions under the ADA. If the laws allow different rights in the same situation, the employee is entitled to whichever provides the greater benefit.

> EXAMPLE: Sam uses a wheelchair due to a back injury that left him paralyzed from the waist down. He needs to have surgery related to his condition and expects to be out of work for two months. Because you know Sam has a disability, you consider whether he is entitled to two months off as a reasonable accommodation. Sam's job is to maintain, update, and troubleshoot the company's website. No one else knows how to do this work and, because the website is relatively new, it requires a lot of work to keep it running smoothly. You decide that it would be an undue hardship to give Sam two months off, and you tell him that the company will have to replace him.
>
> Although you might have been right under the ADA, you were wrong under the FMLA. Sam's disability almost certainly qualifies as a serious health condition, for which he is entitled to FMLA leave (assuming he is otherwise eligible). The FMLA doesn't include an undue hardship defense: An eligible employee can't be denied leave because it would place too much of a burden on the company (unless the employee qualifies as a "key employee," as explained in Chapter 11). You must give Sam his time off and figure out some way to get the work done in his absence.

There are several situations in which the FMLA and ADA are most likely to overlap: when an employee requests a modified schedule, when an employee requests (or an employer proposes) modified job duties, and when an employee is unable to return to work after FMLA leave.

TIP

Count disability leave as FMLA leave. If an employee is covered by both the ADA and the FMLA, make sure you count any time off the employee takes due to his or her disability as FMLA leave, too.

Schedule Changes

An employee can take FMLA leave intermittently or on a reduced schedule, and this might also be a reasonable accommodation for an employee's disability under the ADA. If the employee is protected by both laws, the FMLA provides the greater benefit, because employees are entitled to job protection and benefits continuation during intermittent or reduced-schedule leave. And even if an employer transfers an employee to a different position that better accommodates the need for leave, that position must have the same pay and benefits as the employee's original position. The ADA allows a transfer as a reasonable accommodation (if the employee can't be accommodated in his or her former position), but doesn't give the employee the right to the same pay and benefits, nor to benefits continuation.

> **EXAMPLE:** Najeet is scheduled to begin a ten-week round of chemotherapy and radiation treatment for cancer and needs time off work. She asks to work 20 hours a week for the duration of her treatment. You tell Najeet that you are happy to grant her request as a reasonable accommodation for her disability but remind her that the company provides health benefits only to employees who work at least 30 hours a week. You offer her COBRA coverage, for which she would have to pay the entire premium, until she is able to once again meet the minimum hours requirement.
>
> Uh-oh! In this situation, the FMLA provides a greater benefit, and Najeet is entitled to its protections. She can take the time off she needs for treatment with continued health insurance benefits, regardless of the company's policy on eligibility for coverage. Under the FMLA, Najeet has to pay only her usual share of the premium (if any), not the whole thing.

Job Modifications

The FMLA does not entitle an employee to a different job or to any changes in his or her current job. Instead, the FMLA provides for reinstatement, once leave is over, to the same or an equivalent position: a position that is

"virtually identical" to the employee's former position. In contrast, the ADA may entitle an employee to job modifications or even to a different position in the company as a reasonable accommodation. Here are a couple of ways this issue might play out when an employee has both a disability and a serious health condition:

- **The employee asks for changes to the job.** You must consider whether the requested changes constitute a reasonable accommodation and whether providing them would be an undue hardship. If the accommodation won't work, you must work with the employee to come up with a different accommodation. If you and the employee conclude that time off might reasonably accommodate the employee's disability, your obligations under the FMLA kick in.

> **EXAMPLE:** Carmen is a dispatcher for a delivery company. She works from 6 a.m. until noon. When she arrives, she reviews the schedule to see which deliveries must be made that day, assigns deliveries to drivers, and arranges for the items to be loaded on the trucks. By about 10 a.m., all of the trucks have left the warehouse. Carmen spends the rest of her day processing paperwork from the morning deliveries.
>
> Carmen is diagnosed with depression, for which her doctor prescribes her medication that makes her groggy and disoriented in the morning. Carmen asks if she can change her schedule to arrive at work at 10 a.m. and work until 4 p.m. The FMLA doesn't apply, because she isn't asking for time off. You consider it as a request for a reasonable accommodation, and you deny it as an undue hardship. The essential duties of Carmen's job require her to be there in the early morning. There wouldn't be anything for her to do later in the day. You research whether there are other positions in the company that Carmen might be suited for, but there are no positions for which she is qualified.
>
> You and Carmen talk through some alternatives, none of which will work. Carmen says, "My doctor said that this side effect might go away after I've been taking the drug for a month or so. Some of his other patients have had that happen." You ask Carmen whether she wants to take some time off work and see whether she feels well enough in the morning to resume her job. You explain her right to leave under the FMLA, and she decides to use it.

- **You offer a light-duty position.** If an employee requests time off for a serious health condition/disability, some employers respond by offering

a light-duty position (often, one that doesn't require lifting or other physically strenuous activities). If the employee wants to keep working and accepts the position, that's fine. If, however, the employee is covered by the FMLA, he or she does not have to take the position, and you must inform the employee of his or her FMLA rights. The employee can choose to take FMLA leave rather than working a light-duty assignment, as long as the employee is eligible.

Lessons from the Real World

When an employee's depression causes poor attendance, she isn't protected by the ADA but might be entitled to FMLA leave.

Theresa Spangler worked in the Demand Services Department of the Federal Home Loan Bank of Des Moines. After she was diagnosed with dysthemia (a form of depression), she began having attendance problems. Over the years, she took two leaves of absence for treatment and missed several days of work due to her depression.

After being warned, being put on probation, and facing customer complaints about her absences, Spangler was eventually fired for excessive absenteeism when she called in saying she would be out for "depression, again." She sued the bank for violating the ADA and the FMLA.

The court found that Spangler had no claim under the ADA because she could not prove that she could perform the job's essential functions with or without accommodation. One of Spangler's job duties was to make sure member banks had adequate daily cash, and the court found that regular attendance was therefore an essential function of her job.

The court also found, however, that Spangler might have a valid FMLA claim. Unlike the ADA, which protects employees who can do the job but might need an accommodation, the FMLA protects employees who cannot perform the job's essential functions, at least for a limited time. When Spangler called in and said she would miss work for depression, the company should have treated it as a request for FMLA leave.

Spangler v. Federal Home Loan Bank of Des Moines, 278 F.3d 847 (8th Cir. 2002).

Leave as a Reasonable Accommodation

Here are some things courts have considered when deciding whether leave constitutes a reasonable accommodation:

- **The nature of the job.** If regular attendance is an essential function of the job (as it often is), some courts have found that an employee who needs a significant amount of time off is not a qualified employee with a disability and isn't protected by the ADA or entitled to a reasonable accommodation.
- **How much leave the employee needs.** While many courts have found that an employer is not required to provide open-ended leave, courts are more likely to see a finite period of leave as a reasonable accommodation. If an employee will be able to return to work after two additional weeks of leave (beyond the 12 weeks allowed by the FMLA) for physical therapy following surgery, for example, a court is more likely to find that the employee is entitled to this time off. In fact, courts in some states have found that a leave of up to a year is a reasonable accommodation.
- **How much time off the employer provides in other circumstances.** If an employer grants extended leaves for other purposes, it will be hard-pressed to claim that allowing leave to an employee with a disability is an undue hardship.

Ultimately, the undue hardship test will determine whether you must grant an employee's request for time off under the ADA. Before you decide to deny this type of request, talk to an employment lawyer to find out how courts in your area look at these cases and to make sure you've considered all of the angles before making your decision.

Reinstatement

Once an employee's FMLA-protected leave runs out, the company must reinstate the employee to the same or an equivalent position. If the employee is not able to return to work or perform the essential duties of his or her position, the company's FMLA obligations end. However, if the employee is also covered by the ADA, the company must provide a reasonable accommodation, unless it creates an undue hardship. This means that the company might have to provide additional leave, make changes to the

employee's position to allow the employee to do the job, or even transfer the employee to a different position. And, the ADA requires the company to return the employee to the same job with a reasonable accommodation—not an equivalent one—unless doing so would be an undue hardship. Therefore, if an employee's leave qualifies under both laws, you might not be able to reinstate the employee to an equivalent position.

RESOURCE

For more information on the ADA. The Equal Employment Opportunity Commission, the federal agency that administers the ADA, has a number of helpful resources available on its website, including a fact sheet on how the ADA interacts with the FMLA. You can find these resources at www.eeoc.gov. An excellent resource on reasonable accommodations is the Job Accommodation Network (JAN), at askjan.org.

Consolidated Omnibus Budget Reconciliation Act (COBRA)

COBRA allows employees, former employees, and their families to receive continuing coverage under an employer's group health plan after experiencing a "qualifying event": an event that would end coverage under ordinary circumstances, such as a layoff or reduction in hours. Employees and their families typically have to pay for this continued coverage, but they pay the employer-negotiated group rate, which is often less expensive than an individual rate. This right to continued coverage lasts for 18 to 36 months, depending on the type of qualifying event. COBRA applies to employers with 20 or more employees.

Often, COBRA and the FMLA don't overlap at all. Taking FMLA leave doesn't count as a qualifying event under COBRA, because employers are legally obligated to continue the employee's group health benefits during leave (as explained in Chapter 10). In a few situations, however, an employee who takes FMLA leave might be entitled to COBRA protection:

- **The employee can't return to work after FMLA leave.** If an employee is unable to come back to work when FMLA leave runs out, the employee is entitled to continued health care coverage under COBRA. The qualifying event occurs on the last day of the employee's FMLA

leave. Similarly, if an employee passes away while on FMLA leave, and the employee's family is covered by your company's group health plan, the employee's death is the qualifying event that entitles his or her family members to the protections of COBRA.

- **The employee chooses not to return to work.** As explained in Chapter 10, an employer's obligation to provide continued health benefits ends if the employee provides unequivocal notice of his or her intent not to return to work. But the employee can continue coverage under COBRA. The qualifying event in this situation occurs on the date the employee gives such notice.
- **The employee returns to work with a schedule or position that is not entitled to benefits.** Many companies provide group health benefits only to certain employees (typically, those who work a minimum number of hours per week). If an employee takes FMLA leave and chooses to return to a part-time position, the employee might no longer be entitled to benefits. The qualifying event here, for COBRA purposes, occurs on the last day of the employee's leave.

These rules apply even if the employee failed to pay his or her portion of the premium while on leave or the employee refused coverage during FMLA leave. Neither situation deprives the employee of the right to coverage.

RESOURCE

Need more information on COBRA? You can find detailed information on COBRA's requirements, including the paperwork and notices your company must provide to an employee who is entitled to continuing coverage, in *The Essential Guide to Federal Employment Laws*, by Lisa Guerin and Amy DelPo (Nolo).

Title VII of the Civil Rights Act

Title VII prohibits employers with 15 or more employees from discriminating on the basis of race, color, religion, sex (including pregnancy), and national origin. Title VII applies to every aspect of the employment relationship, including hiring, compensation, benefits, and termination. It also prohibits harassment on the basis of any of the characteristics listed above.

There are a few ways Title VII might overlap with the FMLA. Because Title VII prohibits employers from discriminating in the provision of benefits, an employer might violate Title VII by administering requests for FMLA leave in a discriminatory way. For example, if you routinely allow white employees to take foreseeable leave on short notice while requiring nonwhite employees to provide 30 days' notice, that would violate Title VII. In this type of situation, the employer is using the FMLA as a vehicle for discrimination.

Overlap may also occur when an employee takes FMLA leave for pregnancy and childbirth. Courts have interpreted Title VII's prohibition on pregnancy discrimination to require employers to treat pregnant employees just as they treat other workers who are temporarily disabled by other conditions. This means that you cannot treat employees who take FMLA leave for pregnancy any differently from other employees who use the FMLA, and you might have to provide time off to a pregnant employee who isn't eligible for FMLA leave (because, for example, she hasn't worked enough hours in the past year) if you provide such time off to employees with other types of short-term disabilities.

Parenting and caretaking leave are another potential source of overlap. This issue typically arises when a male employee wants to take parental leave or leave to care for a seriously ill or injured family member. Even in this day and age, some employers still expect women to be the primary parents and caretakers. However, denying a man FMLA leave based on these expectations not only violates the FMLA; it's also gender discrimination, prohibited by Title VII.

EXAMPLE: Connor is an employee at your company. He and his wife, who does volunteer work for a local nonprofit, have a young son who has leukemia. Connor asks to work a reduced schedule while his son undergoes treatment that is expected to leave him fatigued, ill, and unable to care for himself. You respond: "Connor, I'm so sorry to hear about your son, but isn't your wife available to take care of him? We could really use you around here, and if she puts her volunteer work on hold, your family won't lose part of your salary. I'm sure he'll want his mother at a time like this."

Oops. It's not an employer's right to tell employees how to manage their private lives—including which parent should be the primary caretaker, whose job is more important to the family, and so on. If you denied FMLA leave to

Connor because you think his wife should take care of their son, your company might well be facing a lawsuit for violating both the FMLA and Title VII's prohibition on sex discrimination.

Uniformed Services Employment and Reemployment Rights Act (USERRA)

USERRA provides a number of employment-related rights to employees who take time off to serve in the Armed Forces. Such employees may not be discriminated against based on their service; are entitled to reinstatement and benefits restoration upon returning from leaves of up to five years; and may not be fired, except for cause, for up to a year after they return from service.

TIP
Some states have similar laws. Many states have laws prohibiting discrimination or providing employment-related rights to individuals serving in the Armed Forces or state militias. These laws can overlap with the FMLA the same way Title VII and USERRA do, and their protections could be even broader. To find out more about the laws in your state, talk to an experienced lawyer.

USERRA and the FMLA overlap only when determining an employee's eligibility for FMLA leave. As explained in Chapter 3, an employee must have worked for the employer for at least one year, and at least 1,250 hours during the previous year, to qualify for FMLA leave. You must count time the employee spends on leave for military service as time worked when determining eligibility for FMLA leave. When calculating the employee's hours, you can use the employee's schedule prior to taking military leave.

EXAMPLE 1: For eight months, George, a member of the Army Reserve, works full time (40 hours a week) in your company's IT department. He is called for service and takes six months of military leave, then returns to work. After he has been back for a month, George requests FMLA leave to care for his seriously ill wife. Is he eligible for leave?

Yes. You must count the six months George spent on leave as hours worked. This means that George has "worked" 15 months for your company and 2,080 hours (40 hours a week times 52 weeks) in the last year. He is eligible for FMLA leave.

EXAMPLE 2: Now assume that George works a part-time schedule, 20 hours per week. Is he still eligible for FMLA leave?

No. Although George still gets credit for 15 months of work for your company, he hasn't "worked" enough hours in the last year. You must credit George with an entire year of work at his previous schedule—20 hours per week. That means George gets credit for only 1,040 hours (20 hours a week times 52 weeks), which falls short of the threshold for FMLA coverage.

State Laws

In addition to the federal laws described above, there are state laws that might overlap with the FMLA as well. This section describes the types of state laws that might come into play as you administer the FMLA:

- state family and medical leave laws
- workers' compensation statutes, and
- temporary disability or family leave insurance programs.

State Family and Medical Leave Laws

A number of states have adopted their own laws that allow employees to take time off for family and/or medical reasons. These laws fall into a handful of categories:

- comprehensive family and medical leave laws similar to the FMLA that may provide additional protections or apply to more employees
- military family leave laws, which allow employees to take time off when certain family members are called to serve in the military
- pregnancy disability leave laws, which allow female employees to take time off for conditions related to pregnancy and childbirth
- adoption leave laws, which generally require employers to make the same parental leave available to adoptive parents that they make available to biological parents
- small necessities laws, which provide time off for employees to attend a child's school conferences or other school activities or to take a relative to routine medical and dental visits, and

- domestic violence leave laws, which require employers to allow employees to take leave to seek medical care, attend legal proceedings or therapy appointments, or otherwise deal with domestic violence issues.

> **CAUTION**
> **Your state may require you to offer other types of leave.** In this section (and in Appendix A), we discuss only those state laws that might overlap with, or provide leave similar to, the FMLA. We do not cover the many other types of leave laws states have adopted, such as laws requiring leave for voting, military service, jury duty, or donating blood or bone marrow. To find out more about your state's leave laws beyond the realm of family and medical leave, contact your state labor department. (You'll find contact information in Appendix A.)

Each of these categories is explained more fully below. Appendix A provides basic information on each state's family and medical leave laws, including which employers are covered, what the eligibility requirements are, and so on.

> **TIP**
> **Remember to designate FMLA leave.** If any time an employee takes off pursuant to a state law also qualifies as FMLA leave, designate it as such and provide the required notices (explained in Chapter 8). If you don't, the employee may be entitled to additional leave.

Comprehensive Family and Medical Leave Laws

About a dozen states currently have laws that require employers to provide family and medical leave. These laws are quite similar to the FMLA, in that they typically provide a certain number of weeks of parenting, caretaking, or medical leave to eligible employees. However, these laws differ from the FMLA in the following important ways:

- **Some apply to smaller employers.** For example, Vermont employers must provide parental leave if they have at least ten employees, and leave to care for a seriously ill family member if they have at least 15 employees. In these states, smaller employers may be covered only by the state law, not the FMLA.

- **Some cover more family members.** In California, for example, an employee may take leave to care for a domestic partner with a serious health condition. When an employee takes leave to care for a family member who is not covered by the FMLA, it doesn't count as FMLA leave. This means, for example, that an employee in California could take 12 weeks (the state law maximum) of family leave to care for a seriously ill domestic partner and still have 12 weeks of FMLA leave left to use.
- **Some may allow longer periods of leave.** In Connecticut, for example, employees are entitled to 16 weeks of family and medical leave in a two-year period. If an employee needs 16 weeks at once, this provides more leave than the FMLA requires.

Whether leave taken pursuant to one of these state laws counts as FMLA leave depends on whether both laws apply. When an employee takes leave for a reason that's covered by state law but not by the FMLA (for example, to care for a grandparent, in Hawaii), the FMLA doesn't apply, and the employee's leave doesn't use up any of his or her FMLA entitlement. If, however, the employee's leave is covered by both laws (for example, that Hawaiian employee takes leave to care for a parent), the time counts against both the employee's FMLA and state leave entitlements.

If your company does business in a state with a comprehensive family and medical leave statute, keep these tips in mind:

- **Start by figuring out which laws apply.** If the employee's leave is covered only by your state's law, you don't have to deal with the FMLA at all, and vice versa.
- **If both laws apply, the leaves run concurrently.** If an employee takes leave covered by both the FMLA and your state's law, the employee uses up both types of leave at once. If the employee uses all leave provided by state law while on FMLA leave, no additional leave is available, even for reasons covered only by state law.
- **If only one law applies, the employee will be able to "stack" leave.** If an employee's time off counts only under one law and not the other, the employee will still have leave available. This means that the employee could take significantly more than 12 weeks of leave in a 12-month period, if the employee is eligible.

EXAMPLE: Oregon's family and medical leave law allows eligible employees to take up to 12 weeks of leave per year for various reasons, including caring for a family member with a serious health condition. The definition of "family member" includes a parent-in-law. If an employee in Oregon took 12 weeks of leave to care for a child with a serious health condition, that leave would use up both the employee's FMLA and state leave entitlements, and no leave would be available for the rest of the year. If, on the other hand, the employee first took 12 weeks of leave to care for his or her mother-in-law, that leave would count against the state leave entitlement only. The employee would still have 12 weeks of FMLA leave to use in the same year.

Military Family Leave

In the last couple of years, some states have passed laws that require employers to give some time off to employees with family members serving in the military. Some of these laws apply only to certain family members (for example, spouses), and most apply whether the family member is subject to a federal or state call to active duty. Typically, these laws provide only a small amount of leave.

These laws may overlap with qualifying exigency or military caregiver leave under the FMLA. For example, Minnesota allows certain family members to take one day off to attend military events. If the employee is the parent, spouse, or child of the servicemember, that leave would also count as qualifying exigency leave. If the employee is the servicemember's grandparent or sibling, however, the leave would be covered by state law only. Similarly, some state laws allow employees to take leave during a family member's deployment, but don't limit the circumstances under which the employee may take leave. In these states, an employee who uses leave for a family member and a reason that qualifies under the FMLA would be using both types of leave; however, if the employee took time off that didn't fall into any of the qualifying exigency categories, that time would count only against the employee's state law entitlement.

Pregnancy Disability Leave

Some states require employers to provide time off for pregnancy disability: the length of time when a woman is temporarily disabled by pregnancy and

childbirth. Typically, these laws don't provide for a set amount of time off per year or per pregnancy. Instead, they require employers to provide either a "reasonable" amount of leave or leave for the period of disability, often with a maximum time limit. For example, Louisiana requires employers to allow a "reasonable period" of leave for pregnancy disability; the statute goes on to say that this period shouldn't exceed six weeks for a normal childbirth but might be as long as four months for a complicated childbirth, depending on the circumstances.

Because pregnancy is a serious health condition under the FMLA, leave an employee takes under a state pregnancy disability leave law typically runs concurrently with FMLA leave. If your state's law provides for more than 12 weeks of pregnancy disability leave, the first 12 weeks will use up the employee's FMLA allotment. Although the employee may be entitled to take more time off, the employee won't necessarily be entitled to continued health insurance if the state law doesn't require it.

Adoption Leave Laws

A handful of states require employers to offer the same leave to adoptive parents as to biological parents. Generally, these laws don't require an employer to offer parental leave. However, those employers that choose to offer some form of parental leave must make it equally available to adoptive parents. A couple of these states set an age limit: For example, New York employers that provide parental leave must allow adoptive parents to use it, but only if they are adopting a child who is no older than preschool age or, if disabled, no older than 18.

The FMLA provides leave for adoption, so any time an employee takes off pursuant to one of these state laws would also count as FMLA leave (and you should designate it as such).

Small Necessities Laws

Some states require employers to allow time off for various family needs, such as attending school functions, taking a child to routine dental or medical appointments, or helping with eldercare. These laws have come to be known as "small necessities" laws, to recognize needs that don't take up much time but are important to employees. Here are a few examples:

- In Illinois, employees can take up to eight hours off in any school year—not to exceed four hours in a single day—to attend a child's school conferences or classroom activities, if those activities can't be scheduled during nonwork hours.
- In Washington, DC, employees can take up to 24 hours off per year to attend a child's school-related events, including parent-teacher association meetings, student performances, teacher conferences, and sporting events, as long as the parent actually participates and is not just a spectator.
- In Vermont, employees can take a total of 24 hours of leave per year for school activities; to attend or accompany a child, parent, spouse, or parent-in-law to routine medical or dental appointments or other appointments for professional services; or to respond to a medical emergency involving the employee's child, parent, spouse, or parent-in-law.

Many of these laws apply to situations not covered by the FMLA (such as school conferences or routine doctor's appointments). In this situation, the leave provided by a small necessities law would be in addition to FMLA leave, and the two laws wouldn't overlap. However, there are limited situations in which the FMLA might also apply. For example, if your company does business in Vermont, and a parent takes small necessities leave to respond to a child's medical emergency, that might also qualify as FMLA leave (depending on whether the child has a serious health condition).

Domestic Violence Leave Laws

Some states allow employees to take time off for issues relating to domestic violence. In Colorado, for example, employees can take up to three days of leave to seek a restraining order, obtain medical care or counseling, relocate, or seek legal assistance. These laws may apply to employees who need to help a family member, such as a child, who has been a victim of domestic violence, as well.

Whether leave taken under one of these statutes qualifies as FMLA leave depends on whether the employee has a serious health condition or is caring for a family member with a serious health condition. An employee who takes time off to appear in court to testify against her abuser might not qualify for FMLA leave; an employee who is hospitalized following a violent incident

probably does. When an employee takes domestic violence leave, you should find out whether a serious health condition is present. If so, you should designate the leave accordingly.

Paid Sick Leave Laws

Recently, several states and a handful of municipal governments have passed laws requiring employers to provide a minimum amount of paid sick leave. Typically, employees accrue paid time off at a rate set by the law, which they may then use when they are ill. State laws requiring paid sick leave are covered in Appendix A, along with all other state family and medical leave laws.

Putting It All Together

Now that we've reviewed the most common types of state laws that provide leave for family and medical reasons, it's time to see how they might work with the FMLA when an employee needs time off. Here are a few examples that will help you see how the process works.

> EXAMPLE 1: Joan works for a company in California. She and her domestic partner, Betty, are expecting a baby in a couple of months; Joan is carrying the baby. Joan's doctor puts her on bed rest for the last four weeks of her pregnancy. Joan also wants to take some parental leave after the baby is born. What are her leave rights?
>
> Under California law, Joan can take up to four months of pregnancy disability leave, taken concurrently with her 12 weeks of FMLA leave (as leave for a serious health condition). However, she gets an additional 12 weeks of leave under the California Family Rights Act (CFRA), which doesn't cover pregnancy disability. If Joan is disabled for the last four weeks of her pregnancy and another four weeks after the baby is born, she has used up eight weeks of FMLA leave. However, she is still entitled to 12 weeks of CFRA leave, which she can use for any purpose covered by that law—including time to bond with her child. This means Joan can take 24 weeks off in one block and still be entitled to job reinstatement (12 weeks of FMLA and pregnancy disability leave, plus 12 more weeks of CFRA leave). In fact, if she is disabled by pregnancy and childbirth for the full four months, she can take up to seven months of job-protected leave before returning to work (four months of pregnancy disability leave, the first 12 weeks of which are also FMLA leave, plus 12 more weeks of CFRA leave).

EXAMPLE 2: Carla works for a company in Hawaii. Carla's boyfriend batters her son, who is hospitalized for his injuries. Under Hawaii law, Carla is entitled to up to 30 days of unpaid leave per year to deal with domestic violence issues. Hawaii also has a comprehensive family and medical leave law, which allows employees to take up to four weeks off per year to care for a family member with a serious health condition. What are Carla's leave rights?

If Carla takes three weeks off to care for her son, that time counts against her state family and medical leave entitlement, her FMLA entitlement, and her domestic violence leave entitlement. If, after her leave is over, Carla needs an additional week off to relocate her family and seek a restraining order against her boyfriend, that leave is not protected by either the FMLA or Hawaii's leave law. However, it is protected by the state's domestic leave law, which allows time off for these purposes. Carla is still entitled to one week of state family leave and nine weeks of FMLA leave in the same 12-month period, but her domestic violence leave is used up.

EXAMPLE 3: David, a single father of three children, works for a company in Vermont. Vermont law allows him to take up to 24 hours of leave per year to participate in a child's school activities, take family members to routine medical or dental appointments, or respond to a family member's medical emergency. Vermont also has a comprehensive family and medical leave law that provides up to 12 weeks of leave in a year for the same reasons covered by the FMLA. What are David's leave rights?

If David uses his 24 hours of leave to attend parent-teacher conferences and take his children to regular medical and dental checkups, he still has 12 weeks of FMLA leave and state family and medical leave left to use. Because school activities and routine appointments are not covered by those laws, this time off doesn't count against his state or federal family and medical leave entitlement.

EXAMPLE 4: Maek works for a company in Rhode Island. He has cerebral palsy and needs time off work occasionally for reasons related to his condition. Rhode Island law allows employees to take up to 13 weeks off every two calendar years for family and medical reasons, including the employee's own serious health condition. What are Maek's leave rights?

If Maek needs 13 weeks off in one year, the first 12 weeks use up his FMLA entitlement for that year; the final week is covered under state law only. Maek

302 | THE ESSENTIAL GUIDE TO FAMILY AND MEDICAL LEAVE

is not entitled to any additional state leave for the rest of that year or the following calendar year. However, Maek does have an additional 12 weeks of FMLA leave to use in the following year (when that leave year starts depends on how the company calculates its 12-month FMLA period; see Chapter 7). Maek's condition may also qualify as a disability under the ADA, in which case he may be entitled to additional time off as a reasonable accommodation.

Workers' Compensation

Most employers in most states are required to carry workers' compensation insurance (workers' comp), which provides reimbursement for medical bills and partial wage replacement to employees who are unable to work due to a work-related injury or illness. Typically, state law provides that an employee's injury or illness is covered by workers' comp if it is related to work, whether it occurs at the workplace during normal work hours or not. For example, injuries are typically covered if they happen during a workshift, while the employee is running a work errand, while the employee is traveling for business, or while the employee is attending a required work function (such as a company picnic or team-building event).

If an employee's serious health condition is due to a work-related injury or illness, both the FMLA and workers' comp might apply. In this situation, the employee would be entitled to up to 12 weeks of unpaid, job-protected leave under the FMLA, and to partial wage replacement, reimbursement for medical bills, and perhaps some retraining or occupational therapy under workers' comp.

TIP

An employee who is out on workers' comp leave probably has a serious health condition under the FMLA. Under the laws of many states, an employee becomes entitled to temporary disability benefits under workers' comp only after being out of work for a specified waiting period (typically, at least three days). And, an employee seeking workers' comp benefits is usually being treated by a doctor. This adds up to incapacity of more than three days with continuing treatment by a health care provider: a serious health condition. The upshot for managers is this: Whenever an employee is out of work and receiving workers' comp benefits, you should designate that time as FMLA leave.

Workers' Comp Medical Inquiries

As explained in Chapter 9, employers have limited rights to request medical information under the FMLA. The employer may require the employee to submit a medical certification from a health care provider, giving some basic facts about the serious health condition that necessitates leave. However, the employer may not request additional information. Although the employer can, with the employee's consent, contact the employee's health care provider, this is only for the limited purpose of clarifying and authenticating the information on the medical certification form.

The workers' compensation statutes of most states allow quite a bit more contact between employers and health care providers. If an employee is on FMLA leave for a workers' comp injury, and the state's workers' comp law allows direct contact between the employer and the employee's health care provider, the FMLA doesn't prohibit that contact. In other words, the employer can still communicate with the health care provider in any way the workers' comp statute allows.

Workers' comp is, of course, a very detailed and complicated system, which varies greatly from state to state. Our purpose here is not to explain your obligations under workers' comp law, but to highlight the areas where your obligations under the FMLA and workers' comp are most likely to overlap: light-duty assignments and reinstatement.

Light Duty

Under the FMLA, an employee with a serious health condition is entitled to leave for up to 12 weeks, until he or she is once again able to do the original job or one that is nearly identical to it. The employee doesn't have to come back early to a different position or "light duty" work, even if he or she is capable of lesser tasks or responsibilities.

Workers' comp is different. If the company offers a light-duty position that the employee is medically able to perform, the employee typically has to accept that position or lose his or her benefits under workers' comp. This is true even if the employee is on FMLA-protected leave.

An employee who decides to accept a light-duty position rather than remain on FMLA leave doesn't give up the right to be reinstated to his or her former position. However, the employee's right to reinstatement lasts only until the end of the 12-month FMLA leave year; if the employee is still unable to perform his or her old job by that time, the employee no longer has a right to return to it.

Reinstatement

Unlike the FMLA, workers' comp laws often don't place a time limit on how long an employee may be off before returning to work. But they don't necessarily give an employee the right to be reinstated, either. Although employers may not fire or discipline employees for making a worker's comp claim, some states do not explicitly prohibit an employer from firing an employee who is out with a workers' comp injury (for example, because the employer has to fill the position and cannot wait any longer for the employee to recuperate). (Some states do require reinstatement, however; check with a lawyer to find out how your state deals with this issue.)

An employee who is out with a workers' comp injury that is also a serious health condition under the FMLA is still entitled to only 12 weeks of job-protected leave. The fact that the employee has a workers' comp injury does not extend this protection. If the employee is unable to return to work after 12 weeks, the laws of some states allow the employer to terminate employment, unless the employee has a disability that requires reasonable accommodation (see "Americans with Disabilities Act (ADA)," above).

CAUTION

Talk to a lawyer before you fire someone with a workers' comp claim. Although the laws of your state may allow you to fire someone who is out on workers' comp leave (after the employee's FMLA leave entitlement has run out), that doesn't mean it's a good idea. Whenever you fire an employee who has exercised a legal right, you risk a retaliation lawsuit. Before you fire someone who is using workers' comp, consult with an experienced employment attorney.

State Disability Insurance and Paid Family Leave Programs

A handful of states (California, Hawaii, New Jersey, New York, and Rhode Island) have temporary disability insurance programs that provide partial wage replacement (typically funded by payroll deductions) to workers who are temporarily unable to do their jobs due to disability. California, New Jersey, and Washington also have paid family leave programs, which provide partial wage replacement to workers who need time off for parenting leave or to care for a seriously ill family member. (Washington's paid family leave program is on hold for now, due to budget constraints.)

An employee who has a serious health condition, has a family member with a serious health condition, or takes time off to bond with a new child may be entitled to payment from one of these programs, depending on the state's eligibility requirements. However, these laws do not give employees any substantive rights to a particular amount of time off or to job protection. Instead, they provide some pay to employees who are otherwise entitled to time off, whether pursuant to the FMLA or some other law.

Although you may have some administrative duties associated with these programs, these benefits are really between the employees and the state. Your job is mostly to let employees know that the program exists and perhaps to provide the necessary forms. It's the employee's responsibility to file those forms with the state and handle things from there. Of course, when an employee takes time off for a temporary disability, you should investigate whether the leave qualifies as FMLA leave and, if so, designate it as such.

Common Mistakes Regarding Other Laws and Benefits—And How to Avoid Them

Mistake 1: Confusing the ADA's requirements with the FMLA's.

Avoid this mistake by taking the following steps:

- Figure out which law applies. An employee with a serious health condition doesn't always have a disability, and vice versa. If only one law applies, you don't have to comply with the other.

- Apply the most beneficial provisions to each situation. If both laws apply, the employee is entitled to the maximum protections available. This may depend on what the employee wants. If, for example, an employee qualifies for FMLA leave but wants to work with a reasonable accommodation, you must provide the accommodation. Conversely, if the employee could work with a reasonable accommodation but wants to take FMLA leave, you must provide leave.
- Remember that undue hardship doesn't apply to the FMLA. This is a common source of confusion: Although the ADA doesn't require an employer to provide a reasonable accommodation if it poses an undue hardship, no such defense applies to FMLA leave. The employer has to provide the leave, no matter how difficult it might be. (The employer might not have to reinstate "key employees" if that would cause grievous economic harm to the company, however; see Chapter 11.)
- Consider additional time off or job modifications for employees who can't return to their old jobs. Although the FMLA entitles an employee to return to his or her former position after using up leave, the ADA might entitle the employee to additional protections, such as more leave or changes to the job, as a reasonable accommodation for the disability. If it appears that an employee won't be able to return to work after completing FMLA leave, it's time to start thinking about reasonable accommodations.

Mistake 2: Forgetting to designate leave taken concurrently under the FMLA and other statutes as FMLA leave.

Avoid this mistake by taking the following steps:

- Always consider the FMLA when an employee takes time off for his or her own illness or injury. Some companies outsource their workers' compensation claims handling, then neglect to designate this time off as FMLA leave. Or, if an employee has had an obvious disability (for example, having to use a wheelchair) from his or her first day of work, you might be so

accustomed to allowing the ADA to guide your actions that you forget to consider the FMLA when the employee needs leave.

- Think "FMLA" when an employee uses state temporary disability insurance programs. Any time for which the employee is reimbursed by one of these programs (in the states that have them) is almost always FMLA leave.

- Designate parenting leave—whether taken pursuant to state law, company policy, or otherwise—as FMLA leave. Parenting leave is FMLA leave, plain and simple.

Mistake 3: Getting confused as to whether state leave laws apply.

Avoid this mistake by taking the following steps:

- Learn the coverage and eligibility requirements of your state's leave laws. Your first step is always to figure out which laws apply. Many states have different standards than the FMLA. Whenever you're faced with a leave situation, start by determining which laws cover your company, the employee, and the reason for leave.

- Count leave only against the law that covers it. Sounds simple enough, but many managers have mistakenly counted state leave against an employee's FMLA entitlement when the reason for leave isn't covered by the FMLA. For example, if your state allows employees to take time off to care for grandparents, domestic partners, or in-laws, that time off cannot count against the employee's FMLA leave entitlement because the FMLA doesn't apply to leave for those reasons.

- Pay careful attention to record keeping. If your company is subject to both the FMLA and a state leave law, you must designate leave under every law that applies and keep careful track of the employee's leave usage under each law. If an employee's leave is covered by one law and not the other, for example, you'll have to keep records of that fact so you and the employee know how much leave is still available for what purposes.

Do Other Laws Apply?

Americans with Disabilities Act (ADA)

Applies if:

- Employer has at least 15 employees.
- Employee has a disability: a physical or mental impairment that substantially limits one or more major life activities.
- Employee can perform the job's essential functions, with or without a reasonable accommodation.

Overlaps with the FMLA if:

- Employee has a serious health condition that also qualifies as a disability.

If the ADA and the FMLA both apply:

- Employee may be entitled to a reasonable accommodation instead of, or upon returning from, leave.
- Employee is entitled to take FMLA leave, if eligible, rather than accept a reasonable accommodation "light duty" position.
- Employee may be entitled to more leave than the FMLA requires as a reasonable accommodation.

Consolidated Omnibus Budget Reconciliation Act (COBRA)

Applies if:

- Employer has at least 20 employees.
- Employee receives benefits from employer's group health plan.
- Employee has a qualifying event that would otherwise end health coverage.

Overlaps with the FMLA if:

- Employee does not return from FMLA leave for any reason.
- Employee returns from FMLA leave to a position that does not offer health benefits.

If COBRA and the FMLA both apply:

- Employee (and/or employee's dependents, if covered by employer's group health plan) may receive continued benefits for 18 to 36 months, but must pay the entire premium.

Do Other Laws Apply? (continued)

Title VII

Applies if:

- Employer has at least 15 employees.

Overlaps with the FMLA if:

- Employer makes FMLA decisions on the basis of race, religion, or other protected characteristics.
- Employer treats men and women differently in administering the FMLA.
- Employer treats pregnancy leave different than other types of FMLA leave.

Uniformed Services Employment and Reemployment Rights Act (USERRA)

Applies if:

- Employee needs or takes leave to serve in the Armed Forces.

If USERRA and the FMLA both apply:

- Time the employee spends on military leave protected by USERRA counts as months and hours worked for the employer, for purposes of calculating employee's eligibility for FMLA leave.

State Family and Medical Leave Laws

Apply if:

- Employer meets the coverage requirements of the state law: Some apply to smaller employers than the FMLA.
- Employee meets the eligibility requirements of the state law: Some require less time-in-service for eligibility.
- Employee is taking leave for a reason covered by the state law: Some allow leave for a wider variety of family members or for different conditions from the FMLA.

Overlap with the FMLA if:

- Employer is covered by both laws, employee is eligible for leave under both laws, and employee is taking leave for a reason covered by both laws.

If a state family and medical leave law and the FMLA both apply:

- Time the employee takes off counts against the employee's leave entitlement under both laws.

Do Other Laws Apply? (continued)

State Workers' Compensation Laws

Apply if:

- Employer is required to carry workers' compensation coverage (almost all are).
- Employee suffers a work-related injury or illness.

Overlap with the FMLA if:

- Employee's work-related injury or illness is also a serious health condition.

If a state worker's compensation law and the FMLA both apply:

- Employee cannot be required to accept a light-duty position; however, employee's workers' compensation benefits may cease if the employee chooses not to work light duty.
- Employee who cannot return from work after FMLA leave may still have some reinstatement rights under the state workers' compensation law.

State Temporary Disability Insurance and Paid Family Leave Programs

Apply if:

- Employee works in California, Hawaii, New Jersey, New York, Rhode Island, or Washington.
- Employer is covered by the program, and employee is eligible for benefits from the program (in all states but Washington).
- Employee is temporarily unable to work due to disability or, in California, New Jersey, or Washington, takes leave for parenting or to care for a seriously ill family member.

Overlap with the FMLA if:

- Employee's temporary disability is also a serious health condition under the FMLA.
- Employee in California, New Jersey, or Washington is taking parenting leave or leave to care for a seriously ill family member that is also covered by the FMLA.

Do Other Laws Apply? (continued)

If a state temporary disability insurance program and the FMLA both apply:

- Time for which the employee is on leave and receiving compensation from the insurance program counts against the employee's FMLA leave entitlement.
- Employee may not be able to fully substitute paid leave, and employer may not be able to require employee to substitute paid leave, for time during which the employee is receiving compensation from the state program. However, employer and employee may agree that employee can use enough paid leave to bring the employee's total compensation to his or her usual salary. (See Chapter 8.)

Record-Keeping Requirements

Why You Should Keep Records.. 315

Keeping Track of Company Workforce FMLA Data... 316

Individual Employee Records.. 316

Medical Records 318

Review by the Department of Labor (DOL).. 321

Now You're Ready! 322

Common Mistakes Regarding Record Keeping—
   And How to Avoid Them.. 322

Chapter Highlights

☆ Keep all FMLA documents and forms organized and readily accessible, for at least three years.

☆ Keeping accurate, organized records will help you:
- track employee hours for FMLA eligibility determinations
- track employee leave time taken and still available
- remember the dates that employees will return to work after leave
- remember when to request recertification of an employee on leave (see Chapter 8)
- show others (including the U.S. Department of Labor) that you have complied with the FMLA
- justify FMLA designations or other decisions, and
- protect confidential medical records.

☆ The three types of records you need to keep under the FMLA are:
- company-wide FMLA data
- individual employee FMLA records, and
- confidential medical records.

B y now, you probably realize that you have to handle a lot of paperwork under the FMLA, what with notices, forms, and so on. While it may seem like a lot to keep track of, you need to keep accurate records calculating employee FMLA eligibility, leave taken, and available leave time. You also need to keep the documents that employees taking FMLA leave are required to give you. Keeping all of these documents together in an organized, easily retrievable manner will make your job much easier as you try to administer employee FMLA leaves and will help you stay out of legal trouble, too.

In this chapter, we tell you what documents you need to maintain and give you some suggestions about the best way to keep them. Good document control will ensure that you meet all your obligations under the FMLA. It will also make it easier to respond if an employee ever challenges leave decisions or if a governmental agency conducts an investigation, as you will be able to quickly pull all of the documents that show that you followed the law.

Why You Should Keep Records

If your company is covered by the FMLA, the law requires you to "make, keep, and preserve" detailed records of FMLA leaves taken by employees, including copies of all notices given to, and received from, employees taking leave. Good organization of records is not just the law—it is also a good business practice. Thorough, accurate records help you keep track of how much leave each employee has taken or is eligible for, return dates for employees on leave, and other important information.

Keeping accurate records will also help you avoid or fight legal battles. You may have to show certain documents to the employee, his or her spokesperson, or even to the Department of Labor (DOL) if the agency decides to examine your company's FMLA practices. And, if any employee challenges your company's FMLA practices, you may have to gather certain documents to show that you provided adequate notices, denied leave based on adequate documentation, or treated the employee consistently with company policy and past practice. By putting all such records in separate files for each employee, you will be able to pull the exact document you need in any of these situations.

While the FMLA doesn't insist on a particular form or order for keeping the records, whatever form they are in must be clear and identifiable by date

or pay period. They must be kept for at least three years and readily available for inspection, copying, and transcription by the DOL upon request. Records kept on a computer system have to be available for transcription or copying upon request by the DOL.

TIP

Do a regular checkup. Keeping orderly FMLA records doesn't do you much good if the information is out of date or otherwise inaccurate. Be sure to periodically update the records so that they reflect leave taken by an employee, any changes in employee hours or FMLA status, or any other new data. A good way to do this is to review and update the files at the time of six-month or annual employee reviews.

Keeping Track of Company Workforce FMLA Data

If your company is covered by the FMLA, but none of its employees are eligible for FMLA leave (because, for example, none of them has worked for your company for 12 months), you only need to keep basic payroll data, including:

- payroll records showing that your company is covered by the FMLA
- documents describing employee benefits (whether kept in hard copy or electronic form), and
- documents describing your company's paid and unpaid leave policies (whether kept in hard copy or electronic form).

Keep all of these company workforce records together for easy review. These records can be kept in your company's usual human resources area. The manager in charge of FMLA compliance should be tasked with controlling, updating, and maintaining of these records.

Individual Employee Records

If your company has employees who are eligible for FMLA leave, you also need to keep records relating to those employees. These records include:

- basic payroll and identifying data for each employee, including:
  - name and address
  - occupation

- rate of pay and terms of compensation
- daily and weekly hours worked per pay period
- additions to or deductions from wages, and
- total compensation paid
- charts showing the dates FMLA leave is taken by each eligible employee (for example, from time records or requests for leave)
- charts of FMLA leave time available to each employee
- for FMLA leave of less than a full day, records of the hours of leave taken
- copies of notices of the need for FMLA leave given by each employee, if in writing
- copies of all general, eligibility, rights and responsibilities, and designation notices given by your company to each employee taking FMLA leave
- records confirming a family relationship, for employees who take leave for parenting or caring for a family member with a serious health condition
- copies of all certification forms for qualifying exigency leave
- records of premium payments for employee benefits
- subsequent notices issued to any employee on leave informing the employee of a change in FMLA information
- status reports received from employees on leave
- records of any dispute between an eligible employee and your company regarding designation of leave as FMLA leave, including:
    - any written statement of the reasons for designation from either your company or the employee
    - any written statements of the reasons for the disagreement from either your company or the employee, and
    - a written statement of how the dispute was resolved
- initial notice to a key employee that he or she might not be reinstated
- final notice to a key employee that reinstatement is denied
- notes, memos, letters, emails, or other documents that refer to the reason for any decision to grant or deny FMLA leave, including designation decisions, and
- confirmation that an employee has elected not to return from leave.

These records should be organized by employee but kept in a file separate and apart from the employee's regular personnel file. Each employee's FMLA file can be kept next to his or her personnel file. The manager in charge of

FMLA compliance should oversee the control, updates, and maintenance of these files, with the assistance of each employee's immediate supervisor.

If your company is a joint employer with another company (see Chapter 2), your record-keeping duties depend on whether your company is the primary or secondary employer. As a primary employer, you have to keep all of the records listed above. As a secondary employer, you have to keep only the basic payroll data listed above.

If your company isn't required to keep overtime or minimum wage records for its FMLA-eligible employees (for example, because thay are exempt employees), you don't have to keep records of actual hours worked, provided that both of the following are true:

- Your company treats any employee employed for at least 12 months as eligible for FMLA leave.
- Your company reaches written agreement with any employee taking intermittent or reduced-schedule leave as to the employee's normal schedule or average hours worked each week.

Under regulations adopted in 2013, special rules apply to airline flight crew employees. In addition to keeping records of hours scheduled for airline flight crew employees, airline employers must maintain records that establish the applicable monthly guarantee for each category of employee covered by the guarantee. These records include relevant collective bargaining agreements or employer policies that establish the monthly guarantee.

> **TIP**
>
> **For the sake of accuracy and convenience, your company should keep records of hours worked by all employees.** This will make it easier for you to track employee FMLA eligibility, intermittent and reduced-schedule leave taken, and FMLA leave available.

Medical Records

When an employee requests FMLA leave for the employee's own serious medical condition, a family member's serious health condition, or a family member's military service-connected serious illness or injury, the employee

has to give you certain documents containing medical information upon request. These medical records or any other documents containing medical information must be treated as confidential and kept in files separate and apart from your company's usual personnel files. Such records include:

- medical certifications
- recertifications
- medical histories of employees or their family members created for FMLA purposes
- fitness-for-duty certifications received from the employee when returning from FMLA leave, and
- second and third opinions you requested to verify a medical need for leave.

And, if the ADA also applies, you must keep the medical records in conformance with ADA confidentiality requirements. Under both the FMLA and the ADA, your company can disclose medical information only in the following circumstances:

- You can inform supervisors and managers of necessary restrictions on an employee's work or duties and any necessary accommodations.
- You can inform first aid and safety personnel if the employee's physical or medical condition might require emergency treatment.
- You must provide the information to government officials upon request.

(42 U.S.C. § 12112(d)(3); 29 C.F.R. § 1630.14(c).)

EXAMPLE: Your employee, Cara, has disclosed to you that she is HIV-positive and needs to take intermittent leave to attend medical appointments. One of your company's managers later asks you if you have noticed that Cara seems thin and listless. You tell the manager privately that Cara is ill but "doesn't have full-blown AIDS," so you hope she will be able to get treatment for her condition. You figure that a fellow manager who has expressed concern for an employee may be told about the employee's condition, as long as it is done privately. Have you acted lawfully?

Unfortunately, no. Cara's diagnosis is confidential medical information. You cannot disclose confidential medical information just because a manager is genuinely concerned, unless the manager needs to know because of restrictions on the employee's ability to work or the manager is a first aid provider at the worksite and the employee's condition may require emergency care.

CAUTION

The ADA's confidentiality rule applies to employee medical records even if the employee is not disabled. All employee medical records should be treated as confidential, regardless of whether or not the employee has a disability as defined by the ADA (see Chapter 12).

The confidentiality of employee medical records is also protected by the Health Insurance Portability and Accountability Act (HIPAA). (42 U.S.C. § 1320d.) In general, HIPAA bars an employer from discussing an employee's medical condition with the employee's health care provider unless the employee has consented to the discussion. There are exceptions to this general rule when health care is provided to the employee at the employer's request (for example, where the health care provider is retained by the employer in connection with the employer's medical benefits for employees).

You may need to ask for certain medical information covered by HIPAA in order to determine if a leave request is FMLA-qualified. You can ask the employee to complete an incomplete medical certification or for a second opinion from a health care provider, and you may contact the health care provider in certain circumstances. (See Chapter 9 for a full discussion of how you can legally verify the medical reason for the leave.)

The 2010 amendments to the FMLA and regulations adopted in 2013 by the Department of Labor require your company to comply with the Genetic Information Nondiscrimination Act ("GINA"). Under GINA, all employers must treat any records that contain "family medical history" or "genetic information" as confidential, including records related to FMLA leave. An employer is allowed to disclose employee and/or family member genetic information in a manner that is consistent with the requirements of the FMLA.

RESOURCE

Learn more about GINA. GINA prohibits employers with 15 or more employees from discriminating against employees and applicants on the basis of genetic information. You can find a discussion of GINA and how to avoid violating the genetic discrimination law in *The Essential Guide to Handling Workplace Harassment & Discrimination*, by Deborah C. England (Nolo).

SEE AN EXPERT

Get some record-keeping help. Consult an attorney with expertise in the ADA, HIPAA, and state medical records confidentiality laws to find out how you must handle employee medical records under these laws, as well as under the FMLA.

Review by the Department of Labor (DOL)

Another important reason to keep accurate records of FMLA leaves is because you may have to show these records to the DOL. You don't have to submit records to the DOL unless the DOL requests them. The DOL can ask to examine your company's FMLA records only once in a 12-month period, unless it suspects that the company may have violated the FMLA. DOL investigations occur in two circumstances:

- **Employee complaints.** Most frequently, DOL investigations are triggered by employee complaints, which the agency keeps confidential. The DOL won't tell you the name of the complaining employee, the nature of the complaint, or even if a complaint was made.
- **Industry investigations.** The DOL also selects certain types of businesses or industries to investigate because the agency believes there is a high rate of FMLA violations in the business or industry (for example, in industries that employ a high percentage of employees who don't speak English or have a lot of younger workers).

In a typical investigation, the DOL will do the following:

- **Examine the records listed above.** Even if investigating just a single complaint, the DOL may look at all your records. It may also take notes about, make transcriptions of, or make photocopies of the documents reviewed.
- **Interview certain employees.** Usually, these interviews will happen on company premises, but not always. The purpose of these interviews will be to verify the information in the records you presented and to confirm employees' particular hours.
- **Meet with your company representative.** The DOL will meet with someone with authority to make decisions and commit your company to corrective actions (for example, your FMLA compliance manager, if that person has such authority, or a company officer) if a violation is found.

Your company may (and probably should) be represented by an attorney during the investigation. And, after a finding is made, your company has the opportunity to present additional facts to the DOL for consideration. The DOL won't reveal information from your company's records to any unauthorized person.

Now You're Ready!

Congratulations! You've educated yourself on what the FMLA requires of your company and what it offers your employees. You have all of the tools you need to assess, administer, and track FMLA leave requests and time off, including forms, charts, posters, and sample policies. Now you and your employees can move forward together with the goal of keeping your workplace family-friendly, healthy, and operating smoothly.

Common Mistakes Regarding Record Keeping—And How to Avoid Them

Mistake 1: **Losing track of the amount of FMLA-protected leave time an employee has available.**

Avoid this mistake by taking the following steps:

- Keep the payroll and leave records listed in this chapter organized and readily accessible.
- Consult those records whenever an employee requests FMLA leave.
- Update the information in the records periodically (for example, at the time of each employee's annual review).

Mistake 2: **Granting (or denying) an employee's requests for intermittent leave because you have lost track of how much leave the employee has already taken and when.**

Avoid this mistake by taking the following steps:

- Keep hourly or daily payroll and leave records for employees taking intermittent or reduced-schedule leave, depending on how the leave time is taken.

- Keep an updated intermittent or reduced-schedule leave chart for each employee taking such leave, including a running total of leave time taken and when (see Appendix C for a sample).

Mistake 3: Improperly disclosing confidential employee medical information.
Avoid this mistake by taking the following steps:

- Keep each employee's medical information in a separate file (not in the employee's personnel or FMLA file).
- Reveal medical information only when allowed by the law.

Managers' Checklist: Record Keeping

☐ I have collected all FMLA forms and documents for the employee and have put the documents into a file separate from the employee's personnel file, including:

    ☐ payroll records (showing FMLA eligibility or noneligibility)

    ☐ charts showing FMLA leave time taken and FMLA leave time available (for intermittent or reduced-schedule leave, in hours or days, depending on how the leave was taken)

    ☐ general, eligibility, rights and responsibilities, and designation notices provided to the employee

    ☐ notices and other documents provided by the employee, and

    ☐ periodic reports of employee status while on leave.

☐ I have kept a chart showing the running total in hours or days (depending on how the leave was taken) of intermittent or reduced-schedule FMLA leave time taken by the employee taking such leave.

☐ I have kept all employee (or employee family member) medical information in separate files.

☐ I have treated medical records and the information in them as confidential, barring others from gaining access to them except supervisors and managers to provide necessary accommodations or first aid personnel if a condition might require emergency medical treatment.

Glossary

Adoption. The legal process of transferring the rights and responsibilities of a child's biological parents to persons other than the child's biological parents.

Alternative position. A position to which an eligible employee may be temporarily reassigned during a period of intermittent or reduced-schedule leave for planned medical treatment; it must have the same pay and benefits as the employee's original position.

Americans with Disabilities Act (ADA). A federal law that prohibits discrimination against qualified employees with disabilities and requires employers to make reasonable accommodations to allow such employees to do their jobs.

Cafeteria plan. A benefit program through which employees choose from a menu of benefits, such as health coverage, life insurance, disability insurance, and so on.

Certification. A document, to be completed by the employee, a health care provider, or both, verifying certain facts about an employee's need to take leave for a serious health condition, military caregiver leave, or qualifying exigency leave.

Chronic serious health condition. A serious health condition that requires periodic visits for treatment (at least twice per year); continues over an extended period of time; and may cause episodic, rather than continuing, incapacity.

Consolidated Omnibus Budget Reconciliation Act (COBRA). A federal law that requires employers to provide continued coverage under a group health plan to employees and their dependents after an event that would otherwise terminate their coverage.

Contingency operation. A military operation that:
- the secretary of defense has designated as an operation in which members of the armed forces are or may become involved in

military actions, operations, or hostilities against an enemy of the United States or an opposing military force, or

- results in the call or order to, or retention on, active duty of members of the uniformed services pursuant to particular sections of the United States code or any other provision of law during a war or national emergency declared by the president or Congress.

Continuing treatment. At least two treatments by a health care provider, a nurse or physician assistant acting under the direct supervision of a health care provider, or a provider of health care services acting on the orders of, or referral by, a health care provider; or at least one treatment by a health care provider that results in a regimen of continuing treatment under the provider's supervision. In either case, the employee's first (or only) visit to the health care provider must take place within seven days of the onset of incapacity; if an employee is not under a continuing regimen of treatment, the employee's two visits to the health care provider must occur within 30 days of the onset of incapacity.

Covered active duty. The type of military duty for which a family member may take qualifying exigency leave, covered active duty is military duty as a member of the National Guard, Reserves, regular Armed Forces, or, in some circumstances, a retired member of the regular Armed Forces or Reserve, during deployment to a foreign country. For those in the Guard or Reserves only, the servicemember must be serving or called to serve in support of a contingency operation and pursuant to a federal call or order to active duty.

Covered veteran. Someone who was discharged or released from military service under conditions other than dishonorable within five years before the first date the employee takes FMLA leave to care for that veteran (not including the time between October 28, 2009 and March 8, 2013).

Department of Labor. The federal agency responsible for administering and enforcing the FMLA.

Designation notice. A form you must give the employee, stating that time off will be treated as FMLA leave (among other things).

Discriminate. To treat similarly situated employees differently.

Domestic partners. An unmarried couple granted certain of the rights and privileges enjoyed by married couples by the laws of the state in which they reside.

Eligibility notice. A notice you must provide to the employee, within five business days after learning that the employee needs FMLA leave, indicating whether the employee is eligible for FMLA leave and, if not, providing at least one reason why the employee is not eligible.

Employee with a disability. An employee who has a long-term physical or mental impairment that substantially limits a major life activity, has a history of such an impairment, or is perceived by the employer as having such an impairment.

Equivalent position. A position that is virtually identical to the position an employee held prior to taking FMLA leave, with equivalent pay, benefits, and other terms and conditions of employment to the employee's former job.

Essential job functions. The fundamental duties of a position: those things that the person holding the job absolutely must be able to do.

Exempt employee. An employee who is not entitled to extra pay for overtime hours worked under the Fair Labor Standards Act ("FLSA").

Family member. A spouse, child, or parent. For purposes of military caregiver or qualifying exigency leave, adult children are included; for all other types of FMLA leave, only children who are under the age of 18 or are at least 18 and incapable of self-care due to a physical or mental disability are covered. For purposes of military caregiver leave only, next of kin are also family members.

Fitness-for-duty certification. A signed statement from a health care provider indicating that an employee is able to return to work following FMLA leave; you may require that the fitness-for-duty certification address the employee's ability to perform the essential job functions.

Flexible savings account (FSA). An account into which employees may set aside pretax income for medical expenses not paid by health insurance (such as co-payments, premiums, and expenses that are outside of the employer's plan) or for dependent care expenses.

Foreseeable need for leave. A reason for taking FMLA leave that is anticipated or known in advance, such as planned medical treatment or the birth or adoption of a child.

Foster placement. The legal process of awarding the care, comfort, education, and upbringing of a child to someone other than the child's biological parents.

Full-time employee. An employee working 40 hours per week or more.

Group health plan. Any plan of, or contributed to by, an employer to provide health care to employees, former employees, and their families, including self-insured plans, vision plans, dental plans, and other health care plans, whether they are components of a single health care plan or administered separately.

Health care provider. A medical doctor, doctor of osteopathy, podiatrist, dentist, optometrist, chiropractor (only for manual manipulation of the spine to treat a subluxation of the spine—that is, misalignment of vertebrae—identified by X-ray), physician assistant, clinical psychologist, nurse practitioner, nurse midwife, clinical social worker, Christian Science practitioner, or other provider from whom the employer will accept medical certification for purposes of substantiating a claim for health care benefits.

In loco parentis. In the place of a parent. This refers to someone who takes or intends to take on a parental role for a child by providing day-to-day care or financial support.

Incapacity. Inability to work, attend school, or perform other regular daily activities due to a serious health condition, treatment for the condition, or recovery from the condition.

Independent contractor. A person who contracts to perform services for another person or company but does not have the status of an employee; a freelancer or consultant.

Inpatient care. Care that involves an overnight stay at a hospital, hospice, or residential medical care facility.

Integrated employers. Companies that have common management, interrelation between operations, centralized control of labor relations, and common ownership or financial control.

Intermittent leave. FMLA leave taken in separate blocks of time for a single qualifying reason, such as a course of treatment spread over months or flare-ups of a chronic illness.

Joint employer. A company that shares control with another company over the working conditions of the other company's employees.

Key employee. A salaried employee among the highest-paid 10% of the company's employees working within 75 miles of the employee's worksite.

Leave year. The 12-month period during which an eligible employee is entitled to 12 weeks of FMLA leave (or 26 weeks, for military caregiver leave).

Light duty. Work that is less demanding (physically, mentally, or because it requires fewer hours of work) than an employee's usual position, due to an employee's medical restrictions.

Military caregiver leave. Leave to care for a family member who suffers or aggravates a serious illness or injury in the line of duty on active duty.

Moonlighting. Working for another employer while on leave.

Multiemployer health plan. A health plan established pursuant to a collective bargaining agreement, into which at least two employers make contributions.

Next of kin. For purposes of military caregiver leave, an employee is "next of kin" to a covered servicemember if the employee is a blood relative and the servicemember has so designated the employee for purposes of military caregiver leave. If the servicemember has not designated anyone next of kin, the nearest blood relative is next of kin, in the following order or priority: (1) blood relatives who have been granted legal custody of the servicemember; (2) siblings; (3) grandparents; (4) aunts and uncles; and (5) first cousins.

Overtime. Hours worked over and above 40 hours in a week (or eight hours in a day, in some states) and requiring premium pay under the FLSA.

Parenting leave. Leave following birth, adoption, or foster placement, including time to bond with a new child.

Part-time employee. An employee working fewer than 40 hours per week.

Pregnancy disability. Disability due to pregnancy, childbirth, or related conditions.

Primary employer. A joint employer that has authority to hire and fire the employee seeking leave, place the employee in a particular position, assign work to the employee, make payroll, and provide employment benefits.

Qualified employee with a disability. An employee with a disability who can perform the job's essential functions, with or without a reasonable accommodation.

Qualifying exigency leave: Leave taken to handle the following matters when a family member is on covered active duty or called to covered active duty in the military:

- short-notice deployment
- military events and related activities
- child care and school activities
- financial and legal arrangements
- counseling
- rest and recuperation
- postdeployment activities, and
- parental care.

Reasonable accommodation. Assistance (technological or otherwise) or change to the workplace or job that allows the employee to perform the essential functions of the job.

Recertification. A subsequent certification of a serious health condition.

Reduced-schedule leave. FMLA leave taken by working fewer hours per day or fewer days per week than usual.

Regulations. Interpretations of a law written by the federal agency responsible for its enforcement and administration. The FMLA regulations are issued by the federal Department of Labor.

Reinstatement. Restoration of an employee to his or her original position or an equivalent position when the employee returns from leave.

Rights and responsibilities notice. A notice you must give to the employee, setting out the employee's FMLA rights and obligations.

Salaried employee. An employee earning the same amount each week, regardless of how many hours the employee works or the quality or quantity of work performed. To be salaried, the employee must earn at least $455 per week.

Second opinion. A second certification of a serious health condition, from a health care provider of the employer's choosing.

Secondary employer. A joint employer that does not have the authority to hire and fire the employee seeking leave, place the employee in a particular position, assign work to the employee, make payroll, or provide employment benefits.

Serious health condition. An illness, injury, impairment, or physical or mental condition that involves (1) inpatient care at a hospital, hospice, or residential medical care facility; (2) incapacity for more than three full days with continuing treatment by a health care provider; (3) incapacity due to pregnancy or prenatal care; (4) incapacity or treatment for a chronic serious health condition; (5) permanent or long-term incapacity for a condition for which treatment may not be effective (such as a terminal illness); or (6) absence for multiple treatments for either restorative surgery following an injury or accident or a condition that would require an absence of more than three days if not treated.

Serious illness or injury. For purposes of military caregiver leave, a serious illness or injury is one that may render a current servicemember unfit to perform the duties of his or her office, grade, rank, or rating, and for which the servicemember is undergoing medical treatment, recuperation, or therapy; is otherwise in outpatient status; or is on the temporary disability retired list. For a veteran, a serious illness or injury is (1) a continuation of a serious illness or injury (as defined above) incurred or aggravated when the veteran was in the military, which rendered the veteran unable to perform the duties of his or her office, grade, rank, or rating; (2) a physical or mental condition for which the veteran has received a Veterans Affairs Service Related Disability Rating (VASRD) of 50 percent or greater, at least in part because the condition requires caregiver leave; (3) a physical or mental condition that substantially impairs the veteran's ability to get or maintain a substantially gainful occupation due to a service-related disability (or would create such an impairment without treatment); or (4) an injury (including a psychological injury) for which the veteran has been enrolled in the Department of Veterans Affairs Program of Comprehensive Assistance for Family Caregivers. A serious illness or injury must either be incurred or aggravated in the line of duty.

Spouses. A couple whose marriage was valid in the state where it took place.

Status report. An employee's report to the employer, while on FMLA leave, on his or her status and intent to return to work.

Substitution of paid leave. Using accrued paid leave provided by the employer's policies during FMLA leave.

Temporary disability insurance. A state insurance program that provides partial wage replacement while an employee is unable to work due to a temporary disability, including pregnancy.

Termination. End of employment by any means other than resignation, retirement, or disability.

Third opinion. A third certification of a serious health condition, from a health care provider chosen jointly by the employer and the employee, which breaks the tie when the first and second medical certifications conflict as to whether there is a serious health condition.

Title VII. The federal law that prohibits discrimination in employment on the basis race, color, national origin, sex (including pregnancy), and religion.

Undue hardship. A reasonable accommodation that would cause significant difficulty or expense, considering the nature and cost of the accommodation, the size and financial resources of the business and the facility where the employee works, the structure of the business, and the effect the accommodation would have on the business.

Unforeseeable need for leave. A reason for FMLA leave that is not known in advance, such as injuries caused by an accident, a sudden illness, premature birth, or another medical emergency.

Uniformed Services Employment and Reemployment Rights Act (USERRA). A federal law that provides certain job protections to members of the uniformed services, including the right to take leave for military service.

Workers' compensation. An insurance program run by the states, which provides wage replacement, reimbursement for medical bills, and other benefits to employees who suffer work-related injuries or illnesses.

Worksite. The company location where an employee works, which may include a "campus" of buildings grouped together or unconnected buildings used by a company within a reasonable geographic vicinity (for example, within the city limits).

State Laws and Departments of Labor

California 336

Colorado 339

Connecticut 341

District of Columbia 343

Florida 345

Hawaii 346

Illinois 348

Indiana 350

Iowa 351

Kansas 352

Kentucky 353

Louisiana 354

Maine 355

Maryland 357

Massachusetts 358

Minnesota 360

Montana 361

Nebraska 362

Nevada 363

New Hampshire 364

New Jersey 365

New Mexico 367

New York 368

North Carolina 369

Ohio 370

Oregon 371

Rhode Island.. 373

Tennessee... 375

Vermont... 376

Washington... 377

Wisconsin.. 379

State Departments of Labor 380

This appendix summarizes basic information about each state's family and medical leave laws. We have included only laws that apply to private employers; laws that apply to government employers are not listed here. If your state is not included, it has no applicable leave laws as of 2014.

We have not included all state leave laws, only those that provide for family and medical leave. For example, we have not included state laws that require employers to give leave for military service, jury duty, or voting.

The following categories of laws are included (each is explained in more detail in Chapter 12):

- **Family and medical leave laws.** These laws provide leave similar to the FMLA, such as leave for the employee's own serious health condition, leave to care for a seriously ill family member, and parental leave.
- **Military family leave laws.** These laws allow employees to take time off when certain family members are called to serve in the military.
- **Pregnancy disability leave laws.** These laws provide leave when a woman is disabled by pregnancy, childbirth, and related conditions.
- **Adoption leave laws.** These laws provide leave for adoption, generally by requiring employers who offer leave for childbirth to make the same leave available to adoptive parents.
- **Small necessities laws.** These laws provide leave for activities relating to a child's school and/or to take a child or elderly relative to routine medical and dental appointments.
- **Domestic violence leave laws.** These laws provide leave for an employee who has been, or whose family member has been, a victim of domestic violence.

We provide some basic information on each law, including which employers are covered, which employees are eligible for leave, how much leave must be provided, and for what purposes. We have not included every detail about every law such as what constitutes a "serious health condition" under the state's rules, what a medical certification must include, whether employers have posting or record-keeping requirements, and so on. To find out more about your state's laws, including information on recently passed laws, contact your state's department of labor (contact information is at the end of this appendix). If you have any questions about how the FMLA interacts with your state's laws, consult with an experienced employment lawyer.

California

Family and Medical Leave (Cal. Gov't. Code § 12945.2)

Covered Employers: Employers with at least 50 employees.

Eligible Employees: Employees who have worked for at least one year and at least 1,250 hours in the 12 months preceding leave.

Types of Leave: For the birth, adoption, or foster placement of a child; for the employee's own serious health condition; or to care for a family member with a serious health condition. Disability for pregnancy, childbirth, and related conditions is not covered. If both parents work for the same employer, they may be limited to a total of 12 weeks of leave for the birth, adoption, or foster placement of a child.

Amount of Leave: 12 weeks in a 12-month period.

Family Members: Same as FMLA, plus domestic partners and children of domestic partners.

Paid Sick Leave (Cal. Lab. Code §§ 245–249)

Covered Employers: All employers.

Eligible Employees: Employees who have worked at least 30 days in a year since beginning employment.

Types of Leave: Employees may use paid sick leave:
- for preventive care for the employee or a family member
- for the diagnosis, treatment, or care of an existing health condition of the employee or a family member, or
- for specified purposes if the employee is a victim of domestic violence, stalking, or sexual assault.

Amount of Leave: Starting on July 1, 2015, employees accrue one hour of paid sick leave for every 30 hours worked, subject to a cap of 48 hours or six days. Employers may limit the amount of leave an employee may use in one year to 24 hours or three days. Employees may begin using paid sick leave after 90 days of employment.

Family Members: Parents, children, spouse, registered domestic partner, grandparents, grandchildren, and siblings.

Military Family Leave (Cal. Mil. & Vets. Code § 395.10)

Covered Employers: Employers with at least 25 employees.

Eligible Employees: Employees who work an average of 20 or more hours per week.

Reasons for Leave: While a spouse is on leave from deployment during a period of military conflict; the spouse must be a member of the National Guard or Reserves who has been deployed during a period of military conflict, or a member of the U.S. Armed Forces who has been deployed during a period of military conflict to an area that the president has designated as a combat theater or combat zone.

Amount of Leave: Up to ten days of unpaid leave in a qualified leave period (the time during which the spouse is on leave from deployment during a period of military conflict).

Pregnancy Disability Leave (Cal. Govt. Code § 12945)

Covered Employers: Employers with at least five employees.

Eligible Employees: All employees of covered employers.

Reasons for Leave: Disability relating to pregnancy, childbirth, or related conditions.

Amount of Leave: A reasonable period, not to exceed four months.

Small Necessities Law (Cal. Lab. Code § 230.8)

Covered Employers: Employers with at least 25 employees.

Eligible Employees: All employees of covered employers.

Reasons for Leave: To participate in activities at the child's school or day care.

Amount of Leave: Forty hours of unpaid leave in any 12-month period, not to exceed eight hours in a single month. If both parents work for the same employer, employer may prohibit them from using this leave at the same time.

Domestic Violence Leave (Cal. Lab. Code §§ 230 & 230.1)

Covered Employers: All employers; employers with at least 25 employees must provide leave for a broader set of reasons.

Eligible Employees: Any employee who is the victim of sexual assault or domestic violence.

Reasons for Leave
- **All Employers:** For the employee to obtain a restraining order or seek other judicial relief for the employee or his or her child.
- **Employers With 25 Employees:** For the employee to:
  - seek medical treatment
  - obtain services from a rape crisis center or domestic violence shelter or program
  - get counseling, or
  - engage in safety planning and/or relocate.

Amount of Leave: None stated. The law does not create a right to leave beyond that provided in the FMLA.

Temporary Disability Insurance

California has a state temporary disability insurance program, funded by withholdings from employees' paychecks. Eligible employees who are unable to work due to a temporarily disability (including pregnancy) can receive up to 55% of their usual wages. For more information, go to the state's website, www.edd.ca.gov/Disability.

Paid Family Leave

California's temporary disability insurance program also funds paid family leave. Eligible employees may collect the same benefits available for a temporary disability for up to six weeks in order to care for a seriously ill parent, spouse, domestic partner, or child, or to bond with a new child. For more information, go to the state's website, www.edd.ca.gov/Disability.

Colorado

Family and Medical Leave (Col. Rev. Stat. § 18-13.3-203)

Covered Employers: Employers covered by the FMLA.

Eligible Employees: Employees who are eligible under the FMLA.

Reasons for Leave: To care for a domestic partner or a partner in a civil union who has a serious health condition.

Amount of Leave: Same as allowed by the FMLA.

Family Members: Domestic partners or partners in a civil union. Same-sex spouses who were legally married in a state that recognizes same-sex marriage qualify as partners in a civil union under Colorado law.

Domestic Violence Leave (Col. Rev. Stat. § 24-34-402.7)

Covered Employers: Employers with at least 50 employees.

Eligible Employees: Employees who have worked at least 12 months and have been the victim of domestic violence, sexual assault, domestic abuse, or stalking.

Reasons for Leave: For the employee to:
- seek medical treatment or counseling for the employee or his or her children
- seek a civil protection order
- seek new housing or make an existing home secure, or
- seek legal assistance or attend court-related proceedings.

Amount of Leave: Three days in a 12-month period.

Adoption Leave (Col. Rev. Stat. § 19-5-211)

Covered Employers: All employers.

Eligible Employees: All employees.

Leave Provided: Employer that provides parental leave following the birth of a biological child must make the same amount of leave available to adoptive parents. This requirement does not apply to stepparent adoptions.

Small Necessities Law (Col. Rev. Stat. §§ 8-13.3-101–104)

Covered Employers: Employers with at least 50 employees.

Eligible Employees: All employees of covered employees.

Reasons for Leave: To attend academic activities for or with the employee's child.

Amount of Leave: 18 hours of unpaid leave in any school year, not to exceed six hours per month.

Note: This provision is scheduled for repeal on September 1, 2015.

Connecticut

Paid Sick Leave for Service Workers (Conn. Gen. Stat. §§ 31-57r and following)

Covered Employers: Employers with at least 50 employees.

Eligible Employees: All service workers employed by covered employers. Service workers include nurses, restaurant and hotel staff, security guards, retail clerks, and many other job classifications, as listed in the law.

Reasons for Leave: Employees may use paid sick leave:

- for preventive medical care or for their own injury, illness, or health condition
- for the preventive medical care or the injury, illness, or health condition of a spouse or child, or
- to handle matters arising from domestic violence or sexual assault, including medical care, counseling, relocating, obtaining services from a victims' services group, or attending legal proceedings.

Amount of Leave: Employees are entitled to accrue one hour of paid sick leave for every 40 hours worked, up to 40 hours of paid sick leave per year.

Family and Medical Leave (Conn. Gen. Stat. §§ 31-51kk to 31-51qq)

Covered Employers: Employers with at least 75 employees, to be determined annually on October 1.

Eligible Employees: Employees who have worked for at least one year and at least 1,000 hours in the 12 months preceding leave.

Reasons for Leave: For the birth, adoption, or foster placement of a child; for the employee's own serious health condition; to care for a family member with a serious health condition; or for organ or bone marrow donation.

Amount of Leave: 16 weeks in any 24-month period. The 24-month period begins on the first day of an employee's leave. Spouses who work for the same employer are entitled to a total of 16 weeks for the birth, adoption, or foster placement of a child and to care for a parent with a serious health condition.

Family Members: Same as FMLA, plus parents-in-law, domestic partners, and domestic partners' children.

Military Family Leave (Conn. Gen. Stat. § 31-51ll)

Covered Employers: Employers with at least 75 employees.

Eligible Employees: Employees who have worked for at least one year and at least 1,000 hours in the 12 months preceding leave.

Reasons for Leave: To care for a spouse, child, parent, or next of kin who is a current member of the Armed Forces and incurred a serious illness or injury in the line of duty.

Amount of Leave: 26 weeks in a single 12-month period. Like the FMLA, state law provides a per-servicemember, per-injury leave entitlement.

Pregnancy Disability Leave (Conn. Gen. Stat. § 46a-60(a)(7))

Covered Employers: Employers with at least three employees.

Eligible Employees: All employees of covered employers.

Reasons for Leave: Disability relating to pregnancy, childbirth, or related conditions.

Amount of Leave: A "reasonable" leave of absence.

Reinstatement: Employee is entitled to be restored to the same or an equivalent position, unless the employer's circumstances have so changed as to make this impossible or unreasonable.

Domestic Violence Leave (Conn. Gen. Stat. § 31-51ss)

Covered Employers: Employers with at least three employees.

Eligible Employees: All employees of covered employers.

Reasons for Leave: Employees who are victims of family violence may take leave to:
- seek medical care or psychological or other counseling
- obtain services from a victim assistance organization
- relocate, or
- participate in civil or criminal proceedings.

Amount of Leave: Up to 12 days of unpaid leave per calendar year. Employees may also use accrued paid leave during this time off, including compensatory time, vacation time, personal days, and so on.

District of Columbia

Family and Medical Leave (D.C. Code §§ 32-501 and following)

Covered Employers: Employers with at least 20 employees.

Eligible Employees: Employees who have worked for at least one year and at least 1,000 hours in the previous 12 months.

Types of Leave

- **Family Leave:** For the birth, adoption, or foster placement of a child; for the permanent placement of a child for whom the employee permanently assumes and discharges parental responsibility; or to care for a family member with a serious health condition.
- **Medical Leave:** For the employee's own serious health condition.

Amount of Leave: Sixteen weeks of family leave plus 16 weeks of medical leave in any 24-month period. Leave for birth, adoption, or placement of a child must be taken within 12 months of child's arrival. If two family members work for the same employer, they can be limited to a total of 16 weeks of family leave and can take no more than four weeks of such leave at the same time.

Family Members: Same as FMLA, plus anyone related by blood, custody, or marriage, and anyone sharing the employee's residence with whom the employee has a committed relationship.

Paid Sick, Family, and Domestic Violence Leave (D.C. Code §§ 32-131.01 and following)

Covered Employers: All, but leave depends on size.

Eligible Employees: Employees who have worked at least one year for the employer without a break and at least 1,000 hours in the past 12 months.

Reasons for Leave: For the employee's or family member's physical or mental illness, injury, or medical condition; for the employee's or family member's medical care, diagnosis, or preventive medical care; for employee or family member who is a victim of stalking, domestic violence, or abuse to get medical attention, utilize services, seek counseling, relocate, take legal action, or take steps to enhance health and safety.

Amount of Leave:

- Employers with 100 or more employees must provide at least one hour of paid leave for every 37 hours worked, up to seven days of leave per year.
- Employers with 25 to 99 employees must provide at least one hour of paid leave for every 43 hours worked, up to five days of leave per year.
- Employers with fewer than 25 employees must provide at least one hour of paid leave for every 87 hours worked, up to three days of leave per year.

Family Members: Same as the FMLA plus domestic partners, parents-in-law, grandchildren, children's spouses, siblings, siblings' spouses, a child who lives with the employee and whom the employee has responsibility for, and a person with whom the employee shares a mutual residence and committed relationship.

Small Necessities Law (D.C. Code §§ 32-1201 and following)

Covered Employers: All employers.

Eligible Employees: Employees who have worked for the employer for at least 12 months.

Reasons for Leave: To participate in school-related events, including activities sponsored by either a school or an associated organization such as a parent-teacher association. Activities may include meetings with a teacher or counselor as well as student performances and sports activities in which the employee is a participant, not merely a spectator. Employer may deny a request for leave only if it would disrupt the employer's business and make the achievement of production or service delivery unusually difficult.

Family Members: Those who may take leave include not only parents, guardians, and stepparents, but also a child's aunts, uncles, and grandparents.

Amount of Leave: Twenty-four hours of unpaid leave in any 12-month period.

Florida

Domestic Violence Leave (Fla. Stat. § 741.313)

Covered Employers: Employers with 50 or more employees.

Eligible Employees: Employees who have been employed for at least three months and are victims of domestic or sexual violence, or who have a family or household member who is a victim of domestic or sexual violence.

Reasons for Leave: Leave is allowed to:

- seek an injunction
- get medical care or counseling
- get services from a victims' rights group, shelter, or rape crisis center
- relocate or make the home more secure, or
- seek legal assistance.

Amount of Leave: Up to three days of leave in a 12-month period. Leave may be paid or unpaid, at the employer's discretion.

Hawaii

Family and Medical Leave (Haw. Rev. Stat. §§ 398-1 to 398-11)

Covered Employers: Employers with at least 100 employees.

Eligible Employees: Employees who have worked for at least six consecutive months.

Types of Leave: Employee may take leave to care for a family member with a serious health condition or to care for a newly born or adopted child. Leave is not provided for employee's own serious health condition. Leave for a new child must be taken within a year of the child's birth or adoption.

Amount of Leave: Four weeks in any calendar year. Spouses who work for the same employer do not have to combine leave; each is entitled to four weeks.

Family Members: Same family members as FMLA, plus parents-in-law, grandparents, grandparents-in-law, and reciprocal beneficiaries.

Pregnancy Disability Leave (Haw. Admin. Rules § 12-46-108)

Covered Employers: All employers.

Eligible Employees: All employees.

Types of Leave: Employees may take leave while they are disabled due to pregnancy, childbirth, and related conditions.

Amount of Leave: A "reasonable" period of leave, as determined by the employee's physician.

Domestic Violence Leave (Haw. Rev. Stat. §§ 378-71 to 378-74)

Covered Employers: Employers with at least 50 employees.

Eligible Employees: Any employee who has worked at least six consecutive months and who is—or whose minor child is—a victim of domestic abuse, sexual assault, or stalking.

Reasons for Leave: Leave is allowed to:
- seek medical attention
- obtain victim services
- get counseling
- temporarily or permanently relocate, or
- take legal action.

Amount of Leave: A "reasonable period," up to 30 days in a calendar year if the employer has at least 50 employees, or up to five days for smaller employers.

Temporary Disability Insurance (TDI)

Hawaii has a state temporary disability insurance program. Eligible employees who are unable to work due to a temporarily disability (including pregnancy) can receive compensation. Employers may self-insure by adopting a particular type of sick/disability leave program. For detailed information, go to the state's TDI website, www.labor.hawaii.gov/dcd.

Illinois

Military Family Leave (820 Ill. Comp. Stat. §§ 151/1 and following)

Covered Employers: Employers with at least 15 employees.

Eligible Employees: Employees who have worked for the employer for at least 12 months, and at least 1,250 hours in the past 12 months; and are the spouse or parent of someone who has been called to military service lasting longer than 30 days with the state or the U.S., pursuant to an order of the governor or president.

Reasons for Leave: To spend time with a spouse or child while that person's federal or state deployment orders are in effect.

Amount of Leave:

- Employers with at least 50 employees must provide up to 30 days of unpaid leave.
- Employers with 15 to 49 employees must provide up to 15 days of unpaid leave.

Small Necessities Law (820 Ill. Comp. Stat. §§ 147/1 and following)

Covered Employers: Employers with at least 50 employees.

Eligible Employees: Employees who have worked for at least six consecutive months immediately preceding the leave request, and for at least as many hours per week, on average, as one-half of a full-time position.

Reasons for Leave: To attend school conferences or classroom activities relating to their children if they cannot be rescheduled during nonwork hours.

Amount of Leave: Eight hours of unpaid leave in any school year, with no more than four hours in one day.

Domestic Violence Leave (820 Ill. Comp. Stat. §§ 180/1 and following)

Covered Employers: Employers with at least 50 employees.

Eligible Employees: Any full-time or part-time employee who is a victim of domestic or sexual violence or has a family or household member who is a victim of domestic or sexual violence.

Reasons for Leave: Leave is allowed to:

- seek medical treatment
- obtain services from a victim services organization
- get counseling

- engage in safety planning, relocate, or otherwise take steps to increase the victim's safety, or
- seek legal assistance or remedies.

Amount of Leave: Up to 12 weeks of leave in a 12-month period; the law states that it does not intend to create rights beyond those provided by the FMLA.

Pregnancy Disability Leave (775 Ill. Comp. Stat. § 5/2-102)

Covered Employers: Employers with at least 15 employees.

Eligible Employees: All employees of covered employers.

Reasons for Leave: As a reasonable accommodation for pregnancy, pregnant employees may be entitled to leave necessitated by pregnancy, childbirth, or medical or common conditions resulting from pregnancy or childbirth.

Indiana

Military Family Leave (Ind. Code §§ 22-2-13-1 and following)

Covered Employers: Employers with at least 50 employees in at least 20 calendar workweeks.

Eligible Employees: Employees who have worked for at least 12 months, and at least 1,500 hours during the last 12 months, for the employer; and are the spouse, parent, grandparent, or sibling of someone ordered to active duty for 90 days or more.

Reasons for Leave: For military family reasons:

- during the 30 days before the family member's active duty orders are in effect
- while the family member is on leave during active duty, or
- during the 30 days after the family member's active duty orders are terminated.

Amount of Leave: Up to ten days each year.

Iowa

Pregnancy Disability Leave (Iowa Code § 216.6(2))

Covered Employers: Employers with at least four employees.

Eligible Employees: All employees of covered employers.

Reasons for Leave: Disability relating to pregnancy, childbirth, or related conditions.

Amount of Leave: Unless employee is otherwise entitled to time off via sick leave, disability leave, or temporary disability insurance, employer must allow employee to take leave for the period of time she is disabled by the above conditions or for eight weeks, whichever is shorter.

Kansas

Pregnancy Disability Leave (Kan. Admin. Regs. § 21-32-6)

Covered Employers: Employers with at least four employees.

Eligible Employees: All employees of covered employers.

Reasons for Leave: Disability relating to pregnancy, childbirth, miscarriage, abortion, or recovery from any of these conditions.

Amount of Leave: A "reasonable" period of leave.

Domestic Violence Leave (Kan. Stat. Ann. § 44-1132)

Covered Employers: Employers with at least four employees.

Eligible Employees: Any employee who is a victim of domestic violence or sexual assault.

Reasons for Leave: Leave is allowed to:
- seek a restraining order, injunctive relief, or any other relief to help ensure the health, safety, or welfare of the victim or the victim's children
- seek medical care
- seek services from a domestic violence program or shelter, or from a rape crisis center, or
- make court appearances.

Amount of Leave: Up to eight days per calendar year.

Kentucky

Adoption Leave (Ky. Rev. Stat. § 337.015)

Covered Employers: All employers.

Eligible Employees: All employees.

Reasons for Leave: For placement of an adoptive child under the age of seven.

Amount of Leave: Reasonable personal leave, not to exceed six weeks.

Louisiana

Pregnancy Disability Leave (La. Rev. Stat. §§ 23:341 and 23:342)

Covered Employers: Employers with more than 25 employees.

Eligible Employees: All employees of covered employers.

Reasons for Leave: Disability relating to pregnancy, childbirth, or related conditions.

Amount of Leave: Up to six weeks for normal pregnancy and childbirth; up to four months for more disabling pregnancies.

Small Necessities Law (La. Rev. Stat. §§ 23:1015 and following)

Covered Employers: All employers.

Eligible Employees: All employees.

Reasons for Leave: To attend, observe, or participate in conferences or classroom activities relating to their children (in school or day care) if they cannot be rescheduled during nonwork hours.

Amount of Leave: Sixteen hours of unpaid leave in any 12-month period.

Maine

Family and Medical Leave (Me. Rev. Stat. tit. 26, §§ 843 and following)

Covered Employers: Employers with at least 15 employees.

Eligible Employees: Employee who has worked for at least 12 consecutive months and works at a site with at least 15 employees.

Types of Leave: For the birth or adoption of a child; for the employee's own serious health condition; to care for a family member with a serious health condition; to be an organ donor; or for the death or serious health condition of a family member while on active duty.

Amount of Leave: Ten weeks in a two-year period.

Family Members: Same family members as FMLA, plus domestic partners, children of domestic partners, and siblings.

Military Family Leave (Me. Rev. Stat. tit. 26, § 814)

Covered Employers: Employers with 15 or more employees.

Eligible Employees: Employees who have worked for at least 12 months, and at least 1,250 hours in the past year; and are a spouse, domestic partner, or parent of a state resident who has been deployed for military service lasting longer than 180 days.

Reasons for Leave: For family military leave:
- during the 15 days prior to the family member's deployment
- during the family member's deployment, if the family member is granted leave, or
- for 15 days following the period of deployment.

Amount of Leave: Up to 15 days of leave per deployment.

Domestic Violence Leave (Me. Rev. Stat. tit. 26, § 850)

Covered Employers: All employers.

Eligible Employees: Any employee who, or whose parent, spouse, or child, has been a victim of violence, assault, sexual assault, stalking, or domestic violence.

Reasons for Leave: For the employee to:
- prepare for and attend court proceedings
- receive medical treatment or attend to medical treatment for a victim who is the employee's child, spouse, or parent, or

- obtain necessary services to deal with a crisis caused by domestic violence, stalking, or sexual assault.

Amount of Leave: "Reasonable and necessary" leave. Employer does not have to grant leave if the employee's absence would cause undue hardship; the employee doesn't request leave within a reasonable time under the circumstances; or leave is impractical, unreasonable, or unnecessary under the circumstances.

Maryland

Adoption Leave (Md. Code [Lab. & Empl.] § 3-801)

Covered Employers: All employers.

Eligible Employees: All employees.

Leave Provided: Employer that provides paid parental leave following the birth of a child must make the same amount of leave available to adoptive parents.

Military Family Leave (Md. Code [Lab. & Empl.] § 3-803

Covered Employers: Employers with at least 50 employees.

Eligible Employees: Employees who have worked for a covered employer for the last 12 months and for at least 1,250 hours in the last 12 months.

Reasons for Leave: Employees may take the day off when an immediate family member leaves for or returns from active military duty outside of the United States.

Amount of Leave: One day.

Massachusetts

Small Necessities Law (Mass. Gen. Laws ch. 149, § 52D)

Covered Employers: Employers with at least 50 employees.

Eligible Employees: Employees who are eligible under the FMLA.

Reasons for Leave: Employee may take leave to:

- participate in school activities directly related to the educational advancement of the employee's child, such as parent-teacher conferences or interviewing for a new school
- accompany the employee's child to routine medical or dental appointments, and
- accompany an elderly relative (someone who is related to the employee by blood or marriage and is at least 60 years old) to routine medical or dental appointments or appointments for other professional services relating to the relative's care.

Amount of Leave: Twenty-four hours in any 12-month period. This leave is in addition to FMLA leave.

Parental Leave (Mass. Gen. Laws ch. 149, § 105D)

Covered Employers: Employers with at least six employees.

Eligible Employees: Employees who have completed the employer's probationary period, or if there is no probationary period, employees who have worked for the employer for three months.

Reasons for Leave: For birth or adoption of a child.

Amount of Leave: Up to eight weeks of leave. If employer's policies provide for longer leave, the additional period of leave is treated as protected under this law, unless the employer notifies the employee otherwise before leave commences.

Domestic Violence Leave (Mass. Gen. Laws ch. 149, § 52E)

Covered Employers: Employers with at least 50 employees.

Eligible Employees: Employees who are victims of abusive behavior (domestic violence, stalking, sexual assault, or kidnapping) or family members of such victims.

Reasons for Leave: Employee may take leave to:

- seek medical care, counseling, victim services or legal assistance
- obtain housing
- get a protective order
- appear in court or before a grand jury
- meet with a district attorney or other law enforcement official
- attend child custody proceedings, or
- deal with other issues directly related to the abusive behavior against the employee or the employee's family member.

Amount of Leave: Up to 15 days in a 12-month period.

Minnesota

Family and Medical Leave (Minn. Stat. §§ 181.940 and following)

Covered Employers: Employers with at least 21 employees.

Eligible Employees: Employees who have worked at least half-time for one year.

Types of Leave: For the birth or adoption of a child.

Amount of Leave: Six weeks. Leave must begin within six weeks of the child's arrival; if child has to stay in the hospital longer than the mother, leave may begin within six weeks of the child's discharge.

Military Family Leave (Minn. Stat. §§ 181.947 and 181.948)

Covered Employers: All employers.

Eligible Employees: Employees with a grandparent, parent, legal guardian, sibling, child, grandchild, spouse, or fiancé on active duty.

Reasons for Leave: Leave is available:
- to attend a send-off or homecoming ceremony for the family member, or
- if a family member is injured or killed in active service.

Amount of Leave:
- To attend ceremony, only time necessary may be taken, up to one day per calendar year.
- If a family member is injured or killed, up to ten days of leave.

Small Necessities Law (Minn. Stat. Ann. § 181.9412)

Covered Employers: Employers with at least two employees.

Eligible Employees: Employees who have worked for the employer for at least 12 months.

Reasons for Leave: To attend school conferences or other school-related activities for the employee's child, if they cannot be scheduled during nonwork hours.

Amount of Leave: Sixteen hours of unpaid leave in any 12-month period.

Domestic Violence Leave (Minn. Stat. § 518B.01(23))

Covered Employers: All employers.

Eligible Employees: Employees who are victims of domestic abuse.

Reasons for Leave: Leave is available to seek an order for protection from domestic abuse.

Amount of Leave: "Reasonable" time off work.

Montana

Pregnancy Disability Leave (Mont. Code Ann. §§ 49-2-310 and 49-2-311)

Covered Employers: All employers.

Eligible Employees: All employees.

Reasons for Leave: Pregnancy-related disability.

Amount of Leave: "Reasonable" leave of absence for pregnancy.

Reinstatement: Employer must reinstate employee to the same or an equivalent position, unless the employer's circumstances have changed so much that it would be impossible or unreasonable to do so.

Nebraska

Military Family Leave (Neb. Rev. Stat. §§ 55-501 and following)

Covered Employers: Employers with 15 or more employees.

Eligible Employees: Employees who have worked for at least 12 months for the employer, and at least 1,250 hours during the past 12 months; and are the spouse or parent of someone called to military service of at least 179 days, for the state or the U.S., on orders of the governor or the president.

Reasons for Leave: For family military leave while state or federal deployment orders are in effect.

Amount of Leave:

- Employers with 50 or more employees must provide up to 30 days of leave.
- Employers with 15 to 49 employees must provide up to 15 days of leave.

Adoption Leave (Neb. Rev. Stat. § 48-234)

Covered Employers: All employers.

Eligible Employees: All employees.

Leave Provided: Employer that provides parental leave following the birth of a child must make the same leave available to parents who adopt a child under the age of nine or a special needs child under the age of 19. Employer does not have to provide leave for stepparent or foster parent adoptions.

Nevada

Small Necessities Law (Nev. Rev. Stat. §§ 392.920 and 392.4577)

Covered Employers: Employers with at least 50 employees for time off provision; all employers for nonretaliation provision.

Eligible Employees: All employees.

Reasons for Leave: Employees may take time off to:
- attend parent-teacher conferences
- attend school activities during school hours
- attend school-sponsored events, and
- volunteer or otherwise be involved at the child's school.

Amount of Leave: Four hours per school year.

Nonretaliation: No employer, regardless of size, may fire, or threaten to fire, an employee who appears at a conference requested by an administrator of his or her child's school, or who is notified, during work hours, of an emergency regarding the child.

New Hampshire

Pregnancy Disability Leave (N.H. Rev. Stat. § 354-A:7)

Covered Employers: Employers with at least six employees.

Eligible Employees: All employees of covered employers.

Reasons for Leave: Disability relating to pregnancy, childbirth, or related conditions.

Amount of Leave: The period of time during which the employee has a disability relating to the above conditions.

Reinstatement: Employee is entitled to be restored to the same or a comparable position, unless business necessity makes this impossible or unreasonable.

New Jersey

Family and Medical Leave (N.J. Stat. §§ 34:11B-1 and following)

Covered Employers: Employers with at least 50 employees.

Eligible Employees: Employees who have worked for at least one year and at least 1,000 hours in the previous 12 months.

Types of Leave: To care for a family member with a serious health condition, or to care for a newly born or adopted child. Leave for a new child must begin within one year of the child's birth or adoption. Employees are not entitled to leave for their own serious health conditions.

Amount of Leave: Twelve weeks in any 24-month period.

Family Members: Same family members as FMLA, plus parents-in-law and partners in a civil union.

Domestic Violence Leave (N.J. Stat. §§ 34:11C-1 and following)

Covered Employers: Employers with at least 25 employees.

Eligible Employees: Employees who have worked for the employer for at least 12 months, and at least 1,000 hours in the 12 months prior to taking leave.

Types of Leave: Employees who are victims of domestic violence or sexual violence, or whose family members are victims, may take leave to:

- seek medical attention or recover from physical or psychological injuries
- seek help from a victim services organization
- seek counseling
- participate in safety planning, relocate, or take other steps to ensure the future physical safety and economic security of the employee or family member victim
- seek legal assistance or prepare for legal proceedings, or
- attend court proceedings.

Amount of Leave: Up to 20 days in a 12-month period.

Temporary Disability Insurance (TDI)

New Jersey has a state temporary disability insurance program. Eligible employees who are unable to work due to a temporarily disability (including pregnancy) can receive up to two-thirds of their wages, up to a maximum amount.

Paid Family Leave

New Jersey's temporary disability insurance program also funds paid
family leave. Eligible employees may collect the same benefits available
for a temporary disability for up to six weeks to care for a seriously ill
family member or bond with a new child. For information on New Jersey's
TDI and paid family leave programs, go to the website of the New Jersey
Department of Labor and Workforce Development, http://lwd.state.nj.us.

New Mexico

Domestic Violence Leave (N.M. Stat. §§ 50-4A-1 and following)

Covered Employers: All employers.

Eligible Employees: Employees who have been victims of, or whose family members have been victims of, domestic abuse.

Types of Leave: Employees may take leave to:
- seek an order of protection or other judicial relief
- meet with law enforcement officials
- consult with attorneys or victim advocates, or
- attend court proceedings relating to the domestic abuse.

Amount of Leave: Up to 14 days of leave per year. Leave may be taken intermittently or in increments of up to eight hours per day.

New York

Military Family Leave (N.Y. Lab. Law § 202-i)

Covered Employers: Employers with 20 or more employees at one or more sites.

Eligible Employees: Employees who work an average of 20 or more hours per week; and are spouses of someone who is a member of the National Guard, Reserves, or Armed Forces, and is deployed during a period of military combat to a combat theater or combat zone of operations.

Reasons for Leave: While the spouse is on leave during deployment.

Amount of Leave: Up to ten days.

Adoption Leave (N.Y. Lab. Law § 201-c)

Covered Employers: All employers.

Eligible Employees: All employees.

Leave Provided: Employer that provides parental leave for the birth of a biological child must make the same amount of leave available to adopt a child who is preschool age or younger, or up to age 18, if the child is disabled.

Temporary Disability Benefits (TDI)

New York has a state temporary disability insurance program. Eligible employees who are unable to work due to a temporarily disability (including pregnancy) can receive up to 50% of their wages. For detailed information, go to the state website for workers' compensation, www.wcb.ny.gov. Select "Employers/Businesses," then "Disability Benefits."

North Carolina

Domestic Violence Leave (N.C. Gen. Stat. § 50B-5.5)

Covered Employers: All employers.

Eligible Employees: All employees.

Amount of Leave: Employer may not fire, discipline, demote, or refuse to promote an employee who takes "reasonable time" off work.

Reasons for Leave: To obtain or attempt to obtain an order of protection from domestic violence for the employee or a minor child.

Small Necessities Law (N.C. Gen. Stat. § 95-28.3)

Covered Employers: All employers.

Eligible Employees: All employees.

Reasons for Leave: To attend or otherwise be involved in a child's school.

Amount of Leave: Four hours of unpaid leave per year.

Ohio

Military Family Leave (Ohio Rev. Code § 5906)

Covered Employers: Employers with at least 50 employees.

Eligible Employees: Employees who have worked at least 12 consecutive months, and at least 1,250 hours in the previous 12 months, for the employer.

Reasons for Leave: To care for a parent, spouse, child, or person for whom the employee is a legal guardian, who:

- is called to active military duty to last more than 30 days, or
- is injured, wounded, or hospitalized while on active military duty.

Amount of Leave: Up to ten workdays or 80 hours, whichever is less.

Oregon

Family and Medical Leave (Or. Rev. Stat. §§ 659A.150 and following)

Covered Employers: Employers with at least 25 employees.

Eligible Employees

- **Parental Leave:** Employee must have worked at least 180 days for the employer before leave is scheduled to begin.
- **All Other Types of Leave:** Employee must have worked at least 180 days for the employer and at least 25 hours per week during the 180 days immediately preceding the start of leave.

Types of Leave

- **Parental Leave:** For the birth or adoption of a child, or the placement of a foster child.
- **Serious Health Condition Leave:** To care for a family member with a serious health condition or for the employee's own serious health condition.
- **Bereavement:** To deal with the death of a family member.
- **Pregnancy Disability Leave:** For prenatal care or pregnancy disability.
- **Sick Child Leave:** To care for a sick child who does not have a serious health condition but requires home care. Employer does not have to allow employee to take sick child leave if another family member is willing and able to care for the child.

Amount of Leave: Twelve weeks within any one-year period, with the following additional entitlements:

- An employee who takes 12 weeks of any other leave may take an additional 12 weeks of pregnancy disability leave.
- An employee who takes 12 weeks of parental leave may take an additional 12 weeks of sick child leave.
- An employee may combine these entitlements to take up to 36 weeks of leave: 12 for pregnancy disability, 12 for parental leave, and 12 for sick child leave.

Two family members (including spouses) who work for the same employer are each entitled to 12 weeks of leave, but the employer does not have to allow them to take this leave at the same time unless (1) both have serious health conditions; (2) one has a serious health condition and the other needs to care for him or her; or (3) one has a serious health condition and the other needs to care for a child who has a serious health condition.

Family Members: Same family members as FMLA, plus parents-in-law, domestic partners, grandparents, grandchildren, and the parents and children of domestic partners.

Military Family Leave (Or. Rev. Stat. §§ 659A.090 and following)

Covered Employers: Employers with at least 25 employees.

Eligible Employees: Employees who work an average of 20 or more hours per week.

Reasons for Leave: Employee may take military family leave when spouse or same-sex domestic partner is called to active military duty or deployed.

Amount of Leave: Employee may take up to 14 days of leave per deployment:
- after notice of spouse's or same-sex domestic partner's call to active military duty but before spouse or same-sex domestic partner is deployed, and
- while spouse or same-sex domestic partner is on leave from deployment.

This time off counts against the employee's total leave entitlement under the state's family and medical leave law.

Domestic Violence Leave (Or. Rev. Stat. §§ 659A.270 and following)

Covered Employers: Employers with six or more employees.

Eligible Employees: Employees who have worked an average of 25 or more hours per week for 180 days; and are the victims of, or the parent or guardian of a minor child who is a victim of, domestic violence, stalking, or sexual assault.

Reasons for Leave: Leave is available to:
- seek legal remedies or the assistance of law enforcement, including a protective order
- seek medical treatment or recuperate from injuries
- attend counseling
- obtain services from a victim services provider, or
- relocate or make the home safe.

Amount of Leave: "Reasonable" leave.

Rhode Island

Family and Medical Leave (R.I. Gen. Laws §§ 28-48-1 and following)

Covered Employers: Employers with at least 50 employees.

Eligible Employees: Full-time employees who average at least 30 hours of work per week and have been employed for at least 12 consecutive months.

Types of Leave

- **Family Leave:** For the employee's own serious illness or to care for a family member with a serious illness.
- **Parental Leave:** For the birth or adoption of a child.

Amount of Leave: Thirteen weeks in any two calendar years.

Family Members: Same family members as FMLA, plus parents-in-law.

Military Family Leave (R.I. Gen. Laws § 30-33-1)

Covered Employers: Employers with at least 15 employees.

Eligible Employees: Employees who have worked at least 12 months, and at least 1,250 hours in the last 12 months, for the employer; and are the spouse or parent of someone who has been called to military service lasting more than 30 days in the state or the U.S., by orders of the governor or the president.

Reasons for Leave: For family military leave while federal or state orders are in effect.

Amount of Leave:

- Employers with 50 or more employees must allow employees to take up to 30 days of leave.
- Employers with 15 to 49 employees must allow employees to take up to 15 days of leave.

Small Necessities Law (R.I. Gen. Laws § 28-48-12)

Covered Employers: Employers that have at least 50 employees.

Eligible Employees: Full-time employees who average at least 30 hours of work per week and have been employed by the same employer for at least 12 consecutive months.

Reasons for Leave: To attend school conferences or other school-related activities for the employee's child.

Amount of Leave: Ten hours of unpaid leave in any 12-month period.

Procedural Requirements

- **Notice:** Employee must provide at least 24 hours' notice of need for leave and must make a reasonable effort to schedule leave so as not to unduly disrupt employer's operations.
- **Paid Leave:** Employee may substitute accrued paid vacation or other appropriate paid leave.

Temporary Disability Insurance (TDI)

Rhode Island has a state temporary disability insurance program, funded by withholdings from employees' paychecks. Eligible employees who are unable to work due to a temporarily disability (including pregnancy) can receive $74 to $770 per week for 30 weeks. Employees may also receive salary, paid sick leave, or vacation time from their employer while receiving temporary disability payments, and may receive benefits while working part-time due to a temporary disability. For detailed information, go to the state's TDI website, www.dlt.ri.gov/tdi.

Temporary Caregiver Insurance Program (TCI)

Starting in 2014, Rhode Island expanded its temporary disability insurance program to include a small amount of paid family leave. Employees may receive up to four weeks of partial wage replacement when they take time off to bond with a new child or care for a seriously ill child, spouse, parent, grandparent, parent-in-law, or domestic partner.

Tennessee

Family and Medical Leave Law (Tenn. Code § 4-21-408)

Covered Employers: Employers with at least 100 full-time employees at the jobsite or location where the employee works.

Eligible Employees: Employees who have worked full-time for at least 12 consecutive months.

Types of Leave: For pregnancy, childbirth, nursing an infant, and adoption.

Amount of Leave: Up to four months.

Vermont

Family and Medical Leave Law (21 Vt. Stat. §§ 470 and following)

Covered Employers
- **Parental Leave:** Employers with at least 10 employees.
- **Family Leave:** Employers with at least 15 employees.

Eligible Employees: Employees who have been continuously employed for one year, for an average of at least 30 hours per week.

Types of Leave
- **Parental Leave:** (1) During the employee's pregnancy and following the birth of an employee's child, (2) within a year after the initial placement of an adopted child up to 16 years old.
- **Family Leave:** For the employee's own illness or to care for the employee's family member.

Amount of Leave: 12 weeks in a 12-month period. Spouses working for same employer are entitled to 12 weeks each; they need not combine leave.

Family Members: Includes all family members covered by FMLA plus parents-in-law and employee's civil union partner.

Small Necessities Law (21 Vt. Stat. § 472a)

Covered Employers: Employers with at least 15 employees.

Eligible Employees: Employees who have been continuously employed for one year, for an average of at least 30 hours per week.

Amount of Leave: Twenty-four hours in a 12-month period; not more than four hours may be taken in any 30-day period. Employer may require employee to take at least two hours of leave at a time.

Reasons for Leave: For the employee to:
- participate in school activities directly related to the academic educational advancement of the employee's child, stepchild, foster child, or ward
- attend or accompany a family member to routine medical or dental appointments
- accompany the employee's parent, spouse, or parent-in-law to appointments for professional services related to their care and well-being, and
- respond to a medical emergency involving a family member.

Washington

Family and Medical Leave Law (Wash. Rev. Code §§ 49.78.010 and following)

Covered Employers: Employers with at least 50 employees.

Eligible Employees: Employees who have worked for at least a year and at least 1,250 hours during the previous year.

Types of Leave: For the birth, adoption, or foster placement of a child; for the employee's own serious health condition; or to care for a family member with a serious health condition. Parental leave must be taken within one year of the child's birth, adoption, or placement.

Amount of Leave: Twelve weeks in a 12-month period. Spouses who work for the same employer may be limited to a combined total of 12 weeks of leave for the birth, adoption, or foster placement of a child and care for a parent with a serious health condition.

Military Family Leave (Wash. Rev. Code §§ 49.77.010 and following)

Covered Employers: All employers.

Eligible Employees: Employees who work an average of 20 or more hours per week, and are the spouse of a member of the National Guard, Reserves, or Armed Forces deployed or notified of a call to active duty during a period of military conflict.

Reasons for Leave: Employee may take leave only:
- after spouse has been called to active duty and before actual deployment, or
- while spouse is on leave during deployment.

Amount of Leave: Up to 15 days of unpaid leave per deployment.

Pregnancy Disability Leave (Wash. Admin. Code § 162-30-020)

Covered Employers: Employers with at least eight employees.

Eligible Employees: All employees of covered employers.

Reasons for Leave: Disability relating to pregnancy, childbirth, or related conditions.

Amount of Leave: For the period of disability. This time is in addition to the time provided under the FMLA and Washington's family and medical leave law.

Domestic Violence Leave (Wash. Rev. Code §§ 49.76.010 and following)

Covered Employers: All employers.

Eligible Employees: Employees who have been, or whose family members have been, victims of domestic violence, sexual assault, or stalking.

Reasons for Leave: For the employee to:
- seek legal assistance
- seek medical assistance
- get services from a domestic violence shelter, rape crisis center, or other social services program
- get counseling, or
- engage in safety planning or relocate.

Amount of Leave: Reasonable leave.

Family Members: Child, spouse, parent, parent-in-law, grandparent, or person the employee is dating.

Family Leave Insurance

In 2007, Washington passed a law that would allow eligible employees to collect benefits of up to $250 per week for up to five weeks when they take time off to care for a new child. However, the program has been suspended until at least 2015 due to budget shortfalls.

Wisconsin

Family and Medical Leave Law (Wis. Stat. § 103.10)

Covered Employers: Employers with at least 50 permanent employees.

Eligible Employees: Employees who have worked for more than 52 consecutive weeks and at least 1,000 hours in the preceding 52 weeks.

Types of Leave

- **Family Leave:** For birth, adoption, or to care for a family member with a serious health condition; does not cover foster care placements.
- **Medical Leave:** For the employee's own serious health condition that makes him or her unable to do the job.

Amount of Leave

- **Family Leave:** Up to eight weeks total, consisting of up to:
  - six weeks in a calendar year for birth or adoption (leave must begin within 16 weeks of the child's birth or placement), and
  - two weeks in a calendar year to care for a family member with a serious health condition.
- **Medical Leave:** Two weeks in a calendar year for the employee's serious health condition.

Family Members: Same family members as FMLA, plus parents-in-law and domestic partners.

State Departments of Labor

Alabama

Department of Industrial Relations
Montgomery, AL
334-242-8055
www.labor.alabama.gov

Alaska

Department of Labor and Workforce
Development
Juneau, AK
907-465-2700
www.labor.state.ak.us

Arizona

Industrial Commission
Phoenix, AZ
602-542-4515
www.ica.state.az.us

Arkansas

Department of Labor
Little Rock, AR
501-682-4500
www.arkansas.gov/labor

California

Labor Commissioner's Office
Department of Industrial Relations
San Francisco, CA
415-703-5300
www.dir.ca.gov/DLSE/dlse.html

Colorado

Department of Labor and Employment
Denver, CO
303-318-8441
www.colorado.gov/CDLE

Connecticut

Department of Labor
Wethersfield, CT
860-263-6000
www.ctdol.state.ct.us

Delaware

Department of Labor
Wilmington, DE
302-761-8000
www.delawareworks.com

District of Columbia

Department of Employment Services
Washington, DC
202-724-7000
www.does.dc.gov

Florida

Department of Economic Opportunity
Tallahassee, FL
850-245-7105
www.floridajobs.org

Georgia

Department of Labor
Atlanta, GA
404-232-7300
www.dol.state.ga.us

Hawaii

Department of Labor and Industrial
Relations
Honolulu, HI
808-586-8844
www.hawaii.gov/labor

Idaho

Department of Labor
Boise, ID
208-332-3570
http://labor.idaho.gov

Illinois

Department of Labor
Chicago, IL
312-793-2800
www.state.il.us/agency/idol

Indiana

Department of Labor
Indianapolis, IN
317-232-2655
www.in.gov/dol

Iowa

Divison of Labor Services
Des Moines, IA
515-281-3606
www.iowaworkforce.org/labor

Kansas

Department of Labor
Topeka, KS
785-296-5000
www.dol.ks.gov

Kentucky

Labor Cabinet
Frankfort, KY
502-564-3070
www.labor.ky.gov

Louisiana

Louisiana Workforce Commission
Baton Rouge, LA
225-342-3111
www.ldol.state.la.us

Maine

Department of Labor
Augusta, ME
207-623-7900
www.state.me.us/labor

Maryland

Department of Labor, Licensing,
and Regulation
Baltimore, MD
410-767-2241
www.dllr.state.md.us/labor

Massachusetts

Labor and Workforce Development
Boston, MA
617-626-7100
www.mass.gov/lwd/

Michigan

Department of Licensing and
Regulatory Affairs
Lansing, MI
517-373-1820
www.michigan.gov/lara

Minnesota

Department of Labor and Industry
St. Paul, MN
800-342-5354
651-284-5005
www.dli.mn.gov

Mississippi

Department of Employment Security
Jackson, MS
601-321-6000
www.mdes.ms.gov

Missouri

Department of Labor and Industrial
Relations
Jefferson City, MO
573-751-3215
www.labor.mo.gov

Montana

Department of Labor and Industry
Helena, MT
406-444-2840
www.dli.mt.gov

Nebraska

Department of Labor
Lincoln, NE
402-471-9000
www.dol.nebraska.gov

Nevada

Office of the Labor Commissioner
Las Vegas, NV
702-486-2650
www.laborcommissioner.com

New Hampshire

Department of Labor
Concord, NH
603-271-3176
800-272-4353
www.nh.gov/labor

New Jersey

Department of Labor and Workforce
Development
Trenton, NJ
609-659-9045
http://lwd.state.nj.us/labor

New Mexico

Department of Workforce Solutions
Albuquerque, NM
505-841-8405
www.dws.state.nm.us

New York

Department of Labor
Albany, NY
518-457-9000
888-469-7365
www.labor.ny.gov/home

North Carolina

Department of Labor
Raleigh, NC
919-807-2796
800-625-2267
www.nclabor.com

North Dakota

Department of Labor and Human
Rights
Bismarck, ND
701-328-2660
800-582-8032
www.nd.gov/labor

Ohio

Division of Industrial Compliance
and Labor
Reynoldsburg, OH
614-644-2223
www.com.ohio.gov/dico

Oklahoma

Department of Labor
Oklahoma City, OK
405-521-6100
www.ok.gov/odol

Oregon
Bureau of Labor and Industries
Portland, OR
971-673-0761
www.oregon.gov/boli

Pennsylvania
Department of Labor and Industry
Harrisburg, PA
800-932-0665
www.dli.state.pa.us

Rhode Island
Department of Labor and Training
Cranston, RI
401-462-8000
www.dlt.state.ri.us

South Carolina
Department of Labor, Licensing, and
    Regulation
Columbia, SC
803-896-4300
www.llr.state.sc.us/labor

South Dakota
Department of Labor and Regulation
Pierre, SD
605-773-3101
www.dlr.sd.gov

Tennessee
Department of Labor and Workforce
    Development
Nashville, TN
615-741-6642
www.state.tn.us/labor-wfd

Texas
Texas Workforce Commission
Austin, TX
512-463-2222
www.twc.state.tx.us

Utah
Labor Commission
Salt Lake City, UT
801-530-6800
800-530-5090
www.laborcommission.utah.gov

Vermont
Department of Labor
Montpelier, VT
802-828-4000
www.labor.vermont.gov

Virginia
Department of Labor and Industry
Richmond, VA
804-371-2327
www.doli.virginia.gov

Washington
Department of Labor and Industries
Tumwater, WA
360-902-5800
800-547-8367
www.lni.wa.gov

West Virginia
Division of Labor
Charleston, WV
304-558-7890
www.wvlabor.com

Wisconsin
Department of Workforce Development
Madison, WI
608-266-3131
www.dwd.state.wi.us

Wyoming
Department of Workforce Services
Cheyenne, WY
307-777-7261
www.wyomingworkforce.org

Company Policies Regarding FMLA Leave

Family and Medical Leave Policy..387

How Your FMLA Policy Affects Company Obligations..397

    Definitions...397

    Clause 1: Leave Available...398

    Clause 3: Notice Requirements 398

    Clause 6: Substitution of Paid Leave...398

    Clause 7: Parenting Leave..399

    Clause 8: Military Caregiver Leave 399

    Clause 9: Intermittent or Reduced-Schedule Leave......................................399

    Clause 11: Health Insurance..399

    Clause 12: Other Benefits...400

    Clause 13: Premium Payments..400

    Clause 14: Status Reports 400

    Clause 15: Moonlighting..401

A s explained throughout this book, your company's policies can affect its rights and obligations—and the rights and obligations of its employees—regarding FMLA leave. What you say in your FMLA policy and other company policies relating to leave is therefore very important.

This appendix explains how various policy choices affect your responsibilities under the FMLA. Here, we provide:

- A sample FMLA policy. As explained in Chapter 2, covered companies must include accurate, complete information about the FMLA in their employee handbooks, written policies, or other documents describing leave, wages, absences, and similar matters. The policy we provide will help you meet this obligation.
- A guide explaining how your company's FMLA policy affects its rights and obligations. You will have some choices to make when creating your company's policy; this section explains the ramifications of these choices. Use the guide in conjunction with the sample policy.

This material will help you draft a family and medical leave policy that complies with the FMLA, but remember that you may have additional obligations under state laws. Appendix A summarizes each state's family and medical leave laws. If the family or medical leave law of a state in which your company has employees is more generous than the FMLA or your policies, you must comply with the state law.

As a practical matter, if your company has employees in more than one state, it may be simpler to draft your family and medical leave policy to comply with the most generous of the state laws that apply and adopt that as the companywide policy. This way, you won't have to draft separate policies for offices in the different states. You should consult with a lawyer for help devising a family and medical leave policy that meets both the FMLA's requirements and the legal requirements imposed by the state(s) where your company does business.

RESOURCE

Get this policy—and all other forms in this book—online. You can find a digital version of this sample policy, as well as other FMLA forms, podcasts, updates, and more on Nolo's website. (See Appendix C for information on accessing this book's companion page.)

Family and Medical Leave Policy

It is our policy to grant family and/or medical leave to employees eligible under the Family and Medical Leave Act of 1993 ("FMLA") or any other applicable law.

Definitions

Alternative Position: A position to which an eligible employee may be temporarily reassigned during a period of intermittent or reduced-schedule leave. The alternative position will have the same pay and benefits as the employee's original position.

Child: For purposes of FMLA leave that is not military family leave, the son or daughter of an eligible employee who is under 18 years of age, or 18 years or older and incapable of self-care as a result of physical or mental disability. For purposes of this policy, "child" includes the eligible employee's biological child, adopted child, foster child, stepchild, or legal ward. It also includes a child for whom the employee assumes or intends to assume the role of parent by providing day-to-day care or financial support. For purposes of military caregiver or qualifying exigency leave, "child" includes children of any age.

Eligible Employee: An employee who has: (1) been employed by the company for at least 12 months; (2) worked at least 1,250 hours in the 12 months immediately preceding the start date of requested family or medical leave; and (3) worked at a worksite within a 75-mile radius of 50 or more employees of the company as of the date of the leave request.

Equivalent Position: A position: (1) with pay equivalent to the employee's original job; (2) with benefits equivalent to the employee's original job; (3) with job duties and responsibilities substantially similar to the employee's original job; (4) with a schedule that is the same as or equivalent to that of the employee's original job; and (5) located at the same worksite or one that is geographically proximate to the employee's original worksite.

Family Member: The eligible employee's spouse, child, or parent. For purposes of military caregiver leave, "family member" includes next of kin.

Health Care Providers: Doctors of osteopathy, podiatrists, dentists, optometrists, chiropractors (only for manual manipulation of the spine to treat a subluxation of the spine—that is, misalignment of vertebrae—identified by X-ray), physician

assistants, clinical psychologists, nurse practitioners, nurse midwives, clinical social workers, and Christian Science practitioners.

Key Employee: A salaried employee in the highest-paid 10% of the company's employees working within 75 miles of the employee's worksite.

Military Caregiver Leave: Leave to care for a family member who suffers or aggravates a serious illness or injury in the line of duty on active duty.

Military Caregiver Leave Year: The 12-month period beginning on the first date an eligible employee takes military caregiver leave.

Next of Kin: For purposes of military caregiver leave, an employee is "next of kin" to a covered servicemember if the employee is a blood relative and the servicemember has so designated the employee for purposes of military caregiver leave. If the servicemember has not designated a next of kin, the nearest blood relative is next of kin, in the following order or priority:

- blood relatives who have been granted legal custody of the servicemember
- siblings
- grandparents
- aunts and uncles, and
- first cousins.

Parent: The eligible employee's biological, adoptive, or foster parent, or an individual who assumed the role of parent by providing day-to-day care or financial support when the employee was a child.

Parenting Leave: Leave following birth, adoption, or foster placement of an eligible employee's child, including bonding leave.

Qualifying Exigency Leave: Leave taken to handle the following matters when a family member is on active duty or called to active duty in the military:

- short-notice deployment
- military events and related activities
- child care and school activities
- financial and legal arrangements
- counseling
- rest and recuperation
- postdeployment activities, and
- parental care.

Reinstatement: Restoration of employee to his or her original position when the employee returns from family or medical leave.

Serious Health Condition: Illness, injury, impairment, or physical or mental condition that involves one of the following: (1) inpatient care at a hospital, hospice, or residential medical care facility; (2) incapacity for more than three full days with continuing treatment by a health care provider; (3) incapacity due to pregnancy or prenatal care; (4) incapacity or treatment for a chronic serious health condition; (5) permanent or long-term incapacity for a condition for which treatment may not be effective (such as a terminal illness); or (6) absence for multiple treatments for either restorative surgery following an injury or accident or a condition that would require an absence of more than three days if not treated.

Serious Illness or Injury: For purposes of military caregiver leave, a serious illness or injury is one that may render a current servicemember unfit to perform the duties of his or her office, grade, rank, or rating, and for which the servicemember is undergoing medical treatment, recuperation, or therapy; is otherwise in outpatient status; or is on the temporary disability retired list. For a veteran, a serious illness or injury is (1) a continuation of a serious illness or injury (as defined above) incurred or aggravated when the veteran was in the military, which rendered the veteran unable to perform the duties of his or her office, grade, rank, or rating; (2) a physical or mental condition for which the veteran has received a Veterans Affairs Service Related Disability Rating (VASRD) of 50 percent or greater, at least in part because the condition requires caregiver leave; (3) a physical or mental condition that substantially impairs the veteran's ability to get or maintain a substantially gainful occupation due to a service-related disability (or would create such an impairment without treatment); or (4) an injury (including a psychological injury) for which the veteran has been enrolled in the Department of Veterans Affairs Program of Comprehensive Assistance for Family Caregivers.

Spouse: A person to whom the eligible employee is legally married in any state (or country, if the marriage could have been entered into in at least one state).

Twelve-Month Leave Year: The rolling 12-month period measured backward from the first day that an eligible employee takes family or medical leave.

1. Leave Available

[*Option 1—if company policy provides for more than 12 weeks of leave*] An eligible employee may take up to ____ weeks (____ days) of family or medical leave in the 12-month leave year for any of the following reasons:

- because the employee's own serious health condition makes the employee unable to work
- to care for a spouse, child, or parent who has a serious health condition
- to care for a newborn, newly adopted child, or a recently placed foster child, or
- for a qualifying exigency related to a family member's active duty or call to active duty.

[*Option 2—if company policy does not provide for more than 12 weeks of leave*] An eligible employee may take up to 12 weeks (60 workdays) of family or medical leave in the 12-month leave year for any of the following reasons:

- because the employee's own serious health condition makes the employee unable to work
- to care for a spouse, child, or parent who has a serious health condition
- to care for a newborn, newly adopted child, or a recently placed foster child, or
- for a qualifying exigency related to a family member's active duty or call to active duty.

If you have questions about how much leave time is available to you, please contact

_____ .

An eligible employee may take a one-time leave of up to 26 weeks in a single 12-month period for military caregiver leave. This is a per-servicemember, per-injury entitlement; it does not renew every year.

2. Serious Health Condition—Examples

Here are some examples of serious health conditions for which an eligible employee may take family or medical leave (Note: this is not an exhaustive list, but is for purposes of illustration):

- A condition requiring inpatient care, such as medically necessary surgery.
- A condition that results in incapacity for more than three full days and treatment by a health care provider, such as a stroke.

- Incapacity due to pregnancy or prenatal care, such as hypertension requiring bed rest.
- A chronic condition, such as epilepsy.
- A condition for which treatment may not be effective, such as terminal cancer.
- Absence for multiple treatments for restorative surgery, such as skin grafts following a burn.
- A condition that could require an absence of more than three days if not treated, such as kidney disease requiring dialysis.

3. Notice Requirements

To request family or medical leave, you are required to give notice of the need for leave at least 30 days in advance of the start date of the leave if the need for leave is foreseeable. If you fail to do so, we may delay the start of your leave. If the need for leave is unforeseeable, or you are using qualifying exigency leave, you must give as much notice as is practicable under the circumstances, usually the same or the next business day after you learn you will need leave.

To request family or medical leave, inform _____ that you need leave, when the leave will begin, and the reason for the leave (for example, for a serious medical condition or for parenting leave).

[*Option—if the company requires written requests for other types of leave*]
You must submit the reasons (for example, for a serious medical condition or for parenting leave) for the requested leave, the anticipated duration of the leave, and the anticipated start date of the leave in writing within the notice period described above. We will provide a form for this purpose.

4. Certification

You may be required to provide a form from a health care provider certifying the need for leave when you request leave for your own or a family member's serious health condition or for a family member's serious illness or injury for which you need military caregiver leave. We will request certification from you in writing and provide you with a form to be used for this purpose. The company also has the right to seek a second opinion and periodic recertifications if you take leave for a serious health condition.

You may also be required to submit a certification form when you request qualifying exigency leave, along with a copy of your family member's active duty orders or other military documentation. We will provide you with a form to be used for this purpose.

The company may also require that employees provide documentation or certification of parental status when requesting parental leave, qualifying exigency leave, or military caregiver leave. Such documentation includes, for example, birth certificates, adoption decrees, court orders, or a statement signed by the employee.

5. Notice and Designation of Leave

Soon after you request FMLA leave, we will provide you with notification as to your eligibility for leave and a statement of your rights and responsibilities under the FMLA. If we determine that you are eligible for FMLA leave, we will provide you with a designation notice informing you whether or not your leave is approved as FMLA leave and, if so, how much time will be counted against your available FMLA leave time, if known. If the amount of FMLA leave you will need is unknown when we provide the designation notice, we will provide you with an accounting of the time counted against your available FMLA leave time, upon your request, no more often than every 30 days. These notice forms will also provide information about other requirements that may apply to you during or after your leave.

6. [*Option*] Substitution of Paid Leave

FMLA leave is unpaid leave. However, under this policy, if you are an eligible employee who has accrued paid time off, you [Option 1] may [Option 2] must use these benefits to receive pay for all or a portion of family or medical leave.

If you take paid sick leave, vacation leave, or other leave for a reason that qualifies for family or medical leave under the FMLA, the company will designate that time off as such and will count it against your 12-week leave entitlement.

In order to use accrued paid time off, you must meet all requirements of our paid leave policies. Your reason for leave must be covered by the paid leave program. In addition, you must meet all the usual notice and other requirements in order to use paid leave. If you don't meet these requirements, you may be ineligible to substitute paid leave (but you will still be eligible for unpaid FMLA leave as long as you meet the notice requirements set forth in Section 3, above).

7. Parenting Leave

An eligible employee taking parenting leave must complete this leave within one year of the birth, adoption, or foster placement of the employee's child.

[*Option 1*] Married parents of a new child who are both employed with the company may take a combined 12 weeks of leave in connection with the birth, adoption, or foster placement of their child and for a parent's serious health condition.

[*Option 2*] Parents of a new child who are both employed with the company may each take 12 weeks of leave in connection with the birth, adoption, or foster placement of their child and for other FMLA purposes.

8. Military Caregiver Leave

An eligible employee may take up to 26 weeks of military caregiver leave in the 12-month period beginning on the first day of leave; this may be different from the usual 12-month leave year. Any unused portion of the 26-week leave is lost; it may not be used for other types of FMLA leave, nor carried over to a new 12-month period. Employees who are eligible for military caregiver leave may take no more than 26 total weeks of FMLA leave for all purposes during the military caregiver leave year, and no more than 12 of those weeks for all other types of FMLA leave in the 12-month leave year.

[*Option 1*] Employees who are married to each other and need military caregiver leave may take a combined total of 26 weeks of leave for military caregiver leave, parental leave, and leave to care for a parent with a serious health condition in the military caregiver leave year.

[*Option 2*] Employees who are married to each other and need military caregiver leave may each take up to 26 weeks of leave in the military caregiver leave year.

9. Intermittent and Reduced-Schedule Leave

An eligible employee may take leave all at one time or intermittently—that is, hours or days at a time—for his or her own serious health condition, to care for a family member with a serious health condition (for example, to attend doctor appointments or chemotherapy), or for military caregiver leave, if it is medically necessary to do so. An eligible employee may also take leave in the form of reduced

hours for his or her own serious health condition or to care for a family member with a serious health condition, if it is medically necessary to do so (for example, to recover from an illness or medical treatment).

An eligible employee may take intermittent or reduced-schedule leave for a qualifying exigency related to a family member's active military duty or call to active duty.

If you need intermittent or reduced-schedule leave for planned medical treatment, we may temporarily reassign you to an alternative position that is better able to accommodate your need for intermittent or reduced-schedule leave. You must make a reasonable effort to schedule your intermittent or reduced-schedule leave so it doesn't unduly disrupt the company's operations.

[*Option 1*] Intermittent and reduced-schedule leaves are not available to employees seeking parental leave.

[*Option 2*] The company will consider requests for intermittent or reduced-schedule parenting leave on a case-by-case basis and will grant such requested leave if the leave does not create an undue hardship to the operations and work schedules of the company.

You may take intermittent leave in increments of [Option 1] one hour [Option 2] [*If your company allows employees to use leave in less than one-hour increments for other types of leave, include that time frame here (for example, 30-minute increments).*]

10. Employees Who Work Part Time or Irregular Hours

An eligible part-time employee or an employee who works variable or irregular hours may take intermittent or reduced-schedule leave in proportion to the amount of time he or she normally works. For example, if you usually work 20 hours per week and need a work schedule reduction to ten hours per week due to a serious health condition, that amounts to one-half of your normal working hours. You would use up your 12-week leave entitlement in 24 weeks under that reduced-schedule leave.

If your schedule varies from week to week, the leave workweek is measured by calculating the weekly average hours worked in the 12 months prior to the start of the leave. We will calculate this average and put it in writing for your review and signature.

11. Health Insurance

During an approved family or medical leave, the company will continue your health care benefits. You must continue to pay any share of the premium for which you are currently responsible by the usual due date of payment. If your premium payments are more than 30 days late, we may discontinue your coverage for the rest of your leave. If you choose not to return to work at the end of your leave, you will be required to reimburse the company for its share of the premiums paid during your leave.

12. Other Benefits

[*Option 1—if the company does not allow employee benefits to continue or accrue during other types of leave, including paid leave*] With the exception of health care benefits, discussed above, employee benefits will not continue or accrue during the period of your family or medical leave. These benefits will be restored when you return from leave at the same level as before the leave.

[*Option 2—if the company allows employee benefits to continue and/or accrue, but only during paid leave*] If your family or medical leave is paid leave, discussed above, all employee benefits will continue and accrue during the period of the paid family or medical leave.

[*Option 3—if the company allows employee benefits to continue and/or accrue during all types of leave*] In addition to the health care benefits discussed above, employee benefits continue and accrue during the family or medical leave period. You will be required to reimburse the company for the portion of the benefits premiums for which you are usually responsible for but which the company paid during the leave.

13. Premium Payments

Any premium payments for which you are responsible during the leave period must be paid on or before your regular payday. If you fail to make timely payment of the premiums, your benefit coverage, including insurance coverage, may be discontinued.

14. [*Option*] Status Reports

You must periodically contact the human resources manager during your leave and inform the manager of your status and intent to return to work.

15. [*Option*] Moonlighting

You may not work for another employer while on family or medical leave. Such outside employment is grounds for immediate termination.

16. Reinstatement

When you return from family or medical leave, you have the right to return to your former position or an equivalent position, except:

- You have no greater right to reinstatement than you would have had if you had not been on leave. If your position is restructured for reasons unrelated to your leave, for example, you have no right to reinstatement to the exact same position you held before leave.

- The company is not obligated to reinstate you if you are a key employee— that is, if you are among the highest-paid 10% of our workforce—and reinstating you after your leave would cause the company substantial economic harm. If the company classifies you as a key employee under this definition, you will be notified soon after you request leave.

Two weeks prior to your intended return date, you should notify the human resources manager of your intent to return to work. And, if anything has changed concerning your return to work while you have been on leave, you should notify human resources of the change.

If you are returning from leave for your own serious health condition, the company may ask you to provide a fitness-for-duty report from your health care provider before you return to work. We will provide a form to be used for this purpose.

How Your FMLA Policy Affects Company Obligations

As we've explained, if your company's leave policy is less generous than the FMLA, you must follow the FMLA with respect to FMLA-eligible employees or FMLA-qualified leaves. Here are a few areas of particular importance; review them while using the sample policy above to create your own policy.

Definitions

Your company may define terms more broadly than the FMLA. If it does, it may extend the FMLA's protections to employees who would not otherwise be eligible.

- **Eligible employee.** Your company can offer family and medical leave to employees who don't meet the FMLA's eligibility requirements (12 months' employment/1,250 hours in 12 months preceding leave). However, such a decision has ramifications. For example, you can deduct reduced-schedule FMLA leave time (less than a full week of leave) from an eligible, exempt employee's pay without affecting the employee's exempt status. But, if you grant reduced-schedule leave to an exempt employee who is not eligible under the FMLA and deduct his or her pay, you risk eliminating the employee's exempt status and violating the Fair Labor Standards Act.
- **Family member.** Your company can also elect to include in its family and medical leave policy family members not included under the FMLA, such as domestic partners. But, you cannot deduct the leave granted for such individuals' care from the employee's available FMLA leave time.
- **Twelve-month leave year.** The rolling leave year method is the most ad-vantageous to employers because it limits employees' ability to be out of work for more than 12 weeks in any 12-month period. However, you are free to calculate the leave year using one of the alternative methods. In fact, some state laws may mandate a different calculation.

Clause 1: Leave Available

Your company can offer more leave than the FMLA's 12 weeks (or 26 weeks, for military caregiver leave). You may want to consider this option if your company has employees in more than one state, including a state that requires you to provide more leave time. By offering the leave time required under the state law to all employees in all states, you can adopt a single, uniform leave policy for all company locations.

Clause 3: Notice Requirements

Your company can require employees seeking family and medical leave to comply with the usual and customary notice requirements and procedures (for example, requiring that the employee notify you of the need for leave in writing) that it imposes for other types of leave requests.

However, you cannot require more notice (in other words, more than 30 days for foreseeable leave) or more information (in other words, more than leave dates and general statement of reason for leave) than the FMLA requires. And, you cannot impose stricter requirements on employees seeking family or medical leave than you impose on employees seeking other types of leave.

If an employee doesn't give the required leave notice, you can delay the start of an employee's leave, but only if you have informed the employee of the duty to provide notice.

Clause 6: Substitution of Paid Leave

If your company has a paid leave policy, an employee's use of it during family or medical leave is subject to the policy's terms. For example, if your company offers paid sick leave for the employee's own illness, you must allow an employee taking FMLA leave for his or her own serious health condition to use the paid sick leave available. However, you do not have to let the employee use that paid sick leave policy to care for family members, since the sick leave policy does not provide for that.

Remember, it's not really a substitution, but an overlap. The employee isn't using paid leave instead of FMLA leave but is using the two types of leave

at the same time. So, don't forget to deduct the paid leave taken from the employee's available FMLA leave time.

Clause 7: Parenting Leave

Even though the FMLA requires you to offer only 12 weeks of combined parenting leave to married employees when both are employed by the company, your company can offer 12 full weeks of leave to each parent.

Clause 8: Military Caregiver Leave

As is true of parenting leave, the FMLA allows you to limit married employees who are both employed by your company to a combined total of 26 weeks of leave for military caregiving, parenting, and caring for a parent with a serious health condition. However, you may choose to offer each parent the full 26-week entitlement.

Clause 9: Intermittent or Reduced-Schedule Leave

Your company can allow employees to take intermittent or reduced-schedule parenting leave, but the FMLA doesn't require it. On the other hand, you can impose restrictions on the leave that you usually can't impose on intermittent FMLA leave, such as requiring the employee to take the leave in larger increments than those used by your company for payroll.

Clause 11: Health Insurance

You can terminate an employee's health coverage if the employee is required to pay a portion of the premium and fails to do so within 30 days (after being given notice). However, the date that an employee's coverage officially terminates depends, in part, on your policies for other types of paid leave. If your company has an established policy that allows it to terminate coverage retroactively to the date of the missed payment, it may do so. If it doesn't have this type of policy, it may terminate coverage effective 30 days after the missed payment. And remember, you may need to continue health coverage even if the employee fails to make payments, to ensure that the employee's benefits are restored upon reinstatement.

Clause 12: Other Benefits

If your company usually allows employee benefits to continue and accrue during other types of leave, you have to follow that practice when an employee takes FMLA leave. If your company usually does not continue employee benefits during leave, you do not have to continue benefits (other than health benefits) during FMLA leave. However, regardless of company policy, you must restore all employee benefits to the employee upon return from leave. The benefits must be restored to the same level as before leave and without any requalification. For this reason, it may be easier and less costly to simply continue the benefits during leave, regardless of company policy on other types of leave.

You have to follow your company's policy regarding the continuation and accrual of benefits during paid leave for employees who substitute paid leave for FMLA leave. So, if your company's employee benefits continue to accrue during paid leave, they must also continue to accrue during an FMLA leave that is taken as paid leave.

Clause 13: Premium Payments

You can require employees to pay premiums for benefits during FMLA leave, but you must inform them of this requirement in your policies and you must also inform them when premium payments are due and the possible consequences of failing to pay.

Clause 14: Status Reports

You can request periodic status reports during an employee's FMLA leave, asking whether the employee intends to return and, if so, when. Just make sure you are reasonable: Don't ask too often, and don't ask for more information than is allowed. Avoid the appearance of bullying the employee to return from leave earlier than the employee is ready to. Don't try to get additional medical information via the status reports.

Clause 15: Moonlighting

You can prohibit an employee from working for another employer during FMLA leave, as long as your company has a uniform policy against moonlighting that applies to all employees.

Using the Interactive Forms

Editing RTFs 404

List of Forms and Podcasts 405

This book comes with interactive files that you can access online at:
www.nolo.com/back-of-book/FMLA.html

To use the files, your computer must have specific software programs installed. Here is a list of types of files provided by this book, as well as the software programs you'll need to access them:

- **RTF.** You can open, edit, print, and save these form files with most word processing programs such as Microsoft *Word*, Windows *WordPad*, and recent versions of *WordPerfect*.
- **PDF.** You can view these files with *Adobe Reader*, free software from www.adobe.com. Government PDFs are sometimes fillable using your computer, but most PDFs are designed to be printed out and completed by hand.
- **XLS.** You can use this spreadsheet with Microsoft *Excel* and other spreadsheet programs that read XLS files.
- **MP3.** You can listen to these audio files using your computer's sound system. Most computers come with a media player that plays MP3 files, or you may have installed one on your own.

TIP

Note to Macintosh users. These forms were designed for use with Windows. They should also work on Macintosh computers; however, Nolo cannot provide technical support for non-Windows users.

Editing RTFs

Here are some general instructions about editing RTF forms in your word processing program. Refer to the book's instructions and sample agreements for help about what should go in each blank.

- **Underlines.** Underlines indicate where to enter information. After filling in the needed text, delete the underline. In most word procssing programs you can do this by highlighting the underlined portion and typing CTRL-U.
- **Bracketed and italicized text.** Bracketed and italicized text indicates instructions. Be sure to remove all instructional text before you finalize your document.

- **Alternative text.** Alternative text gives you the choice between two or more text options. Delete those options you don't want to use. Renumber numbered items, if necessary.
- **Signature lines.** Signature lines should appear on a page with at least some text from the document itself.

Every word processing program uses different commands to open, format, save, and print documents, so refer to your software's help documents for help using your program. Nolo cannot provide technical support for questions about how to use your computer or your software.

> CAUTION
> **In accordance with U.S. copyright laws, the forms and audio files provided by this book are for your personal use only.**

List of Forms and Podcasts

To download any of the files listed here, go to:
www.nolo.com/back-of-book/FMLA.html

The following files are in rich text format (RTF):

Title	File Name
FMLA Policy	Policy.rtf
FMLA Leave to Care for a Family Member	LeaveForm.rtf
FMLA Hours Worked	WorkHours.rtf
FMLA Leave Tracking	Tracking.rtf
Request for Medical Certification	MedCertifRequest.rtf
Notice to Key Employee of Substantial and Grievous Economic Injury	NoticeEconInjury.rtf
Notice of Termination of Group Health Coverage	CoverageTerm.rtf

The following files are in portable document format (PDF):

Title	File Name
Family and Medical Leave Act Poster (English)	Fmlaen.pdf
Family and Medical Leave Act Poster (Spanish)	Fmlasp.pdf
Notice of Eligibility and Rights & Responsibilities (Family and Medical Leave Act)	WH-381.pdf
Designation Notice (Family and Medical Leave Act)	WH-382.pdf
Certification of Health Care Provider for Employee's Serious Health Condition	WH-380-E.pdf
Certification of Health Care Provider for Family Member's Serious Health Condition	WH-380-F.pdf
Certification of Qualifying Exigency for Military Family Leave	WH-384.pdf
Certification of Serious Injury or Illness of Covered Servicemember for Military Family Leave	WH-385.pdf
Certification for Serious Illness or Injury of a Veteran for Military Caregiver Leave	WH-385-V.pdf
Does the FMLA Apply to My Company?	Apply.pdf
Is the Employee Eligible for FMLA Leave?	Eligible.pdf
Leave for a New Child	ChildLeave.pdf
Military Family Leave	MilitaryLeave.pdf
Duration of Leave	LeaveDuration.pdf
Giving Notice and Designating Leave	LeaveNotice.pdf
Medical Certifications	Certifications.pdf
Managing FMLA Leave	ManagingLeave.pdf
Reinstating an Employee	Reinstatement.pdf
If an Employee Doesn't Return From Leave	EmployeeDeparture.pdf
Record Keeping	RecordKeeping.pdf

The following spreadsheet is in Microsoft *Excel* Format (XLS):

Title	File Name
Calculating Intermittent/Reduced-Schedule Leave	CalculateLeave.xls

The following files are Audio (MP3):

Title	File Name
FMLA: Policy and Enforcement	PolicyandEnforcement.mp3
FMLA: Management and Requirements	ManagementandReqs.mp3
FMLA: The Human Side	TheHumanSide.mp3
The Essential Guide to Family and Medical Leave: Scenario 1	Scenario1.mp3
The Essential Guide to Family and Medical Leave: Scenario 2	Scenario2.mp3
Recent Changes to the FMLA	FMLAChanges.mp3

Index

A

Abuse of FMLA leave, 265
Abuse of intermittent leave, 234–236
Active duty, defining for military
    caregiver leave, 115–116
ADA. *See* Americans with Disabilities
    Act
Administration
    overview, 2, 218–219
    intermittent and reduced-
        schedule leave, 146–149
    by PEOs, 24
    primary employer responsibilities,
        26
    See also Benefits; Certifications;
        Employees' notice
        requirements; Record keeping
Adoptive parents leave, 84, 87–88,
    298
Air France, Moreau v., 23
Airline flight crews
    FMLA leave usage rules, 137,
        138, 148–149
    special "hours of service"
        eligibility, 44–45
*Alameda-Contra Costa Transit
    District, Sims v.,* 199
Alaska Airlines, Tellis v., 75
Allen Health Systems, Inc., Smith v.,
    240

Amendments to FMLA, 3
American Standard, Inc., Thom v.,
    130
Americans with Disabilities Act
    (ADA)
    overview, 282, 283–284, 308
    and employee's serious health
        condition, 11
    on essential job functions, 68–69,
        263–264
    and FMLA, 283, 285–288,
        305–306
    medical record privacy
        requirements, 319–320
    reasonable accommodations,
        239, 263–264, 284, 286, 287,
        289–290
    and reinstatement, 249, 267,
        289–290
    undue hardship test, 249, 284,
        285, 287, 289–290, 306
Antidiscrimination laws, 11, 283,
    291–293, 309, 320
Aubuchon v. Knauf Fiberglass, GmbH,
    95
Authenticating or clarifying medical
    certifications, 200–203
*Automation & Modular Components,
    Inc., Saroli v.,* 161
Avon Products Inc., Byrne v., 8

B

Ballard Spahr Andrews Ingersoll, LLP, McFadden v., 224
"Banked" hours and multiemployer health plans, 227
Baptist Memorial Health Care System, Moorer v., 175
Beaver v. RGIS Inventory Specialists, Inc., 168
Benefits, 224–230
    overview, 224–225, 274
    company policy on, 227–228, 395
    insurance coverage, 227–228, 258
    lawsuit for benefits promised in employee handbook, 14
    paid leave from another source, 158–159
    and premium payments during leave, 228–230
    reimbursement from employees, 270–273
    and reinstatement, 258–260
    retirement benefits, 259
    See also Health insurance benefits
Bereavement leave, 84
Bocalbos v. National Western Life Ins. Co., 87
Bonuses and reinstatement, 256–257
Brenneman v. MedCentral Health System, 171
Brewer v. Jefferson-Pilot Standard Life Insurance Company, 10
Brothers and sisters, 72

Buyers of company and FMLA obligations, 28
Byrne v. Avon Products Inc., 8

C

Cafeteria plans, 225–226
Calendar year calculation for FMLA leave, 127, 135
California, 29, 66, 296, 305
California Family Rights Act (CFRA), 70–71, 300
Cancer, 65
Casey's General Stores, Wierman v., 63
Cavin v. Honda of America Manufacturing, Inc., 167
Certifications, 181–209
    overview, 6, 182, 183, 197
    authenticating or clarifying medical certifications, 200–203
    common mistakes, 206–207
    company policy, 391–392
    for continuing serious health conditions, 271
    DOL forms, 184–190
    employee deadline for returning certification, 195
    employer request for, 10, 190–196
    fitness-for-duty, 147, 164–165, 205, 252–255
    foreign language certifications, 198
    incomplete or insufficient certifications, 198–199
    inconsistency in requesting certifications, 191, 192–193

and intermittent leave, 234–235
managers' checklist, 208–209
for military caregiver leave, 113, 118, 185–189
oral requests for, 196
parental, 85–86
procedures and deadlines for requests, 193–194, 196
of qualifying exigencies, 189–190, 199–200
recertifications, 203–205
record keeping, 198
for serious health condition leave, 55–56, 59–60, 77, 183–185, 200–203
verifying employee's qualifying condition, 190–191
yearly request for, 203
CFRA (California Family Rights Act), 70–71, 300
Child, defining for military qualifying exigency, 108–109
Children. See Parenting leave
Chronic serious (episodic) health conditions, 63–64, 184, 192–193, 232
Clarifying or authenticating medical certifications, 200–203
COBRA (Consolidated Omnibus Budget Reconciliation Act), 272, 283, 290–291, 308
Commute time, 43
Companies covered by FMLA, 17–33
overview, 5, 17, 18, 19, 28
calculating the size of your company, 19–21
common mistakes, 32–33

FMLA compliance manager, 201, 321
joint employers, 22–28, 318
posting requirements, 29–30
workforce records, 316
See also Employee eligibility; Employers
Company policies
overview, 9, 11, 12–13
on bereavement leave, 84
on company-provided paid leave, 156–158
on employees' notice requirement, 172, 174, 215
on fitness-for-duty certifications, 253–255
on intermittent leave, 89, 234–236
on leave year, 129–131
pay docking rules, 146
on reduced-schedule leave, 89
on using paid time, 90
Company policy sample, 385–401
overview, 386
for certification, 391–392
for health insurance and other benefits, 395
for intermittent or reduced-schedule leave, 393–394
for leave duration, 390
for military caregiver leave, 393
for notice and designation of leave, 392
for notice and paperwork requirements, 391
for parenting leave, 393
for part-time employees, 394

for premium payments, 395
for reinstatement, 396
for serious health condition leave, 390–391
for substitution of paid leave, 392
terminology, 387–389
Compassion for employees, 6–7, 84, 218
Compassion of manager, 6–7, 84, 218
Connecticut, 296
Consolidated Omnibus Budget Reconciliation Act (COBRA), 272, 283, 290–291, 308
Consultant as replacement for employee on leave, 220
Continuing treatment, 60–62
Cooper v. Fulton County, Georgia, 196
Counseling as qualifying exigency, 109, 111
Counting forward calculation for FMLA leave, 126, 127, 131, 135–136
Couples. *See* Spouses; Unmarried couples
Crosfield Catalysts, Kelley v., 85

D

Deadlines for reinstatement, 251–252
Delay of FMLA leave, 174–175, 177, 195, 214–216, 241
Denial of FMLA leave, 174, 176–177, 206
Departments of labor, state, 380–383. *See also* U.S. Department of Labor
Depression of employee, 287, 288
Designation notice, 164–166. *See also* Notice and designation of leave

Designation Notice form (DOL), 165
Disabilities, 192–193, 283–284. *See also* Americans with Disabilities Act
Disability income, 158
Disability insurance, 158–159
Disability insurance, state, 305, 307, 310–311
Disciplining an employee during leave, 238–240, 242
Discrimination
against fathers caring for their new child, 97
inconsistency in requesting certifications as, 191, 192–193
laws against, 11, 283, 291–293, 309, 320
DOL. *See* U.S. Department of Labor
Domestic partners, 70–71, 296
Domestic violence leave laws, state, 299–300

E

East Baton Rouge Parish School Board, Smith v., 249
Economic injury, substantial and grievous, 266–269
EEOC (Equal Employment Opportunity Commission), 68
Eligibility notice, 161–162. *See also* Employee eligibility
Emotions, dealing with, 6, 7
Employee complaints, DOL response to, 321
Employee eligibility, 35–51
overview, 5, 36, 37

12 months of employment rule, 40–42, 50

50 employees within 75 miles rule, 37–39

1,250 hours in 12-month period requirement, 42–44, 45–46, 50, 142–143, 145, 293–294

airline flight crew special "hours of service" eligibility, 44–45

common mistakes, 49–50

determining work site, 39–40

eligibility, 22, 29

managers' checklist, 51

manager's flowchart, 49

work hour record keeping, 46–48, 49–50

See also Companies covered by FMLA; Employees' notice requirements

Employee handbooks, 30–32, 160, 194, 385–401

Employees

advising not to work while on FMLA leave, 137

choosing not to return to work, 270, 272–273, 291

circumstances beyond the control of, 271

DOL interviews of, 321

inability to return to work, 270–271, 290–291

individual employee records, 316–318

joint employees, 20, 38, 42

medical privacy rights, 184, 198, 206–207

not returning from FMLA leave, 262–263, 270–273

overtime policies and hours worked measure, 43, 145, 148

part-time employees, 139, 144–145, 394

and planning for workload coverage during leave, 221–223

response to others' FMLA leave, 218–219

See also Essential job functions; Exempt employees; Firing an employee; Substitution of paid leave

Employees' notice requirements, 167–176

overview, 167, 241

additional information from employee, 170–171

company policy, 174, 391

company policy on, 174

employee's failure to give notice, 174–175

foreseeable leave notice, 171–172, 214–216, 233

methods of employee notification, 167–170

notice based on employer observations, 175–176

notifying employees of FMLA leave availability, 11, 28–33, 155, 160–161, 177

unforeseeable leave notice, 172–173, 217–218

Employers

designating FMLA leave when appropriate, 77–78

integrated employers, 27, 28
joint employers, 26–27
mistakes and, 166
notifying employees of FMLA
    availability, 11, 28–33, 155,
    160–161, 177
overtime policies and hours
    worked measure, 43
reimbursement from employees,
    270–273
request for certification, 10,
    190–196
restructuring and layoffs during
    an employee's FMLA leave,
    260–261
substantial and grievous
    economic injury, 266–269
See also Joint employers;
    Managers; *entries beginning
    with* "Companies" or
    "Company"
Employers' notice requirements,
    153–166
    overview, 154, 155
    common mistakes, 176–177
    company policy, 392
    counting time off as FMLA leave,
        155–160, 176
    designation notice, 164–166
    eligibility notice, 161–162
    general notice, 11, 28–33, 155,
        160–161, 177
    managers' checklist, 178–179
    and overlapping state laws, 295
    rights and responsibility notice,
        162–164, 229, 254, 266

See also Notice and designation
    of leave
Episodic health conditions, 63–64,
    184, 192–193, 232
Equal Employment Opportunity
    Commission (EEOC), 68
Equivalent position, reinstatement
    into, 247–250
Essential job functions
    and ADA, 68–69, 283–284
    and fitness-for-duty certifications,
        165, 253–254
    FMLA and ADA overlap,
        285–289, 305–306
    and intermittent or reduced-
        schedule leave, 142
    job modifications under ADA,
        286–288
    light-duty positions, 287–288,
        303–304
    and reinstatement, 263–264,
        289–290
Exempt employees
    as key employees, 266
    overtime work by, 47, 48, 145–146
    record keeping for, 318
    restarting after FMLA leave,
        255–256

F

Family and Medical Leave Act
    (FMLA), 1–15
    overview, 2–3
    and ADA, 283, 285–288,
        305–306
    amendments and regulations, 3

and COBRA, 290–291
on intermittent or reduced-schedule leave, 139
manager obligations, 4–9
medical record privacy requirements, 318–321
on military caregiver leave, 113
and military family leave, 103
posting requirements, 29–30
requirements, 3–4
and state family and medical leave laws, 300–302
and Title VII of the Civil Rights Act, 291–293, 309
and USERRA, 293–294
as win/win for employer and employee, 7
written policies, 30–32
Family leave, paid, 158
Family member's military duty, 4. *See also* Military caregiver leave; Military family leave
Family member's serious health condition leave, 69–76
overview, 69, 77
certification of condition, 185
defining "caring for," 74–76
identifying family members, 70–72
proving a family relationship, 72–73
siblings and change of care for terminally ill mother, 74
Fannin Regional Hospital, Kaylor v., 233

Federal Home Loan Bank of Des Moines, Spangler v., 288
Federal laws, 282–294
COBRA, 272, 283, 290–291, 308
HIPAA, 201, 320–321
overlapping with FMLA, 11–12
Title VII of the Civil Rights Act, 283, 291–293, 309
See also Americans with Disabilities Act; Family and Medical Leave Act
50-employees rule, 19–21
50-employees within 75 miles rule, 37–39
Financial arrangements as qualifying exigency, 109, 111
Firing an employee
fire-at-will rights, 261–262
during leave, 10, 238–240, 242, 261–262
with workers' comp claim, 304
Fitness-for-duty certification, 147, 164–165, 205, 252–255
Fixed-period year calculation for FMLA leave, 127
Flexible schedules vs. FMLA leave, 149
Flexible spending accounts (FSAs), 226–227
FMLA. *See* Family and Medical Leave Act
FMLA-eligible employees flow chart, 49
FMLA lawsuits
overview, 9

for benefits promised in employee handbook, 14
bonuses and FMLA leave, 257
and certification, 191, 192
company interfering with employee's FMLA rights, 224
continuing treatment clarification, 62
custody battle leave request, 85
employee's information requirement for leave eligibility, 95, 167, 168, 171, 173, 175
and employee's notice of need for leave, 8
employee's reasonable effort to reschedule foreseeable intermittent leave, 233
employer failure to provide FMLA information, 30, 31, 130, 161
employer failure to request certification, 199
essential job functions, 142
father caring for premature infant, 96
firing an employee during FMLA leave, 240
firing an employee for abusing leave, 265
intermittent leave availability, 140
joint employee status, 23
oral request for certification, 196
phone calls not included as "caring for," 75
pregnancy-related serious health condition, 63

recertification requests, 205
reinstatement issues, 249, 252, 268
siblings and change of care for terminally ill mother, 74
status report requests, 238
traveling to retrieve an adopted child, 87
for unlawful firing, 10
FMLA leave
    overview, 5, 306–307
    delay of, 174–175, 177, 195, 214–216, 241
    denial of, 174, 176–177, 206
    and holidays, 137–138
    leave year calculations, 125–129, 134–136, 150
    leave year method choice, 129–131, 149–150
    retroactive designation of, 159–160, 166
    See also Employee eligibility; Intermittent leave; Military family leave; Parenting leave; Reduced-schedule leave; Serious health condition leave
FMLA leave duration, 123–152
    overview, 124, 125
    applying leave year consistently, 131
    common mistakes, 149–150
    company policy, 390
    leave year calculations, 125–129, 134–136, 150
    leave year method, 129–131, 149–150
    managers' checklist, 151–152

military caregiver leave, 118–119,
132–136

nonmilitary caregiver leave, 132,
133–136

state law overlap, 296–297

time off as FMLA leave, 136–138,
155–160, 176

FMLA leave duration for intermittent
and reduced-schedule leave

overview, 138–139

administration of, 146–149

exempt employees, 145–146

flexible schedules vs. FMLA
leave, 149

and overtime hours, 145

part-time employees, 139,
144–145, 394

qualifying/eligibility for, 139–143

FMLA leave management, 211–244

overview, 212, 213

common mistakes, 241–242

disciplining or firing an employee
during leave, 10, 238–240,
242, 261–262

and employee benefits, 224–230

implementing plan for covering
employee's duties, 223–224,
241

intermittent leave, 231–236

managers' checklist, 243–244

options for covering employee's
duties, 218–223

scheduling leave, 213–218,
231–232

status report requests, 236–238,
395

See also Reinstatement

Foreign adoptions, 86–88

Foreign language certifications, 198

Foreign-language FMLA posters, 29

Foreseeable leave notice, 171–172,
214–216, 233

Foster child placement leave, 84–85,
88–89

FSAs (flexible spending accounts),
226–227

Fulton County, Georgia, Cooper v.,
196

G

Gemini, Inc., Thorson v., 192

General notice, 160–161

Genetic Information
Nondiscrimination Act of 2013
(GINA), 320

Gilead Sciences, Inc., Peters v., 14

Glossary, 325–332

Group health plan, 225–227, 229–230

H

Hatchett v. Philander Smith Coll., 142

Health care providers, identifying,
59–60

Health conditions. *See* Serious health
condition leave

Health insurance benefits

and ADA/FLMA overlap, 286

and COBRA, 272, 283,
290–291, 308

company policy on, 227–228,
395

group health plan, 225–227, 229–230

for key employee that will not be reinstated, 268

recovery of costs if employee doesn't return from leave, 272

Health Insurance Portability and Accountability Act (HIPAA), 201, 320–321

Highest-paid 10% of employees, 266

Hoge v. Honda of America, 252

Holidays, 137–138

Honda of America Manufacturing, Inc., Cavin v., 167

Howard Memorial Hospital, Terwilliger v., 238

Human resources manager, 10

I

Illinois, 299

Incapacity as serious health condition, 58–62, 64

Incomplete or insufficient certifications, 198–199

Industry investigations by DOL, 321

Ineligibility for FMLA leave, 162

Ingram Constr. Co., Inc., Willard v., 96

In loco parentis, 71–72, 81, 110

Inpatient care as serious health condition, 57–58

Insufficient or incomplete certifications, 198–199

Insurance coverage, 227–228, 258. *See also* Health insurance benefits

Integrated employers, 27–28

Intermittent leave

abuse prevention, 234–236

company policy, 89, 234–236, 393–394

employee rescheduling for company convenience, 233

and employees' ability to perform essential functions of the job, 142

and employee's work hours, 45–46

and fitness-for-duty certification, 147, 164–165, 205, 254–255

leave management, 231–236

medical necessity for, 119, 139–141, 184, 185, 232

for military family leave, 112, 119

mismanagement of, 241–242

and parenting leave, 88–90

for pregnancy incapacity, 93

record keeping, 322–323

transferring an employee to another position, 232, 233–234, 242

See also FMLA leave duration for intermittent and reduced-schedule leave

Intranets, 29, 161, 164

Invacare Corp., Taylor v., 31

Invitational travel authorization (ITA), 187–188

Invitational travel order (ITO), 187–188

J

Jefferson-Pilot Standard Life Insurance Company, Brewer v., 10
Job descriptions, 68
Job modifications under ADA, 286–288
Joint employees, 20, 38, 42
Joint employers, 22–28
    overview, 22, 32
    employer responsibilities, 26–27
    identifying joint employer companies, 22–24
    integrated employers, 27–28
    primary and secondary employers, 25–27
    and record keeping, 318

K

Kaylor v. Fannin Regional Hospital, 233
Kelley v. Crosfield Catalysts, 85
Key employee issues, 265–270, 274
"Kin care" laws, 76
Knauf Fiberglass, GmbH, Aubuchon v., 95

L

Labor Department. *See* U.S. Department of Labor
Labor union employees, 4
Labor unions and multiemployer health plans, 227
Laws
    overview, 280–281, 282
    common mistakes, 305–307
    determining applicability, 282, 308–311
    GINA, 320
    obligations under other laws, 6, 9, 11–12
    and reinstatement, 263–264
    See also Federal laws; State laws
Lawyers, consulting with
    for ADA issues, 289
    denying FMLA leave based on a second opinion, 202
    for disciplining an employee on FMLA leave, 239, 262
    for DOL investigations, 322
    for firing an employee on FMLA leave, 262
    firing an employee with a workers' comp claim, 304
    for FMLA designation based on employee behavior, 176
    for multistate companies, 131, 386
    for recovery of benefits costs if employee doesn't return, 273
    for state laws on parenting leave, 90
    for state posting requirements, 30
Layoff periods, 42
Layoffs and restructuring during an employee's FMLA leave, 260–261
Leave. *See* FMLA leave
Legal arrangements as qualifying exigency, 109, 111
Light-duty positions, 287–288, 303–304
Louisiana, 298

M

Managers
    overview, 4–6
    of companies covered by FMLA, 32
    compassion for employees, 6–7, 84, 218
    identifying a serious health condition, 55–56
    See also entries beginning with "Companies" or "Company"; entries beginning with "Employers"
Managers' checklists
    overview, 15
    certifications, 208–209
    companies covered by FMLA, 28
    employee doesn't return from leave, 278
    employee eligibility, 51
    leave duration, 151–152
    leave management, 243–244
    military family leave, 121–122
    notice and designating leave, 178–179
    notice and designation of leave, 178–179
    parenting leave, 98–99
    record keeping, 323
    reinstating an employee, 275–277
Manager's flowcharts
    FMLA-eligible employees, 49
    serious health conditions, 76
Marital status. *See* Spouses; Unmarried couples
McDonnell Douglas Corp., Sepe v., 44

McFadden v. Ballard Spahr Andrews Ingersoll, LLP, 224
MedCentral Health System, Brenneman v., 171
Medical inquiries and workers' comp claims, 303
Medical necessity for intermittent or reduced-schedule leave, 119, 139–141, 184, 185, 232
Medical privacy rights, employee's, 184, 198, 206–207
Medical record privacy requirements, 318–321
Mental conditions and military caregiver leave, 114–115
Mental disabilities, 192–193
Mergers and FMLA obligations, 28
Michigan Dept. of Human Services, Romans v., 74
Mid-Atlantic of Fairfield, Neel v., 268
Miesel Sysco Food Service Co., Woodman v., 62
Military caregiver leave
    overview, 4, 103, 113, 126, 165
    certifications, 113, 118, 185–189
    company policy, 393
    family members covered for, 116–118
    invitational travel authorization or order, 187–188
    leave duration, 118–119, 132–136
    leave year, 126
    for married couples, 91, 97, 119
    servicemembers covered by, 113–116
    state laws on, 297

Military events and related activities as qualifying exigency, 108, 111

Military family leave, 101–122
overview, 102, 103–104
for brother or sister, 72
intermittent or reduced-schedule leave, 112
managers' checklist, 121–122
common mistakes, 120
substitution of paid leave, 112–113
See also Military caregiver leave; Qualifying exigency leave

Military personnel and USERRA rights, 293–294

Military service
and 12 months of employment rule, 40
and 1,250 hours in a 12-month period requirement, 43
and USERRA rights, 283

Minnesota, 297

Modified schedule. *See* Reduced-schedule leave

Moonlighting, company policy on, 264, 396

Moorer v. Baptist Memorial Health Care System, 175

Moreau v. Air France, 23

"More than three days" requirement, 59

Multiemployer health plans, 227

Multiple births in the same year, 83

Multiple condition as serious health condition, 58

Multiple treatments as serious health condition, 64–65

N

National Western Life Ins. Co., Bocalbos v., 87

Neel v. Mid-Atlantic of Fairfield, 268

New Jersey, 305

"Next of kin" for military caregiver leave, 116–117

Notice. *See* Employees' notice requirements; Employer's notice requirements

Notice and designation of leave, 153–179
overview, 154, 155
common mistakes, 176–177
company policy, 392
counting time off as FMLA leave, 155–160, 176
designation notice, 164–166
eligibility notice, 161–162
general notice, 160–161
managers' checklist, 178–179
and overlapping state laws, 295
rights and responsibility notice, 162–164, 229, 254, 266
See also Employees' notice requirements

Notice and paperwork requirements
overview, 5–6
company policy, 391
and company policy, 13
FMLA guidance on, 7

Notice of determination of substantial and grievous economic injury, 266–269

Notice of Eligibility and Rights & Responsibilities form (DOL), 162, 163

O

1,250 hours in 12-month period requirement, 42–44, 45–46, 50, 142–143, 145, 293–294
Oregon, 297
Outsourcing work of employee on leave, 220
Overtime policies and hours worked measure, 43, 145, 148
Overtime work by exempt employees, 47, 48, 145–146

P

Paid sick leave laws, state, 300
Paid time off. *See* Substitution of paid leave
Parent
    as family member for FMLA leave, 71–72
    identifying, 82
    in loco parentis, 71–72, 81, 110
    parental certifications, 85–86
    See also Parenting leave
Parental care for parent of military servicemember as qualifying exigency, 110, 111
Parenting leave, 79–99
    overview, 80, 81, 83
    adoptive parents leave, 84, 87–88, 298
    birth of the child, 83–84
    common mistakes, 96–97
    company policy, 393
    foster child placement, 84–85, 88–89
    identifying child as family member, 71
    illness of a new child, 95–96
    intermittent or reduced-schedule leave, 88–90
    managers' checklist, 98–99
    military caregiver leave, 118
    as military family qualifying exigency, 108–109, 111
    one-year limit, 217
    parental certification, 85–86
    parents working for the same company, 90–92, 93–94, 96–97
    and serious health condition leave combined, 93–96
    serious health condition leave vs., 97
    state laws on, 295, 298
    state paid family leave programs, 305
    substitution of paid leave, 90
    timing of, 86–88
    and Title VII provisions, 292
    See also Pregnancy or prenatal care
Part-time employees, 139, 144–145, 394
Pay docking rules, 146
Penalties for not posting FMLA information, 29–30
PEOs (professional employer organizations), 24
Permanent or long-term incapacity as serious health condition, 64
Peters v. Gilead Sciences, Inc., 14

Philander Smith Coll., Hatchett v., 142

Physical care, 74

Policies. *See* Company policies

Postdeployment activities as qualifying exigency, 110, 111

Pregnancy or prenatal care
  as serious health condition, 62–63, 84, 89, 93–95
  state laws on, 297–298
  and Title VII provisions, 292

Premium payments, company policy on, 228–230, 395

Primary employers, 25–27

Privacy rights, employee's, 184, 198, 206–207

Professional employer organizations (PEOs), 24

Psychological care, 74

Public employers and schools, 4

Q

Qualifying exigency leave, 104–113
  overview, 103, 104, 107, 112, 120, 132
  certifications, 189–190, 199–200
  for child care and school activities, 108–109, 111
  for counseling, 109
  covered active duty, 104–106
  employee notice requirement, 172
  family members included in, 107
  for financial and legal arrangements, 109, 111
  intermittent leave for, 140–141

for military events and related activities, 108, 111

misdesignation consequences, 166

for parental care for parent of military servicemember, 110, 111

for postdeployment activities, 110, 111

for rest and recuperation leave of military servicemember, 109, 111

for short-notice deployment, 107, 111

R

Raises and reinstatement, 256

Raybestos Products Co., Vail v., 265

Reasonable accommodations under ADA, 239, 263–264, 284, 286, 287, 289–290

Reasonable safety concerns, 147, 254

Recertifications, 203–205

Record keeping, 313–324
  overview, 6, 314, 315–316
  certifications, 198
  common mistakes, 322–323
  company workforce records, 316
  and DOL investigations, 321–322
  employee work hours, 46–48, 49–50
  for FMLA and state laws, 307
  and HIPAA, 201, 320–321
  holding records for three years, 316

individual employee records, 316–318

intermittent and reduced-schedule leave, 146–147

job descriptions, 68

managers' checklist, 323

medical records, 318–321

proof of a family relationship, 72–73

Reduced-schedule leave

company policy, 393–394

and employees' ability to perform essential functions of the job, 142

and fitness-for-duty certification, 147, 164–165, 205, 254–255

medical necessity for, 119, 139–141, 184, 185, 232

for military family leave, 112, 119

and parenting leave, 88–90

as reasonable accommodation under ADA, 286, 289

See also FMLA leave duration for intermittent and reduced-schedule leave

Reinstatement, 245–278

overview, 6, 246, 247

and ADA accommodations, 289–290

benefit restoration, 258–260

common mistakes, 273–274

company policy, 396

deadlines for, 251–252, 273

in equivalent position, 247–250

fitness-for-duty certifications, 252–255

FMLA and workers' comp claims, 304

managers' checklists, 275–278

pay restoration, 255–256

planning for, 236

See also Essential job functions

Reinstatement not required, 260–270

overview, 260

employee cannot perform an essential job function, 263–264

employee not returning from leave, 262–263, 270–273

firing an employee during leave, 238–240, 242, 261–262

fraudulent FMLA leave, 264–265

key employee issues, 265–270, 274

restructuring and layoffs, 260–261

temporary employment as original intent, 262

termination for cause, 261–262

Rescheduling leave, 217

Rest and recuperation of military servicemember as qualifying exigency, 109, 111

Restorative surgery, 65

Restructuring and layoffs during an employee's FMLA leave, 260–261

Retirement benefits, 259

Retirement during FMLA leave, 271

Retroactive designation of FMLA leave, 159–160, 166

RGIS Inventory Specialists, Inc., Beaver v., 168

Righi v. SMC Corp., 169, 173

Rights and responsibility notice, 162–164, 229, 254, 266

"Rolling year" calculation for FMLA leave, 128–129, 136

Romans v. Michigan Dept. of Human Services, 74

S

Safety concerns, 147

Salaried employees. *See* Exempt employees

Same-sex partners, 82, 95

Same-sex spouses, 82, 90–91, 93–94, 96–97. *See also* Spouses

Saroli v. Automation & Modular Components, Inc., 161

Scheduled time vs. time actually taken for intermittent or reduced-schedule leave, 148

Schedule modifications. *See* Reduced-schedule leave

Scheduling leave, 213–218, 231–232

Schools and public employers, 4

Secondary employers, 25–27

Second opinion certifications, 201–202

Seniority, 260

Sepe v. McDonnell Douglas Corp., 44

Serious health condition leave, 53–78
   overview, 54–55, 56–57, 67, 76
   certifications, 55–56, 59–60, 77, 183–185
   for chronic serious health condition, 63–64
   common mistakes, 77–78
   company policy, 390–391
   conditions not covered, 65–67
   employee's serious health condition, 68–69, 167–168, 183–185
   episodic conditions, 63–64, 184, 192–193, 232
   fitness-for-duty certifications for reinstatement, 252–253
   identifying a serious health condition, 55–56, 168
   for incapacity for more than three days and continuing treatment, 58–62
   inpatient care, 57–58
   manager's role in identification of, 55–56
   for multiple and undiagnosed conditions, 58
   for multiple treatments, 64–65
   parenting leave vs., 97
   for permanent or long-term incapacity, 64
   and state domestic violence leave laws overlap, 299–300
   and substance abuse, 66
   and workers' compensation, 302
   See also Family member's serious health condition leave; Pregnancy or prenatal care

75 miles rule, 50-employees within, 37–39

Shadyside Hosp., Victorelli v., 140

Short-notice deployment as qualifying exigency, 107, 111

Siblings, 72

Sick leave laws, state, 300

Sims v. Alameda-Contra Costa Transit District, 199
Sisters and brothers, 72
Small necessities laws, state, 298–299
SMC Corp., Righi v., 169, 173
Smith v. Allen Health Systems, Inc., 240
Smith v. East Baton Rouge Parish School Board, 249
Society for Human Resource Management, 218–219
Sommer v. Vanguard Group, 257
Spangler v. Federal Home Loan Bank of Des Moines, 288
Spanish-language FMLA posters, 29
Spouses
    as family member, 70
    and military caregiver leave, 91, 97, 119
    as parent, 82
    and parenting leave for parents working for the same company, 90–91, 93–94, 96–97
    same-sex spouses, 82, 90–91, 93–94, 96–97
    See also Parent
State departments of labor, 380–383
State family and medical leave laws, 294–302
    overview, 294–297, 307, 309
    adoption leave, 298
    California Family Rights Act, 70–71
    comprehensive laws, 295–297
    domestic violence leave, 299–300
    and FMLA, 29, 300–302, 307

    on FMLA leave to care for domestic partners, 70–71
    "kin care" laws, 76
    on leave year method, 131
    military family leave, 297
    paid family leave programs, 305, 307, 310
    on paid leave, 158–159
    paid sick leave laws, 300
    on parenting leave, 90, 92
    pregnancy disability leave, 297–298
    on rights of servicemembers, 293
    small necessities laws, 298–299
State laws, 294–305
    overview, 12, 335–379
    on deductions to amounts owed to employees, 273
    disability insurance, 12, 305, 307, 310–311
    overlapping with FMLA, 11, 12
    posting requirements, 30
    workers' compensation, 12, 158, 263–264, 302–303, 310
    See also State family and medical leave laws
Status reports, 236–238, 395
Substance abuse treatment, 66
Substantial and grievous economic injury, 266–269
Substitution of paid leave
    overview, 156, 256
    company policy, 392
    and continuation of benefits, 228
    employee's information requirement, 169–170
    for military family leave, 112–113, 119

paid leave from another source,
158–159

paid leave provided by your
company, 156–158

for parenting leave, 90

and premium payments, 228–230

and recovery of health insurance
costs if employee doesn't return,
272

Successor in interest and FMLA
obligations, 28

Suspension, employee, 42, 43

T

Taylor v. Invacare Corp., 31

Teachers, 148

Tellis v. Alaska Airlines, 75

Temporary employment and FMLA
leave, 262

Temporary replacement for employee
on leave, 220

Terminology, 325–332, 387–389

*Terwilliger v. Howard Memorial
Hospital,* 238

Third opinion certifications, 203

Thom v. American Standard, Inc., 130

Thorson v. Gemini, Inc., 192

Time increments for intermittent or
reduced-schedule leave, 147–148

Time off as FMLA leave, 136–138,
155–160, 176

Title VII of the Civil Rights Act,
283, 291–293, 309

Transferring an employee to another
position for intermittent leave, 232,
233–234, 242

Travel time, 43

Treatment, continuing, 60–62

12 months of employment rule,
40–42, 50

U

Undiagnosed condition as serious
health condition, 58

Undue disruption, 217

Undue hardship created by ADA
accommodation, 249, 284, 285,
287, 289–290, 306

Unforeseeable leave notice, 172–173,
217–218

Uniformed Services Employment
and Reemployment Rights Act
(USERRA), 283, 293–294, 309

Unionized workplaces, 4

Unmarried couples
domestic partners, 70–71, 296
and parenting leave, 91, 95
same-sex partners, 82, 95

U.S. Department of Labor (DOL)
on airline flight crew and FMLA
leave usage, 138
airline flight crew terms, 44–45
certification forms, 184–190
Designation Notice form, 165
examining company records,
321–322
FMLA approved poster, 29
FMLA regulation updates, 3
on military caregiver leave, 126
on military family leave to assist
servicemember's parent, 110
*Notice of Eligibility and Rights &
Responsibilities,* 162, 163

on recertifications, 205
on status report requests, 237
USERRA (Uniformed Services
  Employment and Reemployment
  Rights Act), 283, 293–294, 309

V

Vail v. Raybestos Products Co., 265
Vanguard Group, Sommer v., 257
Vermont, 295, 299
Veterans Affairs Program of
  Comprehensive Assistance for
  Family Caregivers, 188–189
Veterans Affairs Service and military
  caregiver leave, 114–115
Victorelli v. Shadyside Hosp., 140

W

Washington, 305
Washington, D.C., 299
Wierman v. Casey's General Stores, 63
Willard v. Ingram Constr. Co., Inc., 96
*Woodman v. Miesel Sysco Food Service
  Co.,* 62
Workers' compensation, 12, 158,
  263–264, 302–303, 310

☷ NOLO *Online Legal Forms*

Nolo offers a large library of legal solutions and forms, created by Nolo's in-house legal staff. These reliable documents can be prepared in minutes.

Create a Document

- **Incorporation.** Incorporate your business in any state.
- **LLC Formations.** Gain asset protection and pass-through tax status in any state.
- **Wills.** Nolo has helped people make over 2 million wills. Is it time to make or revise yours?
- **Living Trust (avoid probate).** Plan now to save your family the cost, delays, and hassle of probate.
- **Trademark.** Protect the name of your business or product.
- **Provisional Patent.** Preserve your rights under patent law and claim "patent pending" status.

Download a Legal Form

Nolo.com has hundreds of top quality legal forms available for download—bills of sale, promissory notes, nondisclosure agreements, LLC operating agreements, corporate minutes, commercial lease and sublease, motor vehicle bill of sale, consignment agreements and many, many more.

Review Your Documents

Many lawyers in Nolo's consumer-friendly lawyer directory will review Nolo documents for a very reasonable fee. Check their detailed profiles at **www.nolo.com/lawyers/index.html**.

Nolo's Bestselling Books

Dealing With Problem Employees
$49.99

Smart Policies for Workplace Technologies
Emails, Blogs, Cell Phones & More
$34.99

Essential Guide to Federal Employment Laws
$49.99

The Manager's Legal Handbook
$49.99

The Employer's Legal Handbook
$49.99

Every Nolo title is available in print and for download at Nolo.com.

AUG -- 2015
342 6764